About the author

Hugh was born in a small village on the edge of the Peak District and spent his childhood there. Leaving school at fifteen with no qualifications, Hugh decided to join the Army as an apprentice and after graduation, was posted to West Germany for three years.

Returning to England and after discharge from the Army at age twenty-one, Hugh moved to London and worked for twenty-four years in the banking sector in the City of London. After that, Hugh then moved on to join the Civil Service.

Hugh now lives in Surrey and runs his own gardening business.

The Hendeca Association

Hugh Willowbrook

The Hendeca Association

Olympia Publishers
London

www.olympiapublishers.com
OLYMPIA PAPERBACK EDITION

A CIP catalogue record for this title is
available from the British Library.

ISBN: 978-1-84897-672-6

This is a work of fiction.
Names, characters, places and incidents originate from the writer's imagination. Any
resemblance to actual persons, living or dead, is purely coincidental.

First Published in 2016

Olympia Publishers
60 Cannon Street
London
EC4N 6NP

Printed in Great Britain

Prologue

The day began like any other. The sun slowly rose over the horizon, and began casting its rays on the earth below it, starting to give its light, warmth and energy. Winter seemed very far away on this early morning in mid-August, but it was approaching steadily, giving no hint of what was to come. The air would become fragrant and warm as the temperature rose, full of the wonderful aroma of the early autumn. Later the harvest would continue to be gathered in. But for now in the cool of the early morning, the cobwebs on the hedgerows were still hung with tiny droplets of dew that shined in the early light. But the earth's orbit around the sun was changing its axis and the days were becoming gradually shorter, and the nights gradually cooler, but on this lovely mellow day it was hard to imagine that winter was getting ever nearer.

The creatures of the night were already gone, replaced by the creatures of the day. The sun's warmth would begin to grow and the dew would slowly evaporate, leaving the cobwebs invisible once again. On the telegraph wires and in the hay barns the young swallows would continue to strengthen their wings for the long journey they would soon begin. The first leaves had already started to fall and berries ripened on the hedgerows.

For those few who were really tuned in to it, there was a sense of change in the air, giving the feeling of being on the edge of something, evoking a sense of nostalgia, of things long forgotten but suddenly remembered by a sound or a smell, triggering memories of other times. It was intoxicating, invigorating and melancholy. It was the English countryside at its very best.

For the lucky few who had a car, a gallon of petrol had reached the outrageous price of five shillings and eleven pence. A pint of milk would set you back eight pence ha'penny, and six eggs two shillings and three pence! A new film had just come out called "Dr No", about a British spy named James Bond, and for One Shilling and three pence you could go and see it. While you were watching it, you could munch on the new cheese and onion crisps, or the equally new After Eight Mints, or both! Another film called "Lawrence of Arabia" had won an Oscar and was "Coming Soon"!

More and more homes now had the ever more popular "TV" in the corner of their living rooms and families would settle down in the evening to enjoy shows like "Z Cars", "Steptoe & Son", and "The Saint". In the towns the new "Push button Panda" crossings began to appear on the roads, helping you to wend your way to shop at the new "Safeway" supermarkets. A little known Liverpool group called "The Beatles" had failed their audition with Decca records.

This was England, and like the approaching winter, for some, life was about to dramatically change forever.

This year was 1962…

Chapter One

In Oslo, Norway, the sun was also rising, having never really set. A little girl and her parents were about to leave their home and travel to England to visit relatives. It was something that they had not done before and was to change the lives of many people in the years to come. They had no idea of what was about to happen that August day as the sun rose in the sky and cast its rays of light and warmth on the earth below.

Freya was excited. She was going to England with her parents today to visit her Uncle and Aunty, who she had never met before. She had not slept very much and had been awake long before the alarm clock had rung at six a.m. She was so looking forward to the journey, riding on the train, then sailing on a ship. She had never been on a ship, spending all her life living with her mum and dad on the outskirts of Oslo, the capital city of Norway. She had packed her bags the night before, helped by her mother and was eager to get started on the adventure. She took no toys, only her Troll, who went everywhere with her. He was her constant companion and had been since she was a baby. Her mother had made him while expecting Freya and the first photograph of the baby Freya had the Troll next to her, to keep her safe. Some of the children at Freya's school said that Trolls did not exist, they were only Scandinavian folklore. Freya did not care what they said, they knew nothing. She knew different.

Freya was six years old and an only child. Her father worked for the Government, and was a keen athlete as a Cross-Country Skier. Freya was proud of her dad and was herself quite good on skis or skates. She was a typical Norwegian girl, with Blond hair and deep blue eyes and a love of the outdoors. She was also very intelligent, with a thirst for knowledge that put her top of her class every year. She was quick to learn, possessing an intuition and instinct about people and life that was the envy of her school friends. She just seemed to know what was for the best without thinking about it. She was a happy-go-lucky girl who had a bright future ahead of her.

Her name was chosen from Norwegian mythology. Freya was the beautiful daughter of Niorn, God of the seas, and given to her when her parents saw what a beautiful baby girl she was. She was part of a small family. All her grandparents had died before she was born and the only relative that she knew of was her father's younger brother who lived in England with his English wife. She was looking forward to meeting them.

It was mid-August , 1962 and the visit to England was to be for a week so as for Freya to be back home in good time for her to return to school for the autumn term, which was her favourite as her birthday was in November, when she would be seven this year. She enjoyed school and was eager to go back and learn more. Little did she know as she and her Troll looked out of the train window, watching the mountains and countryside giving way to houses and streets as they travelled to board the ship that she would not be coming back to Norway again.

The ship was a cross channel ferry, and seemed huge to Freya as they went aboard. She was eager to explore but her mother held her hand to prevent her getting lost. Her mother knew that if Freya had her way, she would be up on the bridge asking the Captain if she could steer the ship! She was an only child like Freya and wished that she could have had more children but at the moment money was tight and it had taken a long time to save for this trip, but maybe next year, it might be possible. There were a few cabins available for those who could afford them, but Freya and her family would have to make do with the rows of benches below deck. After a while, the ship got underway and with a blast on the ships horn, the vessel headed out of the harbour and made her way out to the open sea and turned her bows south-west towards the British Coast. Freya looked back as the Norwegian coast receded in the distance and waved her Troll's arm to say goodbye. She was always careful to keep her Troll in the shade, as she knew that Trolls did not like direct sunlight, preferring darkness and twilight. It was the first time she had left Norway and she felt both excited and apprehensive at the same time. Freya and her parents stayed up on the deck for a few hours, enjoying the sea air as the weather was warm and the sky blue. At Lunch time, they ate the sandwiches that Freya's mother had made and washed them down with water. As the afternoon wore on, the sky began to cloud over and the breeze freshen, so they all went down below deck to sit on the benches. Freya looked out of the port hole for a while, but the sea air and the excitement of the day soon made her feel sleepy and she fell asleep. Her father lifted her feet up on the bench, took off her shoes and put her coat under her head and with her Troll under her arm, she slept the rest of the voyage and only awoke as the ship was approaching the harbour.

England! She was actually in England. She could speak English quite well, as it was taught at her school. Freya watched and listened to all the activity going on around her as the ship made its final approach to the docks. The loudspeakers burst into life and said "Harbour Stations, Harbour Stations, hands to Harbour Stations" Freya and her family were still below decks and like everyone else, they had gathered their possessions together and sat waiting for the instruction to disembark. Freya peered through the porthole, which was on the left side of the ship, the port side as her father had told her, and watched men out on the deck throwing lines to the waiting hands on the dockside to secure the ship. In no time at all the ship was tied up and gangplanks were in place for the foot passengers to leave the ship. Freya and her parents made their way slowly off the ship and down the gangplank to the dock side. Customs came next and Freya's parents handed their Passports over, the official behind the desk peered down at them, then down at her. He said, "Two adults, one child and a Troll, everything is in order, Welcome to England" and stamped the Passports and handed them back to her father. They moved away from customs and found the car hire desk. As Freya's Uncle lived in a rural part of England, a car was necessary to get around. They were led out to a car park and given the keys to a Morris Traveller. Freya's father was just about to sign for the vehicle when Freya called out in alarm,

"Don't sign for this, daddy, the steering wheel is on the wrong side of the car!"

Her father burst out laughing and said,

"It's OK, Freya, in England they drive on the left side of the road."

"Why," said Freya, completely astounded. "We don't at home."

"I know, but here is different from home, come on and jump in!"

Freya climbed in the back seat as the luggage was put in the back and the doors closed. Her mother sat on the left side, where the steering wheel ought to be and her father got in the right side and started the car. It was late evening and the light was fading into dusk.

"Is it much further?" asked Freya from the back seat.

"A couple of hours or so and then we will be there," said her father.

They joined the traffic leaving the docks and there was a big sign at the dock gates that said "KEEP LEFT".

Freya was kneeling on the back seat and looking between the front seats as they moved through the town, the street lights glowing in the gathering darkness. After a while she lay on the rear seat and was soon fast asleep with the rhythm of the car. Soon her mother was also nodding in the front seat, and her father wound down the window a little to stay alert. Soon they left the town far behind and were out in the country. The sun finally dipped below the horizon and darkness descended, which again was a strange thing for the Olsen family as it never really got dark at home at this time of year. Freya's father was the only one awake to witness it. The little van travelled on and on, the flat countryside giving way to more hilly terrain. They were heading for the northwest midlands area of England and her father would not be sorry to get to his brother's house and get to bed. The roads became more and more narrower and twisty, and the hills more steeper. Soon they were the only car on the road as the time approached midnight. Her father concentrated on his driving. He was not far from his destination now, the little village of Elfington. After a while he saw a road sign which said "Elfington- seven miles."

Not far now. The road sloped steeply downhill, descending into yet another valley. A new sign appeared, with a red triangle on it and the words "Steep hill, one-in-six." The road had dry stone walls on each side, and were heavily wooded beyond the walls, the branches hanging over the road. It was like driving into a long tunnel! The road continued to descend, twisting left and right as it did so. Her father's eyes opened wide, as he turned a corner and a car appeared suddenly, travelling the other way, its headlights blazing, blinding him. It was travelling fast and was on the wrong side, his side, the left side of the road. Her father swung the wheel of the van sharply to the left, trying to avoid the car, but still blinded by the lights, he hit the dry stone wall on his left side. The other car, too late, tried to move to its own side of the road, but could not do so in time. The vehicles collided, each hitting the other on the right wing with a loud bang. They bounced off each other and both then hit the stone wall on their left, before passing each other. The oncoming car skidded to a halt, leaving black rubber marks on the road. Freya's father was not so lucky. The long journey and unfamiliar vehicle had slowed his reactions. Frantically he swung the wheel sharply back to the right, stamping again hard on the brakes as he did so. Freya's mother's eyes had snapped open and she tried to grab the dashboard to steady herself from the violent motion of the car. Freya also awoke on the back seat as she slid first one way and then the other, smashing her head many times as she did so. The van hit the right hand stone wall with another loud bang. The speed and weight of the car, passengers and luggage was too much. The little van went straight through the wall, stones flying everywhere and plunged down the steep side of the valley, hitting several small fir trees as it went. Her mother screamed. Her father shouted Noooooooooooooooo . Freya called for her mother but was thrown violently against the front seats and bumped her head hard again, temporarily stunned. The van hit a large tree with a mighty bang the body of her mother went flying straight through the windscreen and landed on the ground, and did not move. Her father was trapped behind the steering wheel and was still. The van was hissing with escaping steam from the radiator, the bonnet crushed completely. For a few moments nothing happened. Then Freya's eyes fluttered open. The back doors had burst open and the luggage had flown out. With the last of her energy Freya raised herself up over the back seat and looked back the way they had come. A figure was walking unsteadily towards the van, stepping over the stones where it had smashed through. It was a man, Freya could tell. The man stopped a few feet from the wreckage, looked for a long moment and then turned and started to walk back up to the road. Freya tried to call out but her eyes had started to close. In that brief moment, before she passed out again, she saw the man's face clearly. As she slipped down the back seat, she could smell a funny smell but did not know what it was. It was petrol. In the distance a car engine started and drove slowly away, but the Olsen family could not know he would not be going to get help, but to run away to leave them to die!

Chapter Two

The ambulance had called ahead and the emergency doctors and nurses were waiting for it. As soon as the vehicle emerged from the darkness and stopped, the rear doors were thrown open and the three bodies were wheeled quickly inside, the whirling blue light on the roof of the ambulance casting a strange pulsating light over the scene. The doctors and nurses worked with ordered urgency, focusing all their attention on the tasks at hand. It was quite rare for three badly injured people to require the services of the Accident and Emergency Department in the small market town of Abbotsbury. The senior doctor on duty that night was dealing with his first multiple emergency since his promotion from the junior ranks. He had telephoned the Consultant as soon as the ambulance had radioed in, and he was on his way, but it would be some time before he would be there. At the moment, he was in charge and, if he was honest, he was scared. No one had the time or need to look out of the windows, all their attention was focused on the three casualties that had just arrived. Had anyone done so, they would not have noticed two shadowy figures moving silently through the grounds towards the accident and emergency dept.

It was Dr Tom Thornton, senior doctor on duty that night, who moved from bed to bed, issuing terse instructions to the junior doctors and nurses, trying his best to keep his voice calm, drawing on his limited experience. He took a deep breath to steady himself, but he could see that the situation was grim. The senior nurse on duty that night was Sister Penny Grey, a very experienced lady whose quiet and calm manner helped to settle the others. Dr Thornton once again thanked his lucky stars that the beautiful and competent Sister Penny had transferred over to be on his team. He would need all the help he could get this night.

"I'm afraid she's dead," said one of the junior doctors, his voice low and full of regret, standing away from the bed, and looking down at the lifeless body below him, the long blond hair cascading over the pillow. It had been over ten minutes since the ambulance had arrived and despite the emergency team's best efforts, they could do no more. Dr Thornton moved over to check, but his colleague was sadly correct. No pulse, no heartbeat, no life. Nothing. With a sigh, he closed the blue eyes and drew the sheet over what once had been a lovely face. What a waste. He wondered if he would ever get used to death. He doubted it.

Shaking himself from his pity, his face ashen, he turned back to the other two beds, Sister Penny Grey watched as he worked, knowing that he would probably blame himself for something that he could not have prevented. The body in the next bed was male and still the centre of frantic activity. The junior doctor treating this patient was using the heart machine again and again, trying to get the heart started. The burns would be dealt with later, others were doing chest compressions while a nurse was squeezing a bag at regular intervals to provide oxygen. Dr Thornton took over the machine, while the junior doctor studied the monitor. Nothing. Again, no pulse or heartbeat. "How long has it been?" asked Dr Thornton, sweat on his forehead. "More than twenty minutes now," came the reply. Never one to give in, Dr Thornton continued on for a further five minutes before reluctantly accepting that it was hopeless to continue.

Dr Thornton sighed. It was no good. They had lost this one as well. He hurried to the final bed. Please let this one live he said to himself as he swiftly approached the final group of nurses and doctors. They parted to let him get to the bedside and take control of the treatment.

Outside the emergency room, around the corner from the main entrance, and sitting in the darkness on the lower stairs of the fire escape, were two figures. They sat perfectly still and could not be seen from inside, even if someone looked directly at them, their spotted coats blending into the shadows perfectly. They had come as soon as they could. But not soon enough for two of the casualties. From where they sat they had a clear view of the third body and could see the frantic activity going on around it. They focused all their attention on that bed, their green eyes locked on to the figure in the bed, eyes growing brighter and brighter as they transferred their huge mental power and energy to save the dying human. They knew that it was this body that was unknowingly transmitting the very weak but unique distress signal that they had received from many miles away. The two figures were in the form of what the humans called a Lynx. A medium-sized but very powerful cat. They had chosen to be this animal because they would have no predators to worry about and they could move around without being seen, could climb trees and they just liked the way it looked. They could not exist on this planet in their natural form, because they were not from this planet. The visitors from another galaxy watched as a male human who seemed to be in charge approached the bed.

Dr Thornton again took over the heart machine, while others performed their checks and duties. The monitor was flat. "How long?" shouted Dr Thornton, all pretence at being calm gone.

"Twenty-three minutes," came the reply. Dr Thornton tried again with the machine. He knew he should stop now, but he just could not give in again. He kept going. Finally he stood back. "How long?" he asked in a tired voice.

"Twenty-seven minutes," said the junior doctor also in a quiet voice. "You did your best," he said. "We all did."

"Our best was not good enough," said Dr Thornton bitterly, and began to turn away from the bed, his head down. Three in one night. Call yourself a doctor he thought angrily to himself.

"Beep."

Dr Thornton spun around in disbelief, as if he himself had been on the receiving end of the electric shock he had just been giving the body on the bed, his open white coat swinging like a cloak such was the speed of the turn.

"Beep."

Dr Thornton stared at the monitor. A spike had appeared, followed a few seconds later by a second.

"Beep", "Beep", "Beep" the noise was getting a little more regular to match the spikes on the screen.

Yes! Incredible as it was, she had come back from the dead, which for 27 minutes or more, she had been. "She's back! We have a pulse," he yelled, "get those drips going again." The others needed no second bidding. They sprang into action like they also had been electrocuted.

The pulse was getting stronger now, the spikes on the screen coming at regular intervals.

Dr Thornton looked down at the body on the bed and smiled. He had done it! How, he had no idea and cared less. The child was alive. Sister Penny Grey saw the smile and knew that only Dr Tom would have carried on for so long, trying to save the child's life. She had been right about him.

Outside the window, the two pairs of eyes glowed less intently than before, but they were still locked on to the child in the bed, transferring huge amounts of energy in to the frail body. They stayed there until the child was moved to the intensive care ward. The two figures finally moved their gaze from the bed and looked at each other. The smaller one nodded slowly. Now they must go. Silently, just as they had arrived, they melted away again through the grounds like shadows, heading back the way they had come, up onto the wold once again. They were not seen. They were never seen. They had done as much as they could for now. When the darkness returned again to the planet called Earth, they would return. The very special little girl they knew was called Freya would live.

Freya was floating. It was pitch black and she could see nothing at all. There was nothing to see. She was alone. She tried to speak, to call for help but no sound came from her mouth. She could sense she was moving very slowly, like a leaf falling from a tree, spinning this way and that on the wind. She did not feel scared, she did not feel anything, she was just floating. As she turned and twisted in the darkness, a tiny light far far away in the distance caught her eye. She tried to think what it could be, but did not know. She felt herself begin to float very slowly in that direction, the motion beyond her control.

The light was getting a little brighter as she moved effortlessly towards it. Eventually she could see it was a lamp of some sort, and there were two figures sitting next to it, one on either side of the light. Closer and closer still she drifted. The movement slowed and finally stopped altogether. Freya's eyes widened in surprise. She could see two cats, looking directly at her.

But they were not like any cats she had seen before. They were quite a bit larger than ordinary cats and they had tufted ears. The most unusual thing she noticed were their eyes. They were green and seemed to be glowing. The cats' faces were kindly and they seemed to be smiling at her. Freya smiled back, but was not sure if they could see her. The cats started to reach out their paws and beckon her forward towards them and the light.

Freya started moving again, but so very slowly now, still towards the light and the strange cats. They were reaching toward as far as they could, stretching, stretching, their paws open wide. Slowly, slowly, Freya floated gently forward. Closer, closer. She was almost able to touch the paws, only a few inches more. The movement stopped again. Freya floated motionless, just beyond reach of the cats and the light. Time stood still. The movement started again, but this time Freya was going slowly backwards, away from the light. The smaller of the cats suddenly leaped forward and grabbed one of Freya's hands.

The larger Cat grabbed the tail of the smaller cat and started to pull them both towards the light. The face of the cat that was holding her hand was much closer now and Freya could see it clearly. It was a beautiful, kindly face, but with a frown at the moment, as the cat concentrated on what it was doing, its eyes still glowing bright green. Freya was moving forward again now, pulled by the power of the cats. The light was glowing much brighter as they got nearer to it. Suddenly the larger cat gave a mighty tug and Freya and the smaller cat shot forward and landed in heap on top of the bigger cat, knocking over the light. The light went out. It was dark again.

He had been dreaming happy dreams, until the shrill bells of the telephone next to his bed had awoken him from his sleep. He was the duty Inspector, at home but on call, but not really expecting to be called at one o'clock in the morning by the desk sergeant at Abbotsbury police station. He listened, grunted a reply then replaced the telephone and looked at it with dislike. Fully awake now, he yawned and carefully slid out of bed, so as not to disturb his wife more than he had already and headed for the bathroom. He did not see the half open eye of his wife watching his retreating back. There were times when being a policeman's wife lost its appeal.

This was one of those times. She turned over, away from the faint glow of the landing light and tried to get back to sleep.

Quickly getting dressed and going downstairs, he had a glass of water, put some fruit and a bottle of water in a bag and headed outside, closing the front door as quietly as he could. He climbed into his police car and headed off to the accident that the sergeant had described to him. It didn't take him long as the roads were deserted at that time of night. An ambulance raced past him, blue lights flashing, going the other way towards Abbotsbury. When he arrived, the fire men were damping down the car which had crashed through the dry stone wall and hit a large tree. As he got out of his car and put on his cap, he was approached by the senior constable, who had been sent out from the police station, together with a junior colleague.

He had his note book in his hand ready to make his report. The area around the burnt out vehicle was lit by hastily rigged lights supplied by the fire service. He returned the constable's salute and asked, "What have we got then?"

"Road traffic accident, sir, probably involving a second vehicle, at approximately 00. 30 this morning. Three people travelling in the vehicle. No sign of the second car. It seems to be a family, one male, one female and one child, all taken to hospital. The vehicle caught fire but that is now out and the lads are just damping down. That's about it for now, sir." The constable ended his report and looked up from his notebook, waiting for the Inspector to speak.

"Hit and run, then," he said.

"That would be my guess, sir," said the constable, nodding his head to confirm his words.

"Let's have a look then," said the inspector, moving off towards the vehicle, which he could now see was a Morris traveller van. Half way there, he paused and looked back, trying to imagine how the accident had unfolded, creating a mental picture of events. Who was going in what direction, and how fast.

Together, they walked carefully around the van, their feet snapping a few dry twigs that littered the woodlands floor, noting the damage to the left and right sides. The Inspector crouched down and looked at the right side wing and bumper. It was scratched with red paint. "That must belong to the other car," he said, "we will have to find that, and the person driving it." The constable made a note to check all garages for any damage to a red car, and all the GP's surgeries and the hospitals for anyone with a sudden injury. Together, they moved around to the back of the car, its back doors had burst wide open from the impact of the crash. The Inspector crouched down again, looking at the ground. "Bring a torch over here," he ordered the constable. The constable passed one over and together they looked at the marks left on the ground. They were like nothing either of them had ever seen before. They started at the back of the van and moved away for about twenty feet. "That's where the body of the little girl was found, sir," said the constable, consulting his notebook again. The inspector scratched his head. The tracks were quite deep in the earth, as if something heavy had made them. Between the tracks were two grooves. "If I were a betting man," said the Inspector, "I would say the little girl was dragged from the back of the van by whoever or whatever made these tracks. Make sure the police photographer gets a good shot of these."

"Very good, sir, maybe it was the driver of the other car," said the constable, looking around to see if there were any more tracks. He could see none.

Inspector Pitt had been a policeman for a long time, all of it in or around this area. Whatever had made those tracks was not a human. He sighed. It was going to be a long night, thankfully the sun rose early at this time of year. He started to move back towards his car to have a think when a voice called out. "Radio, Sir," said one of the other police officers.

He walked over to the man and took the handset. "Inspector Pitt Here," he said.

"This is Sergeant Smith again, Sir. I just got a call from the A & E at Abbotsbury, both of the adults are dead, and the child is touch and go."

"OK. Sarg, understood. Let me know if you hear anything else. "

"Roger, Sir," said Smith. "Out." The radio went quiet.

Inspector Pitt looked around and found the senior constable nearby. "That was Smith back at the station, and the news is not good. Both adults are dead, the child is hanging on, just about. "He sighed. "Put a call through to the Superintendent at his home and let me know when you get him. We will need more men and kit, this hit and run just turned into a murder investigation!"

The police car drove slowly along the road, checking the numbers as they went. "It will be on the left side," said one of the two policemen in the car, who was on that side. They came to a stop at the end house, the only one showing a light in the window. It was number twenty nine. They parked outside, walked to the front door and knocked, the noise sounding very loud in the quiet of the night.

Lars Olsen had been dozing in his chair. It was well passed two a.m. and his brother, sister-in-law and niece had still not arrived from Norway. His wife Rose, had gone to bed some time ago. He awoke with a jump as there was a knock at the door. At last they are here, he thought as he hurried out to the hall to greet his guests, a smile of welcome on his face. The smile froze as he opened the door to see two policemen standing on the path.

"Mr Lars Olsen?" said one of them, looking up at the giant in front of him.

"Yes, that's me, what is it, has something happened to my brother and his family?" asked Lars anxiously, looking from one to the other. "Tell me."

"There's been an accident, Sir, your brother's vehicle was involved in a collision with another car earlier this evening, your brother and his family have been taken to Abbotsbury Hospital," said the second policeman.

"Are they hurt," asked Lars, a shocked and worried look on his face.

"We don't know yet, Sir," said the first policeman.

"I must go to the hospital and see if they are OK," said Lars. "Can you take me, I have no car?"

"Of course, Sir," said the other policeman, "Will your wife be coming too?"

"No," said Lars without hesitation, knowing she would be more of a hindrance than a help at a time like this. "I will leave a note for her."

Lars quickly scribbled a note and left it on the doormat, as if it were post. He grabbed his wallet and keys and hurried down the path to the police car and with blue light flashing they sped away into the night. Upstairs in bed, Rose slept on, unaware of the events unfolding around her.

It was now fully daylight, and the lights supplied by the fire service had been turned off and were being packed away. The road would remain closed for a while longer, but as it was a Sunday morning traffic would be light. Inspector Pitt was sitting in his car, reviewing his notes and trying to get his tired mind to focus on what had happened a few hours earlier. The luggage had been found scattered in the woods where it had been thrown when the back doors had burst open, and a quick look through it revealed a couple of books in a foreign language. The handbag of the female had been found a little later and in it were two passports. They now knew who the victims were and where they were from. The back page of the man's passport had been filled in with the next of kin details, in case of emergency. This would certainly qualify, thought Inspector Pitt. A car had been sent to the address in the passport and the family notified. The victim's brother had been taken to the hospital by his officers.

There was not much else to do here now, the Morris traveller van would be taken away for examination, the drystone walls repaired in due course and the search for the second vehicle would begin. Every garage, petrol station, M. O. T. test centre and anywhere else that they could think of would be visited and checked. All foot patrols would be on the lookout for any red vehicle, particularly one with damage to it. They had to find that car. It could not have gone very far after the crash it had been involved in. They would also make sure that any one attending a doctor or hospital with recent injuries would be noted and the police informed.

Inspector Pitt closed his note book and went to find the sergeant that had been sent out to help him. There was nothing else he could do here. He would go home, get some sleep and prepare his report for the Superintendent. With one last look around the crash site, Inspector Pitt headed for home. As he drove along the empty lanes, a thought popped into his mind. The poor buggers who had been involved in the crash had been from Norway and no doubt had been here to visit their brother and his family. It was a long way to come to end up dead. At least the little girl had somehow survived, at least for now. Welcome to England.

Lars Olsen had come to England for a new life. Not that there was anything wrong with his old one in Norway, he just fancied a change and a bit of adventure. A few of his friends had gone to London and had said that it was a good place to go. All had found work there and unlike his older brother, he was not married and so he decided to see if the grass really was greener on the other side of the hill.

He was big and strong. Six feet five inches tall and a muscular build, with blond hair and blue eyes. He had noticed a few admiring looks from a few of the English women he had met so far. Being a lover of the countryside, he had avoided the big cities and had headed instead for the midlands. He had some savings, but a job was needed. He read all the local papers and one day noticed that there was a vacancy for a Milkman in a small village called Elfington.

This was right up his street, as it would be outdoors. He had never fancied factory or mill work, of which there was plenty. He found a working telephone box, and making sure he had plenty of pennies with which to make the call. His first attempt failed, because he had pressed button "A" before he had received an answer. He lost his 4d.

The second try worked and he secured an interview for the same afternoon at two p.m.

Wearing his best clothes he arrived early at Elfington dairy. The Manager was impressed with what he saw, the job suited a strong man, as Elfington was a village that straddled a valley. There were lots of steep hills to climb. Lars was hired. He would start the following Monday at five a. m. The manager gave him a quick tour of the dairy and introduced him to some of the men who had just finished their rounds. As he crossed the yard, he noticed a pretty young woman looking at him through a window. Lars smiled at her. She smiled back. Lars was a happy man as he waited for the bus to take him back to Abbotsbury later that afternoon.

The following Monday, Lars reported for work at four thirty a. m. having cycled the eight kilometres, or five miles as they said in England from Abbotsbury. The first week he was shown the round by a colleague, learning who the customers were and what they had. He was a quick learner and by week two he was on his own. He loved it. Even when the weather was bad, he enjoyed being outside. Back at the dairy, he would see the pretty woman who had caught his eye most days. He asked who she was. Her name was Rose and she worked in the office.

After a month, it was clear that this was the job for him. The dairy manager was happy with his work and Lars was confirmed a permanent member of staff. He had noticed a Cottage for rent as he was out on his round and decided to move to the village. This would save him a five-mile cycle ride every morning and afternoon and give him an extra hour in bed! Lars took the cottage, paid his deposit and moved into number twenty-nine Druids Way.

There was some furniture, a bed and a cooker. The toilet was outside, next to the coal bunker.

It was a modern one, with a flush. He considered himself lucky. Many houses still had a toilet at the top of the garden, which consisted of a piece of wood, with an oval hole cut into it. The wood was placed on top of a stone "Pit" into which the Poo would go. This would be emptied twice a year by men from the council. He was grateful he would be spared that. All in all, it would do very nicely indeed.

That first evening in his new home, Lars wrote a long letter to his brother and sister-in-law back in Norway, telling them his new address and all about the cottage. He went out to post his letter, there was a post box at the end of the road and then decided to take the short walk into the village for a well-earned pint of beer. There were several pubs in Elfington and he went to the nearest one to see what it was like. He intended to try them all over the weeks ahead and choose a favourite. Being a Saturday, the pub was quite busy, so Lars got his pint and went outside to sit and enjoy the summer evening. He quickly realised that he knew a few of the people who were also sitting outside, they were customers of his and Lars spent an enjoyable evening chatting to them. It was dark when Lars walked back to his cottage and went to bed. As he switched off the light and lay back in his bed, he drifted off to sleep thinking it would be nice to have someone to share the cottage with. As his eyes closed, a face appeared in his mind. It was the girl who worked in the dairy office!

The next morning Lars awoke and walked to the bedroom window and opened the curtains. The view was spectacular. As his cottage was the last on his side of the road, he was next to the moors, or Wold as the locals called it. In the far distance, grey rocks thrust out of the ground, tall and magnificent. He wondered how many millions of years they had been there. In a way, they reminded him of home, of Norway. He swept his gaze fully left and right, enjoying the rugged beauty of the landscape. Lars pushed the window open fully and took a deep breath of fragrant air. Fantastic. For a while longer he lingered there, at one with the world. Finally he moved away from the window and made his way to the bathroom, a happy and contented man.

The next few months went by and summer moved into autumn. Lars had settled into village life. He tried all the pubs in the village and had decided he would make the "Time Flies" his favourite. It was on the edge of the village, not too far from his cottage, with the same breath-taking views of the wold. There had been a pub on that site for hundreds of years, so the landlord told him. There were supposed to be a secret tunnel from the pub to somewhere in the village, so smugglers could avoid being caught when smuggling contraband and paying tax on it. No such tunnel had ever been found, despite extensive searches being carried out. It was, the landlord said, just another story with no truth in it.

The pub was reasonably big, with one large room that had a stone fireplace at each end. It was cosy, friendly and welcoming. Lars enjoyed his visits there. It was in the Time Flies that Lars got to know the girl from the dairy, the girl called Rose.

Chapter Three

Rose was an only child. She had been born in Elfington and grew up there. In any village in any country, anywhere in the world, everyone knows everyone else. The village folk knew your history just as well as you knew theirs. It is almost impossible to keep a secret for long in a small community. Anyone who has lived in a village will know this to be true. Everyone knew Rose. They knew where her dad worked, where her mother shopped and the whole history of the family. The currency of any village or small community is the same the world over. Gossip!

Her father was well liked and respected, a kind, helpful and hard-working man who would do anything for anyone. Her mother, however was known as stuck-up, not very bright and above all, lazy. She used her husband's kindness to her own advantage, making him do most of the things she couldn't be bothered with. The village folk hoped that Rose would take after her dad. They were disappointed. She had inherited a keen mind from her father, but her mother's "why should I bother" attitude. She had been blessed with a pretty face, which she used to her advantage when at the village school, the local boys would fall over themselves to try and win her attention. They all indulged in the local pastime of "going for a walk" which could last for hours. Rose made it crystal clear to them all. Forget it! If they could not entertain her in a manner that she hoped to become accustomed, they could look elsewhere for a girlfriend. She quickly realised that boys were easy to manipulate to get what she wanted, the problem with the local boys was they were all poor and therefore unable to give her what she was looking for, which was basically an easy life.

Every year her school reports read the same. "Could do better" "Lacks motivation" and "Must try harder" were to be found at regular intervals. She did not care. She would find a rich husband and live a good life. Hard work was for mugs. At age eleven she sat and failed her eleven plus exam. It would have surprised most people, not least her teachers that Rose was quite bright, the problem was she just didn't try. Rose read magazines, as the stories were short and there were plenty of pictures. Books were left well alone. She would have to concentrate on them, and that required effort. The next four years at the secondary modern school were much the same. She left at the first opportunity at age fifteen with no qualifications whatsoever. Many other children did the same, the difference between her and them was most had tried their best. Rose had not tried at all. Her father had managed to get her a job at the local dairy, as a filing clerk. He hoped she would do her best to make the most of it. Her mother was pleased that Rose was in the office, clearly better than some of the village girls who had got work in the mills or factories nearby. The position at the dairy was a dead end job and boring. This suited Rose down to the ground. It was inside, mostly sitting down and she did not have to engage her brain at all. Perfect.

Things continued much the same for the next few years, except for when she was just past eighteen her father died suddenly. He had worked as a coalman, for the local coal merchant, delivering bags of coal in all weathers. When he got home, he would then have to do most of the house work and usually cook the evening meal. He loved his wife and daughter and would do anything for them. He was fifty-two

Rose was almost twenty when one day she saw the dairy manager showing a new man around. He was tall, blond, powerfully built and handsome. She casually enquired who he was and was told he would be joining the dairy the following Monday to take over the milk round in Elfington. He was single, from Norway and was called Lars Olsen.

Rose was immediately interested in the new man from Norway. She found out that he had moved to the village from Abbotsbury and rented a cottage in Druids Way. She saw him around the dairy and would smile at him. He would always smile back. She hoped their paths would cross in the village but they never seemed to. She even volunteered to do the shopping on Saturday mornings, much to the surprise of her mother, but she never seemed to bump into him. It was only when she overheard a conversation in the post office that she learned that he usually went to the "Time Flies" pub on Saturday evening for a drink. She had never been there, she didn't usually go to pubs as she would have to go with someone and get involved in conversation. That required effort. But she decided that she needed to do something soon, as a man like that would not be on his own for long. So the next Saturday evening she put on her best dress, high-heeled shoes, brushed her freshly washed hair and with carefully applied make-up in place, she looked at herself in the bedroom mirror. She had to admit, she looked stunning. With her best perfume liberally applied, handbag and light jacket in hand, she set off early for the "Time Flies". Lars Olsen wouldn't stand a chance!

It was late summer and as she was early she sat outside at a table and pretended to read a magazine she had brought with her. A few early drinkers who knew her nodded as they passed by. She nodded back but returned her gaze to her magazine to discourage conversation. Half an hour passed and there was no sign of him. Her drink was almost finished but she did not want to get another in case she missed him. Ten minutes later she spotted him approaching and casually crossed her legs, allowing her dress to ride up more than it should. As he neared her table, she looked up from her reading as if in surprise and pretended to drop her magazine on the ground. He stopped by her table and bent down to pick it up, not failing to noticing her stocking-clad legs as well as a glimpse of cleavage as he straightened up. He smiled with genuine surprise and handed it back to her. He noticed her almost empty glass and asked if she would like another drink. She pretended to hesitate before accepting his offer. He went inside and returned with drinks for both of them and sat down at her table. She removed her sunglasses, looked him in the eye and smiled.

They spent the rest of the evening together, chatting and enjoying the twilight, only going inside when darkness fell. He told her about his life in Norway, his desire to come to England and see life in a different country. She asked about his hobbies and interests and he seemed pleased that she shared many of them. At the end of the evening he asked if he could walk her home, assuring her that there would be no funny business when they got there. Lars was a gentleman and she would be safe with him. Rose agreed. They walked slowly through the village streets together, enjoying the smells of the late summer air, chatting as they went. Eventually they arrived at her front gate and Rose thanked him for a very enjoyable evening, moved close to him and gave him a kiss on the cheek. Before he bade her good night he asked if he could see her again, having already established that she was not with anyone else.

Rose said that she was considering going to the cinema next Saturday evening at Abbotsbury and he could take her there if he wanted. Lars wanted. It was a date! Not wanting to push his luck and spoil the moment, Lars did not try to kiss her again but waited until she was safely inside the house and the front door was shut, before making his way to his cottage.

Behind the closed front door, Rose leaned back against it and let out a long sigh. He liked her, she could tell and she genuinely liked him. All she had to do now was box clever, play her cards right and he was in the bag! She removed her high heels with pleasure and carried them in her hand as she climbed the stairs to her room, smiling to herself. The evening had gone even better than she had dared to hope. Job done.

It started seemingly by chance one Saturday evening. Lars walked to the Time Flies for his usual visit and as he approached the door, he was pleasantly surprised to see the girl from the dairy sitting at one of the tables, reading a magazine. She had not noticed him and he could not resist going over to her. She looked up as he approached and accidently dropped her magazine to the floor. Lars bent down to pick it up, noticing a pair of shapely stockinged legs as he did so. The girl also leant forward to try and pick the magazine up and in so doing revealed a milky-white cleavage from the top of her dress. Lars picked up the magazine and handed back to the girl. She smiled and said "Thank you", uncrossing her legs as she did so, making the dress ride a little higher still up her legs, which showed the hint of a stocking top. She quickly smoothed her dress down and looked embarrassed. Lars pretended not to notice, even though he had got an eyeful.

Lars found himself asking if she was meeting anyone and when she said no, he asked if she would like another drink, she hesitated before accepting , appearing to not have regained her composure. Lars went inside the pub and returned to her table with the drinks and sat down. Although he knew her name, he pretended not to and he introduced himself. She smiled and said, "Hello, Lars, I'm Rose Butler."

Lars smiled back at her and raised his glass and said, "Cheers, Rose," and she did likewise, the glasses clinked and they each took a sip of their drinks. Lars was still in shock at the unexpected meeting and was trying to think of something to say. She was beautiful, with brown hair and brown eyes. She was looking directly into his eyes and he was getting tongue-tied. A slight evening breeze blew and he could smell her perfume wafting his way. She raised an eyebrow and said, "Are you the strong silent type or am I scaring you?" Lars took a long drink of his beer and smiled back at her. "No," he said hurriedly, "it's just that I am not used to being this close to a beautiful young lady and I cannot find the words."

She leaned back in her chair and said, "I'll take that as a compliment, thank you, tell me Lars, how did you come to this part of England?"

"Well," said Lars, "I was heading for the south of England in my longboat for a few days of looting, when I got blown off course and ended up here. I even lost my horned helmet on the beach!"

Rose laughed and said, "You can row a whole longboat on your own? You must be very strong!"

Lars stuck out his chest and nodded. "We Vikings are very tough people." Rose nodded her head. She could see with one eye that Lars was very muscular. She asked, "How big are your arms?" Lars thought for a moment and said, "In your English measurements, eighteen inches, my neck also is the same."

Rose seemed impressed and said, "A girl would be safe with you then?" Lars nodded. "Yar, it is true, you are safe with me!"

Rose had the soft, gentle accent of the area, which all the village people had. It was very appealing and Lars was glad he had come to this North Staffordshire area and not gone further south. He began to relax, helped by the beer. He looked at Rose and said, "So, pretty lady, tell me about Rose Butler, am I safe with her?"

Rose looked directly into his eyes and said, " I think you will be, Mr Viking!"

The next Saturday Lars called for Rose and they caught the bus to Abbotsbury to go to the cinema. She had again made a special effort and looked beautiful. Lars felt very happy as he sat next to her for the five-mile journey. They arrived at the cinema and Lars went to buy the tickets while Rose went to examine the sweets and ice creams. "Two please," said Lars to the lady behind the glass screen.

"Stalls or circle?" She asked. Lars looked bewildered. He had never been to an English cinema before.

"Stalls," he said. Two tickets appeared from a slit in the steel counter. Lars slid a ten-shilling note towards the lady and she gave him his change. Lars took the tickets and went to find Rose. She had decided on fruit gums which were in a box, and some of the new "After Eight" mints. Lars paid for them and they made their way to the entrance doors. A man in a bow tie and black suit took their tickets and tore them in half and then waved them through. They went inside and took their seats. At the back of the cinema were a group of young men, sitting in the back row. They had long hair and leather jackets with silver studs in them. Tight jeans, together with pointed shoes completed their outfits. They were the local "Hard men". Two had their legs over the seats in front. Most seemed to be smoking, adding to the cloud that hung in the air. They were noisy and would call out now and then. When Rose had entered, one had said in a loud voice, "Cor, darling, you can come and sit next to me!" His pals sniggered and laughed. They saw Lars glaring at them and didn't say anything else.

Lars and Rose sat in the middle of the auditorium, well away from the rabble at the back. The lights dimmed and the short film began, lasting about an hour. The lights came up again and the curtains closed for the interval, before the main feature film. Two ladies appeared with trays of ice cream, popcorn and more sweets. Lars looked around and was surprised to see so many people inside. He also noticed that there was an upper seating area. That must be the "Circle" the ticket lady had mentioned. He had missed that when he had arrived. Next time they would go up there, away from the noisy dim wits on the back row. Lars went and bought two tubs of ice cream and they sat in their seats, eating them. Rose thought that Lars's ice cream looked like a thimble in his big hands. She was enjoying the evening. She felt safe with him. She had been here many times before with other men, by now they would have had their hand on her leg, waiting for the lights to dim before trying to move the hand higher. Lars had not tried anything like that. He was a perfect gentleman. She also knew that if the riff raff at the back had been foolish enough to make trouble, Lars would have been more than capable of protecting her. His wide shoulders were touching hers, such was his size.

After a while, the lights dimmed again and the curtains opened. Before the main feature, a western, were the adverts. The Pearl and Dean's music blared out. Adverts for Gin, cigarettes and local traders flashed up on the screen. The music blared out again before the main film began. Lars was riveted to the screen. After about half an hour he felt something touch his hand. It was Rose's hand. She looked at him and smiled. Lars smiled back and they held hands for the rest of the film. The time seemed to fly by. It was almost a shock when the good guys won and the bad guys were in the jail. The lights came up and people started to leave. There was a lot of noise as the seats flipped up with a squeal of springs. They joined the crowd as it slowly made its way outside. It was dark and the real world seemed strange compared with the one they had just left. They made their way to the bus stop and Lars took Rose's hand again. She did not resist. Lars felt on top of the world as they walked together down the darkened streets. There were a few others waiting for the bus back to Elfington. Lars decided he would push his luck a little further and put his arm around Rose's shoulders. She leaned against him and put her arm around his waist. The air was fragrant with the smells of the country at summer time. There was the smell of hay, flowers and Lars took a deep breath and sighed contentedly. There was also the added fragrance of Rose's perfume. The bus arrived all too soon, and they boarded and set off for home. It seemed no time at all until they were alighting in the village.

Again they held hands as they made their way to Rose's house. Rose could sense Lars getting tense as they approached the front gate. She correctly guessed that he was not sure what he should do now. She took the lead. As they stopped by the gate, she turned and put her arms around his neck and standing on tip toe, kissed him on the lips. Lars put his arms around her and she sank back into her shoes and put her head on his chest. They stayed like this for a long moment before she released him and stood back. "Thank you for a lovely evening," she said. She meant it. It had been a very enjoyable date. He looked down at her and said, "It was my pleasure to be with you, we must do it again."

"Yes," said Rose.

"In the meantime, are you free tomorrow?" asked Lars hopefully. Rose shook her head. "Sorry, but I don't want to leave mum on her own, not now dad has passed away. " Rose lied smoothly.

She had nothing to do tomorrow and she didn't care much if her mother was on her own or not. She just didn't want to appear too eager, even if she actually was. There was an old saying that Rose was fond of. Be mean and keep 'em keen!

Lars nodded, disappointed. Having had a taste of romance, he was hungry for more. "Maybe next Saturday? He asked hopefully. Rose pretended to think about it. "OK, " she said. "You can choose what we do." Lars smiled, happy again.

"We can go to the Time Flies, if you like?" Rose nodded.

"It's a date, Mr Viking," she said. She kissed him again, this time on the cheek before turning and going through the gate. She paused by the front door, turned again and waved. "Goodnight," she whispered.

Lars whispered back. "Sweet dreams."

Rose opened the door and went inside, without looking back. She locked the door and removed her shoes . As she climbed the stairs she smiled to herself. This was the second date and things were going really well. All she had to do was take it nice and steady and who knows what might happen!

A few miles away from the crash site, two exhausted bodies were fast asleep in their secret hideaway. Their green eyes were tightly closed and gentle snoring could be heard from them both. They would sleep throughout the day as they would need to return to the hospital again, when darkness fell once more. The little girl they had saved would have further need of them. The hospital staff would provide medical help and other comforts to the child's body. But there was another dimension that needed to be dealt with and only they could help with that. It had always been their intention that they would never get involved with any aspect of life on this world, until they were completely sure that the humans were ready for contact with them, and this visit was no different from the other times they had been here. The humans were not ready. Their mission was now as it had always been. To watch, observe, monitor, and report back on what they had found. But not to contact, never to contact, even if the human was unaware that they had even been contacted, as it was in this case. But this case was different. This child was different, special. She had the one in a billion unique gene. She did not, and would not, ever have known she had this small but vital difference from everyone else, had it not been for the car crash that had almost ended her young life. It had been this inbuilt "distress call" that had activated itself from deep within her mind. The Cats also had it, as had all of their species. Thousands of years earlier, others of their kind had been here on this world and somehow left their DNA behind. Who and when did not matter, only that it had been done. They were called Gallownians and knew that what they had just done had not happened by random chance.

There were many millions of worlds that they could have been on, but they were here. Now. They knew that some things were meant to be. The universe was vast, and yet the universe had put them here at this time. It was meant to be. Call it what you will. Fate, synchronicity, luck. Whatever. The child called Freya was very special. She was the only human they had ever connected with. She was part of them now. She would not know it yet, she was far too young but as she grew older she would find that she had gifts that no one else had, she would be able to do things that others could not do, and know things that others did not know. Their job now was to ensure that she fully recovered and was able to grow and to evolve, and for that to happen she would need a safe and stable home in which to grow. With her parents dead the Gallownians would have to ensure that she had this. It was vital that she understood what had happened. But not yet. She was not ready. So they slept on, regenerating themselves for the work that lay ahead. The universe had decided it would be so. Back at the hospital, a little girl lay unconscious in her bed, unaware that she was the first. The first of a new kind, a new life form. The first of many.

Lars Olsen sat in a waiting room at Abbotsbury Hospital. It was starting to get light outside and he glanced at his watch. It was nearly six a. m. He was in a state of shock. When he had arrived with the police men, he had been met by a Doctor Thornton. There was another man with him. He introduced himself as the duty registrar, but said he had only just arrived himself and that Doctor Thornton would be the best one to explain what had happened. They had come in this room and it was then he had learned that his brother and sister-in-law were dead. Lars could not believe his ears. There must be some mistake, there had to be. The little girl, Freya was alive. Just. Lars thanked the gods at least she had survived. Dr Thornton had said that his brother and sister-in-law would have died instantly. He and his staff had tried everything they could to revive them, but sadly they had failed. They would have felt no pain. He was absolutely sure about that.

He said he was very sorry for his loss. Lars believed him. Dr Thornton looked terrible, pale and seemed close to tears. Lars noticed that the doctor's hands were shaking slightly. Lars thanked him for what he had done. At least his niece was alive. She was the only family he had left now, he realised with a start that he had not counted his wife as family. The doctors had left him alone then and when they had gone, Lars put his head in his hands and wept. His massive shoulders heaved, he called their names and cried out. Why! Why them. Anders, his big brother, who he had looked up to and admired so much, was gone. Marit, his sister-in-law, a real woman, a real wife, a mother. Not like Rose, he thought, not for the first time. Also gone. At least they would be together. They didn't deserve this. No one deserved this. He felt huge guilt, they were coming to see him. If they had stayed in Norway they would be alive now. It was his fault they were dead. He had killed them, just as surely as if he had been there himself.

Eventually the sobbing subsided. There was a tap at the door, Lars looked up to see a nurse standing there, holding a cup of tea in her hand. The British thought that a cup of tea could solve anything. She came in and put the tea down next to him and put an arm around his shoulders. Her hand was warm, her concern real and her voice low and soothing. She stayed with him for a long time, he drank his tea and she went to get another. He cried again. After a while the nurse said, "Would you like to see your niece, Mr Olsen, you won't be able to stay long, but I am sure Doctor Thornton would allow a few minutes."

Lars nodded. "Thank you," he said, he noticed for the first time she had a name badge on her dark blue uniform. It read Sister Grey. "Please call me Lars, OK?" Lars said.

Sister Grey nodded, and gently took his arm, "Come with me." She walked with him down a long corridor. He noticed the floor was red and very shiny. There were bits and pieces of hospital equipment here and there. The main thing that he would always remember was the antiseptic smell.

They entered a room in which were four beds, three were empty. Lars was guided to a chair and asked to sit down. He could hear a machine giving out a regular beep, beep, beep noise close by. There were curtains drawn around the bed and he could not see what was beyond them. The curtains moved and Dr Thornton appeared through them, together with the nurse who had brought him here. Dr Thornton sat down next to Lars and said in a quiet voice, "Freya is asleep, Mr Olsen, so please don't make any noise." Lars nodded. Dr Thornton stood and said, "This way." Lars went with him through the curtain.

The little girl called Freya Olsen lay in the bed. She was connected to monitors and drips. She looked so small and pale. Her blond hair, what could be seen of it, her head bandaged seemed almost white against the pillow. Lars looked down at her, tears rolling down his face, it was the first time he had met her. His niece, his flesh and blood, now his responsibility. The nurse took his hand and squeezed. Dr Thornton put a hand on his massive shoulder and patted him gently. They stood there for a few minutes, just looking down at her. Dr Thornton whispered, "Better let her sleep, she had been through a lot. You can come back later and see her again."

Lars nodded. Before he turned to go, Lars said in Norwegian, "Do not worry, little one, Uncle Lars is here and I will care for you now." They moved away and went outside the curtain.

Dr Thornton said, "With all the drugs she has in her, she should sleep for many hours."

Lars nodded his head. "She knew I would come, she knew I was there. She will sleep now," said Lars as they moved out into the corridor again. As the curtain closed behind them, a pair of eyes opened momentarily, then closed again. Lars had been right. Somehow, Freya had sensed he was there for her.

Sister Grey went with him back to the waiting room, where a policeman was waiting. "I'll have to leave you for a while, Mr Ols—, I mean Lars," said Sister Grey, but I will come back." She went out and Lars sat down next to the policeman.

"I'm very sorry, Mr Olsen," he said, taking out his notebook, "do you feel up to answering a few questions?

Lars shrugged. "Why not, I am not going anywhere."

"Thank you," said the policeman and proceeded to ask a few questions, saving the most difficult one until the end. "We have your brother's and sister-in-law's passports, but would you be able to formally identify them?" Lars looked at him for a long moment, then nodded his agreement.

He stood up on shaky legs. "Let's get it over with," he said in a quiet voice. The policeman stood and they walked out of the waiting room to find Sister Grey. She was in her small office, and looked up as they appeared in the open door. She did not have to ask what they wanted, the look on both their faces said it all.

She rose from behind her desk and moved to the door. "This way, Lars, they are in the chapel of rest." Lars and the policeman followed her down the corridor and then down another.

They came to a pair of doors, with a cross on each one. Sister Grey took his hand again and said in a low voice, "Would you like me to come in with you, Lars?"

Lars shook his head. "No, thank you, Sister, I must speak to them alone, I must tell them that little Freya will be safe with me and that I will care for her."

Sister Grey released his hand and said, "There is a bell inside, ring it when you have finished."

Lars looked at the policeman and said, "Please let me stay alone, once you have what you need."

The policeman nodded. "Of course, Sir, it's just a formality, for the records." Lars straightened his back, took a deep breath, and opened one of the doors, and followed by the policeman, went inside, closing the door quietly behind him.

Lars awoke with a start, aware that someone had touched his arm. It was Sister Grey, she had a plate with two sandwiches on it and a cup of tea. She also had something under her arm. She put the tea and plate down and said, "This, whatever it is, was brought in with your niece, she was holding it so tightly that we had trouble getting it away from her." She held it out to Lars. "What is it?" she asked.

Lars smiled for the first time since he had arrived at the hospital. "It's a troll," he said, taking it from her. It was looking a bit worse for wear, there was soil on its feet, and some of its fur was singed. He carefully placed it on the chair next to him. "I'll keep him here until I can take him to Freya, she will be pleased to see him."

Sister Grey nodded. "Is there anything I can do, Lars?" she asked, sitting down next to him.

"Yes," said Lars. "Would it be possible to use a telephone? I must let my wife know what has happened."

"Of course," said Sister Grey, "have your food and then come to my office, you can call from there, bring your friend too if you like!" nodding towards the troll. Lars nodded and reached for the plate, suddenly very hungry. Sister Grey turned to leave, thinking that the sandwich looked like a stamp in his big hands.

As she moved towards the door, Lars said, "Thank you, Sister Grey, you have been so kind, I will not forget this."

Sister Grey smiled. "It's no trouble, Mr Ol—" she corrected herself, "Lars" and left the room. On her way back to her office, she sighed and thought what a terrible thing to have happen to such a lovely man. She would be going off duty soon, but would return on Monday morning. She hoped that the little girl would have improved a little by then. She would pray that it would be so.

Lars appeared ten minutes later at her door, with the troll under his arm. He had no telephone at home, but a lady down the road wouldn't mind fetching Rose. He rang the number and said he would ring back in fifteen minutes. Rose was there when he called again. He told her what had happened and that he would stay at the hospital until Freya woke up. He did not want her to be alone. Rose said she was very sorry to hear the news and would wait at home for him. He was on a week's holiday anyway, so there was no work to worry about. Lars put the phone down and asked if he could go back to sit in Freya's room. Sister Grey went out to find out. Lars picked up the troll and held it tightly to his chest and wept again.

Sister Grey came back after ten minutes. "Sorry I was so long," she said, "I couldn't find Doctor Thornton."

Lars said, "No problem, I was chatting to my friend," indicating the Troll, who was sitting on a chair next to Lars. Sister Grey smiled. She had in fact found Dr Thornton straight away, but had heard Lars as she returned to her office, so she had waited around the corner for a while. She knew the importance of grieving, of letting out your emotions. She had been in nursing for many years. Lars left the Troll in the office and walked to the intensive care unit with Sister Grey. Not for the first time since he had arrived at the hospital, Lars thought it was a pity his wife was not like Sister Grey. They arrived at Freya's bed just in time to catch Dr Thornton before he went off duty. Again the three of them stood together looking down at Freya. A little more colour had returned to her face.

Doctor Thornton said, "She is doing better, getting stronger, but I am keeping her sedated for now. If this keeps up, I may move her out of intensive care in a day or so, but that will be up to the consultant when he does his rounds tomorrow. She is a fighter, that's for sure."

Lars said, "We Vikings are a determined people, she cannot give up, even if she wanted to." Doctor Thornton had to agree. Lars was allowed to sit in a chair in the corner of the room, out of the way of the hospital staff who were constantly in and out, checking and monitoring the little girl. He would remain there until she awoke. It did not take long before the warmth of the room and the stress of the past twelve hours caught up with Lars again. His head slipped to one side and he was soon asleep again and dreaming.

Rose had slept all night, only waking at eight a.m. There was no Lars, maybe he was downstairs, seeing to the guests. Rose climbed out of bed and put on her dressing gown. The cottage was silent. Rose frowned. Not what she would have expected with four other people in it. She moved along the landing to the second bedroom, where the guests were staying. The door was open, the room empty and the bed still made. Puzzled, Rose went down stairs and saw the envelope on the door mat. It was Sunday so there was no post. She picked it up and recognised Lars' handwriting. She opened the envelope and quickly read the note.

Shit, she thought, that's all we need. Why couldn't they watch where they were going!

She would have to make her own breakfast now. She moved into the kitchen and filled the kettle. The kitchen was spotless, as was the rest of the cottage, ready for the visitors. It was a good job that Lars liked cleaning as she certainly did not. Nothing wrong with a bit of dust here and there. The cupboards were all full as they had stocked up for the guests. Might as well tuck in, thought Rose, they won't be needing it now.

She would have a good fry up. Lars could wash up when he came back! She thought about going around to her mother's, but quickly decided against it. Her mother was even more lazier than she was and would expect Rose to cook a meal for them both. No, she would stay in and await news from Lars. He would have to return sooner or later for a change of clothes and a shave. Meantime, breakfast!

Chapter Four

Rose walked slowly back to the cottage from the neighbour's house. She had pretended to be shocked, in front of the neighbour, but as she made her way home her mind was working as to how she could use this new turn of events to her advantage. She had thought that Lars family had only been involved in a minor traffic accident and would only have a few cuts and bruises. But they were dead. It was good that the little girl had somehow survived. When she was better they could pack her off back to Norway.

Rose had just about got back inside the cottage before the neighbour who had taken the call headed for the pub to spread the gossip. Such is the way in a small community. The news would be around the village within the hour.

Rose sat in the front room and thought back to when the letter had arrived from Norway. Lars had been excited and had asked Rose if it would be possible for them to come and stay at the Cottage. She had agreed at once, much to the surprise and delight of Lars, who she sensed had been expecting a "No chance" answer. She had had her own reasons for agreeing so quickly. Over the last few months she had noticed that Lars had changed towards her, he seemed almost disinterested in what she said or did, and would do his, or rather her chores before heading down to his gym in the shed most evenings. After a while Rose began to worry. Had she overdone the threats? Was her hold over him less strong that it used to be? She knew that you could only threaten someone so much, as there would come a point when the underdog would turn and say, "Do your worst, I don't care anymore" and then her power over him would be gone. It was only the threat of what she would do, what embarrassment she could inflict on him if she did not get her own way that kept him in line. She did not want to kill the goose that laid the golden egg.

For the first time since she had got married, she had felt a stab of fear. What if he left her? What if he returned to Norway? What if… She had better start being a bit nicer, if only for a while to keep him in his place. It never entered her head to talk to him as an equal, to do her fair share of the house work or to treat him not so much as a servant, but as a husband. For her to act like a wife. With her plan in place she brightened up. You didn't keep a dog and bark yourself!

So she had pretended to be pleased they were coming, and said she was looking forward to meeting them at last. So long as he did all the cleaning and preparations for the visitors that is. Lars was more than happy to do it, and did not go down to his gym so much, instead he would be washing curtains, sheets, blankets and doing anything and everything that needed to be done. The garden was tended, the windows cleaned and the cupboards full. Looking around the room, she saw that it was spotless. Now they would never see it. Pity, but there you go. She had had a bath and washed her hair, even though it had only been a month or so since the last time she had done it. What a waste of energy! Never mind, she had agreed to them coming, and it was not her problem that they had not looked where they were going. She had made the gesture and that would be enough to use against Lars if he started being difficult.

Her position was secure once again. She smiled to herself. He would do as he was told, or else!

Back at the hospital, Lars was dreaming again, as he dozed in the corner of the intensive care ward. His mind took him back to his early dates with Rose. After their trip to the cinema, Lars saw Rose more and more often. They walked around the village and stopped to chat here and there with villagers they met. Everyone knew Lars, even those who did not get their milk from him. He was a gentle giant and well-liked by all. Everyone knew Rose too, and had to admit that she had grown up into an attractive young woman. But they also knew her family and although her father had been a popular man in the village, her mother was not. Nearly all feared that Lars was making a big mistake and would be happier with someone else. Rose would not make him happy. But as the weeks and months passed by, the giant blond Norwegian and the smaller dark-haired local girl were seen together more and more. Autumn had passed into winter, and winter into spring. During the winter months Lars had fallen in love with Rose. For him, she was the one. There could be no other. It was over the Easter weekend that Lars produced the ring he had bought in Abbotsbury and asked Rose to marry him.

She had appeared to be surprised, but Lars suspected she had been expecting it. She said yes. They had a small quiet wedding in the summer, at Abbotsbury Registry Office. Lars' brother and his family could not afford to come over to England and Lars could not afford to pay for them, so they agreed to visit the new Mr and Mrs Lars Olsen in the future. As Rose's family were not well off, Lars paid for nearly all of the wedding expenses. He did not mind. He had Rose. After a short four-day honeymoon in Blackpool, Rose moved in with Lars at number twenty-nine Druids Way to begin their married life together.

Lars stirred in his sleep, as his mind moved on to what had happened after the wedding. At first things went well, Lars did his milk round and Rose continued to work in the office. The walks together around the village began to get less and less frequent, and finally stopped. Lars would go on his own once in a while, when he had the time. The villagers noted this and talked among themselves. Told you she didn't like walking, they said. Told you she wouldn't keep it up for long, they said. They were right.

The chores around the cottage were shared. At first. But as the first few months went by and the autumn leaves began to turn brown once again, Lars found himself doing more and more, while Rose did less and less. She said she was tired. She said she had a headache. She said she would have an early night. Lars accepted this and carried on. Women were strange creatures, after all. Living with one was a new experience for him and he did not know if this was normal or not. He was afraid to ask the men at the dairy, in case it was not normal and he was the odd one out. He knew that his new mother-in-law was a bit on the lazy side. On their infrequent visits to her, Lars had noticed that her house was somewhat untidy. She did not seem to mind. She was fond of saying, "It's only a bit of dust," or "It's only a bit of dirt," or whatever it was. Washing up was left until there was nothing clean left, then only a few things were done. Lars wondered if all of it ever got washed. He doubted it.

After a year, Rose came home one Friday evening and told Lars that she had been made redundant. Lars was shocked. There had been rumours for a while, that this might be in the wind, but Lars had thought that he and Rose would be safe. Only much later did he find out that Rose had volunteered to go. But at least he had a job. They would have to manage until Rose could find something else. Rose did not look. She said she would be a housewife instead. But even though she was home all day, Lars still found himself doing most of the chores around the house.

Lars was getting more and more frustrated. This was not the life he had imagined it would be. His escape lay at the bottom of the garden. When Lars had first moved in, he had patched up the old but quite large shed that came with the cottage. Over the months that followed he had made it into a gym for himself. There were no machines, but plenty of free weights that he had bought second-hand after seeing an ad in the local paper. He kept his skis in there and during the winter months he was to be seen skiing on the slopes and paths of the wold. He also used them in bad weather to deliver the milk. They were short cross-country skis, and together with a sledge he had made himself, was able to reach the remotest customers who were surprised but delighted to see him approach with the milk and bread loaded on his sledge.

When the evening meal that Lars had prepared was over, and he had done the washing up, Rose would retire to the front room, and settle down in front of the T V set. Lars knew that he must not make too much noise doing the washing up. It was usual for Rose to shout from the living room, "Do you have to make so much racket!" and get up to turn up the T V. Lars watched little television, so he would escape down to the shed and vent his anger and frustration on his weights. He would do his workout and at the end, would put on a pair of old boxing gloves and spend the last ten minutes hitting the punch bag that hung from the rafters. He always felt so much better when he had finished. One of the men at the dairy had joked once that if Lars ever lost his temper he would kill someone. One of the positives of this situation was that Lars was in superb physical condition, something that was not lost on one or two ladies in the village to whom Lars delivered the milk.

He remembered with a smile one morning when he was outside a house when the door suddenly opened and a young lady stood there in her dressing gown. She had smiled and bent down to pick up the milk from the step, the dressing gown had gaped open, revealing what lay beneath it, which was not a nighty. Lars got a glimpse of a well-shaped breast, before the lady stood up again. She had not tried to close the gown but had looked at Lars and raised an enquiring eyebrow. Lars had coughed, picked up the empties, turned away and headed down the path. The message had been clear enough. It's here if you want it. But Lars had been faithful to Rose. He was a married man, that meant something to him. There was little or no intimacy between him and Rose these days and there were times when he was lying in his bed at night that he thought about that morning and the lady in the dressing gown.

It was just as well that Lars, for all his physical power was very well balanced and placid. He could not hold a grudge for more than ten minutes. The term Gentle Giant was very well suited to him. Placid he might be, but stupid he was not. He knew that Rose was using him, and he felt very disappointed and disillusioned that he was giving so much to the marriage and Rose was giving so little. What was the old saying that the English said? Oh yes. "Marry in haste and repent at leisure!" Still, they were married and he would do whatever it took to make it work. Things never stayed the same for long, and Rose might yet become the wife he had hoped she would be. He still loved Rose, but wondered if she loved him, or indeed ever really had.

With a sigh, he closed the shed and headed up to the cottage to wash. He had to be up early in the morning.

The two Gallownians set off once again at sunset, the shadows growing longer as the Sun slid below the western horizon and gave way to the night. They made their way once again to Abbotsbury Hospital, making sure that they were not seen by anyone. It was quite a long way, but fortunately the Hospital was on the edge of the town next to the moors and by the time they arrived and made their way through the grounds and up the fire escape to the ward where Freya lay, it was dark. The Hospital, however was ablaze with lights which further helped them to stay undetected in the shadows. Once again they took their positions and quickly re-connected their minds with the little girl's and were pleased that she had responded well to the work they had done the night before. Her physical wounds were being treated by the Doctors and nurses. It was the mental wounds that they were helping to fix. It did not take long for them to be aware of the negative waves of emotion coming from the large human man who slept in the chair in the corner of the ward. Lisa the female lynx, continued to connect with Freya and help her mind and emotions to recover, while Bob the male, turned his attention to the man to see what could be the cause of all this negative energy. Bob soon connected with Lars and entered his thoughts. He soon realised what the problem was.

The man's mind was in turmoil, jumping from one thing to another, then back again. His racing thoughts were all connected with the care of Freya after she was well enough to leave the hospital and go home with him. The problem was that this may not be possible because of someone called Rose. Rose would not agree to this, Rose would not agree to that. Rose would not care for the child. Rose would not be interested in anything to do with being a parent. Rose would make no effort whatsoever to love the girl. Rose was incapable of loving anything except herself. Rose did not love him. There was no one in Norway to take in the girl. He could not allow his only niece to be put into an orphanage, either here or in Norway. The cats knew all about Norway. Their first visits to this world had been to there.

It was his duty to care for his brother's child, but he would not be allowed to care for her alone. The authorities on this planet would insist on there being a woman in the house. A capable woman who could take the place of Freya's mother. But Rose would not be interested. He would plead, he would do anything. He would even beg. But in his heart, the man called Lars knew that no matter what he promised to do, the woman called Rose would have none of it.

He had to go to work to pay for everything. Which meant he could not care for the girl and take her to school while he was away. He would work extra hours, get an extra job, get two extra jobs, work day and night so long as he could keep Freya with him. She was his blood. She was his only family. She was his only link to home. She was his brother's daughter. But Rose would not allow him to do anything. Rose was only interested in herself. And so Lars racked his brains to find a solution to a problem that did not have one. Surely there must be a way to keep Freya with him. But the more he went over and over the situation, the more desperate he became.

The man called Lars stirred in his sleep, but his mind kept going around and around. He was beside himself with worry. But what could he do? Rose would never agree to take the child. Rose would not agree to… And so it began again. Bob had learned enough, and disconnected himself from the man's mind.

It was clear to Bob that the little girl whose life they had saved from certain death would require a little more help yet. Bob turned to Lisa and transferred the thoughts of Lars into her mind. She did not take long to reach the same conclusion as Bob had done. This human woman called Rose was the key to the child's future happiness and without her Freya would not be able to follow the path that the Universe had set out for her. Lisa told Bob that Freya was in no danger now and would awaken during the next day.

They looked at each other and silently agreed what must be done. They did not have much time, and it would require a change of form, something that took a lot of energy. They must leave at once and gather what power they could as tomorrow they had a new task to complete. It was vital that they had enough energy to complete their new mission. Tomorrow they had to see someone. Tomorrow when the Sun rose once again in the east, they had to ensure that the child would have a home to go to, and an

Aunty to love her as well as an Uncle, and guide her until she was able to make her own way in the world alone. As they made their way back up to the wold, Lisa put a couple of paws in a freshly dug flower bed, but as she was so tired, she thought no more about it. Tomorrow they had to visit the woman called Rose.

Freya found herself standing on a path, which seemed to stretch off away from her far into the distance. She couldn't see how far because of the thick fog that swirled around her. There were trees each side of the path, evenly spaced out, stretching out until they too were lost in the fog. She could smell the fog, damp and cold, yet she was warm and dry. She started to walk forward down the path into the greyness, which seemed to part to let her pass, swirling away from her as she moved through it, reforming again behind her. It was quiet, yet peaceful. She did not feel afraid. She felt relaxed and confident, eager to see what was at the end of the path. Her feet made no sound on the path as she continued along it. It ran straight and true, on and on as if without end.

After walking on for a while, she noticed something in the far, far distance, distorted by the fog but definitely there. Freya walked unhurriedly onwards, the fog thinning as she approached whatever it was ahead of her. Suddenly a shaft of sunlight shone down and revealed in more detail what it was she had seen. Gates. Two big gates attached to two large pillars. The pillars were white, the gates black and made of wrought iron. The gates were closed. Freya walked towards the gates until she stood in front of them. She looked up at them as they towered above her.

Somehow she knew she must wait. How she knew, she did not know, only that she must. The area around the gates was bathed in sunlight, the fog still all around but not where she stood. She turned and looked back the way she had come, but the fog had grown even thicker and Freya knew she should not look back, but forward. What had gone before was past and could not be changed. Freya knew that. She must look to the future. She turned again to face the gates, which had silently opened inward while she had not been looking. Still she did not move. A little girl alone in the fog. She waited.

Movement. She could see movement. Something was approaching her from beyond the gates, coming slowly closer. The fog still swirled all around and it was also inside the gates where the movement continued. Freya strained her eyes, trying to see what was approaching her. She could now make out four shapes, two tall ones in the centre, two much smaller ones on the outside. Suddenly the fog parted and Freya could see more clearly. The smaller shapes on the outside were the two cats with the kind faces she had met before, when she had been floating towards the light. In the middle were her parents!

It was her mummy and daddy! They were there! Freya ran forward as the group passed through the gates and she threw herself into their arms and hugged them with all her might. She clung on to them as they kissed her and stroked her hair, speaking to her, telling her she was safe and they would always love her. After what seemed like a long time, they released her and Freya stood back and the cats came closer. Freya knelt down and hugged them one after the other, stroking their fur and their heads. The cats licked her face and purred with pleasure. Their faces beaming and filled with delight. Finally, Freya got to her feet and looked up at her mummy and daddy, waiting for them to speak again.

Her father knelt down and touched her face gently with his hand. "It's so good to see you again, Freya," he said, "we almost lost you for a while, but our new friends here helped us to get you back."

Her mother also knelt down and after giving her another hug, said, "We missed you so much, we just had to see you again. Our friends were kind enough to allow us this chance. This is Bob, and this is Lisa," gesturing to the two cats. The larger one held out his paw and said, "Hello, Freya, how lovely to see you as well." Freya shook the offered paw and turned to the smaller cat. She took the paw of the female and said, "Thank you for saving me, Lisa."

Lisa smiled and said," It was our pleasure to help you, you are a special little girl." Her father and mother stood and taking one of Freya's hands each, they walked to the side of the path where there was a bench. They sat down and Freya sat between them with the cats sitting on the ground, facing the bench.

Freya looked at the cats and said, "How can I hear your voices but you have not spoken?"

Lisa smiled and said, "We communicate using our thoughts directly to your mind, it is not necessary for us to speak as you do."

Freya nodded, understanding completely. She said, "You must be special cats to be able to do that!"

Her mother said, "They are very special cats, we are very lucky that they were able to help us."

"What has happened?" asked Freya. "We were driving to Uncle Lars and Aunty Rose's house and that's all I can remember, will we be there soon?"

Her father said, "We had an accident in the car, and Mummy and I were not able to complete our journey. Our new friends here were able to save you. "

"But what about you and mummy," said Freya, aren't you saved as well, I mean you are here now!"

Bob the cat said, "We were not able to save them as they used to be, as you used to know them, but they are still here, just on a higher level. They will exist in your mind and in your thoughts whenever you wish them too. You can also visit them every night in your dreams and tell them what you have been doing during the day. They just cannot be as they used to be anymore. "

Freya nodded, not completely understanding but trying to comprehend the situation.

"Are you dead?" asked Freya, in a small voice, looking at her mother and father. "But you are here, I can see you, touch you, hear you. I want to be with you all the time" she said. "Why can't I?" "Why can't we be together as we were before?" She looked at the cats and said, "If you are special cats, you can make it happen!"

Lisa said, "We can do many things, but we cannot change destiny. What has happened was meant to be. Even before you were born, this moment was going to happen. Every being has two lives. Your mummy and daddy are now starting their second life, a higher existence, while you must continue to live your earthly life. You will never be alone. They will always be nearby, to help and guide you. You will know when they are near, when you see the special number. It is a number that has much value in our world. It is also a number that holds special meaning for you."

"What is the special number?" asked Freya, curious to find out.

"It will become clearer to you soon," said her mother. "But please understand that although daddy and I will not be able to be physically with you anymore, we will not be far from you. Do not worry about us. We feel no pain. We know you will not forget us, and we will not forget you. We will still be there for you, when you have need for us. Uncle Lars and Aunty Rose will care for you, just as we would have done. They will love you and provide for you, just as we would have done. They have our full support and approval. They are waiting for you now. You must go to them and be happy. We really want you to be happy. Do not feel guilty that you have survived and we did not. We must go with Bob and Lisa. It is just how the Universe has decided it will be. "

"We have a gift for you, to remind you that we are close by, and that we will always love you," said her father. He gave Freya a small package, gift-wrapped in gold paper and tied up with a gold ribbon. "Open this on your next birthday and wear it whenever you can and think of us."

"We brought it from our home planet," said Bob. "It, like you is unique. Take it and remember us. Its size and shape is special. You will learn why when you are older."

"Thank you," said Freya, putting the package in her pocket.

Her parents and the cats sat with Freya for a long time, telling her things, explaining and reassuring her that all would be well. Freya tried to understand, but it was hard for a six-year-old to grasp what had happened. But finally Bob and Lisa got to their feet and Freya knew that the time was nearly up.

"We have one final thing to tell you," said her mother, looking directly into Freya's eyes.

"Trust us. What we have said to you is true. Trust in the bounty of the Universe. Trust in yourself. Trust your own judgement. Trust your instincts. Trust that we are close. Trust. This is not the end. This is the beginning of a new life for all of us. Trust in the Universe. It will never let you down. Trust. "

Freya nodded. She felt that somehow she understood. She was ready for what came next. As if by some unspoken command, Freya and her parents stood and together with the cats, walked slowly back towards the gates. Freya held her parents' hands again, the cats followed behind.

At the entrance to the gates, Freya knew that this was the final goodbye. She did not cry, because deep inside her she understood that her life must continue in another way, and her parents must leave her here. She wished it could be different. She wished she could turn back time and put things back the way they had been before. Deep down she knew that she could not.

They all hugged each other one final time, and then , with the cats leading the way, her mother and father slowly walked back through the gates and into the fog. Just before they were lost from view, they turned and waved. Freya waved back. The gates started to slowly close as the figures were lost in the mist.

The gates closed completely. Freya was alone again. She turned around and noticed that the fog was rapidly closing in towards her, getting thicker and thicker. Freya was not afraid. She had some inner strength that had not been there before. The fog was her friend. Once again she knew she must wait. Quickly the fog was all around her and she could see only its swirling greyness. She knew that this part of her journey was over, now she must go forward and face whatever lay ahead.

For a brief final moment more, Freya lingered, standing quite still in the fog. Then, taking a deep breath, she stepped forward and vanished in to the fog.

It was late Sunday afternoon, but Lars felt that he had been in the hospital for days. Earlier he had been for a quick stroll around the town and down by the Railway Station had found a cafe that was open. He found that he was starving and consumed a large breakfast before returning to the ward. Freya was still in a drugged sleep. Dr Thornton had said that when the consultant did his rounds in the morning, and was happy with what had been done, he would probably reduce the medication and Freya would awaken. Meanwhile, Lars sat back in his chair and continued to wait. Just in case she should wake early, he did not want Freya to awaken alone. But soon he became sleepy again, the meal and his fatigue making him doze and as the sun started to slide down lower in the western sky, he fell asleep again and began to dream once more.

But his dreams were not happy ones. He now knew that Freya would live, and all being well would be a healthy girl. But after she was well enough to leave hospital, what then? Where would she go? He would, of course like to be a guardian to the girl, and care for her. It was his duty, his brother and his wife would expect nothing less. Vikings take care of their family. But they had not met Rose, and now they never would. Lucky them. They did not know what she was like. She would not accept any responsibility whatsoever.

Rose would not want the child to be brought home. He was certain of that. But he could not allow his only niece to be placed in an orphanage. He just could not allow that. But what could he do. As he slipped further in to an exhausted sleep, his mind was whirling around and around, trying to find an answer. But try as he might, he could find none. As darkness fell once again, Lars Olsen racked his brains to try and solve his problem, but the problem had no solution. The problem was Rose.

They arrived promptly at Nine thirty on Monday Morning. Rose was not long up and in her dressing gown. She ignored the first knock, and the second. The third knock was reluctantly answered. "What do you want?" She asked indignantly, looking at the two smartly dressed visitors standing on the door step. There was a man and a woman. The man carried a briefcase. The lady had a clipboard. They looked every inch "Official". Just as they were supposed to. The man answered. "Mrs Olsen? Good morning. So sorry to disturb you." He held out his hand "We're from the Children's Department. May we have a few moments of your time?"

"It's about your niece, Freya," added the lady visitor.

Rose looked from one to the other, completely bewildered. "The Children's Department?" She asked, reluctantly shaking the outstretched hand, then shaking the hand of the lady as well.

The two visitors nodded their heads in unison. "That's correct, Mrs Olsen. We're here on a preliminary visit, just to see if you will be taking the child in, or if we will have to make arrangements with the orphanage," said the lady.

"It won't take long," added the man.

Rose, still not quite with it said, "Orphanage? Surely the child will return to Norway?"

"I'm afraid not," said the man. "There's no relatives there to look after her, we will, of course need to speak to your husband also, but as we know he's at the hospital and as we were in the area anyway, we thought we would see what you said."

"I see," said Rose, not seeing at all. "You'd better come in then," opening the door wider and standing aside. "I'm afraid you'll have to take me as you find me, I wasn't expecting anyone."

"Thank you, Mrs Olsen," said the lady with a smile, stepping inside the cottage, followed by the man, who closed the door behind him. They went into the front room, where the rare visitors they got these days would be entertained, and sat down. Rose did not offer refreshments. She was still confused, caught off guard by this sudden turn of events. She had no way of knowing that that was exactly what the visitors had intended. She also did not realise that there had been no contact whatsoever with any form of "Officialdom." She did not know that the wheels of government turn very slowly, or that the visitors were not what they seemed. The visitors, on the other hand were very happy with how things had gone so far. They had gained entry to the cottage and most importantly, made skin contact with Rose once each. That might well be enough already, but to be sure another handshake would be required. Normally they could change a human mind with just a look, but in their weakened state, they must make actual contact with this woman to be quite sure.

The visitors chatted about what it would entail to look after a child, the extra effort required, mostly by Rose herself. She would bear the lion's share of the duties. Extra cooking, washing, cleaning, taking and collecting the child from school were just some of the many things that Rose would have to attend to. And there would be an increased financial burden as well. Rose sat, listening as the lady with the clipboard went through these and other points. It was beginning to dawn on her that having a child around was a lot of work. Work that she, Rose would be expected to do. Work that she could well do without. Rose knew what decision would be made about the child, no matter what Lars said. Freya would go to the Orphanage. Definitely.

Finally after about half an hour, the visitors concluded their business and asked that Rose talk to her husband and consider what they had said. Rose nodded her head. The Orphanage seemed by far the better option. Not for the child or her husband, but for herself, which was the only thing that she was concerned about. As the visitors stood to go, they again shook hands with Rose before taking their leave. As she closed the door, Rose noticed that the man had hairs growing out of the tops of his ears. Like Tufts.

A man who lived across the road and had seen the visitors arrive through his lace curtain, was now in his front garden, pretending to sweep the path so he could see who had visited number twenty-nine It would be something he could tell his pals about in the Post Office later on. The visitors saw him and walked across to his gate, asking for directions back to the village. He told them the way and they both insisted on shaking his hand while thanking him for his kind help. They walked off down the road in the direction he had indicated. He watched them go and was surprised when they turned left instead of right as he had said. By going left they would go down an alley that only led onto the moors. He waited for them to realise their mistake and reappear and take the correct road. They did not come back.

After five minutes the man went inside, suddenly feeling a wave of fatigue wash over him. He sat in his chair and was almost instantly asleep. He woke twenty minutes later and went to make a cup of tea. While the kettle boiled he peered out of the front window behind the lace curtain. Nothing. Not even a cat or dog was to be seen. The kettle boiled and he moved back into the kitchen. His memory of the last hour had gone. He would never get it back. Across the road in number twenty-nine, Rose Olsen was also feeling suddenly weary. She had finished her breakfast and was sitting in an armchair in the front room, thinking about what the visitors had told her. The note that Lars had left for her the night before was on the coffee table. Just as she started to fall asleep, she remembered thinking it was a bit strange that both of the officials had had green eyes.

Rose awoke in her armchair and for a few moments she did not know where she was. Her eyes focused on the clock on the mantel piece. It said it was eleven o'clock exactly. She looked down and wondered why she was still in her dressing gown at this time of the morning, then she noticed the note lying on the coffee table. She picked it up and read it again, suddenly remembering that she was alone and that Lars was at the Hospital. Then she remembered the phone call of the previous morning and gave a gasp of horror. Her brother-in-law and his wife were dead, and the little girl's life was hanging by a thread. Yet here she was on a Monday morning at eleven o'clock and still in her dressing gown. How could that be? She got up from the chair and suddenly felt dizzy.

She held on to the sideboard for a moment and steadied herself. A wave of nausea swept over her and she felt as if she was going to be sick. She started to retch, over and over again. It would not stop. Her eyes were dripping with tears from the dry retching. She pulled a tissue from the pocket of her dressing gown and dried her eyes, taking several deep breaths to calm herself. Rose had no way of knowing that she was just starting to release a lifetime of negative emotion. Finally the retching subsided and finally stopped. Rose walked slowly into the kitchen and drank a glass of water straight down, burping loudly at the end. Pardon me, she thought, as a wave of warmth swept over her, making her face flushed. She immediately felt better.

She looked around the kitchen, as if seeing it for the first time. It was spotless, but she could not remember cleaning it. She opened a cupboard and saw the shelves stocked with tins, but could not remember buying any of it. She felt disoriented, lost, like a stranger in her own home. Rose shook herself and stood upright. She knew what she would do. She would dress and go to the hospital and take Lars some sandwiches and a change of clothing. He would need a shave by now too.

Rose left the kitchen and went slowly upstairs to change, holding carefully on to the bannister rail as she climbed. She did not realise that she had, for the first time ever thought of someone else's needs and not her own. She had no memory of her visitors earlier that morning and never would have. The Rose Olsen that had awoken that morning had gone forever. A new Rose now had taken her place. A much better Rose.

As she began to select her clothes, she ran her tongue over her teeth and wondered why they were furry. She walked into the bathroom and reached for her toothbrush, a second wave of nausea swept over her again and she had to hold on to the sides of the sink as the retching started again. Like the first time, it went on for a long time before subsiding again. Rose felt drained. As before, once the retching had stopped, a warm pleasant sensation swept over her, making her feel happy.

She wiped her eyes and then looked at the reflection in the mirror. A chubby face that had perhaps, once been pretty looked back at her, the eyes red and moist from the violent retching. It was a strange face. She touched her cheeks with her fingers, turning left and right, noticing the double chin and the bags under her eyes. It was like seeing a stranger. Feeling unsettled and unsteady, she reached for the toothpaste and began to clean her teeth, looking with surprise at the blood dripping over the handle of the toothbrush and splashing into the sink. She had no memory of when she had cleaned them last. She would have been surprised to learn that it was just after Easter, six months ago! She finished her teeth and with a last look in the mirror, returned to her bedroom and began to dress. She had a busy day ahead.

Chapter Five

Freya opened her eyes. Images swam before her, vague and unfocused. She closed her eyes again against the brightness that was around her. She could hear something. It had a familiar sound to it, but she was not sure what it could be. She opened her eyes again and they began to focus a little better. She was lying in a bed. The bed was in a room of some kind. The light seemed so bright. She moved her head slightly and tried to see what else there was in the room. The noise was still there, and she turned her head towards where she thought it was. Her eyes came into focus for a brief moment, long enough for her to see what was making the noise. It was a person. Someone else was in the room with her. She could not make out who it was, only that it was a man. A man in a chair. The noise came again and finally Freya identified what it was. It was the sound of snoring! As her eyes closed again and she sank down into the blackness, she wondered who it was making the noise, but her mind was unable to process the thought and the darkness took over once more. In his chair in the corner of the room, Lars Olsen also slept on.

Freya awoke again, how much later she did not know. Again she had trouble focusing her eyes and getting her bearings. She could not hear the noise from before. She looked towards the place where the man had been, but the chair was empty. Had she imagined it? She did not know. Freya moved her head and noticed for the first time that there was something stuck in her arm, which was connected to a bottle on a stand by a tube. Where was this place? Her mind was so slow. Gradually she began to understand. She was in a hospital. Which meant she was alive. She began to try to say the words but her mouth and lips were so dry she could only croak. There was movement at the foot of the bed and as she turned her head to see what it was, the shape came in to focus and moved nearer.

It was the man. She looked at him as he came closer. He was big and blond with blue eyes and looked like her father. He had a smile on his face. "Papa?" croaked Freya. The smile faded. The man moved away and she could hear him calling for someone. Soon a new face came into focus, a lady this time. She was wearing a white cap and Freya could feel something cool and wet on her dry and cracked lips and in her mouth. She swallowed gratefully and moved her mouth. She tried to speak again. "I'm alive" she said. The lady frowned and turned to the man who looked like her father but was not.

"What is she saying?" asked Sister Grey. The man moved closer and put his ear closer to Freya.

Freya tried again. "I'm alive," she said.

The man smiled and replied, "Yes, little one, you are alive. You are safe here. I am Lars, your uncle." The man turned to the lady with the white cap and said in English. "She said she is alive."

The Lady smiled and nodded. "Yes, you are alive and going to get better," she said in English. Freya frowned, not quite understanding. "Why is the lady speaking English?" croaked Freya in Norwegian. Lars replied in the same language.

"Because you are in England, little one, don't you remember?"

Freya licked her lips as more drops of water were put in her mouth by the lady in the white cap. "England? Why am I in England?"

"Do not worry about that, little one," said Lars taking her tiny white hand in his huge one. "You must rest and get well. I will be close by. Trust me."

Freya smiled as she started to drift back into sleep. "Yes, I understand, that's what Mummy and Daddy said and the Cats."

"What did she say?" asked Sister Grey, looking at Lars.

"Something about her mother and father and cats," said Lars.

"Cats?" asked Sister Grey.

"That's what it sounded like," said Lars.

"She's confused and needs to rest. So go back to your chair and I'll have one of my nurses sit with her. "

Lars nodded and with a last look at Freya, walked back to his chair and sat down. His mind was whirling. He had held the child's hand and in so doing had bonded with her. There was no way in hell he would ever put her in to an orphanage. Never! Lars sat back in his chair and took a deep breath. Whatever it took, Freya was coming home with him! Sister Grey was writing on one of the charts that hung on the bottom of the bed. She noted the time that Freya had first woken and also amended one of the items of information that had been filled in incorrectly from before. Colour of eyes. Green.

Monday morning had dawned clear and bright. The easier ways of the weekend at the hospital had gone and in its place was the sharper routine of the working day. Dr Thornton and Sister Grey walked up the corridor behind the flapping white coat of the Consultant. They made their way first to the intensive care ward where Freya slept her drugged sleep. Of Lars there was no sign. He had been asked politely but firmly to remove himself to the waiting room as the Consultant was due in soon and would be doing his rounds. The five feet two inch nurse had encouraged the six foot five inch Lars that she would not take no for an answer. He went.

He sat in the waiting room as the Consultant and his followers swept by the window. Sister Grey signalled that they would come back and see him a little later. He nodded his understanding and stayed in his seat.

The Consultant picked up the chart from the bottom of the bed and scanned the pages. He turned to Dr Thornton and said, "Humm, this girl is lucky to be alive. How the hell did she survive a crash like that and get out of a burning car? You did very well to save her, Dr Thornton."

"That's just it, Sir, I don't know what I did. She was slipping away like her parents when suddenly she started to pick up. I have never seen anything like it. I'd like to take the credit, but somehow, she just came back to life!"

"Well, what ever happened, she's getting stronger. We can start to reduce the medication, little by little. I'll look in again tomorrow." He wrote on the chart before handing it back to Sister Grey.

"Right, Sister, let's go to the wards." And with that he left the room and with white coat flapping once again headed off down the corridor, with Sister Grey and Dr Thornton following on behind.

As they passed the waiting room again, Sister Grey looked through the window at Lars and gave a thumbs up sign.

He nodded his thanks and sat back. Thank the gods she was going to be OK. He knew that Sister Grey would be back before she went off duty later. So he sat back in his chair and waited.

Rose locked the front door and headed for the bus stop. She carried a heavy bag, full with clean clothes, underwear and toiletries. There was also a plastic container full of rolls and a flask of tea.

As she walked down the road she wondered how the child was doing and how Lars was bearing up. What a mess. She arrived at the bus shelter and thankfully set the bag down and waited for the bus to Abbotsbury. As it was Monday, they were not frequent. Only market day on Wednesday was there a decent service. At least the weather was still good, warm and sunny.

It was not long before someone else entered the bus shelter and waited for the bus to Abbotsbury. It was Mr Jenkins, an elderly gentleman who had lived in Elfington all his life. He moved closer to Rose and said, "I was so sorry to hear about your brother-in-law and his wife, terrible news."

"Thank you, I am just going to the hospital now," said Rose, not the least surprised that he knew what had happened. She had also lived in the village all her life, and knew all too well just how efficient the village grape vine was. You could not keep a secret here for long.

"I hope the little lass gets better soon," prompted Mr Jenkins, who was hoping that Rose would reveal some more details that were not already known and that he could gossip about over a pint later in the evening.

"I'm sure she will, thank you," said Rose, who could now thankfully see the bus approaching in the distance and began to get the fare from her handbag.

Mr Jenkins nodded, trying not to look too disappointed, now that he had not learned anything new to pass on. Never mind, he could always make something up, he thought.

The bus stopped and they got on, Rose sitting near the front by the window and kept her head turned away from the other passengers, looking at the landscape so as to discourage any conversation, as the bus went along. The journey should not take long as it was about five miles to Abbotsbury and some of the bus stops were empty and the bus continued uninterrupted.

Rose did not feel like talking. She felt a little dizzy and hoped she would not be sick on the bus. She was still trying to take in the enormity of what had happened over the weekend and what it meant for her and Lars. One thing was for sure. Life was never going to be the same again!

The Bus pulled into the town centre with a squeal of brakes and the driver turned the engine off, signalling to those who did not know, that this was the end of the line. Rose waited until all the other passengers had alighted before getting off the bus and making her way towards the hospital. It was getting hotter as she walked along, the sun still having power in the late summer afternoon. Rose was soon out of breath, but she did not know why.

The hospital was on the edge of town, next to the moors, which was why she had not taken the train, and it took Rose a while to reach the gates, her legs letting her know that they were not used to this much exercise. Rose wondered how much exercise she had done before today, she had no memory of doing any at all. That would have to change, she thought. She walked into the cool of the hospital entrance and looked at the signs that pointed this way and that, telling the visitors that the X-ray department was to the left and the wards were to the right. Rose turned right and started to walk down a long corridor. The floor was painted red. The walls were pale green. The smell was universal. Even a blind man would know that he was in a hospital without being told.

As she walked along, she noticed that other corridors joined on to the main one she was on. As she approached one junction, a bed came around the corner pushed by a porter. There was an old lady in the bed covered by a red blanked. Rose moved aside to let them pass. In the distance a man approached on crutches, moving around a wheelchair that had been abandoned by the wall. The hospital was a busy place. Finally Rose saw a door with a sign over it that said "Ward Sister's Office". Rose headed for that. As she approached the door a tall slim lady emerged wearing a light coat as if going outside. She saw Rose and turned towards her and said.

"Can I help you? You look lost!"

Rose smiled and said, "Thank you, I am lost. I am trying to find my husband. He's here somewhere. His family were brought here over the weekend after they were involved in an accident. "

The tall lady nodded. "You must be Mrs Olsen then."

"Why yes, I am," said Rose in surprise. "How did you know?"

"I am Sister Grey. I was just going off duty. I was here when they were brought in. I will take you to where you husband is. He will be pleased to see you. Just follow me." And Sister Grey guided Rose to the Intensive Care Unit, where they found Lars asleep in his chair.

As the two women had walked along, Sister Grey had said, "I am so sorry that we could not save your brother-in-law and his wife, but they were just too badly injured in the crash. It was a miracle that the little girl survived. She will need a lot of care and attention for quite a while before she is well enough to go home."

Rose nodded. "At least she is still alive!

"Thank goodness for that," agreed Sister Grey, as they approached the Intensive Care Ward.

She touched Lars gently on the shoulder and he awoke with a start, but smiled when he saw who it was. The smile vanished as Sister Grey moved to one side and he saw Rose. What was she doing here, he thought angrily. Probably run out of clean plates and wants me to go home and wash up!

Sister Grey saw the look and noticed that they did not attempt to kiss or even touch each other.

So that's how it was.

"Well then, I must be going. I'll leave you two to chat. I'll be back tomorrow to see how little Freya is doing." And with that Sister Grey walked out of the door and was gone.

Rose looked at Lars and said, "I had to come. I have brought you some clean clothes and your razor. Food too!"

Lars was surprised. "Thank you." He could not remember the last time that Rose had done anything for him. A sound from the bed made them both turn towards it. Freya's eyes were open and she was looking at them. They moved to the bed, one on each side.

Rose looked down at the small child in the bed. She looked pale and wan. There was a drip in one arm and she was wired up to a monitor which stood next to the bed. She had a bruise on her head which was turning yellow and blue below a bandage on her head. Her golden blond hair was spread out over the pillow. Her arms were outside the sheets and Rose could see cuts on both of them. The small white hands were still. She was battered and bruised. But alive. Only her eyes moved as they followed Rose as she moved closer and gently stroked Freya's hair. Lars looked on, astonished.

Freya smiled. The plump lady had a concerned look on her face.

"You must be Aunty Rose. They said you would come. They said you would take care of me."

"Who said?" asked Lars in surprise.

"Mummy and Daddy said, and the Cats," replied Freya

"Cats?" asked Rose puzzled.

"Yes, there are two of them. They saved me."

Rose's heart was breaking as she gazed at the small, battered girl. She could feel the tears welling up and falling down her cheeks and making darker circles on the white sheet.

She took the small white hand in hers and said, "The Cats were right. As soon as you are well enough, you will be coming home with Uncle Lars and me."

Freya squeezed Rose's hand gently, her eyes starting to close again. Before she drifted off to sleep again, she whispered. "Thank you. I'm getting better already!"

Lars nodded to Rose and they both moved away from the bed and back to the chair in the corner. Lars was frowning. "You should not get the child's hopes up. We both know that you have no intention of having the girl at home with us, as much as I would like to have her."

Rose looked at Lars and was shocked. "I do want to have her with us. She is your flesh and blood, we must do what's right for her."

"Really? I can't see you getting her ready for school on a wet and cold day, and washing and ironing her clothes. You don't even do it for me. There's no way you would shift yourself away from the telly, and we both know it," said Lars bitterly, the stress, strain and emotion causing him to speak his mind. Sod the consequences. What could she do to him that would be worse than this?

Rose was silent. Then she reached for her bag and took out the clothes and food she had brought with her and gave them to Lars who took them and put them on the chair.

Rose said, "Why not go and have a wash and shave, then change your clothes. You'll feel better then. When you come back you can have some food. I'll keep an eye on Freya. And Lars, I will prove to you that I mean what I say. By the time Freya is ready to leave here, you will see that I have changed."

Lars took the clothes and toiletries and headed for the washroom. He was too tired to argue at the moment, but he was not convinced. It would be a miracle if Rose had turned over a new leaf, and he didn't believe in miracles.

Inspector Pitt sat at his desk, a frown on his face. His officers had checked every garage, petrol station, car repair shop and MOT station in and around the scene of the crash. They had found nothing. The search had been extended to Abbotsbury and surrounding areas, but again nothing. The car had vanished. He knew that it could not have gone too far in a damaged condition and would have attracted attention in the daylight. It had to be fairly close by. But, as yet, it had not been found. His men would keep looking and talking to people. Someone must have seen it. Someone knew where it was. The local paper was due out on Thursday. Details of the crash and the car the police were looking for would be on the front page. He hoped that would bring results.

The local newspaper did indeed come out on Thursdays, and Bob and Lisa tried to read it every week. It helped them to know what was going on. Information is power. The car crash was on the front page in some detail. But for them, it would read differently. But it was not that story that caught their eye. It was an article inside on page seven

PANTHER ON THE LOOSE.

"Tracks that are believed to belong to a wild panther have been found at Abbotsbury Hospital. Mr Wilfred Hanson, head gardener at the hospital, found them in a flower bed on Monday morning and reported it to us the same day. The police had been informed and have advised that pets should be secured at night and that those readers with cats might wish to consider not putting them out at night until this matter is investigated.

In a separate development, another witness, who does not want to be identified, said he saw a "Panther-like Cat" up on the wold, with a rabbit in its mouth, when he was walking his dog. The creature was jet black and powerful looking. "

Lisa and Bob looked at each other in dismay. Lisa said, "It must have been me, I was so tired from giving my energy to the child that I must have got careless."

Bob nodded. "Everyone makes mistakes, even us! But there is no harm done. No one saw us and if the humans want to look out for a black panther, good luck to them!"

Lisa agreed but they both knew they had made a mistake, but had got away with it. Another lesson learned!

Lars returned from the washroom feeling almost human again. A wash, a shave and clean teeth had done wonders. The fresh clothes Rose had brought felt good. He felt a bit guilty about what he had said earlier, even though it had been true.

Rose was sitting next to the bed, looking at Freya, even though she was asleep. She stood and walked towards Lars as he returned to the room. "You look a lot better," she said.

"I feel better, thank you for coming and bringing everything, it was a nice surprise. I wasn't expecting you."

"I know, but I had to come and see you, and to say how sorry I am about your brother and his wife. I can't imagine how you must feel. "

Lars nodded, his face sad. "At least I have little Freya."

"We have little Freya," said Rose. "I meant what I said before. I really do want to bring her home with us. I know what you must think of me, and I don't blame you. But since the accident I have had a lot of time to think. To look at myself. I didn't like what I saw. I can only say that I will really try to be a good Aunty to the little girl. And more of a wife to you."

Rose looked up at Lars, tears running down her face. For the second time that day, Lars was completely shocked. Rose didn't cry. Rose didn't show emotion. Rose didn't care. He stepped forward and put his arms around Rose who clung to him, her head against his chest. He was lost for words. This was totally unexpected. They had not embraced for so long, Lars could not remember when the last time had been. Finally they stood back from each other and Rose wiped her eyes. "I don't know what's come over me today, I'll try and do better," said Rose as she blew her nose.

Lars looked at her and said, "I like this Rose better than the one I left at home on Saturday. I hope she is here to stay. I need her."

Rose nodded as she began to put Lars' dirty clothes in her bag to take home.

"She's here to stay. I can't explain it, but it's like I've suddenly woken up and realised what I've got, what I have to loose. Try to believe me, Lars, I know it will take time to convince you, but please give me a chance to prove myself."

Lars lifted his hand to her face and gently tilted her chin up until she was looking directly into his eyes. He held her gaze for a long moment, looking for deceit, for lies. He could find none. A miracle had happened. Finally he smiled down at her. "Agreed!"

From the bed, two green eyes took in the scene at the foot of her bed. She smiled. From the depths of despair, a little ray of hope had appeared. The eyes closed again. Freya slept on.

Lars stayed at the hospital for a few more days and nights, while Rose made the journey to the hospital each day, bringing food and clean clothes for Lars. He could have walked into Abbotsbury to eat, or even got the bus home for a rest, but until Freya was really out of danger, he opted to stay at the hospital. To be close. Freya continued to improve and after two more days in the intensive care ward, she was moved to an ordinary ward. The drips and monitors were gone and she was starting to eat some solid food again. They had placed her in a small ward of four beds, and hers was nearest the nurse's table. The other women in the ward were all recovering from minor surgery and all made a fuss of her like she was their own child.

They took it in turns to sit and watch over her, while Lars snoozed in the chair next to the bed. Sister Grey was ever present, as this was another of the wards for which she was responsible. Now that the intensive care ward was empty, she could spend more time here. Thankfully the intensive care ward was little used.

It was on a Friday lunchtime that Rose returned once again with supplies. She also bought the local newspaper. Making sure that Freya did not see, she took Lars to one side and showed him the headlines.

FAMILY SLAIN. TWO DEAD IN HORROR CAR SMASH. CHILD'S LIFE HANGS IN THE BALANCE.

There was a picture of the accident, of the wrecked Morris Traveller Van. The story began with, "The family of popular local milkman Lars Olsen were killed in a tragic car crash late on Saturday night."

"Police scouring county for the other car that was involved. Inspector Pitt of Abbotsbury Police appeals for information".

Lars looked up, unable to read any more. The local press had done their work only too well, a reporter had even come to the hospital and tried to speak to Lars. Now everyone would know.

Rose took the paper from him and put it in her bag. "Don't worry, Lars. The locals will gossip about it for a while until something else takes their attention. "

Lars nodded, knowing that she was right, but still feeling angry that his family were the talking point of the general public. It didn't help.

He said, "I'm glad you're here, I have news to tell you. The authorities have released the bodies of Anders and Marit. I can take them home, back to Norway whenever I wish. Sister Grey has kindly let me use her telephone and I have arranged for the local Undertakers to make the necessary arrangements. They will do everything, contact the authorities in Norway and I can travel with them. But I need to know that you will continue to visit Freya and be there for her while I am gone. "

Rose nodded at once. "Of course I will Lars, you can count on me." And strangely enough, Lars knew he probably could. A week ago, he would not have trusted Rose to open the curtains in the morning, let alone to visit his only living relative in hospital. Since Rose had first visited the hospital on Monday afternoon, she had changed. The fact that she had come at all was completely out of character for her, and to have brought clothes and food was beyond belief. Rose just didn't do that. Yet, here she was, for the fifth day in a row, bringing things in for him.

Who was this strange woman, who looked like Rose but actually seemed to care? Was she an imposter? A fake? He didn't know. Somehow the Rose he had met and married had returned, just when he needed her. His prayers to the Gods seemed to have been answered. Maybe it wouldn't last, maybe she would revert back to her old ways again. He hoped not. Things had changed for him also. He had Freya to take care of. Things would not, could not, go back to the way they had been just one week ago. In any case Freya would be under the care of the hospital for a while yet, she would be fed and looked after, whether Rose had a relapse back to her old ways or not. He knew he could rely on Sister Grey.

Lars smiled and said, "Thank you, Rose. It is a weight of my mind to know you are here with Freya. I will return as soon as I have done what needs to be done. "

Freya awoke just then and they moved over to her bedside. She was able to sit up now. Close by her bed, in the shade was her Troll. Sister Grey had brought it up from her office when she had moved Freya out of the intensive care ward. He was too grubby to be allowed in there.

But here he was, and Freya was so glad to have him with her. He was a reminder of happier times. Before.

The weekend passed and Lars got the call from the funeral people on Monday. The arrangements had been made. He would leave on Wednesday morning.

He could not know that another pair of eyes had already read the local paper's headlines and knew that Inspector Pitt would find no trace of the other car. It was where he would never find it. He had managed to nurse it back to its hiding place before anyone saw him or the car. He had been very lucky. With only a few cuts and a sore leg, he had escaped injury. Within a few weeks the police would move on to other crimes and things would settle down as before. He had got away with it.

And so it was that Lars began the journey back to his homeland, together with his brother and sister-in-law, retracing the route they had taken on their way to see him. He would never have imagined two weeks ago that he would be doing this. You never know what is around the corner. How true that was. He had been away for almost four years and had always wanted to return home for a visit, but not like this.

The next week was a busy one. Lars stayed in his brother's house while he was in Norway. He arranged for Freya's clothes and toys to be shipped to England. The house was rented and furnished. He gave the landlord the keys back at the end of the week. He visited his brother's employer, his bank and somehow got through the funeral service. There were people there he had not seen in many years. The little church was packed. Anders and Marit were well known and respected. They were not regular church goers, but it did not matter.

On the final day he went to Freya's school and saw the head teacher. They had of course heard the awful news by then and Freya's class had made a get-well card for her and the pupils had all signed it. Lars was really touched. He told the head teacher that Freya would, at least in the short term, be staying in England with him to fully recover. What would happen after that, he did not know. It was, he told himself, down to Mrs Rose Olsen. The future was uncertain, but if he had to choose between Freya and Rose, he knew which way he would go.

When everything was finally done, and after a last visit to the grave, Lars Olsen picked up his suitcase and headed back to England. What happened next was in the hands of the Gods.

While Lars was away in Norway, Rose kept her word and visited Freya every day. She had done her best to explain to Freya where Uncle Lars had gone. Freya had seemed to understand and knew that her mother and father were gone, and that she must face life without them. It made Rose realise that Freya had never asked her where they were or why they did not come to see her. How did a six-year-old deal with that?

Sister Grey was magnificent. She had spent a lot of time with Freya when Rose had returned home, even staying on after her shift was over. She had helped Freya to wash and to start to walk around the ward, slowly at first, but a little more each day. By the end of the week Freya had even been outside for a short while on a warm afternoon with Rose and Sister Grey. They had sat on a bench in the grounds of the hospital, not far from the ward. The Troll had stayed behind. Freya had explained that they must not be taken out in the sunlight. After twenty minutes they had returned indoors, but it had done Freya good to go out. There was more colour in her cheeks now and she was eating well.

It never ceased to amaze Sister Grey how young children seemed to bounce back from serious injury. They recovered much quicker than adults did. Freya in particular was a star patient. She did everything that Dr Thornton asked her to do, eating when she wasn't really hungry in order to gain strength. Drinking lots of fluid and engaging with everyone, to the limit of her English. Sister Grey also got to know Rose a little better. She could tell that Rose was not used to being around children, but did her best anyway. Lars had mentioned that they did not have any children of their own, a situation not of his making, Sister Grey was sure.

It would not be long now before Freya would be allowed to go home. When Lars returned she should be nearly ready. Sister Grey would miss Freya. There was something about that child, a fierce determination to get well, and not to be too sad. Lars would be a fantastic Uncle, she was sure. Rose would have a lot to learn.

Lars returned to the hospital on Thursday afternoon, still carrying his suitcase. He looked worn out, but was pleased to see how much better Freya looked. He had brought the card the children had made with him and gave it to Freya. He had a lump in his throat and his eyes were moist as he watched Freya sitting in her bed, holding the card in her little hands and reading what her class mates had written. He was surprised when Rose took his hand in hers and gave it a squeeze. He smiled at her, pleased by the gesture.

He was not used to Rose showing affection. He stayed until the end of visiting hours and for the first time went home with Rose. They rode the bus home in silence, each lost in their own thoughts. It was dark when they finally arrived at the cottage.

Lars went into the kitchen and started to fill the kettle, but was surprised when Rose took it from him and told him to sit down and she would make the tea. Lars did as he was told, too tired to protest. Old habits die hard, he was so used to doing everything himself.

Lars was surprised to see that the washing up had been done. He had almost expected it to be waiting for him. He was also half expecting Rose to say that she had been thinking while he had been away, and perhaps it was not such a good idea for the child to come here after all.

The tea appeared, together with a plate of ham sandwiches. Rose came and sat down and watched him eat. The bread was fresh, she had bought it that morning. Rose was so glad he was back, she had missed him more than she had realised.

There was a pile of mail to be looked at, most of which were cards from people in the village saying how sorry they were to hear of the crash and the loss of the two people. But they could wait until the morning. All Lars wanted to do was sleep and he went up to bed and slept like a log, the morning could wait. Rose locked up and went up a little later. She looked down at the sleeping Lars and thanked her lucky stars that he was home, safe and sound. She knew that she had a lot of work to do to earn his trust again. She was worried that if she did not measure up, Lars might take Freya back to Norway and stay there with her. She would do her best to prevent that.

She climbed into bed and lay next to Lars. Her mind went back to before the accident. How had she treated him like she had? How had he put up with it? How had she suddenly changed? She did not know the answers. Out of something terrible, something good had also happened. She had been given a new direction in life, one that she never had thought possible. One that a few weeks ago she would not have wanted. But now, she saw things in a totally different light. She would make this work. She had to. There was no going back to the way things had been before, for any of them. She set her alarm clock and turned off the light.

Chapter Six

Lars awoke to the smell of bacon in the air. He turned in the bed but Rose was not there. Yet again he was surprised. She had never cooked breakfast before, or indeed any meal that he could remember. He had slept well. He looked at the clock. Nine o'clock. He had slept for nearly twelve hours. He put on his dressing gown and went downstairs. Rose was in the kitchen. She looked up as he approached and smiled. "Good Morning! You look like you had a good sleep." Lars nodded. "I did, thank you. I needed that."

"Tea?"

"Please."

Rose put a mug of tea next to him and sat down. "I've had mine, so when you have had your tea, go and wash and I will prepare yours, then we can catch the eleven o'clock bus to Abbotsbury. "

Lars sat and drank his tea, watching Rose as she moved about. As she moved past him he took her hand, stopping her. "What has happened to you, Rose? You never did these things for me before. What has made you change?"

Rose looked down at him and shook her head. "I can't explain it to myself, let alone to you. After I got your phone call on the Sunday morning, I was fine. But the next day, just before I came to see you at the Hospital in the afternoon, I came over all weary. I must have fallen asleep for a while because I woke up in the front room with a fuzzy head and felt like being sick. It passed after a while and then I just started to do things. It was really strange. It was as if I had been reprogrammed. I just knew what I had to do. Ever since then, I just feel so energised. I look at things in a different way than I did before. I know it sounds strange, but that's what it feels like. "

Lars let her hand go and stood up. "Then it seems that some good has come from this after all. I did not like the Rose that was here before very much. This new model seems much improved. Is she here to stay or just visiting?"

"She is here to stay, if you want her to," said Rose, in a small voice, looking at the floor. Lars lifted her chin again, as he had at the hospital, and looked in her eyes. He saw no deceit, no lies. Just Rose. Rose as she had been when he had first seen her. By some miracle the girl he had fallen in love with had returned.

"I want her to."

"Thank you, you don't know how good that sounds. Now go and wash!"

Lars kissed her on the cheek. "Yes, Ma'am!" and went back upstairs. Rose turned and walked to the kitchen window and for a long moment looked out towards the moors. The sun was shining. She took a deep breath. It was going to be a nice day. She had been given a second chance, she knew. She did not intend to waste it. It came as a surprise to realise that she did not like the old Rose much either. She thought of her own mother and saw herself. As she had been. She would not go back to that.

Rose turned back to the cooker and began to prepare the breakfast for Lars. How many men would have put up with her the way he had, she asked herself. Not many. She would make it up to him. Starting with breakfast!

They caught the eleven o'clock bus and arrived at the hospital around noon. It was almost lunch time and the trolley was doing the rounds, its smells making the patients mouths water, well most of them, anyway. Dr Thornton was waiting for them.

"Good News, Lars," he said. "The consultant has been around this morning and he has agreed with me that Freya can be discharged tomorrow morning. "

Lars and Rose exchanged a look. "Are you sure?" said Rose in surprise.

Dr Thornton nodded. "Physically she is ready to go, emotionally we don't really know. But we think she will get stronger in a home environment rather than a hospital one. We haven't told her yet, we thought that you might like to do it."

"Thank you, we'll go and see her now," said Lars.

Dr Thornton nodded and moved off, and Rose and Lars went into the ward to find Freya tucking into Shepherd's Pie. She was sitting in the chair next to her bed, with a table in front of her. She smiled as she saw them approach. "What's it like?" asked Lars, sitting on the bed.

"Good," said Freya, shovelling the minced meat into her mouth.

Lars looked at Rose and gave her a "You can tell her" gesture.

"Well," said Rose, sitting next to Lars, "I'll have to see if you like the way I do it."

The fork stopped midway between the plate and Freya's mouth.

"I can leave?"

"Yes," said Lars. "In the morning. Dr Thornton says you are strong enough to try Aunty Rose's cooking!"

Freya was thoughtful for a moment.

"If I come to your house, will I be able to have herring?" she asked in a serious voice.

"Well, I don't have any at the moment, but I am sure I could get some," said Rose, caught unaware.

Freya put down her fork and touched Rose's hand. "Don't bother, I don't really like them!" and smiled at their worried faces.

Lars and Rose visibly relaxed. Freya had made a joke! Dr Thornton was right. Freya was ready to take the next step on the road to recovery.

Lars and Rose spent the rest of the day with Freya and left at the end of visiting time. Rose had helped Freya choose what clothes she would wear in the morning. Her suitcase had been brought to the hospital by the police after they had recovered it from the crash site. After they had gone, Freya lay in bed and was suddenly apprehensive. Apart from a couple of trips out to the hospital grounds, Freya had been in the hospital all the time. She was used to it, there were always doctors or nurses around if she needed them. It was safe, secure. No one could hurt her in here. Suddenly the thought of going out into the world without them was a bit daunting. She had no idea what lay beyond the Hospital grounds. It also hit her that she was not going back home to Norway. There was no home in Norway, not any more. The reality of her situation was suddenly clear. She would not be going back to her old school, or see her old friends, at least not for a while, until Uncle Lars and Aunty Rose decided what to do. She reached out and cuddled her troll. He would look after her, he always had. She would have to put him in the suitcase if it was a sunny day. Just before she settled down, a single word popped into her mind. Trust! She trusted Uncle Lars and Aunty Rose. What would be, would be. She finally fell asleep with her troll in her arms. Tomorrow would be a big day!

On Saturday morning, Lars and Rose arrived after Breakfast at nine o'clock. Lars had managed to borrow a car from a friend at the dairy and parked it in the near-empty car park. Freya was ready. She was dressed and sitting in her chair holding on to her troll when they walked into the ward. When Rose saw her, her heart was full of emotion. It reminded Rose of the Films about the Second World War, when the children were being evacuated. Freya sat in her chair, swinging her legs, which did not touch the floor, ready to be shipped out. All she needed was a label on her coat and a gas mask, and it could be 1940. It made Rose aware of the responsibility she now had to bring up this child. No wonder Lars had doubted her, when she said she had wanted to have Freya home with them. Rose took a deep breath and went to collect Freya, while Lars picked up the suitcase.

"All ready?" asked Rose.

Freya nodded. She was scared, but didn't want to show it. She had already said good bye to the other ladies in the ward, there were only two of them now, and they waved to her as she walked out with Lars and Rose. Freya waved back, then with shoulders back and head held high she marched out of the ward without a backward look. Along the long corridor, down the stairs and down another long corridor and then they were out of the main entrance and into the fresh air. Lars had noticed the upright stance of Freya and it bought a lump to his throat. The child was apprehensive, but trying to be brave. He thought of his brother and sister-in-law back in Norway. At rest. They could no longer care for her, it was down to him now. He hoped with all his heart that Rose was up to it. Time would tell. They reached the borrowed car and Rose and Freya got in the back. Lars put the case in the boot and got behind the wheel.

"All aboard for Elfington!" he said in a cheerful voice.

Rose joined in the game. "Two ladies and a Troll to go to twenty-nine Druids

Way, driver!" Freya smiled and relaxed a little.

"Very good, madam." And with that Lars started up and took the road to Elfington.

It was much quicker in the car than on the bus and Freya was looking out of the window at the English countryside as they went along. She saw yellow fields in which farm workers were loading bales of straw on to a trailer, pulled by a red tractor. Other fields had black and white cows munching on the green grass. It seemed very odd to Freya to be on the wrong side of the road, but in this country, the left side was the right side! They arrived in Elfington and drove through the Village and Rose pointed out various places as they passed by. Lars had done a slight detour to avoid taking the road on which the crash had happened. Rose noticed and gently touched Lars on the shoulder, catching his brief smile in the rear view mirror.

A few weeks ago this journey would not have taken place, Rose thought to herself. Somehow there had been a big change in her that she could not understand. She never would. She was only glad that it had happened. Freya held her Troll on her lap so he could see out too. It was a cloudy day and he would be OK. Finally they pulled in to the curb and stopped outside Number twenty-nine Druids Way. Freya looked out at the cottage that would, for a while at least, be her home. It looked a nice cottage, friendly and welcoming. They all got out and walked down the path. Rose unlocked the door and went in, followed by Freya. Lars brought the case in with him. Across the road the lace curtains twitched!

Rose helped Freya out of her coat and took her into the living room, while Lars took the case upstairs. Freya looked around the room. A fire was burning low in the grate, with a fine mesh guard around it. It was cosy and inviting. She sat in an armchair and clutched her Troll while Rose went to put the kettle on. Lars came in and sat next to Freya. "Welcome, Little one, we hope you will be happy here with us."

"Thank you, Uncle Lars, for looking after me," said Freya. Lars nudged her gently with his elbow.

"We Vikings stick together!" He said with a smile.

"Can I be a Viking too?" Said Rose coming in with a tray of tea and biscuits. "What do you think, Freya?" Asked Lars.

"Yes, you can be, as long as I don't have to eat herrings!"

Lars and Rose burst out laughing. It was agreed.

They had just finished their tea and biscuits when they heard the clip clop of horses going down the road, and the sound of some sort of horn. Freya went to the window and looked out. There were horses going by the cottage and men with red coats and black hats riding them. Other men on foot followed behind.

"Where are they going?" asked Freya, watching them go by.

"They are going up to the wold to see if they can catch a fox," said Rose.

"Why?"

"Because that's what they do sometimes," replied Rose.

Freya turned away from the window and sat back in her chair. "I hope the Fox gets away," she said.

Chapter Seven

Hugo the Fox awoke with a start, instantly alert. He had been dreaming. He had been riding on a horse across the moors, chasing after humans who ran away from him in all directions. He had been wearing a red coat and had in his hand a large net on a long pole with which he captured the fleeing humans and put them in a bag. His face broke into a smile. If only! He listened, turning his head left and right, trying to identify what had woken him. He could hear nothing. After a while, he lay back on his bedding. He felt hot. It was dark in the room, but he could see reasonably well even so. He stretched and yawned, still a little puzzled as to what had awoken him. He felt unsettled, but could not explain why. Something was wrong. He could feel it, sense it. There was something different about today. The air was very stale. It should not be. Perhaps I will be caught, he thought to himself, as he stood up.

It was a Saturday. He didn't know it was Saturday, he just knew that six sunrises after the bells in the village rang in the evening, that was the day they might come. The humans usually hunted on this day, if the weather was not too bad. The huntsmen would be gathering in the village, about three miles away and he knew they were there for one reason only, to try and catch him. They had been chasing him and his brother for a long time, but they had always managed to escape. To them, it was just a game, he never gave any thought to what would happen if he was actually caught one day, he just knew that he would not be. The humans did not know that he had a brother, an identical twin. They only knew that the fox they hunted more than any other had distinctive white ears. Hugo had been looking forward to a little lie-in, as he knew that the hunt would not start much before noon. It never had, and humans were creatures of habit. As he stood there he wondered, not for the first time, why it was that humans always had to be chasing him, setting traps or shooting at him, his brother and his fellow foxes. He sighed. It was just what they did, and he just had to accept it. He began to feel hot once again. He sniffed the air, it was even more stale than before. It should be fresher than this. He would go outside and have a look around. He rose from his bedding and stretched. It was his turn to be hunted today, as his brother was still away.

They were predictable in their ways, the humans. Always coming from Village and up on to the Wold the same way. He tried not to worry. They were only humans after all, and he was smarter than they were.

As he trotted along the tunnel that led to the surface he could imagine how it would be at this time of the morning. Still. Quiet. Calm. The Moorlands, or as Hugo and his brother always called it, "The Wold". It had always been their home, and their parents and grandparents before them. It was a magical place, he thought, as it changed through the seasons. It could be kind, cruel or just normal, but whatever the Wold did, he loved it. He felt connected to it, part of it. He would not leave it because of the humans. He took an imaginary deep breath and could almost smell the earthy, autumn smell, a combination of wood, leaves, heather and other things. Lovely, he thought, the best time of the year. There would be a slight mist lingering from the night before. It would still be cool this early, but he always loved this time of year, the colours of the leaves, the smells of the wold and the lovely sunsets. But the air was getting more stale by the minute and he knew that something was very wrong.

As he approached the entrance to his home, it was dark as night, when there should have been daylight streaming in. Something was blocking the entrance, something big and solid. Hugo moved closer and touched the object. It was a very large rock, which had been jammed in to the entrance of his home. He pushed against it, but it did not budge. He tried again, putting all his strength into it, but it was too big, and he was too small. He leaned his back against the rock and sighed. The humans had done this, no doubt about it, he could smell them. With a sinking feeling in his tummy that he had not had before, he turned and trotted back down the passage.

John Stagg was not in bed. He had been up for hours, preparing for the hunt. It would be his last, as he was selling his farm, and moving away. Today would be a special day! He smiled. Today he would get the one thing he wanted most of all, that fox! Two years ago, John remembered when he was out with the hunt, he had seen a very young and thin fox with distinctive white ears for the first time, John and the others had chased after him, thinking that this would be easy. The fox had led him and his fellow hunters a merry dance, always one step ahead for hours, sometimes waiting for John to catch up before trotting off again. Finally, as if tired of the game, the fox had disappeared. John, hot, sweaty and cross, had sworn then that he would get that fox if it was the last thing he would do. For such a young fox, he has the knowledge and cunning of one much older, thought John, as he rode back to the village with the hunt.

John came out of his daydream and hurried off. That was all in the past. Today was going to be the day he got what he wanted, and he wanted that fox more than he could say. It had eluded him and others for far too long. So he had prepared for this hunt carefully, making arrangements and spending more money than usual. He would not be denied his prize. He looked at his watch. Nine o'clock. Good, he thought as he headed to the stables. No time to waste day dreaming, he had lots to do as the hunt would start early today, at ten o'clock!

That's what I heard earlier, thought Hugo. The humans had never done this before, maybe they are not so dumb after all! Thank goodness my brother is away, at least he is not being hunted today.

Right, Hugo thought. I'll just have to use plan "B" and go out the back door! So off he went, down tunnels that were not used much these days and made his way to the rear entrance. But again, before he got there, it was dark when it should be lighter. I don't believe it, thought Hugo, as he approached the rear exit. They had found that one too. It also was blocked by a huge rock. He again tried to move it but it did not budge. He leaned his back against the rock and sighed. He was trapped! For the first time in his life he felt something else. Fear. Real heart-stopping, gut-wrenching, mind-numbing fear. It was not a game anymore. This was real.

John Stagg rode his horse down the high street of the village, together with 10 others and then turned north up Druids Way, the road that lead up on to the moorland. He looked down at the village people, smiling and waving as he went. It was ten o'clock exactly. How important I must look to them, he thought as he moved along. John Stagg was convinced that he was held in high regard by the village folk, sure in his own mind that they looked up to him, envious of his good looks and wealth. The village people who looked back at him saw a fat, ugly and mean man who was loud and crude, As he clip-clopped his way past the butcher's shop, Mr Benton, the butcher looked out of the window and made a mental note to ensure that Mr high and mighty Stagg paid his long-outstanding meat bill before he left the village.

John Stagg was blissfully unaware of any of this as he moved along. He knew that his men had been out earlier, blocking up the holes on the Wold where he believed the Fox had his home. Just to be on the safe side, he had ordered every hole to be blocked up for half a mile around where he thought the Fox's home was. He did not give a thought for all the animals he had trapped underground, that was their hard luck! So long as he had trapped the Fox, that was what he wanted. He had hunted foxes up here for many years, as had his father before him. He had caught them all. All except one, that is and today was going to be the day. He knew that there were other foxes in other parts of the moors a few miles away, and he could have chased them, but compared to this fox, with its distinctive white ears, they were easier to catch, he knew, no challenge there for a man of his skill. No, it had to be this fox. For much too long, it had led him a merry dance all over the wold, making him look foolish in front of his friends . No more.

This was going to be the day he finally won the battle. He never stopped to consider that it was a very one-sided contest, with him having men, horses, and dogs on his side, while the fox only had his wits and cunning. He did know that this fox was the best of the best, skilled, cunning and resourceful at evading him and his men. But not today. As he rode along he imagined his two brothers, riding in from the west and east, and the dogs heading in towards him. It had taken a long time and a lot of money to arrange this hunt, but it was worth every penny. The Wold ahead of him was big, he knew, but by the time they all met up in the middle, the fox would have been caught and he could move away a happy man. Even the weather was perfect.

It was indeed a special day!

Lady Veronica Spar Butterfly, known as Ronnie to her owner John Stagg, trotted along with the hunt, looking every inch the pedigree that she was. A wire-haired fox terrier, with a powerful body and strong jaws, bred by humans to catch and fight foxes when they had been cornered by the hunt, usually in their "Earths" as the humans called the foxes' home. She was smart and knew what was expected of her if they caught a fox. She also knew she had no intention of fighting with a fox or anything else. Although bred to be fierce, she was in fact easy going, just wanting to be left alone to do her own thing, a fact she was careful to keep hidden from the other dogs and especially from Mr Stagg. She was fully grown and had lived all her life on the farm owned by him. She did not like John Stagg. If she did but know it, she was not alone. He was loud and cruel and when she was young she had tried to escape from the farm but had been caught and brought back. She had been beaten and made to understand that she could expect more of the same if she ever tried to run away again. She was his property, his possession and she would do as she was told. He had tried to make her savage and fierce, and she had played along, growling and snarling when she thought he was looking her way. She had been lucky so far, in never having to go down into a fox's earth. All the foxes that had been caught had been out in the open on the moors. She had watched recently as things had started to be packed away. She did not know why this was happening, but knew it was not the usual routine of the farm. Something was going to change and she had sensed that this could be her chance to escape again.

She did not know that John was moving, but she knew that this would probably be the best chance she would get. She did not know where she would go or how she would survive, but she was sure that she would think of something when her chance came. She was a free spirit, belonging to no one. Her life was her own and she had no intention of wasting any more of it on John Stagg, or any other human. So, on this early autumn morning, she trotted along with the horses and watched and waited for her chance to come.

Hugo sat in the den, thinking. So much for the humans being creatures of habit. So much for him being smarter than they were. He was cross with himself for being trapped so easily, he would not make that mistake again, if he ever got out of this mess! He was thinking about why the humans had trapped him below ground. They could not hunt him here, he thought. Then it suddenly came to him. When the hunters were in position, they would unblock both entrances together and send dogs in the back way, forcing him out the front door and right in front of the hunters. Very Clever, thought Hugo, as he watched a faint shaft of light from the vent in the ceiling

It was clear that the hunters had changed their tactics today and he was powerless to escape them. What could he do? He had to get out of his home below ground and get out on to the Wold. At least he had a chance up there. But how? Again he looked at the shaft of light, dust particles swirling around in it. Slowly his eyes followed the thin shaft. The vent! The vent went up to the surface didn't it? Quickly, he jumped up and studied the vent. It was narrow, but he might be able to make it big enough for him to wriggle up. The soil was very dry. Fully alert now, and with his hopes rising again, he began to scratch at the soil, using his front legs while standing on his back legs. Large chunks of soil and stones dropped into the den, and after a while, he carefully put his head and shoulders into the vent. It was a very tight fit. He looked up and could just see a faint speck of light far above his head. With difficulty, using his elbows and knees, he began to slowly wriggle his way up towards the light and freedom.

Twenty minutes later, Hugo's head emerged above ground and very carefully looked around. He was tired after wriggling slowly up the vent. He was covered in brown soil and it had got in his ears and up his nose. He sneezed. He finally climbed all the way out, shook himself and took a deep breath. It was so good to be out in the fresh air again. He was in the middle of a large patch of thick gorse bushes and brambles where humans could never go and it was why they had missed this small hole. He could not afford to rest yet, so he crawled slowly out, the brambles catching his coat and making small painful cuts. Finally he was free and without hesitation he moved off up towards the higher Wold. He looked up at the sun and judged it was approaching ten o'clock and in the distance he could hear a hunting horn being blown. So much for the humans always starting at eleven he thought again. It was going to be a warm day, he could tell, with autumn still not quite in control. He walked slowly past the gorse bushes and heather and up on to the Wold, enjoying being free again. To his right, in the far distance was a wood. He knew the humans called it "The Old Wood", as it had been there for as long as anyone could remember.

Also, ahead in the distance and near the old wood, huge rocks rose up from the wold, dominating the whole area. He knew the humans called these rocks "The Craggs". They were grey in colour and he remembered his father saying there were caves there, but he had never found any when he had bothered to look. The thick gorse bushes, heather, brambles and ferns grew right up to the rocks themselves in places.

He moved on, taking his time, enjoying being free once again, conserving his energy and keeping his wits about him, still angry with himself at being so easily trapped below in his home. He knew he could never live there again, now that the humans knew where it was. He and Jago would have to make a new home somewhere, but that was for later, he must focus on the here and now and survive this day.

It was his plan to watch the humans from the high ground and try and sneak around behind them and enter the village and hide somewhere while the humans tired themselves out up on the Wold, looking for him. He had done this before and the humans had never thought to look behind them. He moved to his left, heading east, with the sun directly ahead of him, keeping below the top of the hills so as not to show himself. He had not gone very far when he saw some huntsmen in the far distance headed directly towards him. Oh dear, thought Hugo, they really are out in force today. He doubled back and headed west, towards and then passing through the edge of the old wood, with the sun behind him now and started going around in a circle the other way. Before he got more than a mile or so past the old wood, he again heard the sound of a hunting horn in the distance. Hugo headed up hill and when he was near the top he hid behind a rock and peered over the top, careful not to show too much of himself. He could see for miles out to the west and once again he saw, emerging from a small stand of trees far in the distance, huntsmen on horses, their red jackets visible. They too were heading his way! The only route he could go was North, up onto the very high wold, where it was rocky, with thicker heather and gorse bushes. He knew he could still escape the huntsmen, as after a few miles the wold sloped steeply down and the horses could not go there, so, with butterflies in his tummy and fear in his heart, Hugo headed north.

He headed slightly downhill for a while into a small fold in the land and at the bottom jumped into Willow brook, which was only a few inches deep at this time of year, and splashed his way along for half a mile or so. He Jumped out and heading up hill, until he was once again high up. He paused and looked down below. A gentle wind was blowing from the south, the view spectacular on this clear day. Hugo lay down and took a rest. He would head a little further North and find somewhere to hide for a few hours while the hunt tried to find him. A bumble bee was buzzing slowly towards him, going from flower to flower, gathering pollen to take back to the bee hive. He kept very still, as he knew that it was movement that always gave animals positions away. Many animals he knew either ran or flew away in alarm when they saw humans coming their way. If they had only stayed still, they would not have been seen.

The bee landed on his nose! Hugo looked down his nose and focused his eyes on the bee. It turned left and right looking for pollen. Finding none, it flew off to the north to a clump of heather. Hugo watched it go, adjusting the focus of his eyes to longer distance. Something caught his eye, far away in the distance. Movement! There was something moving towards him. Slowly he raised himself up, so he was standing. There! There was a line of humans walking slowly south towards him. He could faintly hear dogs barking now, and straining his eyes he counted fifteen men, together with some dogs, about two miles away, spread out in a long line directly ahead of him. Hugo swallowed hard, the wind ruffling his fur as he watched the line walk slowly forward. He was surrounded!

Hugo quickly considered his options. They were fast running out. He knew if he stayed where he was he would almost certainly be caught, simple as that but where could he go? He racked his brains and suddenly he jumped up. He knew where he could go and be safe. A mile away there was a small water fall which had a little cave behind it, which could not be seen through the water as it cascaded over the rocks. The water would hide his scent from the dogs. He had found it by chance years ago and had filed it away in the back of his mind as a place he could use in an emergency, and this definitely counted as that! Off he ran, no thought of conserving energy now and in a little while he came to Willow brook again. He jumped in and this time headed south, going up stream, splashing his way along, leaving no trail behind. He felt more confident now, sure that this would be a safe place for him to hide until the hunt had given up and gone home. Faster and faster he ran, eager to get to the safety of the hidden cave where he could rest.

He rounded a corner of the brook and there it was, directly ahead.

Hugo splashed to a halt and looked up at the water fall with its secret cave. Only it was not a secret cave now! The summer had been a dry one and the usual mighty waterfall had been reduced to a trickle, the cave behind it clear for all to see! Hugo's heart sank. He stood in the shallow brook and panted for breath, wet, tired and out of ideas! All around him, the hunt was slowly closing in! What would he do now?

Ronnie was resting with the horses, while the humans scanned the wold with field glasses, looking for movement. She could not understand what they said, but some words were repeated many times. Fox they said, today they were going to catch the Fox. She guessed that was what the humans called the creature they usually chased after. Ronnie had seen one only once before, far in the distance. A shape not too different from her own, four legs, but bigger with a long bushy tail and a pointed face. She hoped that the "Fox" had found a safe place to hide so she could start to look for a suitable chance to run away.

She heard her name being called and jumped up and ran over to where John Stagg was. He was watching his men remove a large rock from a hole in the ground. John picked her up and took her to the hole and pointed inside and said, "Go in, Ronnie, and chase him out."

Ronnie did not understand a word and wondered, not for the first time, why humans thought she did. All she could hear was a noise coming out of John Stagg's mouth, which meant nothing to her at all. She ran down into the hole anyway and growling for the benefit of the watching men, disappeared underground. She ran down a long tunnel, twisting left and right and suddenly arrived in a larger den. The floor was covered in earth from a hole in the ceiling. She looked up. Faint daylight could be seen far above. So that's how the fox got out, thought Ronnie. Very clever. So she looked around and saw another tunnel and ran down that, finally emerging above ground, blinking in the sunlight. She shook herself and looked up at the hunt leader.

He picked her up and pushed her back down the tunnel, where she retraced her steps and emerged out of the front tunnel where John Stagg was waiting. When he saw Ronnie reappear, he gasped and said, "Where is the Fox! Ronnie shook herself again and then sat down and waited while John, who was not looking a happy man, rode off to the other entrance and spoke to the men waiting there.

"He can't be down there," said the hunt leader, scratching his head, "or Ronnie would have chased him out." John frowned and scratched his head as well. It was true, he thought, the fox has somehow managed to get out. Well, he has only one place left to run, and we have it surrounded. Feeling somewhat better, John smiled again and mounted his horse.

"I'll say one thing for that fox, he's not making this easy, but then I never thought it would be." And with that John and his men spread out and began to move up to the higher ground. The hunt was on again!

Hugo was starting to get very frightened. Never before had he been hunted like this. He racked his brains, trying to think of something he could do, somewhere he could go to escape. He had never felt so alone, so vulnerable. He did not want to die this day. He wished his brother were here, would he ever see him again? He noticed movement from the top of a tree and looked up. He could see several grey squirrels looking down at him, they all seemed to be smiling. Hugo frowned and glared up at them. They were no threat to him, he knew. He had heard of stories about the Greys before, and none of them were good. They were aggressive newcomers to the Wold and had lost no time in pushing other animals around, especially the smaller Red Squirrels.

Hugo turned his back on the Greys and took a long drink from the brook, his throat suddenly dry, then began trotting back down stream, heading back the way he had come. He had no time to waste on them now. He had to survive this day and suddenly the thought that this day might be his last, made him very angry. There was so much that he wanted to do, places to visit and things to learn. It suddenly hit home that this was not a game anymore, it was war! How dare these humans chase him? Who did they think they were, treating him like this?

With his face set in a grim line, Hugo broke into a run, splashing through the water very quickly, his energy levels high now. On and on he ran, jumping out of the water and heading instinctively upward, towards the higher ground, knowing, but not now caring that the huntsmen were also heading that direction. Suddenly he tripped over and went crashing to the ground. He picked himself up and looked to see what had tripped him up. It was a long strand of Ivy that had stretched between two trees. Muttering to himself, he stepped over the ivy and continued on his way. He knew that his chances of survival were slim, but he had not yet given up hope. 'Never give up and never give in, adapt!' Were his mottos and with his brain working overtime, he headed ever upward to the high Wold.

John Stagg continued to ride slowly north, together with the other huntsmen. He was not pleased with the way things were going so far. His expensive ploy of blocking all the holes in this area had not paid off. Still, he thought, he had plenty of men and horses, not to mention the dogs approaching from the north. The ground was sloping upward most of the time, away up ahead was the top of the moors, huge grey rocks, thrusting high into the air in places, some smaller ones lower down. Getting close to them on horseback was impossible, as the base of the rocks was covered in thick gorse bushes, together with heather, it was impenetrable in places. That's why I brought Ronnie, thought John as he rode closer to the top. We drive the fox in there, surround it and she can go in and finish the fox off, once and for all. John smiled again, he would yet prevail!

Hugo could see the huntsmen approaching as he crouched in the gorse bushes. He knew that they would have to dismount soon and start walking on foot. He looked at the huntsmen intently. They were mostly wearing red jackets and black hats, invited specially for this last hunt, consequently, they were not young men, indeed, some were quite old. One thing they all had in common was the fact that they were all overweight and clearly not fit. Already some were red in the face and puffing and blowing from the effort of riding up the slope.

I feel sorry for the poor horses, thought Hugo, as he moved ever deeper into the gorse bushes. One thing that he knew was going to be a problem was the dog that they had brought with them. He knew the reputation of these dogs and kept well away from them on the few times they had brought them on the hunt. The dog was super fit and in very good condition, being well fed and exercised regularly. Hugo had been down to the farm and had had a good look around, being careful to keep downwind at all times, so as not to allow his scent to carry on the breeze and alert the dogs. The dog they had brought was slightly smaller than he was, with a cream, brown and grey coat. The fur around the dog's face must have been cut, giving the dog a square-looking face. The strangest thing of all was the fact the dog only had half a tail! Know your enemy, his father had told him, and use his weakness against him. Which was why he knew that his main threat came from that dog. Thankfully they had only brought one, the rest of the bigger bloodhounds which were approaching were not so good in this type of terrain.

Hugo crawled and wriggled deeper and deeper into the gorse bushes until to his surprise he came to a small clear flat space, at the very top of the wold, where the grey rocks towered over him. This is it then, thought Hugo, this is where I will make my last stand against the dog. It made him sad to think that he had been forced into this situation by the humans, as he still did not wish to fight and hurt the dog. Focusing his mind on the job at hand, Hugo started to look around and make his plans.

Ronnie trotted along with the hunt, as it moved ever upward to the top of the moors. The hunt had been out for more than two hours already, and they had never come up this high before. The sun was beating down on the huntsmen, out of a clear blue sky. She could see that John Stagg and his pals were getting hot, tired and grumpy. Jackets were unbuttoned, collars undone and several were muttering that it was one thing to ride along for an hour or so on flat moors, it was quite another to get hot and sweaty up here!

They dismounted from their horses and had a rest, while John Stagg waited for his brothers to arrive from the east and west, and for the other dogs to arrive from the north.

Twenty Minutes later, the top of the wold around the tall rocks was surrounded by men and dogs. John's brothers and the dog handlers reported that nothing had got through their lines, but the brothers both said they had seen a glimpse of a fox in the far distance with distinctive white ears, running away from them. Fantastic thought John. The plan had worked! The fox must be trapped inside the circle! He ordered everyone to start walking slowly forward, but after five minutes the gorse was so thick that progress ground to a halt. One of the hired men tried to push his way forward , but got his foot caught in a root, and fell over, twisting his ankle as he did so. Ronnie tried not to smile as the man was carried off, down the wold by two of the other huntsmen, to have his ankle treated by the village doctor. On a Saturday afternoon, he would be lucky!

Ronnie suddenly realised that this was her chance! She knew that she would be sent into the gorse to find the fox and fight with it, as the humans could go no further. All she had to do was somehow avoid the fox and hide until John and his huntsmen gave up and went home. She would be free! Ronnie knew she would have to put on a good show for John to make him believe she was fighting the fox, but he could not see what she was doing in the thick gorse bushes, so if she made plenty of noise, that should do the trick. The fox, she thought, would hear her approaching and hopefully be smart enough to keep out of her way and with a bit of luck, they could both go free!

In the small clearing, Hugo was ready. He had looked around and found a small tree trunk that had fallen over. He stood next to it and it was more or less the same colour as he was. If he kept still he would not be seen. He also knew that the only way in to the clearing was the way he had come, which meant that the dog would also have to come in that way. He had found some more ivy growing nearby and tied it between two gorse bush roots, making a trip wire. He also made it easier to enter the clearing by bending back a few branches. The dog would easily pick up is scent. He then got down and lay next to the tree trunk. He had just finished when he heard growling noises heading his way. The enemy was coming!

John Stagg's mood had changed from delight to anger as he watched one of his men being carried off down the wold with a twisted ankle. He was hot, sweaty and cross. No doubt he would get the bill for the man's time off work. Never mind, he thought grimly, I am so close to getting my prize that it does not matter. "Ronnie" he bellowed, looking around. He had arranged his men and dogs around the crags to form a circle around it. No one could get out. If the fox tried, it would be shot.

Ronnie ran over and looked up at John. It's the last time I'll see that ugly face she thought to herself, as he picked her up and started speaking to her. She could not understand a word, as always. She did hear one word that she knew, and that was "Fox".

John finished speaking and placing Ronnie back on the ground pointed into the thick gorse. Ronnie did not need telling twice. She raced off, growling and snarling for all she was worth into the gorse weaving her way in and was soon lost from view. She pushed her way in to the very thick gorse and headed in a circular route, away from the rocky centre. After a few minutes, she reversed course and with increasing difficulty, headed in to the centre of the gorse, making lots of noise as she went. Outside, John Stagg and his huntsmen were watching and listening with smiles on their faces.

"That's a good dog you have there," said one of John's brothers, who was standing nearby as they heard the snarling and growling coming from the bushes.

John nodded his head, enjoying the moment. He had waited years for this and after a few unexpected setbacks, he was finally getting what he wanted, with lots of his pals to witness the event. It would be a shame he would not be able to see the fox's body, but it could not escape from there. He straightened himself up and beamed around at everyone. Wonderful!

Hugo could hear the dog approaching. It was making a lot of noise as it came. Hugo wondered if the dog was trying to warn him that it was on its way. Why would it do that thought Hugo, surely it would not try to help me? He tightened his grip on the ivy trip wire, keeping it loose on the ground so it would not be seen until the last moment.

The dog was very close now and as it got to within a few feet, Hugo pulled the ivy tight. The dog, who was running quite quickly, tripped and flew through the air, letting out a loud yelp as Hugo sprang out from behind the tree trunk and jumped on the dog's back as it flew past and put his front legs around the dog's neck so it could not bite him. He also let out a loud bark as they crashed to the ground together and skidded on the earth, straight towards the rocks at end of the small clearing.

Both their heads hit something solid at exactly the same time before they reached the rock face and they both thought the same thought as they faded into darkness. What have we hit? There's nothing here. That was their last thought as they were both knocked out at once and lay still, side by side at the foot of the rock!

John Stagg and the men surrounding the front of the thick gorse heard the yelp and the bark quite clearly, then the silence that followed. They looked at each other, then they looked at the gorse. Nothing. Not a sound could be heard. It was John Stagg that finally spoke. "They've killed each other, must have done," he said, with a surprised look on his face. He had wanted the fox dead, but had wanted the dog back, so he could show it and its wounds off to the other huntsmen.

"I think you are right," said one of John's brothers, who was eager to go back down to the village and to the pub. "We would hear them if either one was still alive. You've lost the dog, but got what you came for." There was a general murmur of agreement by the other men, who were now hoping to be able to start back down the wold and go for a drink. John Stagg slowly nodded his head. That was it! He had won! He had won! Wow, he had got that fox, after all these years of trying! He felt strangely empty, as it had happened so quick. But there could be no doubt about it, He, John Stagg, had got the fox that no one else could catch. He would be the talk of the Village after this! He could now move away a happy man. He looked around at the waiting men, a beaming smile on his red face.

"That's it, lads," he said. "Mission complete. Pass the word to pack up and meet at the pub, the drinks are on me!"

The other men needed no second bidding. They turned and started walking away, leading the horses back down the slope and looked forward to the celebrations to come. It was a pity about the dog, but it was only a dog. No one cared about the fox, plenty more where he came from. In ten minutes, the men, horses and other dogs had gone, and the Wold was empty and still once again.

The unconscious bodies of Ronnie and Hugo lay where they had fallen, close to the rock face. There was only the fading noise of the departing men and dogs to hear, except… for the faint sound of rocks grinding together. A watcher, had there been one, would have seen the rock face had split open and a small door had appeared from nowhere. Unseen hands pulled the bodies of the two animals one by one through the door and inside the rock. Then the door closed behind them, again with a faint grinding sound until the rock face was again as it had been before. Ronnie and Hugo were gone!

Chapter Eight

Freya had gone up to her new bedroom. For the first time since she had arrived in England, she was really alone. Lars had brought up her suitcase and Rose said she would be along soon to help her unpack. The room was cosy but had a slight musty smell to it. This was the room that her father and mother would have shared with her. They would never see it now. The ceiling was low and the windows small. It looked out on to the back garden, where Freya had noticed a large shed. Beyond the grey dry stone wall that marked the boundary of the garden was the moors, or Wold as they seemed to call it around here. It reminded Freya of home. But it was not home. This was not her room. This was not her bed. She walked slowly around the room, touching the furniture, the walls, the bed. Her room was gone, just like her mummy and daddy. A large wave of emotion swept over her, and she started to cry. She wanted things back the way they had been. Her life was in Norway, not here. Her friends were there, her school, everything. It was where she belonged. It was familiar, stable, real.

She knelt on the floor and cried into the bedspread. Why had this happened to her? Why had the car crashed? Why were her parents not here to care for her? Why?

The little girl with the blond hair and the green eyes sobbed her heart out, needing to cry, releasing trapped emotion that needed to get out. She did not hear the bedroom door open. Rose entered and went over to Freya and gently knelt down and held her. Rose was crying too now, but for a different reason, purging her own soul. They clung together for a long time, each feeling the warmth of the other, feeling the need within each to release the negative energy. Finally they were both cried out and it was over. Rose and Freya sat on the bed, side by side, Rose's arm around the slim shoulders of Freya, Freya's arms around the waist of Rose. They just sat there, each glad of the company of the other, lost in their own thoughts.

Lars, downstairs, had been about to go up when he heard the sound of sobbing. Two people. He took his foot off the stair and returned to the kitchen. They did not need him at the moment. He started to prepare some lunch, knowing that Rose and Freya should be left alone. He rubbed his eyes with his hand. He must have something in them to make them water like this. He was a man, a Viking. Vikings do not cry.

The lie came easily.

The fox with the distinctive white ears trotted along at a steady pace, eyes and ears alert for any sign of danger. Today was the day the bells in the village would ring before the darkness came. He did not know it was the church bell ringers announcing the evening service. The hunt would have been yesterday. He would be home soon and would sleep in his own den tonight. He was glad it had not been his turn to be chased by the huntsmen, as the day before was when they were most likely to come, and with nice weather, they would surely have tried again to catch him or his twin. His name was Jago. Hugo was his brother. They took it in turns to be the one who was chased, so the other could rest and relax. They were identical, and just as smart as each other at evading the humans. When they were young, they would take it in turns to be chased, swapping over at a pre - arranged spot. The humans never knew.

Suddenly Jago stopped, a strange feeling of un-ease passing through him. Something was wrong. Very wrong. Jago moved off again, more quickly now, a feeling of dread in his stomach, and headed towards his home.

Hugo opened his eyes, and slowly looked around him. He kept his body still and just moved his eyes. He was lying in some sort of basket. The basket was in a dimly lit room. There were no windows. The room's ceiling, walls and floor were all made of rock. He appeared to be underground, in some sort of cave. But whose cave? Whose basket? How did he get here? Where is "Here"? He had no idea of what the time was, or if it was day or night. He closed his eyes again, and tried to recall what he was doing earlier. The last thing he could remember was grabbing the dog that had been chasing him and skidding across the ground with his arms around its neck. He remembered the rock face looming large in front of him and thinking he was not going to stop in time, then blackness. He opened his eyes again and took another look around.

He was alone in the room, but had no idea how long he had been there. He slowly sat up in the basket and tried to move his legs and neck and found that apart from being a little stiff, he appeared to be in one piece. He gently climbed out of the basket and stood on the floor of the room. Just as he looked towards the door, it slowly opened and a large powerful Cat-like creature padded silently in. It did not open its mouth, but to his great surprise, Hugo could hear a voice in his head. It was a low, gentle voice. "Ah, I'm so glad you are awake. Allow me to introduce myself. I am called Bob. Bob Cat. Welcome to our hideaway."

When the door had opened, Hugo had tensed, fearing the worst, knowing the only way out of the room was through that door. He had looked at the newcomer in disbelief, his heart sinking at the sight of this large and powerful cat. Would he have to fight it now to escape?

The visitor was quite a bit bigger than a normal cat, and had spotted fur and short tail. Hugo could see at once that the cat was powerfully built. But the most unusual thing about the car was its face. It pushed the door open wide and came into the room and sat on the floor, facing Hugo. The cat smiled. It was a friendly face, kindly looking, intelligent, with tufted ear tips and green eyes. Without knowing how or why, Hugo instantly knew that he was safe, this creature would not harm him. He looked back at the cat and waited. "We brought you both here and cared for you, after your mishaps outside," said the voice in his head.

The cat had not moved, its mouth had still not opened, but somehow Hugo had again heard what it had said. It had said "We" meaning more than one, and both! Where is here? Thought Hugo, "And how can I understand what you say when you are not my kind, and have not spoken?"

"I am what the humans on this planet would call a telepath, I can communicate with you by using my thoughts," said the cat, its green eyes shining, as it looked directly at Hugo. Again its mouth had not moved. The cat called Bob went on.
"There is a power within every creature to do this, but yours, like most others, were dormant, I have temporarily turned it on, so we can communicate together. As I said before, I am Bob, you are quite safe here. You may leave whenever you wish. But I hope that you will stay for a little while and we can continue to share our thoughts. "The dog is here?" thought Hugo, "and you say "We". Are there more of your kind here?"

"Yes, the dog is here and with my companion. The dog was also injured as you were. It is recovering. We are the only two of our kind here in this place. As you and I are both male, I thought it best to choose you. My companion is female, as is the dog. You are underground, in our secret place, below the Wold. We call it our hideaway. We saw what had happened to you and could not leave you like that, so we brought you here, to recover before you return to your world outside. "What's a planet?" thought Hugo. "I live up on the wold." Bob smiled again and looked at Hugo. "There is much for us to explain to you, but to answer your question, the wold as you call it, is a very small part of what is called a Planet, your Planet is called Earth. "

"My Planet is called Earth?" repeated Hugo. "Isn't your planet called Earth as well? I must be dreaming. It is impossible for me to communicate with other creatures. I can only talk in a limited way to my own kind."

"All will be made clear in due course, I am sure you have many questions but first, you must be hungry. Let us go and join the others." Hugo nodded, suddenly realising he had not eaten for ages.

Hugo looked at the cat again for a long moment, still a little unsure of what he should do, then shrugged his shoulders, and followed the cat called Bob out of the room.

Jago approached his home with caution, senses on full power, as they always were when humans had been around. He could tell immediately that the humans had been here recently, the smell of them was almost overpowering. There was also the smell of horses and of at least one dog. He moved quietly, to a patch of shade beneath a bush and lay down, listening and looking around carefully. He could see no sign of the hunt now, or detect any traps they may have left. I hope Hugo managed to give them the slip, he thought as he moved slowly forward again.

He arrived at the front entrance of his home and saw a large rock nearby, and lots of hoof prints and human foot prints on the ground outside. And again the smells. Humans, horses and dog! They have found our home, he thought, we will have to move now. He was tempted to go inside straight away, but decided to go around the back and check there. There was another large rock near the back door and again many hoof and foot prints. And again the smell of humans and dog, together with the horse droppings. He swallowed hard. Had they trapped his brother below and captured him? He waited a little longer then, with a final look around, he very slowly and carefully went below to see what had happened.

There was a strong smell of dog, and Jago saw a pile of soil and stones under the air vent. That's how he got out thought Jago, hugely relieved that at least his brother had managed to get out from underground and not be trapped. But where was he now? It was mid-morning and he should be here, ready to tell him how he had outsmarted the humans once again. But the place was empty. Was he hurt somewhere, and needed help? Or was he dead! They did not have much, just this den, their freedom and each other. Now the den was lost to them and Hugo missing. Was he alone now? Jago had to know, and so he quickly made his way outside and began to search for his twin brother.

Hugo the fox followed Bob the Cat down a short tunnel and found himself in a large chamber. In the chamber there was another Cat just like Bob but slightly smaller. Next to the second Cat sat the Dog that had been chasing him. In the corner of the room a large fire burned cheerfully in the fire place. There was a low wooden table near the fire and the Dog and the new cat were seated around it. Bob indicated that Hugo should sit at the end of the table, facing the Dog, while he sat opposite the other cat. It did not escape Hugo's notice that he and the dog were seated as far apart as possible, with two powerful cats between them. It seemed that these cats were smart enough to know that dogs and foxes did not usually get along, and would rather be safe than sorry.

The room was lit by several lamps that were placed on ledges in the rock walls, and gave the room a cosy feel. The floor of the chamber was covered in a fine light sand. The Dog's eyes had not left Hugo since he had entered the room and taken his seat. The Dog's body language did not suggest it was anything other than relaxed and Hugo gazed back across the table in a like manner, studying the Dog with interest now that he could see it clearly for the first time. Bob looked at Hugo and said, via his mind that the other Cat was his companion and was called Lisa. Lisa Lynx. Lisa smiled at Hugo and told him, again via her mind that the Dog was a female and the humans had called her Veronica, or Ronnie for short. Hugo inclined his head slightly in the direction of the Dog and the Dog acknowledged it and gave a slight nod back. The Cats had watched this and seemed satisfied that there was no danger of trouble between the two newcomers. Lisa rose from the table and left the room and vanished into another tunnel, reappearing again quickly with two large bowls of hot soup, two spoons and two mugs of water, which were put in front of Hugo and Ronnie respectively. "Please eat," said Lisa, "you must both be very hungry after your ordeal today."

Both Hugo and Ronnie suddenly realised that they were starving and tucked into the soup without delay, not bothering with the spoons, which they did not know how to use anyway. The cats just sat and watched, the only sound in the room was the slurp of soup being eaten. When they had both finished and drunk their water, they sat back in their chairs and sighed with satisfaction. Bob and Lisa beamed with pleasure, their short tails moving back and forth.

While the visitors had been eating, Bob and Lisa had been exchanging thoughts between themselves and now turned their attention to their guests once more. They explained that while Hugo and Ronnie could not communicate directly between themselves, they could talk to each other via their hosts. Bob and Lisa smiled again as they revealed to their respective guests that they were both asking the same questions at the same time. What had happened to them? Where were they? And how had they got here?

And most importantly, who were these strange cats with whom they could communicate with just by thinking? This could not be real, they must be dreaming. Foxes and Dogs do not communicate with beings from another planet that look like some sort of strange cats. Until today, neither of them had the faintest idea that there were any other planets. Foxes lived wild on the moors, dogs live under the control of humans. That's how it was. Or was it?

The cats smiled and assured both their guests that they were not dreaming and this was indeed real. It seemed that the cats could communicate to both Hugo and Ronnie at the same time, and Lisa told Hugo that before he and Bob had arrived, Ronnie had told her that she did not want any trouble with him and had only been chasing him because the humans had made her do it. She had tried to warn him by making a lot of noise and had been taken completely by surprise when Hugo had tripped her up and jumped on her. Bob now took over the contact and told Ronnie the dog that Hugo had told him that he did not want to harm Ronnie either, he just wanted to get away from the humans and be left alone. Setting the trap for Ronnie was all he could think of as the humans had cut off all his escape routes and got him cornered and he could not get out of the thicket. What he did not know was, what had happened next, how did they end up here and what was going to happen to them? Both Ronnie and Hugo looked at Lisa as she continued the story. "You will not be harmed, please be sure of that. You are both now uninjured and are free to go whenever you wish. It is still the same day outside, but darkness has fallen. When you had your accident, we could not leave you there as we felt responsible for your problem. You both bumped your heads on something that belongs to us and you were knocked out. You could not see it, as we do not want the humans to be aware of us. It is hidden in a special way. We decided to bring you in here and help you recover. You are underground, below the rocks. We are pleased to tell you that you are the first animals on this world that we have had the chance to communicate with. To find two compatible animals at the same time is quite amazing."

"We are not quite what we appear to be," said Bob. "We are not from this world and we have taken the form of Cats because we like how they look. There used to be wildcats like us in this part of your world long ago, but not now. We like the cat shape and are able to move around outside without fear of attack. We do not allow ourselves to be seen by the humans and are not usually outside in daylight. We come from another world far far away and are here on this visit to study the animal and bird life here on your planet. When we return you back to your own lives again, you will remember nothing about us or of ever being here. We are able to do this to be sure that no one will know of us or of this place. We know that you have no way to verify what we have told you is true. We ask that you trust us. What we have revealed to you is true. We are called Gallownians." Ronnie looked at Lisa and told her that she had nowhere to go. She could not return to the Farm as they thought that she was dead, and she wanted them to continue to think that. She had wanted to escape and now she had, and for the first time in her life she was free of human control. She had not a clue what she should do next, or where she might go. The only thing she did know was that there was no going back. Not now.

This was relayed to Hugo who nodded. He explained to Bob that he had always been free, but the humans had a nasty habit of chasing him at regular intervals, and trying to kill him! Today they had almost got their wish. He had been scared to death, and was so relieved to know that the dog, Ronnie had not wanted to harm him. But he could not return to his home either, not now the humans knew where it was. He would have to try and find somewhere else to live that the humans did not know about, but of course they, or others like them would return to hunt him again. And again. One day they would succeed. He was fed up of the endless cycle of being hunted. Then there was his twin brother. He told Bob about Jago who was to return home the next day and would be looking for him. For him too, there was no going back to the way things had been before either. If his memory of this place and of them had to be erased, he could not prevent that. But at least for a little while he was safe, warm, fed and dry. And alive.

Lisa passed this on to Ronnie who nodded in agreement. Life had changed for both of them. She was too tired to think beyond the here and now. Bob and Lisa looked at each other. They had much to consider before the Sun rose tomorrow. The future of these two animals lay in their hands.

Bob and Lisa looked at their respective guest and said that they should return to their rooms and rest. But just before they did, there was one more thing that they wanted to show them. It was to reassure them that the outside world was still there and they could go back to it whenever they wished to. The Cats rose from their seats and gestured to Hugo and Ronnie to follow them. Bob led the way and the two guests followed him, Hugo behind Ronnie with Lisa bringing up the rear. The cats had evidently decided it was safe to let them walk together, without the fear of them fighting. Hugo wondered what had happened to the dog's tail, most of it seemed to be missing. The answer came immediately from Lisa, behind him. The humans had cut most of her tail off when she was very young. It seems that they like that breed of dog to look a certain way! Hugo was shocked. His tail was long and full, he was proud of it. He felt sorry for the dog, who he now realised was completely on her own. He knew that there were no other dogs of her type at the farm or anywhere around. He wondered what she would do in the morning. It was a pity that he would not remember any of this.

Bob was leading them down a tunnel, away from the one where they had woken up. It was tall and wide with a sandy floor. It occurred to Ronnie that it was big enough for humans to fit into. There were no lights in the walls and they moved along in pitch darkness. It did not matter. They could all see well enough to find their way easily. The rock was quite smooth and as far as they could tell uniformly grey in colour. After a couple of minutes they entered a chamber, which was wide but narrow. There was a slight breeze coming from somewhere, the air fresher and cooler. Bob walked to one side and pulled a lever that was sticking out of the rock floor. There was a faint grating noise and then Bob began pushing the rock wall, which to their great surprise began to move to one side, revealing a gap in the wall of the cave, beyond which was the outside! The cool night breeze blew in, ruffling their fur, as they gazed out at the night sky beyond. The air was fragrant with the smells of the wold at night and both Hugo and Ronnie took deep breaths of it. Lisa motioned them forward and all four of them stood on their back legs and put their front paws on the ledge and looked out.

The view below was spectacular, lights twinkled in the distance. The darkened wold stretched out before them, and the cats told their guests that the lights were from a small settlement of humans called Elfington. They were looking out from the rocks on top of the wold to the outside world below. Conversation was not needed. The view before them said it all. Magnificent. Wonderful. Magical. They all just looked, drinking in the beauty of what lay in front of them. The Dog and the Fox were thinking the same thing. What they had been told was true. The proof lay right before them. It had never crossed either of their minds to doubt it.

Finally Lisa broke the silence.

"It's really quite beautiful, isn't it? We never get tired of looking at it. It is one of the many beautiful things that you have here on your world." Ronnie and Hugo just nodded. Ronnie, never being off the farm before, or out at night, had never seen the village from here before and it was breath-taking, magical. She could not get enough, she had not known that there was a village. They drank in the view, their fatigue forgotten for a while. They could see some small lights moving in the distance. They were told they belonged to a device the humans used to move around in. They both felt completely safe and secure here, with these strange cats. They could look out at the world beyond, but the world could not see in. It was indeed a secret hideaway.

That was almost true. Unknown to Hugo and Ronnie, a pair of human green eyes was looking directly back at them from a bedroom window on the edge of the village. Bob and Lisa exchanged a look, but said nothing to the others. Only they knew who the eyes belonged to. If it was not for the owner of the green eyes, they would have already left this world, and none of this would have happened. Clearly, it was meant to be.

Finally Bob moved over to the lever and waited, the others taking the hint and moved away from the secret window. The slab of rock slid back into its place again, and the wall looked just as it had before. Lisa led the way down the tunnel and back to the main chamber. The fire had died down and Ronnie and Hugo knew that it was time to return to their rooms for the night.

They could hardly keep their eyes open. They were escorted back and each went inside and closed the door. So much had happened to them today, their tired minds could not take it all in. They were physically and mentally drained and knew they must sleep. Strange as it may seem, they both had no fear whatsoever of being attacked, and there was a calmness in the air that made them relax. As each of them drifted off to sleep, they both had the same thought. I don't want to leave!

When their unexpected, but very welcome guests had gone to their rooms for the night, Bob and Lisa returned to the main chamber and sat by the dying fire, looking into its flickering light, as if for inspiration. The fire gave them many things, warmth, comfort, contentment and peace of mind. But it did not give them the answers they sought. They needed to talk, to think and plan. They needed to discuss what to do next. They should, of course simply let Hugo and Ronnie go, erase their memories and be done with it. They had repaired the injuries of these animals and that should be the end of it. They had never connected with any animal before and now they had two of them all at once. Their sudden encounter with these two animals had caught them off guard and they needed to evaluate their options. This could be an opportunity to really learn about some of the creatures in this part of the world and would be a valuable addition to the information they had already collected. On the other hand, should they alter the status quo of these creatures, did they have the right to change the evolution of the animals on this world, because any change to these two, would undoubtedly ripple out to touch many others . They must be careful of what they do here. The time remaining to them was short. They did not want to return to their own world leaving chaos and problems behind here.

Clearly Hugo and Ronnie were intelligent animals, choosing not confrontation and aggression, but going out of their way to avoid it. They were not cowards. They were smart. Only a fool looks for trouble. Also they had not put themselves in that position, the humans had forced it upon them, and when they were beyond human control, their own common sense had kicked in and they had both tried to limit the impact they had on the other. Another plus in their favour was their ability to communicate with them. Bob and Lisa were sure that with time and training, Hugo and Ronnie would be able to use telepathy to talk to each other, even though they were different species and different genders. There was real potential here. But should they tamper with the lives of others, or leave things alone. They looked back into the fire, but again, it gave them no solutions.

This visit had been so full of surprises, unlike their previous ones. Their encounter with the little girl, Freya had also been unexpected, but necessary, for without it the child would be dead. It had pleased them both to sense that she had been looking out, directly at them at exactly the time that they had been looking at her. She could not know they were there. Not yet anyway. She would now be getting the sleep that she needed so much. It occurred to the cats that perhaps the Universe was trying to tell them something. It was not random chance that the child, her Aunt and now these two animals had all come into contact with them, and that they had been able to receive the thoughts of the cats. The odds of that happening were billions to one. No. The Universe was sending them a message. But what message were they being sent? They both agreed that it was not coincidence that things had turned out as they had. It was not "One of those things". It was meant to be.

So Bob and Lisa looked at each other and nodded. It was agreed. Assuming that Hugo, his brother and Ronnie wanted to stay, they would be allowed to. But time was short. The Gallowians could not hold this form for too much longer. Their encounter with Freya, and the change of form that had been needed to restructure the woman had taken vital energy from them, rewarding as it had been. In the time that they had left, they would do what they could. If at the end they concluded that the animals would be better off as they had originally been, that they had not learned enough to be able to live undetected and look after themselves and this place, the gifts that they had been given would be erased and no harm would have been done. They would not remember any of it.

With the fire all but out, the two cats moved away to their rooms to rest. Nothing could be done until the Sun rose once more. It was out of their hands. Either a second form of intelligent life would be born, or an existing one would continue. What would be, would be. Only the Universe knew, and it would keep its secret safe.

Ronnie lay in the basket that was in her room, finally alone. She had only known her small kennel at the farm. Her mind was whirling from the events of the day. She had achieved her goal and escaped. But never in her wildest dreams could she have imagined that she would be where she was now.

She could not go back, that much was certain. She had not given too much thought to what might happen if she managed to escape. She had guessed correctly that there were other villages or similar places in the area and if she managed to find one of them, she might have been taken in by some other humans and kept as a pet, but then she would not have been free, as she had wanted to be. But being free had its own problems, like how to find food and shelter. Being here she had both, at least for now. The strange "Cats" outside would in all probability do what they had said and erase her memory of this place and them and she would find herself out on the moors and on her own. A thought occurred to her. If that did happen, she might meet the fox again and have no memory of meeting him before! A dog could go crazy thinking things like that.

Of one thing she was certain. The fox, Hugo could have killed her, no question about it. He had set a trap and she had been caught in it. Although she was strong and powerful in her own right, he had been in a position to inflict a fatal bite, from which she would not have recovered. But he had chosen not to do that. That told her something. He had also said, via the cat, Bob, that he did not want to hurt her, and strangely, she had accepted that to be true. Again her mind started to speed up, as her fatigue swept over her. The fox had said he had a twin brother, so she would be on her own against two of them, what if the other fox was not like his brother and attacked her. What if they were allowed to stay and when the cats left they locked her out and she could not get back in? What if they locked her in and left her here with no food and water? What if...

With a sigh, Ronnie tried to calm herself down. She was exhausted, both physically and mentally. She needed rest. Whatever was going to happen in the morning, she would deal with it then. Her eyes closed and she fell into a deep sleep.

Hugo had got into his basket and lay on his back looking up at the stone ceiling.

What a day. He thought back over the events of the day and marvelled that he had managed to survive. He had avoided being caught, and killed, by the humans, but it had been a very close run thing. If that dog had been as savage as the humans had wanted her to be, then things could have been very nasty indeed. The dog, Ronnie had deliberately made noise to let him know she was coming. She had not needed to do that. She could have approached quietly and avoided his ambush, and then he would have had to fight her. She was smaller, but powerful and had a mouth full of sharp teeth to equal his own. A fight with her could have gone either way. He could have been killed or seriously injured, and unlike the humans, there were no places up here on the wold to get him better.

The dog had said, via the cat Lisa, that she did not want to fight him and he had to accept that as being true. He was worn out. Stress was as much a drain on him as physical activity, and he had had both in large measure. His world, until today had been limited to how far he could see from the top of the wold. He had no real concept of what lay beyond that. Now these strange cats had said that there was much more than he could ever have dreamed of. Could it really be true? He was too tired to think. This place was incredible, and to think that he had lived on the wold all his life and never known it was here.

One decision he had made. In the morning he would ask if he could stay here, together with his brother. The cats might allow it. The dog would have to make up its own mind. If they said no, then his brother and he would have to find a new home up on the surface, and the cycle of being hunted would begin all over again. He thought suddenly of the dog. It could not go back to where it came from. Dogs did not live in the wild, like he did. They belonged to humans. He wondered what it would do if they could not stay here. Would he trust it enough to let it live with him and his brother? As his eyes closed he thought that he just might. What a day it had been. Hugo slept. You had to be alive to sleep.

It was hard to know if it was morning or night when you were underground. There were no windows and no clocks. Bob and Lisa were up and about, but as usual they made no sound. The fire was re-lit and burned brightly. Breakfast was being prepared. One of the advantages of being in the form of a cat was that you could eat solid food and drink liquid drinks.

It was things like this that they would miss when they left and returned to their real shape. Where they came from there was no food or drink. Only energy and matter.

It was Hugo that appeared first. He entered the large chamber and said, or rather thought "Good Morning" to his hosts. To his surprise he found that he was already getting used to "Thinking", rather than speaking. He sat by the fire and accepted a bowl of something the cats called "Tea". It was hot and brown in colour. He let it cool before giving it a try. It was amazing that he could just accept being here with two large cats, as if he had been doing it all his life. They had that effect on him. Lisa went to check on her other guest.

Bob came and sat opposite him and raised an eyebrow.

"You have something to ask me, do you not?"

"Yes, what time is it?"

Bob smiled. "Nearly eight o'clock, human time. The Sun has risen. But that's not what I meant." It was Hugo's turn to smile.

"I know. You must have read my mind. Can you do that?" he asked.

"A little. But you had better tell me what's on your mind, so that I have the full picture." Said Bob

And Hugo took a deep breath and asked if he, and his brother could stay. He told Bob he was tired of being hunted, shot at and having traps set for him. He would do whatever Bob and Lisa said. He did not want things to go back the way they had been. Last night, they had given him a glimpse of another world, another life. He had expanded his mind, raised his expectations and did not want to shrink back to being what he had been before. He wanted to know more. To learn, and above all, be safe. His fate was in their hands, or rather paws.

He stopped and took a sip of his tea. He found that he liked it. It was good.

Bob had said nothing. When Hugo was finished, he nodded and got up.

"Lisa and I will give you a decision after breakfast, but first, finish you tea and come and eat!"

Hugo followed him to the table and sat down. He would have to be patient. Not something that he was particularly good at.

Lisa had met Ronnie in the tunnel, just as she was coming out of her room. She asked Ronnie to follow her and took her into a room that she had not been into before. Lisa told her that it was called a "Kitchen", a human word for a room where food was prepared and cooked. Ronnie was fascinated. At the farm, she had been given a bowl of cold meat and biscuits once a day and some water. She had no idea that it was possible to make other things, to make them warm. She watched as Lisa made a big pot of something she called "Porridge". Lisa told her that this meal was called "Breakfast" by the humans and was the most important meal of the day.

To Ronnie, it was a dreamworld. She began to imagine what things she could create in a place like this.

She looked at Lisa and it all just flowed out of her in a rush.

"I don't want to forget any of this. I want to know more. Please let me stay. My future is here, I know it. There is nothing for me outside. I cannot go back. I would like to go forward."

Lisa nodded and said. "I will speak to Bob and we will let you know our decision after breakfast. But first help me to finish this."

Ronnie went over to where Lisa was stirring a cream-coloured, lumpy liquid. Ronnie took the spoon and with difficulty gently stirred the mixture round and round. As Lisa went to get the bowls, she noticed that Ronnie's tail was wagging!

When the porridge began to boil, Ronnie and Lisa lifted the pot off the little fire and put it on a small cart that Lisa had produced, together with four bowls and four spoons. The cart was pushed into the main chamber where Ronnie saw Hugo the Fox sitting at the table with Bob. As strange as it seemed, it felt the most natural thing in the world to Ronnie. She realised that she had no fear of the Fox and he seemed to have no fear of her. She was glad.

Greetings were exchanged between the animals and they all sat down to eat. While the food was cooling Bob and Lisa exchanged thoughts between themselves.

The meal was eaten in relative silence. One of the many advantages of having a conversation by using your mind was that you could eat and "Talk" at the same time. Ronnie and Hugo both said that they had slept well and had been comfortable. Bob and Lisa said that they had discussed the future of the visitors at considerable length and had both agreed on what they would like to do. They stopped short of saying what that was. Finally the meal was over. Hugo and Ronnie said that they had enjoyed their porridge and thanked Lisa for providing it. Lisa collected up the bowls, spoons and mugs and pushed her trolley back into the kitchen and then rejoined Bob at the table.

For a while, both cats looked at their visitors without saying anything. Then they looked at each other, nodded and it fell to Lisa to put them out of their misery.

"Both of you have come to us unexpectedly. Both of you have shown respect to us and to each other.

You have demonstrated your intelligence and compatibility by co-existing here without any sign of aggression or violence. Had any of these conditions not been satisfied, you would have been kept separate and returned to the outside world with no memory of us or of ever being here.

Both of you have shown an interest in us and in each other. Both of you have asked to stay." Hugo and Ronnie looked at each other, then back to the cats.

"Bob and I have agreed that your presence here and the manner of your arrival is a sign from the Universe. This meeting between us was meant to be. If you, and Hugo's brother are prepared to work hard, to learn, study, listen, observe and take instructions from us without question, we are prepared to teach you all we can in the time left to us. If, at the end of this time, we decide that you are ready to survive here without us, and that the humans or anyone else will never discover this place and its secrets, you can stay. But remember, with knowledge comes responsibility. You will both have taken a quantum jump in your development. If all goes well you will be many thousands of years in advance of where you should be, far, far ahead of the humans. They cannot be allowed to know about your gifts."

Ronnie and Hugo were overcome with relief. They both had beaming smiles and were beside themselves with joy.

"But," said Lisa. "If at the end of the allotted time, we conclude that you are not ready, and your discovery and the discovery of this place is possible, we will erase your memories and return you outside, with or without your agreement. We have to ensure that the humans have no knowledge of us, of you or of this secret place. For if they did, their whole concept of the galaxy would forever change. They are not ready to deal with visitors from another world, they are too hostile, primitive and war-like to accept that there is superior life on other worlds. They must not know of us. Ever!"

Ronnie and Hugo had gone quiet, realising the seriousness of Lisa's words.

Bob concluded the conversation.

"Will you accept our terms? He asked."

Hugo looked at Ronnie, who in turn looked back at him. This was a chance of a lifetime, for both of them. To make it work they would have to trust each other completely. As would Hugo's brother. There could be no doubt, not even a tiny bit. If they were to make a success of this, they would have to work together for the good of all. If they could not, then they would all fail, and all the wonders they would have learned would be lost to them, they would go back to being just another fox and dog. They could not let this chance of security, knowledge and safety slip through their paws. They would try.

They nodded to each other and turned back to face Bob and Lisa. "We agree!"
Bob and Lisa also nodded. "Then we are all agreed then," said Lisa. "That just leaves us one small detail to take care of."

Hugo and Ronnie looked puzzled. "What small detail?" They asked.

Lisa smiled. "We must go and find Hugo's brother. He is in for the shock of his life, and will have some serious thinking to do!"

Chapter Nine

Lisa and Ronnie decided to stay behind, while Hugo and Bob went off to find Jago. Bob led Hugo down yet another long tunnel, which was either flat or sloped slightly down. It was wide and high and its sides were quite smooth. The floor was covered by a fine sand. I wonder how it was created, thought Hugo, as they walked along, side by side. It was made by water, millions of years ago, flowing down from the wold to the valley, came the reply.

Hugo was surprised. Not by the answer, which he accepted as probably true, but by Bob being able to read his every thought. He was just not used to it yet. Bob smiled in the darkness as they continued along the tunnel. "You will soon be able to shield the thoughts you wish to keep private. It is just one of the many things that we will teach you."

"Thank you."

Hugo tried to keep his mind on walking down the tunnel and after fifteen minutes, they arrived at what seemed to be a dead end. The tunnel had suddenly widened out into a large cave. Hugo was astonished to see three carts or trucks parked at one side, two were loaded with fire wood, branches and small logs, while the third was empty. He looked at Bob and raised an eyebrow. Bob gestured at the Trucks. "We made them on an earlier visit when we found this place. We use them to move firewood and other things up to the living area."

The trucks were made entirely of wood, with slightly sloping sides which made them wider at the top. Even the wheels were made of wood. Hugo was impressed. He suddenly realised what Ronnie had worked out earlier. This whole underground world was human size. The carts, the tunnels, everything. Humans had once lived here, he was sure. How had he missed something so obvious?

Bob nodded. "Yes you are correct, we took the form of humans on a previous visit, but that was hundreds of earth years ago."

"Where are we exactly?" Hugo asked. Bob just smiled. He did that a lot.

"You will be surprised! Watch!"

Bob walked to one corner of the cave and reached up, pulling down some sort of long tube. When it was hanging straight down, he folded two handles out, one at each side. There was an oblong "Slot" between the handles and Bob stood on his back legs and putting a paw on each handle, peered into the slot. He then began to turn the tube slowly in a circle, going around with it until he was back where he had started from. He stepped back and gestured to Hugo to have a go.

Hugo, not having a clue as to what he was doing, just copied what Bob had done. He put a paw on each handle and looked into the oval slot.

He jumped back in alarm. "What did I just see?" He asked. Bob just said one word.

"Outside!"

Carefully, Hugo put his paws on the handles again and looked into the slot.

He could see trees, heather, gorse and grass, all bathed in bright sunlight. He was staggered.

It was like standing in a hole in the ground, with only your head showing. Amazing.

"Turn the tube slowly" said Bob.

Hugo did as he was told and went around in a full circle until he was looking at the same things again. Finally, he stepped back and dropped back onto all four legs.

"What is that?" He asked in wonder.

"The humans call it a Periscope. It enables you to see outside without being seen. Clever, isn't it?"

Hugo nodded his agreement.

"Did the view look familiar?" Asked Bob.

"Yes, but I can't quite work out where it is."

"You soon will," and with another quick look through the periscope, Bob folded it away.

He moved to what looked like a solid rock wall and reaching up, began to move bits of the rock to one side. Suddenly, a large section of the Wall seemed to fall outwards, letting light and fresh air stream into the cave. Hugo could see dust swirling in the beams of light that spilled into the cave, as it had done in his den when he had looked at the beam of light from the vent. Was it only yesterday?

He also noticed a wooden barrel next to the entrance, with a watering can next to it. There was a tap in the side of the barrel.

Bob explained. "That is something we have added. The barrel was here before, we supplied the contents."

"What's in it?" Asked Hugo.

"Something that will erase our scents, so we cannot be traced back to here."

The wall had gently lowered itself down so as to form a ramp. But there was still something else between the ramp and the outside world. Bob walked down the ramp and gestured for Hugo to join him. On doing so, Hugo could now see what was hanging down, like a thick curtain. Ivy.

Bob carefully put his head through the Ivy and had a good look around , then, satisfied, he pushed himself completely through the curtain and was gone.

Hugo, hesitated for a moment, then pushed himself through the curtain and stepped outside, instantly knowing where he was. He gasped with surprise. They were in a sunken gully, once a sizable stream but long since dried up in the Old Wood!

Bob had sat down a few feet from the curtain of Ivy and was watching Hugo's surprise with much amusement.

Hugo was only a few feet from the entrance and looked back at the Ivy but could not see through it. There was nothing to show that that piece of bank was any different from any other. He had walked past this spot hundreds of times and had noticed nothing.

Finally he looked at Bob and said, "That is the best kept secret I have even seen. I had no idea that there was anything there. Amazing!"

Bob nodded his agreement. "Normally we only come here at night, when there are sure to be no humans around, but we must find your brother urgently." Hugo nodded his agreement.

Bob went back through the Ivy and returned with the watering can in his mouth. He sprinkled the liquid around the entrance, then went back inside and closed the door to the secret cave, then reappeared. "Better to be safe," he said. Hugo agreed. Being safe was second nature to him.

"What about tracks?" Asked Hugo.

"Mine are the only ones to worry about, and I am careful where I put my paws, we are lucky it is dry. If we erased all tracks around the entrance, it would look odd that there are tracks everywhere else but not here," said Bob.

"Good thinking," said Hugo. These cats think of everything, he thought to himself.

"We try!" Said Bob.

"Now, you take the lead and let's try to find your brother."

So Hugo set off with Bob following behind, both keeping a sharp lookout as they went. They emerged from the shade of the gully, where the branches of the trees on either side reached out and met in the middle, to form a sort of arch over their heads. Ten minutes later they were close to Hugo's home. Bob sat down in some shade under a large oak tree, and let Hugo go on alone, so he could prepare his brother for meeting him and the others.

Hugo decided that if his brother was still around, he would be close by, watching the entrance to their former home to see if Hugo came back. So he sat down at the entrance in full view and waited, noting the hoof prints and human footprints and the trampled ground. After a few minutes he heard a soft "Psst" from behind a bush and saw Jago rising from his hiding place where he had been watching. He came forward, relief clearly on his face and embraced his brother for a long moment. Then they stood back and Jago said, "Where have you been? I thought they had finally caught you. I have been worried sick!"

Hugo nodded and smiled. "They very nearly did catch me. I have such a story to tell you. Come over here in the shade and sit down. You aren't going to believe this!"

After lunch Freya was shown the rest of the house and garden. Rose helped Freya unpack the things that she had in her suitcase. They would have to do until the rest of her clothes arrived from Norway. Freya had a nap during the afternoon and it was decided that an early night was required soon after tea. Rose tucked her in and went downstairs. But Freya was restless, and she felt unsettled and sleep would not come. She was overtired and was unused to the quiet of the house after the hospital ward. Something made her get out of bed and go to the window. She could just about see the garden and shed in the growing darkness and beyond them was the moors. Her gaze moved to the far distance, where, unknown to her, four pairs of eyes were looking back, directly at her! Only two of the pairs of eyes were aware of her gaze. Like hers, these eyes were also green. She looked up at the moors for quite a while and then returned to bed and fell asleep instantly, settled and calm, where she dreamed of her parents who were waiting there for her.

Sunday was a lazy day. The alarm clock was not set, Lars did not shave and everyone wore their slippers. Freya awoke to see sunlight streaming in through a gap in the curtains of her bedroom window.

The room faced north and the rising sun was shining into the room and leaving a long distorted window shape on the lower part of her bed. Her first thought was to make sure that her Troll was safely in the shade.

With that done, Freya slid out of her bed and went over to the window and drew back the curtains and looked out. The branches of the tree next to her window were starting to get bare, and as she watched a leaf gave up its fight to stay attached to the branch and started its journey to join its brothers and sisters in the untidy heap at the foot of the tree. As she watched it slipping and sliding against the branches as it fell, there was a knock on the door and Rose put her head around the door and looked in.

"Morning," she said in Norwegian, which brought a smile to Freya's face. "Can I come in?" lapsing back into English.

"Of course, Aunty Rose."

Rose came in and sat on the bed. "Did you sleep well?"

"After a while. It was so quiet, in the hospital there is always noise."

"Well, when you are ready, come down and have a wash. Uncle Lars is doing the breakfast and he said to tell you that there are no herrings!"

Freya smiled, lighting up the room to rival the sunlight, and together they made their way down the narrow stairs to start the day.

The day passed as Sundays tended to do. Lars had the radio on while he cooked the breakfast and Freya tucked in, to the delight of Rose and Lars. She was introduced to a new breakfast food, called an "Oat Cake", and she loved it! True to his word, there were no herrings to be seen.

As they all sat around the table that first morning, it struck both Lars and Rose that they were a family, a real family and they realised Freya had filled a huge hole in their lives that neither of them had known was there.

Later on Freya just had a little walk down to the end of the road and back before lunch. Lars went with her and she reached up and held his hand. He was surprised and held it gently, it was so small in his giant one, Freya's trust in him was total. He would make sure that he never let her down. He owed his brother and sister-in-law no less. But the DNA flowing through both hands was the same, he thought as they walked along. He was almost right.

The lace curtains across the road twitched slightly as the giant blond man and small blond girl walked along.

Freya was glad to be out of hospital, but missed seeing Sister Grey. After lunch she watched the "TV" for the first time, and was fascinated by it. They had not got one in Norway. Lars and Rose did their best to make her feel welcome and it was with sadness that Lars began his preparations that evening for returning to work the next day. He was wary about leaving Rose alone with Freya, lest she lapsed back into her old ways and left Freya unattended. He had been impressed and very grateful to Rose over the past few days and hoped with all his heart that it was not just a passing phase. Time would tell.

Lars returned to work on Monday, leaving Rose to look after Freya on her own. Rose was nervous about the responsibility she now had, and had had a bout of the dry retching soon after getting up. She was getting them on and off, but always felt better after. The internal re-structuring of Rose was continuing and the negative emotion was being released. She could well imagine how a new mother felt when she returned home from the hospital with a first born child and found herself suddenly alone with no one to ask for help. Freya sensed her uncertainty but said nothing. Grown-ups always knew what to do.

Rose need not have worried. After breakfast at about nine thirty there was a knock on the front door and when Rose went to see who it was, there on the doorstep was Sister Grey! She sighed with thanks at the unexpected but very welcome visitor.

Sister Grey said that she was off duty for a few days and thought she would pop in and see how things were going. She had Freya's medical notes in her bag to drop into the local GP. She could have put them in the internal mail, she knew, but it made a good excuse, as she thought Rose might be in need of some moral support. The look on Rose's face as she had opened the door told her that she had guessed correctly.

Freya was delighted to see her and they all spent the morning washing and mending the Troll who was in need of some repairs and a good wash! Sister Grey stayed until lunch time and then it was time to leave. At the door, Rose thanked her and asked if she could know her first name as Sister Grey was a bit formal now they were out of the hospital environment. Sister Grey smiled and agreed. From that day on, Freya had acquired a second Aunty. Aunty Penny!

And Rose and Penny began the start of a long and close friendship that would develop as time passed, each becoming to the other the sister that they had never had.

Penny Grey made her way down to the village to the GP surgery and handed in the notes to the practice nurse, who was an old friend of hers from way back and with whom she had infrequent contact as patients went in and out of hospital. They chatted and Penny found out that the practice nurse was leaving next year at Easter, to take up a job at an old people's home in Abbotsbury, as the GP was retiring at that time, as he was sixty-two and wanted to take it easy.

Penny was thoughtful. She had been thinking about a change of direction herself, knowing that too much stress and running around were not good over the long term. She had been at Abbotsbury Hospital for ten years and was going to be thirty one next birthday. A quieter job with regular hours, and no night shifts was suddenly very appealing. She asked her friend if the job had been advertised yet and was told it had not.

She asked if the vacancy could be kept quiet for a short while, as she might be interested herself and needed time to think. She also said that she might just know a doctor who was also considering a change of direction as well.

As she walked to the train station for the journey to her home at Wallbridge, she thought to herself that if she had not decided to visit Freya and Rose, she would not have known about the jobs at the surgery.

What a stroke of luck that she had had!

"So, let me get this straight! The humans trapped you underground, but you managed to escape through the vent. Then you were chased up hill and down dale by humans, horses and dogs. Finally you were cornered at the base of the craggs in the thick stuff. OK so far, that sounds like it could well be true, you did well to keep ahead of the lot of them, I'm not so sure that I would have done.

Then, and this is the part I am having trouble with. You set a trip wire for the dog, which you think is trying to warn you it is coming by making a lot of noise, a dog, by the way that is not known for its kindness, trip it up, grab it and you both bump your heads on something you cannot see and both get knocked out.

Then, you wake up in some secret, underground room, in a basket provided by two large cats, that aren't really cats, and just happen to own the invisible thing that you hit, which can take them off to another, what did you call it?"

"A Planet."

"Oh yes, that's right, a Planet, whatever that is, and these cats, who are not really cats then start talking to you via your mind, and they tell you that they are your friends and that the dog is also there, but is a nice doggy really who would never dream of fighting you and only uses its nice sharp teeth for eating.

Then, you meet the dog and it tells you, via your mind that it really is a quiet and shy thing that was only chasing you because the humans forced it. "

"Actually, I can't talk directly to the dog yet, but should be able to soon," corrected Hugo.

"Oh, pardon me for misunderstanding. Then, you spent the night in this secret place, together with two large cats and the nice doggy, and wake up this morning to have a nice breakfast together, before coming out of a secret tunnel that leads to the old wood, a place that we have been to hundreds of times, but never managed to notice it before, and, if that wasn't enough, one of these cats, who is called "Bob" is close by and wants to meet me. "

"That's about it," agreed Hugo. "Look, I know it sounds crazy, but I swear that is what happened to me."

"Come with me now, and meet Bob, then you will see that I haven't lost my mind and that it's all true."

Jago looked at his brother for a long moment, then with a shake of his head, reluctantly agreed to go with him. "I hope I don't regret this," he muttered under his breath, as he followed his brother. He actually felt a little guilty about the way he had spoken to Hugo, but really, it was just so far-fetched that he could not buy into it at all. He was so relieved to see his brother again, and he had spoken more sharply than he should have done. He wondered if the bump on Hugo's head had caused him to imagine things.

He stopped walking and called after his brother. "Hugo."

Hugo stopped and turned to look back.

"I'm sorry. I am just so glad to see you again. I really thought they had caught you."

Hugo smiled. "I know, and thank you. When you see what I have to show you, you will realise that this will be a real opportunity for us to be safe, really safe. For the first time in our lives, the humans cannot get us. Please trust me on this!"

Jago nodded and they continued on. He was still very sceptical, but he did trust his brother and would give him the benefit of the doubt.

Five minutes later, the pair arrived at the spot where Bob should have been. There was no one there.

Jago sat down and watched as his brother looked around. Finally Hugo sat down next to his twin. "He was here!" he said.

"You're sure this is the right place?"

"Yes, positive. This is it!"

"What now?" asked Jago, trying not to sound too smug.

"We can wait for a while, I'm sure Bob will turn up soon!" Said Hugo.

"OK if you say so."

And so they sat and waited. Jago heard nothing, but Hugo heard a familiar voice in his mind. "Tell your brother to look up!"

Hugo turned to Jago and said, "Look up." They both looked up.

There, in the branches of an oak tree, stretched out on a sturdy limb, right above their heads, was Bob.

He smiled down at them and waved his paw.

Hugo waved back, while Jago had leaped to his feet in alarm as if he had been electrocuted, and took a few steps back, ready to leg it if he had to. Neither of them had thought to look up. Hugo turned to his brother. "Don't worry, he won't harm you."

"You sure?"

"Quite sure. If he had wanted to, he could have jumped the pair of us long ago!"

Somewhat cautiously, Jago moved back to Hugo's side, but remained standing. Just in case.

"Tell your brother I'm coming down and not to be alarmed."

Hugo passed this along and they both watched as Bob, in one bound, leaped down from the tree and landed without a sound a few feet away.

They both had noted the power and grace necessary for Bob to do that. They saw the large paws and sleek body and the ease in which he jumped down. Even together, they would be no match against him.

Let's hope he's as friendly as Hugo said thought Jago, or it's curtains for us both.

Jago was in shock. He had gone along with Hugo and his extraordinary story only so far, but now there really was a large cat-like creature standing right in front of him, exactly as Hugo had described. He hadn't really been expecting it. It dawned on him that there might just be some truth in this after all.

Bob looked at the two foxes in front of him. They really were identical to look at, but he could already tell that they were quite different personalities. He looked at Hugo.

"Sorry if I startled you, I just fancied climbing that tree. I saw you coming some distance away. So this is your brother Jago. Please ask him if I can have his permission to switch on part of his mind to enable me to talk directly to him, as I do to you. It won't hurt, I promise!"

Hugo passed this along to his brother and Jago, still not quite recovered, nodded agreement.

The connection was instant, as the brothers were on very similar "Wave lengths".

He could hear a voice. A low, calm and friendly voice, right in his mind. The voice was speaking to him, and he could understand what it said. It was very strange. Only a fox could talk to another fox, and then with limited words. But this voice was from a Cat! And he could hear it. Clearly. He looked at Hugo and suddenly he could hear his voice as well, only he was not speaking. He was thinking!

"It's OK. I know it feels strange, it did when it happened to me yesterday. It's how they communicate. You will get used to it. I told you that they can do this. Good isn't it?" Jago just nodded.

"Hello, Jago. My name is Bob. Do not be alarmed. Your brother is right. My species communicates with their minds. It is a higher form of communication that we have developed. Some creatures on your world are not able to adapt to it. But you are one of the lucky ones. Are you starting to believe what your brother has told you about us?"

"Ye, yes," thought Jago. "I can't believe that I am doing this. It's so, so different."

"You are correct. But you will adapt, as Hugo has. Now you can practice for a while, as I am sure you have many questions for me!"

And so Jago did. Slowly at first, he asked all kinds of things, mainly to confirm what Hugo had already told him, and to try and understand what had happened to Hugo and what it might mean for them both.

Hugo had moved away and sat down in the shade while Jago and Bob got to know each other. He could not hear what was being said, or rather thought, he corrected himself. After a while Jago looked at Hugo and said,
"Bob says we should go back to the Old Wood and use the tunnel to meet the others. What do you think?"

Hugo stood and stretched. "Agreed. Do not worry, there is nothing to fear. I have already been in the tunnel and spent last night in the secret hideaway. As I told you earlier, this could be a real safe home for us, where we will be never be hunted by humans again. Come and see!" Jago hesitated for a moment, then with a nod of his head agreed. He was still quite nervous, but getting calmer. Being with his brother was helping, and he found that he was beginning to get used to being with Bob and being able to communicate with him. Why not give it a try! Besides, Bob had said that lunch would be ready and Jago had only had a small breakfast! He did not want to live alone without Hugo, who had clearly decided that this was the life for him. So far everything that Hugo had told him had turned out to be true, as unbelievable as it had first sounded. Why not?

And so the three of them began to make their way back to Old Wood. It was a beginning!

Jago was having trouble believing here was really here. He was sitting next to the fire with his brother, staring into the flames. It was all true! Everything that Hugo had said had been true. But although he was here in the main chamber, waiting for lunch, it was still hard to believe. They had made their way to the Old Wood and Bob had invited him to try to find the secret tunnel. He went up and down the gully slowly, looking, sniffing but finding nothing. It was just a gully, like it had always been. Bob and Hugo sat and watched. Finally he joined them and admitted defeat.

"Is it really here?" He asked Hugo.

"Oh yes," came the reply, "come and see." And Bob led him to the thick curtain of Ivy and pushed through it and disappeared, followed by Hugo. Jago walked up to it and carefully put his head through, just in time to see Bob lower the ramp and go inside the bank. Hugo turned and said,

"Come on! It's quite safe," then he too trotted up the ramp and disappeared. Jago, hesitated for a moment then he too carefully went through the curtain of Ivy and up the ramp into the tunnel.

Bob worked the machinery and closed the door without it making a sound. Jago was apprehensive. He could not go back outside now. Hugo went over to him.

"Relax, brother. It is quite safe, or I wouldn't be here!"

Jago nodded and looked around, noticing the trucks loaded with fire wood, and the tunnel which Bob was standing next to, waiting for him.

"We are quite safe now, no humans to worry about, come this way!" Said Bob and led the brothers back down the tunnel to the main chamber, at a brisk pace. With a last look around the room, Jago followed his brother into the darkness.

And now he was actually here. He had not met the other cat and the dog, they were in what Hugo had told him was a "kitchen", a room where food was prepared and cooked. He knew that was true. He could smell it.

In fact Lisa had kept herself and Ronnie in the kitchen on purpose, so as to give Hugo's brother a bit of time to settle himself in. It must, she thought to herself, be quite daunting for him, even with his brother to help him along. Finally, the meal was ready and she went out into the main chamber while Ronnie pushed the cart with the food on it. Bob introduced her to Jago, and she was surprised to see just how identical they were to look at, but as she tuned into his mind, after asking if she could do so, she, like Bob realised that they were very different personalities.

Lisa went over to Ronnie and brought her over to meet the newcomer. Ronnie was nervous. She was one dog. They were two foxes, but Lisa had assured her that like his brother, the new fox, called Jago was not going to be a problem. Lisa had also told her that a fox is actually a distant member of the dog family! Ronnie walked over to where the twins were sitting and taking a deep breath, sat down a few feet from them, with Lisa next to her to act as translator.

She need not have worried. Hugo had told his brother all about the chase and what had happened afterwards and Jago told Lisa to tell Ronnie that he was pleased to meet her and she need not have any worries about trouble from him. Lisa did so and Ronnie nodded her head and visibly relaxed, her tail starting to wag slowly. The twins noticed it and they in turn relaxed a little more themselves. Ronnie looked at the newcomer and was astonished at how exactly alike they both were. She turned to Lisa and asked how was she ever going to know which one was which! Lisa told her once she could communicate with them it would be very easy to do, as they were very different on the inside!

Jago, for his part looked at the dog and was curious. He, like his brother had never been this close to any dog before, in particular one that had such a fearsome reputation.

Yet here he was, sitting a few feet away from what, a couple of days ago, would have been a mortal enemy. It was unreal, but then, the past three days had been unreal. He should be getting used to it! He admired the courage that the dog had shown in facing the two of them, and accepting that, like them, she had the power to fight and give a good account of herself, she had the brains to not do so.

It was Hugo who broke the ice completely. He asked Lisa to tell Ronnie to forgive his brother for staring at her, but he was just not used to being around girls! Lisa laughed and passed it on to Ronnie, who also laughed, the tail wagging a little more still. Bob called them all over to the table for the meal and they all went and sat down, Ronnie between Bob and Lisa, while the twins sat across the table from them. They were all hungry and tucked in. Lisa told the brothers that it was something the humans called "Shepherd's Pie". They nodded their approval. Whatever it was called, it was delicious. It was not long before there were five plates being licked clean!

After the meal had been eaten, Lisa produced tea, another new taste for Jago, but he drank it down and enjoyed it. Life underground was not so bad after all. When the tea was drunk, Ronnie told Jago and Hugo about her life on the farm, how she had been taken from her mother when she was still quite young and put into a box and the lid shut down. There had been no food or water in the box, and her tail was still sore from when they had cut off most of it, and after what had seemed an eternity, the lid of the box had been removed and she had found herself on the farm. Ever since she had arrived, she had been waiting for her chance to get away from the humans. She had no idea where she had come from. She had to admit that she had never thought in her wildest dreams that she would end up here with two twin foxes and a couple of cats from another world!

That made everyone laugh, which was just what was needed. They all moved over to the fire and lay down, and spent the afternoon exchanging stories and information about themselves and their lives before fate and the Universe had thrown them together. It was the beginning of a lifelong friendship!

Chapter Ten

John Stagg sat in the front seat of the taxi as it made its way out of Elfington and headed to the main train station at Abbotsbury. The sale of his farm had been completed today and his wife and daughter had gone with the removal vans. He had waved them off, locked up and dropped the keys in at his solicitors, then headed to the pub for a last drink with his pals. That was three hours ago. He had drunk heavily as he usually did as they talked over old times, especially the last big hunt of a few weeks ago.

He settled back in his seat and tried to get his eyes to focus on the passing scenery, while the driver tried to avoid his passenger's breath. He would come back to Elfington from time to time, as his sister and her family were here.

As the car slowed to go around a sharp bend, John glanced to his left, his eyes coming into proper focus for a moment. There, sitting on a slight mound in a field, were three animals, all of whom were looking down at the road. His jaw dropped open. There were two foxes, both with distinctive white ears, one each side of a dog, that looked a lot like his Ronnie! They all seemed to be smiling!

John sat bolt upright in his seat as if electrocuted and gaped, making the driver jump. John blinked and tried to turn in his seat and look back, but the car had rounded the bend and the mound was lost to view.

"You OK, sir?" Asked the driver, who would be glad to see the back of this passenger.

"Er Yes, I thought I saw something back there."

"Well, I can't really turn around on this narrow road, sir", said the driver in the sort of voice that meant he didn't want to.

"It's all right, drive on," said John, not really sure just what he had seen, if he had seen anything at all. As soon as he got to the station, he told himself, he would head straight for the bar. He needed a drink!

Inspector Pitt was in his office, the "Olsen Accident" file open on his desk. He frowned at it in frustration. Despite ongoing inquiries over the last few weeks, there was little progress. In fact, there was no progress at all. He had received photos of the strange tracks he had found at the crash site, which may or may not have already been there. They showed the tracks of something with four toes, clearly an animal of some kind and not really relevant to the case.

Animals did not drive cars.

And that was the problem. There was no other car. It had vanished off the face of the earth. His officers had checked and re-checked everywhere. Nothing. There were no witnesses either, save for the little girl who could remember nothing.

Until he found that car, and the person or persons in it, the case was going nowhere. With a sigh he closed the folder, but the case was still open. He would wait.

Lars set of for work early on Monday morning with mixed emotions. He was glad to be out and doing his work on the one hand, yet not fully convinced that Rose had really changed enough to do all that she would be required to do to look after Freya properly.

She had surprised him, it had to be said, since the accident and he had to give her credit for that, but would it last. Would she tire of being a mother-like figure and return to the lazy and selfish person that she had been before?

The problem was that the bulk of the work necessary to care for a child would fall on the woman's shoulders, it always did, and Rose had no experience to draw on. Her own mother would be worse than useless and Lars did not intend to let her have any involvement in Freya's upbringing. So, he would just have to see how it went. If Rose did not measure up, then he would have to take Freya back to Norway and he would live there with her and somehow sort something out. Freya was his only concern, he owed it to Anders and Marit to make Freya his top priority.

So Rose was still on probation, although she did not know it. He would have been surprised to learn that Rose did know it. The balance of power in the relationship had swung from Rose to him now, and he knew it. So did she.

So he let himself out of the house quietly and set off in the early morning darkness and headed to the dairy. The sooner he started his round, the sooner he could get back home. He quickened his pace.

It was agreed that Freya was now well enough to start school after the half-term holiday at the end of October, and to introduce her to the other children she was taken to visit St Martin's junior school one afternoon in October. After being shown around the building by the headmaster, Mr Mitchell, she was allowed to join the children for the mid-afternoon playtime break in the schoolyard. He introduced her to the children who seemed nice and friendly. They had never met anyone from Norway before and they milled around her while Lars and Rose stood apart with Mr Mitchell. One boy, however was not interested in meeting the new arrival. He was running around the playground pretending to be a spitfire aircraft, arms out to make wings, and making engine-type noises as he swooped around, his socks falling down to his ankles. The spitfire had machine guns on it and he swooped close to the pack of children and mowed them down before flying off again. Finally he got tired and as no one had joined in the game he landed close to the group of children and folded in his wings which, as if by magic, turned into arms.

He was, what you might call "Chunky". Big for his age and somewhat rough in manner, he made his way through the crowd to see what was going on. Freya was sitting down on a low wall and was talking to one of the children when she noticed a pair of scuffed shoes that had not seen polish for a very long time, wrinkled and none too clean socks around the ankles, and a pair of sturdy legs sticking out of a pair of none to clean short trousers, which all the boys wore. She looked up at the newcomer and smiled.

Richard "Ricky" Wild, known to the others as "Munch" as he never stopped eating, looked down and felt his heart stop. His mouth fell open, but no words came out. He just stood there as if poleaxed. He had never seen such a beautiful girl in his short life. He was seven and a half. He tried to speak but could not. Finally he went bright red, to match his hair and turned and walked away, still in shock. Freya was told he was not normally struck dumb, in fact quite the opposite. Freya watched him go inside the school and disappear, so she continued to speak to the others. She did not think any more about it.

Ricky Wild went into the toilet to compose himself. Lessons would start again soon. But his mind would be elsewhere. Ricky Wild was in love!

As Lars and Rose chatted with Mr Mitchell, Rose saw a sour face peering out of the staff room window. She knew who that person was, as Rose had been taught by her when she had come to this school. It was Mrs Hunter. She was a dour, strict and scary woman, who had taught at St Martins for as long as anyone could remember. Rose smiled at her but Mrs Hunter just looked away.

In the staff room, Mrs Hunter turned back to drink her tea, which one of the older girls had served. Another foreigner at the school! That made two now. What was the world coming to, she thought to herself, with a scowl. The girl on staff room duty noticed it and glanced at the clock. Nearly time for lessons to start, thank god. Mrs Hunter put down her cup and saucer, preparing to rise and return to her class. She sniffed. Whatever next, it wouldn't surprise her if they started letting black children into the school! She stood. Of course that jumped-up nobody of a headmaster would probably think that was a good idea too, she thought to herself as she moved to the door, but then people like him had no breeding, no class!

He was the son of a Baker! A local lad who had literally used his loaf to earn a place at grammar school, do well enough to somehow be accepted into a University and eventually become headmaster. A nobody. If there was any justice in this world she should have been appointed Headmistress. No wonder this country was going to the dogs!

The other "Foreigner", a boy of seven, was talking to Freya, introducing himself as Gilbert van den Berg. He had lived in the village most his life, his parents were from Holland. Freya liked him, he was friendly and lived quite close to her. She tried to say his name, but got it wrong. He smiled. "Don't worry," he said, "everyone calls me Dutch. It's easier!"

"OK, Dutch, it's a deal," said Freya with a smile, just as a boy came out and rang a handbell to signal the end of playtime. The children lined up and then went back into the school while Freya joined Uncle Lars and Aunty Rose.

"You seemed to have made some friends already!" said Lars as the last of the children went inside.

"Yes, they seem to be nice," said Freya, pleased that she had met them and had a look around. It would not be so hard to come back after half-term now.

And so they made their way out of the playground and closed the iron gate behind them. As they started to walk down the road towards home, Freya noticed a boy waving from a window.

It was the boy she had talked to earlier. A boy called Dutch!

Freya started school on Monday morning, walking the mile or so holding Aunty Rose's hand, and carrying her school bag in the other. Rose could feel the eyes of the village people watching her as she walked along, joining the other mothers and their children as they all headed towards the school gates. Her mother had brought her here when she was young, until she was able to get out of it by sending Rose with another lady who lived down the road and was taking her own children. Even then, thought Rose, her mother had found a way to avoid doing something she couldn't be bothered with. Like she would have done, before Freya came to them, she told herself and the miracle had happened and she had somehow become changed into a new Rose. She was still not sure how that had happened, but however it had come about, she was quite sure that she preferred this version of herself than the old one.

They arrived at the school gates and they went inside. Mr Mitchell was there to welcome her and to show her where her "Peg" was. It was a metal hook, in a row of others where she could hang up her coat. Freya noted the number was number eleven! The boy she had chatted with before half-term had peg number twelve. Mr Mitchell had noticed that they had seemed to get along and as he was also from overseas, he had asked Dutch to keep an eye on Freya until she settled in. Dutch was happy to do so, his dad had asked him to do so as well!

Gilbert van den Berg had lived in Elfington since he was two years old, and could remember nothing about his life in Holland before that. He had been born in Venlo, which is quite close to the border with West Germany. He spoke Dutch fluently and

German reasonably well, and of course English. He was a bright and eager boy with a thirst for knowledge and was doing well with his school work. He was average size for his age, having had a growth spurt from age four to six, where he had shot ahead of his school friends and his mother had had to buy ever bigger clothes for her rapidly growing son. Then at six, the spurt had come to an end and his school friends had slowly caught up with him, so at age seven, he was more or less where he should be.

His mother ran the house, while his father was employed in the small town of Pondford as a barber. His father was also called Gilbert and he would travel the four miles to the barber's shop on his bicycle except in the very bad weather, when he would get the bus. He had brought his universal skill of barber to England which transcended the language barrier. He, like his son and wife spoke three languages and if that was not enough and an Eskimo had sat in his chair and wanted his hair cut, all the Eskimo would have had to do was point at one of the many black and white photographs of well-groomed men's heads that hung around the walls of the barber's shop and he would have had his hair cut in that style.

He also made a bit on the side in the evenings and week-ends from the local men who needed a trim and they would sit in the wooden chair in the kitchen while enjoying a cup of tea provided by Mrs van den Berg. One thing that young Gilbert would never go short of was a good haircut.

Lars Olsen delivered the milk to his house and would have his hair cut in the kitchen whenever he needed to, and the two men got along very well. Gilbert senior had known that Lars was expecting his brother, sister-in-law and niece for a visit and he was very sad to hear of what had happened to them. Before Lars had returned to Norway with the bodies of his brother and sister-in-law, he had popped in for a trim and told his friend that the child would, at least for the short term, be staying with him and Rose.

He told his son to make sure that when his friend's niece started school after the half-term holiday he should look out for her and make her welcome . Gilbert junior was happy to oblige, and when Freya arrived at the school for a visit prior to starting full time, he ensured that he introduced himself as a friend of his Uncle. He had immediately liked Freya and knew they would get on. He would make sure that he showed her around the village and instruct her in the art of tree climbing. She was only a girl, after all.

Dr Thomas Thornton finished the last of the case notes and closed the file. He was in his office and was tired, having just finished another night shift. The only good thing about working nights was that Sister Grey had shared it with him. She had joined his team about six months ago and he knew that she was a real professional, skilled in all areas of nursing and probably knew as much about medicine as he did. She was calm and in control, no matter what was going on in the ward. The shift ran like clockwork as she oversaw the duties of the nurses under her.

He also knew that his fellow Doctors envied him, not only for having the most skilled and competent ward sister in the hospital to support him, but also for his having the most attractive one as well. He had heard that some of his colleagues had asked her out for a drink or a meal but all had been tactfully declined. It did not stop them from trying again. She always attended hospital social functions, including the Christmas party, but left early, sober and alone. That was one of the reasons he had not tried his luck. Yet. He was also afraid of being rejected and thus spoiling a very good working relationship.

She was sitting in front of his desk now, legs crossed, waiting for him to finish the case notes. Watching him. Cool. Beautiful. Unobtainable. He guessed that she was older than him, but looked younger. He was thirty. Although they had worked together for quite a while, he knew little about her, only that she was single, lived alone in Wall Bridge and was an excellent nurse.

And gorgeous. He looked up.

"That's the lot, Sister." She nodded but did not move. He raised an eyebrow. "Anything else?"

"Yes. I've been thinking that as we have worked well together for a while now, it might be good for us to be a little less formal in private. If you like, you can call me Penny. What do you think?"

Dr Thornton looked at her in surprise, caught unawares.

"Er yes, I think that is a good idea, er, Penny. I'm Thomas, or Tom if you like. "

He had noticed lately, ever since that terrible night when he had lost both parents of the little Norwegian girl that Sister Grey had seemed a little more relaxed around him. A slight softening of attitude. More smiling, less frowning. But he had not been expecting this. She spoke again, looking directly into his eyes.

"It takes me a while to get to know people, to see if they are worth knowing. I'm pleased to tell you that you have passed the test. Congratulations!" She smiled again.

"Well, thank you, er, Penny. You are obviously a good judge of character," he said with a smile of his own.

"I like to think so," she said as she rose to her feet and collected up the notes. "See you tomorrow, Tom."

As she headed for the door, he watched her swaying hips and caught a faint whiff of perfume as she went past him and out of the door. Well, Well, Well!

As Penny walked down the corridor to her own office, she smiled to herself. She liked to think that she was a good judge of people. It was time to tell him she liked him. What he did about that was down to him. He would never know that she had asked to swop shifts to be on his team, to see what he was really like. She liked to take her time. She had been hurt before and had needed some time on her own to recover.

Now she was ready to give Dr Tom a chance to get to know her, if he wanted to. She hoped he would. He seemed a nice chap, not like the other Doctors who had asked her out. It was quite plain what they had in mind! What would be, would be. She would await his invitation.

Tom sat behind his desk, in a state of shock, his fatigue forgotten. He had not been expecting this! She had made it clear she liked him, and now the ball was in his court to make the next move. He needed time to think what move he might make, but he knew that he would make one. The lovely Sister Penny was suddenly not so unobtainable after all!

It was the fourth morning that Rose had taken Freya to school, and now she was certain that Freya had settled in and would be in their care until three p.m. Rose returned home and quickly changed into some old clothes. She found an old shopping bag in the cupboard under the stairs and went outside to find some garden tools and gloves. The weather was dry, but cool and cloudy, good enough for what Rose had to do. A quick check around the house, making sure that the fire guard was in place and she was out, locking the door behind her. She set off down Druids way towards the village and the Church.

The time of day and the time of year was such that she met no one on her journey and she was grateful for that. She was eager to get to her destination without delay. She headed for St Martins Church, avoiding the centre of the village and as the Church clock struck quarter to ten, continued on a little more to the Cemetery next door, the Churchyard being full long ago.

She went in through the gate, just as a car went by, and stopped just inside to get her bearings. To her shame she could not remember where to go, so she walked down the wide path, looking left and right and reading the nearest headstones as she went. She did remember it was not too far from the path but that was all she could recall. Near the end of the path on the left side was a grave that was unkempt and overgrown, by far the worst one on that side, if not the whole Cemetery. All its neighbours were neat and tidy. She walked up to it and stopped, reading the short inscription. She read the words silently to herself, least some one should hear and challenge her right to be here.

HERE LIES HARRY BUTLER. 1905-1957. AGED 52.

For the first time since he had died, Rose had come to visit her dad. It was clear that her mother had not been either, but then Rose had not expected her to. It has been over five years. Rose looked around the Cemetery. She was alone.

She knelt on the grass at the foot of the grave, pushing aside a bramble to do so. She looked at the headstone again, feeling the emotion welling up deep inside her as the tears started to fall. She was barely able to speak.

"Hello, dad", she whispered almost to herself. "I'm so sorry!" She broke down completely, sobbing uncontrollably, shoulders heaving and head down. The dry retching came next, such was the force of the raw emotion pouring out of her. It was worse than the morning when she awoke in her chair, after the visitors she would never remember coming had gone. It just would not stop. She purged her very soul, memories of her father flooding through her mind, and how she and her mother had treated him.

He had been a happy, caring and humble man, asking little from life. A man liked and respected by all who knew him. A man who always put others before himself. A man who would give you the shirt off his back if he thought you needed it more than he did. A man who had loved his daughter and worked himself into an early grave, this grave, trying his best to give her as much as he could. A man who she and her mother had treated so very badly.

She remembered him coming home from being out all day delivering coal, dead on his feet, only to find the washing up waiting for him, before he could start to cook the evening meal, while she and her mother had sat in the front room, doing nothing to help. He never complained, forgiving them every time. She remembered seeing the sadness in his face sometimes when he hadn't seen her watching him. The hard work and the worry of where the money was coming from over the years had just worn him down. Her mother had found him sitting in his chair one morning, dressed to go to work. Dead. Through her tears and retching, she asked him for forgiveness, saying she was sorry over and over again. She shuffled forward, still on her knees and hugged the moss-covered headstone.

She lost track of time. A light breeze blew, making her headscarf flutter slightly, but she did not feel it. She just hugged the headstone, as if it was him.

Finally, the retching and the tears eased and then stopped. She released the headstone and took several deep breaths to steady and calm herself. She wiped her eyes and blew her nose, looking around the Cemetery again. A lone figure, holding a bunch of flowers in her hands, stood on the path, watching her. It was Penny Grey. Rose got to her feet and walked towards her without a word being spoken. The two women hugged each other tightly, and Rose started to cry again, while Penny spoke quietly to her. "It's all right, Rose. Let it all out. I'm here. I've got you."

After a while, the crying stopped. There were no more tears left, and Rose released Penny and stood back. Penny offered her a tissue. Rose had used all of hers.

"How did you know I'd be here?"

Penny smiled. "I called at your house, but you were out, so I thought I'd visit my Granddad. He's over there," nodding towards the other side of the path.

"Well, I'm so glad you're here," said Rose, as they moved back to the graveside again.

"Can I help, or would you rather do it by yourself?" asked Penny.

"No, you are most welcome." And so the two friends worked together, Rose dealing with the brambles and long grass, while Penny peeled the moss from the headstone. After forty-five minutes, the grave looked considerably better, as if someone cared for it. Someone now did.

Penny put the flowers she had bought with her by the headstone, adding a splash of colour, saying her granddad wouldn't mind this time!

They stood back and gathered up the tools and put them in the bag. With a last look at the headstone, they moved back to the path and walked down it together. The sudden shrill call of a seagull made them jump and turn towards the sound, just as a brief ray of sunlight broke through the clouds. Penny stopped and said to Rose, "You see, your dad knows you were here!"

It was exactly the right thing to say.

Rose squeezed Penny's arm and nodded, not trusting herself to speak. She was right.

They parted by the gate, Rose to head home, Penny to catch the train to Wall Bridge. As Penny turned to go, Rose touched her arm again. "Thanks, for everything."

Penny smiled. "Any time, it's what friends are for. Say hello to Freya and Lars!"

Rose Nodded. "Will do, and thanks again. Bye, Penny!"

"Bye."

Rose turned and started to walk back home, while Penny headed down to the Station, thinking how fortunate it had been that a patient had given her the flowers as she had been discharged from hospital that morning, just as Penny had finished her shift. She smiled to herself.

Rose would never know that her granddad was alive and well and living in Stoke!

In fact, Penny had not called at Rose's house at all, but at the GP's surgery to see her friend, when the Doctor had come in from a house call and mentioned he had just seen Rose going into the cemetery.

Penny had chatted to her friend for half an hour, asking more details about the job, then, acting on female intuition, had decided to walk up to the Cemetery, even though she was tired after the night shift.

Village life never changed! Everyone knows everyone. Penny quickened her pace, not wanting to miss the train. She had a rare date this evening. Dr Thornton, Tom, had finally plucked up the courage and was taking her out for a drink!

Chapter Eleven

Ronnie, Jago and Hugo sat in a row directly in front of the fire, ready for their first day of tuition, with Bob and Lisa in front of them but at each end so as to allow the warmth to reach everyone. Bob picked up a stick and on the sand of the cave drew a circle.

This is Earth. You are now sitting on a tiny little piece of it. Later on in your training I will go into more detail about your part of it. But for now, I just want to give you the big picture. Every grain of sand in this room is another planet out there in the Universe, just to give you an Idea of the size of it. Earth is also the size of a grain of sand. Three pairs of eyes looked around at the floor of the room. There were lots and lots of grains of sand. Wow.

And so it began. They had only five weeks to cover as much as they could. They would have to prioritise what was important. They would teach their pupils how to read, write and count. They would learn about measurements, food and where to find it and how to cook it. Also human habits, fuel, earth history, geography, how to tell the time, and about tools that the humans used, like telephones, areoplanes and boats. And a whole lot more. The most important lessons would be about something the Cats called "Field Craft". Or the art of not getting caught!

They would also fully explore the rest of the tunnels and entrances. But first, a little game of "Hide and Seek" would be held outside. Hugo and Jago questioned the need for them to spend precious time doing this as they had lived on the Wold all their lives and had always managed to avoid the humans. You couldn't outfox a fox after all!

Lisa just smiled and said, Come with me and you will see. So, leaving Bob behind to work in the kitchen, the rest went up to the Wold, using the Old Wood entrance. Once there, Lisa and Ronnie moved to a piece of higher ground and watched at first, Jago, and then Hugo went from place "A" to place "B" as agreed beforehand. As Ronnie watched, she understood why Lisa had conducted this little test. When both foxes had arrived at place "B", Lisa and Ronnie joined them.

Well? Asked Jago, what was wrong with that?

A few things, actually, said Lisa. Do you know that you have a distinctive way of walking and by doing it you immediately identify yourselves as "Foxes?" You both walk by putting your paws directly in front of the other, leaving a single line of tracks. Worse still, you both went from A to B using the same track.

If you did that in and out of the hideaway, you might as well as put up sign posts to show the humans where it is!

Hugo and Jago were staggered. They looked at Ronnie who nodded her head in agreement. That was exactly what they had both done! They had no idea that they did that. It would be hard for them to un-learn that habit, they could both see that it had to be done. A lesson learned. They would never question Bob or Lisa again!

During their training, Ronnie had decided to change her name. "Ronnie", or Veronica, was the name the human, John Stagg had given her, and now she was free of him, she wanted to move forward with a name she had chosen. Out of respect for Bob and Lisa, she had decided she would like to be called "Astra". Everyone thought it was a good name and seemed to suit her.

After three weeks of training, Lisa and Bob had decided to show their pupils a new secret. They were pleased with the way their three trainees were learning their new skills and it was time for a reward. It was raining outside and so it seemed appropriate that as it was wet outside, they would show them wet inside!

When breakfast was finished, Bob and Lisa told their friends to follow them and they set off down a tunnel that they had not been down before. Astra, Hugo and Jago had wondered what was down there, but had not explored it without being told to do so. They were learning the skill of patience! They had seen Bob and Lisa disappear down it many times and now they would find out where it went. They were excited and trotted along behind the cats as they made their way down the new tunnel. Like the other tunnels, it was wide and high, big enough for humans to walk through, as indeed they once had, but unlike the other tunnels, this one sloped downwards most of the time.

After about ten minutes, the cats stopped and asked if anyone could hear anything. Three heads nodded. Faintly, but distinctly they could hear the unmistakable sound of water The cats continued on and the sound grew louder as they moved further down the tunnel. A few more minutes later, the tunnel ended, and they found themselves in a vast cavern that took their breath away.

It was pitch dark, but they could all see quite well even so, but when Bob lit two lamps, the light transformed the cavern and brought it to life, adding a magical dimension. It was like entering a world, within a world. That was the only way that they could describe it. On their left, two streams of water entered the cavern near roof level and cascaded down the rock walls until finally joining together and tumbled into a pool on the floor of the cavern, making a gentle and almost musical sound as it did so. The pool itself was quite large and it appeared to be deep.

At the front edge of the pool was some sort of gully into which the water surged and flowed across the floor of the cavern before disappearing into another tunnel on the right side of the cavern. Astra immediately noticed that the gully looked odd and out of place. It was straight and level, nature did not usually do things in straight lines.

Lisa, reading her mind, answered her unspoken question.

"Yes. It is human made. We made it like this, so we could put a boat in the water and transport things on it, we did it a long time ago.

Astra, like the others was awe struck at the sheer magic of the place. She had never dreamed that such a place could exist, or that she would be able to visit and enjoy it. There was something about the water. Its sound, its smell and just the fluidity of it. Then it struck her. The water was free, and like Bob and Lisa, it had no definite shape, able to alter itself almost at will, able to go its own way, create its own path.

Like they were doing. Astra had fallen in love with the place. She felt so calm and peaceful! She walked over to the side of the pool and sat down and just looked at the water as it flowed down the waterfalls and entered the pool. This was a place that she knew she would visit often. It was a place of reflection, in more ways than one. She could recharge her batteries, clear her mind and organise her thoughts. The others came over and sat down next to her and they all just looked and enjoyed the magic that was before them. They stayed there a long time and felt totally energised.

Finally Lisa broke the silence with two words. Look up!

Five heads tilted upward and there was a second gasp from three of them. There was something in the rock ceiling that reflected off the light of the lamps, giving the impression that there were millions of tiny stars twinkling above. There was just so much beauty before them that they felt that they could not absorb all of it at once, least they overloaded their senses.

They drank it all in until they thought they would burst. What a place.

Bob rose and said that they would have to return to the main chamber and prepare the lunch, but they would come back in the evening and they would be given an extra treat. They would go on a boat ride!

The lamps were turned off and the stars vanished with the light, and they made their way back up to the upper level just in time to save the fire going out. The meal was prepared and eaten without much being said, each of them with their own thoughts about what they had seen and experienced during the morning. It was only after the dishes were washed and put away did the questions begin.

"Where does the water come from?" Asked Jago.

"We think it is an underground stream, that has somehow found its way into the cavern," answered Bob, "but as with most things in life, when you need to know the answer to a question, you will endeavour to find it. As you will have noticed, it is water that has created this whole system of caves and tunnels, over millions of years."

"I'm so glad it did," said Ronnie, "I have never seen anything like that cavern before. It's magical. I can't wait to go back tonight!"

"Who were they, the humans who were here before, and why did they leave?" Asked Hugo. He, like the others had wondered about that a lot. If they were here once, they might come back.

"Bob and I will explain all later, when you have seen all there is to see, but I can tell you that the humans who used to come here were known as Druids, and I can assure you that they will not be coming back again!"

The afternoon had passed quietly, everyone waiting for the evening to come so they could continue the adventure that had started after breakfast.

Finally it was time, and they set off once again, and made their way back to the magical cavern. It was just as breath-taking the second time as it was the first, even though they knew what to expect, such was the beauty of the place.

Lisa led them away from the waterfall and moved to the right side of the cavern, where, they noticed for the first time, there were several boats by the cave wall. They were hollowed out tree trunks, long and thin, just the right size to fit into the channel. Together they moved one to the edge of the channel, using thin logs as rollers, and Bob tied it to a post with a piece of rope, before they pushed it into the channel where it rose and fell to the flow of the water. Lisa put a lamp at the front of the boat and lit it.

Carefully they climbed into the boat and sat on the wooden seats. There was a long pole on one side of the boat, which Lisa said they would need for the return journey. There was also a great pile of thin rope at the back of the boat, which Bob tied one end to the post that held the boat in place, and the other end was tied firmly to a metal ring at the back of the boat.

When everyone was ready, Bob untied the short rope and the boat started to move into the tunnel, carried by the force of the water. Slowly they left the cavern behind and entered the tunnel, which was rather like a large pipe, although the walls were not smooth. There was just enough width for the boat to move downstream, the boat having been made to fit the channel. The channel turned this way and that, and Jago noticed that the boat was just long enough to take the gentle curves without getting stuck. Everything had been engineered to fit exactly. The water was not deep, only a couple of feet at the most and the boat glided along silently.

After only five minutes, the boat entered a small chamber, with a higher ceiling and floor space on each side of the boat, which they could have jumped onto if they had wished to. Lisa explained that this was called a "Way point". At the back of the boat, the rope had run out, it had been just long enough to reach here. Jago had noticed that as the boat had drifted down the channel, Bob had put the rope on hooks, that had been set into the walls as they had passed by, thus keeping it out of the water. Clearly a lot of thought had gone into this.

Bob untied the rope from the boat and secured it to a stout post set into the rock floor, while keeping the boat tied up with a shorter piece. There was another large coil of rope on the floor next to the post, no doubt for the next leg of the trip.

"Anyone worked it out yet?" Asked Lisa, turning on her seat to look at the three students in the middle of the boat.

"I think I have," said Hugo, looking left and right at the open space on each side of the boat.

"This is how heavier goods were brought into the hideaway. The old wood tunnel is good for collecting firewood and lighter things, but bigger and heavier goods could be loaded into the boat and floated in!"

"Excellent!" Said Lisa, beaming at Hugo. "That's exactly what this is. A supply route."

"And," put in Jago, "more than one boat could be used at once. It could be unloaded here and the goods could either be left on the side floor for a while, or transferred to another boat and taken up to the magical cavern, while the other boat went back down stream again."

"Well done!" Said Bob, "that's exactly what happened. It is possible to fit at least two boats in here at the same time."

"But," said Astra, who sat listening to the discussion, but had said nothing until now, "The whole hideaway is secret, with very clever ways of hiding the entrances and tunnels, so how could sacks and boxes be loaded into these boats without anyone noticing? And where did the goods come from in the first place?"

Bob and Lisa exchanged a look and nodded in agreement. All three of their pupils had contributed to the discussion, each solving a part of the problem and, most importantly, working together and sharing knowledge, feeding off the thoughts of the others. Working as a group. After only three weeks, it was more than they could have hoped for.

"What time is it?" Asked Bob.

"I don't know exactly," answered Astra, "early evening is about as close as I can get. Why do you ask?"

"When we showed you the "Magical Cavern" as you call it, this morning, why did we not continue and take the boat ride then?" Asked Bob.

"Because it was daylight!" Said Hugo & Jago together.

"Correct!"

"So the goods were brought in under the cover of darkness, when there would be no one around, but where were the goods stored before they were collected and loaded?" Asked Astra, "surely someone would have seen them?"

"The answer to that question lies further on downstream," said Lisa. "Shall we continue?"

Bob tied on the long rope and pushed the boat forward, and slowly they slid into the next section of tunnel and left the "Way Point" behind. As before, everyone was careful to keep their paws away from the edge of the boat, as it bumped its way down the channel. Once again at the back of the boat, Bob was hanging the rope on hooks set into the tunnel walls to keep it from getting wet.

Astra wondered how many millions of years it had taken the water to create this tunnel, and indeed, all the others. Quite a lot, she guessed. Little by little, piece by piece, the relentless water had made its way down to whatever lay ahead. The water had been patient, knowing it would, in the end, win its battle against the rock. Just like the first part of the journey, the channel again wended its way along, curving gently left and right as the water carried them along.

It was very enjoyable, just floating along gently on the current. It was also exciting, as only Bob and Lisa knew just where they were going. Jago turned to watch Bob with the rope and noticed that there was not much of it left, it could only mean another stop was coming up. He was right. The boat entered another "Way Point" chamber, just like the first one and it came to a halt. Bob tied up and secured the rope to a post set into the floor on the right hand side. On the left side another large coil of rope was waiting for the next part of the journey.

A thought suddenly came into Astra's mind, and she quickly shielded her thoughts from the others while she took the time to understand what it was. Like the first "Way Point", there was room on either side to load or unload things, and again there was enough height for humans to have stood upright. It was a marvellous way of travelling and every one was enjoying the trip. Without waiting too long, Bob changed over the rope and once again they continued to float on their way.

The final part of the journey came to an end after a further five minutes of slow progress, and the boat entered a third "Way Point", only this one was much wider than the other two, but not as long, having only the length for one boat. To compensate for this lack of length, there was a second channel that had been cut into the rock, with a wide gap between the two. The second channel, on their left side was clearly man-made, its sides completely straight.

Astra saw her chance to test her theory, and she turned to Bob, who was busy tying up the boat and said casually,

"It must have taken you ages to cut that second channel out of the hard rock!"

Bob nodded absently. "It certainly did, the rock was very hard!"

Astra turned back to face the front of the boat again and shielded her thoughts once more as she considered what she had learned.

She had guessed correctly. Some of the "Druids", in this area at least, had in fact been the Gallownians on an earlier visit to earth, only on that occasion they had taken the form of humans!

The reason for the second channel was obvious. Two boats could be here, side by side, separated by the width of the rock between them, onto which either boat could be loaded or unloaded. What lay beyond this chamber was still unknown, as the water seemed to flow straight into the rock face ahead of them and disappear under it.

They did not have to wait long to find out. Lisa sprang out of the boat and onto the rock platform between the two channels, and Bob passed the long pole to her from the boat. She used it to pull down something from the ceiling and everyone knew at once what it was. It was another "Periscope", just like the one they had all used when they had been in the tunnel that opened into the Old Wood gully. When it was fixed into position, the lamp was blown out and they all took a while to get their eyes adjusted to the darkness again. When Lisa was satisfied that she had her night vision, she folded out two handles and slowly and carefully looked around outside. It was dark outside, but there was half a moon and no cloud so she could see reasonably well. When she was happy that there was no one around, she moved away from the periscope and Bob took her place and continued to scan the outside world.

Lisa turned to the boat and said, "Watch this!" And walked up to the rock face at the far end of the channel and reached down and pulled something on the left side. Immediately the rock face split open and half of it swung inwards, letting a blast of colder air that smelled of rotting vegetation into the chamber. She pulled the door fully open until it was end on and resting on the rock platform. It had opened silently. She stopped to listen for a while and then reached down on the right side and did the same thing, pulling open another half door, this time at the front of the channel in which the boat sat in. More cool air flowed in as this door joined the other until it too was resting on the rock floor between the channels.

The three in the boat peered out, trying to see what lay beyond the doors, but could only see more water ahead. They then turned to look at the doors. They were great slabs of solid rock, at least four inches thick and held in place on metal pins that went into the roof and the floor. They were green with slime at the bottom and were dripping water on to the rock platform. Hugo noticed that the bottom end of each door had been cut at a slight angle so as to avoid hitting the rock platform when they were opened and also to allow the water from the channel outside. Like everything else in this underground world, the attention to detail was fantastic, everything fitting exactly into everything else. Bob had finished his scanning and had folded away the periscope. He nodded at Hugo and said,

"Everything must fit together exactly, or we run the risk of being discovered. I know that it is a chance in a million that someone might notice a small gap here and there, but it is a risk that we cannot take. You must always assume that someone is around. The one time you don't, someone will be!"

Hugo and the others nodded their agreement as Bob and Lisa climbed back into the boat.

Lisa said, "This next part is the most dangerous. If someone comes along unexpectedly, we must pull the boat back inside quickly before we are seen."

At the back of the boat, Bob untied the holding rope and slowly the boat moved forward once again. Jago noticed that Bob was holding the new rope in his paws and letting it out between them. At no time was the boat allowed to be free of control. Slowly the boat emerged out of the channel and when Bob was just clear of the doors, he stopped the boat and everyone listened.

There was the sound of fast-flowing water somewhere off in the distance, but Astra, Hugo and Jago sensed that they had entered a much larger body of water, a lake of some kind, but they could not see what it was as there was a curtain of green blocking their view. When Lisa was satisfied that no one was around, she used the long pole to push the front of the boat to the right, just as Bob released more rope to make the boat move forward again. The front of the boat had swung round and they all realised that they were lying next to a bank on their right hand side. The green "curtain" that had blocked their view, turned out to be the protective screen of branches of a weeping willow tree that hung down and fell into the water, cleverly hiding the entrance to the channels!

Again they waited and listened, and as they did so, Hugo and Jago realised at last where they were.

Directly ahead in the distance was a building. They knew its shape well. It was the Old Mill!

Chapter Twelve

Children, anywhere in the world, are very adaptable, far more so than adults who tend to be more set in their ways, and Freya was no exception. She quickly settled in to her new school, helped by her new friend Dutch. They seemed to have much in common, including speaking three languages, two of which they shared, English and German. She quickly realised that Dutch was "on her wave length" and she had some sort of affinity with him. They sat together in class, and the other children also did their bit to make her welcome. The aeroplane boy, she later learned that he was called "Munch" by the other children, though not to his face by the smaller ones, was also in her class. He always sat at the back of the class and sometimes Freya could feel his eyes on her, although he never actually spoke to her. She did not know that in his mind, she was his girl, and Munch let his pals know that they had better be nice to her or he would want to know the reason why!

Their teacher was a very nice Irish lady called Miss Doyle. She came from a place called Dublin. That was in a country called Ireland. She had a way of getting the best out of her pupils and encouraged them to ask questions and interact with her and with each other. She made learning fun and enjoyable and the children enjoyed her lessons and were fond of her. For reasons no one quite understood, she had a habit of calling the children "Pet".

One thing she was not was a soft touch. If Munch (and it usually was him) or one of his pals started talking or playing around, the soft voice would quickly become sharp and she had a way of looking at you over the top of her glasses that left you in no doubt that she would tolerate no interruptions in her class! Freya was starting to remember some of the children's names and on her second day at school, Miss Doyle gave Freya the job of handing back the drawings the class had made before half-term and she had marked. The children's initials were in the corner of their drawings and Miss Doyle hoped it would help Freya to remember who they were. Dutch was GVDB. Munch was RW. Freya had almost handed out all the drawings when she came across one she was not sure about. With a frown she looked up and asked, "Who is DIM?" The whole class burst out laughing, and even Miss Doyle had a smile on her face. She said, "That one is for Daphne". Freya handed over the drawing to a quiet but better dressed girl who always sat at the front of the class. DIM was Daphne Imelda Marshall.

At play time, Dutch told Freya that DIM was a bit posh and would not go around with the other village kids. She was dropped off and collected by her mother in a car.

Everyone else walked to and from School. Very few families had a car. The Marshall family lived in a big house on the edge of the village. Her father did not have his hair cut in the kitchen. Freya learnt that Miss Doyle would be their teacher until they were nine, then they would get Mrs Hunter, whose voice they could often hear through the wall shouting at her class. They were not looking forward to that.

Mrs Hunter was a dour and miserable woman who seldom had a good word to say about anything or anybody. People tried to like her, but there was very little to like. She had lived alone in the village for quite a long time, moving there since her husband had died. Well, that's what she had always told people, until a man from the village had gone to a football match and had accidentally bumped into her dead husband, who he had once worked with years before. It turned out that Mr Hunter had left his wife because he could not put up with her any more, and was quite surprised that she had listed him as deceased. The man from the village could quite understand Mr Hunter's point of view!

This piece of gossip got around the village in short order, but no one ever told Mrs Hunter, who continued to tell anyone who would listen how hard it was for a widowed woman on her own. As is always the case, the Mrs Hunters of this world were not as smart as they liked to think they were. It is indeed a small world.

The house that Mrs Hunter lived in was somewhat shabby in appearance, mainly because she could not get anyone to do anything to improve it. She had, when she had first moved in asked the local handymen to do a bit of painting, or gardening, or repairing, but in all cases she had found fault with their work and had refused to settle their bills, saying that the work was not up to her standards or that they had not taken the required time to do it properly, as per the regulations. In the end, all had taken only half of what they had quoted for, but vowed not to return again. Word spread and now she could find no one to do anything. Mrs Hunter was her own worst enemy!

Freya was visiting Dutch at his house, and they were sitting in front of the fire in the front room. Before them on the rug was a pile of coins, the proceeds of very busy weekend of hair cutting by Dutch's father. It was Dutch junior's job to count it all up and make a note of how much there was. His father thought it would help his arithmetic skills, and save him the trouble of doing it himself!

Dutch had invited Freya over to help him and for her to learn the strange ways of the British monetary system. He would leave the weights and measures for another time. Freya was interested, having had little contact with money of any kind, either here in England or before in Norway, and was eager to learn, after all, how hard could it be?

Dutch started at the bottom, with a ha'penny. He took one from the pile and handed it to Freya, who looked at it. On one side of the copper coin was the picture of a sailing ship, the date it had been made, and what it was, a Half Penny. On the other side was the head and neck of a lady, Queen Elizabeth the second. Dutch said that the Queen's head was on all the coins and notes, as she was in charge of it all, being Queen. Freya was impressed. She thought that the Queen would be kept busy overseeing it all.

Next came a whole Penny, which Freya had already seen. After that was a funny-looking yellow coin with eight sides. It was called a Three penny bit. On one side was some sort of gate, and the Queen on the other. So far, so good. This was easy. Then Dutch handed her a small silver coin, called a sixpence. It had some sort of thistle on one side, and the Queen again on the other. It was worth six pennies, or two three penny bits, or twelve halfpennies.

"Now it starts to get a bit tricky," said Dutch. "Some coins have two or even three different names!"

"Why?"

Dutch shrugged his shoulders. "Beats me! But a sixpence is also called a Tanner."

"Why?"

"I don't have a clue," was his reply.

"Next we have a shilling," he said, passing one over to her. It was silver again, but bigger than a tanner.

"This is worth twelve pennies, or two sixpences, or four threepenny bits, or twenty-four halfpennies, or a combination of all of them, and if that was not enough, a shilling is also called a Bob!"

"Bob? Why?"

Dutch just looked at her, and raised his eyebrows, saying nothing. This was England, after all. Freya looked at the coin with a frown. "Bob. Bob. That name means something to me, but I don't know why."

"Well, next we have Two shillings, which is also called two Bob, or a Florin!"

Freya opened her mouth, then closed it again, as Dutch said, "Don't ask. In my country, we also have a Florin, or Dutch Guilder."

"Is it the same as two Bob?"

"No."

"Oh."

Dutch called a break then, to allow his friend to think about what she had just been told. There was much to consider, he knew. They looked into the fire for a while, then Freya helped Dutch to put the money into piles, each pile worth a Shilling. Then she nodded. "Right, I've got it. What's next? "

Dutch smiled. "I know it's complicated, but after a while you just get used to it. Anyway, next we come to Half a Crown. You are going to love this coin!" Handing one over to her. "It is worth two Shillings and Sixpence."

Freya looked at the coin in her hand in bewilderment. "Two Shillings and

Sixpence?"

"Yup."

She thought about it for a moment. "So a crown must be worth five shillings!" she said triumphantly.

"Actually no."

"No?"

"As far as I know, there is no crown," he admitted.

"What! There is half a crown, but no crown? In Norway we have crowns, called krone, but they are nothing like this."

"Did you really think they would be?"

Freya rolled her eyes.

Just then Dutch's father came into the room with a tray, on which was a tea pot and cups, together with milk. He knew that neither of them took sugar.

"How are you getting on with the funny money, Freya? Got the hang of it yet?" he asked with a smile.

"Papa, is there a Crown? Freya was just asking why there is half a crown, but no crown. Do you know?"

Mr Van Den Berg set down the tray and scratched his head. "If there is a crown, I've never seen one," he admitted, adding, "and I've lived here quite a long time. Here, have some tea, it will help you think!"

They drank their tea by the fire, and Dutch asked his father if he could show Freya a ten shilling and a pound note, as they had covered all the coins. He went to get his wallet and handed them over to his son. "Carry on, Gilbert, I might learn something."

Dutch junior handed the ten-shilling note to Freya. "This is a ten-shilling note, and worth a lot of money. It is also called ten bob, or half a quid."

"Quid?"

"Sorry, that is another name for a pound note." The ten-shilling note was brown and white and looked like it had value.

"So ten-shillings is four half crowns, or five florins, or twenty sixpences, or forty threepenny bits, or one hundred and twenty Pennies, or a combination of all of them," said Freya.

The two Van Den Bergs looked at each other. This girl was no dummy. "Er, that's correct."

The pound note was green and white and also beautifully designed, like the ten-shilling note. "So a pound note, or quid is worth twenty shillings, or eight half crowns, or ten florins, or forty sixpences, or eighty threepenny bits, or two hundred and forty pennies!"

"You forgot four hundred and eighty half pennies."

"Sorry."

"I really think you have got the hang of the money, Freya. Of course there is a five pound note and a ten-pound one, and even a twenty, but they are worth so much money that I doubt that we will get to see any of them any time soon," said Dutch.

"Well, that only leaves one more thing to tell her about," said Dutch's father.

"What? I thought I had covered them all," said Dutch junior, a puzzled look on his face. "There is something called a guinea."

"I thought that was a small furry animal," said Freya.

Dutch's father laughed. "That is a guinea pig. A guinea is twenty one shillings. It is a recognised unit of currency, but is not spoken of very much, or used for that matter."

"Is there a guinea note?" Asked Dutch junior.

"What do you think?" Replied his father.

"As we are dealing with the British monetary system, I would think not," said Dutch junior.

"You would be correct," smiled his father, turning to Freya. "Welcome to England, Freya!"

There was no rain now, as the boat slid slowly along the bankside, Hugo thought that they would still be very hard to see, even if someone was standing on the bankside, directly over their heads, but, as ever, caution was the name of the game, as had been drummed into the three of them for the last few weeks. Hope for the best, but plan for the worst. Never take things for granted.

Astra watched the building on the land ahead grow larger as they approached. She wondered what it was, where it was, and who lived in it. The noise of a branch, growing out of the bank, scraped against the boat and made them all jump. They were all tense. Up on the wold after dark, there was zero chance of any humans being around, even though they checked anyway. Here, there was more of a chance that someone could be around.

"It's called the Old Mill, because it used to be a Mill, years ago, but now it's empty and abandoned, no one lives there anymore," said Jago. "We are in the lake next to it. We have been here many times, it's on the edge of Elfington Village."

Astra nodded in the darkness. The fox twins certainly got around. She hadn't been anywhere, only the farm she had escaped from. It was a real pleasure to be seeing all these new places now she was free.

Jago reflected that the whole secret tunnel system had been adapted in a very clever and practical way, whoever had done it, knew what they were doing!

Ronnie, heard his thoughts and smiled to herself in the darkness. Shielding her thoughts briefly again, she was ninety-nine per cent sure that she knew who had adapted the tunnels to how they were now, two of the beings responsible were sitting in the boat!

She quickly opened her mind again to the others and joined in the conversation that was going on.

There was a human-made slope leading down from the bank to the water's edge, no doubt for getting in and out of the boat and on to dry land. The boat slowed and then stopped just short of the ramp and again they sat silently and listened. Five pairs of very sensitive ears and eyes scanned the area, heads turning in all directions. Nothing. The only sound they could hear was the noise of the water flowing further along the bank. They were alone.

The boat moved forward again and nudged the ramp. Lisa immediately sprang out and silently bounded up the slope and vanished into the night. The others waited. A few minutes later she re-appeared, like a shadow.

"All clear!"

The boat was secured and everyone jumped out and joined Lisa on the grassy bank. She led the way along the wide strip of grass and headed for the Old Mill. Close up it was quite large, but clearly abandoned. They halted next to the channel where the water surged and roared down the side of the Mill and had driven the big Mill wheel, only now the wheel was still, broken and decaying like the Mill itself. Astra noticed some large round stones, each with a hole in the middle, leaning against the side of the mill. They looked like huge wheels, larger than those in the trucks. She went over to look at them more closely. They all had grooves cut into them, running from the centre outwards. She had no idea what they were. Lisa joined her and said,

"They are called Millstones. They were used to crush the wheat between them and make flour.

The big wheel drove a machine inside the Mill and it turned the stones around. Clever, don't you think."

Astra nodded. It was clever, she thought to herself. She was surprised that Humans had thought of it, on account of them not being very bright. Lisa had heard her thoughts and said,

"Never under estimate the Humans. Not all of them are dumb!"

Astra nodded. Another lesson learned.

Hugo could imagine the Mill as it had once been, busy and prosperous, a vital part of the local community. People would have come and gone, deliveries in and out, the perfect place for the Druids to receive supplies. It would have been easy to put a little aside, which then could have been loaded into the boat when everyone had gone and darkness had fallen. Like now.

They moved away from the noise of the water, Jago noticing that Bob had stayed back a bit. "I didn't want the noise of the water to ruin my hearing," he explained to Jago's un-asked question.

Jago nodded. Smart!

They wandered around, exploring the ample grounds that surrounded the Mill.

There was a wide track on each side of the mill that led down to join the main road between Elfington and Beggars Cross.

Jago watched the water, after it had turned the Mill wheel, meander its way along through the meadow until it joined the River Elf. It occurred to him that a boat could be put into that channel, down below the Mill Wheel and then enter the river itself. It was another way of getting around without being seen. Ingenious!

After a good scout around, they assembled once again by the lake. It was getting cooler now, and there was a thin mist hanging over the still water. The Moon had risen and cast its light down over the land below. A wisp of cloud floated slowly across its face. It was a beautiful place to be.

It was time to go home. Everyone returned to the boat and climbed in. Again, Lisa vanished for a few minutes while the others waited. She returned and climbed into the boat, having had a final check around. Bob sat at the front and pulled on the rope to make the boat move quietly along. They arrived back at the channel entrance and slid beneath the cover of the willow tree, whose leaves were already starting to fall off into the water. Its protection would be diminished in the winter months, but the darkness would take over instead.

Lisa used her pole to push the rear of the boat away from the bank and Bob quickly pulled the boat back into the channel. As soon as the back of the boat entered inside, Lisa bounded onto the platform between the two channels and silently closed both doors behind them. They were safely inside once again.

Bob also jumped onto the platform and lit the lamp again. The two cats looked down at their three students and Bob said,

"We hope you all enjoyed your adventures today!"

Three heads nodded together, knowing that something was coming their way.

"Good!" Said Lisa. "In that case, you can take us back to the Magical Cavern! Bob and I have earned a rest!"

Jago and Hugo moved forward to the front of the boat, with Astra behind them. Bob and Lisa sat further back. Bob gave instructions to the others and Hugo untied the boat and began to pull the boat forward, passing the rope back to Jago, who in turn passed it back to Astra, who, under Bob's watchful eye, began to coil it up. At each waypoint, each of the students changed places, so everyone got to do all the jobs once each. By the time they arrived back in the magical cavern, they were all quite good at it.

The journey was complete. The boat was pulled out of the channel and left to dry. Everyone was tired as they made their way back to the main chamber, where, of course, the fire had gone out.

Everyone had a quick cup of tea, made by Astra, then headed for bed. Tomorrow training would resume again!

Back at the Old Mill, the lake was silent, with not even a ripple to show that anyone had ever been there.

The moon looked down, as before, at the Old Mill by the lake. It would keep the secret of what it had seen to itself. It always did.

The dictionary says that a Druid is a seer, a soothsayer, a person who sees. Someone who speaks the truth and who has an insight of the future. Someone who gives the facts. Someone who would stand up for truth and justice, and speak up for those who have been misled and lied to.

Such people would, of course, not be very popular with the "Authorities", in whatever form they may be, who would like to think that the "Truth" was whatever they decided it would be at any given time.

Down the centuries, many forms of "Authorities" had distorted and manipulated the truth to make it fit what they wanted it to be. Wars have been fought and countless lives lost, based on nothing more than lies.

It is small wonder then, that people who challenge the "Truth", and do not "go with the flow" are soon noticed by the authorities and encouraged to toe the line and keep their mouths shut, or else! Money can be offered, and if that fails, threats can be made to ensure that the troublemakers see the light. If, at the end of the day they are not willing to be sensible, they can, of course simply be killed. It is hardly surprising that speaking the truth and giving the true facts is a very dangerous pastime, and such people would need a safe place to hide out and avoid persecution. Such places are very thin on the ground. They would have to be totally secret and secure, known only to a select and trusted few. It would also have to have a practical element, enabling the Druids to get their hands on food, water and fuel, and to allow the trusted few to come and go without detection.

While being thin on the ground, such a place was found under it! How the Druids came upon the caves and tunnels under the moors, nobody really knows. But find it they did, and they used it and adapted it for years. The secret chambers and tunnels were never found, and no one but the Druids knew of them. It is still a mystery to this day what happened to the Druids, they just vanished. Some say they were captured and killed. Others claim they went overseas or perhaps they went back to their own world, as the humans on this one were not ready for contact, or to accept this "truth".

The tunnels and caves were abandoned by the Druids and the secret of their existence died with them. Until the Gallownians came back to visit the Earth again!

Chapter Thirteen

To the north of Elfington lay the small town of Pondford, and it was here that Dr Thomas Thornton lived alone in a small, furnished one bedroom flat, with a shared bathroom. It was actually the lower half of a small house, his landlord, an elderly widower, lived upstairs. Being a Doctor who worked shifts in an Accident and Emergency department and a bachelor, the flat was often somewhat untidy. But not today. Today he was not working and the flat was spotless. Not since he had moved in had it looked so spick and span. Everything that could be washed, had been. Everything that could be cleaned, had been cleaned to within an inch of its life. There was not a cobweb, piece of fluff or even a speck of dust to be seen. There was a good reason for all this effort. Dr Tom was expecting a rare visitor. A special visitor.

He stood in the living room in a state of nerves not seen since he had sat his final exams to qualify as a Doctor. He checked the room once again. It would have to do. There was no time left to clean anything else. There was nothing left to clean. There were fresh flowers on the table. The flowers were in a new vase which sat on a new table cloth. The brown wooden table had been polished. He moved over to the flowers and adjusted them yet again. There.

That looked better, he told himself. Or were they better before? He reached out for them again when the doorbell stopped him in his tracks . His visitor had arrived!

He had to stop himself from running to open the door, and with an effort he slowed his pace. He opened the door, a smile of welcome on his face to greet his guest. Only it wasn't his guest. It was his landlord who had forgotten his keys again. Tom let him in and returned to the living room, disappointed and anxious, his mind racing. He had food. He had drink. He had flowers. But what if his guest didn't come? What if something had happened? What if his guest was allergic to flowers? Christ, he hadn't thought of that. What if… The doorbell rang again. This was it. Had to be. He walked to the door again and opened it. His guest stood on the doorstep and looked up at him. Dr Tom just stood there, as if suffering from paralysis. His guest raised an eyebrow and spoke first. "Well, Tom, aren't you going to ask me in?"

Penny Grey had arrived!

Dutch was a good teacher, patient and able to explain things as far as he could, and admitting when he did not know. Freya was a willing pupil, with a thirst for knowledge and information. Now she had digested the Imperial money system, she was ready to tuck into the weights and measures.

Soon she knew that there were sixteen ounces in a pound, and fourteen pounds in a stone. twelve inches made a foot, and three feet would give you a yard. Twenty-two of those equalled a chain, or sixty-six feet! A furlong was two hundred and twenty yards. Or one eight of a mile.

Both Dutch and Freya were fascinated by the British way of doing things, their money, weights and measures. It seemed to suit them. It was just so different from what they had been used to in their own countries, especially Freya, as Dutch had lived in England for quite a bit longer than she had. Unlike nearly all the other children, they had the advantage of knowing both the British and continental systems, Imperial and Metric. They were familiar with millimetres, millilitres and milligrams, and all that came after them.

They had to admit that the continental system was much easier, as everything was in tens, hundreds, thousands and so on, whereas here it was twelve pennies to a shilling, sixteen ounces to a pound. Fourteen pounds to a stone, twenty shillings to pound (For the life of them, neither could see why both money and weight had the same name!).

There were also eight pints to a gallon! Or four quarts!

It was all just the British way of doing things, and that was that. The two friends complimented each other very well, wanting to learn and improve themselves, to understand how and why things were as they were. In the years ahead they would grow ever closer, creating a special bond, unique only to them. They gave and received energy from each other and were happiest when they were together.

The number that mattered most to Freya was, of course eleven. Her special number. She saw them everywhere, a random look at the clock would often be elven minutes past the hour, or the telephone number on the side of a van would end in eleven. The bus that ran between Pondford to Abbotsbury, via Elfington and Wall Bridge was a number eleven. It was a great comfort to Freya to see these numbers and to know that her parents were never far from her.

It was evening and outside darkness had fallen a while ago. It had been a lovely day and both Tom and Penny had really enjoyed it. They had talked a lot, each finding out things about the other. Tomorrow they would be back at work, and it would be "Doctor" and "Sister" in front of the others, until they could be themselves again. But that was tomorrow. Tom helped Penny into her coat, noticing the brief thrust of her chest against her blouse as she slipped her arms into the coat. He quickly put on his own and as they moved towards the front door, she turned to face him and said, "Let's say our goodbyes here, rather than in public."

Tom nodded. He had insisted on walking her to the station and she had agreed, touched by his concern. It was nice to have someone who cared. Tom moved forward to kiss her on the cheek, but Penny stepped back and said, "No." Tom stepped back instantly and said, "Sorry, Penny, I..." She looked straight into his eyes for a long moment, as if deciding something. Her hand came up and touched her cheek.

"Not there." The hand moved to her lips, and a finger lightly touched them. "Here." The hand reached out and gently touched his face, her gaze never leaving his. The hand moved again and moved slowly behind his head, and gently pulled his face to hers. Their lips met, briefly at first, then again for a much longer, passionate kiss, before she pulled back and they hugged each other, each holding the other tightly. They stayed like that for a long time, just holding the other, feeling the emotion that surged through them both. A noise upstairs made them part quickly. Up on the landing, Tom's landlord shuffled out and went into the bathroom. Tom smiled at Penny and said, "Let's hope he's gone for a sit down job!"

Penny laughed out loud. "Let's hope so," she murmured reaching for him again.

They walked down the dark streets, damp after a shower, in silence, each lost in their own thoughts. There were not many people about, and their footsteps seemed loud. It was cold and there was the familiar smell of coal smoke hanging in the air. Penny took Tom's arm and held on to him, as if to say "He's Mine!" The walk to the station seemed to go by in a matter of seconds, and Penny waited as Tom bought a platform ticket, before they moved onto the platform and sat on a bench, waiting for the train to come, both hoping it would be late. They sat close together and turned to look at each other.

"Thank you for a lovely day, Tom."

"Thank you for making it so."

"I really enjoyed being with you, you must come to my place next time."

"Thank you. I will look forward to next time."

"You haven't tasted my cooking yet," laughed Penny.

"You haven't tasted mine either," admitted Tom. "The food we just had, my mother made it, I didn't want to poison you!"

I'm sure you wouldn't have, and even if you did, you could always give me the kiss of life," she said in a husky voice.

Tom laughed, just as the points on the track changed with a loud "Clank", followed by the "Clunk" of the signal changing. The train could be heard in the distance, approaching the station.

"I don't want you to go." he said.

"I know. I don't want to go either, so I'll settle for a little of that mouth to mouth, just in case we need it in the future," she said, reaching for him again. "What about the public?" Murmured Tom as Penny's lips found his again.

The steam had long dissipated into the cold night air, and the last few wisps of smoke vanished into the November sky. The points had changed once again and the signal had returned to where it had been before. Dr Tom Thornton stood alone on the platform and watched the red lamp that hung on the back of the guard's van finally disappear far in the distance as the train turned a corner and followed the valley on its way to Elfington, and then to Wallbridge. Finally Tom turned and walked down the now deserted platform and left the station behind in the darkness. He felt a strange sensation, and it took him a moment to identify it. For the first time in his life, he felt incomplete. Penny had gone.

The boy called Dutch was impressed. It was Saturday afternoon, and he had called at his new friend's house to see if she would be allowed out to play. She had been, provided that they stay together, and not go too far. Mr Olsen had made it clear to Dutch that he was responsible for Freya when they were out together.

They had walked off together and Dutch took Freya to a tall tree nearby, so he could demonstrate to her how to climb it. He got about half way up, turned and waved down at his pupil, who waved back. Satisfied she had taken note of what he had done, he made his way down again to stand beside Freya, who had watched from the ground. Dutch was proud of his tree climbing skills, he would soon , probably next year, he told Freya, be able to go even further up.

Freya was invited to have a try, and she walked up to the tree, paused for a moment, then started to make her way up. Dutch called instructions up to her, she was only a girl after all, and everyone knew that they were not good at this sort of thing. He fell silent as he watched Freya literally spring up the tree, reaching and then passing the branch where he had stopped. She continued on, reaching the very top of the tree, where she turned and waved down at Dutch, who waved back in disbelief. After having a good look around, she began carefully to climb down, finally reaching the lowest branch, and sitting down on it. She then shuffled sideways along it until she was clear of the trunk, and holding on with both hands, leaned back and swung upside down for a while, and ending with a back flip, landing lightly on her feet.

She walked over to Dutch, brushing her hands clean as she did so. "Good Tree!"

Dutch nodded, still in shock. "You climbed that very well," he said graciously. "Just like a cat!"

"Meow," said Freya with a smile.

They left the tree behind and had a short walk around the village before arriving back at Freya's house. Her Uncle was in the back garden, stacking logs in a pile near the back door. They helped him until the light began to fade then Dutch said his goodbyes and headed for his home. On the way he reflected on the afternoon's activity. Whichever way you looked at it, Freya Olsen was a very impressive young lady!

Tom was coming around to visit her today, but Penny was much more organised for it than Tom had been. Her small cottage did not need extra cleaning, as it was always neat and tidy. Nor did she need help from her mother to cook a meal, she was a good cook in her own right. It felt good to have a visitor to cook for again. It had been a long time since she had felt like this, part exited, part nervous. The problem she had now, was what to wear? She had tried on, then discarded several combinations of clothes, unable to make up her mind. Thankfully she did not have too many clothes to choose from. Nurses were not highly paid!

Normally she had no problem choosing what to wear, but if she was honest, this visit, this date, was important to her. It mattered. She was starting to get rather fond of Dr Tom.

She stood in front of the long mirror in her bedroom, wearing just bra and pants, looking at her reflection. Tall and slender, willowy, as some might say, with long shapely legs and a slender waist, she had no need of girdles or corsets. Walking up and down stairs and corridors at the hospital kept her fit!

She had never had too much "Up Top", but there was enough for a man to get his hand around, she told herself with a smile! A reasonably pretty face with short brown hair and hazel eyes. Not bad, she told herself. Now, what to cover it all with?

Doctor Tom Thornton emerged nervously from Wallbridge station and, with flowers in his hand, began to follow the directions he had been given by Sister Penny Grey to get to her cottage. He hoped he would be a regular user of this route, as what lay at the end of it was becoming special to him. He thought back to her visit to him of the week before, he had really enjoyed it, and he was sure that she had as well. What a beautiful woman she was, and what a lucky man he was to be invited to her home, something he was sure that few men ever did, though many would like to be.

The day after her visit to him, they were back on shift at Abbotsbury Hospital, and it was back to "Doctor" and "Sister" in front of the others, until they had a moment in private where they could relax a little. She had repeated her invitation to him, and he had waited impatiently for the day to come. It had finally arrived. It was today. It was now.

He turned into her road and looked for number seven. With dry mouth and sweaty palms, he opened the gate and walked up the short path and knocked on the door. It was opened at once, and there she was. God, she looked lovely he thought to himself as he handed over the flowers and gave her a peck on the cheek.

She had finally settled on a simple dress, which fitted her like a glove, showing off her curvaceous figure to perfection. "Wow!" You look gorgeous!" said Tom on seeing her. "Thank you, kind Sir!" smiled Penny, pleased at the compliment, giving him a mock curtsy. "Please, come in!"

Tom stepped into a small but cosy living room and took off his coat. A fire burned brightly in the grate and he could smell the smell of cooking in the air, and it reminded him of his grandmother's house, where there always seemed to be something in the oven. "The meal won't be long, so I'll leave you to have a look around. Drink?"

"Please."

Penny disappeared with his coat and came back with two bottles of his favourite beer, a bottle opener and a glass. "Help yourself, there's plenty more," before vanishing once again into the kitchen, tying an apron around her slim waist as she went.

Tom poured one of the bottles into the glass and looked at some of the photographs as he drank it. There was one of Penny as a girl, holding a rabbit. Another of a wedding, probably Mum and Dad, the bride looking attractive, like his host. There were a few more of her family and one more of her standing next to a man. Tom wondered who he was, but would not ask. If she wanted to tell him about the man in the photo, she would in her own time. He would not pry into her private life. She had mentioned she had had a serious relationship but that it was over quite a long while ago. She had been hurt, he knew. If this was the man, he was a fool to let Penny slip through his hands. Tom would not be so foolish. Women like Penny were few and far between and he would take his time, letting things go at their own pace.

Tom turned as Penny came back into the room carrying a large dish, which she placed on the table, already set for two.

"Cottage Pie suit you? I made it with real Cottage!"

Tom grinned. "A beautiful woman who can cook and tell jokes! I am truly blessed!"

She blushed at the compliment and went back to the kitchen, returning with vegetables and gravy. He poured her a glass of wine and himself the second bottle of beer as the plates arrived and they sat down to enjoy the food she had prepared. "If it tastes as good as it looks, I am in for a treat!" said Tom, his mouth watering.

It did. It was fabulous. They chatted and laughed while they ate and enjoyed it. Later there was a Ginger Pudding, with custard. Tom was in heaven.

Finally, they could eat no more. Tom reached out and took her hand and kissed it.

"That was fantastic! It really was. I cannot remember when I have enjoyed a meal more, or the company. Thank you very much! I'm afraid I'll wake up in a minute and find out that this was all a dream."

Penny rose from her chair and came around the table and kissed him lightly on the lips. "Thank you. They say that the way to a man's heart is through the stomach!"

"How true!"

"I'll just put these dishes in the sink, please make yourself comfy on the sofa and I'll come and join you in a moment."

Tom did as he was asked as Penny cleared the table, refusing his offer of help. After a while she returned and put more coal on the fire before joining him on the sofa. She sat down close to him and again looked into his eyes for a long moment before she spoke in a low voice. "Thank you for being patient with me, it's been a long time since I've had feelings for a man, I need to take things slowly." Tom looked back at her, drinking in her beauty.

"For you I would wait for ever. It's been a long time for me too, since I have had strong feelings for a lady."

"You have them for me?" He leaned forward and kissed her gently. "Yes."

"Good! I was hoping you might!"

She kicked off her shoes and snuggled up close to him, taking his left hand and draping his arm around her shoulders and reaching for his right hand she placed it around her slender waist. Her left hand was around his waist. She whispered to him.

"Hold me, don't let go, just hold me."

Tom was more than happy to comply, very aware that he was holding a stunningly beautiful woman in his arms. He could feel the warmth of her body pressing against him, smell her perfume. He was indeed a very lucky man. After a while, the warmth of the fire, the food and the drink all combined to totally relax them both. They fell asleep in each other's arms. Happy and at peace together.

The five weeks of instruction had come to an end. To the pupils it had simply flown by and they could hardly accept that today was the day that would decide the rest of their lives. Bob and Lisa had done as much as they could in the time they had. They had concentrated on the most important things that Astra, Hugo and Jago needed to learn, the most important of all being. Do not get caught!

For Bob and Lisa too this was an important day. This would be their penultimate day on Earth, and they would miss it. They had grown used to being in form of a cat and they would also miss the three friends that now sat beside the fire that they had started, after eating the breakfast they had prepared. Today they would decide if enough progress had been made to earn the friends the right to stay in the secret hideaway and survive on their own. They had to be sure that the humans would never learn of it, or of them being here. Hugo, Jago and Astra had worked very hard and done well. They each had the ability to read, write and count equal to a human child aged seven. They had learned how to avoid being followed and what they should do if they thought that they might be. They had learned how to start a fire from nothing and to prepare and cook basic meals. In learning these skills, they had developed their telepathic communications and could communicate between themselves quite well, including how to shield their private thoughts and keep them to themselves.

They had also explored all the secret tunnels and entrances to the hideaway and knew how to open and close the doors, and how to use the "Periscope" to check before they went out. They had done all that had been asked of them, but as they sat together waiting for Bob and Lisa to come, they hoped with all their hearts that it would be enough to enable them to stay here.

The thought of going back to what they had been before and of having no memory of what they had learned was too frightening to think about, especially for Astra, who sat between the brothers as she had got used to doing. She felt completely at ease with them now, as they did with her. It was only the humans who had decided that they should be enemies.

Lisa and Bob came into the main chamber and sat together beside the fire and facing the trio of friends. They were not smiling. It was Lisa who began, addressing all three of them together.

"Bob and I have done our very best to train and guide you over the last five weeks and we know that you have worked hard to learn from us the many lessons we have taught you. As you know, we have to be very sure that you will be able to survive here without us and not get caught by the humans and reveal this place to them." She stopped and looked at Bob, who continued.

"I agree with what Lisa has just said, you have all done your best to learn from us, but I have to tell you that you have not reached the required standard that we both think you need to attain to be allowed to stay here without us." He paused to look at the three disappointed faces before going on.

"You have in fact exceeded it," his face breaking into a beaming smile, unable to maintain the false gloom any longer. Three heads that had dropped suddenly looked up, confused and bewildered.

Exceeded the required standard, they thought as one, that means… "You can stay," finished Lisa for them. "Congratulations!"

The cats moved forward to embrace their friends, who had still not quite recovered from the shock and surprise of being allowed to stay. They hugged the cats and then hugged each other, dancing around the chamber in sheer relief. They had done it. They could stay. All the hard work had been worthwhile. They knew that they must continue to extend themselves when the cats left, but for now they could relax and enjoy the moment.

When they had all returned to sit in front of the fire again, Astra moved closer to the flames and gazed into them, suddenly overcome with emotion. She could never have dreamed that she would have ended up here like this. She had come such a long way since that Saturday afternoon in September when she had been forced to chase after Hugo, just over five weeks ago. It seemed a life time ago. She turned to face the others. "Now that we know that we can stay here, there is something that I want to do. It is something that I have given much thought to, and I want to share this moment with you all. The collar around my neck, was put there by the humans, dogs that they 'own' have to wear one. The others nodded in approval. Jago moved over to her and sat down, gazing into the flames, to let her know that he understood how she felt, how they all felt. He looked over at her, correctly reading her emotions and said, "It's time!"

She nodded and replied back, "Would you do the honours?"

Jago said, "It will be a pleasure!"

The others moved closer to watch, sensing what was about to happen.

Gently, Jago undid the collar around Astra's neck, letting it fall to the floor. She picked it up and threw it into the flames, watching it catch fire. There was no going back, there never had been. Now she was completely free!

The final task for the two Gallownians on planet Earth, was to visit Freya for one last time. They waited until well after dark, and then made their way to Freya's new home. They were in no hurry and took their time as they moved down the tunnel to the Old Wood, this being the closest to where they had to go.

Once outside they moved silently through the damp and somewhat chilly night air, their breath coming out as vapour as they went along. There was no moon. They did not need one, being able to see very well in the near total darkness. There were leaves everywhere on the woodland floor, a few blowing around as a brief gust of wind caught them. There were also quite a few Pine trees in this part of the wold, the wind whistling through their needles, making a distinctive sound. The two cats exchanged a look. They would really miss this world.

They went carefully, slowly, as always, savouring the early winter darkness. They did not want to arrive too early. The humans must all be asleep before they could do their work. Tomorrow night would be the night they would leave. There would be a big storm to mask their departure. But tonight it was clear, dry and cold.

They arrived at last at the dry stone wall at the bottom of Freya's garden, where they sat in its shelter and watched and listened, alert for any sign that they had been detected. Far away they heard the distant barking of a dog, the sound carrying on the cold night air. It was not barking at them and after a while it stopped, just as the church clock struck midnight. When they were sure that they had not been seen, they sprang up to the top of the wall and had another look around. You could never be too careful and the job they had to do this night was important. The humans might get lucky and look out of their window just at the wrong time.

Nothing stirred, and they jumped down into the back garden, silently landing on the lawn. Like shadows they moved forward to the tree that was next to the old house. No lights were showing in any of the windows of the houses in this street. Again a slight wait, then they climbed up the tree until they were level with the bedroom window of Freya's room. They could see that the window was slightly open, which was a bonus. They could do part of what needed to be done from where they were, but they needed to get inside Freya's bedroom. Once again they waited and listened. They could hear the ticking of a clock from inside the house. The clock was downstairs and there were two closed doors between them and the clock, not to mention an almost closed window. The clock had a soft tick, not always heard by humans who were in the room in which it was in.

Satisfied, Bob moved along the branch until he could reach the window frame, where he gently pulled it towards him, just enough for him and Lisa to get through. Hearing Freya's breathing had not changed, Bob sprang into the room and landed silently on the floor. Seconds later Lisa's head appeared through the gap and she too landed on the floor without making a sound. The window was left as it was, they may have to leave in a hurry!

The first thing Bob did was to take out the package he had brought with him and looking around the room slipped it in the pocket of a coat hanging on the back of the bedroom door. That done he moved to the bed where Lisa was waiting. They sat down less than four feet from the sleeping body of Freya. Her head was facing them, but she was fast asleep. With the main task completed, they had only to check how well the repair work they had done on the night of the crash was going.

Wasting no time they connected to Freya's mind and were pleased to see how well she had healed. The gifts they had planted in her mind weeks ago were still there, but they saw the repairs had gone well beyond restoring her to her original condition. They had actually had the effect of augmentation. In only a few weeks, Freya's injuries had completely healed, but her body, and to a much greater extent, her mind had continued to evolve rapidly. In the years to come her DNA would continue to accelerate her mental capacity. She would, without doubt be empathic, and telepathic. Just as they were.

She would possess a greatly enhanced intellect. The building blocks had already been there, but now, thanks to their intervention, the possibilities for this special girl were incalculable. As the cats watched, Freya went into Rapid Eye Movement, or REM sleep. As she should. From this time forward she was Augmented, and without doubt the most advanced human being on the planet.

Moving quickly but carefully, Bob and Lisa went back out of the window, deciding not to try to close it in case it made noise. They had been very lucky so far and did not want any problems now. Along the branch, down the tree, across the lawn and over the wall, where they again waited, looked and listened.

Satisfied that they were alone, the two cats vanished into the dark night as silently as they had come.

Ten minutes later, Rose awoke and needed to go to the loo, which was downstairs. On the way she peeped into Freya's room. The child was sleeping soundly. A slight gust of wind moved the lace curtain, attracting Rose's attention. She quietly moved to the window and pulled it closed, and went out of the room, closing the door behind her and made her way downstairs.

As she sat in the chilly toilet she thought how her life had changed since that terrible night in August, and how lucky they were to have Freya with them. There was no going back now, not for any of them.

Lisa and Bob had gone out together, after darkness had fallen, saying they had one last thing that they had to do before they left tomorrow. Astra had noticed Bob had taken something with him in a small bag, but had not asked what it was or where they were going. There would always be much about the cats that would remain a mystery. So Hugo, Jago and Astra were alone, sitting in front of the fire, a taste of things to come. It brought it home to all of them that soon they would be here on their own.

The fire was warm and a sense of peace settled over them all. Astra was completely at ease with Hugo and Jago, and they with her. A little over five weeks ago this would have been impossible, and they had trouble thinking that it was only five weeks ago that their lives had changed forever. It seemed as if they had lived here like this forever. The world was a different place for them now, they knew so much more, and yet they knew that it was a mere fraction of what there was to know. They were like sponges, soaking up knowledge and information, learning, improving themselves. Hugo and Jago had found it very hard to change the way they walked and to stop using the same track each time, but they were getting used to it now. It had never crossed their minds that by doing so they were making it easy for the humans to identify them and to track them. How could they not have seen it themselves?

John Stagg had gone. They had watched him go. They were not sure if he had seen them or not, they just had to see him leave. It was strange to think that it was because of him that they were here now.

It was October now and the nights were drawing in quickly, and the temperatures were much cooler. Winter was on its way. Nearly every night, except when it rained, and when their instruction had ended for the day, they would all go outside to the Old Wood and collect wood for the fire. There was already great piles of it stacked up inside the main chamber, but Lisa and Bob had assured them that they always needed more, as the approaching winter would be very hard. How they knew this, no one asked. They just accepted that it was true. The cats knew many things. They also collected as much food as they could find as well. Nuts, berries, fruit and grains, also potatoes from the fields. The humans were busy gathering them in and left many behind.

The shop in the village often put out unsold food at the back of the store that they could use, as did the butcher and the greengrocer. They had been shown by the cats how to store it and how to make things with it. Astra was particularly good at cooking and baking things and they collected a good stock of everything. For Astra, it was really enjoyable to go out and bring things home. To her home, the first one she had ever had that was really hers. Safe, secure, where no humans could interfere with them. She felt a feeling of freedom, shared by Hugo and Jago. They could determine their own future, plan ahead, free of humans in their own private, secret world. They were so lucky to be able to stay here and live in peace. They could not thank the cats enough for letting them stay. They could never go back to how life had been before. Not now. The cats had given them a future that they could never have dreamed of. They had given them something far far better than a gun, a knife or a trap. They had given them knowledge, and knowledge was power. The power of the mind was a far better weapon.

The humans killed animals for sport. For fun. To pass the time. For nothing. They were cruel, crude, arrogant and stupid. They thought they were smart. They were wrong. It would be their undoing.

Chapter Fourteen

Astra, Jago and Hugo awoke the morning after the Gallownians had left with the realisation that they were now solely responsible for the hideaway and all of its secrets. The Cats had revealed one last secret just before they went. They had all sat by the fire and Lisa began the story.

"Bob and I will be leaving you shortly, but before we go we have one final thing to tell you. We have told you many times that you must never trust a human. Never. But, we can reveal to you now that there is an exception to that. "

The twins and Astra looked at each other in surprise.

Lisa continued. "There is one, and only one human you can trust, and trust completely. This human is known to us, and we can vouch for this person. It may be some years before you and this human make contact. You must be sure that you have the correct one. "

"How will we know?" asked Astra. "What if we get it wrong?"

Bob took up the story. "There will be some small indications, that this person may be the one, but the only way you will be totally sure is that they will be wearing something we have given to them. It looks like this."

Lisa handed them a colour drawing she had made. They all crowded round to look at the picture. "You will be able to communicate with this person as we do with you, and you do with each other, with the power of your thoughts. It will be a great advantage to you to have a human that you can trust and rely on. It will be your ultimate test. Choose wisely. Remember, only the wearer of the item in the picture will be the correct one. The only other help we can give you is that the contact will take place somewhere on the Wold. "

The Cats stood, and spoke with one voice, "We must take our leave of you now, while the storm is here. Remember all we have taught you, and you will be fine. It has been a real pleasure to meet you and learn about you. Do not forget. Everything happens for a reason, nothing is accidental. Enjoy everything. Trust in the Universe."

Standing in front of the log fire that burned merrily, they embraced the three animals for the last time, transferring the last of their energy into them. Then, with a final wave, the cats had gone.

Now, it was the morning after, and it hit the new owners of the hideaway that they were now on their own. But they had each other and, they had the gifts that the cats had given them, the knowledge and wisdom would serve them well. They would continue to learn, study and grow.

After breakfast they all set off down the tunnels to the chamber that was just behind the Old wood exit. There were three trucks loaded with firewood to be moved up to the main chamber. After dark they would bring the empty trucks back, and then go outside to collect yet more fuel. The cats had told them that they should gather as much fuel and food as they could. The winter to come would be severe.

It was time to go. They had stayed far too long already. They could not hold this form on this planet any longer. Their visit to this world had not been the routine one they thought they would have. For the first time ever on this world, they had made contact with some of the beings who lived there. The Universe had deemed it so to be.

Hugo, Jago and Astra had been greatly enhanced by their contact with them. They, in turn would be able to enhance others if they so choose. Now they had been taught how to use and control their special gifts. The human woman, Rose would more than fulfil her role as guardian and role model to the child, and as a wife to her husband.

It had been easier than they had thought to change her. The woman she had now become was inside her all along, it just had to be brought out. The husband, Lars would also benefit by being around the two females. Their gifts would rub off on him and make him an even better man than he already was. The real beneficiary was Freya.

In saving her life, they had changed her life. She had been special even before they had connected with her, and now with the gifts they had given to her, she would live her life on a much higher level to all others. They were in no doubt that she would use her gifts wisely. Freya would discover that every birthday a new gift would reveal itself to her. The universe had selected her. They had been here when she had need of them, and now she would go forward on her own. They had done all they could do. They must go.

With a last look around, they left the cavern and made their way to the space craft.

Yes, mused Bob, as he and Lisa headed down the tunnel that led to the door through which they had brought in the unconscious bodies of Hugo and Astra, and thus begun this new chapter in the development of this world. This visit had, unexpectedly, yielded positive results, unlike the "Druids" visit, which had ended in disaster. They had thought that in the guise of "Soothsayers", or "Seers" that the humans would be receptive to what they had to say. But they had not been ready then, and the humans of this time were still not ready. First contact with them would have to wait a long time.

The animals, however, showed real promise. Hugo, Jago and Astra had, in a very short time bonded together very well and had accepted the concept of Alien life quite easily. And it was all by a quirk of the Universe that they had met them at all!

They had already said their goodbyes to Hugo, Jago and Astra. They were in control of their own destiny for the first time in their lives. They had learned quickly how to use and control the gifts they had received. What happened to them next was down to them alone. They had also been shown how to recognise the only human they could really trust. This person would reveal themselves at the appropriate time. The Universe had deemed it so.

The storm outside was approaching its maximum power. Heavy rain lashed down, lightning flashed and thunder claps rumbled almost continually. The wind howled around the craggs. Even their space craft rocked a little, caught in an extra strong gust of wind. Everyone would be sheltering inside their homes. Perfect. They would not be detected by the humans.

Both Bob and Lisa thought the same thought as they boarded their craft and smiled. There would be no flashing lights as they left, and their ship was not saucer shaped and it did not spin around. The humans had a strange vision of aliens contacting them. They had not parked their craft in the village square for all to see and had not had tea and cake with the vicar and told him that they came in peace and were his friends. The humans here were far from being ready for any kind of contact and may always be so. They would leave as they had come, without being seen. Or so they thought.

As they prepared their ship they could see some of the lights twinkling down in the village. When all was ready they lifted off, leaving a different planet from the one they had landed on when they had arrived. The two Gallownians guided their craft up into the storm and then through it, into calmer air before heading out into the inky blackness of space. There were no man-made objects in orbit. Yet. The planet called Earth was blue below them, like the colour of the child, Freya's eyes, had been before her contact with them. As they moved away from it, they wondered what they would find when they returned again.

They would wait for a while on the dark side of the moon, before commencing their next adventure. They needed some time to rest and regenerate. They also had to wait for the others to return from the planet and join them…

Chapter Fifteen

Sunday afternoon was, weather permitting, when Lars would take his truck cum sledge up on to the wold and follow the track to the Old Wood. He took his saw with him and would look for wood for the fire. He never cut down any living tree. There was always plenty of branches and fallen trees to go around. He had always gone alone. Until now. One Sunday in late October, Freya had asked to go with him and to his continuing surprise, Rose had also said she would like to go. Another first. Lars would remember this day, not only because it was the first time that he would have company and helpers, but also the Cuban missile crisis had just come to a safe conclusion. Lars had been following it in the newspapers, and he was glad that it had come to an end without any missiles actually being fired.

So Lars had agreed, he could do little else. Freya he did not mind, in fact he liked to spend time with her, but so long as Rose did not start moaning, as she had a tendency to do, about why he did things this way , when he should do them that way, all would be well. The jury was still out on Rose, Lars told himself as they set off, Freya riding in the back of what she had christened the "Tredge". He desperately wanted to believe that Rose had really and truly changed for the better, and he had to admit, she had gone a long way down that road, but could someone really change so much? He hoped so.

One thing that he could not doubt, was that Rose was losing weight. She was more or less back to what she had been when he had first met her, more than three years ago, which meant she had lost close to two stone, quite an achievement for one who used to be very lazy.

But he had to admit that since the death of his brother and sister-in-law, she seemed to have much more energy and a positive attitude, neither of which was there before. May be miracles do happen, he thought as he pulled the Tredge along. Time would tell.

Rose walked along side Freya and they chatted as they went along, as females the world over tended to do. That was another change in Rose. She had never had much in the way of small talk before, and apart from criticizing or complaining, tended not to say much.

The Old Wood was quite large and there was plenty of fallen branches and trees to collect. Rose and Freya would drag them to Lars, who would saw them up and stack them in the Tredge. After nearly two hours, it was full and with rope around the wood to keep it from falling off, they set off back down the track home. The temperature was falling and the wind starting to pick up, with clouds forming in angry clumps. Freya and Rose were out in front, with Lars pulling the tredge behind. Rose remembered that her dad had got cheap coal as a perk of his job. If only he was here to see her now!

Lars was in his harness, which helped him pull the load. The harness was connected to a rigid frame of light wood, which kept the tredge a fixed distance from him at all times. He had made everything himself.

As they walked along, Lars marvelled yet again at the way that fate had put the three of them here on this early winter's afternoon. But for the accident, if that was what it had been, Freya would have returned to Norway with Anders and Marit. Rose would still be as she had been before, and be sitting at home watching the TV, no doubt with a box of chocolates next to her, while he would be doing what he was doing now, assuming that he had not given up and returned to Norway when his brother and family had gone back. He would never know what he might have done. Fate had changed all of their lives. Rose had undergone a complete change for the better since the death of his brother and sister-in-law, one that he would never in a million years thought possible. He hoped it was worth it. It had to be.

They reached the back gate of the cottage just in time, as the first heavy plops of rain began to fall. Quickly they covered the logs with a plastic sheet and hurried inside as the rain began to fall heavier.

The sky had darkened, making the approaching night come more quickly. Freya had noticed that the telegraph wires seemed to be green against the dark clouds. The wind continued to strengthen and in the distance, there was the unmistakable sound of thunder. A storm was coming.

During the evening the storm gathered strength and the rain hammered down, with the wind throwing it against the windows of the cottage. Only a fool would be out this night. Inside the cottage it was warm and cosy and after the exercise of the afternoon, Freya began to get sleepy. She went up to bed a little early, partly because she was tired, and partly so she could dream and tell her parents about the adventures of the day!

Rose went up with her, after she had kissed Uncle Lars goodnight, and tucked her in. After she had gone back down stairs, Freya lay back in her bed, with her troll next to her and listened to the storm outside. Suddenly, she got out of bed and went to the window. She opened the curtains a little and looked out towards the Wold and the invisible Craggs. Lightning flashed and the thunder rumbled around, but Freya was fascinated by the power of the storm. For quite a long time she just stood there and waited.

The little girl with the blond hair and green eyes stood in her nightgown and watched the storm rage outside. Just for an instant, there was a brief flash of light, far in the distance, which Freya knew was not lightning. Without knowing why, she whispered two words to herself as she looked out of the window and into the night.

Good Bye!

It was eleventh of November, 1962 and Freya's seventh birthday. Lars and Rose had given her some small gifts, as had Dutch. Her birthday had fallen on a Saturday and Lars had taken the day off work, one of the last days of holiday that he had left. As a birthday treat, Lars and Rose were going to take Freya on a train ride from Elfington to Wallbridge where they would have a meal in a nice cafe there. Unknown to Freya, and as an extra surprise, Penny would be there as well. As it was a special occasion, everyone was wearing their best clothes. It was a cold early winter's day and Freya was putting on her best coat, it still fitted her, but only just. Rose gave her a hanky to put in her pocket and as she did so, her hand touched something hard in the bottom of the pocket.

Puzzled, she pulled it out and held it up for Rose and Lars to see. It was a small box, wrapped in gold paper and tied up with a gold ribbon. There was a label attached to the ribbon, the message written in Norwegian. "What does it say?" asked Rose.

"To our darling Freya, to light your way in the fog of life! Love always, Mummy and Daddy. Xxx," translated Lars.

"It is from your parents, Freya, they knew that you would wear this coat on your birthday and must have put it in there as a surprise!" said Lars. "You'd better open it."

With a look of wonder on her face, Freya took the package back from Lars and gently untied the ribbon and very carefully began to unwrap the gold paper, making sure she did not tear it, conscious of the fact that her parents' hands had wrapped it up for her, which made it very special paper. She would keep it always.

As Rose and Lars watched spellbound, the paper was removed to reveal a small blue box. Freya put the paper and ribbon carefully to one side and then removed the lid of the box. Inside, something was hidden in layers of tissue paper. This too was slowly unwrapped and there was an audible gasp from all three people in the room as they saw what lay inside. It was a stunning piece of jewellery, a necklace. It was a beautiful deep blue in colour and had 11 sides to it, about 1-1/2 inches across and seemed to be made of some kind of clear stone, which also had 11 faces, or angles. Embedded through the exact centre of the stone were two bolts of bright gold, about one third of the length of the stone, making a very clear number 11. From deep within her mind, like a half remembered dream, Freya knew that this was the special number she had been waiting to be revealed to her. Of course! How could she not have guessed it! Her birthday was 11 November! Today.

The piece of jewellery was on a gold chain and as Freya picked up it up and took it completely out of the box, she felt something like a light electric shock going through her body for a brief second. She looked up at Lars and Rose. "Can I wear it now?" she asked.

"Of course," said Lars and as Freya lifted up her pony tail, Rose put the chain around her neck and fastened the clasp. Freya moved to the mirror and gazed at herself as Rose and Lars stood behind her and admired it too. Against her pale skin, the blue stone seemed to glow, the golden figure eleven standing out clearly.

Lars glanced at his watch. "Come, we must go now or we will miss the train!"

And so they moved downstairs and then went out into the cold November weather and headed down the road into the village to the station. Freya was very conscious of the stone around her neck under her coat, feeling it as she walked along. Her parents had bought this for her. They knew she would find it. It made a special day extra special. If only they were here to share it with her.

If anyone had counted the edges, or faces, they would have found that there were eleven of those. It was an Hendecagon. But what no one would ever know was that there was no other stone like it on planet Earth, or indeed anywhere within a hundred thousand light-years. It had come from a planet far, far away, called Gallownia. It was unique and if worn by anyone else, it would still be stunning piece of jewellery, but nothing else. But worn by the one person in this world with which it was compatible with, it was far, far more. As soon as the stone had touched Freya's skin, it had activated itself, recognising her special DNA, and had started to release its hidden power. It had found its one true home and it was the final gift that her parents and the cats could give her before they had passed over to the other side. Its creators had known that somewhere out in the vast Universe there was just one unique match that would unlock its secret power. It was not just luck, random chance or colossal coincidence. It was destiny.

Freya had enjoyed the day. It had been as good a birthday as could be expected, she reflected as she lay in her bed. She had, during the week, received some cards from her school friends back in Norway, and she had been reminded of home, her old home, now gone for ever. The one thing she really wanted, she could not have. Mummy and Daddy back again. Uncle Lars and Aunties Rose and Penny had done their best to give her a nice day and she was grateful to them for that.

She knew that Mummy and Daddy would never be able to celebrate her birthday again, like they had before, yet she truly believed that they had been there with her today, as they had been every day. They were there in spirit, she was sure. She thought back to the events of the day again. Finding the necklace had been a lovely surprise, and she had worn it all day, only taking it off before getting into bed. It now lay close by on the top of the chest of drawers. Then the walk down through the village to the Railway station. As they had walked past St Martins Church, the clock in the tower had struck eleven o'clock, exactly as she had gone past it.

Then, when waiting on the platform for the train to Wall Bridge, she had found a penny coin. It may have been there for a long time, but no one had noticed it. Many, many people must have walked past it but only she had noticed it, almost as if it had been waiting for her, and her alone to find it. She could have been standing anywhere on the platform, it was very long, but she stood where she had noticed it. It was fate. She had put it in her pocket, and would examine it later. The train had chuffed and hissed its way into the station, and as it approached, Freya noticed the number on the front of the black and green engine. It was number eleven!

The train ride was not very long and they had got off at the next stop, and made their way to a nice cafe for lunch. Wallbridge was a smaller village than Elfington but very pretty. Another surprise was that Aunty Penny had joined them for lunch and she had given Freya a gift for her birthday. It seemed strange to see her without her uniform on.

After lunch they had taken a walk to Aunty Penny's house and spent the afternoon there, before catching the train back to Elfington. It had been almost dark when they had got back home again. This was her home now, and she knew that she was very lucky to be here with Uncle Lars and Aunty Rose. It was as if all the "elevens" that kept appearing were messages from her parents, telling her that they were here too, and that they were close.

After tea, Freya had examined the penny she had found. On one side was a lady sitting down, holding a shield in one hand and some sort of fork in the other. Aunty Rose had said that the lady was "Britannia". Underneath the lady was the date the coin was made. It was 1911! Freya imagined that the lady was her mother, with the fork and shield to protect her. On the other side was a man's head, he was facing to the left. That would be her father, looking out for her. The writing around the edge of the coin said he was George V, the fifth. The coin was very worn with years of use. It had survived two world wars and had changed hands thousands of times during its life. It would not change hands again. She had been meant to find it, yet another gift from her parents. The message the coin gave her was clear. It had survived. Against everything the world threw against it, so would she. Freya would keep the special coin for ever and remember this day.

She was getting sleepy and her eyes began to close. Soon she was fast asleep cuddled up to her troll and quickly entered the dream world where her Mummy and Daddy were always waiting for her. They knew what she had done today, as they had been there, but she would tell them all about it again anyway! Freya slept, a smile on her face. Her special coin and necklace on the stand next to her bed. For the first time since that terrible night when her life was changed for ever, she was happy!

Chapter Sixteen

Hindsight was a wonderful thing! Thought Simon Marshall as he drove home after yet another busy day at the office. He was not looking forward to getting there.

Last night, after a couple of glasses of wine and a meal, he had foolishly let slip to his wife that his boss was being sent overseas to one of the company's European offices, and that his job would need to be filled. He had then compounded his error by saying that he had no intention of applying as he was stressed enough already and did not want to go any higher.

Simon, husband of Mary and father of Daphne was an assistant manager of a department of a large Insurance company, a job he could just about cope with. It was a job he had not wanted in the first place, preferring to have stayed where he had been before. He had been happy there. But his wife, ever the social climber, had other ideas. She had spoken to her brother, who was well connected, and he had "Put a word in" the right ear at the Golf club, and all Simon had to do was apply and the job was his.

Under constant pressure from his wife, he had applied and sure enough, he got the job. His wife was thrilled. She was now married to a Manager!

As he approached the outskirts of Elfington, he sighed. Why had he not simply kept his gob shut? She would never have known about the vacancy and he could have stayed where he was. But no! He had blurted it out and now it was too late. His wife had looked at him and said in a tone of voice he knew all too well. "Of course you're going to apply for the position, darling, and I'm sure you will be successful!

She had not said anything further, and had continued to watch the TV, but he knew that she would not forget, women never forget anything. Shit!

Maybe he would be OK after all, as his brother-in-law had recently moved away. He hoped so as he turned into the drive of the house that he couldn't afford and parked next to his wife's car. He couldn't really afford that either. Christmas was just around the corner and his daughter had her heart set on a pony, and he knew that his wife had one in mind from a local stable. Once again, his brother-in-law was well connected there as well.

He climbed out of his car and stretched, dead on his feet, and went inside, looking forward to a glass, or two of wine, a hot meal and a sit down. On entering the living room he stopped dead in his tracks at the sight that greeted him. His wife and daughter were sitting on the sofa with their coats on. They turned to look at him as he came in. Their provider had arrived.

"There you are, darling! You've got five minutes to wash and change. I've booked a table at Luigi's for seven."

He stood there, brief case still in his hand, and his heart sank. He knew that it was a waste of time arguing about it with her, she was not the least bit interested in how he felt. So, without saying a word, he turned and trudged upstairs. He wondered how much the meal he didn't want would cost him.

He sighed again. He couldn't really afford that either.

It had been over two weeks since Tom's visit to Penny's cottage. They saw each other at the Hospital, of course, but it had been extra busy lately and apart from brief chats here and there, they had not been able to spend any real, private time together. Tom had been forced to cover for a fellow Doctor who needed time off, and had to do extra shifts. It was just part of being a Doctor in a Hospital. It would be December in a few days and Tom was keen to see Penny again. He looked up from the patient's notes he was working on to see her approach him. They were on a ward, with people all around them, and there was a group of nurses close by. She had another file of notes in her hand. He greeted her formally.

"Yes, Sister? She handed the file to him. To anyone who might be watching, it would look completely normal. Held in place with a paper clip on the front of the file was a note in her handwriting.

My Place. Friday. 12 noon. P. xxx

Without looking up, he wrote on the paper.

Cannot wait. See you then. Thank you. T. xxx

He handed the file back with a smile and she moved away. He had to stop himself from watching her walk away, and kept his head down. Today was Wednesday. Friday could not come quick enough!

Friday had finally arrived, and Tom caught the train to Wallbridge and made his way to Penny's Cottage. He had bought a box of chocolates with him this time. He was tired after a busy couple of weeks and had really missed being with Penny. Seeing her nearly every day only made it worse. He thought about her a lot. He arrived at the Cottage and before he could knock, the door opened. She had been watching for him. She looked stunning, wearing a skirt and jumper.

"Hi! I know I've said it before, but you really do look gorgeous!"

"Well, thank you, Doctor! Please, come inside. I've missed you," she said with a smile.

Tom stepped inside and as soon as the door was closed she was in his arms, even before he had taken his coat off. "I really have missed you. Kiss me please!"

150

Tom was more than happy to oblige and for the next couple of minutes, they clung together, kissing and hugging. Finally she stepped back, her eyes shining with pleasure. "That's better. Seeing you at work, so close and yet so far away has been agony!" She said, helping him out of his coat.

"I know, I've felt the same. I was like a little boy with his nose pressed against the pie shop window and no money!" Penny laughed out loud. "Funny you should mention Pies, I've got one in the oven!"

"Umm, I can smell it. If I give you these, can I have a piece, I've been good!" and he handed over the chocolates. "Although they may have melted with the warmth of your welcome."

"Thank you. I'll put them in the fridge and then climb in after them, I need to cool down. I am just so pleased to have you here. I love it when I have you all to myself."

Tom gave her a hug. "Thank you. How long do we have before the pie is ready? I have something to tell you." A look of concern appeared on her face. "It's not bad news is it? You haven't met someone else, have you?"

"No and No," smiled Tom. "If you ply me with drink I will tell you everything."

Penny suddenly realized that they were still standing next to the front door.

"I'm so sorry! Please come and sit down and I'll get you a beer."

Tom sat on the sofa, taking the same place as he had before, hoping that she would want to be cuddled. She did. They settled down in front of the fire, Penny snuggled up to him, removing her shoes and curling her legs up. Tom said, "I'm in heaven. I have a cold beer in one hand and a hot woman in the other!"

"What's your favourite?"

"Well, this beer is very good," he said taking a sip. That earned him a mock punch.

"I can do things that the beer can't!"

"I believe you! I've been thinking about what you said, about the GP's job at Elfington, and I have applied for it. I have been working in Hospitals for almost three years now. The Shifts, the weekends and the stress didn't matter before. But now, things have changed."

"What has changed?" asked Penny, hoping he would say what she wanted him to say.

He was serious now. He moved his hand from her waist and gently tilted her head up and looked at the beautiful face in front of him.

"I got to know you! We have worked together for quite a long time, I know, but I didn't know you then. I always thought you were out of my league, out of my reach, far too beautiful to be interested in me. A woman like you could have any man you wanted, you must know that. There are plenty of my colleagues who would jump at the chance to take you out, so what chance did I have?"

"But now?"

"But now I think a might have a slim chance after all. For some strange reason, you seem to like me!"

Penny smiled, and kissed him. "I would say you had more than a slim chance. I do like you, more than like you, in fact. I've lived here not far short of four years and there have been no men in my life. You are the first man I have asked to come here. That's why you are in my home and in my arms, not to mention drinking my beer and eating my food!"

"Thank you. I'm pleased to think my investment in flowers and chocolates had not been wasted!"

He was keeping the conversation light, not wanting it to get too serious, but she continued. "As I have already mentioned, I have been hurt before, and it took me a long time to get over that. Perhaps I will tell you about that one day. Suffice to say, if he was here now, he would have a hand up my skirt and the other one up my jumper, not interested if I want it or not. I don't want a man like that. We both see too much pain and suffering in our jobs, it gets to you after a while. Too many broken bodies, too many broken lives. That's why I want to get to know you, you are not like the other Doctors. They have all asked me out, some more than once, even the married ones! But I don't want them. I want you. When I am here, I want kindness, tenderness, gentleness. I want to be caressed, not groped. I want a man I can trust. Really trust. I trust you. Ask any woman. Trust is very important to us. There was a time when I thought I'd never trust any man again. But you are different, and if you will be patient with me, I think we could have a future together. So I am glad you have applied for the job. I have asked to be considered for the practice nurse's position. Just think. If we are both lucky, we can go behind the screen in your surgery whenever we like!"

She had ended on a lighter note, but Tom could tell, that she had indeed been badly hurt before.

He drew her closer to him. "Let's hope we are both lucky then. To think that we could work together away from the Hospital, and have beer and pies afterwards, that would be really good! She turned his head and kissed him. "Wouldn't it just!"

The lunch had been eaten. It had been wonderful. Afterwards they had gone out for a walk to blow the cobwebs away and to enjoy the weak winter sun. She had taken his arm and had not let go of it, even when they had met some people who knew Penny. She had introduced him as her friend Tom. They both knew that the local "Grape Vine" would swing into action and soon everyone would know about Penny's friend "Tom". They did not care.

As the light began to fade they made their way back to Penny's Cottage. In the distance they could hear the sound of the railway, so much a part of the community. It would be well used in the future, Tom thought, all being well. They went inside and closed the door on the world outside. The curtains were drawn and the table lights lit.

The fire was brought back to life once again. Penny brought in tea and sandwiches and then they made their way towards the fire and the sofa. On the way, Penny stopped and said, "I'll be back in a tick, I just have to pop upstairs."

Tom nodded and sat down, waiting for her to return. He had had quite a day, in fact they both had, revealing things to each other as their relationship developed. She had said she trusted him, that she liked him. They were good things to know. He heard footsteps on the stairs, and got ready to put his arm around her. She appeared before him and removed her shoes, but did not sit down. He looked up and found her looking down at him, not moving. Their eyes met and she smiled, as if deciding something.

She moved closer, then carefully placed a knee each side of his legs and settled herself on the edge of his lap. Again she did not speak, just looked into his eyes in that direct way of hers, that Tom had come to know. "I have had a lovely day with you, Tom, thank you. Remember earlier I said that I can do things that beer cannot?" He nodded. "Well, you seem to have let the genie out of the bottle. I don't want it to go back inside again. It's been in there for four long and lonely years. So, I have decided that I want to do this, for you." Slowly she moved her hands down to the bottom of her jumper, gripped the edge, then slowly pulled it up and over her head, removing it completely. She was wearing nothing underneath.

Tom's mouth went dry. Just inches from his face were two perfect, full, pert breasts.

"Don't move, Tom. Let me do this!"

She raised her arms above her head and arched her back, making her breasts stand out against her ribs.

She turned slightly left, then right, letting him have a long look at them. Lowering her hands down she cupped her own breasts, one in each hand, giving each a slight squeeze, before gently teasing and pulling her nipples, until they were fully hard and erect. Again she lifted her arms above her head and arched her back, watching him watching her. He could not take his eyes off the magnificent breasts in front of his eyes. Not in his wildest dreams had he thought he would be looking at this.

The arms came down again and her left hand again cupped her left breast, while her right hand reached out and pulled his head forward towards it. She guided her nipple into his mouth and then put both hands behind her back, allowing him complete access. Tom slid the nipple into his mouth and began to suck her breast, while his right hand gently squeezed it. He moved his left hand up to her right breast and gently fondled it. A light gasp escaped her lips. "Ohh yes, Tom, this is what I want you to do, I have waited four years!" Tom continued to pleasure her until he felt a light touch as her hand guided him over to the other breast, where he continued his work there.

Her hands had returned behind her back again, and he could hear small moans and sighs coming from her. Her breasts were full, firm and bigger than he had imagined they would be, set against her slender frame. He withdrew his mouth and, as she had done, teased the nipples, while squeezing the breasts, careful not to squeeze too hard. He looked up to see her looking down, watching him, a smile of pure joy on her face. Finally, she could take no more and the hands guided his head away. One final time, she raised her arms and arched her back, and the magnificent breasts strained against her ribs. Tom said, "Don't move" and she stayed still. He gently blew on each nipple, still moist from his lips and was rewarded with a gasp of pleasure from Penny.

Finally she lowered her arms and reached to unbutton his shirt, then sliding her hands inside, while he stroked her arms, back and shoulders. She rested her hands on his shoulders and he watched her breasts swing away from her body, as she leaned forward a little more and kissed him, a long, tender kiss. She eventually leaned back and said in a husky voice. "That was wonderful. Thank you, Doctor!"

"No, Penny, thank you! You are so beautiful, so sexy, so desirable, I can hardly believe you let me do that. I have never experienced anything so wonderful in my life. You are a truly a goddess. Thank you."

She got to her feet, and looked down at Tom's erection, clear to see. "I wonder what that is?" she said with a smile. "Don't button your shirt, I've not finished with you yet."

She put the jumper back on and then sat down next to him, swung her legs around, smoothed down her skirt and lay back in his lap, with her head on the arm of the three-seater sofa. As she looked up at him, she pulled up the jumper and exposed her breasts again, now spread flatter on her chest, nipples still erect.

"If you want more, they are there for you. All I want is gentleness, I don't want to be hurt any more, I have had enough hurt. Caress them, Caress me. That's all I want you to do, just caress me.

She lay in his lap, looking up at him as he ran his hand across her flat stomach and lightly over her breasts. He did not go below the waistband of her skirt, knowing that she did not want him to. He had plenty to play with right in front of him.

She sighed with pleasure. "This is what I am looking for, you do it so well. Thank you."

He looked down at the gorgeous woman lying across his lap. "Dear Penny, please don't thank me, you are amazing, you really are. I am truly blessed to have had this gift that you have given me tonight. I will never forget it. Never!"

"You are such a special man, Tom. So different from, from before. He, his name was Roger, would never have done that for me. He just took what he wanted, then would tell his mates up the pub what he had done to me. That's the difference. He did things to me, not with me, as you just did. Such things are private, secret, only between us. Special. What we just had was my gift to you, and yours to me. But he told his pals everything!"

Her voice was breaking and her lower lip quivering as she relived it.

"God, Penny, what did that swine do to you?"

"I, I can't say, not now, not yet. I don't want to spoil what we have had tonight.

He's in my past, you are my future, if you can put up with me. I'm damaged goods, Tom, that's how I think of myself sometimes, an emotional cripple!" Her voice broke again, the lip quivering. Tom gently pulled her jumper down and bent down to kiss her before he spoke.

"Let me tell you what I see when I look at you. I see a strikingly beautiful, desirable, goddess who has taken pity on a poor and humble Doctor. I see a lady who would stand out in a room full of beautiful women, like a thoroughbred horse would stand out in a group of donkeys. I see a lady of class, with poise and gracefulness. I see a lady who I want to be with, who has this very night given me something very special. I see a lady who had had a bad experience, but that is over now.

There are many women who are lovely to look at, but not nice to be with. There are some who are lovely to look at and nice to be with, but have a lack of intelligence. There are a few, a rare few, who have it all. An extra dimension. You are a very rare, very precious lady who has that extra dimension. You have the personality to make it all work together.

You could, if you chose to, make people feel inadequate, clumsy, foolish. But I know you would never dream of doing that. Your personality compliments all the other gifts you have, that makes you very special. The truth is, I'm under your spell. I am becoming addicted to you. I need my fix of being with you more and more often. If I can't get my fix, then I am not happy. You make me happy, by just being you.

That man who hurt you, Roger, was a fool. He did not know what he had. He only saw your beauty, and was too dumb to see the rest. I can see the whole Penny. The woman of my dreams is lying on my lap. You are not damaged goods, you were just unlucky. Wrong place, wrong time, wrong man. What ever happened to you, was not your fault.

He's gone and he's not coming back. I am here now. Would I be correct if I said that you have never spoken about what happened to you to anyone?" She nodded. "Never."

"Well, when, and if you ever want to, you can talk to me. You said you trusted me. I trust you. You mean so much to me. You said I might be what you have been looking for, I really hope I am. You are everything I want. I want to make you as happy as you make me. "

Penny looked up at him in way he would never forget. Tears were flowing freely down her face. She reached up and clung to him with all her might and sobbed as if her heart would break, purging herself.

For four long years she had kept it all inside, what he had done to her. Tom had, with the gentleness he had shown her, contrasted so much with the horror of four years ago. Then his kind words about her, spoken quietly, but with such sincerity. Her emotions had been very near the surface already, and his touch, followed by his words had been too much. It had triggered something deep inside her. The dam had burst, and all the emotion, pain and anger flooded out of her, as it had needed to do.

Tom just held her tightly, saying softly, "It's all right, Penny, I've got you. Let it out. You're safe with me"!

She cried for a long time, unable to stop and not wanting to. Finally, she was quiet. She just held him, feeling his warmth, his compassion. He reached into his pocket and handed her a hanky.

She dried her eyes, blew her nose and took a deep breath, then turned in his arms, her face very close to his. She kissed him and said in a shaky voice,

"Thank you, Tom. You have no idea what you have done for me. You were right. I told no one about what happened to me, no one. But you, lovely man, you engender such trust that I feel so safe with you. Thank you." She kissed him again, then lay back across his lap and looked up at him.

"I need to finish this, I want you, and only you to know everything, as I said before, the genie is well and truly out of the bottle now. There is no going back, besides, when you know the whole sorry tale, you might not want to be with me. But, if we are to have any future together, you must know it all!"

Tom said nothing, just reached for her hand and kissed it gently.

She took a deep breath and began, reliving it again.

"I had been working, and had gone to his house quite late..."

Tom sat in a damp and musty carriage for the journey home, and thought about Penny and what she had told him. He had wanted to stay, sleep on the sofa, but be near to her if she needed him. But she had insisted she was all right now, kissed him again and he had gone. The first part of the evening had been wonderful, and he guessed, an impulsive move on her part. She was fantastic, and starved of affection for so long, had wanted to taste it again. Trusting and testing him at the same time, wanting him to touch her and wanting to see how he touched her.

What a woman! How had she kept all that hurt and pain inside and told no one. If he ever came across that bastard Roger, he would kill him. Slowly. Being a surgeon would come in very handy. He should have stayed. He felt guilty, but she had said she wanted him to go. So here he was. He did not like it.

She had told him everything. He had not interrupted. He had not asked any questions. He had made no comment. He had made no judgements. He just listened.

She had cried again when she had finished, and it had been hard for him not to join her. How could any man, worthy of that name do that to a woman. His woman, because that was how he thought of her. She had bared her soul to him, so total and complete was her trust in him.

He felt emotionally drained by the events of the evening. He needed rest. She would need his support in the days and weeks to come, and he would give it gladly.

She had got through a dreadful experience, but she was strong and would now start to heal. Her medical training had, and would continue to serve her well. All the things he had said to her were true. He did indeed need a regular fix of her company.

As he made his way towards his flat, walking along the dark and damp streets, he was sure about one thing. He wanted to be with her even more than before. He got home and went to bed. But sleep would not come easily tonight. He should have stayed with her.

Penny had locked up after Tom had gone, and on shaky legs had gone up to bed. He had wanted to stay with her, but he had done more than enough for her already. She got into bed and lay there in the darkness, thinking about Tom, and what she had shown him, and what she had told him. What they had shared. She had not intended to do any of it. The first part, the nice part, she told herself had been an impulse. It was a test of sorts and he had passed with flying colours.

No man had touched her for four long years. Not since she had gone to that place on that fateful night, after a long day at the hospital, to find him waiting for her, much the worse for drink. He drank a lot.

He had wanted sex, not love, but sex. She had said no, but he had insisted, grabbing at her uniform and putting his hand up her skirt. She had said no, and tried to get away, getting more and more frightened. He would not listen. He would not stop. He was like a mad man, clawing at her clothing. No, Roger, no, not now, not like this. He had punched her in the stomach hard. And again. She was winded. He would not stop. He ripped her underwear off and raped her, right there on the living room carpet. She had been having her period at the time. He just laughed. "You should be used to a bit of blood in your line of work," was all he had said.

When it was finally over, he just went up to bed, just like that, leaving her lying on the floor. She lay there for a while, clothes in tatters, bruised. There was blood on her legs, and on the carpet. Finally she had got to her feet and had had a bath, knowing he would be out for the count for hours. She packed the few clothes she kept there and then sat downstairs in the darkness until morning, looking straight ahead, but seeing nothing, feeling nothing. When the first rays of dawn lightened the ground, she left the house and then went to her parents' house, only telling them that her relationship with Roger was over. She never thought about reporting it. Her word against his. She didn't even cry. And she told no one. Until tonight.

But there was something about Tom, his quiet, confident demeanour, soft voice and ways. He had said such nice things to her, not to gain any advantage, she instinctively knew, but he believed them to be true. He realised that her body was hers to give, not his to take. He hadn't grabbed or crushed her breasts. His touch was light.

157

She had enjoyed his touch, and he had enjoyed pleasing her. She had been stimulated, not intimidated. He had left her wanting more, not less. He had awakened something deep in her that she had thought had died that terrible night, and once awakened and experienced again, she wanted more. She had been in a vast, dry desert for four lonely years, but now she had found an oasis. Her birthday was in July, her star sign was Cancer, the Crab. She had gone back into her shell, but he had brought her out. So now her secret was out. She was glad. It had brought huge relief. She was overwhelmed by emotion. Unsettled. Lost and alone. Finally she fell into a fitful sleep.

She awoke at six, after a restless night. Her mind was trying to adjust itself to the emotional roller-coaster that she was on. She wished Tom had stayed. He would be downstairs on the sofa, close by. She needed him to hold her, she needed to hear his voice. Only he would do.

Her parents were not too far away, but they did not know what he knew. Only he could give her what she needed. Living alone had never bothered her before, she just got by on her own, never really thinking about it. Before she had found Tom. She really missed him.

It was Saturday. He would be at home, probably worrying about her. She swung her legs out of bed and pulled on her dressing gown. It was cold in the cottage and would remain so until she lit the fire and it had got going. She went downstairs and sat on the middle seat of the sofa. The place on her right where Tom had sat was empty. The cottage felt different without him. She felt different without him. She pulled her dressing gown closer around her body. Her mind went back four years to that other time when she had sat downstairs in a cold room in the early hours waiting for the dawn. The time after.

Like then, the room was very quiet, just the ticking of the clock on the mantelpiece. Four years ago she had left that room and closed the door on that part of her life in all respects. But now she had got to know Tom and things had changed. He had changed her. She looked around the room. It was the same and yet it was different. This cottage had been her retreat, her sanctuary. The place where she was safe. No man, except her father had been allowed to come here. Until Tom. But she had invited him here. Cooked a meal for him here. Been intimate with him here and confided her innermost secret to him here.

Just as she had closed one door four years ago, Tom had opened a new door for her and she knew that she would gladly step through it so long as he was on the other side waiting for her. She looked at the clock again. Twenty past six. She rose from the sofa. She knew what she would do. Penny headed for the stairs, this time moving with purpose. She would go to him.

Tom had not slept well. His mind was far too active to sleep. He could not relax. All he could think of was Penny, of what she had told him, what she had endured. She was alone and she should have someone with her, not just someone, him. Her friends, or parents would not do. They did not know what he knew and they never would. He looked at the faintly glowing hands on his bedside clock. Nearly six a. m. It was not yet light. He would go to her. He had to. If she wanted to be alone, that was fine, at least he would know that she was all right, and she would know that he had taken the trouble to find out. He could not rest until he saw her again. He got out of bed and headed for the bathroom, hopefully before the landlord got in there, forgetting that he was away for the weekend.

Lars drove his milk float along the dark and empty roads towards Wallbridge, to cover the round for one of his colleagues at the dairy. This would be welcome extra money. He had delivered double the day before on his own round so he would be available to do this. Wallbridge was considerably smaller that Elfington and also, he had a helper.

Freya had wanted to come with him to help, and he and Rose had agreed, as it was Saturday and there was no school the next day. So she sat next to him as they drove along the deserted roads, well wrapped up in her winter clothing, complete with woollen hat with its two long strings hanging down. He checked his watch. A little after six. They drove on.

Penny sat in the cold and musty carriage, impatient for the train to get going to Pondford. It had been late arriving in the first place and now was just sitting there. With a jerk if finally began to move and she looked out of the grimy windows at the dark countryside beyond. She could see a light here and there in the distance as they moved along. The train stopped once at Elfington and again waited, what for, she could not imagine, before jerking into motion again. At last she arrived at Pondford and was out the carriage door and down the platform quickly, before leaving the station and heading for Tom's flat. He would be so surprised to see her.

Tom's train left Pondford station just as another one pulled in on platform two. He caught the end of an announcement saying it was the late-running train from somewhere or other but could not care less. This train was taking him to Wallbridge and to Penny. There were two other men in the dingy carriage, both of whom were smoking. No wonder the carriages stank of smoke.

The train seemed to be going too slow, but it was probably his imagination. After a too long stop at Elfington, it moved off again towards Wallbridge. He felt guilty about leaving Penny alone. He should have stayed, to be there for her. Anyway, he was on his way now. She would be surprised to see him, he was sure.

Finally he arrived at Wallbridge and Tom hurried off to Penny's cottage as it began to get light. In record time he was knocking on her front door, waiting for her to open it. Nothing happened. He knocked again. Still nothing. He was about to knock a third time when the lady next door came out to see what was going on.

"Oh, it's you, Doctor. I'm afraid she went out early this morning, wasn't wearing her uniform though!"

"Oh, er, thank you for telling me, I'm sure I'll catch up with her later, thank you!"

Tom walked down the path and closed the gate behind him. He was more worried now. She could have decided to go to her parents for the weekend, but she could also have decided to go to him! Damn. Now what should he do? He looked up as a milk float turned into the street and headed towards him, taking no notice of it. It was what you expected to see at this time of the morning. The milk float stopped next to him but he ignored it, deciding that he would return to the station and go home to see if she was there. He started to walk when a voice called out. "Doctor Thornton!"

He turned back to see a small girl in a woollen hat and a giant blond man walking towards him. It was Freya Olsen and Lars!

"See, Uncle Lars, it is him," said Freya, as they stopped next to a bewildered Tom. He shook the giant hand that was held out to him and bent down to give Freya a hug.

"Branching out, Lars?" asked Tom. "I didn't think you did this neck of the woods."

"Only today and we are finished already. I helped him. What's a neck of the woods?" asked Freya. "Do you live here?"

"I'll explain later. Aunty Penny lives here, but she went out early, possibly to go to my place. I have to get down to the station and go back to Pondford in case she's there. It's important that I see her, so I will have to dash!"

"The trains are not regular on Saturdays, you could miss her again. Hop in, Tom. We will drive you there, won't we, little one?"

"Oh yes! I've never been to Pondford!"

Penny sat on the cold stone doorstep of Tom's flat. He was not in. No one was in. She did not know that the landlord had gone away for the weekend. She did not know where Tom was. Where could he have gone? His parents? The paper shop? At least it was getting light. Perhaps he had gone to her Cottage to see if she was all right. That would be just like him. She was unsettled, anxious and hungry. She had so looked forward to seeing him. She needed his arms around her. It wasn't even eight o'clock yet. She would wait here.

Freya sat between her Uncle who cared for her and the Doctor who had saved her as they drove along the still quiet roads. Today was turning out to be an extra exciting day! She had already helped Uncle Lars to do his work, and now they had met Doctor Thornton and were going to Pondford, she might even get to see Aunty Penny as well! She would tell her friend Dutch all about it when she saw him again. When they finally got home, Aunty Rose would cook a nice hot breakfast. It was all a big adventure for a little girl.

"I hope we find her, I really like Aunty Penny."

"Everyone likes Aunty Penny, little one, it would be hard not to. She was very kind to me when you were in hospital. A very fine lady!"

"You were very kind to me, Doctor, when I was sick. You saved me. You are a very good Doctor!"

"Well, thank you, young lady. You were a model patient. I'm so pleased to see you looking so well."

OK, Tom, we are nearly there, where do you live? Asked Lars.

"Head for the station, then take the first left..."

Penny was dozing on Tom's doorstep, leaning against the wall. She was getting cold and her bum had gone numb, but at least it was getting light. She opened her eyes and looked up and down the street. Nothing, except a milk float that was approaching. She would give it another half an hour, then make her way home. She was bitterly disappointed not to have seen Tom. She was not looking forward to a weekend alone. Her head began to go down again when she took a second look down the road. The milk float seemed to be going quite fast. She watched it get closer and to her surprise it stopped with a squeal of brakes right by Tom's gate.

Her eyes widened with surprise as the passenger door flew open and Tom jumped out and ran towards her. He was here! Penny got to her feet with difficulty, stiff from sitting in the cold and staggered a little, nearly losing her balance. Tom caught her in his arms and they hugged and kissed each other, not caring who might be watching.

"Thank god I've found you, Penny, I went to your cottage, but your neighbour said you have gone out early."

"I did, to come here and be with you. I didn't want to be alone, but I guessed you had left to be with me. I should have let you stay. It's a wonder we met at all!"

"We might not have, if it wasn't for our friends over there!"

Penny noticed Freya and Lars for the first time. Freya had reached up to hold Lars' hand, unsure what to make of things. On the way here, she had sensed Tom's tension.

161

Penny released Tom and went over to hug Freya and Lars.

"Hello, Aunty Penny! Doctor Thornton was looking for you in Wallbridge, and I saw him. We brought him here, didn't we, Uncle Lars?" Said Freya, looking up at her uncle.

"Ya, we did, little one."

"You are such a clever girl, Freya," said Penny hugging her again. Freya beamed. Wait till she told Dutch!

Tom had come over to join them. "You are a real star, Lars, and you also, Freya. You have saved the day. Thank you so much!"

Lars smiled. "It is nothing. You saved Freya's life. That is much more." "Well, now that we have found each other, I need food!" said Penny.

"We are going home for breakfast, you can come with us, can't they, Uncle Lars?

"Of course! Rose will be happy to see you, we have plenty of food. We are all friends! Come."

Tom looked at Penny. "Sounds good to me. They have a warm fire and hot food. We don't!"

"Why not. As long as I'm with you, I'll go anywhere. Thank you, Freya. Lars, have you got any herring?" said Penny with a wink.

"Yuk!" said Freya.

Tom and Penny had gone. Freya was in the back garden with Dutch, who had called to see if she could play. She was telling him all about her adventures of the morning.

Lars and Rose were in the kitchen. She was washing the dishes, he was drying.

"It was a lovely surprise, Tom and Penny coming in for breakfast," said Rose, passing him a plate.

"Ya. They are such a nice couple. I think they are seeing each other. It is little I did today, after what they both did for Freya. They saved her life."

"And mine," said Rose in a small voice.

"How so?"

"Take this morning. You would not have brought anyone here for breakfast before, because you knew that I would have hated it. I probably would still have been in bed, and it's now 10. 30. And who would you have brought anyway? We had no friends. I made sure of that. I actively discouraged you from bringing anyone here, because I could not be bothered to talk to them. Before that terrible, terrible night of the crash, I had been a lousy wife to you. Lazy, fat and dirty. I'm so ashamed of myself when I look back at myself now. I wouldn't have blamed you if you had looked somewhere else, but you being the person you are, I know you did not. But since the crash, since Freya came to us, something has happened to me. I've mentioned it before."

Lars said nothing, just kept on wiping the plates, letting her speak.

"I've changed. I do things now. I like doing things. We have some real friends, they just left. I really enjoyed having them here. I was not a fit wife, hell, I was not a fit person. But now I want to make it up to you, to be a good wife. You have put up with so much from me. You are a really good man, I'm so lucky. I'll never go back to the way I was before!" She turned to look at him.

"You remember when I came home and said I had been made redundant?" Lars nodded. "I asked for it! I could have stayed. You didn't know that, did you?"

"Actually I did."

"You knew? How long?"

"Not long after it happened."

Rose turned back to the sink and started on the cutlery, silent for a while. "My dad would have got along with you like a house on fire."

"I would like to have met him, I think he would be proud of his daughter now, I am proud of my wife. You are correct. You have changed. I am pleased. You are a good wife now. It is enough!"

"No, Lars, it is not." She turned to face him again.

"After Freya is asleep tonight, come to bed early. I will be waiting for you!" Rose pulled out the plug in the sink and as the water gurgled down the waste pipe, she left the kitchen, drying her hands as she went.

Lars watched her go, then finished his drying. Alone in the kitchen, he smiled. For the first time in years, he found that he was looking forward to bedtime much more than usual.

"So we brought them back here for breakfast!" concluded Freya.

"Seems like you had a busy morning."

"It's nice to have friends here for breakfast, Dr Thornton said he was going to apply to be the new Doctor here in Elfington, and Aunty Penny is going to apply to be the nurse," said Freya.

"Let's hope they are lucky." said Dutch

"Oh, they will be, I'm quite sure. When I was in Wallbridge, helping Uncle Lars, I noticed that some of the houses had funny signs in their gardens."

"Funny signs?"

"Yes, one said, "Husband and dog missing, reward for dog!"

"I don't get it," admitted Dutch.

"The other one said, "A lovely Lady and a grumpy old man live here."

"What does it mean?" asked Dutch.

"I think that the grumpy old man had better not get lost when he takes the dog out!"

"I still don't get it," said Dutch. Adult humour was way beyond him.

Just then Lars came into the garden and the two friends went over to him. When Dutch went home for his dinner, Freya would go up to her room and make a start on a special task she needed to do. Freya had a letter to write.

Chapter Seventeen

Tom and Penny caught the train from Elfington back to Pondford and went to Tom's flat where he packed a bag for the rest of the weekend and then they travelled back to Penny's cottage at Wallbridge. They spent the rest of Saturday and all of Sunday just being together. They talked, walked, ate, cuddled and kissed and then talked some more. They were both off duty until Monday morning. Tom spent Saturday night on the sofa.

Penny was just so glad to have his company. She told him about her childhood, her schools, anything and everything, and he in return told her about his early life. She was so easy to be with, he could just relax and be himself. All too soon it was Sunday evening and Tom, reluctantly had to go home. Penny saw the look on his face and knew what he was thinking. Tom held her in his arms, feeling the warmth of her body, wishing he could stay.

"It's OK, Tom, I'll be fine now. Thank you for everything. I feel so much better now that I have shared my secret with you. I had to tell you, I needed to tell you, to tell you the truth about what had happened. I had to give you the chance to walk away now, if you wanted to. It will take me some more time yet to fully adapt to having a man in my life again, to share things with, to trust. Being with you is so, so different from before. You have brought me back to life, just as you did with Freya. I'm so lucky to have found you."

"I could never walk away from you, not now, not ever. It was a very brave thing that you did, sharing your most private secret with me. I think more of you now than ever. But you are wrong about me saving Freya. That little girl was dead. She had been down for more than twenty minutes. I could do no more for her. I was turning away to call the time of death, when the monitor started to show signs of life. It was nothing I did. She came back from the dead all on her own, I have no idea how. I am very glad that she did."

"It's strange, how that little girl links us together. It was when I was involved with her care that I decided that you may be someone I could be friends with, and now here we are!" said Penny.

"And it was Freya who spotted me when we missed each other yesterday morning. I want to be the man in your life now. So sleep well, Penny, do you have a kiss for me to take home?"

"Oh yes, Doctor!"

Lars Olsen lay on his side, his body supported by one muscular arm, and looked down at the attractive, slender woman he had just made love to. He had been as careful as he could be, it had been a long time. For both of them.

"Who are you? The Rose Butler I met at the dairy and later married would never had done what you have just done. You must be an imposter!"

Rose looked up at her husband and smiled. "You have found me out! I confess. The person you mentioned does not live here anymore!" She lowered her eyes, suddenly serious. "She died the same weekend your family did. Don't ask me how it happened, because I do not know. All I can tell you is somehow, some miracle happened to me, at the same time that Anders and Marit were taken from you. I am not the same woman that you married, and never will be again. I cannot believe how I used to be, and I am so thankful that you stayed with her, in your place, I'm not sure that I would have."

Lars said nothing for a while, staring, but not seeing the room beyond the bed, remembering. He looked down again at Rose as his eyes refocused. "Before Anders and Marit came over, I had been considering going back with them when they returned to Norway. I see that does not come as a surprise to you?"

Rose shook her head. "I suspected that you might."

Lars continued. "But I had decided that I would not. Vikings do not quit when things are difficult. It is not our way, it is not my way." He smiled at Rose's anxious face. "As things have turned out, I can see that I made the right decision. Anders and Marit's deaths were an accident. If we had been happy and content before, it would have made no difference. For reasons I will never understand, the Gods took them from me, but in return they gave me a new wife and little Freya instead. "

"I love that child as if she was my own. You must know that," said Rose.

"I do, and she loves you, as I will learn to do. The old Rose would not have done what you have just done this night. She would not have spoken as you have, or let me speak as I have. The gods have indeed sent me a new wife. You are welcome in my home, and in my heart."

Lars turned to turn off the lamp and as he lay down, Rose moved close to him and held him tightly as she wept, her breasts pressing against his chest. Lars held his wife and thought about the woman in the gaping dressing gown, a few years ago. He had made the right decision there as well!

Sunday morning breakfast was a late and unhurried meal. Rose had prepared eggs, bacon and Freya's favourite, oatcakes, plus crusty bread and tea! Freya tucked in as usual and finally was satisfied. She finished the last of her tea and sat back from the table.

"You are finally full, little one?" asked Lars with a smile.

"Yes, thank you, Uncle. It is just that skiing makes me extra hungry!"

"But you have not been skiing," said Lars in surprise.

"I was last night, with Mummy and Daddy. In my dreams, we do lots of things together." Lars stopped eating and looked at Freya.

"Do you see them often? He asked softly.

"Oh yes, every night. They said for me to say thank you to you and Aunty Rose for looking after me so well, and also that they miss you."

Lars looked at Freya for a long moment before asking, "Will you see them again tonight, little one?"

"Of course, Uncle Lars."

"Then tell them that I," he reached for Rose's hand, "that we miss them very much, and that we love looking after you."

"They know!"

The year was drawing to a close and Christmas was approaching fast. For everyone at twenty-nine Druids Way, this Christmas would be very different.

The school nativity play had come and gone. Freya had not had a part in it, she had joined the school too late to be given one, so she had helped out with the scenery. Dutch had been a shepherd, as had Munch, much to her surprise. DIM was Mary and kept forgetting her lines, despite them being written on cards and sellotaped to places where she could see them. DIM was indeed a good name.

The huge Christmas tree had arrived in England from Norway, a gift from its people, and had been placed in Trafalgar Square in London.

Freya had been asked what she would like "Santa" to bring her, but she could think of nothing she wanted. She had her troll, her coin and her necklace. She could do with a new bicycle, but sensed that her Uncle and Aunty could not afford one, so she would manage with her old one, small though it was.

It was a time of reflection for everyone.

For Freya, Christmas without her Mummy and Daddy would be hard for her to cope with. It would not be the same, would never be the same, but deep down, she knew that they would be with her in spirit and that would have to do. She saw so many "elevens" every day and drew comfort from that.

She had sent cards to her friends in Norway and had received some back. A link back to that other life. Before.

Rose was busy as Christmas drew near. Being busy was a new experience for her and to her, and everyone else's surprise she revelled in it. She was confident that she would cope when it came. Going to and from the school, washing, ironing and cooking took up most of her time.

The old Rose had gone forever, she knew that. The new Rose still did not really understand quite what had happened to her, she was just glad that it had. She now had interest in things that she had hated doing before, and the things that she had enjoyed doing, like eating, watching T V and watching Lars do everything else, held no interest for her whatsoever. How she had got like that, and how Lars had put up with her she could not understand. She still had bouts of the dry retching, but they were getting less and less often. It was, as if she had had a personality transplant, which was not too far from the truth. She was able to fit into clothes she had not worn for years, and even some of them were a bit loose on her. One thing was quite clear. She was happy. Happy and fulfilled. Needed. Wanted. She had a purpose. Her dad would have been so proud.

Lars had mixed emotions. He still mourned the loss of Anders and Marit. At this time of year, the focus was on family and all the family he now had was Rose and little Freya. It was strange to have no letters to write to his brother any more. They had always been close. His big brother and his beautiful wife were gone. He missed them. But he had Freya, and she was the light of his life. She had settled in very well and he and Rose had had contact from and discussions with the adoption people about Freya's future with them. But Lars was troubled.

There were rumours going around the dairy about it possibly being taken over by a rival company, and if that happened, there would be redundancies. There was nothing definite, only rumours. It may all come to nothing, but he worried all the same. His circumstances had changed now, he had Freya to think about. The authorities might not let them keep her if he had no work to do. What little savings he had, had gone. Travelling back to Norway to settle his brother's affairs had been expensive, plus the cost of the funeral. His brother had not had much in the way of savings either, and although there should be a little money left when his brother's estate was finally settled, it would not be much. He felt vulnerable. He had always had a bit put by until now. All he had now was his wages from the dairy to live on. So long as he could keep working, he would be all right. But he did have Freya, and he could put no price on what she brought to him. He loved that child as if she was his own and could not imagine life without her. She had changed their lives in so many ways and was a real ray of sunshine. Then there was Rose. She had changed so much, he still could not believe it. She had not just gone back to how she had been when he had first met her, she was so much better than that!

It was truly a miracle. He had been very close to giving up and leaving her, and return to Norway with his brother and his wife. He had not believed it possible for a person to change as much as Rose had done, yet here she was, up early, getting Freya ready for school and taking her there, and doing all the things she had not bothered doing before. Somehow, she had become the wife he had always wanted her to be.

She had told him that she had been to visit her father's grave and had made a start at clearing it up. She had never done that before. She had also lost close to three stones in weight and now looked like a different woman. Slimmer and, he had to admit, attractive. And now she wanted him in bed, and that, he had to also admit was so much better than the few times when they had made love after getting married. She bathed regularly and the sour smell that she sometimes used to have had gone, together with the folds of flesh that had caused it. It was just such a shame that his brother and sister-in-law had had to die for it to have happened! As the old saying went, "Out of something bad, something good will come". It was true. Something had.

It was Friday, and tonight was the Hospital Christmas Party. For the unlucky ones it meant duty instead of fun. It meant that relationships would be made and lost, and they would only hear about it second or third hand. It meant that the woman or man that they had had their eye on would probably be taken by someone else. It wasn't fair, it just was the way of the world.

Like years gone by, the event was held in the large upper room of a pub in Abbotsbury, frequented by the hospital staff throughout the year. Tom and Penny had finished their shifts and were not on call all weekend. They both had agreed to attend. Penny as a senior Nurse and Tom as a Doctor. They were expected to go. Both had been before. Neither were thrilled at the prospect. Loud music, loud people and a smoky room held little interest for cither of them. But it was the done thing to at least show one's face, even if only for a while. They had hoped to slip away later and meet in the staff room and make their plans there. Both knew that on the Monday morning after the "Do", the post mortem would start. Who had "Got off" with whom? Who had not gone? Who had drunk too much? Who had been sick? Etc., etc., etc.

Penny had gone with her fellow nurses, and Tom had arrived with his colleagues. As is usual at the start of these proceedings, the two groups kept their distance, at first. As the evening wore on and alcohol was consumed, they would start to integrate. People would start to make their moves. Nothing of any importance ever happened before the raffle was called. Until tonight! All the Doctors, Porters, Ambulance Drivers, Maintenance workers were men. All the nursing staff, cleaners and admin people were female. It was 1962 after all.

There was a "Disco" and before people were too drunk to read their tickets, the raffle would be drawn. Neither Penny nor Tom had ever been there when the latter had taken place. Everyone seemed to be watching everyone else, seeing who was sitting with whom. Both Penny and Tom had already had a few "Quick dances" if you could call it that, with various people, usually work colleagues. It was expected. It was when the music slowed down that the evening really started.

Penny was with her nurses, when the D J announced that he was going to slow things down, for a short while. One of her colleagues said to another nurse, "I wouldn't mind getting my hands on that Doctor Thornton. He looks a bit of all right!" The other nurse nodded agreement. Penny saw two men start to head her way, eager to get their hands on her, if only for a few minutes each. Penny had other ideas. She stood and walked directly across the mostly empty dance floor, the night was still young, and head towards the bar, where Tom and his colleagues were. Curious, and hungry eyes followed her graceful body as she made her move. It was noted that she had not gone around the edge of the floor, but straight across, in full view of all. Something different was happening tonight!

Tom was buying a round of drinks as she approached and had his back to her. He heard a voice say, "Aye, Aye, it's somebody's lucky night!" But he was about to pay the barman when he felt a tap on his shoulder. He turned to see Penny standing behind him, his colleagues and half the room watching her.

She smiled at him and said, "They're playing our song, Tom, would you like to dance?" and held out her hand. Tom smiled back, passed the pound note he had been holding to his pal and said, "Pay the man for me, would you," and took her hand and followed her on to the dance floor. There were only three other couples slow dancing this early in the evening. He was about to put his hands on her hips when she moved in very close and, put her head on his shoulder. He put his arms fully around her and just swayed to the music. Penny was sending out a message, loud and clear. He's mine, and I'm his! They could both feel the weight of many pairs of eyes watching them.

Tom held her tightly, knowing that what she had done was as good as putting a notice on the notice board. He also knew what it had cost her. She was a very private person, who did not seek attention. Everyone now knew that they were together, something that she had not previously wanted to be made public. Clearly, that had changed. As the next slow record began she raised her head and looked at him.

"Don't be angry, Tom. I don't want to keep us a secret any more. I don't care who knows. I want everyone to know I'm with you!"

He looked into her eyes and smiled. "I could never be angry with you. I'm surprised, and I'm flattered. The most beautiful woman in this room has just told everyone she wants me, I couldn't be happier. You sure you know what you're letting yourself in for?"

"I know" and as the slow music came to an end, she kissed him lightly on the cheek. They were officially a couple!

They had left the party soon after they had danced together. The music had returned to a faster tempo and the noise and smoke in the room had increased to match it. The mirror ball on the ceiling twirled as the dance floor filled up quickly and as they went to claim their coats they could hear the sound of "Love, Love me do" by the Beatles blasting out across the room.

They both had had quite enough for the evening. Penny had already asked Tom to take her home and to stay at the cottage for the weekend. He had hoped she would.

The train was quite full, it was that time of year and when they arrived at Wallbridge station, Penny took his arm for the walk to her cottage. It was cold inside, the fire had not been lit all day, so Penny pulled an electric fire out from behind a chair and placed it on the hearth, putting all three bars on. "That will have to do for tonight. I need to pop upstairs and powder my nose, so make yourself at home. Keep warm!" Especially your hands! Thought Penny as she disappeared upstairs. Tom drew the curtains and then sat in his usual spot on the sofa as the bars on the electric fire started to glow orange and he could smell burning dust as it warmed up.

A few minutes later and light footsteps on the stairs heralded Penny's return. She entered the room and moved in front of the sofa directly opposite Tom and looked down at him with a smile that he remembered from before. She was wearing her dressing gown, buttoned up to the neck. As before, she looked into Tom's eyes for a long moment, as if deciding something. Finally she spoke in a quiet husky voice.

"When you trained to be a Doctor, you obviously did anatomy classes?" He nodded.

"Did you pay attention?"

"Of course. You cannot practice medicine without knowing where everything is and how it works."

He wondered where she was going with this.

"Good! I want you to find something for me. Something small. Something which I do not know works or not. Do you think you can help me?"

Tom nodded again, completely puzzled now.

"Good. That's what I hoped you'd say." And starting at the top, she slowly unbuttoned her dressing gown and finally let it fall to the floor, watching Tom as she did so.

Tom could not stop himself from gasping aloud as his eyes took in the sight that stood before him.

Penny was naked, except for her high-heeled shoes, black stockings and suspender belt. Tom's mouth went dry as he let his gaze travel up and down her body. A goddess had revealed herself to him and it took every ounce of will power to tear his eyes away from the flared hips, dark pubic hair and flat belly. His gaze lingered on her perfect breasts, the nipples in no need of teasing this time, her excitement and the chilly air in the room doing their work. She watched his eyes move and as he looked at her breasts, she raised her arms above her head and arched her back, as she had done that first time, as she knew he liked her to do, so that her breasts were straining against her ribs. She held the pose until his eyes moved again.

His eyes met hers again and his unspoken question was answered with an almost imperceptible nod of her head. Her cryptic words of earlier were suddenly crystal clear. He knew what she wanted him to do.

She slipped off her shoes and then carefully moved forward to kneel on the sofa, placing one stockinged leg on each side of his legs and then finally lowering herself down to settle her naked buttocks on his knees. She noticed the bulge in his trousers. She would have to do something about that soon. She looked into his eyes again and smiled, indicating where she wanted his hands to start.

Tom moved his hands to her breasts and started to gently squeeze and caress them. He could feel her heart pounding to match his own, giving lie to her composure, and his. He would stay there until she let him know that she wanted him to put his hands elsewhere. No words needed to be spoken now. They both knew each other well enough to do without them.

After a while she raised herself up and off his knees and put her hands on the back of the sofa to steady herself, her breasts now above his head. His hands slid slowly down her body, over her hips and then backwards, until his hands found and caressed her bottom, holding a buttock in each hand. They were smooth and firm. Again he lingered there until a movement of her right leg to a slightly wider position told him that it was time.

Tom leaned back again and with his left hand finding and caressing her right buttock once again, he was rewarded by a gasp from Penny as his right hand found the place she had asked him to find, he started to gently pleasure her. The gasps and moans that followed told him that her secret place worked just fine.

Penny was lying on the sofa with her head in his lap, looking up at him, the dressing gown back in place and closed, with just her nylon clad feet visible.

"Do you think less of me after that, Tom?"

"I could never think less of you, Penny. What consenting adults do in a private and safe environment is their own business. After what happened to you before, I would think that your sex drive was, not surprisingly nil. But now you feel safe enough and confident in yourself to explore your sexuality and, you are confident enough in me, in us, to trust me to treat you like the sexy lady you are. You started down that path before, on the night you confided in me. You just moved it up a few levels!"

"Kiss me," said Penny. So he did. Then Penny continued. "Some people would say what I asked you to do was dirty, shameful and wrong. But I don't see it that way. For me, to expose my very intimate, feminine self to you as I did, means that I am one million per cent secure in my relationship with you. I just wanted to know what it was like, to feel that sensation, to enjoy what you were doing with me, not to me, with my consent, with my approval and with a man that I know that I can really trust. I don't think you know what you have done for me tonight. I am now totally free of what happened before. A new woman. A fulfilled woman. Your woman. "

Tom looked down at Penny and saw a woman totally at peace with herself, and with him. "Thank you. How do you feel now?"

"Happy. Warm. Contented. Satisfied. Tingly. I have never felt like this before. If I get run over tomorrow, I will have had this experience. I'm glowing! Before you came into my life, and discounting you know who, my experience of men, not to mention sex, was very little. I think I scare men away somehow. "

"Shall I turn the fire down?" Laughed Tom. They probably think like I used to, that someone as lovely as you would never be interested in them, that you were way out of their league. I would guess that it is a problem that beautiful women have always had."

"I like it when you say that I'm beautiful. I don't think of myself that way. I'm just me, a nurse, ordinary".

"I would never describe you as ordinary," said Tom. "I told you before, you have it all."

"Soon you will have it all, my darling. Just be patient a little longer. I am not quite ready to go all the way, not quite yet. Not after, well, you know. I will go up now and have a bath. When I'm done, come up and tuck me in. But before I go, kiss me," said Penny.

Penny lay in her bed, the yellow light of the bedside light bathing her in a circle of soft light. Tom sat on the covers and looked down at her. She was wearing a fresh nightgown, but her arms were outside the covers, her hands holding his.

"Your pupils are dilated, Doctor."

"So are yours, Sister!"

Penny said, "Where have you been all my life?"

"Worshipping you from afar," said Tom.

"Well, now you can worship me from close up. I will never forget what we shared tonight. How did you know how to do it so well, you must have had lots of experience with women."

"Confession time, Penny. Trust is a two-way street." He took a deep breath, then continued. "I have never done that before, or anything close to it. My experience with women is practically nil.

"You could have fooled me!"

"You are a very easy person to be with, I can be myself with you. Truth be told, I have never slept with, had sex with, got my leg over, call it what you will, with a

173

woman. Ever. I'm a virgin. How's that for honesty? You trusted me with something very important to you, very sensitive, very private. But you told me, so now you know my secret!"

"Kiss me!" He did. "Again."

Penny lay back and looked up at Tom with moist eyes. "Thank you for telling me. You have never slept with a woman. I have never slept with a man, he doesn't count. Soon you will be in here with me, and I will be your first, and you will be mine. It will be soon. You have been very patient with me, and I respect you all the more for it. You said that I could have any man I wanted. I have decided. It is you. I think I am falling in love with you, Tom. When I am not with you, I think about you all the time. I was beginning to think that after four long lonely years, there was no one in this crazy world for me. Then I got to know you. "

"Where have you been all my life, Penny?"

"Waiting for you." She was getting sleepy. It had been quite a day. For both of them.

He rose from the bed, turned out the light and moved to the door, his shadow on the carpet from the hall light. He turned to look at her.

"Penny?"

"Umm?"

"I'm falling in love with you too!"

"I know. Good night."

Ten minutes later, Tom lay under the covers on the sofa and thought about what they had shared earlier. He smiled in the darkness. There are not many men who don't fantasize about beautiful, shapely nurses, wearing stockings and suspenders, who want you to touch them. Such a creature lay upstairs above his head. He could not believe his good fortune. The few women he had known seemed to see him as a brother or uncle figure, not someone with whom they wanted to be intimate with. That had now changed. As he drifted off to sleep, he remembered what Penny had said. It had all started the night Freya and her parents had been brought in to the hospital. Out of something very bad, something very wonderful had happened. The circle of life.

Chapter Eighteen

Jago, Astra and Hugo kept themselves busy, stocking the hideaway with more food and fuel, taking advantage of the early nights and the dry weather. During the day, or if the weather was wet, they used the time to study and improve themselves! Now they had learned how to read and write, they read as much as they could get their paws on. The cats had left a pile of books that they recommended they should read.

Sitting in front of the fire, with a bowl of tea close by, they soaked up knowledge and warmth in equal measure. Reading was a whole new world to them and they could not get enough. Each night they went to bed a little wiser than they had woken up. There was just so much to know.

They knew that there was a human festival in England on December 25, and they agreed that they would hold their own version of it on that day. They planned to have a lazy day of eating, drinking, relaxing and fun, in honour of the creatures that had given them a new life.

They called it Catmus day!

Chapter Nineteen

Doctor Tom awoke on Christmas morning to find Penny's lips pressed against his. She was wearing her nightie and dressing gown.

"What a wonderful way to wake up," he said.

"Thank you! But, Christmas Day or not, I'm afraid I have some bad news. You are not a well man!"

"I'm not?"

"No."

"What seems to be my problem?"

"That!"

"What?"

"That!" she said pointing to the bulge in the blankets, halfway down the sofa.

"Oh that. You seem very perky this morning!"

"I'm not the only one!"

"What could be causing it?" asked Tom, going along with the banter.

"I'm not sure, I'd better have a look at it, I wouldn't want it to come between us!" she giggled.

"Are you qualified to do this sort of thing?" he asked.

"Oh yes, I am from the flying nurses service, and I just happen to be in the area."

"I see, I wondered why you wore that blue outfit and the funny hat."

Penny pulled the covers down, revealing only a pair of underpants. "Lift up."

Tom raised himself up, and she expertly pulled the pants down. "It looks very swollen!" she said in a concerned voice.

"I noticed that. What could be causing it?"

"It's infected with something, no doubt about it. I need to get whatever is in there out!"

"Is that wise?"

"I think so. Relax. I must say that I have noticed some swelling in this area a few times before, and I think that I must take action!"

"Well, if you think you must," said Tom.

Penny reached out and held him in her hand.

"It's definitely infected. It's very hot!"

"Oh, oh, yes, you may well be right. Tell me, have you done this sort of thing before?"

"Actually no. I've seen plenty of them in my work, but I've never held one in my

176

hand before, not like this anyway. Don't worry, you're in good hands with me!"

"I believe you," gasped Tom.

"Am I holding it right?"

"Oh, that's about it, just move your hand a bit."

"Like this?"

"Oh, yes. Oh, oh, Penny, I'm…"

"So I see. There. I was right all along. There was something in it, quite a lot of something it would seem. There. It's going down already, now I have released whatever was in it!"

The tissue she had held ready to catch the "Infection" was full. She put it in another and handed another one to Tom. "How was that, Doctor?" She asked.

"You have no idea," said Tom.

"It was probably as good as what you did for me a couple of weeks ago," she said.

"Thank you very much. That was a first for me."

"You are most welcome, it was a first for me as well. I wanted to give you an early Christmas present, as Santa only comes once a year." She giggled again.

"Well, that was very kind of you. It's a good job there is no post today, as you had better not open the door in your dressing gown with that in your hand." Penny looked back at Tom as she headed up the stairs.

"I don't have a door in my dressing gown," she said laughing out loud.

Tom lay back on the sofa and shook with silent laughter. This was going to be the best Christmas ever. What a woman!

Christmas and New Year had come and gone, and now they were already starting the third week of 1963.

Lars was back at work and Rose had resumed the school routine as if she had done it all her life.

Freya and Dutch were back in class, grateful that they were still under the care of Miss Doyle, and not Mrs Hunter. Freya and Dutch liked to sit next to each other in class, they seemed to encourage each other to do even better than they would have if they had been on their own. Children often make friends for life, and Freya and Dutch would be no exception. They just got along so well that they could not imagine being without the other.

Tom and Penny were hard at work at Abbotsbury Hospital, aware that if they were lucky in their interviews for the jobs at Elfington, this would be their last winter here. They would not miss it. They had enjoyed a magical Christmas together, the first of many they both hoped, and each had met the others parents, where the newcomer had been warmly welcomed by the families, who were delighted at how happy they both were together.

Their shifts and duties had not been kind to them and they had been able to spend little private time together.

Since Boxing Day, the weather had been very cold by day, and even colder by night, and the weather man on the TV had warned of heavy snow on the way. But they always had a good lot of snow in this part of the world at this time of year, and anyway the weather man had been wrong too many times before for anyone to worry about a few flakes of snow!

It had been twinging on and off most of the day, but for ladies at a certain time of the month, abdominal discomfort was not uncommon, was it? So she had ignored it and carried on with her day, which happened to be Sunday. Lars would not be going to work in the morning, and Freya would not be going to school. They were, for the time being at least, cut off. Outside it had been snowing for nearly two days and this latest dump was on top of a considerable amount that had already been there and not melted. The temperature had not risen above freezing for some weeks now, and it was approaching the end of January. So as they could not go outside, Rose was using the time to do work indoors that had been put off for just these circumstances.

Tea had been eaten and the washing up done. Lars and Freya were in the living room listening to the radio in the firelight while Rose had gone upstairs to sort out some clothes that had now become too big for her. She was sitting on the bed when a sudden sharp pain on her right side made her gasp and clutch her side. She sat there, holding her side and after about ten minutes, the pain subsided and she went back to the pile of clothes on the bed. Fifteen minutes later, the pain came again, in the same place but even more severe than before.

Rose instinctively knew that this was something serious and again held her side, wishing it would go away. She was starting to get frightened, as if it was what she feared it was, she was in big trouble as she could not get out, and worse yet, no one could get in.

The pain eased again and Rose slowly got off the bed and started to go downstairs to take some pain killers. She was half way down when another sharp stab of pain made her cry out sharply and sit on the stairs and lean against the wall. In the living room, Lars and Freya had both heard the cry and came out to the hall together to find Rose half way down the stairs and clutching her side. She was pale and sweating.

"What is the matter?" asked Lars, kneeling on the stairs in front of Rose in case she fell forward.

"I have been having a sharp pain in my right side, low down, on and off for a while, and it is getting worse. Please help me to get to the sofa so I can lie down. "

Lars helped her to descend the rest of the stairs and guided her to the sofa when another sharp pain came again. Freya put cushions under her head while Lars brought a glass of water and two pain killers. Rose swallowed them down and lay back.

Lars said, "What do you think it is?" while already suspecting what Rose had thought.

"It might be a grumbling appendix. Let me lie here and see if the tablets work, hopefully it will go away. Don't worry, Freya, it is probably just Uncle Lars's cooking!" Freya smiled but she too realised that it could be serious.

Lars nodded and beckoned Freya to follow him out into the hall. He had already discounted going down the road and telephoning for an ambulance. There was no way any vehicle could get here in this weather. He was fairly sure that Rose had the beginnings of Appendicitis and knew that she would have to go to hospital and have it out. The local Doctor was old and retiring soon and may not even be at home anyway. Which meant that he would have to take her, snow storm or not, to Abbotsbury hospital. And the only way to do that was to load her and Freya into his sledge and ski there!

"Freya, please go and get yourself dressed in your outdoor clothes and put on an extra jumper. Be sure to put on your thick socks and boots and bring your hat and gloves. When you are ready, get Aunty Rose's outdoor clothes and bring them down here. We will have to take her to Abbotsbury Hospital in the sledge. Do you think you will be able to ride in the back with her and keep her from falling out?"

"Yes, Uncle, I think I can, but can you get there in this weather?"

A cry from the sofa decided the matter. Lars and Freya looked at each other for a brief moment, their eyes meeting. They had no choice in the matter. If Rose did not get to Hospital soon, she could die!

"Go, little one, and get ready." Freya ran upstairs while Lars went back into the sitting room and knelt down besides Rose. She smiled wanly at him. "Sorry, but it's getting worse."

"We need to get you to Hospital and the only way to get you there is in the sledge. Are you able to put on your outdoor clothes if Freya helps you?"

Rose nodded, knowing that he was correct. But to ski five miles in a blizzard pulling a sledge with two people in it was almost impossible, even for him. As if reading her mind, Lars said, "Don't forget, we Vikings are tough! I will get you there, just hang on. Freya will be with you!"

Freya came in loaded with Rose's outdoor clothes and started to help her into them. It was not easy and Rose needed Freya's help with almost everything. The pain was getting worse all the time. Lars quickly got into his own gear and went out to get the sledge ready. When he came back inside, Rose was dressed in an extra pair of thick trousers, extra jumper, thick socks, wellies, hat, scarf and gloves. If there's one thing Norwegians know to deal with, it's cold weather!

Moving quickly now, Lars put the fire guard around the fire and checked that the back door was locked and secure, not that anyone could break in during this weather, but they may be away for some days and he wanted the cottage to be safe while they were out. Returning to the living room, Lars very gently picked Rose up in his arms and carried her out of the front door and laid her carefully on the blankets, brushing away the snow that had settled on them. Freya got in and lay down next to her and Lars wrapped the blankets around them both, finally covering them up with an old plastic table cloth, it was all he had and would have to do. Rose had tried not to cry out while Lars had put her into the sledge, but the pain was too bad and she could not help it. She cuddled up to Freya for warmth and comfort, each giving and receiving energy from the other. The snow was falling a little lighter now and Lars had his snow shoes on his back in case he needed them later. They looked like two tennis rackets with short handles.

Lars pulled the sledge out into the road and he got into the harness, the sledge would be kept a fixed distance from him by a rigid frame of light metal. Lars had made it himself and had based the design on what the mountain rescue people used to bring casualties down the mountains on. He had used it to deliver the milk now and then, but tonight he carried a far more valuable cargo. He planned to follow the roads which would be impassable to traffic and people on such a night like this. Only desperate people would be out tonight and he was certainly one of those. Skis were snapped on and with a pole in each hand he set off in the upright stance of the cross-country skier and started to go down the road, the swirling snow closed in behind them and they were soon lost within it.

They had been travelling for more than an hour, but progress had been slow, mainly due to the fact that it was mostly up hill. Lars was having to use the herring bone style of skiing as he struggled up the hills, with the skis like a letter V to make headway. But more and more often, Lars had to put on his snow shoes, the snow was just too deep. Once they got past Beggars Cross the ground would be flatter and then start to go downhill, and he could make much better time. He was plastered in snow, his breath coming in short gasps, but he kept powering on, knowing that the clock was ticking and he must not delay. The storm had taken a turn for the worse and the snow was falling heavily again, whipped up by the icy wind. Freya lay in the sledge and clung on to Rose who was whimpering with the pain and trying to keep her calm. Freya kept telling her that they were making good progress and they would be at the hospital soon, where it would be warm and safe and the doctors would make her better. All she had to do was to hold on and all would be well, but she knew that Rose was getting gradually worse. Freya raised her head and looked out over the side of the sledge and saw an alien landscape outside. Although it had been dark for some hours, she could see quite well in the whiteness. She was wearing her necklace. The snow had drifted against the stone walls and hedges, and it seemed like she was in a tunnel with high cliffs of snow on each side. The wind had blown the snow into fantastic shapes, as it swirled around her. There were great banks of snow higher than the wall against which it was being blown, with a knife-like edge at the top. Here and there were slight dips in the drifts where there had been a gate way leading into a field. Telegraph poles and the wires were inches thick with snow, the hedges were just round humps of snow. As Freya looked out she saw a large hump in the road, like a massive meringue. She guessed correctly that it was an abandoned car completely hidden under feet of snow. She smiled briefly at the thought that she was starting to think in feet and inches. Not so long ago she would have thought in metres and centimetres. Before. Everything was distorted and she hoped that Uncle Lars had not got lost and they were still on track.

Freya lowered her head again and lay back down. Suddenly, in a flash of thought, she knew what she had to do. Carefully she removed her left glove and unzipped her coat, looking for and then finding her necklace. She held the stone in her hand for a minute or so before withdrawing it, then unfastening Rose's coat, managed to get her hand inside until it was touching her skin. She gently placed her hand on Rose's abdomen and held it there, focusing her mind on keeping her hand in place. Rose seemed to grow quieter after a while and did not call out again.

Lars had been pulling the sledge for over an hour and a quarter now and was starting to tire. Gritting his teeth, he drew on his reserves of strength and kept going. Suddenly he crested the last of the hills and knew that it was downhill from here. If it had been a clear night, he would have seen the lights of the town in the distance, but as he changed back into his skis again, all he saw was a curtain of snowflakes. Energized by this knowledge, he began his descent in to Abbotsbury and knew that he was nearly there. Thirty minutes later he skied to a stop outside the Emergency entrance of Abbotsbury Hospital and released his skis. Freya heard the sound and gently withdrew her hand and started to climb out of the sledge, the table cloth that he had covered them with was thick with snow. Lars, completely caked in snow, reached down and scooped up Rose as gently as he could and pushed through the double doors and out of the storm and into the glare of lights, and the warmth and safety of the hospital, with Freya right behind him. Against all the odds, they had made it!

Sister Penny Grey and Dr Thomas Thornton were on duty. Again. They should not have been, but they could not get out of the hospital, and their relief could not get in. But at least they were together. They were stuck, and had been for two days, together with everyone else who happened to be in the hospital at this time. No visitors could come in and the patients who were discharged could not leave. But it could have been worse. It was nice and warm, and the kitchen staff, marooned as well, continued to prepare all the meals. Thankfully, they had had their delivery on Thursday morning, the last day that the roads were still passable.

The main problem was boredom. There was little, if anything to do. For the first time in living memory, every case note was up to date, all shelves fully stocked and cupboards replenished. So they sat in the staff room, near the Emergency entrance, secure in the thought that there would be no emergency. No one could get there. They were playing cards with two other nurses and a porter, and all jumped out of their skins when the main doors burst open and a giant snowman came in carrying something in its arms. For a full five seconds they all just sat there, looking through the glass window, and gaped in disbelief at the figures before them, then they all sprang to their feet and rushed out to the main entrance to see who it was. Freya appeared from behind the snowman and, on seeing Aunty Penny, she rushed forward and said, "Aunty Penny, come quickly, it's Aunty Rose, she has very bad pain in her stomach, we think it might be her appendix!"

Lars gently laid Rose on one of the trolleys by the wall and tried to speak. He couldn't. His jaw and face were completely frozen!

The trolley was quickly taken into an examination room by the porter and Dr Thornton, while the nurses went ahead to begin getting the scissors out, in case they needed to cut off any clothing, the training kicking in immediately the door had burst open. Penny, meanwhile, was helping Lars out of his coat, hat and ski boots before taking him and Freya into the staff room and into chairs, next to the radiator.

"How on earth did you get here? We're completely cut off at the moment, no one can get in or out!"

"Sledge," croaked Lars, his face starting to thaw a little.

Another nurse appeared and Penny told her to get the kettle on and to make two mugs of tea, both with sugar. Freya started to say that neither of them took sugar but Penny was in Sister mode and said, in a voice that brooked no argument, that for once they were going to have it with sugar and that was that!

The drinks appeared, together with a plate of biscuits and while Penny watched, they sipped their tea and attacked the biscuits. Leaving the nurse to give them a refill, Penny went to find Tom.

He had just finished his examination and Rose was now in a hospital gown and under a red blanket.

She looked over as Penny came in and was able to manage a weak smile. Dr Thornton was washing his hands and spoke over his shoulder.

"Young Freya was right. Acute Appendicitis, it's a miracle it hasn't burst already. I'm going to operate right away, I've sent the porter to wake up the Anaesthetist, and the theatre staff are on standby."

Penny went over to the bed and held Rose's hand, just as she cried out in pain again. "Don't worry, Rose, we will sort you out, no problem. Tom is a good surgeon and you will be in good hands."

Tom, drying his hands, came over and said, "Praise indeed from the good Sister here! OK, Rose, I'm off to scrub up and get ready, Penny will bring you down in few minutes. Don't worry, she would never forgive me if I let anything happen to you!" and with that he left the room.

Penny said, "Lars and Freya are getting thawed out and having a sit down. They are fine and will see you afterwards, I'll keep them out of mischief!"

"Thank you," said Rose as the door opened and two theatre porters came in wearing masks and guided the trolley out of the double doors and down to the operating theatre, glad to have something to do at last.

Penny went with them, suddenly realising that Tom had called her Penny in front of the nurse. She did not care. After the Christmas party, there were not many staff members who did not know they were seeing each other anyway!

They entered the prep room and Penny said, "I'll go now and let my colleagues do their work. See you later, Rose" and with that she left the room and made her way back to the staffroom where Lars and Freya were waiting.

"It's all OK. Rose is going into theatre now and Dr Tom is operating. He said to tell you, Freya, that you were right. It is Appendicitis. Thanks to you both, she is going to be fine. How's your face, Lars? Have you defrosted yet?"

"I'm getting there, thank you," said Lars, working his jaw muscles.

"Right, next stop for you two is the canteen. Hot soup to start with, then what ever you like! I'll see if there is any herring left, Freya! Come on."

Freya pulled a face, going along with the joke and jumped out of her chair with ease, but Lars was stiff after his marathon effort and hc hobbled along behind Freya and Penny. He was wearing surgical booties on his size fourteen feet, kept in place with a thick elastic band around each ankle.

As they went down the empty corridors, memories of that other time flooded his mind. The antiseptic smell was still the same, but there were no wheelchairs or trolleys to be seen. Everything had been returned to its proper place, another first! They came to a junction in the corridor and continued straight on. Lars glanced down the corridor as they passed. Down there, he knew was the chapel of rest. Where he had had to identify Anders and Marit. They were not there now, of course, he had taken them home. But it came as a shock to think that it was only five months ago, it seemed like a lifetime. And now here he was again, back in the hospital. He hoped that there would not be a third time. They arrived at the almost empty canteen and took a tray from the pile and the lady behind the counter put down her magazine and gave them two large bowls of vegetable soup and a plate of bread and butter, having been tipped off by Penny earlier, and who was also having some.

They sat down together and ate the soup and bread. There was nothing else they could do now, only wait.

In the operating theatre, Dr Thornton was gowned up and awaited his patient. He too remembered the other time that the Olsen family had been here and needed his skills. He still did not know how Freya had pulled through. He had been credited with saving her life, but he knew that he had not. She had come back from the dead all on her own. The double doors swung open and the trolley bearing Rose was wheeled in. He took a deep breath.

Show time!

He approached the table and his assistants closed in around him, ready to help as necessary with swabs, clamps and other instruments. As he watched, one of the assistants cleansed the area that was to be operated on with a swab of brown liquid and as that was completed, he noticed something that he had not seen before, but appeared through the brown antiseptic fluid. He adjusted one of the overhead lights slightly so he could see better. There, some sort of faint mark, right over the appendix. He bent forward to have a closer look. It must be some sort of birth mark he concluded, as he was handed a scalpel, strange though, it looked just like a small hand print!

Freya and Lars were back in the staff room, sitting in their chairs next to the radiator and waiting for news. On the way back they had passed the waiting room that they should really be sitting in, had it been a normal day and the hospital rules had not been suspended. It was empty and closed, with the light off. Lars remembered the hours he had sat in there waiting for Freya to awaken. Freya had taken his giant hand in hers, sensing and understanding the emotion he was reliving. He gave the small hand a slight squeeze, grateful for the contact. Penny noticed the movement and smiled to herself, also remembering that other time. She had seen too many "Other times" with other people in her years working at the hospital. You could only take so much. Time to leave.

Penny had left them there, having other things to do. She would return when there was any news to tell them. It did not take long for the heat of the room, and the large meal they had both eaten to have its effect on them. First Lars, then Freya's eyes started to close and before long they were both snoozing, relieved that they had delivered Rose safely and that they could do no more but wait for Doctor Thornton and his staff to do their work. Outside in the dark of the night, the snow continued to swirl around the building and the wind to howl, but the two Norwegians next to the radiator slept on.

Half an hour later, Doctor Tom Thornton peeled off his surgical gloves and dropped them in to the surgical waste bin, together with his hat and mask. The operation was over and had gone very well, Rose was now in the recovery ward with Penny to watch over her. She would make a full recovery, and when the roads were finally cleared she should be able to go home, together with all the other patients and staff that had been stranded here by the storm. He was still amazed that the appendix had not burst much earlier on the journey to the hospital, thankfully it had not, or things would have been a lot more serious than they had been. Rose had been very lucky indeed. He left the theatre and walked down the empty corridors to the staff lounge and as he opened the door, two sleepy heads jerked awake instantly, their eyes full of anxiety.

"Relax. All went well and the operation was a success. Rose is in recovery with Penny. When she is satisfied, she will take Rose to a ward and you will be allowed a brief visit. Freya, you were correct. It was the appendix, and had it burst things would have been very different. Thank goodness you were able to get her here in time."

Lars got to his feet, towering over Tom and shook his hand. "Thank you, Tom. This is the second time you have saved a member of my family. I cannot thank you enough for what you have done."

Freya came over and gave Tom a hug. "Thank you. From now on you will be Uncle Tom!"

He blushed at that, but was pleased as Lars and Freya were more than just patients, they were friends of Penny's and that made them friends of his.

"My pleasure, folks, when you leave school, Freya, maybe you should consider a career in medicine!"

"May be I will. Will I get a white coat like yours?"

"Absolutely, and you will go to a special school to learn how to write so no one can understand it!"

They all laughed at that.

One of the nurses came in and offered everyone a cup of tea, so Tom sat down with the others and stretched out his legs.

"How's your Troll doing," he asked. "You didn't bring him with you I see."

Freya giggled and said, "No. He's fine and at home, looking after the cottage until we get back"!

The door opened again and Penny came in. "Ah, there you are, Tom. Rose is awake and in the ward now and with your permission, I think a short visit is possible."

"Granted."

Penny, Lars and Freya went out and Doctor Tom took his tea and rested the cup and saucer on the arm of his chair. The nurse went out and he was alone. Being stranded here had given him time to think about his future. He was glad he had decided to apply for the GP's job at Elfington. He should hear soon when his interview would be, and if things went well, then he could have a much more normal life and spend more time with Penny, who would be working with him if she was given the practice nurse's job. He had had enough of shift work and if truth be told, he did not want to stay here without Penny. She meant so much to him, perhaps love had really found him. He knew that he meant a great deal to her, she had told him she loved him. It was such a nice thing for a woman to say to a man.

In the ward, a sleepy Rose smiled as Lars and Freya came in. "Hi there! Thank you both so much for all you have done for me, I don't know how I can ever make it up to you!"

Lars smiled and winked at Freya. "We will think of something, won't we, Freya!"

She smiled and said, "Yes. I'm working on it right now!"

Penny said, "Right. Time to let Rose sleep. You can come back in the morning. Say good night."

Lars bent down and kissed Rose, then Freya did the same as Rose drifted off.

They left the ward quietly and went downstairs again and returned to the staff lounge, where they found Dr Tom sound asleep, his tea untouched!

Chapter Twenty

It was Wednesday morning and it had finally stopped snowing and the sun was actually out, very low on the horizon, but there all the same, shining down out of a pale, washed-out blue sky and making the snow have a bad glare to it. The sun gave the illusion of warmth, but the temperature was still below freezing. The wind had died down and was now a mere shadow of its former self, again making it feel warmer than it actually was.

The hospital had received a phone call from the council, to inform them that every snowplough, farm tractor and industrial loader was working flat out to get the road to the hospital open as soon as possible, hopefully by the evening. They were having to move tons of snow, which in places had drifted as high as twenty feet! Progress was slow, but getting access to the hospital was their number one priority. Whoever had thought to build the hospital a mile out of the town had some serious explaining to do! For those stranded in the hospital, it could not happen soon enough.

Rose was recovering well and would be able to go home when the roads were passable again, but until that time, they continued to be stuck. Some of the porters, nurses and doctors had ventured outside and started to clear the yard, and the road that led to the main gate, and try to start the ambulances up. Surprisingly all four did! There was of course the obligatory snowball fight and it did them all good to get outside and let off a bit of steam. The mood was lighter now that they knew that their ordeal was drawing to a close. They had been very fortunate that during their isolation, there had been no emergencies reported, except for Rose, but at eleven-thirty their luck ran out.

The phone rang and a very weak male voice kept calling for an ambulance, saying he had slipped on some ice while bringing some more coal inside and broken his leg and gashed his head the day before. It had taken him hours to drag himself inside, close the door, where he had collapsed in the hall and fallen unconscious. He was cold and weak and it had taken the last of his strength to get to the phone. He was seventy-four. It had not occurred to him to dial 999, but in any case they would have been in no better position to help him either, everyone was snowed in! He managed to tell the nurse his name and where he lived before passing out again. The nurse hurried off to find Sister Grey, finally tracking her down in one of the wards, chatting to Rose, Lars and Freya. She told Penny about the call and she immediately knew who he was, as he had been in the hospital the week before as an outpatient. It was the aptly named, Mr Winter. He sounded in a bad way, but there was no way they could get to him, he lived outside Elfington, near Beggars Cross, some four miles away. Lars, Rose and Freya had actually passed his house on the way there.

Lars and Freya had been listening to the conversation, and Lars said, "I know this man, I deliver his milk. I could go and get him in the sledge. It's stopped snowing and it's daylight, I will be able to do it, it will be easier than before."

Penny nodded. "Thank you, Lars, but we must go now, he could have hypothermia and be dehydrated. I'll come with you."

Lars shook his head.

"There is not room for two in the sledge, and I would struggle to carry two adults on the way back."

"I could do it!"

All eyes turned to look at Freya, who had said nothing until now. "I kept Aunty Rose from falling out of the Tredge and kept her warm, I could do it again. I have met him a few times when I helped Uncle Lars on Saturdays."

Penny and Lars looked at Rose. "What do you think, Rose? He will need to be kept still and warm, as you were."

Rose looked at Freya. "Do you really think you can do it again, Freya?"

"Yes," said Freya, "He's not very big and we must help him. He's a nice old man."

"Lars?"

Lars looked at Rose and raised an eyebrow, silently asking for approval. Rose thought about it for a few seconds. Freya would be safe with Lars, and a man's life might be at stake, as hers had been. They couldn't just leave him there. She nodded.

"As long as Penny and Dr Thornton are happy, then yes."

Leaving Rose to rest, they all went downstairs to find Dr Thornton to get his approval. He was in the staff lounge, having done his stint outside shovelling snow. When Penny had filled him in, he nodded. "Agreed. Normally I wouldn't dream of sending a seven-year-old to do something like this, but as you will be with your Uncle, and you are not just any seven-year-old and used to cold weather, I will allow it. Just do what you did with your Aunty, keep him still and warm and your Uncle will do the rest."

Lars and Freya went off to prepare for their unexpected journey, while Tom and Penny put some things together for them to take with them.

Soon they were ready, Penny handed over a bag with flasks of hot tea, sandwiches, and bandages. She also gave Lars the telephone number of the hospital and told him to call in when they got there and give them details of Mr Winter's condition.

Lars got into his harness and snapped on his skis, while Freya knelt on the blankets in the back, able to see where they were going this time. Tom came out and gave them both a pair of sun glasses. They would need them against the glare.

They set off, Freya waving as they headed down the cleared drive and onto the road, which was still deep with snow. After about three quarters of a mile, they came across the road clearers and after a brief word with the foreman, they headed down the cleared road towards Elfington. They made much better time, the snow was only an inch deep and was flat and they fairly whizzed along. In less than an hour, they had passed Beggars Cross and were close to the short track that led to Mr Winter's house. Lars took off his skis and walked down the track with difficulty, the snow was waist deep! There was a huge drift in the drive which had almost covered the back door, so they made their way to the front. Lars peered through the window and through an open lounge door he could see a pair of legs lying in the hall. The legs were not moving! He hoped that they were not too late. If they were, Freya would not be allowed to go in, they would just turn around and go back. She had had enough of death in her short life already. The front door was locked! So Lars had to force his way through the drift to the back door, which was really at the side of the house, while Freya stayed in the sledge at the front.

Finally he made it, and thankfully it was not locked and he went inside, calling out as he did so. Mr Winter was lying in the hall, the telephone receiver hanging on its cord nearby. Quickly Lars knelt next to him and checked for signs of life. He was alive, cold and unconscious. The pulse was weak but the breathing was steady.

Lars got to his feet and went into the lounge and unlocked the front door and got Freya inside with the bag. "He's alive and we need to get him warm."

They returned to the hall and Lars got coats from the rack and covered Mr Winter up and put a cushion from the lounge sofa under his head, while Freya held his hand and talked to him. "Wake up, Mr Winter, wake up. Help is here. Wake up."

Mr Winter's body moved slightly and he opened his eyes. The first thing he saw was a little blond girl with a serious face and green eyes looking down at him and holding his hand.

He frowned. "Who, who are you?" he managed to croak.

"I am Freya. I am here with my Uncle. We have come to help you!"

Lars replaced the phone back on its stand and got one of the flasks from the bag and poured a cup out and handed it to Freya.

"Get him to drink this."

Gently, Freya brought the cup to his lips and he took a sip. Then another. Little by little with Freya's help he drank it all. Lars knelt down next to Freya.

"Hello, Mr Winter It is me, Lars, your milkman. You remember me!"

"Lars? Yes. I remember you. Thank god you have come. I thought I was a goner!"

"Where does it hurt, Mr Winter?"

"Leg, right leg and my head!"

Lars could see there was a lump on Mr Winter head and gently he felt along his leg. As he got below the knee, he gave a cry of pain.

"There! That's where it hurts!"

Lars got to his feet and stepped over Mr Winter and went into the kitchen to find a knife or a pair of scissors, while Freya gave him a second cup of tea and some biscuits. He found a pair of scissors in a drawer and went back into the hall. He thought

189

Mr Winter was looking better, with a little more colour in his cheeks. The tea and company were working their magic. Lars carefully cut the right trouser leg up to the knee. There was no bone visible, but there was quite a bit of swelling and discolouration on the shin.

He looked at Mr Winter. "I think it could be broken, are you able to stand on it?"

"No. It won't take any weight at all."

"OK, any other injuries?

"Only a lump on my head and my wounded pride!"

"Well, the lump will be looked at, together with your leg at the hospital. The pride you will have to mend yourself. Can you sit up now?"

"Yes I think so, if you help me."

Lars helped him to sit up with his back against the bannister and Freya opened a packet of ham sandwiches and while Mr Winter tucked into them, Lars rang the hospital and reported in. Penny answered it and she had Tom with her. They were pleased that he and Freya had got there, and that Mr Winter was eating, drinking and talking. The phone was passed to Mr Winter who told Penny what had happened. They agreed that he would have to come in to the hospital on the sledge and be checked over, and if his leg was broken, have it set in a plaster cast.

Lars was told how to put Mr Winter leg in a temporary splint for the journey, and Mr Winter told Freya where there was some string.

He lay back against the bannister and continued to eat his sandwiches and drink more tea. He reflected how lucky he was that he had been rescued by these two wonderful people. It had been a chance in a million that they were at the hospital with a sledge and that Lars could ski.

He had lain in the hall all night, cold, alone and frightened, listening to the wind howling around his house. He had been in pain and had really thought that he might die. His mind had started to play tricks on him, telling him that no one would come. Then he had passed out. When he came round, he found that he had wet himself and he was so embarrassed and angry, but he could not help it.

He passed out again and when he opened his eyes again he thought he had died and gone to heaven, because there was an angel looking down at him and smiling. The angel was holding his hand and she had a halo.

It took him a moment to realise that the "Angel" was in fact a little blond girl who had somehow come to help him, and the "Halo" was the hall light shining behind her head! He was alive!

He would not forget this. Ever. Young Freya and her Uncle Lars had saved his life, no doubt about it.

Twenty minutes later, he was lying in the back of the tredge, covered up and with Freya next to him to stop him rolling around or falling out. The pain was manageable, thanks to the tablets Lars had given him. His house was secure, the keys in his pocket. So they set off back to the hospital before the light faded and more snow started to fall. It was bitterly cold still. It did not take as long as Mr Winter thought it would. They met up again with the snow clearers and they were quite near the hospital by now. It would be open for business again very soon! Once again Lars pulled into the emergency bay and removed his skis, this time, people were waiting for him, a stretcher ready. As Mr Winter was whisked away, Lars looked down at Freya and smiled. "We make a good team, little one, yar?"

"Yar! Let's go and see Aunty Rose and tell her all about it," said Freya.

"Good idea! But let's tell her about it in the canteen, I'm starving!" Said Lars

Mr Winter lay back against the pillows and looked down at his right leg, encased now in plaster. He had broken it in two places, what the hospital called the "Tib" and "Fib", whatever they were. He had had to have an operation to set the leg properly. That had been yesterday.

Today was a rest and recover day. He could do with it. Outside it was still freezing, and although the main roads were slowly becoming passible in places, there were piles of snow everywhere. In here, he was warm, had been fed and was safe. He was not alone any more. His body would heal fairly quickly, but his mind might take a bit longer. The experience had shaken him badly. He closed his eyes and thought back to the night he had spent lying on his hall floor, cold, alone, in pain, listening to the wind and feeling his strength slowly fading away. His thoughts had wandered, would he now be reunited with his wife, son, daughter-in-law and granddaughter. They had all been taken from him during the Second World War. He thought about them a lot. Now, perhaps it was his time to go too. He didn't want to go yet, he wanted to live on, but no one could get to him in this weather. As he had passed into unconsciousness again, he went back in his mind to that terrible day when they were taken from him.

He had lived with his wife, son, daughter-in-law and granddaughter on the Island of Jersey, in the Channel Islands. He had owned a small Jeweller's shop in the town of St Helier, and his family had helped him to run it. He did well and enjoyed the Island life. It was a lovely place to live. Then came the War. The Germans could not be stopped and some of the people had started to leave the Islands to go to England. Just in case. He did not go. Why would the Germans come here? There was nothing here for them to come for. Just a few small Islands, that's all. No, they were safe here. The Germans would not come. He was sure.

His wife and son were not so sure, and urged him to think again. Boats were sent from England and more and more of the Islanders were leaving. France had fallen and also the Low Countries. German aircraft had been overflying the Islands more and more often. But still he would not go, and they would not go without him. The

Germans would not come, there was nothing for them here.

But he was wrong, and he had, through his stubbornness, condemned them all. The Germans did come, and they came quickly. Before he knew it, white bed sheets were hanging out of every window, his included, and Jackboots were marching down the streets. But it was not so bad at first. Being occupied by the Germans would not last long, and he would just carry on as before until the British came and things got back to normal.

At first, things stayed more or less the same, sure, there was a curfew, some things were rationed, and they all had to register, but the Germans he came across seemed polite and friendly. All he had to do was sit out the war and all would be well. He was wrong about that too. After only two years or so, people started to be removed from the Island to the continental mainland. Small groups here and there. Quietly. They were needed for work in Germany and other occupied countries, they were told. They would be treated well. They would be paid. There was nothing to worry about. They would be allowed to return to the Islands soon. It was only a temporary measure. It soon became clear that the people who were being taken all had one thing in common. They were Jewish people. People like him.

By a stroke of good fortune, if you could call it that, he was out on a valuation of some jewellery when they came for his family. He returned to the shop to find it closed and empty. He asked next door. What had happened? Where were his family?

He was told they had been told to pack quickly, only one case. They would be given clothes when they arrived at their work places. Everyone had gone, even little Rachel, his granddaughter. She was only three.

He ran down to the harbour, but there was a road block across the Weighbridge with armed soldiers.

The Germans were not so friendly now.

Desperately, he ran down an alley and into a shop at the end. He could see the docks through the window. There! There they were, walking down the quay to the ship that was waiting. His son was carrying the case and Rachel was pushing her little pram with her dolly inside. There were soldiers everywhere, keeping the people back. Only those on the list were allowed through. The Germans had lists for everything. He saw them go down the gangway and disappear into the ship. His last memory was of little Rachel pushing her dolly in its pram into the ship, going past a soldier in a coal scuttle helmet.

Soon the gangway was pulled up and the ship left. That was 1942. He never saw them again. Somehow he had survived the occupation, hiding out with the few friends that he had left. Finally, the war ended and the British came back. He had tried to find out what had happened to his family, and by sheer luck, he found someone who had somehow survived the camps and had seen them. His son had been separated from the rest of his family and had been put to work cutting down trees. He had managed to last almost two years before he had died. The Germans had told the truth about one thing. His family had been taken to an occupied country.

Occupied Poland to be exact. A place called Auschwitz. The others had been taken at once to the "Showers". They had not come out again.

They were gone. Part of him had died that day. He had prayed for their souls and then sold the shop and moved to England. He had money and bought a nice house in a little village called Elfington. That had been in 1947. He had lived alone ever since.

Then he had slipped on the ice while bringing in more coal from the shed outside. Managing to drag himself inside and close the door, he had passed out in the hall and stayed there all night. With the last of his strength he had managed to call the hospital. It never crossed his mind to call 999. He had a letter from the out patients department next to the phone and had managed to call the number on it, before passing out again. When he opened his eyes again, he thought he was dead. He saw an angel kneeling next to him, a smile on its face and halo around its head.

But he was not dead, and it had not been an angel he had seen but a little girl with her Uncle. They had, somehow managed to get to him and save his life.

He opened his eyes and wiped away the tears. He owed his life to them and would be forever in their debt. He would never forget. Never.

Chapter Twenty-One

Tom and Penny had finally been relieved and had decided to go to Penny's cottage. They emerged from the hospital like bears from hibernation, blinking in the glare of the snow, unused to being outside. One thing that they did remember was the bitter cold. They had had to travel by road, as the radio had told them that the trains were not up and running. How unusual. One thing in their favour was that some of the outlying villages were still cut off, the steep hills in and out of them just too dangerous to travel on, but Wallbridge was on a main road and the buses went through there. They finally got to her front door, frozen and dying to go to the loo, the bitter cold doing its work all too well. Once inside, they discovered that there was no power! So they had to go to plan "B" which was to try and get to Tom's flat, as they reasoned that Pondford, being a small town was more likely to have electricity than a small village like Wallbridge. So once Penny had packed a bag to last for a few days, they again made their way to the Bus stop, this time luck was on their side and one came along after only fifteen minutes.

The main roads were, while not exactly clear, passable with care and so they arrived at Pondford Bus garage in the middle of the afternoon, with the light starting to fade. They got to Tom's flat and were very relieved to find the electricity was working. So after a welcome mug of tea, made without milk, and with the electric fire doing its best to put some heat in the chilly rooms, Tom headed out to the shops to buy what supplies he could, while Penny got the coal fire going. It was fully dark when he returned with two heavy bags of shopping to find a fire burning cheerfully in the grate and the curtains drawn. While Tom thawed out in front of the fire, Penny prepared a simple but very welcome meal of sausages and mash. Tom had a bottle of wine in the cupboard and they shared that with the meal.

It was so good to get away from the hospital and be alone together. They cuddled and kissed while they watched the TV and enjoyed an episode of "Z Cars", followed by a new programme called "That was the week that was", which it certainly had been! Penny shared a box of "After Eights" that Tom had bought for her, and as it had passed that time, they judged it would be all right to eat some of them.

They were tired after the day's events and decided to have an early night. Penny headed off to Tom's bedroom, where the electric fire had been on for a while, and Tom started to get the blankets to make up the sofa for himself. As he brought them into the living room, Penny's voice called out from the bedroom, and he went in to find her in his bed, with the covers turned down on the empty side next to her.

Only the bedside light was on, and Penny looked up at him and asked, "Care to join me?" In a quiet voice while patting the empty space. Tom went over and sat on the bed and took her hand as he looked at her, his eyes full of questions.

"You sure you want me to?"

A squeeze of his hand accompanied her words. "Yes. Very sure. Your waiting is over, Tom. I want you in here with me. I want you to love me."

Tom nodded, and with trembling hands and a dry mouth, he quickly got undressed and slid into bed, where Penny immediately took off her nighty and reached out to cuddle up to him. They kissed and ran their hands over each other's bodies, getting warm quickly. As Penny pressed against him, she could feel him becoming aroused and she slid her hand down his body to find and hold him, until he was fully erect. Wasting no time now, she moved and straddled him, the bedclothes falling from her, revealing her exquisite body and still holding him in her hand, positioned herself over him before guiding him inside her, then gently sinking down onto him until he was fully inside her, gasping as she went ever lower.

Tom had watched her in fascination as she had lowered herself onto him, the sensation like nothing he had ever felt before. The goddess that was Penny Grey had said that she wanted him to love her, and now he was about to experience the one thing that he had never had. The love of a beautiful woman, given freely to him. She saw his eyes travel from where they were joined to her breasts and, while continuing to rise and lower herself slowly, lifted her arms up and arched her back, thrusting out her breasts, wanting to give him as much pleasure as she could, wanting this first time to be extra special, for both of them. She took her time, wanting it to last as long as possible, while he ran his hands over her body, fondling her breasts as she continued to move up and down on him. At last, she leaned forward to kiss him, her breasts flattening against his chest, his hands moving up and along her back and down to her bottom where they were joined. Between kisses she whispered to him, "Love me, Tom. Love me. That's what I want, only you, Tom, only you, just love me."

She raised herself up again, her hands now on his shoulders, breasts hanging free, and began to move her hips more quickly, pushing herself down on him with increasing urgency, her breathing coming in gasps in between moans of pleasure as Tom held her hips in his hands, helping her in her movements, his own breathing and gasps of pleasure matching hers. Finally, he could wait no longer and she cried out as he exploded inside her as she continued to move, not wanting the pleasure he was giving her to stop. She lowered her body down again, to lie on top of him once more, wanting to keep him inside her as long as possible, hearing him whispering his thanks, over and over again. She whispered back to him, her lips next to his ear.

"Thank you, darling, that was my first time of being loved by a real man. You belong to me now, and I belong to you." They stayed like that until she felt him start to fade, then gently raised herself off him and lay down beside him, holding him close to her. Tom covered Penny with the bedclothes and held her close to him, lightly stroking her hair and her back, his breathing like hers, still not back to normal. Outside, in the bitter cold, a few flakes of snow drifted past the window in the darkness of the night, but in the glow of the bedside light, Doctor Tom Thornton held the most precious thing in the world close to him and marvelled at the gift she had given to him. He was in no doubt that, after what had happened to her four years ago, she had needed to draw on a huge amount of courage to face having sex again, and he felt very humble that she had chosen and trusted him to show her how wonderful and glorious it could and should be. The last time had been with a man, if you could call him that, who had forced her to have sex, this time she had given him her love, there was a huge difference between the two. He had never felt so happy in his life, the final mystery of what "IT" was like had been solved. It had been worth the wait. Like the goddess he held in his arms, he was complete.

Rose Olsen was discharged from the Hospital two days after the road to it had been cleared enough to allow staff in and patients out, getting some of them home to remote areas however, was something else! Tom and Penny had already gone the day before, and had said their goodbyes before heading off together. Rose, like Freya before her owed her life to Doctor Tom, who waved her thanks away with his usual modesty, saying it was all in a day's work, and when she was fully better, he and Penny would call in to their house for another free breakfast. Rose would hold them to that.

Before they left, the Olsen family went to see Mr Winter and spend a little time with him. He in turn thanked Lars and Freya again for saving his life and they told him that he was most welcome. They all signed his plaster cast and then said their farewells, he would remain in hospital for a while longer, until it was possible to get him safely home and for care to be arranged, care that could actually get to his house!

They left the same way as they had arrived, Rose and Freya in the Tredge, and Lars on his skis. There was still little traffic on the roads, and apart from a few startled drivers who came across a large man pulling a sledge with two people in it, Lars made good time on the way home. The minor roads around Elfington were still not cleared, but they got home safely and were relieved to find the power was still on. Rose was escorted to the Sofa by Lars and Freya, with strict instructions to stay there, or else!

Rose lay back and watched the three bars on the electric fire glow orange, and ignored the smell of burning dust, while Lars and Freya moved around the house, getting the fire going and the kettle on. The little blond girl who had lost both her parents in the most brutal of ways , and the giant blond man who had lost his brother and sister-in-law in the same way . They had both moved on, outwardly at least, from that terrible time, and were making the best of the life they now had.

There was no doubt that they had saved her life, and if that was not enough, Lars and Freya had saved Mr Winter as well! She was so glad to be home, and even gladder to be alive, she thought as a mug of tea was put on the table next to her. She looked around the room, and her eyes fell on a photo of her and Lars taken less than a year before. She remembered one of the people who had visited them from the Children's Department, the real one, although she had no memory of the first visit, who had come to have a look around and meet her and Lars as they began the process of adoption for Freya, asking who the lady standing next to Lars was.

The man had been very surprised when Rose had said that it was her. The woman in the photo looked like a complete stranger to her now. The old Rose. Before.

Lars and Freya came in with their tea and Rose held out her arms to them as the emotion of the last few days over came her and she could not stop her tears. So much had happened in the last week. Lars and Freya put down their mugs and while Lars knelt beside the sofa, Freya climbed up on to the seat next to her Aunt and Rose pulled the two blond heads close to hers, kissing them both in turn.

"Thank you both so much for saving me, I don't know what I would do without you, I really don't!"

Lars and Freya looked at each other in some surprise, then turned back to Rose as Lars spoke for both of them. "You are very welcome. We Vikings look after our own. We do not want to be without you. We both need you in our home, we both need what you give to us. We are a family. So when you are better you can take your place again in our family, with us. Is that not so, little one?"

Freya nodded, moved by his words. They were home.

Penny Grey left the Elfington Doctors Surgery with a spring in her step and smile on her face. She had just had her formal interview for the Practice Nurse's Job, and had got it!

Her friend and outgoing job holder had sang her praises to the GP who knew her quite well anyway from her visits to the surgery to see her friend and that, together with a glowing letter of recommendation from the Matron of Abbotsbury Hospital had been more than enough. The interview had been a mere formality and the GP was quite sure that he had made the right choice. The Matron had even said in her letter that Penny would have been her choice to be appointed to Matron's rank, when she herself retired in a few years' time, and knowing the Matron as he did, the Doctor was convinced. Penny's years in Nursing and her time at Abbotsbury Hospital had put her head and shoulders above the other three applicants.

Penny would serve her notice at the Hospital and start her new job after Easter. Tomorrow it would be Tom's turn to be interviewed. His would be a much more formal affair, and he would have to sit before a panel of people, one of which would be the outgoing GP whose influence would be vital. She also knew that he was up against stiff competition from at least one other very good doctor.

But that was tomorrow. Today was her day and she had been successful. Penny made her way in the bitter cold weather to the one and only telephone box in the village and hoped that it had not been vandalized. The ice on the pavement and on the roads was hard packed and the sun glinted off it. There was snow piled up everywhere, and it was still very icy underfoot. Each day the temperature rose to two or three degrees above freezing and where the sun, when there was any, caught the ice, a slight thaw took place, only for everything to quickly re-freeze at night time. Anywhere that the sun did not shine remained frozen solid!

She reached the phone box and found it to be working. The box smelled of cigarettes, but then they all did and taking her four pennies from her pocket, she put them in the slot and dialled the number of Abbotsbury Hospital. When they answered, she pressed button "A" and heard her four coins drop down inside the black box to which the phone was connected. She asked for Doctor Thornton. He came on the line quickly, as he had been waiting next to the phone in the doctors' lounge before going on duty. Penny had taken the day off. She told him the good news and he was thrilled for her. He said, "Well done, Penny, I knew you would get it! One down and one to go. My turn tomorrow."

"You will be fine, darling, I'm sure. You can call me tomorrow and tell me how you got on. "

"I will, but today is your day, so very well done. I am so proud of you. "

The pips went then and they said their goodbyes and ended the call. Penny left the phone box and decided to go and see Rose, who was up and about quite well after her operation of a few weeks ago.

Penny would spend the rest of the day with her and then go with her to collect Freya from school. Lars would be home soon, one advantage of starting work so early. So she made her way through the village whose citizens she would get to know very well indeed when she began to serve them as the new village nurse!

Doctor Thomas Thornton sat on a hard wooden chair in front of the panel of four men, who would decide who the new General Practitioner for the Elfington and district area would be. The panel was made up of the outgoing GP, the Vicar, who was aptly named Reverend Hope, a consultant from somewhere or other and another retired Doctor.

Tom was the third and last candidate to sit before them. The interview was being held in the waiting room of the surgery. He had already handed over a sealed letter of recommendation from his boss at Abbotsbury Hospital, the senior consultant himself. Tom hoped that it was a letter of recommendation, rather than a letter saying don't employ this man, he's hopeless!

Tom sat upright in his chair, wearing his best suit, recently cleaned, and tie. His shoes had been shined to a high gloss, in fact he had brought them in a separate bag and changed into them after arriving, not wanting to get them dirty. He had also made sure he had had his hair cut, availing himself of Dutch senior's kitchen a few days before. He thought that the interview was going well so far, he had been able to answer all the questions the panel had asked him, and thought they seemed impressed. The panel would choose the new Doctor after he had left and the three contenders would find out the result by post.

Finally it was over, and he thanked them for seeing him and after shaking hands all round, Tom left the surgery and headed down to the station, after changing his shoes again, not so much to keep them clean now, but his wellies had much better grip on the icy pavements. Tea and biscuits were served by the GP's wife and then the panel got down to business.

One candidate was discounted quickly, as being too young and inexperienced, although the Vicar had voted for him as he had said he was a regular church goer. It did not occur to him that he would say that, wouldn't he, to get his vote! So now it came down to two. Both were strong candidates, and there was little to choose between them. In the end, it came down to two things, both of them letters. One had had a slightly better letter of recommendation than the other, and the outgoing GP had said he had received a letter from a local person, who had been treated by one of the candidates and had wanted to say they had received superb treatment while under his care.

The consultant, who knew Tom's boss quite well, had voted for Tom, as he knew that getting praise out of him was like getting blood out of a stone. The retired Doctor favoured the other candidate and voted for him. The Vicar abstained, as his favourite had already been discounted. So it fell to the outgoing GP to have the casting vote. He took his time, giving frank and fair comments to both of the candidates, either of which would make a fine replacement for him and serve the community well. It was the letter from the local person that was the deciding factor in a very close run contest. The outgoing GP took a deep breath and announced that the new General Practitioner for Elfington and district was going to be...

Dr Thomas Thornton!

The panel was thanked for their service and reminded that they should not reveal the result until the letters had been sent out. They nodded their agreement and went about their business. The Vicar returned to his church. The retired Doctor was invited to join the consultant for a spot of lunch at the nearby Golf Club, the consultant being a member. He had started to go a bit more often now that the loud mouth John Stagg had buggered off down south!

The outgoing GP went upstairs to his study and sat behind his desk, glad that the panel was over and sure that the right decision had been reached.

He pulled open a drawer and took out the letter to which he had referred to the panel and read it again. He smiled as he got to the end. It simply said "Yours hopefully, Miss Freya Olsen. Aged seven".

He remembered the story in the paper last year, it had been front page news, the crash and the loss of the parents, and the little girl, who had been brought back from the dead by one Doctor Thomas Thornton!

What he did not know, and never would, was after Freya had finished her letter, she had taken her special necklace in her hand and rubbed the blue stone all over the paper, before sealing it in an envelope.

She was not sure why she had felt the need to do that, only that she must. She marked the envelope "PRIVATE AND CONFIDENTIAL" and had delivered it by hand herself.

When the GP had opened and read the letter, he was impressed by the neat writing and the fact that she had taken the trouble to support Dr Thornton's bid to succeed him. What he had forgotten, and would never remember, was that after reading the letter and putting it in the drawer of his desk, he had suddenly felt very sleepy and had had to be awakened by his wife twenty minutes later to eat his lunch. The seed had been planted that day, and today it had flowered.

Freya had tapped into a tiny fraction of the power that her special necklace held and was still not yet aware of the immense power that it contained. The power of the Universe!

Penny cuddled up to Tom again as he returned to bed after getting out to go and collect the mail. It was Saturday morning and they were in Tom's flat in Pondford. They were both off duty for the weekend and were here, rather than Penny's cottage for one very good reason. That reason had just been delivered by the postman. Tom had put the letter on the bedside table and turned his attention to cuddling and kissing Penny, there was, after all nothing more important to him than her and her happiness. He had already noted the postmark. It was Elfington. This was it. But whatever the letter said, it would say the same thing ten minutes later.

It was Penny who cracked first. With a final kiss, she reached across him, her breasts crushed against his chest, and took the letter from the table and handed it over. "OK let's get it over with, Tom. Please open it and put me out of my misery."

He nodded and tore open the envelope, then handed the letter over to her.

"You do it."

Penny took the letter, opened it out and started to read it out loud. "Dear Doctor Thornton,

Further to your recent interview for the position of General Practitioner for the

Elfington and district area, I am delighted to inform you that the Panel has decided to offer the position to you."

She stopped reading and threw her arms around Tom. "You got it, you got it. We can be together now, no more hospital, no more stress, no more night shifts, no more weekends apart, no more crazy life. You did it, Tom, this will be the start of a whole new life now. A normal life, like other people have. I just can't believe it. I've got you, I've got the nurse's job, and now, the final piece. You will be the GP. Congratulations, darling, I'm so proud of you."

Tom just held her close, feeling the warmth of her body, her breasts pressed against his chest, his mind whirling, unable to speak. He had hoped against hope that he would be successful, but had steeled himself in case the news was not good. But now, now he would see Penny every day, live above the surgery in the rooms that came with the job. Live a different life, be able to do things like normal people. He silently thanked the gods for this latest piece of good fortune. To have a goddess like Penny in his life was more than he ever dreamed possible, and now this as well. His cup runneth over. The relief was immense. He had done it!

He ran his hands down Penny's back and over her bare bottom, as she started kissing him again. As if reading his mind, she released her grip on him and lay back, watching him, wanting him, needing him, her heart full of love for him. Gently Tom raised himself up on one arm and ran his other hand over her breasts, squeezing and teasing her before moving to be over and above her. In a quiet voice he said, "I don't know about you, practice nurse Grey, but I feel a little celebration might be in order."

She put one hand on his shoulder, and reached down to find and hold him with the other. "I feel you may be right! As I have always said, a good doctor should have a good nurse under him!

Chapter Twenty- Two

They were in the viewing room, looking out at an alien landscape, not that they could see much of anything, only the white curtain of swirling snowflakes. It was early February and Catmus day seemed a long time ago to them now. Only a couple of days after that the weather had become very cold and it had not got any warmer. Snow, snow and yet more snow. The cats had warned them that this winter would be severe. As usual, they had been right.

Astra smiled to herself as she thought that this was the first year that they had known that days, weeks and months existed, and even though they now knew what day and month it was, that knowledge was not a whole lot of good to them at the moment. They could not go outside whatever the day and month was!

They had not been able to go outside for weeks, the weather was just too bad, even for them. So they used the time to study, and improve their reading and writing skills. Every day they thanked the Universe for guiding them here. They were so lucky. They had enough food, water and fuel. And they had each other. They were warm, safe and free. Every few days they came here to look out at the world beyond and see if anything had changed. Today, like the last time, and the one before that, nothing had.

Astra did not need to ask the twins the obvious question, she already knew the answer. It was no.

No they would not have survived this winter if they had been in their old home. They would have either starved or frozen to death. With a last look outside, they closed over the stone window and shaking themselves to get rid of the snow that had blown in and settled on them, headed back down the tunnel to the welcome warmth of the fire. Eventually spring would arrive, but for now they had seen enough of winter.

Chapter Twenty- Three

On 27 March 1963, Dr Richard Beeching published his report on the country's railways. It made grim reading. In it, he recommended closing about thirty percent of the rail routes, and if that was not bad enough, he also recommended closing half of the railway stations!

Of course reports and recommendations were one thing, actually implementing them was something else. The people who used and worked on the railways were at first alarmed, none less than those on the Elfington valley line, but then they reasoned that the government wouldn't actually take any action, so they did not worry too much. They should have.

It was the Sunday after the report came out that the Olsen family made their way to Mr Winter's house. He had invited them to take tea with him at three O'clock. The day before the clocks had gone forward to British Summer Time and the "extra" hour was a welcome sign that the savage winter they had just endured was finally behind them. As they walked through the village they saw blossom on some of the trees and daffodils and crocuses were making up for lost time and were finally able to force their way up through the ground now that the frost had finally relented. Spring was in the air.

They arrived promptly at three and Mr Winter was waiting for them. He was still on crutches, but in cheerful mood as the plaster cast was due to come off in a few more days. They went inside and followed him through the hall where Lars and Freya had found him two months earlier and were ushered into the front room where a fire burned cheerfully in the grate and there was a table loaded with sandwiches and cakes, which Mr Winter confessed had either been bought in the village shop or made by his neighbour.

The visitors were invited to help themselves as and when they got hungry. He started to make his way to the kitchen to make some tea, but was intercepted by Rose who said she would be happy to do it while he entertained his other guests.

The conversation was light as they sat before the fire, Freya doing most of the talking, telling Mr Winter about her school work, her friend Dutch and about Uncle Tom and Aunty Penny who would soon be taking over the doctor's surgery in a few weeks' time. Mr Winter sat and smiled, really enjoying the company and the chatter of the little girl who still looked like an angel, with or without a halo. Lars also sat and smiled. For him, this was a very enjoyable way to spend an afternoon. He was proud of his niece and also his wife, who came into the room with a tray with the teapot on it, together with a jug of milk. Not so long ago the old Rose would not even have bothered coming, let alone actually doing something! Not that she would have been invited any way!

While they drank their tea and discussed the weather, Mr Winter brought the conversation around to the real purpose of his invitation.

Firstly, he thanked them again for saving his life. He was in no doubt that that was what they had done. Without them, he would not be sitting here now and enjoying their company. To show his gratitude, he asked them to follow him outside for a few minutes as he had something to show them before it got dark. His visitors rose to their feet and followed him, two of them knowing what was coming, or at least part of it. Mr Winter led them out the back door and into his huge garage, via a side door, turning on the light as he went in. There was a musty smell inside, and old oil stains on the floor. The garage was large enough for at least two cars. There was a vehicle at the back, covered with a dust sheet. Mr Winter turned to Freya and asked her if she would be so kind as to look behind the car and see what she could find. Freya, with a quick look at Lars and Rose, walked behind the car to find a girl's bicycle waiting for her! She gasped with surprise and ran over to it and carefully wheeled it out so everyone could see it. The rear wheel clicking as it moved. It was pink, and had three gears, a saddlebag and a bell. She could hardly take her eyes off it. Mr Winter spoke. "This is for you, Freya, a small token of my thanks for helping your Uncle to save me. Do you like it?"

Freya looked up at the old man with tears in her eyes and putting her new bike back on its side stand, rushed over and hugged him. He could not hug her back, as he needed both hands on his crutches, but his face said it all. Lars and Rose smiled with delight, they had known about the bike, as Mr Winter had asked Lars if he and Rose would agree for him to buy it for Freya, and to ask what sort of bike she was looking for. Judging by the look on her face, he thought that he had got the right one. Finally Freya released Mr Winter and they all crowded around the bike, admiring it. Freya could not believe it was hers. Santa had not been able to bring one at Christmas, but as Lars had pointed out, the change of address could have confused him. Mr Winter said she could take it home this evening. Wait until she told Dutch! He already had a bike, now they could go riding together. She was so happy, what a kind man Mr Winter was.

But Mr Winter had another surprise, one that Lars and Rose did not know about. He turned to Lars and asked if he would be so kind as to remove the dust sheet from the vehicle. Lars did so, and looked in admiration at the Hillman Minx that was revealed. It was about five years old, but he could tell, in very good condition. Mr Winter produced a set of keys and invited Lars, Rose and Freya to climb inside. Lars wondered why he was doing this, maybe it needed to be taken to the garage for servicing. He could do that. But that was not the reason.

Mr Winter leaned against the car and looked down at his guests. Lars was behind the wheel, Rose next to him and Freya in the back. Rose said,

"You have a lovely car here, Mr Winter, you will enjoy driving it again when your leg is better."

Mr Winter smiled at her and said, "Actually I won't. I don't drive any more, my eyesight is not what it was. I was thinking, it is such a pity to let it sit in here, and not be used. So I have decided to give it to you!"

Three jaws dropped open, three pairs of eyes went wide. Rose gasped in surprise. There was silence for a few seconds, before Lars found his voice again. "Mr Winter, tell me you are joking. This is a valuable car, worth hundreds of pounds. You cannot seriously be saying you are giving this to us. We cannot accept it, it is too much!"

Mr Winter was serious. He looked at each of them in turn and said, "But for you, I would not be here, enjoying this spring day and your company. You saved my life. Please let me do this for you. As I said, I do not use the car any more, and it is doing nobody any good just sitting in here. I really want you to have it. I will be offended if you refuse this gift."

Lars turned to look at Freya in the back, Freya looked at him and Rose, knowing that it would be they who would decide, but she nodded her acceptance anyway. Rose looked at Mr Winter again.

"Are you really sure? I mean it's a car! The bicycle for Freya was very generous, but this, this is... "

"A car," he finished for her. "A car that I do not use, and even if I sold it, you don't get much for them these days, so, please tell me that you will accept it."

Everyone looked at Lars, leaving the decision to him. He licked his lips, then nodded. "On behalf of the Olsen family, I accept. Thank you. Thank you so much. I cannot believe your kindness. Thank you."

Mr Winter beamed. "That's settled then. Now, I don't know about you, but I feel I could manage a sandwich and a cake. Shall we go back inside? I have all the documents ready." They all climbed out and Mr Winter received another hug from Freya, a hug and a kiss from Rose, and hug and very firm handshake from Lars. As they followed Mr Winter back inside, they did not see the tear that fell from his eye. His family had been taken from him, many years ago. Now he had been sent a new one.

It was after dark, even with the extra hour, when Freya, Lars and Rose said their goodbyes to Mr Winter and headed for home, full of sandwiches, cake and tea. They were also still in shock after the surprises that the afternoon had had in store for them. Freya was pushing her new bike, glad that it was dry, as she did not want to get it dirty or wet. She still could not believe it was hers. She had thought that she would have to wait for Santa's next visit, but as the saying goes, Christmas had come early. She was a very happy little girl as she pushed her new bicycle down the dark streets that Sunday evening. She deserved to be.

Walking behind her, Rose and Lars were equally still coming to terms with the events of the afternoon. They had known about the bike, but that dear, kind, and generous gentleman had given them his car!

In Rose's handbag was an envelope containing the car documents. In Lars's pocket were two sets of keys.

It was a miracle. After the terrible events of last year, 1963 had seemed to be going the same way when Rose had become ill, but since then, everything seemed to be going in the right direction. Rose had recovered, Mr Winter was on the mend and now this. They owned a car! There were few houses in their street that had one. Lars had said that he would call round and collect it after work the next day, unless he awoke and found himself in his bed, and it all had been a dream!

Mr Winter had hobbled to the end of the drive and waved them off, sorry to see them go. He had had a fantastic day and was so glad he had been able to help them, and that they had accepted his gifts. He watched them until they turned the corner at the end of the road and they were lost to view. Even in the darkness, he had been able to see them quite well. It was strange, he told himself with a smile, how his eyes had suddenly improved again. Who would have thought it!

Chapter Twenty-Four

There are some people who are known as "Romantics" and are able to convince themselves that the object of their desire is what they believe them to be, not what they actually are.

Young people with this condition some times change their attitude as their young minds develop and they gain experience and knowledge of the world and about human nature. Some do not. Munch was one so afflicted. He had a "Crush" on Freya and to his simple child's mind, she was his girl. Like others before him, he credited the girl of his dreams with virtues that she may or may not actually have. Kindness, moral excellence, goodness and many others were given to the female they idolise, especially, as in the case of Freya, they were physically attractive. She could do no wrong, think no bad thoughts and in Munch's mind, be as much "in love" with him as he was with her.

So he appointed himself her guardian and protector, ready to leap to her defence and strike down anyone who would dare to say a bad word about his heroine. She was, simply perfect. The fact that he had not ever spoken to her and knew nothing about her was beside the point. Freya had come from Norway, where ever that was, to Elfington to be with him, it was obvious. Well, it was to him at least. So as the spring of 1963 went on, and the weather finally started to improve, Munch decided that he would begin to keep an eye on her. She would expect him to.

So with his gang of three other village children, at weekends and holidays he would start to follow her.

Freya had noticed them at once. She noticed everything, without even trying. She did not know it, but she was a scanner, subconsciously noticing things on the edge of her vision while looking at something else. She filed all this away in the back of her mind. At weekends, and now over the Easter holidays, everywhere she seemed to go, Munch and his gang were never far away. It was easy enough to give them the slip and at first it was fun to do so, while never giving them any indication that she had seen them at all. It was a case of mind over matter. She didn't mind and they didn't matter!

But after a while, she was starting to get fed up with them and would have to come up with a plan to stop them doing it. She headed to Dutch's house to see if he could play, hoping he would be able to come up with an idea. He was quite smart, for a boy! He was in and his parents welcomed her inside. It was not very warm and she was glad to be inside next to Mrs Van den Berg's fire. Dutch was playing with his toy farm yard and she sat on the carpet next to him and helped to move the toy cows, pigs, sheep and tractors and other farm implements around while Munch and his gang shivered in the bushes nearby, until they got fed up and went home. Serve them right!

Freya was starting to get angry, something that was almost unknown for her. Munch and his gang were really becoming a pest. What had at first been a game, a bit of fun, was getting out of hand. He would just not give up, and try as she might Freya could not think of a way to stop them from following her. To burn off some of her frustration, she decided to go for a bike ride alone. Munch and his followers did not have bikes, he probably could not balance on one anyway! Freya mounted up and, not caring if Munch was watching or not, she headed out of the village towards Beggars Cross, passing Mr Winter's house, the old mill and the lake as she went. It was up hill, but she just dropped her three-speed-geared bike down to Number two and getting off the seat, powered her way upwards, glad to be free of company and on her own. Even if Munch and his crew had owned bikes, they would not have been able to keep pace with her anyway!

She arrived at Beggars Cross and turned right, towards Withycoombe , which the finger post told her was one and a half miles away. To have turned left would have taken her to Wallbridge, and to go straight on would have led to Abbotsbury. Freya smiled as she peddled along the twisting country road. She was getting used to Miles, pints, feet and shillings. And keeping on the left side of the road. A thought flashed through her mind. She remembered on her first evening in England arriving at the docks and seeing, together with a big blue and white arrow, a big sign which said KEEP LEFT. That seemed a long time ago.

Freya cycled along, enjoying the countryside that unfolded all around her. She passed through the tiny hamlet of Kingham, where she saw a farmer unloading milk churns from a cart and putting them on a stand, waiting for them to be collected and taken to the dairy. Maybe that very same milk would end up on her Uncle's milk float tomorrow morning, she thought as she waved to the farmer, who touched his cap in reply as she whizzed past. Uncle Lars had been wise to come here to look for work, instead of heading for the larger towns and cities where life was lived at a much faster pace. Sunlight flashed through the trees as she went along and the roadside undergrowth was starting to grow, not yet threatening to encroach on the road itself, which was narrow enough as it was. She coasted down the hill into the small village of Withycoombe, passed the few shops and the one pub, crossing the bridge over the river Elf. The village was picturesque, popular with the hikers and walkers. The pub was olde worlde, with a thatched roof and a waggon wheel outside the front. Colourful hanging baskets hung from hooks, and now that it was starting to get a bit warmer, there were plenty of tables and chairs outside for people to enjoy a drink outside.

Once across the river, she was already heading out of the village again, so she slowed down and turned around, stopping half way across the bridge to look down into the slow moving water flowing along. The river would flow down the valley, turning this way and that, just like the railway line, all the way to Abbotsbury, passing Elfington and WallBridge as it went.

Freya mounted her bike again and started the journey home, passing the pub on her left for the return trip to Beggars Cross and Elfington. Another black and white finger post told travellers that Beggars Cross was one and three quarters miles down the same road that she had cycled down earlier. She smiled and wondered if anyone else had noticed the difference. Back along the road she went, legs pumping and ponytail flying out behind her. The farmer had gone, but the milk churns were still there, but the stand was in the shade so the milk would be kept cool. She turned left at Beggars Cross, noticing the extra sign, directing travellers to Cropwell Manor, which lay just beyond Elfington. It was a country manor, with extensive gardens and some attractions, like rowing boats on the lake and a small fun fair. She had not, as yet visited it. Freya stopped peddling and coasted downhill towards Elfington village and home. It was amazing, she thought, how different things were when you looked at them from a different direction.

Freya jammed on her brakes, the back wheel skidding sideways and then to a stop as her mind grasped the importance of what she had just thought!

How different things were when you looked at them from a different direction! A light bulb had just come on in her mind and as she once again continued on her way, an idea began to take shape in her brain. She completed the rest of the journey and arrived home. The frustration she had left home with had completely gone, partly due to the exercise, but partly due to the idea that she was thinking about. Freya Olsen had plans to make.

Doctor Thomas Thornton and Sister Penny Grey had finished their last shift at Abbotsbury Hospital, and had said their final goodbyes. They could go. It was the Thursday before Good Friday and they had a very busy holiday weekend ahead of them. The weekend before, they had had a joint farewell drink up in a local pub for the closest work colleagues and friends.

So now, carrying the gifts they had been presented with earlier, they walked out of the main entrance for the last time and out into the Easter sunshine. They paused for a moment and looked back, remembering the years they had served. The lives saved and the lives lost, the people they had met and the friends they had made, three of which would be helping them over the bank holiday weekend. The most important event that had happened in the hospital was that they had found each other. As they made their way down the drive that led to the main road, Penny reached out for Tom's hand and held it. An ambulance swept past them, blue lights flashing and bell ringing, heading for the A and E department. Others would deal with the patients that it contained now. They carried on walking down to the railway station hand in hand. They did not work there anymore. They were free.

Tom and Penny spent all Good Friday at Tom's flat, packing boxes and deciding what to take and what to throw away. On Easter Saturday reinforcements arrived in the form of Lars, Rose and Freya. The car that Mr Winter had given them was coming in useful already. Although the flat was furnished, Tom had lived there for five years and had accumulated a large amount of "stuff" which he had kept in case he might need it someday, but actually never had. That was taken first to the rubbish dump and left outside the locked gates, it was of course, closed over Easter.

Then came the first of many trips to Elfington, where the car was unloaded before returning to Pondford to collect another load. The old GP had already moved out and into a new house in the village to start his retirement, but would continue to hold surgeries for a while longer until Tom and Penny were fully settled in.

When the pile of boxes was larger at the surgery than the one left in the flat, Tom called a halt for lunch. They all walked the short distance into the town and Tom treated everyone to a chip shop lunch. Freya tried a meat and potato pie, chips, gravy and mushy peas and polished the lot off, together with a mug of tea. Vikings, even small ones liked their grub!

When everyone was full, they headed back to start work again. By evening the flat was cleared. Tomorrow they would all return to start the cleaning!

Lars, Rose and Freya drove home, while Tom and Penny spent their last night in his flat. They were both worn out and after a quick wash and light meal, they went to bed and quickly fell asleep in each other's arms.

The Olsens also had an early night. Rose cuddled up to Lars, happier than she could remember, glad to part of something, rather than apart from it. Freya, cuddled up to her Troll and was soon fast asleep, quickly slipping into R. E. M. sleep, her body paralyzed to prevent any injury, as she dreamed. As always, her parents were there, waiting for her.

The next day, operation "Spring Clean" swung into action. Everything that could be cleaned, was cleaned. Windows, floors, woodwork, everything. Finally, Penny was satisfied. It would do. Tom then announced that they were all invited to his parents' house, where a buffet lunch awaited them. With Lars being guided by Tom, and the ladies in the back of the car, they headed to Toms parents' house. They spent the rest of the afternoon and early evening there, and really enjoyed the visit. Freya was presented with a giant Easter egg in a box, and Lars, Rose and Penny received somewhat smaller ones.

It was dark when they finally drove back to Elfington, via a garage where Tom paid for the car to be filled with petrol, a small thank you for all that his friends had done. Tom and Penny were dropped off at Penny's cottage at Wallbridge. Tomorrow, Easter Monday, the Olsen family could have a day to themselves, while Tom and Penny sorted things out in the rooms above the surgery.

The new GP and his nurse had to be ready for business when the surgery opened its doors again on Tuesday morning.

Practice Nurse Penny Grey stood next to her friend and out-going practice nurse in the dispensary. It was a long narrow room that was completely lined with shelves that held the drugs and medicines that the doctor would prescribe to his patients, as there was no chemist in Elfington. Part of Penny's new job was to dispense the medication that Tom would authorise.

There was a stable door that opened into the waiting room, and when the surgery was open, the top half of the door was swung inward and Penny would wait for the patients to emerge from the consulting room and hand over their prescription paper. The door was completely closed at the moment, but the two nurses could hear the low buzz of conversation of the patients who waited beyond it. Penny would shadow her friend for just a week before carrying on alone. She looked down at her new pale-blue uniform with its wide black elasticated belt and silver clasp. The only things she had brought with her from her time at Abbotsbury hospital were her old "upside down" watch, her comfy flat black shoes, and her vast amount of knowledge and experience. She was excited and a little nervous, but most of all, she was happy. Tom, her Tom, was just in the other room, and the thought that he was so close to her during the working day, not to mention the night brought a smile to her face. This job was by far the best she had ever had.

Behind the closed door of the consulting room, Dr Tom sat behind the desk and checked that he had everything that he needed again. The outgoing Doctor was also there, sitting next to him, but a little behind. He too would "sit in" for a week before Tom went fully solo. Not that he had any doubts about Tom's ability to do the job, but more to guide Tom and pass on his "local Knowledge" about some of the patients. He would, however cover the surgery on a Saturday morning for a while and also take over when Tom was on holiday or if he was sick.

The hands of the clock, which was hidden by a screen so that the Doctor could see it but the patients could not, (A Doctor should never look at his watch when he was with a patient) told Tom that it was now nine o'clock. With a brief look at his fellow professional, who nodded, Tom rose and walked to the door and opened it on the stroke of nine. Eighteen faces looked up from the waiting room. A full house.

"Good morning, everyone. I'm your new Doctor, Doctor Thornton. Who's first?"

As Tom went back inside the consulting room, followed by his first patient, the top half of the door of the dispensary swung inward and was clipped into place, revealing two figures in pale-blue uniforms.

The surgery was open for business!

Chapter Twenty-Five

It was two weeks later before Freya could put her plan in to effect. On a cloudy Saturday morning, Freya told Aunty Rose that she was going for a walk with Dutch and would be back in time for lunch. She left the house at ten thirty having given her followers time to assemble behind the usual bushes on the edge of the wold.

She looked neither left nor right, just set off down the road and into the village. She paused outside the grocer's shop as if looking for something in the window, but she was just using the window as a mirror to make sure that Munch and co were there. They were, pretending to read the notice board next to the phone box. Satisfied, Freya moved on and headed out of the village and down a track that wound its way gradually upwards towards a different part of the wold.

She walked on at a good pace, never looking behind her and after three quarters of an hour the track went between some large rocks, switching first left, then right before heading into a small stand of birch trees. She was briefly lost from view of the followers, who, to avoid possible detection, would have to let her go fully around both corners before they could do so themselves. It was eleven twenty and Freya was right on schedule. As soon as she turned the first corner, she quickly stepped off the track and into the ferns and bracken, making her way through the silver birch trees to hide behind the large rock, where Dutch was crouching down, waiting for her, together with their two bikes!

Five minutes later, Munch and his three gang members came down the track and peered around the corner to make sure that Freya had gone. The track was empty so they made their way to the next corner and peered around that before vanishing down the track. Dutch and Freya gave them five minutes before emerging from their hiding place and mounted their bikes for the fifteen minute downhill ride back to the village. Phase one was complete!

As they free wheeled down the track, the sky was getting ever darker and the wind was starting to get up. They arrived back in the village just before noon, well pleased with their morning's work. They wondered if Munch and his gang had yet realised that Freya was not there, and they were over an hours walk from the village. Time to begin phase two. Cycling through the village, they made their way to where they knew two of the gang lived. They were immediately lucky as the mother of one of the gang was cutting the front hedge and was standing on the pavement. Freya and Dutch stopped for a chat. It would be bad manners not to, after all! The mother asked if they had seen her Jimmy on their travels, as dinner was almost ready and it looked like rain. Jimmy had not taken a coat. Freya said that she had seen him earlier with Ricky Wild and a couple of others, heading up to the wold. The mother was not pleased.

"I've told him not to hang around with that boy, he's nothing but trouble. If you see him again, tell him to come straight home." Freya and Dutch said they would if they saw him, but they were heading for home as it was dinner time and looked like it was going to pour down with rain. They cycled off and the mother watched them go. Such nice children, those two.

Turning into a different road, they again were lucky as the father of another of the gang was walking down the road with his dog. He waved to them and as they stopped, asked if they had seen his Steven, as it was almost dinner time. Again Freya said she had seen him with some others earlier heading up to the wold.

The man was not happy. He thanked them and continued on, hoping that the dog would hurry up and have a shit so he could get back home before it started to rain. He had five bob on a horse that was running in a race that was being shown on the telly. It was nearly twelve twenty.

Dutch and Freya decided to abort the mission then as the first plops of rain were starting to fall. Two out of three would be quite enough! They headed home and Dutch peeled off down his own road and Freya waved goodbye to him. They were both safe indoors when the rain really started to lash down.

Up on the wold, Munch and his crew had continued on until ten to twelve before it dawned on them that they were a long way from home! Somehow Freya had disappeared. Quickly they turned around and started back as the clouds gathered over their heads. But they were starting to get tired and could not go too fast. It was well after one o'clock when four soaking wet children arrived back at their respective houses to face the music that they knew was awaiting them. To say that they were in big trouble was an understatement. Munch actually got away with it, sneaking in the back door and up to his room before his mother could spot him. The others were not so fortunate. Two of them got a clip around the ear, and all three were told not to hang around with that oaf Ricky "Munch" Wild again, or else!

After dinner, Freya helped with the dishes as the rain lashed against the window. She smiled to herself. She would not want to be out in that! Score one for the Vikings!

From that day on, she was never followed again.

It was on a warm and pleasant early afternoon day in May that Lars returned home a somewhat worried man. The rumours about the future of the dairy were going around again. It was not the first time that such rumours had done the rounds, and there was little to worry about. Probably. This time there was talk of the dairy being taken over by a bigger rival based in Pondford. If that were to happen, jobs were sure to be lost, particularly if you worked for the smaller company that was being taken over. He sighed. Time would tell. There was nothing he could do except wait, and keep his ear to the ground. But he had to admit that such rumours were unsettling none the less.

He arrived home and let himself in. Rose was out at her father's grave, but would be back in time to go and collect Freya from school. He made himself a mug of tea and a couple of sandwiches and sat down to eat his lunch. Just when things had been going so well, Freya settled at school, Rose a new woman and Tom and Penny installed in the Doctors surgery in the village. When Rose came in he would tell her what he had heard. He thought back twelve months as he ate his food. This time last year he would not have mentioned it to her, knowing what she would say, knowing that she would not have cared less. He was the provider, and it was nothing to do with her! If he lost his job, he would just have to go and find another one. Simple. And that would have been that. She would have returned her attention back to the TV, cross that he had distracted her from looking at it.

How things had changed since then. He still had trouble believing it. Rose was a new woman all right, in all respects, four and a half stone lighter, now a trim, and he had to admit, sexy nine stone, with a positive attitude and a smile instead of a frown, together with a willingness to do things for him, Freya and for others. Amazing. And not only that. There was also a willingness on her part in their personal relationship which had certainly not been there twelve months ago. Then, she had no interest what so ever in any physical contact with him, nor he with her.

But now, she wanted that physical contact, and more. She wanted him in bed and he wanted her. She was slender, firm and desirable. And clean. A real woman. A confident woman. A partner. A wife, who, job or no job would stand by him and support him, rather than wash her hands of him and his problems.

He heard a key in the lock and the front door opening, and Rose came in, a smile on her face as she bent down to kiss him, giving him a momentary glimpse of her breasts down the front of her shirt. Smaller, firmer, sitting snugly in her bra, as she did so.

"Hello, Lars! Had a good day? I've been doing a bit of work at dad's grave. You've had your lunch, good. I'll have to go and get changed before I go and collect Freya. "

He nodded and stood up, towering over her.

"I'll come with you, Rose, and I can tell you what I heard at the dairy today."

She nodded and went to wash her hands in the kitchen. The new and improved Mrs Rose Olsen was home.

Rose Olsen cuddled up to her husband and thanked her lucky stars that she had a man like him in her life. They had just made love and she lay next to his warm body, feeling fulfilled and complete. Although he did not know it, she too was thinking back to how things had been twelve months ago. Certainly not like this, that was for sure.

Then he did not touch her, and she did not blame him. Back then she had not wanted him to. Being intimate with her husband was, like everything else, just too much of a bother. He paid the bills, did the housework, and did as he was told. That had suited her just fine.

She sighed. Was that life only twelve months ago? It seemed a life time. She still had no clue what had made her change from how she was then to how she was now. It just happened. Thank god it had. Ever since Freya had survived that terrible night when she had lost her parents, she had started to change. Ever since then she had grown closer and closer to Lars, and when he had taken her to hospital in a terrible snow storm and undoubtedly saved her life, she knew that she loved him. Really loved him. It was today, when she had called in to see her mother on her way home from the grave that she had suddenly realised just how far she had come.

Her mother had a new "gentleman friend" and he had been at her mother's house when she had called. He seemed a nice enough chap, friendly and well mannered, clearly smitten with her mother and eager to please her. You poor sod, she had thought. You just don't know what you are letting yourself in for, but you soon will. Rose had to suppress an overwhelming urge to take the man to the front door, open it and tell him run like hell, while he still could, because it would not be long before her mother would switch her charm off and start giving him the "treatment", just like she had done to her dad, and just like Rose had done to Lars. Before. Her mother was a founder member of the "Be mean and keep 'em keen" club. The man might just as well have had "MUG" branded on his forehead.

Rose had not stayed long. She had seen enough. She had made her way home, but on the journey she had a small bout of the dry retching, triggered by a reminder of what she had used to be like. It quickly passed and the warm afterglow washed over her as it always did. She had released a further bit of negative energy that had been trapped down inside her. Soon there would be none left.

Rose fell asleep holding the man that she had nearly lost. She was indeed a very lucky woman.

Simon Marshall sat in his new office reading a report from one of the companies' "in house" investigators, concerning a possible fraud by a firm that was insured with them. It was one of the new things that he now had to do since his promotion. On his desk was a framed photograph of his wife Mary, and his daughter Daphne. It seemed to him that they looked back at him in expectation. Nothing new there. The extra salary was most welcome, and he had hoped to pay down his overdraft at the bank and maybe start to put a bit away for a rainy day. That had been his plan. His wife, however had other ideas. Angrily he turned the photograph away from him so that he could not see them.

Earlier that week he had arrived home to learn that his wife had already ordered a new three-piece suite, in leather, from Italy, for the lounge, and when he had protestcd that the one they had now was less than five years old, she had merely said it was dated, whatever that meant, and any way it would not match the new decor she wanted, the painters would be here in two weeks' time, just before the new carpet was due to arrive. One had to maintain one's standards, she had said, now they had gone up in the world.

His heart had sank. Why couldn't she just be satisfied with what she already had, instead of always wanting more, bigger, better.

He put the report away in his drawer and got ready to go home. If that's what it was. He hoped against hope that they would not be eating out yet again, he was totally fed up with doing that. Not that anyone was interested in what he wanted. Every restaurant they went to, he always chose the cheapest item on the menu, and never had a starter or sweet, trying to keep the bill down a bit. His wife and daughter had no such inhibitions and always had all three courses. No wonder Daphne was getting podgy. So he just sat there and watched them stuff their faces, trying to look as if he was enjoying himself, while wishing all the time that he was anywhere but here. When they were finally full, he would settle the bill and drive them home. Last night he had dropped his keys on the door mat as he was about to unlock the door. Angrily, as he bent down to pick them up, a thought crossed his mind. That's what he was to them. A door mat!

Chapter Twenty- Six

Munch was bored. It was Saturday afternoon and he was on his own, something that he was not used to. Ever since that Saturday when he had followed Freya up on to the wold, and had got home late and soaked, his gang had deserted him. They were not allowed to play with him anymore. His elder brother Jimmy and his father were in the village, drinking, and when they staggered home would be plastered. His mother had gone for a nap on the sofa after giving him his dinner.

He could go into Elfington himself and see who he could find to hang around with, but friends were few and far between at the moment, and it was a hot afternoon and he could not be bothered. An idea popped into his head, they did on rare occasions and he knew what he could do to amuse himself. He had spent the morning shooting his toy gun, which had a roll of caps inside it and made a realistic bang when he pulled the trigger. But he had run out of caps and anyway, it was only pretend. He wanted to kill something, anything. Bird, rabbit, fox, it didn't matter to him. He was bored, so some wildlife had to die. He would take his dad's .22 air rifle and go up to the old wood and see if he could shoot something. He knew that he should not take the gun out by himself, but no one would know and he would put it back in its place long before anyone knew it had gone.

He went to the cupboard where the gun was kept and took it out, together with a handful of bullets, and made his escape out of the back door, closing it quietly before heading up onto the wold, following one of the many tracks that criss-crossed the moors. After half an hour he entered the old wood and slowed down to see what he could shoot at. He was hot and sticky and the rifle was heavy. After a further ten minutes decided to have a rest on the bank of a dried up stream and see if a suitable target would present itself. He sat down and leaned back against the trunk of a large tree. It was much cooler in the wood and he looked around to see what he could see. He could hear bird song from the tops of the trees, but he could not see what was making it. A sudden flapping of wings made him look up and to his right, as a pair of wood pigeons squabbled among themselves before flying off, one chasing after the other.

He leaned back again and let his eyes sweep around the wood. Nothing. He would sit here for a while before heading back. At least it would be downhill on the way home. A slight breeze stirred the branches of the trees ahead of him and by pure chance Munch noticed something sitting on the end of a low branch not too far away. It was a medium to large bird of some sort, and the breeze had caused the branch on which it was perched to sway, making the bird extend its wings for a moment to keep its balance. It was that movement that had caught his eye.

He guessed, correctly that it was a young bird, not long out of its nest and its inexperience had caused it to perch too near the end of the branch, and the wind, together with the bird's weight was causing the branch to rock and sway much more than it would have done, if the bird had moved further along the branch nearer to the tree trunk. The bird had its back to Munch and did not see the boy slowly raise the rifle to his shoulder and take careful aim.

"Phut."

The bird fell from the branch like a stone and dropped into some bushes below. "Yes!"

Munch put the gun down and got to his feet, then set off to claim his prize, congratulating himself as he went. "What a shot!" Just wait until he told his mates about this! He did not know that just as he had fired, another zephyr of wind had moved the branch again and in so doing had saved the bird's life. The branch had dipped slightly and the bullet which would have killed it had just grazed the bird's head and knocked it unconscious.

Munch arrived under the tree where the bird had perched to find to his dismay that it had fallen into a patch of brambles and nettles, and try as he might, he could not get close enough to reach the bird. After getting himself scratched and nettled, he finally admitted defeat and extracted himself from the brambles and collected the gun, before making his way back home, scratching his nettled legs as he went. He never noticed that one of the small pieces of wood that lay on the ground on the other side of the gully had a very small hole in it and unseen eyes underground had watched the whole thing.

When they were sure that the boy had gone and that there were no more humans around, Astra and Jago went outside into the gully, while Hugo kept watch with the periscope. They moved quickly, not wanting to be outside for too long, as during the summer months if the weather was good, humans tended to walk through the woods during the day, particularly at the weekends. They reached the bird, expecting it to be dead, but to their delight found that it was still breathing, but unconscious, with a nasty gash on its head.

They judged it to be a young owl of some sort, but not one they had come across before. Just as they were deciding what to do, they heard three blasts on a whistle that only they could hear. It was Hugo giving them the danger signal. Astra unfolded a sack they had brought with them and gently rolled the bird on to it, quickly taking one end each in their mouths, they went as swiftly as they could back to the secret entrance where Hugo waited to close the door before returning to the periscope. The humans he had seen were still a good way off and he was satisfied that they had not been seen. He secured the periscope and went to join the others who had transferred the bird on to one of the trucks that were always parked there.

"What sort of bird is it?" He asked.

"Some sort of owl, I think. I'll have to check the book." Replied Astra.

"What can we do to help it?" asked Jago, peering down at the still unconscious owl.

"Let's clean the wound, bandage it and let the bird rest, we can do no more than that for now," Said Astra.

"I like its ears, they remind me of the ones that Bob and Lisa had," she continued.

Hugo and Jago looked at each other in puzzlement. They didn't think birds had any ears, but this one clearly did.

They set off for the main chamber, pulling the truck behind them, with Astra riding in the back to keep an eye on their patient. When the owl awoke they would try and communicate with their new guest.

It was early evening when the owl opened her eyes, although she did not know it. She had a splitting headache, which only got worse if she tried to move her head, around which something was tied. She was in some sort of enclosure, lying on something soft and propped up at an angle. Her eyes started to close again, but not before she had seen a Fox sitting close by, looking at her.

She opened her eyes again. There was still something tied around her head, but at least the pain in her head was less than before, or was she just getting used to it. She did not know. What she did know was that the Fox was still sitting close by, looking at her as before. She wondered why the Fox had not eaten her by now, as that was what she had been told they did. She could not know that this Fox was not the same one as she had seen before, and that they were special creatures. Only later would she realise just how special. Her young brain reasoned that she was in the Foxes den and that the reason they had not eaten her yet was that they were not hungry. She tried to remember what she had been doing before waking up here, where ever "here" was. Slowly it came back to her. She had been sitting on a branch in a tree when suddenly her head seemed to explode and she felt herself falling before everything went black. She closed her eyes and slept again. She did not know that both of the Foxes had tried to connect with her unconscious mind but had not been successful. So while Jago took his turn to sit with the owl, Astra and Hugo discussed what to try next. They had been told by the Cats that all beings, even humans, were able to be contacted, it was just a matter of finding the correct "Frequency".

To demonstrate this, they had been shown a human gadget called a "Radio", which had a dial on the front of it. By carefully turning the dial, the Radio was able to "receive invisible waves" and they had been astonished by the various "Stations" as they were called that the radio could receive. It was a crude but effective way of demonstrating how the Cats were able to communicate with them. The radio had two "Bands" one of "Long waves" and another of "Medium waves", but the mind uses infinitely more powerful thought waves , and has but one spectrum of many millions of waves and it was just a matter of finding the correct one. Every creature on planet earth 'Vibrates" at a slightly different frequency, but once you have found the correct one, like a path through a forest, the more you travel down that path, the easier it becomes to do so. Astra knew that even the twins, identical to look at, but very different in personality, vibrated in a slightly different way to each other. Every creature was unique. The radio could only "Receive" a limited number of stations. It could not transmit. But the mind was able to do both, and over the five weeks of their instruction, they had "Fine-tuned" their minds to each other so well that they did not have to think about doing it. But Dogs and Foxes are of a similar design, but birds are quite different. So they each sat with the owl and, being close to it and able to see it helped them to go through endless vibrations until they got lucky.

Astra and Hugo agreed that as owls "hoot" in a lowish tone, they would continue to stay on a low frequency. Astra relieved Jago and started on the next set of frequencies, while the twins had a cup of tea. After an hour, the owl opened her eyes again, the pain in her head now just a dull throb, to see a dog sitting close by and looking at her, just as the Fox had done. Astra knew that females could communicate with other females much quicker than male to female or vice versa, as could male to male.

So it fell to Astra to establish the first contact with the owl. She asked it how it was. The astonished owl, hearing a strange voice in its mind, instinctively replied, "Thirsty!"

Ten days after the owl had been brought inside the hideaway, she was well enough to go back outside and return to the wild. She still had no idea where she was, only that it was underground and safe. Strange as it may seem, she was already feeling an affinity with these animals, a bond, a connection. She knew beyond any doubt that they would never harm her. She just felt so comfortable being around them. Once again, out of something bad, and being shot was just about as bad as it could get, something good had happened. The circle of life.

Once the dog, Astra, had been able to make contact with her mind, the twin foxes had also been able to communicate with her as well, it was just a matter of "fine tuning their minds" they had said, or rather thought! The contact was limited at first, as she did not have the vocabulary needed for in-depth conversation. Yet, somehow, after only ten days, she could understand perfectly what they were saying to her, even though there was no actual sound. She understood that to ensure the secrecy of the hideaway, she would be taken back to where they had found her and her memory of them and this place would be erased. They had told her they had the power to do that. It would not hurt, and she could go back to being an ordinary owl once again.

Or she could stay, and be one of them, continue to learn what they knew, and join their family of special creatures. There was only one condition. She must keep this place secret. She had thanked them for their generous offer and asked for a while to consider what she would do. She was only young and had little experience of life. A life that would have been over already if not for the kindness of these animals. She flew through the tunnels on silent wings to the place they called the "Magical Cavern". It was easy to see why they called it that. She perched on the edge of the pool and watched the two waterfalls tumble down the rocks and into the dark pool. Although she could not see her reflection, she knew that if she could, it would show her just the same as she had been before, on the outside at least. But on the inside, she was very different. She had only experienced just a tiny bit of what she could be. The sight and sound of the water was very calming. Although it was pitch black in the cavern, to her it was as light as the day outside. The outside to which she could return and forget about the last ten days as if they had never been.

This was a place to think, to relax, to consider what choice she should make. She thought back over the last week and all that had happened to her. Hugo, Jago and Astra could have simply left her where she had fallen to die. Sooner or later, and being unconscious she would not have known, she would have been found and eaten, either alive or dead. The laws of nature are simple. The weak or old do not last long. Only the strong survive, or the lucky. Her rescuers could have eaten her themselves, but they had evolved way beyond other primitive animals, and instead they had brought her inside their secret place and helped her to get well again. They had also taken the time to communicate with her and now they were offering her a choice. She would make the decision. These were very special animals indeed. They had not revealed how they had come to be here, or how they could do all the special things that they could do. If she chose to go back outside, she would never know. She owed them so much, not least her very life! So she watched the water, and listened to the sound it made while she made up her mind.

A sound from the tunnel made her turn her head, while her body remained where it was. They could not do that! It was the others. They had guessed she would come here. They walked over to her and sat down in a semi-circle, saying nothing, waiting for her to communicate with them. She looked at each of them in turn. Ten days ago they would have been the enemy. Now they were her friends. She had made her decision.

"I cannot thank you all enough for saving me. This last week while I recovered made me realise that I had, by pure chance found all of you and this magical place. If I returned back to the wild, all of this, and all of you would be lost to me for ever. I would just be an ordinary owl again. But here, I am a special owl with special friends. There is so much more for me to know. I cannot go back. I must go forward. As you have said, nothing in life happens by accident. The events that brought me here were no coincidence. It was meant to be. I would like to stay with you." She did not know how much of what she had just thought had got through to the others, she hoped enough had.

The twins and Astra beamed with pleasure. They had been hoping she would stay. They had got used to her being around and would have missed her if she had left.

"As you are now part of our family, you will have to choose a name." said Hugo.

The owl seemed to understand and thought for a while. "There is a word that keeps coming up when you tell me the story of how I came to be here. I was lucky that the humans did not kill me, I was lucky that you saw what had happened and lucky that you brought me here and made me well again. So, I would like to be called Lucky! "

The others nodded their approval. It was a very good name. She had indeed been lucky.

Lucky continued. "You have given me the chance of a whole new life here with you, you could simply have left me where I was and I would never have known any different. But you have given me this chance and I will never let you down, or betray your trust in me. I want to learn, and grow, just like you have done. We can do it together!"

Astra spoke for the others. "You are most welcome, Lucky. We have much to show you, and to teach you. Let's return to the main cavern and make a start!"

And so Lucky the eagle owl joined the family of special animals. She did not yet appreciate that she would become the most advanced bird on the planet.

May passed into June, and June into July. The school sports day had come and gone, and Freya had won the hundred yards' race, the egg and spoon race, and the three-legged race, together with Dutch. She knew that she could have won every race, but some inner voice had warned her that it was better if she did not attract too much attention to herself. So the high jump bar was knocked off, the hurdle knocked down and the bean bag dropped. On purpose.

There was a surprize winner of the mothers' race, Rose Olsen! She had been there, with Lars to support Freya, and had had no intention of participating. But she had been encouraged to have a go, as she was as near to being a mother as made any difference any way, and there were only four other mothers in the race!

So cheered on by Lars, Freya, Mrs Van Den Berg and Dutch, she had lined up with the others. It was only fifty yards and when the starting pistol went off, she flew down the track to be an easy winner. She was delighted. There were some people who, not having seen her for quite a while, did not recognize her at all, so much had she changed. It was the first time that Rose had attended the school sports day since she had been a pupil there. Then she had been a very reluctant participant, who had come last in the few events she had been forced to do. She had hated sports. The new Rose loved it.

Soon the summer holidays would start, and Freya realised that she had been in England for almost a year. Wait till she told her parents about her wins and about Aunty Rose.

There was an extra spectator to watch the sports day. Perched high in an oak tree that over looked the playing field, was Lucky the eagle owl. She watched in fascination as the races were run. One child in particular caught her eye. A blond girl who had done well, winning three events, and, Lucky thought, could have won more. The child had an Aura about her that kept drawing Lucky's eyes back to her. As the sports day drew to a close, the girl had suddenly turned and looked up at the Oak tree, directly at her! Lucky knew that there was no way that any human could possibly know that she was there, but the blond girl looked right at her for a long moment, before turning away and joining her family . When the humans had gone, Lucky flew back to the hideaway. She would tell the others about what she had seen. And about the blond girl.

Freya joined the others and they began their journey home. Just for a moment there, she had felt that she was being watched. It was a strange feeling, like some inner sense had detected something. She thought that someone was hiding up in the oak tree, but she could see no one, and anyway, why would anyone hide up there? They had all had a lovely family day, and on the way home, they decided to call in to see Mr Winter, who was delighted to see them and hear all about the sports day. His leg was healing well, the plaster cast had gone and he was getting around with a stick. The Olsen family had regular contact with Mr Winter, Lars worked in his garden once a fortnight, and Rose did a few hours cleaning each week. She also walked down to the village to collect his prescription from the Doctors surgery and would have a chat with Penny, and Tom if he was about. They had settled in really well and it was nice to have them close by in the village.

When Lars did the garden, Freya would come with him and help, while Mr Winter would sit in a chair outside and enjoy the company and the summer sunshine. He insisted on paying Lars and Rose for the work they did for him, and Freya would get a shilling for her efforts each week. Once again, out of something bad, something good had happened. Far in the distance, hidden from view by the summer leaves, the Old Mill by the lake stood alone. Empty and abandoned. Waiting.

Chapter Twenty-Seven

The schools broke up for the summer break, and Lars took his two weeks' holiday straight away. Money, as always was tight, but it was possible to have a couple of days out.

Wednesday was Market day in Abbotsbury, and the first Wednesday in August the Olsen family set off in the car, collecting Dutch and his mother on the way. The town was busy, everyone for miles around seemed to be there, the local farmers using the market to meet their friends and neighbours and to catch up on the latest gossip. Rose and Dutch's mum went off together, and would meet up with the others at a cafe later for lunch. Lars, Dutch and Freya headed for the cattle market. Freya and Dutch were fascinated by all the animals, mostly cows and calves, but there were also sheep, pigs and a few goats in the pens.

There was a lot of noise, most of it coming from a large permanent enclosure, where a metal gate would open, a cow would come out, be prodded with a stick to go around the enclosure a couple of times by a man wearing a cloth cap and wellies, before disappearing out of the enclosure through another metal gate in no more than thirty seconds, all accompanied by the non-stop and almost unintelligible voice of the ruddy-faced auctioneer, who ran all his words together. The only word Freya could identify was "bid", the rest was complete gibberish. But the farmers who lined the enclosure seemed to be able to understand it, and with a flick of a hand bids would be made and the hammer would bang down and a cow would change hands.

Lars bent down and said to Dutch and Freya, "Don't wave your hands about, or you might end up buying a cow!" They immediately put their hands in their pockets, Lars included. They could not afford to buy a cow, and had nowhere to put one. Freya had five shillings, earned from working in Mr Winter's garden, Dutch had half a crown, which his dad had given to him the night before. Neither of them got pocket money, they had no need of it. They watched the auction for a while then continued to explore the market. A while later a loud squealing made them turn their heads. A young pig was being pulled along by its ears by two men, and the pig was not going quietly. As they watched the pig being dragged past them, it suddenly managed to break free and made a run for it. It streaked past Freya and Dutch, chased by the two men. Freya suddenly realised that the pig was heading for a dead end, they had not long been down there and unconsciously reached to hold her necklace in her hand and she thought to herself "That's a dead end! Go left, go left!" And as if by magic, the pig swerved to the left, shot through the market and out into the high street to vanish in

225

the crowd.

Freya stood still and watched the pig disappear. Had she done that? Had the pig actually heard her thoughts and understood? Surely not. But this was not the first time that she had thought something, then seconds later watched it actually happen. When she got home, she would have to sit down and think about this. She turned to Dutch and said, "Good luck, piggy," and he nodded his agreement.

Soon they had seen all that there was to see in the market and so they headed out into the high street and made their way to the cafe where Mrs Van Den Berg and Rose were already waiting for them, enjoying a cup of tea. It was a lovely summer's day, so they sat outside and enjoyed a leisurely lunch, watching the people go by. Dutch spotted Miss Doyle, their teacher from school in the crowd and she waved to them. Freya wondered where the pig was and if it had been caught yet. She hoped not.

When lunch had been eaten, they all moved off together, heading for a shop called "Woolworths". It was a big shop and was busy. Dutch went to the toy section and got excited when he saw that there was a model Aeroplane on the shelf, but his joy was short lived as the model Lancaster World War Two bomber was a large one and cost four shillings. He only had two and sixpence. He turned away from the counter and joined the others, Freya saw his face and asked what was wrong. He told her about the model.

She put her hand in her pocket and counted out three sixpences and held them out to her friend.

"Here you are, Dutch, take this and go and get it. I can watch you build it!"

"Are you sure, Freya? I may not be able to pay you back for a while."

Freya smiled. "I don't want it back, silly. You're my best friend. You can have it. Now, let's go and buy it before they sell out!"

They made their way back to the counter and Dutch pointed to the large box and asked the man if he could have it. He put his half-crown on the glass topped counter, together with the three sixpences and the man handed over the large box to the excited boy. He was lucky. It had been the last one they had.

They joined the adults, who examined the box that Dutch proudly held under his arm. Freya watched his joy and was happy that she had been able to help her friend. She realised then just how much he meant to her. They looked at the rest of the shop, Rose bought Freya an Enid Blyton book. It was called "The Wishing Chair". She was thrilled. They left the shop and headed back to the car. They had all had a really nice day. Dutch and Freya would always remember their holiday visit to Abbotsbury Market.

On the drive home, Freya said to Dutch, "I wonder if they caught the piggy?" Dutch said, "Bound to have. Pigs are valuable, they won't let it get away."

But he was wrong. Against all the odds, the pig was still free!

A few days after the visit to Abbotsbury Market where the pig had escaped, £2.6 million was stolen from a train in Buckinghamshire. The robbery would forever be known as the Great Train Robbery. The pig however, knew nothing of this robbery, in fact it didn't know much about anything, except that it was alive and free. For now at least. The pig was a male, and like most pigs of either gender, was quite bright. When he had been taken to the market, he instinctively knew that the humans who had brought him there did not have his best interest at heart, and when he had managed to escape from them, he knew that he had to make the best of his bid for freedom, there would be no second chance. So he had started to run, but then he had heard a voice, quite clearly in his mind telling him to "Go Left" and strangely, he understood what that meant! Without hesitation he obeyed the voice, somehow knowing that the voice was trying to help him escape. It did. He shot down the market street and out into the main road. He turned left again, it had worked once, so why not? And avoided the hands that tried to grab him as he ran.

Arriving at the end of the High Street, he tried left a third time and shot down a smaller side street as fast as he could go and just kept going. The street gave way to some houses, which in turn gave way to fields. As the noise of the market faded away, he could see in the distance open country and he headed for that. He was getting tired, but fear drove him on. Avoiding cars and people as best he could, he made it to the green fields on the edge of town disappeared into them. Now he slowed down. Running down the side of a hedge, he came across some long grass under a tree at the far end of a field, and lay down in it, hidden from view and gasping for breath. He had a good view of the way he had come and took a rest and gathered his wits. To his great surprise, no one seemed to be after him and after five minutes he realised that he had got clean away. He had made it! He was free.

The pig stayed in the long grass under the tree for the rest of the day. He had no idea where he was, where he would go, or where he had come from. He realised that being pink in a green field, he would attract attention if he moved, so he waited for darkness to come. In the far distance he could just make out part of a tall building, but it looked incomplete and showed no lights. When it was fully dark, he got to his feet and carefully headed towards the old building, following a narrow track, for no better reason than he had to head somewhere and that was as good as anywhere! There was a full moon, which helped him see where he was going. No one seemed to be around.

After what seemed to be a long time, he was close to the building he had seen. He approached carefully. The narrow track he had been on had brought him to a small road. He waited. No one seemed to be here. He crossed the road and entered the strange buildings. He did not know that he had arrived at the ruins of Edgewell Abbey. Almost at once he found an old stone trough full of water, and he had a long drink from it, the first for many hours. Perhaps this might be a good place to stay?

It is true that pigs will eat almost anything, but only when there was anything to eat! Carefully he explored the ruins. They were quite extensive, but most only had one or two walls standing and none had a roof. There was one very tall wall, which went to a point at the top. It was that which he had seen from under the tree. Beyond the tall wall he found a small orchard of apple trees, but again the grass was long and it was clear no one came to pick the fruit. There were many apples that had dropped to the floor and he helped himself. Better and better. Water and food. Now he needed somewhere to hide.

Next to the orchard and at the extreme edge of the ruins, he found a collection of abandoned farm machinery. They were old, rusty and had not been used for a long time. There was a flat trailer with flat tyres and surrounded by tall grass. That would do nicely. Carefully he crawled under the trailer and lay down. There was a hedge on one side of the trailer and no one could approach from that direction, so he lay behind one of the wheels, facing the way he had come. He would be able to see any approach. Satisfied, he stretched out on the dry earth and exhausted by the events of the day, he fell asleep at once.

He had no way of knowing that pigs did not behave in the way he had done. He had had about three seconds of mental contact with Freya and that very brief connection had been enough to change him into the logical and careful pig he now was. Had he not had that contact, it would have been more than likely that he would have been recaptured quickly. He would probably have run into someone's garden and been trapped there, eating the plants in blissful ignorance of what would happen to him next. But now he was free, he had known to get away from the town, lie low until darkness and then find food, water and shelter. Ordinary pigs do not think to do those things. But things do not happen by accident. Somehow he had heard a voice in his mind, and somehow he had understood what the voice was saying! How could that be possible? The voice was human, and the words meant nothing, yet he had understood what they had meant! How could that have happened? He did not know, but he did know that the voice had helped him escape. The voice had changed him. He felt different within himself. It was strange. The voice he had heard in his mind had belonged to a little human girl. The pig slept on. Free.

The friends in the hideaway knew nothing about the escape of the pig from the market until the Thursday of the next week, when they saw the local newspaper. There on the front page was a picture of a pig's head, underneath was the headline "HAVE YOU SEEN THIS PIG?"

The story below the headline told of the pig's dramatic escape from the market the week before, and it concluded that at the time of going to press, (Tuesday) the pig was still at large, somewhere in the Abbotsbury area.

Jago, Hugo, Lucky and Astra looked at each other and thought the same thing. Now, everyone would know about the pig, and its chances of staying free much longer were slim. Being free, and safe was so vitally important to them, that as one mind they knew they had to try to help the pig if they could. But first, they had to find it!

Astra went to get the big map of the Wold that the cats had left behind, and they unfolded it on the table and gathered round to study it. Abbotsbury was clearly marked, being the largest town in the area. The newspaper story had said that the pig had not been seen since its dramatic escape. Quite how it had managed to do that was a miracle. It must be hiding somewhere, but how could it be, pigs don't hide, they don't think they have to. So, assuming that it had not been run over, where had it gone?

Being pink should make it easy to spot, but no one had seen it. This little piggy had gone to Market, then changed the script of what should happen to it next.

"There!" thought Astra, "I would go there," pointing at Edgewell Abbey on the map.

"Why?" Asked Lucky. "What is there?"

"Not very much, but the story said that the pig turned left when it left the market, so if we assume that it turned left again, that would put it there!" thought Astra, pointing to a spot on the map. "If the pig had gone right, or even straight on, it would have been in the centre of town and loads of people would have seen it, but there is no report of that, so I would guess it would want to head out of town and away from humans, which would bring it to the Abbey. A good place to lie low for a while. "

Hugo was not sure. "This is a pig, not brain of Britain! They are not known for their logical thoughts, are you sure it would go there?"

Astra nodded firmly. "Yes, I know it's only a pig, but I have a feeling that this animal is a lot smarter than we think. I recommend we start our search for it there at Edgewell Abbey." The others nodded. It was agreed.

The pig awoke the next morning, just as the sun was rising, unsure where he was. Then he remembered. He was hiding from the humans after his escape. He looked around his little shelter. It looked different in the daylight, but he was sure that so long as he did not go wandering about in the open during the day, he should be all right. He felt lonely and unsettled. Until yesterday there had been a routine, and the company of his fellow pigs. The humans had fed him regularly and well, there was always plenty to eat and drink, and a hut to go into if it was wet. They had wanted for nothing. He had been happy and had not given a single thought beyond the next day, when he was sure he would be given more food and drink. He had trusted the humans to continue to look after him, after all, they always had. Now he was alone, but alive! He had been very fortunate so far, while the rest of his fellow pigs, some of which were his brothers and sisters had not been. Now he knew why he had been fed and looked after. Now he knew the truth. If he were caught, the humans would simply put him back into the system, which until yesterday, had worked perfectly for them. Was he the first to escape? Probably.

He stayed under the old trailer all day. With so much time on his hands, his mind wandered, going over the events of the day before. Against all the odds, he had made it here, where ever here was. He was hungry and thirsty, but knew he must wait for darkness. How did he know to do that? Before he could come and go as he liked, but now he knew he could not. Later on that day he heard the sounds of humans and he watched them through the tall grass. Had they found him already? He would not go without a fight. But they did not come close. They wandered through the ruins, looking at the walls and floors, unaware that he was nearby. Some had dogs with them, who immediately found his scent and barked and pulled at their leads, but fortunately, all dogs must be kept on a lead and they could not hurt him. Again, he was lucky. But somehow, deep down he knew that nothing that had happened to him had been by accident. It was more than just luck. It was destiny. So he stayed under the trailer all day and when it was quiet and dark, he emerged carefully and, using the same roundabout route to avoid leaving an obvious trail, he drank from the trough and ate in the orchard. He stayed out most of the night, keeping close to the walls and away from the road, before returning to his hideout. The weather was dry and settled and he left no tracks. For a whole week he remained there, undetected. But he knew that his luck could not last much longer. The trough was all but empty, and the fruit all but gone. Tonight he would finish the last of the water and fruit, then he would move on under the cover of darkness. He had been at the abbey eight nights. Time to go.

As darkness descended over the wold, Lucky flew on ahead of the others, who set off on foot. Hugo had remarked that although Lucky had only been with them for three months, he could not imagine being without her. The others had agreed. She was a fine addition to their special family.

Lucky, unaware of the praise she was getting, arrived at Edgewell Abbey just as the last of the daylight had gone. It had been easy to find, the tall wall stood out with its empty arched windows, and the lights of Abbotsbury shimmering and twinkling in the back ground. She had not been here before, and perched on the very top of the arched wall so as to have the best view all around. A slight breeze ruffled her feathers, reminding her of the time before when she had been shot, then rescued by her now very good friends. They had helped her then, she must try and help the pig now, if it was here. She had a feeling that it was. It had already been free for eight days, no small achievement. Her very sharp eyes scanned the ground, missing nothing as she waited for the others to arrive.

Half an hour later and she had not seen the pig. It would not be hard to spot, being large and pink. The others had arrived by now and Lucky had positioned them around the ruins. Astra was next to a stone water trough, Hugo was near the narrow road, while Jago was lying on a low stone wall at the far end of the ruins. Such was the development of her mental powers, Lucky had been able to communicate with all of the others without leaving her perch.

A sudden noise made her turn her head, but it was only an apple falling from the tree and hitting the ground. Suddenly, another movement caught her eye. There it was, no mistake. She could see it very clearly. It had emerged from under an old trailer, no wonder she had not seen it before! It was the pig, Astra had been right, it was moving slowly, heading for the water trough. Clever, she thought. Quickly, she alerted the others. No sooner had she done so that the pig suddenly stopped and looked around, almost as if it had heard her thoughts. But that was not possible. The pig stayed still for a couple of minutes, then resumed its way to the water trough. Lucky told Astra that the pig was still coming her way. Immediately, the pig stopped again. Lucky was very intrigued. Twice now it had suddenly stopped when she had used her mind to contact the others. This was no ordinary pig. It was almost thinking like they did. Time for a little test.

On silent wings, she glided down to a much lower level, much closer to the pig. She could see it was looking completely bewildered. Instantly, she connected to the pig's mind. That also should not happen so easily, or so quickly. This was a very special animal indeed.

"Hello! I hope you can hear me. My friends and I are here to help you. We know of your escape from the humans. We are not humans, we are free creatures who have also escaped from them. We are free of their control. Do not worry, we will not harm you, we are not here to catch you, we are here to help you. You must trust us. If you have heard me, and understood, please take one step forward. "

The pig did not move for a few seconds. Then it moved forward. One step only.

"Thank you. Please continue to the water trough, you must be thirsty. We will meet you there and introduce ourselves. Then you will see we mean you no harm. Do not be afraid. Please go now."

The pig moved slowly forward, looking around as if to try and see who or what it was that had been able to speak to his mind, without making an actual sound. Just as the human girl had been able to do. He could see no one. Who were these "Free creatures?" How had they found him? Why had they found him? Strange as it may

231

seem, he no longer felt afraid. The voice was calm and friendly. He arrived at the water trough and had a good drink, his throat dry. When he raised his head from the trough he jumped. Lined up behind the trough were three creatures that he had never seen before. Two of them looked the same, both had white ears. The other one was different. Perched on the end of the water trough was another much smaller creature, different again.

The smallest creature looked directly at him with big round eyes. "Hello again. My name is Lucky. These are my friends, Astra, Hugo and Jago. We have much to tell you. There are many humans looking for you now, you cannot stay here. You can come with us, we live in a safe place. But first, let us go back to your hiding place under the old trailer, and we can explain ourselves to you and answer your questions."

The pig looked at them all, one by one, then turned around and led the way back to the old trailer. Without knowing how or why, he believed what the small creature had said to his mind. He felt safe with them. He had no idea where they had come from, or why they had come, or how they could speak to him as they did. He was about to find out.

The pig sat in front of the fire in the main chamber of the hideaway, next to his new friends. He still had trouble believing he was here. He was not really sure where "here" actually was. He did know that he was safe and among friends.

His mind returned once again to the events of the evening. He had been lying under the old farm trailer, as the darkness had come once again, alone, hungry, thirsty and frightened. Just like all the other nights that he had been here. The care free world he had once known was but a distant memory. He knew that he had to leave this place, the food and water were all but gone, and surely someone would find him sooner or later. But where would he go? And how would he survive? He had done very well and been very fortunate to have avoided capture so far, but he was alone and lost in an environment to which he was not suited to cope with.

Then they had found him, these strange, special creatures who were so different from him, yet the same as him. They were all hiding from the humans that had, or would harm them, or even kill them, given the chance. It was impossible, yet all of the special creatures had been able to communicate with him straight away, and even more strangely, he had been able to understand them and communicate back to them, without making a sound! How? How could he do that? How could anyone do that?

Right from the first contact with the small creature, called Lucky, he had felt safe among them. How, he did not know, he just did. And after a brief chat with them, he had decided to go with them to the secret place they had said they lived in where the humans could never find them. At the end of the day, it all came down to trust. Did he trust these creatures? Could he trust these creatures? Yes. Somehow he just knew that he could.

He did not know what to expect, but now he was actually here with them, warm, safe and full of food and drink, just as they had said he would be. The creature called Astra had shown him something they called a "Newspaper" whatever that was, and she had said that the picture on the newspaper was what he actually looked like. He gazed at the picture with interest. So that's what his face looked like. He had had no idea before. He had also been told that he was a creature the humans called a pig. Astra was called a Dog, the twins, Hugo and Jago were Foxes and Lucky was a bird called an Eagle Owl.

There was more information with his picture, called a story, and it was this story and his picture that had first made them aware of him. This "Newspaper" had now been seen by a great many humans, some of whom would be actively hunting for him. It was clear to him that they had found him just in time. The fire was warm and friendly, its glow adding its light to that of the small lamps that were placed around the room. For the first time since he had been loaded into the truck and taken to the market, he felt totally safe and secure.

Lucky said she was puzzled by how easily they had all been able to communicate with him, as it had been much harder for the others to contact her at first. The pig told them that their contact with his mind was not the first contact of this type that he had had. He told them about his escape from the market, and a voice in his mind, telling him to go to the left and avoid a dead end where he would probably have been caught again.

The others looked at each other in shock. The cats had told them that there was a human somewhere who was known to them and that they could trust, but they were surprised to think that this human was so close, and had probably been at the market and warned the pig. This information tied in with what Lucky had told them about the girl he had seen at the school sports day, the one who was not like the others. Was it the same person? Probably. Now they knew that the human the cats had told them about was young and female. And lived close by. Interesting.

That explained why they could all communicate with the pig so easily. The cats had explained it was like a path through a forest, once travelled down it was easier to do so another time. They were all getting tired, they had had an eventful evening! Hugo turned to the newcomer and said that he should start thinking about choosing a name for himself. The pig nodded and said that he had already had one in mind. He had taken refuge under the old trailer for many nights, and as he had come and gone he had seen an old rusty metal plate, fixed to the end of the trailer. Most of the words were too faded to see, but one was readable, but as he could not yet read, he did not know what it said. He had asked Astra what the word was, as she had stopped to look at it.

Astra told him that the plate was put there by the humans who had made the trailer long ago. It had been made by a company called BARNABY & CO. So if the pig wanted to use that name, he would be called Barnaby, or Barney for short. The pig nodded. He liked the name. It would always remind him of his time at the Abbey. "Yes," he said. "I am a free creature like you. Please call me Barney."

And so it was. Barney the pig joined the group of special creatures who lived in the secret hideaway beneath the wold.

Chapter Twenty-Eight

Towards the end of the second week of Lars's holiday, the Olsen family decided to go for an evening walk, having spent an enjoyable afternoon at Mr Winter's house. They went around the edge of the Village before entering the fields that were there. It was a lovely summer evening, one of those magical ones that only happen very rarely. The air was warm and full of the intoxicating smells of the countryside at this time of year, added to which was a touch of a fragrant bonfire, making a combination of aromas unique at this time on this one special evening. If this blend of pleasant smells were ever to be recreated again in the future, it would evoke wonderful memories of this first, special, magical time.

They walked along, enjoying the evening air and letting the beauty of the English countryside wash over them. They followed a narrow path down the side of a field full of black and white cows, and climbed over the stile that lead into a larger field which was dotted with hundreds of bales of hay. In the middle of the field was a blue tractor and trailer, onto which an elderly farmer was slowly loading the bales.

He was wearing a faded blue boiler suit which was tucked into wellingtons, and on his head was an old cloth cap. He was only a quarter of the way down the field, and they could see that he was hot, tired and struggling. As they got closer, Freya asked, "Can we help him, Aunty Rose, he will never get it done on his own!"

Rose turned to Lars. "What do you think, Lars? Fancy a bit of hay making?"

Lars smiled. "Why not? As you English say, we must make hay while the sun shines!" Yet again he was surprised that Rose would suggest such a thing, having already walked for a mile and helped out in Mr Winter's garden. This time last year, well, he knew the answer to that.

They approached the farmer. "Good Evening! Need a hand?" The farmer turned to face them and removed his cap to wipe his brow. "Evening. I wouldn't say no, thank you. It might rain tomorrow and I really need to get all of this in!" "Right then, we will help you. I am Lars. This is my wife Rose and our niece Freya." They all shook hands.

"I'm Alan Briggs, and I'm very grateful to you all. If I may suggest that the ladies ride on the trailer and stack the bales, and we pass them up to them?"

Lars shook his head. "If Rose and Freya could stack the bales, that is good, but you take a rest and drive the tractor and I will pass up the bales."

The farmer nodded, looking at Lars's powerful body. "That would be great." He turned to Rose and Freya. "Just stack them the way I was doing and that will be just fine."

Rose and Freya were helped up on to the trailer, Lars was handed a pitchfork, and Alan called up to them, "When I call out, hold on to something while we move, I don't want you falling off!" And he climbed onto the tractor and called out, "Hold on!"

"OK," came the reply from Rose, as she and Freya sat down on a bale of hay and held on to the orange string that kept it together.

"This is going to be fun, Aunty Rose," said Freya with a smile. Rose nodded. She was really enjoying herself. The tractor jerked into motion and travelled a small distance to allow Lars to pass up the first of the bales. The farmer was impressed at Lars's strength as he lifted the bales with the pitch fork as if they were nothing. To him, they were nothing.

And so the Olsen family went to work and within half an hour, the trailer was fully loaded and Alan climbed off the tractor and threw some rope over the load to keep it in place, while Freya and Rose climbed down the wooden back of the trailer into the waiting arms of Lars.

Alan thanked them again and asked if there was any chance they fancied a bit more, as he just had to go and take this load to the barn and return with an empty trailer. Everyone said yes, so while Alan moved carefully over the field back to the farm, they started to stack the bales into piles. Rose and Freya could manage one bale between them, Lars carried one in each hand! By the time Alan returned with an empty trailer, there were three large stacks of bales waiting to be loaded. He was impressed. "I thought you would have a break while I was gone, but you have been working very hard, I'm so grateful to you for helping me!"

"This is so much fun," said Freya. She was having the time of her life, running around the field and carrying the bales with Rose, squealing with joy. Lars looked at Rose and smiled at her. She had straw in her hair and it was stuck to her shirt. She did not care. She too was really enjoying the evening. In no time at all the second trailer was loaded and the field was empty. When Alan put the lights of the tractor on, they realised that the daylight was starting to fade. Time to go home.

Lars picked Freya up as easily as he had the bales of hay and put her on his massive shoulders. She loved it.

Alan came over and thanked them once again. Lars said he was very welcome and they started to turn away when Alan said, "Haven't you forgotten something?"

They looked at him in surprise. Rose said, "I don't think so, Alan. We have all that we came with. We must get Freya into bed, it's way past her time."

Alan pulled out his wallet. "I mean you must let me pay you for all your hard work, it's the least I can do."

Lars shook his head. "There is no need, Alan, it was fun, but we must go now before it gets dark."

Alan put his wallet away. "Well, if you are really sure, thank you very much, but you must let me give young Freya something for all her hard work."

Lars looked at Rose, who nodded. "That would be OK, she has worked very hard!"

"You all have, so young lady, this is for you." Reaching into his pocket and pulling out some coins. He selected two and handed them up to Freya, whose eyes widened in surprise. He had given her two half crowns. Five shillings. She had never had so much money before. She held the coins out to Lars and Rose asking if she could accept them. They nodded.

"Thank you, Mr Briggs. If you need my help next year, I live at twenty nine Druids Way!"

Everyone laughed as they said their goodbyes. When they reached the stile, they turned to wave to Alan as he drove along towards his farm, he waved back, tractor headlights on.

The sunset was magnificent as they made their way up the fields and onto the road. Clouds tinted with pale pink hung low on the horizon as the sun began to disappear. Birds were singing and the heat of the day was starting to cool. Freya was enjoying her ride on Lars's shoulders, she could see so much further from up there. In the gathering twilight the Olsen family made their way home, once again enjoying the magical aroma as they went. It was almost dark when Freya was lifted down onto the path of their cottage. They went inside and Rose went to put the kettle on while Lars and Freya flopped down on to the sofa. Freya showed her coins again to Lars, who looked at them and lifted her onto his knee and gave her a hug and a kiss. "You have done very well, little one, Aunty Rose and I are very proud of you."

Freya put her arms around him and hugged him as Rose came into the room with a tray of drinks and some biscuits. "Hey, can I have one of those?" she asked as she sat down. Freya climbed off Lars's knee and went to hug Rose. Over Freya's shoulder Rose saw Lars smile and give her a thumbs up sign. She smiled back and gave him a thumbs up as well.

It was a perfect end to a perfect day. It was a day that none of them would never forget. Soon the tea was drunk and the biscuits eaten. Freya kissed Lars goodnight as she always did and went up to her room with Rose. Soon she was tucked in bed next to her troll, her coins on the bedside table.

Rose looked down at her, the blond hair spread over the pillow, the sight triggering a memory of the first time she had seen Freya in intensive care at Abbotsbury Hospital. Nearly a year ago. A life time.

"I really enjoyed that," she said to Freya.

"Me too! Wait until I tell Dutch about it!"

Rose smiled and turned out the light. "Sleep well, you must be tired out!" But Freya was already asleep, telling her parents about her adventures.

Rose went down stairs to find Lars also asleep. She looked down at him with genuine love in her eyes.

The magical aroma wafted into the room and she took a deep breath of it, it truly had been a day to remember!

Lars had been back at work for more than a week when Rose and Freya made their usual Thursday morning visit to Elfington Village to buy supplies. They walked down the roads with their shopping bags, as did many others. Wednesday had been half day closing, due to the market at Abbotsbury. After stopping at the post office and the newsagent's, they made their way to the butcher's shop.

Benton's butchers had been in the village for as long as anyone could remember. But unknown to the village folk, business was not as good as it could be, and Mr Benton was starting to worry. He was a big jolly man, and looked exactly like what you would expect a butcher to look like, everyone liked him. His son now worked in the shop as well, but truth be told, there was not much for the two of them to do. Which was why Rose and Freya found the son behind the counter when they went in, and Mr Benton senior sitting on a stool at the back, in front of his sandwich board sign, a piece of chalk in his hand, ready to write a witty message on the black surfaces of his sign to lure the customers in. The trouble was, he could not think of a witty message to write. He had been sitting there for half an hour, racking his brains for some eye catching message to write, but nothing would come. It was not unusual for him to spend a lot of time on this with nothing to show for it. It was not something that he was good at, and never would be.

While Rose was being served by his son, Mr Benton sat on his stool, deep in thought, his jolly face unsmiling. Freya walked up to him through the sawdust on the floor, and when he noticed her, his face changed back into its usual jolly condition. A ray of sunshine had penetrated the gloom.

"Hello, young Freya! How are you today?" he asked, pleased to see her, as most people were.

"Very well, Mr Benton, thank you. Are you going to write a message on your sign?" she asked.

"I am, when I can think of something witty to say to attract the customers in," he said, scratching his head and pushing his straw hat to the back of his head.

"What is the special offer this week end?" she asked.

"Ducks! I've got a load of ducks to sell."

Freya thought for a moment, then asked for a pencil and paper. Mr Benton went behind the counter and handed them to her, more out of hope than of expectation. Freya was not yet eight years old.

Freya went over to the counter and wrote on the paper in capital letters, then went back to Mr Benton and handed the pencil and paper back to him.

He took them and read what she had put, his face breaking into its usual jolly smile.

"Wonderful! This is just what I need. Thank you, Freya, you've saved the day."

He went behind the counter and showed his son what Freya had put, as Freya joined Rose, who asked, "What have you two been up to over there?"

"Just helping Mr Benton with his sign. He's selling Ducks this weekend," she said, as if that would explain everything.

"Well, we must get this meat home, so say goodbye."

They turned towards the door, but Mr Benton said, "Wait a second please, if you would," and went over to the till and rang up "No Sale" to open the draw. He took a coin out and closed the draw again.

Coming around the counter, he handed the coin to Freya. It was a sixpence.

"Oh, I can't take that, Mr Benton, I was glad to help you," said Freya.

But Mr Benton was determined.

"Please take it. Without you, I would have sat there all day. I'm very grateful to you."

Rose looked at Mr Benton. "Are you sure, Mr Benton?"

"Oh yes. And if you can think of any more like that, just you let me know!"

Rose nodded and Freya reached up and took the sixpence and thanked him as they left.

Mr Benton went over to his sign and, with his tongue sticking out as he concentrated on his words, started to write in his best writing.

Five minutes later, the sign was on the pavement.

"MOUTH WATERING DUCKS FOR SALE - SWIMMINGLY GOOD PRICES!" said one side.

"BUY A PLUMP DUCK, NO BIG BILL!" said the other.

Mr Benton commented to his son, "Smart girl that Freya, She will go far, you mark my words."

Just then Freya reappeared at the door.

"Mr Benton?"

"Yes?"

"What's next week's special going to be?"

"Chickens!"

"Right. I'll be in touch by Tuesday, is that all right?"

"Done!"

The first anniversary of the crash that killed Freya's parents and put her in intensive care fell on a Sunday, and Tom and Penny had invited Lars, Rose and Freya to join them for Sunday lunch at their rooms above the surgery. For all of them, that day had changed their lives in ways they could never have imagined. There was a duck in the oven that Penny had bought from Benton's Butchers.

Tom and Penny had settled into the routine of running the surgery like ducks to water. They saw each other every day and worked so well together that their patients were full of praise for the way that they were looked after. The old Doctor was more than happy with his replacements.

The surgery was slightly set back from the road and was reached by a short gravel drive. It was also surrounded by thick hedges, which made it quite difficult for the local gossips to know if Penny had actually gone home or not after the evening surgery was over. It was usually not. Professionally and personally, she had never felt happier. Tom also was really enjoying being in General Practice, not to mention having Penny all to himself. He was settled and content, but he knew that without Penny, on duty or off, he would be miserable and incomplete. Which was why he intended to take action on this special day to ensure that his happiness, and hers, continued.

So he had made his plans and now it was time to put them in to practice. He went downstairs to his consulting rooms and asked Penny to join him. He sat behind his desk and indicated that she sit in the chair at the side of his desk used by the patients. As usual, she looked gorgeous and his mouth went dry as he looked at her. He told himself that faint heart never won fair lady so he put his well-rehearsed plan into action. No going back now.

"I've been thinking of making a change here at the surgery, and I want to know what you think, as it will mean you will have a new role on top of your current duties."

"OK. Tom, what new role would I have?" she asked.

"Well, it's a very important role and it's one only you could do, but I will fully understand if you decide that you don't like it, so don't be afraid to say no."

Penny nodded, interested. She could not think what the new role could be.

"Go on, Tom, you've got my attention!" she said with a smile.

Tom expertly slid off his chair and knelt on one knee in front of Penny, a manoeuvre he had practiced many times to be sure he got it right.

Penny had gone quiet, suddenly realising what might be about to happen.

Tom reached for her hand and took it in his, kissing it while from his jacket pocket, he produced a small box and opened it to reveal a ring.

He looked up at Penny and said, "I love you, Penny, will you marry me?" Less than half a heartbeat later, he had his reply.

"Yes, Tom, yes I will!" she gasped. Tom took the ring from the box and put it on the correct finger of her left hand. Penny looked at it, and then at Tom who was still on one knee before her. She slid off her chair to kneel in front of him and threw her arms around him and hugged him as hard as she could.

Tom held his fiancée and whispered, "This is the new role I want you to do, be my fiancée! Oh, Penny, you have made me the happiest man on the face of the earth! I wanted to ask you on this special day, as you told me that it was this day last year that you decided to get to know me, remember?"

"I remember! It is a decision that I have never regretted. Oh, Tom, I love you so much, thank you for asking me, for choosing me. I will make sure you don't regret it! I had thought that this day would never come for me. Now you are officially mine!"

Penny released Tom and he got to his feet and helped her up and looked into her happy face. "I've always been yours, Penny, I've always wanted to be. There could never be anyone else for me, never! Only you. "

"I'm so happy, Tom. I've got you and this wonderful job here, I get to see you every day. What more could a girl want?"

"How about a kiss from your future husband?"

"Oh yes Doctor!"

The local paper had been about to give the "Have you seen this pig?" story one more week, as nothing else of interest was happening, when something of huge interest and importance actually did happen. They found out from impeccable sources something far more dramatic than a story about a pig. The front page and several others were cleared so that they could carry this new story. The banner headlines said it all;

ELFINGTON VALLEY RAILWAY TO CLOSE!

The Beeching report, which most people had long forgotten about, had come back to bite them! If the story was true, the last train would run on the line on thirty first March 1964!

It was unthinkable that the railway would close. It had always been there, and always would be. Many local people relied on it for their jobs , more still relied on it to get to their jobs , and some relied on it to connect to the main lines to get to Stoke, Derby, Nottingham and beyond. Surely it could be saved, surely something could be done. The railway was part of the fabric of their community, the railway had taken the troops off to wars and brought the lucky ones home again. Special trains brought day trippers to Cropwell Manor.

The mail, the milk and other goods all came by train. They needed it. There must be some mistake.

The unions would not stand for it, the voters would not stand for it. A hornet's nest had been stirred up. The pig that had escaped from Abbotsbury market three weeks ago was completely forgotten. Barney was free and clear!

Chapter Twenty-Nine

Lucy the dog had lived at the "Time Flies" public house for just over a year, and she was very happy to be living there. Cream in colour, she was a mongrel dog of medium size with a friendly nature and was very well liked by the customers of the pub who made sure that she was not starved of food or affection. At night when the pub was closed, she had the run of the building and was as content as a dog could be.

Today was Monday, although she did not know that, but she did know that today the landlord of the pub and her owner was going into the village to resupply the kitchen. The noisy lorry from the brewery had already been and gone, replacing the empty barrels and bottles with full ones for the week ahead.

The landlord had a Morris Traveller van, brand new last year and his pride and joy. He had made a special "Shelf" behind the back seats for Lucy to lie on, separated from the seating and the rear loading area by wire grills. It was her special shelf and she lay on it now, waiting, as the landlord closed the rear doors prior to the trip into Elfington Village. It was the second of September, and although the leaves were starting to turn brown, the sun still held considerable power and today the sky was a clear blue and the weather continued to be settled for the time being.

As the landlord closed the rear doors and moved around to the driver's door, he realised that he had left his pipe inside. So as the van was parked in the shade, he went back inside the pub to find his pipe, leaving the keys dangling in the ignition.

The three men had been watching the landlord from behind a stone wall, waiting for him to go. They had been drinking in the pub the night before, and as was usual for them, had drunk far too much, got far too loud and finally the landlord had had enough and had put them out. They had returned this morning to try and be allowed to drink in the pub again, if that plan failed, then they would pretend to leave, hide somewhere for a while then go back and when the landlord was not around, vandalise and/or steal something, just to teach him a lesson.

They climbed over the wall and walked past the van, and seeing the keys dangling in the ignition, abandoned plan "A" and decided to pinch the van and go for a joyride in it. The landlord would probably have said no to their request anyway, most of them did. Moving quickly, they piled into the van and the one who could drive, albeit badly and with a provisional licence, got behind the wheel and started the engine. With the doors hardly closed, he crunched it into gear and headed out of the carpark, spinning the wheels as he did so, just as the landlord came out of the pub, pipe in mouth and watched in disbelief as his lovely van, with a madly barking Lucy on her shelf, headed out of the car park, turn right into the lane and speed off.

That was their big mistake. They were not from the Elfington area and were only there at all because they had been banned from all the pubs where they lived and wanted to let the landlords of those pubs calm down for a while and, hopefully allow them back in again. So they did not know that had they turned left, they would have linked up with a road that led down into the village and been free and clear to make good their escape. But by turning right, they were going nowhere fast. The lane quickly became a track, which in turn became a path, which only went one way. Up on to the wold.

But nothing that happens in life is accidental, everything having a reason that sometimes is not clear for a long while later. So something as simple as turning left or right can, like throwing a stone in to a pool, ripple out and start a chain of events in motion that can go way beyond the initial event. Such was the case that Monday morning, as the van lurched down the ever narrowing lane with Lucy barking madly on her shelf, going to nowhere!

Finally, fifteen minutes later the van was on a path only just as wide as the vehicle was, the journey came to a sudden stop. The van had run out of petrol. Getting more fuel was one of the things that the landlord had meant to do today. So the thieves simply coasted to a stop right out in the middle of the wold and got out and left the van there, keys still in the ignition, slamming the doors behind them for good measure. All the windows, except one that was partly open, were shut. They had no idea where they were, so they simply carried on walking down the path that they were on, as it led away from where they had come from, laughing and joking as they went. As luck would have it, they came to the hamlet of Withycoombe after about an hour's walking and quickly found the only pub there and spent the last of their dole money on beer.

Sitting outside in the hot sunshine, the yob called Roger reflected that they had had a really good day and that would teach that old bugger who ran the "Time Flies" pub a good lesson. He never gave a thought about the dog that they had left shut in the van!

"There's something down there, right in the middle of the wold," said Astra, as the sun flashed off a shiny surface again. Her eyesight was superb, enhanced even more by her contact with the Gallownians, but whatever the object was, it was just too far away, even for her. "What do you think, Lucky?" she asked.

Lucky the owl hopped on to the ledge of the partly open viewing room, her private entrance and exit from and to the hideaway and focused her eyes. Astra watched her in fascination as those huge pupils grew smaller to compensate for the bright sunlight outside. "It's a human vehicle of some kind," she reported after a few moments.

"What? Out in the middle of the wold?"

"That's what it looks like," confirmed Lucky, turning her head to look at Astra, while keeping her body still. Astra had come with Lucky to open the "Window" in the viewing room a few inches so as to allow Lucky to come in and out. They did not normally open the viewing window in the daylight, but until they could think of something else, it was the only way, but she needed help to open the stone panel. The viewing room was in the shade of the craggs, with the sun behind the rocks. The twins were out in the Old Wood, cleaning the lens of the periscope.

"Are there any humans with it?" asked Astra, as another flash of sunlight reflected their way. They could not know that a very distressed Lucy was desperately trying to get out of the van and so rocking it slightly.

"Don't see any, I'll go and have a look if you like," replied Lucky. Astra nodded her agreement and on silent wings, Lucky the owl launched herself out into the air currents and glided down to the distant object, growing smaller as she headed towards the mystery vehicle.

In next to no time, Lucky landed on the roof rack of the van, only to take off again as the red hot metal burned her feet! Settling on a bush close by, she immediately saw the dog, now motionless on the shelf, trapped inside the van. Her heart sank as she imagined how hot it was inside there. A quick check of the doors and windows made her realise that she could not open any of them, as they were designed for human hands, not an owl's beak or claws. But she had to try and do something. She could not leave the dog in the van to die a slow and painful death. She knew that the dog was still alive, but unconscious, as she had been when she had been shot.

She looked around and saw a large rock that had been disturbed by the wheels of the van and fluttered down to land on it as an idea formed in her mind. She managed to get her claws to grip it and tried to take off, but the stone was just too heavy. She tried again, moving it a little this time and, with a final herculean effort, managed to take off, with much flapping of wings, slowly gaining height over the van. It was a great strain to keep going up and when she could go no higher, she used the last of her strength to position herself over the windscreen of the van before letting the stone go. It took mere seconds for the stone to shatter the windscreen and fall through inside the van. As Lucky descended again, she could feel a wave of super-hot air escape from the van. Avoiding the metal bonnet of the van, which she knew would be red hot, she perched for a second on a windscreen wiper before hopping through the hole in the glass to stand on the dashboard. The heat in the van was almost unbearable. Turning around carefully, she pushed her body against the bigger pieces of glass to make the hole bigger, so she could get out easier and of course let more, cooler air inside.

Hopping onto the back of the front seat, then the back seat, she looked through the wire grill at the dog, which was still breathing, but very shallowly. The heat inside the van was making her feel dizzy, and Lucky knew that she needed to get more air flowing through the van. She noticed that a window on the side of the van was open a little, and it was designed to slide.

She moved over to it and gripping the plastic knob she pulled with all her might, and was fortunate that the van was quite new and well oiled, and slowly the window slid open as far as it would go. She immediately noticed a better flow of air and tried to open the other side, but it would not budge. She needed help now, knowing she could do no more on her own. Quickly hopping to the side window, she went out of it and launched herself up into the air, heading for the Old Wood, where she knew Hugo and Jago were. She hoped that they were not inside the tunnel, as time was quickly running out for the dog!

Lucky arrived just as the twins were heading back inside, and although they were keeping a good look out, she landed next to them and made them jump, so silent was her approach. "You scared the hell out of us!" complained Hugo.

"Sorry, but this is an emergency," and she quickly told the twins about the dog in the van. They looked at her with admiration. "You did very well, Lucky, but we must try and get the dog out quickly," said Jago and they raced off, following Lucky who guided them to where the van was. Once they arrived, Lucky went over to a small babbling brook that flowed nearby and enjoyed a well-earned drink of cool water, before returning to the viewing window and updated a worried Astra, who had waited for her, sensing that something urgent had kept Lucky from returning. With Lucky safely inside, Astra quickly closed the window and ran down the tunnels as fast as she could, with Lucky in hot pursuit to go to the Old Wood entrance and help the twins. She hoped that they could get the dog out and it would not be dead. She could not imagine what it must be like to be trapped in heat like that.

The twins arrived at the van panting hard and Jago immediately jumped up and through the side window and checked on the dog. It was still unconscious, but alive. He quickly looked around the inside of the van and concluded there was no way to open the wire grill from this side, but he noticed that the mechanism that opened the rear doors seemed to suggest a twisting motion. He had always been the more practically minded of the two brothers. He quickly went out through the side window and joined Hugo at the back of the van. Standing on his rear legs, he reached up and gripped the silver handle in his mouth and twisted it to the left. Nothing happened. So he twisted it to the right and it turned easily until it was pointing up and down, rather than side to side. Changing his grip on the handle again, he now started to pull the door towards him and it opened a few inches before he lost his grip and it closed again. Hugo, seeing this, waited until the door moved again and managed to get his paws inside and try to squeeze in. Jago, let the handle go and started to push against the door. Hugo managed to get inside the rear platform and push the door from there and it swung open fully and they heard a sound as a small metal bar clicked in place, holding the door open.

Jago jumped onto the rear platform of the van to join his brother, who had spotted the catch on the door of the wire grill and lifted it up and pulled the grill open. Wasting no time now, the twins pulled the dog off the shelf, Hugo had its collar in his mouth, Jago had grabbed the dog's tail. This was no time for niceties.

The dog dropped down on to the loading platform and the twins pulled the dog until it was lying on the track, in the shade of the van. Its body was hot to the touch. They had to cool the dog down quickly and they dragged the dog between them to the brook that Lucky had drank from and lay it on the sandy bank. Jago began gently splashing water over the dog's body, steam rising from its coat, while his brother was guiding water into the dog's mouth. Still the dog did not move, but the twins did not give up, and a few minutes later they were rewarded with a pink tongue emerging from the dog's mouth and began to weakly lap at the water, while Hugo continued to guide water towards the dog's mouth.

After a long time, the dog opened its eyes and tried to raise its head, but was far too weak and it flopped down again to rest on the sand. The dog's body was soaking wet, but much cooler and the twins looked at each other with a smile. Hopefully the dog would survive!

Astra and Lucky had arrived at the Old Wood entrance and after a careful look around with the newly cleaned periscope, Astra opened the door and carefully went out in to the gully for a further check around. Satisfied that there were no humans around, she parted the ivy to allow Lucky to fly out and head to the van. Astra closed the door and followed her. The twins had pulled a travel blanket out of the van and dragged it to the brook, where they carefully rolled the dog into it, just as Lucky arrived back. She was delighted to find the twins had managed to get the dog out of the van and that it was alive, but only just. She circled overhead, keeping watch as the twins took an end each in their mouths and started to carry the dog back towards the Old Wood, meeting Astra on the way. They had a rest in the shade of a tree and Astra checked the dog over, and was able to establish contact with it without difficulty, a dog to dog and female to female contact was easy for her to do. The dog was, like her, a girl. She reassured the dog that it was among friends and that they would care for her, and the dog seemed to relax and slept as she was carried into the Old Wood and into the secret entrance, only waking briefly to drink more water and allow the others to dry her coat.

She was loaded into a truck and taken down the tunnels to the main chamber, where she managed a light meal and yet more water, before just managing to climb into Astra's basket and fall into a deep sleep. Astra had noticed the collar that the dog had. It reminded her that not that long ago she had a similar one around her neck, the property of a human. No more.

The others gathered together and Astra told them that the dog should make a full recovery, and in a few days' time, should be ready to return to where ever it had come from, if it wanted to. They still had no idea how the dog had come to be trapped inside the van, or indeed, how the van had come to be where it was. All that would be revealed later, when the dog was better. Astra looked at the twins and Lucky and said with emotion in her thoughts, that they had done a fantastic job, a real team effort, each one of them helping the other, working together, using their brains and gifts for the good of others, and in so doing, had saved the life of another living being. The cats would have been so proud of them, as she was.

As a special reward for their splendid work, she would now go into the kitchen and join Barney, who had missed all the excitement, and make them a large cottage pie for their evening meal! That was greeted with smiles all round, it was one of their favourites. Before Astra went, she had one more thing to tell them. The dog had a name. She was called Lucy.

Lucy the dog was now well enough to leave. She had met Barney and had been told all about his escape by Astra. For him also, there was no going back. Ever. She had recovered quite quickly and had told Astra that she wanted to go back to her old life at the pub, where the humans were kind to her. But she did not want her memory erased and to forget her new friends who had undoubtedly saved her life. It was Barney who came up with a solution that should suit everyone. Lucy could keep her memory of the hideaway and of them, but also be able to return back to her old life.

While Lucy was not close by, Barney told the others of his plan. Lucy had no idea where she was, other than it was somewhere on, or rather under the wold. She had been asleep when they had brought her in, and she had not been outside since. Even if she wanted to, and they were all sure that she would not want to, she could not lead anyone back to the Old Wood entrance, simply because she did not know there was an entrance there, or anywhere else.

Barney suggested that Lucy be blindfolded, with her consent, of course and taken outside and only when they were a good way away from the Old Wood, would the blindfold be removed. She did not know how to get into the hideaway, and did not need to. They would escort her back to the pub called "Time Flies" and reunite her with the humans. At the moment, Lucy could only communicate with Astra, as until they knew whether she was staying or going, the others had not "tuned their minds" in to hers. They agreed that to keep things simple, Astra would be the only one to communicate with Lucy. Barney went on.

The cats always told us that knowledge is power. If Lucy was agreeable, we could enable her to understand the human language, and to read and write it. The cats had shown them how they could do that, and how they could empower others with that gift. With her able to do that, she could listen to the humans who came to the pub and if she heard something of interest, she could let them know. Barney was sure that he could come up with some sort of signals that Lucy could make to let them know she had something to tell them. In short, Lucy would be a secret agent!

Hugo, Astra, Jago and Lucky thought it over. They were reminded by Barney that nothing happens by accident and that it would be foolish not to take advantage of the chance to keep an eye, and an ear on what the humans were up to. The others agreed. Lucy was called over and Astra told her what they wanted her to do. She agreed at once. When Astra had told her how they had got her out of the van and brought her here, she was overcome with gratitude. If it would help the creatures who had saved her life, she would be more than happy to do it, and, it would be very interesting to actually be able to understand what the humans were saying. It was a deal!

Lucky suggested that Lucy skip supper, Barney said he would eat hers, and when she was outside, she should roll around in the mud a bit, to appear to the humans that she was hungry and dirty. To appear back among them clean and well fed might seem strange. This was passed on via Astra and Lucy nodded her agreement. That owl was a very smart bird indeed. So while they waited for darkness, Astra used her powers to enable Lucy to begin to understand what the humans said. Reading and writing would come later. Lucy was delighted with her new gifts. Over time, she would be able to read, write and understand the humans. She was a very very lucky dog indeed.

They set off for the pub when darkness had fallen. Barney said his goodbyes in the hideaway. He was too light in colour to go near humans, no one had yet thought of a solution to this.

Lucy was wearing her blindfold and being guided by the others. She knew when she was outside by the smell of the air and the coolness of the night. A mile from the Old Wood, the blindfold was removed and they made much better time. She had a quick roll in some mud and it was half past ten when they arrived in the lane behind the pub, hidden by the stone wall. They said their goodbyes and then Lucy trotted off down the lane, she paused to look back, but already her new friends had vanished, as if they had never been. She went to the back door of the pub and barked and scratched at the door, which was opened by an astonished Landlord, who was overjoyed to see her again, and knelt down to greet her, not minding the mud getting on his clothes. His Lucy had come back! Calling for his wife, Lucy the dog went inside the pub to begin her new role as a secret agent for her secret friends who lived up on the wold!

Chapter Thirty

The Director that was head of the division that Simon Marshall worked for was hosting a dinner party at a posh hotel for his senior managers and their wives. Since his recent promotion, Simon was now one of the lucky ones. Daphne was in the care of a baby sitter and so here he was with Mary who, unlike him was really enjoying herself, not least because of the attention she was getting from the Director, who could not keep from looking down the front of her low cut dress and what was inside it. She revelled in his attention and was flirting openly with him. Simon appeared not to notice, although he and others did. He knew he would not mention her behaviour when they got home, as she would say he was exaggerating, as usual and she was only promoting her husband's interests to the Director as a good wife should.

Yeah, right!

The Director was a thirty-something former Rugby player called Quentin Drummond, who was single and had a reputation as a ladies' man. Simon believed it. There were seven other senior managers and their wives attending the dinner party and Simon was getting to know them. The Director had brought his secretary with him, a very nice lady who was approaching sixty and had been with the company for many years. She had been appointed to be his secretary by the Chairman himself, mainly to keep an eye on the Director and report back on what he was up to. Quentin knew this, but did not mind too much. The Chairman was also approaching sixty and soon he and his spy would retire and then things would change. He would wait. Meanwhile he would feast his eyes on the charms of Mrs Mary Marshall.

Simon could never see the point of events like this, it was in his opinion a waste of time and money, but as the company was paying for the meal, drink and taxi home, he was drinking quite a bit to pass the time. It made a welcome change for him not to have his hand in his own pocket for once!

Before she knew it, the long summer holiday was over and Freya found herself back at school. She did not mind as she liked school and was always eager to learn. She really liked the way Miss Doyle taught the lessons, making them fun and interesting. Freya also liked sitting next to her special friend Dutch. In his bedroom at home was a fully completed model Lancaster bomber that he had bought at Abbotsbury Market the day the pig had escaped. He and Freya had made it during the holiday. He had to admit that she was quite good at model making, for a girl anyway.

Freya had told Dutch about Mr Benton and his Ducks. Since then she had done more work for him, this time it was Chickens. Mr Benton was a shrewd business man and knew the value of advertising his products. Clever slogans could make a big difference to his sales and therefore his profits, and if young Freya could come up with something clever and catchy, then he would tap into that. He was smart enough to know what he was good at, and what he was not. He looked out of the shop window and gazed at his advertising board that stood on the pavement.

TASTY CHICKENS GOING CHEAP, said one side, while on the other was, OUR DELICIOUS CHICKENS AREN'T FOWL!

Freya had even thrown in a suggestion for a sign to put in the window for something he always stocked.

CRACKING EGGS ON SALE HERE.

He turned his attention back inside as his son handed over a chicken and half a dozen eggs to a new customer who had just moved to the village. She had said that it was the sign outside that had tempted her to come in. He smiled. Freya had just earned herself a shilling. Business was improving and he was happy. He was not so happy about the story in last week's paper about the railway closing. He hoped that something could be done to keep it running. If it did close, that would not be good for business. He wondered what had happened to that pig that had escaped from Abbotsbury Market a few weeks ago. Probably got run over and taken home by some lucky sod! He was wrong.

Barney the pig was at that very moment being fitted for a harness that Astra had designed, to enable him to pull the trucks they used when they went outside to collect logs and food, it would be his contribution to the collecting process. He had been told that something called winter was approaching and that they must stock up with things to sustain them if the weather was too bad to go out. He, like Lucky had never experienced a winter. Neither of them had been born when the last one was here, and he was looking forward to seeing what it was like. One thing he and Lucky both knew. If it had not been for their friends Astra, Hugo and Jago, neither of them would be alive now to experience it. They also knew they were incredibly fortunate to be here, safe and among such nice animals, and to have been given such wonderful gifts by them, and be part of this special family.

Time waits for no one, moving relentlessly onward into the future. Most children yearned to get older quickly, and when they got there, they often yearn to be young again, especially the females! Too late, they quickly realise that school is very much easier than work. Freya did not yearn to get older, she just enjoyed being the age and size she was, taking each day as it came and enjoying everything it gave her. She did yearn to get wiser, and would soak up knowledge and information like a sponge, whether consciously or sub-consciously. She did not realise that she had a photographic memory and once a piece of information was learned, it was never forgotten. She was wise well beyond her years and had an air of confidence about her that many of the other children lacked. She had poise and grace, and was taller than all her class mates, even the ones older than her. The seat on her new bike had had to be raised twice already, by an inch each time. Mrs Hunter hated her, seeing trouble ahead. Mrs Hunter liked to intimidate people, adults and children alike, it made her feel good to shout or stare them down, to bully them with her aggressive manner and attitude, and belittle them with her superior knowledge and class. She could see with one eye that Freya Olsen was going to be a hard case to intimidate, unlike her Aunty Rose, who she had reduced to tears many times when she had been a pupil here. Still, Mrs Hunter liked a challenge and soon Freya and that other foreign boy would be in her class. She would soon show them both who was boss. No foreign "Blow in" would ever get the better of her!

Freya could sense Mrs Hunter's hostility. She could almost see the waves of negative energy emanating from her like a heat shimmer on a summer's day. She did not worry. It would be good experience for her to deal with such a miserable woman. She was confident in herself and her ability. She had an inner strength that few children of her age, or indeed any age had. What would be, would be. She would deal with whatever came her way. She felt different from the other children and could sense their insecurity and fears. Within her mind, an inner evolution was just starting to take place and would not stop. The very D N A of her brain was being altered in a way that no human's ever had before. But it did not stop there. Her body was also undergoing significant change, her strength, reflexes, hearing, eyesight, reaction, co-ordination, everything was starting to be enhanced and would continue to improve. She was light years ahead of her class mates in every respect but was mature enough to handle it without appearing condescending or superior. She knew that above all she must not attract attention to herself. But to the outside world, she was just a normal girl who would soon be eight years old. Everyone liked her and she liked everyone. But Dutch was her special friend and they would always be close. But even he would never know her secret.

At the moment she was studying geography in her own time at home, particularly capital cities of countries. This was something that she should start to learn next year, but she had realised that she was lacking in this area when Mr Winter had come to her house recently for Sunday lunch and after the meal he had told them about his life on the Island of Jersey before and during the war and the occupation of the Channel Islands by the Germans. Freya was fascinated. She knew that her own country of Norway had also been occupied by the Germans, her father and Uncle Lars had been school children during those years. But the story that Mr Winter told them was truly remarkable.

It had all started at the end of June, 1940 on their sister Island of Guernsey. The Germans had just flown in and landed at the airport! Soon, all the main Islands were occupied, the only part of the British Isles to be so during the Second World War. At first, it was not too bad. Things were rationed and there was a curfew between ten p.m. and six a.m., and the kids had to learn German at school, but mostly, life just went on, although driving on the right hand side of the road took some getting used to but after a while it did not matter. No-one had any petrol! But as the years passed and the tide of the war turned against the Germans, things started to change for the worse. Everything started to run out. The ration was cut, and cut again, and yet again. Food and fuel, medical supplies and petrol, clothing and soap. Bread, milk, and sugar were in real danger of running out completely. Soon, every rabbit, dog, cat, squirrel, pigeon and even rats had all been caught and eaten. People were thin and gaunt, underweight and ill with things that a healthy person would overcome easily. The Islanders were starving to death. There was a huge German garrison on the Islands, and since the D-Day landings, nothing was coming in. There was silence in the Olsen house as Mr Winter relived the war years. He touched on the fact that his family had been taken to the camps on mainland Europe and that he had, by pure chance been out when the Germans had come to take them away. He had been sheltered by friends until liberation, no easy task on a small island and if he had been caught, he and those sheltering him would probably have been shot. Freya was wise enough not to ask what camps his family had gone to. She had also read about those places.

But the Islanders were in peak condition when compared to the slave labourers who were made to build the defences that still stand to this day. He also left out the details about them. Finally the Islanders were saved from certain starvation by the International Red Cross. The civilian authorities had begged the Germans to try and get help from the International Red Cross, and finally they did so.

On the twenty seventh of December 1944, an old Swedish ship called "Vega" arrived at Guernsey and then moved on to the other Islands. The "Vega" delivered Red Cross parcels and everyone got one. Starvation had been avoided. Just. The Islanders were overcome with joy. Milk. Sugar. Tea. Coffee. Chocolate. Forgotten luxuries had come back to them. The "Vega" came every month after that until liberation on ninth May 1945, when the Islands were once again free and back in civilian control. The war was finally over.

There was silence again when Mr Winter finished his story. Freya rose from her chair and went over to Mr Winter and gave him a hug. "We are your family now," was all she said. Lars and Rose nodded their agreement. Both seemed to have something in their eyes and went out to make a pot of tea. Mr Winter asked Freya if she knew where the Channel Islands were. "Of course," she said and went to get her map.

She opened it and pointed. "There it is," she said. Like many before her, she had pointed at the Isle of Wight. Mr Winter smiled and shook his head and showed her where they really were, just off the coast of France. She was amazed, as were Lars and Rose. Freya had learned much that afternoon, not least how incredibly valuable senior citizens were. They had seen so much, experienced and lived through things she could only guess at. Education was a very valuable part of the complexity of life. But only a part. Experience of life she would learn as she travelled through it. But to tap into the knowledge of someone like Mr Winter was of great value, and she would avail herself of it as much as she could, and enjoy his company at the same time. He was the nearest thing to a grandfather that she would ever have and he would always have a special place in her affections, and she in his.

Later that evening, as Lars drove Mr Winter home to his house, he realised that Freya had been right when she had said that Mr Winter was a part of their family. He was an important person to them all, wise and kind, and Lars knew that he could talk to him about anything if he needed to. He had only got to know him since his rescue during the severe winter, only ten months ago, but it seemed much longer than that. He felt privileged to know such a man and he knew that Freya, and Rose were very fond of him. Once again, out of something bad, something good had come.

Freya was not the only one to sense that Mrs Hunter was trouble. Mr Mitchell, the Headmaster of St Martins School had known it for a very long time. He was a quiet, caring and popular man, both with the children and their parents. The first thing he had done on being appointed Headmaster was to put the school cane in a desk draw and lock it. No child would be caned in his school! It came as no surprise that Mrs Hunter hated him. She had actually taught him at this very school, many years ago, an experience he and many others had not enjoyed. He had been clever enough to go to Grammar school and from there to University. Now he was back as Headmaster, he was enjoying it even less. She had not changed at all down the years, and was still the same sour, nasty, bitter woman he remembered as a boy.

Why, he asked himself for the hundredth time, didn't she just retire and go home and stay there. She was already over the age that she could. He should have been more careful what he wished for!

When Mr Mitchell had returned to her school as a teacher, (she always thought of it as her school) Mrs Hunter had been appalled. And when he had been appointed Headmaster, beating her for the job, she was outraged. How could the board of Governors have been so stupid? Could they not see that she was by far and away the most experienced person in the school? Apparently not. He was a nothing. A nobody. His father had been a Baker for god's sake. A common working man! Entirely the wrong class. She was far superior to him at every level, anyone could see that! She never called him Headmaster, and tried to undermine him whenever she could. He was polite, respectful and courteous to her, as indeed he was to everyone and was a popular Headmaster.

He could hear her voice through the wall as she shouted at her class. She was teaching, if you could call it that, in what had always been the Headmaster's classroom, where the children in their final year were taught by the Headmaster himself as they prepared for the eleven plus examination. He had offered the room to her to teach her class in, and she had accepted, mistakenly thinking that it was his way of acknowledging her superior status in the school. It was not. It was simply the furthermost room from the Infants' classroom. Now they could not hear her booming voice. Good! Mr Mitchell smiled to himself. Score one for the commoner!

Half-term came quickly and Lars took the last of his holiday so he could earn some extra money potato picking. It was a hard, back-breaking and dirty job, walking behind the tractor for hours on end in all weathers.

There were no toilets, except behind the nearest hedge, for men and women alike. Lunch was a half hour break while you ate your sandwiches and had a drink. But the extra money would be very useful, so he put his name down. Once again, Lars was surprised when Rose said she would like to do a few days with him, if Dutch's mum could look after Freya. Freya asked if she could help as well, some of the bigger children were allowed to, so long as their parents were there to keep an eye on them. So Lars did five days, Rose did Monday, Wednesday and Friday, and Freya did Monday and Friday. Wednesday was spent at Dutch's house. The work ended each day at four o'clock. No one had the slightest idea that during the night, the potatoes that they had missed were being collected by someone else.

Barney would pull the truck, Lucky would perch in a nearby tree and keep lookout, and Hugo, Jago and Astra would collect the spuds and load the truck. No one saw them. All tracks were carefully erased. Well before dawn they were back inside the Old Wood entrance with a fully loaded truck. Before the next night came, they would have unloaded the truck and be ready to return to the field again. Unlike the humans, they were not paid! Winter was approaching and they must store as much as they could. There were five of them now.

Soon the clocks would be put back one hour and the darker nights would soon be upon them. Freya loved the dark, she also loved the fog which was common at the time of year. They were both her friends, wrapping themselves around her like a cloak. She moved through them both with joy, knowing that they would protect her and keep her safe and secure. She had no fear of them at all.

But there was still a fog in her mind, concerning the accident that had taken the lives of her parents, and nearly taken hers. Freya was sure that somewhere deep in her mind she knew what had really happened that night, and who had driven the other car, which the police had never found, and may never find. Try as she might, she could not remember. Freya could not know that the Cats, Bob and Lisa had deliberately blocked her mind from remembering what had happened. For now. Deep in Freya's sub-conscience, a clock was ticking away, and when she was ready to deal with the trauma of that night, the fog that concealed the truth would lift and she would be able to shine a light into the gloom. But she was not yet ready. So for now, the fog remained impenetrable, and like the fog and darkness outside, it was her friend too.

At the hideaway, everyone was also happy to embrace the fog and the darkness, as they kept the humans away and enabled the augmented friends to go out and forage for more food and fuel. Both Lucky and Barney had settled down very well to their new lives and were a great help to their special friends, helping them where ever they could. They felt so happy, so wanted and so safe.

Astra made weekly visits to see Lucy when the pub had closed and the humans were asleep. There was an old cat flap in the back door which was quite large and could be secured from the inside by the humans and was always locked shut each night before the humans went up to bed. Lucy had watched how they did it, and from then on, when she wanted to go out, or when Astra wanted to come in, Lucy unlocked the flap, always securing it again before sunrise. The humans never knew, and they would never see the two dogs stretched out in front of the fire in the main bar, silently using their telepathic minds to talk to each other without making a sound. Astra teaching Lucy how to read and write a little more each visit. So far Lucy had heard nothing of any real importance that would affect her friends in the hideaway up on the Wold.

Lucy was really enjoying her role as a secret agent and had learned a lot about the humans who came to the pub. Now she could understand what they were saying, she was surprised to find that most of them seemed dissatisfied with their lot in life, always wanting more, bigger, better and more expensive "Things". As far as Lucy could tell, they all had enough to eat and drink, work to do, a house to live in and were in good health, yet it never seemed quite enough for them.

She had noticed that the male humans, when together in a group, spent a lot of the time complaining about the females, who they could not understand. The females, when they were together in a group, did the same, complaining about the men. The male humans were, in Lucy's opinion the simplest of the two groups. The females were more complex, their minds in a constant state of flux, jumping from one thing to another then back again, continually changing, making and then discarding plans, before reinstating the original plan again.

The males' simple minds could not cope with the continually changing females. The females could not understand why they could not!

The special friends, thanks to the gifts that the Gallownians had passed on to them, had clarity of thought, instantly seeing the path to follow, without the need for debate. Both Astra and Lucy were very aware of the changes that had happened to them. Their 'dog kind' had not changed much for millions of years, then suddenly they had undergone a massive evolutionary jump from primitive animals to very advanced new life forms, moving way ahead of the humans who slept above their heads.

The two dogs looked no different from others of their breed, the changes were all inside their minds.

So as they lay together before the dying embers of the fire, they enjoyed the mental telepathy between them that no human could ever hope to understand. No human except one.

Mrs Mary Marshall, husband of Simon and mother of Daphne, sat across the table from her lunch date and considered the proposal that had just been put to her. The meal was over and dessert had been consumed. Her eyes were bright and her heart was beating quickly as she gathered her thoughts.

This was the third such lunch date she had had with this particular person and she knew that the other two had been building up to this. Across the table from her, Quentin Drummond sat and waited. He had suggested that as his flat was close by, Mary might like to come with him and have a coffee there.

Mary knew what he wanted, and it did not involve drinking coffee. She looked at her watch, one that Simon had bought for her. She had an hour and a half before she would have to pick up Daphne from school. It was enough. She looked at Quentin and smiled. "That would be acceptable," she said in a husky voice.

He smiled back and rose to his feet and went off to settle the bill. Mary watched him count out some banknotes and hand them to the manager of the restaurant. She took a deep breath to steady herself and then stood and followed him out of the door and into the street. There was no going back now.

It was the last day at school before the Christmas Holiday, and the children had enjoyed a special lunch and would go home earlier than usual. There would be no afternoon lessons today!

Freya and Dutch were putting on their hats and coats in preparation for going outside. There was an air of excitement in the school, and the talk was of Father Christmas and what he might bring. Each child had been given a gift from the School to take home, Freya and Dutch had already given each other a small gift, and on impulse, Freya gave Dutch a Christmas kiss on his cheek, making him blush, just as Munch came out of the boy's toilet and saw it. He stopped dead in his tracks as Freya and Dutch went past him together and out of the front door.

He went bright red and felt hot tears prick his eyes as he reached for his own coat. He brushed them away so no one could see. What the hell did she think she was doing? Everyone knew she was his girl, even though he still had hardly spoken to her. A rage swept over him, making him clench his fists in anger. How could she do this to him? Him, who worshipped the ground she walked on. How could she?

It is said that love and hate are opposite sides of the same coin, and in an instant, like a switch being thrown, the coin turned over so the "Hate" side was now face up.

His blood boiled and there was a roaring in his ears as he roughly pushed past some other children and went outside. The Bitch. After all he had done for her. Of course, her and Dutch were both bloody foreigners and would stick together. Obviously, he was not good enough for her, well, they had better both watch out from now on. They were probably laughing at him right now. Nobody was going to make a fool out of him!

Lars, Freya, Rose, Dutch and his mother were already walking down the road, when Freya suddenly turned around, sensing the wave of negative energy being directed her way, to see Munch staring after her, a scowl on his still red face. She turned her back on him and continued walking with the others. She instinctively knew that something had changed in Munch, and not for the better. She made a mental note to keep an eye on Ricky "Munch" Wild from now on!

Chapter Thirty-One

Mr Benton watched out of his window as the children and their parents streamed past his shop for the last time this year. They were early, but he knew that it was the last day of term and they always came out early. He was keeping his eye out for Freya, as he owed her some wages for her work for him and wanted to settle up before he closed up the shop for Christmas.

Outside on the pavement stood his Blackboard, and as it was nearly Christmas, there were two messages on each side to lure the village folk inside.

OUR VENISON IS NOT DEAR! and BUY A PHEASANT FOR A POULTRY AMOUNT! adorned one side, while on the other side were the messages,

GOBBLE UP OUR PLUMP TURKEYS!, together with YOU WON'T BE ABLE TO BEAT OUR CHICKEN DRUMSTICKS!

Mr Benton was a happy man. In the two weeks before, Freya had contributed some other gems.

One week it had been TRY OUR TONGUE, IT SPEAKS FOR ITSELF! That had been Mr Benton's favourite. Another was PIG OUT ON OUR CHEAP PORK!

Last week it had been WE CAN MEAT YOUR BUDGET! and PRICES CUT TO THE BONE!

The girl was a genius and Mr Benton was more than pleased with her efforts. Since Freya had begun to compose her slogans for him, he had noticed a sizeable increase in customers and profits. Wonderful!

As he continued to watch for Freya, a car pulled up and parked alongside his blackboard. A man got out and approached the shop. It was his friend, Larry Lamb who ran the local driving school.

"Afternoon all," he said as he came inside. "You've outdone yourself this week, Fred, with that board of yours, it's brilliant!"

Fred Benton beamed at his friend. "One tries one's best," he said modestly, adding "How's business with you?"

Larry Lamb shook his head. "Not good, Fred. Maybe you can dream up a catchy slogan or two for me?"

Just then Mr Benton saw Freya, Rose and Lars coming down the high street, he waved and when they saw him, he beckoned them over. He moved out from behind the counter and said to his friend, "Wait here. There's someone I'd like you to meet."

Lars, Freya and Rose came inside, and Mr Benton's face broke into a smile. "Hello, everyone, and merry Christmas," he said. "Thanks for all your hard work,

Freya, this is for you," handing her an envelope. Freya opened it and found a Christmas card. Inside the card was a ten shilling note! "I included a bonus," he added when he saw her eyes go wide. She turned to her Aunty and held the note up to show her. Rose raised an eyebrow at Mr Benton, who nodded and said, "Worth every penny, Mrs Olsen. She's a very clever girl and has helped me out no end." He turned to his friend and introduced him. "This is my friend, Larry Lamb, he runs the local driving school." Larry Lamb shook hands all around. He had watched them come in, this giant man, the bright girl, and the slim attractive woman "Nice to meet you all," he said. Fred Benton made a show of looking around before whispering to his friend. "Freya is the brains behind the slogans!" he confided to his friend, who looked impressed. Larry Lamb nudged Fred. "I should have known that you did not think of them, they are far too clever for you to have been responsible!"

Fred Benton pretended to be hurt as he moved behind the counter as more customers came in.

Larry Lamb headed for the door. "Nice to have met you all, but I must be off now, a very merry Christmas to you," he said as he went outside. The Olsen's said their goodbyes and followed him out onto the pavement, and started to make their way home, Freya clutching her money in her hand. Larry Lamb drove past them and tooted his horn and waved, and received waves in reply.

As he drove home, he remembered that he had forgotten to collect his meat, his mind thinking about what Fred Benton had told him. If that child was as good as he said, maybe she could work her magic on his business. As of today, the number of students he had was… zero. It was worth a try.

As his car turned a corner and disappeared, Freya smiled to herself. Over the Christmas break, she would begin to work on promoting Mr Lamb's driving school. She had no doubt he would be in touch. She had planted the idea in his mind as she had shaken his hand!

It was December 29, and the evening meal had been cleared away and everyone was in the back room, the TV was on but Freya was working on Mr Lamb's promotional material, a writing pad on her knees. She had not heard from him as yet, but knew that he would be in touch soon. She looked up. Uncle Lars and Aunty Rose were sitting on the sofa and had been watching the telly, but now their eyes were closed. Freya smiled. She had planted a thought in their minds that they were tired and soon after they had nodded off. They had been like that for fifteen minutes. Freya would wake them soon, as there was a program on the telly she knew that they wanted to see, but she would not move from her chair to do it, but use her mental telepathy.

She was continuing to develop and focus her mental powers, something she knew only she had. One of many special gifts. She looked around the cosy room. In the corner was a Christmas tree, decorated with tinsel and shiny balls that reflected the flickering light of the fire and the TV. She felt secure and safe here. Snug. Santa had been four days earlier and left some presents for her. Mr Winter had spent most of Christmas day with them and had also brought presents for everyone. She had made a special card for him at school and he was delighted with it. She had drawn a group of Islands and joined them together with bridges. It was her version of the Channel Islands! On Boxing Day they had walked down to the doctor's surgery and spent the afternoon and evening with Tom and Penny. It had been another lovely day, with yet more presents. They had said that they would soon finalise the date for their wedding and that Freya would be a bridesmaid! Yesterday Dutch and his parents had come over in the afternoon and they had had another super day. It had been six days since she had last seen her friend and she realised that she had really missed him. He meant a great deal to her, and she did not like being parted from him for too long. He had said that he had missed her as well, and she knew he meant it.

Freya looked across at the sleeping adults and focused her mind on Uncle Lars first, telling him to wake up. A few seconds later he stirred and his eyes opened. He looked around, glancing at the clock.

"That was lucky, Freya, just in time for the program! I don't usually nod off." He looked at Rose, who was also waking up. "Stay here, I'll go and make some tea," and he went out to the kitchen. Rose stretched.

"Have you been nodding too?" she asked Freya, who shook her head. "Well, I'll just go and pay a visit before the program starts" and she went outside, a wave of cool air from outdoors entering the room as she did so. Freya smiled to herself. She was pleased with her evening's work, and not just with what she had written on her pad. It was a pity her mental powers did not work on the telly, you still had to get up to change it to the other channel or adjust the volume!

Jago, Hugo & Astra sat alone by the glowing log fire in the main chamber, each looking into the flames, enjoying the warmth and each other's company. The others had gone to bed and it reminded them of the first night that they had been alone here, after the Cats had left. So much had happened since that night. They were the originals, the ones who had met and been trained by the Gallownians, and who had in their turn, met and trained the others. It all seemed a long time ago now, yet it was only a little over one earth year since the Cats had said their goodbyes and returned to their own world.

Since then, their family of special animals had grown. Now there were six of them, if you included Lucy who, although back living with the humans, was very much part of them. They had come such a long way together during that year. They had enjoyed their second "Catmus Day" and had retold the stories to the others of how it had all begun. They all wondered who the mysterious human could be that the Cats had said they would meet one day and that this was the only human who, like them had been altered by being in contact with an alien race of beings. From what Barney and Lucky had told them, they were reasonably sure that this altered human was a young female. Perhaps the blonde girl that Lucky had seen? But that was all they knew for now. They did not know when the contact would happen or what form it would take. The Cats had only said that it would happen up on the wold.

Outside the hideaway it was night time, the wold covered by darkness that was their friend. Out of this darkness one day would come the special human to find them. They would know this person by something that they would bring with them, something given them by the cats themselves which was unique. This sign would bear the special number. A number very important to all of them. The special, magical number. The number eleven. But they knew that it would not be yet. It was not the time. They would wait.

It was not until third of January 1964 that Mr Larry Lamb knocked on the door of twenty-nine Druids Way. Rose showed him in to the front room and went to retrieve Freya from her bedroom. Lars was out delivering the milk. Mr Lamb came straight to the point of his visit. His friend Fred Benton had told him what Freya had done to help him bring in more customers and he had suggested that Freya might be able to work her magic for him. The trouble was, his business was teaching people to drive and was totally different from what Mr Benton did. He had no shop for people to pass by, so something different would be required for him. He had a small advertisement in the local paper every week, which was the only way he could think of to tell people about his driving school. He was a good instructor, with many years of experience, and a good reputation. But he was not good at much else.

So there it was. He took a sip of his tea that Rose had provided and added that if Miss Freya was able to help him, it would of course be with the approval of Rose and her husband. Rose looked at Freya, who had not spoken up to now. "Well, Freya, what do you think? Can you help Mr Lamb?"

Freya nodded slowly, as if Mr Lamb's visit was a total surprise to her and had caught her unaware.

"I think I might, I'll have to think about it. This is a different kettle of fish from what I did for Mr Benton," she said, throwing in one of the phrases that Dutch had taught her. "I will need to prepare a list of questions for you, so I can fully understand your requirements and focus on them." Mr Lamb nodded, already impressed. "Can you give me your address and I will be in touch, if Aunty Rose and Uncle Lars think it would be all right for me to try, of course."

"Yes, yes, of course," said Mr Lamb, looking at Rose, who said that she would speak to Lars about it when he got home and they would let him know soon. Mr Lamb nodded. "That would be best, I think. Thank you for the tea, Mrs Olsen, and I hope to hear from you soon, Miss Freya." He finished his tea and Rose showed him out. When he had gone, Rose came and sat down next to Freya and gave her a hug. "Your fame is spreading, Freya. If you think you can help him, I don't think Uncle Lars will mind, Mr Lamb seems a nice man. I have no objection."

Freya smiled. "Thank you, Aunty Rose. I think I will be able to do something for Mr Lamb. If Uncle Lars agrees, I would like to try." She got up from her chair. "But first, I had better go and bring some logs in for the fire!" Rose watched her go out of the room. What a lovely child. She has a bright future ahead of her, I am sure, she thought to herself. She had no idea how right she was!

Easter had come early. The winter had, when compared to last year's, been reasonable. There had been snow of course, there always was in this part of the country, but it had been no more than usual. It was mid-March and soon the clocks would go forward to herald the arrival of spring. Already there was some blossom here and there and Freya had seen some lambs skipping about in the fields. The perfect time of year to launch Mr Lamb's driving school. Lars had agreed with Rose that Freya could have a go at helping Mr Lamb and she had posted her list of questions to him the next day. She had already had it written out even before he had knocked on the door! A week later he had sent it back and Freya had only to make some minor changes to what she had thought of over the Christmas holidays.

Now she was ready to reveal to him what she had put together. She had decided that the best way to promote a business like his was by way of leaflets, hand delivered to selected houses in Elfington, Wallbridge and Withycoombe, at least to start with. She could deliver them herself, and had designed a postcard-size leaflet, which she hoped would do the trick. One of the questions she had asked Mr Lamb was who signed up for his lessons the most, men or women. As she had correctly guessed, there were more women than men. This was the "Swinging Sixties" and women were on the move! They were starting to be more independent and learning to drive, even if they did not have a car of their own was all part of their progress. They could always use "Daddy's"!

On one side of the leaflet she had drawn a cartoon. It showed a car, with a smiling sheep standing next to it. The sheep actually looked a bit like Mr Lamb, and it was saying, with the aid of a bubble above its head that pointed to its mouth, "Ewell pass with us!" The sheep was white with a black face and had a badge pinned to it with the word "Larry" on it. Sitting in the driver's seat of the car was a young smiling lady, who was clearly enjoying herself. In the back ground you could see the Beggars Cross finger post with the place names clearly visible, indicating that he covered all those areas. It was very well done, Dutch had helped with that, as he was quite good at drawing things. On the other side of the leaflet was a poem that Freya had composed herself.

The whole concept gave the impression that Mr Lamb's driving school was value for money and it was fun to do. Freya was pleased with her work and hoped that Mr Lamb would be. She could plant a thought in his mind, telling him to like it, but she would not. She used her growing powers sparingly. Freya had asked Mr Lamb to call and have a look at what she had produced and he was due soon. Lars and Rose were also going to be there, as they were keen to see what she had been up to these last few weeks.

Freya nodded her approval at her work. It was as good as she could make it. Not bad, she thought for an eight and a half-year-old. There was a knock at the door, and Lars went to open it. Mr Lamb had arrived.

Larry Lamb sat next to his friend Fred Benton near the fire in the "Time Flies" public house and took a long drink from his pint of bitter. He set the glass down on the table and licked his lips in appreciation.

"Well, Fred, you were right. The girl's a genius! I must say I had my doubts at first about approaching her, after all, she's only a kid and foreign as well. But, as I am sure you know, when you speak to her you forget how old she is and talk to her as if she's much older." Fred Benton nodded. He knew what his friend meant. There was something about Freya Olsen.

She was so calm, serene even. When she looked at you in that direct way of hers you felt as if she could see right into your very soul. It was her eyes, he decided, yes, that was it. Her eyes were like a cat's. Watchful and untroubled, yet shrewd and confident. One thing they had both noticed was obvious. When she grew up she would be a stunningly beautiful young woman, as only ladies from the Nordic countries could be. And smart. Very smart. When he had said she would go far, it was not just a figure of speech. He actually meant it.

Larry Lamb passed over the leaflet that Freya had been delivering for him this past week. It was postcard-size and reasonably thick and immediately gave you the impression of quality. The cartoon on one side was much as it had been originally, only an artist friend of the printers had done a little work on it and had improved it. Behind the signpost there were now a few lambs in a field, and perched on one of the finger posts of the sign were a couple of birds.

They all had an interested expression on their faces as they gazed towards the car. The sheep now looked even more like Larry Lamb himself, and was holding a pair of "L" plates in its hoof. Fred chuckled as he looked at it, he couldn't help it. He turned the card over and read the poem.

"Our message is clear, it isn't a ploy,

The lessons are fun,

It's really sheer joy.

Through country and village,

We'll pass you on,

You can't help but notice, we're better baa none!

Ewe'll pass with us, it won't be a shock, as one of our pupils,

You're in the best flock.

It's value for money,

We charge the least,

We are simply the best.

So you won't get fleeced!"

Again Fred Benton chuckled to himself. Fantastic. Freya had done a wonderful job. He was a master butcher, and Larry was a very good driving instructor. Neither of them had a clue about advertisement or promotion. She did. After the poem were Larry's address and telephone number. Fred put the leaflet in his shirt pocket. He would put it up in his shop. "If this doesn't get you lots of pupils, I don't know what will. How many new ones have you got since this hit the streets last week?"

"Six already, and they are all women, Freya was right about that too, although I only get paid for teaching five of them," said Larry.

Fred raised an eyebrow. It was not like Larry Lamb to do anything for free.

"Freya's Aunty is taking lessons with me. That's the deal she wanted for designing the leaflet and delivering it. I'm more than happy with that. She's done a really good job, Fred, you were right about her!"

Fred Benton drained his glass and set it down on the table. "Well, as I recommended her to you, you can get them in again!"

Larry Lamb got to his feet without protest and headed for the bar. Fred reached down to stroke Lucy the dog, who had been sitting close by and listening to their conversation. She wondered who this clever girl called Freya they had spoken about was. Although she didn't know it then, she would soon find out!

Chapter Thirty-Two

There had been protests, strikes and heated debates in parliament, but despite this the Government had implemented the Beeching plan. In full. Blue bells had appeared in the woods, green leaves on the hedges and trees, and birdsong filled the air in the early spring of 1964.

But on 31 March, the last ever trains travelled along the Elfington valley line. On the morning of 1 April, the valley was silent of man-made train noise. The signals remained where they had last been set, the signal boxes unmanned and empty. The gates of the level crossings remained across the rail tracks. A few passengers arrived at stations, only to find them empty and locked. At Elfington Station, someone had removed the time table from behind the glass as a souvenir. It would not be needed again. Ticket office staff, porters, maintenance workers, station managers, cleaners and many others that serviced the railways did not report for work. There was no work to do.

The unthinkable had actually happened. On 1 April 1964 the railway had closed and it was gone for ever. It was no joke.

The first of April was also a memorable day for another reason for the Olsen family. Lars and his colleagues reported to the dairy as usual for work to find the gates to the yard shut and locked. The dairy had closed! Some lucky men, told in advance that they still had jobs, had been put on a bus and taken to Pondford from where the milk rounds for Elfington and Wallbridge would now be serviced. The dairy had been taken over by a larger one based in Pondford and there were not enough jobs for everyone, both groundsmen and office staff alike.

A grim-faced dairy manager gave each redundant person an envelope that contained a letter of explanation, a reference and three weeks' wages in lieu of notice, together with money for any untaken holiday. Their P 45 would be forwarded to them later. He thanked them for their past service, said he was very sorry and wished them well. He wisely stayed on the inside of the locked gates, before going back into the empty office to wait for them to go home. He had a job at Pondford to go to.

Lars and the other men stood outside the gates in the darkness and talked amongst themselves for a while, trying to take in this completely unexpected turn of events. It was a horrible feeling to be made redundant, to be on the outside looking in to what had been their place of work for many years. Eventually, as it began to sink in, the men drifted off home to break the news to their families, most of whom were still in bed. It was ironic, there had been no rumours about this at all!

Lars headed back home in a state of shock, his mind in a whirl. He just could not believe what had just happened. Completely out of the blue his job had gone! Just like that. Gone. All those years, all that hard work, for what? An envelope with three weeks' wages and a letter.

He felt very bitter, angry, resentful and most of all, betrayed. He had worked so hard for them. He had been happy here and suddenly, at a stroke, it was all gone. He stopped walking. He could not go home, not yet. Rose and Freya would not even be up yet and he did not want to disrupt their morning routine. But where could he go? Elfington was a small village. There was no cafe. He couldn't even go and sit in the railway station. It too had closed this day. He felt completely lost and alone. He thought about going to Mr Winter's house, but it was too early even for that.

The cemetery. He would go there and think things through. To take it all in, to adapt. No one would be there at this time in the morning and there was a bench to sit on. So he walked on in the dark of the early morning. Now he knew how the railway workers were feeling. He arrived at the cemetery and let himself in through the side gate, which squeaked in protest, and found the bench and sat down, suddenly tired. He just sat there, all alone, in the dark, thinking about nothing, thinking about everything. It had been such a shock. No one had seen this coming.

It was completely silent in the grave yard. He put his head in his hands, for the first time in his life, he was at a complete loss. He could have been the only human being on the planet at that moment. He prayed to the Gods to help him, give him strength to go forward. He had never felt so alone. A thought sprang into his mind. Freya! The adoption was not yet complete, and now he had no work. He could not lose her now, it was more than he could bear. She meant everything to him and Rose. He could not imagine life without either of them. Those fools at the dairy had no idea what they had done. A job was more than just earning a living, important as that was. It gave you purpose, a reason for being, a feeling of being part of something, a status in society, a sense of belonging. Of being wanted, useful.

Then he heard the first birdsong of the new day as the sun started to rise, a few shafts of light shining down through the clouds. The birdsongs increased, as more birds joined in, and the weak spring Sun rose above the horizon. He stayed there for a long time. Hearing the church clock striking the quarter past, half past and three quarter past and the hour. At half past eight, Lars raised his head and sat up straighter. He was a Viking. He would not give up. Ever. He would find new work. He had to. He was big and strong and could turn his hand to anything. His spirits rose again as the shock of the redundancy wore off. The birds did not give up, no matter how harsh the weather was, they just got on with it. So would he. He got to his feet, feeling better. Time to go home and wait for Rose to get back from taking Freya to school. What was it that Freya sometimes said, Trust in the bounty of the Universe. That was it. He hoped that the Universe was listening.

Alan Briggs parked his old van outside Elfington Post Office and climbed out. He was not a happy man. The man he employed to help him run his farm had managed to break his leg and would be off work for between six months and a year! Why couldn't the stupid bugger watch where he was going! He had not been the best of workers in the first place, but was better than nothing. Getting good workers was not easy, farming was hard graft and now he had to try to find someone else.

He had written out a notice on a postcard to go in the Post Office window and as he approached the door, it opened and Rose and Lars Olsen came out. Since they had helped him last summer, Alan had bumped into them from time to time in the village and always had a word.

"Hello, Rose! Hello, Lars! Fancy seeing you. On holiday again, I'll bet," he said, his weather-beaten face breaking into a smile.

"Hello, Alan, nice to see you. No holiday today, I'm afraid. The dairy closed yesterday, and I am out of work!" said Lars.

Alan just stared at them, stunned. "The dairy? Closed? Why? We have always had a dairy in the village, ever since I can remember. What happened?"

Lars explained about the takeover. Alan took off his cap and scratched his head. "I don't know what the world is coming to, first the railway's gone, and now the dairy!" He stopped speaking and looked at Rose and Lars, the smile returning to his face.

"I was just going to put this in the window, but maybe meeting you has saved me the trouble and expense." He handed the postcard to Lars and he and Rose read it together.

WANTED. TEMPORARY FARM WORKER TO PROVIDE SICKNESS COVER FOR REGULAR HELPER MIN 6 MONTHS, PROBABLY LONGER. MUST BE ABLE TO DRIVE. GOOD RATES OF PAY. CONTACT MR ALAN BRIGGS AT THE OLD WOOD FARM FOR INTERVIEW, OR TELEPHONE PONDFORD 24211.

Alan looked at Lars and smiled. "Now where do you think I'm going to find a big strong man who can drive and who I can trust to work hard?" He asked.

Lars just looked at him, then down at the card in his hand, then at Rose. He had a lump in his throat.

"When can I come for an interview?" he asked.

"You had that last August when you gave me a hand. The job is yours!" said Alan.

Lars looked at Rose, who threw her arms around the old farmer and gave him a hug. "Thank you, Alan, I don't know what to say!"

Lars held out his hand and Alan took it. "I accept. Thank you so much, I do not have the words to say how grateful I am. When would you like me to start?"

Alan pretended to think about it. "What are you doing tomorrow?" and they all laughed. Lars had got a new job. He had been unemployed for two days.

Alan chatted with them for a while before driving off, pleased that he had managed to fill the vacancy so quickly and with such a quality worker.

Lars and Rose made their way home, unable to believe their good fortune. Lars turned to Rose and said, "Little Freya was right. She always says Trust in the bounty of the Universe! And now look what has happened!"

Rose nodded. "I think I will make her a special Cottage pie for tea."

Lars smiled. "Make it a big one. We farmers need our energy!" They both laughed, the strain and tension melting away. Lars had a new job! It was 2nd April, 1964.

When Freya heard the news and had read the card, she was very happy. She knew the universe would not let her down. Mr Briggs telephone number ended in eleven!

A pet should be forever, not just until you get bored with it. Many people who get a new pet and find that it is not for them, find it another home where it will be cared for. Some however, do not.

The puppy had been brought home as a Christmas gift for a spoiled little girl, who always got what she wanted. The first six weeks of its life had been full of joy and wonder. It was with its mother and four other brothers and sisters. There was warmth and happiness. It had plenty of milk, lots of fun and could sleep whenever it wanted. He would play until he became tired and he would just drift off to sleep. The world was a place of wonder and mystery. The world was safe and secure.

He enjoyed learning about solid food and was growing into a happy, inquisitive and contented little dog.

Then one day one of his sisters was taken away and did not return. He was puzzled. Where had she gone to? A few days later one of his brothers also disappeared. He began to wonder what was happening. Then, without warning he was picked up and put into a cardboard box and taken away. It was dark in the box and he was frightened. He never saw his family again. After what seemed like ages, the box was opened and light flooded in. He was picked up and placed in the arms of a human girl.

The girl opened the box with a squeal of delight and looked inside. It was a small mongrel dog but was cute and lively. She never gave a thought that it had been taken from its mother and the other puppies in its family after only a few short weeks, or that it was hungry and thirsty. And scared.

The girl's parents had bought him a nice new collar of red leather, which looked good against its light-coloured coat. The girl played with it a lot at first, feeding it chocolate, sweets and biscuits. She took it out for walks and showed it to her friends.

All was well for a while. The Christmas holidays came to an end and the girl went back to school. Then the novelty started to wear off. The walks became more infrequent and the attention it received was less. The puppy found itself either shut in the kitchen for long periods or shoved out into the back garden, come rain, snow or wind. He would spend hours shivering by the back door, whimpering to be let back in. He was confused. One minute he was the centre of attention, the next he was rejected and left out in the rain and cold.

He also started to chew things as he grew, he just couldn't help it, and this did not go down well with the mother, who hadn't really wanted the thing in the first place. He had also peed on the floor a few times when he was unable to get outside. The mother found out from a friend that the Vet's fees were quite high when their dog had had to visit the surgery. Perhaps getting the dog had not been such a good idea in the first place.

It was, of course left to the girl's mother to care for the dog, something that she had seen coming as soon as the dog had entered the house. It was a job she did not want. The fact was that the family had never had a dog before and knew next to nothing about them and what they needed. She started to nag her husband about the dog and after a while he was forced to take action, just for a quiet life. They had had the dog for three months now. It was enough. The dog had to go.

The puppy did not know that he had out stayed his welcome until, when the girl was at school, he was put in another cardboard box and loaded into the boot of the family car. The nice red collar was unfastened and removed. He would not be needing it where he was going. An hour's drive later the box was opened and the puppy found himself alone at the side of a lay-by in the middle of the moors, watching the car drive away. The little girl was told that a new home had been found for the dog in Abbotsbury. She didn't really mind. It was only a dog anyway. She had a nice new doll to play with.

Alone, starving and scared out of its wits, the puppy (It had never been given a name, it was just the dog!) was left to fend for itself. It drank from puddles, got soaked when it rained and was soon filthy from the mud and goo of the moors. There was nothing to eat. It wandered about, getting weaker and weaker, wondering why this was happening to him and why he had been abandoned. He had been good. He had tried his best. He pined for his mother. The world was not such a nice place anymore. At night he would try and sleep under a bush but the nights were long and cold, and there were strange noises and cries by unknown creatures to keep him awake. By the end of five days and nights he was at a low ebb. He found a pile of rubbish left by some campers, but there was nothing to eat. There was a sodden and filthy old duvet, and now, too weak to stand, he lay down on it and fell asleep, not caring if he woke up again.

It was early the next morning and completely by chance that Lucky found him, more dead than alive. A quick check revealed that the puppy was breathing but only just. She quickly flew to the hideaway and got the others, and Hugo and Jago arrived as soon as they could, with a truck pulled by Barney, who was taking a chance that he would not be seen. As gently as possible, and with Lucky flying overhead to keep watch, they carried the puppy back to Old Wood and into their secret world, where Astra was waiting. The cold and filthy animal was cleaned and dried by Astra in the back of the truck as Barney pulled it along the tunnels to the main chamber. Gently the wretched creature was lifted out of the back of the truck and put in Astra's basket right next to the fire and was covered by a warm blanket. It was still breathing but now unconscious. Astra decided to get into the basket with him and cuddled up close to his back to help get him warm. They stayed like that for hours, the life of the puppy hanging in the balance. Only the Universe would decide if it would be death or life.

By evening the puppy briefly awoke and opened its eyes and tried to lift its head, but could not. Astra called for some hot milk and climbing out of the basket, she placed the puppy's head gently on a cushion and spoon by spoon forced the hot milk into the puppy's mouth. It was almost too weak to swallow, but Astra would not give up. The puppy managed about twelve spoons before it could take no more. Astra climbed back into the basket again and cuddled up to the puppy's back. It felt a little warmer and its breathing a little more even. The puppy awoke again a few hours later and was able to take more hot milk. Barney, Lucky, Hugo and Jago stayed close by all night, making sure that the fire was well supplied with logs, as they all waited and sat close to the basket, concentrating their thoughts onto the puppy, supplying it with their energy, willing it to get better. They could do no more. The puppy, still semi-conscious, had no idea where it was, or who these strange new creatures were, but instinctively knew it was among friends. Astra stayed in the basket all night. By morning it became clear that the puppy would recover. It was still very weak, but would get no weaker. From now on it would start to get stronger. The danger was past. The Universe had decided. It would be life.

It was Lucky who thought of a name for the newcomer. She had told the others where and how she had found the puppy quite by chance as she was flying along, her super sharp eyes missing nothing on the ground below. They called the puppy Tog.

Tog recovered quickly, physically at least, and as the spring gave way to summer, he began to explore the hideaway and the secret tunnels, but always with at least one of the others with him. He was not keen to venture outside very much, and would not go out in the dark. His treatment at the hands of the humans had scared him badly, and his confidence was low. Being with the others had, over time helped him and gradually he became more lively and was able to help them gather in supplies. His tail began to wag more often. Everyone liked him, it was impossible not to, and he got along with all the others very well, but Lucky would always be his best friend. They liked to go to the magical cavern and enjoy the peace and tranquillity it gave them.

But try as he might, Tog worried that he was unworthy of being there and that the others were just being kind by letting him stay. As the summer wore on Tog worried more and more until finally he could stand it no longer. He asked Lucky to accompany him to the magical cavern, and Lucky went with him, knowing that there was something weighing on his mind. She thought she knew what it was. She was right.

They sat together by the side of the pool and listened to the trickle of the water as it ran down the wall and into the pool. The flow was considerably less than it had been in the spring. The summer had been a dry one. Lucky waited for Tog to tell her what was on his mind, and gradually it came out.

Tog was scared that he had no gifts to offer the others and that they might not want him to stay in the hideaway. He could not face going out into the world alone, perhaps to be given to another family of humans who would not care for him and he would be rejected again. He knew he could not cope with that. He had heard the others talk about another dog called Lucy, who he had not met, that had been saved by Lucky and the others, but had chosen to go back to live with the humans. Tog could not return to the family that had thrown him out, even if he knew where they were, which he did not.

Lucky listened in silence, not interrupting, until Tog had finished. She looked at her young friend and smiled. "It might surprise you to know that I thought much the same when I first came here, what could I possibly offer these super animals, who were far superior to me in all respects? Like you, I thought that they were just being kind when they said I could stay and that I could just contribute whatever I could, what could I contribute? But it did not take me long to realise that they meant it, as I am sure that you know, the others are incapable of telling lies." Tog nodded.

"So I just did what I could and they were happy with that. So my advice to you is this. Just be yourself, contribute whatever you can and be happy. You know what the others say, "Trust in the bounty of the Universe" and just take each day as it comes. Nothing happens by accident. I was meant to find you, just as I found Lucy. You were meant to be here with us. The Universe is vast, and earth is but one small planet among billions. It was not by chance that I found you and brought you here. You are part of something wonderful, something very special. You are part of our family. You already have a special gift which you give to us all every day, did you know that?" Tog shook his head, he could not think of what it could be.

"You give to us the gift of joy, just by being you. We are all happier when we are near you. We are all pleased to be around each other, but we are all delighted to be around you, such is your unique personality. Without you, we would all be less, and with you being a valued member of our family, we are all more than we were before you came to us. You give us more than you would ever know. Tog, my friend, you are still young, as indeed am I, so who knows what gifts will come your way as you grow up. Who knows what the Universe has in store for you? Never doubt the value you have. So just continue to be you, and trust. That is all the advice I can give you. That is all the advice you need."

Tog sat next to his extra special friend and watched the water trickle down the rocks and listened to its musical sound. The water did not know what awaited it when it left here, it just flowed along and trusted.

As he would. He could never have imagined that as he lay on the sodden duvet on the wold that he would end up here, yet, the Universe had chosen him to join this special group of creatures and be part of their family. Lucky was right. He was meant to be here. It was his destiny.

He looked at his friend and smiled. "Thank you, Lucky, I needed to hear that. You have made me feel so much better. I feel special, wanted. Thank you."

Lucky smiled back. "You are special. Unique. In the whole Universe there is only one creature like you, with your knowledge, experience and personality. Now, I think Astra has made some scones for tea, we should go back before the others eat them all, especially Barney. Come!" Together the two friends made their way back to the main chamber just in time for tea. Lucky had been right. There were scones, and lots of them. Tog joined the others and tucked in, feeling totally at peace, his doubts all but gone. He belonged.

They had never imagined that there was so much to it. Freya and Dutch had been in the back garden of Freya's house, swinging on the knotted rope that hung from the tree next to her bedroom window, when Lars came out of the house and went to his shed, which was in fact a mini gym that he had created in there.

Curious as ever, they stopped swinging and went over to the shed just as Lars opened the door. They looked inside as Lars went in. He turned and waved them in. "Come and have a look if you want to, but please don't try to pick up any of the weights, as some are very heavy and you may hurt yourselves."

"Yes, Uncle Lars," answered Freya, for both of them.

The shed was a large one, and it was laid out in such a way as not to put too much weight in one spot.

There was a padded bench at one end, the base of which could be raised up at an angle, lots of weights, some small ones and some bigger. At the far end was a big punch bag hanging down from a roof beam.

On the walls were some posters of champion body builders flexing their huge muscles, and there was a diagram of a man without any skin, showing the various

272

muscles in the human body, and what they were called.

They were both fascinated. "Can women do weight training?" asked Freya.

"Of course they can, little one, but they tend to use lighter weights and will not get as muscular as men do, they have a different body type."

"Why?"

"Men are naturally more muscular, a woman's body tends to have more fat tissue, it's just how nature designed us!" he laughed.

"Could we do this, Mr Olsen?" asked Dutch.

"You could, under my supervision, but as you are growing naturally, you would have to be careful not to over train."

"How much do you do?" he asked.

"Usually three times a week, and for about 45 minutes or so each time, including warming up and warming down, but the exercise is only one part of the story. You must eat a good diet and also get enough rest, as your body is organic and must be able to grow. It is easy to do too much and then you will not grow."

He went over to a shelf and took down a file, then sat on the bench to study it. "What is that?" asked Freya, looking over his shoulder.

"This is how I keep track of what I do, and when I do it, and what weights I used, so all body parts get their fair share of work, and I don't miss any of them out. Now, you can watch me if you wish, but save your questions until the end, as I must concentrate and count how many exercises I do."

And that was how it started. Freya and Dutch watched Lars as he warmed up, bending, stretching and twisting and running on the spot, then he did his workout, making notes in his folder as he went. When he was finished, he spent five minutes stretching, twisting and bending again. When he had finished that he sat on his bench and answered all their questions while drinking a bottle of water.

Both Dutch and Freya were hooked, and so began an interest in weight training and fitness that would stay with them for the rest of their lives. In the weeks and months that followed, under the expert tuition of Lars, they learned all there was to know about body building, diet, nutrition, rest and relaxation.

They learned all the names of the muscles and where they were in the body, and what exercises to do to work a particular group, that would put a medical student to shame. They learned about the importance of water, and being hydrated, about protein and carbohydrates, and fruit and veg, and what foods to eat more of and what they should avoid.

They were willing pupils and needed no prompting to do their workouts, always under the watchful eye of Lars. Early in the tuition, an extra pupil asked to join the program.

It was Rose.

Once again, she surprised Lars, and he was more than happy to enrol her. Like Freya and Dutch, she was amazed at how scientific and structured the training was, and like them she really enjoyed doing the movements. Lars was a good teacher, explaining and demonstrating the exercises, as they progressed.

Soon there were four files on the shelf in the shed, and Lars was pleased at the progress they were all making.

One morning when Rose was alone in the house, Lars was at work and Freya was at school, she stood naked in her bedroom in front of the full length mirror and looked at her body. She looked, and indeed was a completely different woman than she had been two years ago. She was almost five stone lighter than she had once been, and looked fantastic, she had to admit. She had a slender and firm body, but she had kept her curves. She ran her hands lightly down over her flat belly, or abdomen as they said in body building speak, and smiled. She could faintly see the outline of her abdominal muscles beneath her skin.

The dry retching had gone, together with the lazy, dirty and stupid woman she had once been. The old Rose was no more. In her place was a willowy, sexy and intelligent young woman, full of energy, who had never felt so alive, so wanted, so loved and so happy.

Chapter Thirty-Three

Mrs Hunter was in a particularly bad mood as she made her way to school. She had slept badly, partly due to having one too many gins the night before. Thank goodness that the term was drawing to a close. She could have a rest from the little monsters that she had the misfortune to have to teach. Woe betide any of them if they got on the wrong side of her today! With relief, she arrived at the school and went to the staff room for a much needed cup of tea before her first class of the day. She was ready to vent her pent-up anger on the first child that displeased her. But to her disappointment, she could find no one to pick on. The children were always on their best behaviour in her classes, having seen what would happen to them many times before, if they were stupid enough to bring themselves to her attention. This meant that the next class would have to be extra careful if they were to make it to lunch time.

Freya was in the next class that came in and took their seats quietly. She sat by the window as she usually did, Dutch sat next to her. The lesson this morning was revision on Capital Cities of Europe, which Freya knew off by heart anyway. The weather outside was warm and sunny, the sky a pale blue and through the open top windows the smells of summer wafted in to the room. Freya wished she could be outside, rather than stuck in the classroom. Still, not long until lunchtime. From where she sat, Freya could see the main gate and noticed that a group of four adults were approaching the school. She did not recognise any of them and wondered why they were here. She saw the headmaster walk across the playground and greet them and usher them inside.

Freya quickly turned her attention back to the lesson, not wanting to incur the wrath of Mrs Hunter who she sensed was in a particularly bad mood this morning, she could almost see the waves of negative emotion radiating from her. The lesson began. After twenty minutes something caught Freya's eye outside. A large bird had just landed in the tree outside her window and was lost in its leaves. Freya quickly turned her head back to the book open in front of her and was just in time to avoid being seen by Mrs Hunter, and the lesson continued, but somehow Freya knew that the calm would not last for much longer. She was right.

Outside, in the tree, Lucky was perched on a branch, high in the tree. She had been flying back to the hideaway and for reasons she could not explain, had had the urge to fly down to the school and land in the tree, which was next to a large window. She could just about see that there was a group of children inside being taught by a grumpy-looking woman. She hopped to a lower branch, then to a lower one still, which gave her a much better view of the class inside, but without being seen herself. She focused her mind on the class inside and quickly tuned in to the conversation and began to listen to what was being said. To her delight she found it was geography, one of her favourite subjects and one she was very familiar with.

She could not stop her gaze moving to rest on a little girl with blond hair who was sitting by the window. There was something about her that was different to the others in the classroom. Then she remembered. She was the girl that had attracted her attention at the sports day. The aura she projected was still there, only now much stronger. A slight gust of wind moved the branch on which she was perched and she had to briefly extend her wings to keep her steady. Like when she had been shot, she was too near the end of the branch

Out of the corner of her eye, Freya caught the movement in the tree and turned her head towards it. She caught a quick glimpse of the bird she had noticed earlier and in her mind she said, "Hello, Mr Bird, How are you today?" Outside in the tree, Lucky heard the message and before she could stop herself she replied, "Hello, Little girl. I am very well, thank you." Freya jumped in surprise. The bird seemed to have heard her thoughts and replied to them! But how could that be? She quickly turned her attention back to the class. Too late! Her movement had been spotted by Mrs Hunter. "Freda Olsen! Were you looking out of the window!" said Mrs Hunter in a loud voice. The rest of the class was silent. Mrs Hunter now had the victim that she had been looking for. They all knew what was coming next. While they were sorry for Freya, they were very glad it was her and not one of them.

"Yes, Mrs Hunter."

"How dare you gaze out of the window in my class while I'm trying to educate you? You ungrateful child. I suppose you'll be telling me next that you don't need to pay attention as you already know all the answers!'

"Yes, Mrs Hunter."

"Really! We'll just have to see if you do, won't we? Come down to the front and leave your book on your desk. "

Freya rose to her feet and walked to the front of the class and stood in front of the blackboard.

She looked small and pale next to the blackboard. Freya was wearing a thin summer dress that had been mended a few times and pumps on her feet that were now too small for her and almost worn out, but she stood upright and calmly looked at Mrs Hunter with confidence, which only served to anger Mrs Hunter even more. "Well, children, Freda here says she knows the answers and does not need to pay attention!"

Mrs Hunter smiled at the class as if they were her friends. There were a few nervous smiles among the class but not many. Even Munch was quiet. Freya did not try to correct the incorrect pronunciation of her name. Mrs Hunter often called her Freda, probably deliberately to see if she dared to correct it. Freya never did.

Mrs Hunter turned to face Freya, the book of answers open in front of her. A smile flickered across her face for a moment as she remembered something from long ago. Some years before a boy had stood exactly where Freya stood now, trembling and terrified, so much so that he had wet himself. Mrs Hunter sighed. Happy days! Now she could unload all her pent-up anger and venom on this little girl. A foreign girl at that. This was going to be good. She began in a deceptively calm voice.

"So, if I were to ask you to name the capital city of the Irish Republic, what would that be?"

"Dublin, Mrs Hunter."

"And France?"

"Paris."

"What about Italy?"

"Rome."

"Belgium?"

"Brussels."

"Spain?"

"Madrid."

"Portugal?"

"Lisbon."

"Denmark?"

"Copenhagen."

Outside in the tree, Lucky hopped down to an even lower branch and now had a better line of sight to Freya. Her eyes were locked on Freya, her concentration total. She was surprised to be able to hear the girl's thoughts so easily. The class nervously looked on. Freya would get one wrong soon, they knew.

Mrs Hunter's mild tone had started to change. Her voice grew louder. Freya just stood there, calm and relaxed, her green eyes looking right back at Mrs Hunter.

"Let's move a little further afield, shall we?" said Mrs Hunter. "What is the capital city of Poland?"

"Warsaw."

"Hungary?"

"Budapest."

"Austria?"

"Vienna."

"Greece?"

"Athens."

"Sweden?"

"Stockholm."

"Finland?"

"Helsinki."

"Norway?"

"That would be Oslo," said Freya with a slight smile.

Mrs Hunter's voice was getting ever louder. Her face was turning red and there were two white specks of spit at the corners of her mouth. In the next classroom, Miss Doyle could hear Mrs Hunter's voice getting very loud through the wall. She heard it most days. Mrs Hunter usually shouted at the children.

"Germany?"

"Pre or post second world war?"

"Don't you get clever with me my girl," thundered Mrs Hunter, "answer the question."

"Pre-war was Berlin," said Freya.

"And post war?"

"That would be Bonn."

The rest of the class watched spellbound. They were beginning to sense that they were witnessing something very special. Their eyes moved from Mrs Hunter to Freya and back again, as if they were watching a tennis match. No one noticed the bird in the tree outside the window. No one but Freya.

"Russia?"

"Moscow."

"Turkey?"

"Ankara."

"Malta?"

"Valletta."

"Estonia?" Mrs Hunter had finished the lesson material and was now making the countries up from memory. It was now a battle of wills, hers against the child, and she was losing. She could not allow that. Mrs Hunter never lost.

"Tallinn."

"Latvia?"

"Riga."

"Lithuania?"

"Vilnius."

"Ukraine?"

"Kiev."

"Bulgaria?"

"Sofia."

"Tunisia?"

"Tunis."

"Jordan?"

"Amman."

"United States of America?"

"I thought this was capital cities of Europe, Miss?" Said Freya.

"Silence. Answer the question! Answer the question!" screamed Mrs Hunter, whose face was going from red to purple, her eyes bulging out behind her glasses.

Flecks of spittle flew out of her mouth. She had moved from sitting to standing, but could not remember getting up. She took a step towards Freya.

Many of the children were getting quite distressed now, more than a few had tears in their eyes. The tension in the room was electric. They could feel the raw hatred and venom in Mrs Hunter's voice. Only Freya remained calm.

"It's Washington D. C."

"What's D C stand for?"

"District of Columbia."

"Japan?"

"Tokyo."

"Chile?"

"Santiago."

"Argentina?"

"Buenos Aires."

"Brasil?"

"Sao Paulo."

"Colombia?"

"Bogota."

"Burma?"

"Rangoon."

"Jamaica?"

"Kingston."

"Venezuela?"

"Caracas."

"Kenya?"

"Nairobi."

"Peru?"

"Lima."

"Philippines?"

"Manila."

"Iran?"

"Tehran."

"Iraq?"

"Baghdad."

"Nepal?"

"Kathmandu."

"Ethiopia?"

"Addis Ababa."

"Thailand?"

"Bangkok."

"Cuba?"

"Havana."

Mrs Hunter was getting desperate. The child knew them all. She had one last card to play. She would ask for capital cities of countries where it was not the biggest or most obvious one. No child would know them. Not many teachers would either. She took another step closer. Almost within striking distance. Freya moved for the first time, taking a step backwards. Mrs Hunter's face was purple with rage and hatred. Her voice was beyond a scream. This child must be broken. Must be. Must be.

Nearly all the children were crying now, even Munch's lip was quivering. They had never experienced such pure hate, such fury, such venom before. Their childish emotions could not cope with it.

"Canada?"

"Ottawa."

"Australia?"

"Canberra."

"South Korea?" Mrs Hunter's right hand started to rise.

The classroom door opened, breaking the spell. Miss Doyle strode in, a worried look on her face. "Is everything OK, Mrs Hunter, I heard shouting?"

"Mind your own business," screamed Mrs Hunter, all self-control gone.

Suddenly the class stood up as the Headmaster entered the room, followed by the four adults Freya had seen earlier. He took in the scene before him and approached Freya and said quietly, "Please take your seat," and looking at the rest of the class said, "Sit down, Children." They sat.

He turned to Mrs Hunter and said, "What's going on here, you should not shout at the children."

Mrs Hunter gave him a terrible look and spat out the words. "Don't you tell me what to do, you jumped up student!" She took a deep breath. "My father was an Officer!" There was complete silence. The children looked at the teachers. The visitors looked at the Headmaster.

The Headmaster looked at Mrs Hunter. No one looked out of the window. If they had, they would have seen nothing. The bird had gone. It was Miss Doyle who took charge.

"With your permission, Headmaster, I think the children should go out early and play before lunch."

The Headmaster nodded. He had gone pale.

"Please go with them, Miss Doyle, and ask cook for something to give them."

Miss Doyle stood by the door and the class filed out. When the last one had gone, the headmaster turned to the visitors and said, "My apologies. It seems Mrs Hunter is not well today."

He then turned to Mrs Hunter and introduced the visitors. "These ladies and gentlemen are from the Schools Inspectors' office."

Mrs Hunter flopped down into her chair, like a puppet that had just had its strings cut. She looked up again at the Headmaster, and said quietly, "Shit!"

Out in the playground, Miss Doyle and Cook were comforting the children and giving them drinks of iced water. Many of them were still distressed. Dutch was standing next to Freya, who seemed completely unfazed by the whole episode. Miss Doyle came over. "Are you all right, Pet," she asked, a concerned look on her face.

Freya nodded. "Yes, Miss Doyle."

"What happened in there?"

Dutch answered. "Mrs Hunter caught Freya looking out of the window and then asked her loads and loads of questions about capital cities, trying to catch her out, but when Freya knew them all, Mrs Hunter started shouting and screaming at her!"

"You poor child," said Miss Doyle, bending down and giving Freya a hug, "No child should have to endure that sort of thing. You are a very brave girl." Then she whispered in a friendly tone in Freya's ear, "But do try and remember not to draw to much attention to yourself if you can possibly help it," before giving her another hug and then getting up.

Freya looked at Miss Doyle in puzzlement. Had she heard right? For once she was not sure. Miss Doyle smiled at her, winked, and then moved away. Freya watched her go. It would seem there was much more to Miss Doyle than meets the eye!

Two days after the "Mrs Hunter" incident with Freya, St Martins School closed for the summer holidays. Although she did not know it, Mrs Hunter would never teach there again. Or anywhere else. Freya was also unaware that she had earned her place in history at St Martins School and Elfington Village. The story of what had happened that day had spread around the village and surrounding areas like wildfire. There were too many people who had suffered at the hands of Mrs Hunter down the years for Freya to be thought of no less than a saviour. Future classes of children would be spared the trauma of being "Taught" by this nasty old woman and the story would be told and retold for ever, and those who had been in the class that day and witnessed it would gain special status just by having been there. There was a collective opinion that Mrs Hunter could not come back from this, and they were right.

She might have got away with it had it not been for the visit of the schools inspectors. During the summer holidays meetings would be held and decisions made about the future of St Martins School.

Freya herself just shrugged the whole thing off and spent a very enjoyable summer with Dutch, and together they would be out and about the village and wold on their bikes or on foot. They were frequent visitors at Mr Winter's house and worked in his garden, while he watched from his chair on the path. Some days they would cycle out to the Old Wood Farm and find where Lars was working and help him with whatever he was doing that day. They helped with the haymaking, weeding the rows of crops in the fields and lots of other things. Mr Briggs was more than pleased with his new helper, who did three times more than the idle sod he was replacing.

Lars himself took to his new job like a duck to water. He missed his milk round and his mates at the dairy, there were a lot of memories of his years there, but he was still outside and earning better money than he was before. Alan Briggs was a great man to work for, and he and his wife soon became good friends.

Rose continued with her driving lessons and Lars took her and Penny, who had also enrolled with Mr Lamb, out some evenings and at weekends. Tom had a car which he had inherited with the job, but it was a big and powerful Humber and Penny correctly thought would be too much for a learner to handle. It would be very useful for the practice nurse to be able to drive, especially now the railway had closed.

She and Tom had set a date for their wedding, 11 May 1965 and Freya was to be a bridesmaid. The Tokyo Olympic Games had come and gone, with everyone singing the catchy song, "Good Morning Tokyo." The days and weeks passed and before anyone realised it the summer had passed by and it was September and the new school year was starting again.

A pet's life is entirely in the hands of its owners. It can have a happy life or a miserable one. How much it is fed, what it is fed, when it is fed, together with if it is exercised and for how long is down to them. Not only that, the pet can be cared for or neglected, loved or hated, treated as one of the family or ignored as a waste of time and money.

The pet has no control over its own destiny whatsoever. The vast majority of pets are loved, wanted and cared for. A small minority are not. Andy the Greyhound was one of the unlucky ones. He was not a pet. He was an investment, bred purely and simply to make money for his owners. He had no idea that his future was only secure if he could win the greyhound races he was entered into and win money for his owners. He did not know that all the care and attention he and his fellow greyhounds were getting was subject to them all performing to a very high standard. There is no such thing as a free lunch.

Born in a kennel with many others of his breed, he was at first cared for very well. No expense was spared on his wellbeing. He was fed good food, exercised regularly and had access to a vet if he needed to. It did not take his owners long to realise that there was a problem with him. He could not run as fast as his brothers or sisters. He tried his best, but was always last in any race he was entered into. He had no clue that his well-being and future depended on his lap times. His owners decided to give him a little more time to improve, as he came from a long line of champion dogs. From now on, his training would be harder, his food would be less and his time at the kennels shorter if no improvement was forthcoming.

Andy the greyhound was on borrowed time.

Mary Marshall resumed her affair with Quentin Drummond as soon as Daphne was back at school. She had seen very little of him during the summer holidays, he had gone to Spain for two weeks, while she, Simon and Daphne had gone to Cornwall. Most of the other villagers went nowhere.

Now things were back to normal and she was excited as she drove to his flat on the far side of Abbotsbury, the area known as Churchwell. It was a quiet residential area with a mixture of houses, bungalows and flats. As usual, Mary parked around the corner from Quentin's flat and walked back to it. She did not want any of the neighbours to see her car, although it was almost certain that no one she knew, or knew her would see her here. There were twelve flats in his block and no one would know to which one she was visiting. She now had her own key. She was so wrapped up in her own thoughts that she did not notice the Lamb's School of Motoring car driving slowly past her as she turned into his block of flats. Lots of learners were brought here to practice their three point turns and reversing skills, as the roads were quiet and wide.

She also did not notice who was driving the car. Penny Grey recognised her at once as she drove by, as Mary had called into the surgery to collect a prescription only the day before. Fancy seeing someone she knew around here! What a small world it was.

Autumn 1964 was, like other autumns before it, a very busy time for the friends at the hideaway as they gathered in as much food and wood as they could before the winter set in. Already the days were getting shorter and the nights longer, but for the augments, that gave them more time to forage for the things they needed. Tonight everyone was in the magical cavern and climbing in to the boat, ready to set off downstream to the Old Mill lake, but as usual they all took a few moments to look yet again at the splendour and beauty of this special place, especially Tog who was in his usual state of excitement, his tail wagging so much that the others feared that it might fly off and end up in the pool! Even after six months, he was still in a state of wonderment and awe of the caverns and tunnels in which he lived with his special friends, to whom he owed everything, including his very life. But the magical cavern was the very best of them all, and he loved coming here.

The others smiled at each other. Now he had got his confidence back and had stopped worrying that he had nothing to offer the others, he had come on by leaps and bounds. Tog was such a happy dog, and a joy for everyone to be around. As usual, he was right at the front of the boat, enjoying every second of the adventure as the boat wended its way downstream through the tunnel. At each of the waypoints, there were piles of logs stacked on the stone bank, some from the previous year, ready to be taken upstream to the main cavern, in case there was another severe winter. Finally they reached the end of the tunnel and stopped behind the doors that gave access to the lake beyond. In the second channel was another boat, already loaded with wood, ready to be taken up stream later on.

Tonight the friends were foraging for fruit, berries and acorns for Barney. Hugo and Jago sprang up on to the centre shelf of rock and carefully opened the right side door part way and waited for Lucky to fly out and have a look around. The other waited in the darkness, which for them was not dark at all. After five minutes she came back as silently as she had left.

"All clear, no one around."

The door was opened fully and the boat slid quietly out to wait beneath the branches of the willow tree, which still had most of its leaves. Again, Lucky flew off and perched in a tree that gave her a good view of the area. No one could get anywhere near without being seen and heard by her. Satisfied, she gave the all clear again, and the boat began to move slowly along the bank towards the ramp. It was completely dark now and there was no moon. Perfect.

Suddenly they all heard Lucky's voice as she broke into their thoughts. "HOLD IT! CAR APPROACHING!" Immediately, Barney began pulling the boat back behind the cover of the willow tree and then manoeuvred it back into the channel. Hugo and Jago half closed the door and then they all waited. They could hear the engine now as it approached. What would humans be coming here for at this time of night?

Lucky, invisible in her tree, watched the lights of the car bounce around as it moved down the rutted track, before it turned right to drive along the wide strip of grass in front of the Old Mill, with the lake on their left. She too wondered what these humans were up to, they hadn't come here at this time of night in the pitch dark for the good of their health, that much was clear.

The car stopped, but its engine continued to run and its lights stayed on. The driver got out. Lucky could see it was a large male. He was carrying a sack. The sack was moving and she could hear faint cries from inside it. There was something alive inside the sack! The man moved in front of the car, using its headlights to see and then as he started to swing the sack back and forth, Lucky knew what he was going to do.

On the third swing forward he let the sack go. It flew from his hand and out over the lake, hitting the water with a loud splash and immediately started to sink. Lucky could see the sack still moving and could hear the cries from within it. The man looked out over the dark water for a moment as the ripples spread out from where the sack had hit the water, but unable to see much made his way back to the car, got in and began to drive slowly along the grass strip to the track on the other side of the mill that lead back to the road. The car had hardly started to move when Lucky swooped down from her tree and managed to get her claws into the last inch of sack, just as it sank beneath the surface of the lake. It was so heavy that it nearly pulled her under with it, but she would not let it go and with a fantastic effort, managed to fly towards the ramp, dragging the sack with her, wings flapping wildly and calling for the others to come and help her. Out of the corner of her eye she noticed the car had joined the main road and vanished into the night.

She just managed to make it to the ramp before her strength gave out and pulled the sack clear of the water before collapsing on to the ramp, gasping for breath. There was no noise or movement from the sack now. The boat approached and Lucky managed to withdraw her claws from the sack.

"Quickly, open the sack, there is an animal in there," she cried.

The sack was ripped open and there inside, next to some large stones, were four kittens. They were silent and unmoving, so young that their eyes were still shut. Their fur was sodden and matted into dripping peaks. Gently but quickly the kittens were lifted out of the sack and Astra, Jago, Hugo and Tog took one each and tried to blow air into the tiny bodies. Barney, knowing he would only be in the way, passed four dry and empty sacks to the others and the kittens were each placed in one and very gently rubbed dry while they were being revived.

Tog, completely out of his depth, just copied what the others were doing, and to his immense joy his kitten finally started to move, water coming out of its mouth and nose. The others, seeing his success continued their efforts, but try as they might, the other three did not respond. After a long while, they reluctantly stopped trying to revive the tiny creatures. They were dead. Three pairs of eyes that had never opened and seen the world, now never would, their short lives over before they had even begun.

With great sadness, they watched Tog continue to dry his kitten, which was moving and crying more and more. At least this one would live.

Barney, Astra and Tog immediately returned upstream in the boat with the kitten which Tog had wrapped in a clean dry sack. He took no part in pulling the boat, just cuddled the kitten in his paws and held it close to his body for warmth, while the others got the boat back to the magical cavern in record time and then they moved quickly to get back to the main cavern. Then Barney made the fire up and then headed back to the magical cavern to go back and collect the others, while Astra heated some milk for the kitten. While it was warming up, she moved Tog's basket closer to the fire and held the kitten while he climbed in. Gently, she handed the tiny frail creature back to Tog, who held it close to him once again to keep it warm.

Their eyes met. Six months ago Astra had cuddled up to a barely alive little dog to keep him warm and restore him to life. He who had been saved was now saving another. The circle of life.

Back at the Old Mill, the twins had found a suitable spot to bury the three kittens. While Lucky kept watch, they dug a deep hole and, wrapped in a clean dry sack, the three tiny bodies were laid to rest. There would be no foraging this night. Not now.

Lucky flew back up the tunnels and met up with Barney on his way down in the boat. She landed on one of the seats and they drifted back down to the lake in silence. No communication was necessary. While she was gone, the twins sat by the grave and kept the dead kittens company as their tiny souls were released back to the Universe. They too were silent, just listening to the sounds of the night that the kittens would never hear. After a while Lucky reappeared and reluctantly, the twins left the kittens to continue their journey alone, and went with her back to the ramp and got in the boat. Barney guided the boat back behind the willow tree and then into the stream. The door was closed and the lake by the Old Mill was silent once again. It was over.

At last everyone was back in the main cavern and Astra gave everyone a large bowl of hot soup to warm them up. The kitten was fast asleep, cuddled up to Tog, having drank some hot milk. Tog just lay back in his basket with the kitten in his paws. The only sound was the crackling of the logs on the fire but all the friends were talking silently between themselves.

The Cats, Bob and Lisa had been right, as they usually were. The humans were a very long way from being ready for first contact. Despite the veneer of sophistication, it would take very little for them to revert back to the savages they so recently had been, and some of them still were. No wonder the Cats had made so sure that they were able to remain here undetected after they had left. The events of the evening had brought it home to all of them that they must never relax their watchfulness, or become careless. One lax moment could spell ruin for them all. The question they had all asked themselves had been answered by Lucky.

The question was, of course, why? Why do some humans do such terrible things? The answer was simple. Because they can.

Lucky came over to the basket and looked at his friend as he held the kitten. "Remember our conversation of a few months ago in the magical cavern?" Tog nodded. "Well, you have acquired a new gift to add to the ones you already have." Tog looked puzzled.

Lucky continued. "You have this night given this tiny creature the most precious gift of all. The gift of life.

Now you can see that your place here with us was no mistake, your value is equal to ours, not less. Never forget that. When this kitten grows up, it will look to you for help and guidance. I can think of no one better to provide it. Well done, my friend." Tog smiled at his special friend. Lucky was right. Tog felt very humble as the others came to congratulate him. Any lingering doubt that he had of not being as valued as the others had vanished. He felt accepted. He always had been.

As the kitten, a female, moved in her sleep, Tog announced that he had thought of a name for her.

He would call her Millie.

Chapter Thirty-Four

It was time. She could not resist any longer. It had been getting stronger and stronger. The night was calling to her and she could wait no more. Now she was tall enough to climb out of her bedroom window and down the old Oak tree, the same tree that the Cats, Bob and Lisa had used to climb in to visit her room on their last night on earth, although she would never know that.

She already had had the strength and the eyesight, and now she had the height. It was time. Lars and Rose would not awaken until long after she got back. Wearing dark clothing and a dark woollen hat, and of course her special necklace around her neck under her clothes, she climbed out of her window, pulling it almost closed behind her and down the tree and onto the lawn. Moving like a shadow, she vanished into the night.

Most humans can see reasonably well in the dark, though few bother to try, even when there is Moonlight and starlight to help them. When darkness falls and temperatures drop, most can be found behind closed curtains with the lights on.

Freya was not like most humans. She had found, to her delight, that she could see clearly in the dark, even on the darkest winter's night. This was a gift that she had told no one about, knowing that other people did not have this gift and would wonder why she had. She wondered why herself. Why was she different than others? She did not have an answer. All she knew was that the darkness held no fear for her, the night, like the fog was an old friend, and she intended to visit it as often as she could.

One of her favourite times of day was twilight, when the Sun began to slide below the western horizon and the hustle and bustle of the day gave way to a more gentle pace. There was a magical quality to the hours of darkness, it was a time of peace, a time of rest and renewal, as if the very earth itself was releasing some of the energy it had received from the sun during the daylight hours, and it was travelling up through the soles of her feet and into her body for her to use whenever she needed it.

Everything was so different during the hours of darkness. Sounds carried much farther, the smells of the earth seemed stronger, the air fresher and cleaner. The Aura of the planet changed. There was no need to rush. There was time to slow down and enjoy just being. Freya could just melt into the night and become part of it, embrace it, connect with it and be enriched by it.

The later the hour, the better she liked it. She was always aware of other creatures, particularly humans who may be out, long before they could ever be aware of her. She moved silently, without effort, and was invisible when she stopped. No human ever saw her and few animals.

She could crisscross the Village without hardly ever crossing a road, using the many alleys and tracks that were there. There were only a handful of streetlights in the village. She did not need them. She was like a pale shadow.

A stroll through the silent Village left her invigorated and energised. She would return to her room the same way as she had left it, using the tree near her window and the tree swing rope. Uncle Lars and Aunty Rose never knew she had left the house. Only the night knew and it would not tell.

A few days after her rescue, Millie opened her eyes. Two tiny blue eyes peered out of her fluffy black face and focused on Tog looking down at her. In those few seconds, they bonded and Millie snuggled closer to his warm body. Tog called for Astra, who appeared from the kitchen with another bottle of warm milk. She handed it to Tog who gently guided the nourishment into Millie's tiny mouth. Millie drank it down and then closed her eyes again to sleep. All she needed was being provided. She was warm, fed and safe. Her needs were simple. Millie would continue to grow quickly and in a short time was out of the basket and jumping around the hideaway and into everything. She was a delight to have around and as she grew, she began to explore the tunnels, but never far from Tog.

Everyone took their turn to keep an eye on her to give Tog a break. Millie would grow up in a safe and loving environment, the first to be altered from birth and have no memory of what it was like to be ordinary. For her, it was completely normal to live with other types of creatures and not fear what they might do. The world outside the hideaway was unknown to her and she had no recollection of anything before opening her eyes and seeing Tog. The hideaway was her world and she thrived on its protection and the love of the creatures who lived in it. Communicating telepathically, and learning to read, write and understand the humans and their ways was all she knew. All she needed.

The new school year began again at St Martins School, but with major changes. Mrs Hunter had been "encouraged" to retire. She had not wanted to, but she had been told in no uncertain terms that she could retire with dignity, or be sacked! Eventually she had had to accept defeat, as the board of governors, acting on strong recommendations from the schools' Inspectors had made it crystal clear that her days at St Martins School were over. She had, of course no one to blame but herself, but she did not see it that way. She blamed Freya Olsen.

The second change was that Mr Mitchell had also stepped down as Headmaster, and had left the school to pursue a career as a college lecturer. He would be greatly missed by pupils, teachers and parents alike, but the Inspectors had felt he had lost control of the staff and he had to admit that he had. There was great sympathy for him in as much as no one would be able to control the Mrs Hunters of this world.

The new Headmaster was Mr Fuller and it did not take long to see that he was everything that Mr Mitchell was not. He was a poor teacher and a man who did not bother to consult his staff on anything. He was the new Headmaster, and he would decide what was what and that was all there was to it!

Miss Doyle was less than thrilled to be working with him and was sure that they would not get along. She was right. But she put up with him, knowing that she herself would not be teaching at St Martins for ever. She was sure that Mr Fuller's appointment was because he knew the "right" people and she was right about that too. She thought he was very ambitious and would only stay here until his network of contacts could secure him advancement to something bigger and better elsewhere. Right again. Miss Doyle had many talents that she chose not to reveal.

She was a very bright lady and one of a large group of people, who thought Freya Olsen should get a medal for giving Mrs Hunter a chance to show her true colours and to shoot herself in the foot. It was a pity it had not happened years ago! Freya Olsen would make a splendid Head Girl when the time came.

A further change to take place at the school was the arrival of a student teacher to assist Mrs Stratton, the Infants' teacher. Her name was Miss Fiona Foster, an attractive young lady who was good with the children. It was hoped that once she had settled in, Mrs Stratton could be released now and then to teach the older children.

Now that Mrs Hunter had actually gone, the school was a different place and the whole atmosphere had improved. It just went to show how one miserable old woman had affected the whole school. Freya was treated as a heroine by the other children, someone who had liberated the poor oppressed children from the wicked witch! It was not that far from the truth. The exception was Munch, who although just as glad to see the back of Mrs Hunter as anyone else, was unwilling to give her any credit for it, and just glowered at her and said negative things about her whenever he could. He was big for his age and getting bigger all the time, no surprise to most people as he never seemed to stop eating. Although only nine, he was feared by most of the other children, who thought it wise to keep him happy, lest they be singled out for a spot of bullying. Miss Doyle had thought that he was already making the transition from stupid oaf to a menacing thug. She would keep an eye on him.

Freya also noticed how most of the other children were wary of him and six weeks into the new School year, she saw an opportunity to bring him down a peg or two. Just before the half-term break, Dr Tom and Nurse Penny arrived at the School to give Freya's class their next inoculation, the dreaded jab! After lunch and before the next lesson had started, Tom and Penny set up their clinic in the staff room and when they were ready, the lucky children were lined up in the corridor outside in alphabetical order before being called in. This meant that Freya was about half way down the queue, while Dutch was second to last and Munch last of all.

Penny had told Freya what to expect and she had told Dutch.

During the lunch time, Freya and Dutch had been busy recruiting a few trusted friends to help them with their plan and by the time the bell was rung they were ready. One by one their names were called by Penny and in they went. After the first half had gone in Dutch nudged Munch and said in a worried voice, "It looks like they are using a big needle!" Munch looked up in time to see the first of their recruits emerge from the staff room holding his arm and hurrying away. Munch had gone quiet.

The line shuffled forward and a second recruit came out, also holding her arm. Freya's turn came and when she came out there appeared to be tears on her cheeks, which were actually a few drops of water from the sink inside the staff room. She too did not speak but hurried away. Dutch looked at Munch with a concerned look on his face. Munch had gone pale. The line continued to move forward and finally Dutch went in, leaving Munch alone in the corridor. When he came out, he could see that the plan had worked. Munch was nowhere to be seen! Penny came out and called his name. "Richard Wild?"

But Ricky "Munch" Wild had gone. A search was carried out and he was eventually found, hiding behind the shed in the corner of the playground. Mrs Stratton coaxed him out and he was marched back inside the School and into the staff room, but not before most of the School had seen him through the windows!

Penny checked off his name and ushered him over to where Doctor Tom was waiting. Tom held out a dish to Munch on which sat a lump of sugar! After he had taken it he joined the rest of his class, where Miss Doyle, who knew a bully when she saw one, played her part. As he took his seat she looked at him over the top of her glasses and said, "At last! Thank you for joining us, Master Wild. Pray be seated and we will finally begin!" This prompted much sniggering from the rest of the class and Munch went bright red and sat down. He sulked for the rest of the afternoon. Freya smiled to herself. Score another one for the Vikings!

Chapter Thirty-Five

Freddy Piper was only four years old. He would not get to five. He was back in Elfington to spend his last few days at home in familiar surroundings, as the Doctors at Abbotsbury Hospital could do no more for him. Doctor Thomas Thornton rose from the wooden chair by the side of the bed and closed his bag, his face grim. He doubted that Freddy knew that he had been there at all.

He hated losing a patient, especially one so young who had spent much of his short life in and out of hospital.

He went out of the back room where Freddie's bed was and into the hall to get his coat, together with Freddie's mother. "Thank you, Doctor" she said. Tom nodded. "I'll come again in the morning, of course, but please call me if…"

"If he gets any worse," finished Mrs Piper for him. "Don't worry, Doctor, I know where you and Penny are if I need you. You have both been fantastic since you took over the practice, I'm very grateful to you both." She wiped away a tear, adding, "but we have to face it. We're going to lose him." Tom touched her arm. "Keep your chin up. I'll see myself out." And he was gone. Out in the street, he paused by the front gate to compose himself and took a few deep breaths when he heard a familiar voice say, "Are you all right, Uncle Tom?"

He opened his eyes to find Freya standing next to him, a bunch of leaflets in her hands, across the street he noticed Dutch delivering the other side, the second wave of Freya's promotion of Lamb's school of motoring. "Yes, thank you, Freya. I've just been to see a patient of mine who is not very well."

"But you will make them better, yes?"

Tom sighed. "I wish I could Freya, I wish I could," was all he could say. "I'd better get back to the surgery. Give my best to Lars and Rose," and he walked off down the street.

Freya watched him go. It was not like him to be downbeat. She made a note of the house number and continued on with her delivering, careful not to go to the house Dr Tom had just left. She finished her side of the street and joined Dutch, who was waiting for her and they made their way home for lunch.

It was Saturday and the first weekend of the half-term break. Lars was home from his half day at the Old Wood Farm and as Freya took off her coat she asked, "Uncle Lars, who lives at number twenty-one Coleman Street?"

"Mrs Piper," replied Lars at once. A very nice lady who was a good customer of mine when I was at the dairy. Why do you ask?"

"I saw Uncle Tom leaving there just now, he looked upset. He said he had been to see a patient who was not very well."

Lars thought for a moment. "It must be young Freddy. Yes, I remember now. He's been in and out of hospital a lot. Mrs Piper was adjusting her milk requirement all the time. I'm not sure if you have seen him, he's missed a lot of school." Freya thought back and had brief memories of a thin pale boy in the infants', who was missing more than he was there. "Yes I do remember him now," she said. "Uncle Tom said he wished he could help him, he's already saved me and Aunty Rose, and he can make Freddy better as well."

Lars bent down and gave Freya a hug. "Tom is a very good doctor, he did save you and Aunty Rose, but sometimes people are too sick to be saved. I'm sure Tom will do his best."

Freya kissed her Uncle and he let her go to wash her hands for lunch. As she turned on the tap she made a decision. Tonight, Freddy Piper would get some special help.

The clocks went back one hour that weekend, and Freya intended to make the most of it. They adjusted all the clocks in the house before they went to bed. Freya had gone up much earlier, of course but did not go to sleep. She had made sure that her Uncle and Aunty would enjoy a long and sound night's sleep tonight. She would not. She had work to do. As soon as she could, she went out of her window, down the old Oak tree and vanished into the night. Like a shadow she moved silently through the darkness, completely at home there. Soon she was in the alley behind Coleman Street and trying to work out which one was number twenty-one, when she noticed a wooden gate with twenty-one painted on it, to help the dustmen. She smiled to herself. She would accept all the help the Universe gave her this night. Avoiding the gate, she climbed over the brick wall with ease and stood in the shadows in the small rear garden. There had been rain that afternoon and there was a damp, earthy smell in the air. A sudden down draft of air added the distinctive smell of coal smoke to the mix. She could see it was coming from the chimney of number twenty-one. Mrs Piper would not be going to bed tonight. There were no lights from the upstairs of the house, but Freya could see light showing behind the curtains that were drawn across the patio doors of the back room of the house.

As she stood there, the Church Clock of St Martins struck the half hour. Half past midnight. Like a cat that part of her was, Freya moved down silently down the garden, using the stepping stones set into the lawn, and stood on the concrete next to the patio doors. Through a small gap in the curtains, she could see the room beyond. The bed took most of it up. On the left side of the bed, next to a small table light was Mrs Piper, slumped in an armchair, dozing. The bed was in the shadow of the table light, but Freya could see a slight, frail figure lying in it, hooked up to a drip of liquid that was going into his right arm, to help ease the pain that his small body could not cope with. Freddy. Freya took a deep breath. It was like looking at herself, two years ago, only it was her in the bed and Uncle Lars dozing in the chair and it was Abbotsbury Hospital and not Coleman Street. She knew at once that she had no time to loose. Concentrating on Mrs Piper first, Freya focused her thoughts on her, it did not take long to send the exhausted lady into a deep sleep from which she would not awaken until Freya had gone. She knew that Mrs Piper lived alone with her son, Uncle Lars had told her that her husband had run off with a woman from Pondford soon after Freddy was born, leaving his wife to care for their sick son alone.

Sensing that there was no one else in the house, Freya reached for the door handle and pressed it down. The door was not locked! Gently pulling it towards her, Freya stepped over the sill and into the room, quickly closing the door behind her. She stood perfectly still. Neither Mrs Piper nor Freddy moved. One was in a deep sleep, the other on the edge of a coma from which even Freya could not wake him from. She glided over to the bed and sat on the wooden chair next to it.

Freya's eyes snapped open and she looked at the clock on the mantel piece. Five thirty. She had put that clock back one hour to the correct time before she had started to help Freddy. Subconsciously she had been trying to keeping track of the time. She could not stay too long. Freya had taken Freddie's left hand in both of hers and closing her eyes, she concentrated on him, letting her special energy flow into him. She had not seen the golden "eleven" of her necklace start to glow, going from gold to orange, then from orange to bright red, as its healing powers flowed through her and into him.

The hours went by and Freya had just sat there, letting the cosmic energy restore the child back to life. Outside the room the night had run its course, clouds had drifted across the new moon and the creatures of the night had gone about their business. Just like she had. She had been aware of the clock on the mantelpiece chiming the quarter, half, three quarters and the hour. She knew that she had got here just in time. Freddy had been slipping away, entering the void between life and death, where she herself had floated before the Cats had pulled her back from the dark and into the light. She had pulled him back from that dark place and returned him to the light. The Universe, in placing her here, had decided it was not his time to die.

Time to go. Freya released Freddie's hand and lay it gently on the bed. Such had been the intensity of the contact with him, her fingers had left faint imprints on both sides of his hand, almost like light burn marks. It could not be helped. They would fade quickly. She rose to her feet, feeling completely drained, but also feeling a deep sense of achievement. Freddy Piper would live.

She must go now. A quick look at Mrs Piper, who had not stirred during the long night, ensured that she would awaken later with no memory of what had happened here. One last look at Freddy. He was smiling in his sleep. As silently as she had come, Freya opened the patio doors and vanished into the garden, over the wall and made her way home, drawing on her last reserves of energy which she knew would always be there for her to use when she needed to. Up the Oak Tree and back through the window, dropping lightly back into her room. Quickly taking off her clothes and into her nightie, she was asleep almost before her head hit the pillow, just having time to cuddle her Troll in her arms.

Mrs Piper opened her eyes in alarm in response to a hand touching her arm. Quickly she turned towards the bed and saw Freddy looking at her, and automatically noticed that his drip was almost empty. She blinked her eyes, her brain not quite understanding what she was seeing. Freddy was looking at her! She sat up and took his hand. He squeezed it. She looked at her wristwatch. Seven thirty! It could not be. She looked at the clock on the mantelpiece. Six thirty! She was dreaming. Or going mad. Or both. She returned her gaze back to her son. He smiled at her again and spoke for the first time in days, a voice she had thought she would never hear again. "Hi, Mum! Can I have a drink please, I'm thirsty!" Mrs Piper put her arms carefully around her son, mindful of his drip and hugged him. "Oh, Freddy! What has happened to you? You, you are alive!"

"Of course I'm alive, mummy. I feel better now. What did you do?"

Mrs Piper just hugged him and whispered, "I prayed for a miracle, Freddy. I think I got one!" Then she burst into tears.

It was ten o'clock when Tom stopped his car outside number twenty-one and switched off the engine. It was raining and grey and overcast. The weather matched his mood exactly. He reached for his bag which was sitting on the wide leather seat next to him and steeled himself for what he might find behind the front door. He knew there was nothing in his bag that would help, but he took it anyway. He sighed. Better get it over with. Not for the first time he blamed himself for not being able to save this boy. He knew he could not save them all, but he so wanted to. He opened the car door and walked briskly to the door and rang the bell, trying to stay under the porch. The door opened and a smiling Mrs Piper invited him inside. Why would she be smiling at a time like this? "Is everything all right? How's Freddy today?"

"Come and see, Doctor!" Tom followed her into the back room, not bothering to remove his coat, something was wrong. Freddy was lying back on his pillows, as he had been the day before, but unlike then his eyes were open! He turned to face the door as Tom entered the room. "Hello, Doctor. How are you today?"

Tom just stood there and gaped, his mind unable to believe what he was seeing. "I—, I'm fine, thank you. How are you?" he stammered.

"Much better, thank you. Mummy says it's a miracle. I felt so bad before, but now

I feel better. Thank you for making me well!"

Tom was just about to say "It wasn't me" but stopped himself. His training kicked in and he quickly took off his coat. He turned to Freddie's mum. "What happened?"

She walked around the bed and sat in her armchair. "I don't know, Doctor. I woke up here in my chair and Freddy was awake and asking for a drink! It's a miracle, that's all I can say. Somehow I slept all through the night and woke up at seven thirty, or rather six thirty now the clocks have gone back. I have never done that before, and there he was, awake and thirsty. I can't believe it, I just can't!"

Tom opened his bag and then turned to Freddy. "Right, young man, let's have a look at you!" and he began his examination, while his mind was reeling. This could not be happening. It just could not. The child was all but gone. Tom reached for Freddie's left wrist and froze. The marks were very faint, but still there. He gently turned the wrist over and again, there they were. Very faint but still recognisable. He had seen marks like these before. On Rose Olsen's appendix. And on Old Mr Winter's broken leg. Now here they were again. Exactly the same. Imprints of small fingers! Human fingers, like those of a woman. Or a girl.

Tom looked at Mrs Piper. "Have you had any visitors since I was last here? Any one at all?"

"No, Doctor. No one. My parents are on their way now, I rang them this morning, but since last night no. It's like I said, he just got better all by himself. It's a miracle!"

Tom looked at Freddy. "Your mother is right. Well done, Freddy, you have improved. Keep it up! Now you must rest and continue the good work. I'll come and see you again later." Freddy smiled and touched Tom's hand. "Thank you so much, Doctor Tom."

Tom rose from the chair and indicated to Mrs Piper to follow him into the hall.

When they were there, she asked. "Is he really better, Doctor? I mean, will it continue?"

Tom scratched his head. "In all my years in medicine, I have never seen anyone recover from where Freddy was yesterday, to where he is now. But I do have to admit he's much better today. If you don't mind, I'll contact my colleagues at Abbotsbury and ask them to come and give him the once over. But be prepared, Mrs Piper, in case Freddy relapses. Call me if there is any change, any change at all. "

"I will, and thank you so much, Doctor, for all you have done."

Tom put on his coat and walked back to his car. He sat in it for a long while, listening to the rain beating on the roof, trying to get his racing thoughts to slow down. He was delighted that Freddy had taken a sudden and totally unexpected turn for the better, and hoped it would continue. But, he knew that no one had ever recovered like he had, so much and so quickly. It was medically impossible, yet there he was.

He thought back again over the times he had seen those marks. Only two people were linked to all three cases, himself being one of them. He knew that he was a good Doctor, but not that good. No one was that good, able to bring someone back to life like that. That only left...

He started the engine and began to make his way home. He would not mention his suspicions to anyone, as there was no proof. But he knew, he knew! In one week's time he should be able to find out how it had been done, as he and Penny were expecting guests. The Olsen family were coming for Sunday Lunch!

Sunday lunch had been eaten and enjoyed by all. It had been a nice joint of beef from Benton's Butchers. The conversation had eventually come around to the miracle recovery of Freddy Piper. Both Tom and Penny had visited him during the week, and Tom had contacted the old Doctor that he had replaced, to also pop in and make his own assessment, as he had been treating Freddy for much longer than Tom had. Later he had come around to the surgery and had a chat with Tom. Like him, he had never seen such a turnaround in a patient before. Neither had the specialist who had done a very rare house call on Tom's insistence. They had both been staggered by what they had found.

Tom had looked at Freya during the conversation but her face had given nothing away. Freya had used the half-term break to recover herself. The weather had been mostly wet and she had not gone out much. As soon as she had arrived at Tom and Penny's she knew that something was wrong with Tom. His aura had changed completely. She also knew why. He knew. Or rather he thought he knew. Somehow he had linked her to the recovery of Freddy, she could not work out how, but she knew he had. She would have to find out just how much he actually knew, and what he only suspected and take the necessary action. Outwardly Tom was his usual self, but he didn't fool Freya. So when Tom invited Freya to join him downstairs in his consulting room for a moment to ask her opinion on something, she agreed at once.

Tom went behind his desk and sat in his large leather chair, and invited Freya to sit in the smaller chair at the side of the desk that the patients used. For a moment, Tom had a twinge of doubt. Could he be wrong? No. He had spent a good deal of time wondering how he would go about this, he was a University educated Doctor and surgeon, Freya was a little girl who was not yet nine years old. He had decided on the direct approach and try to get her to slip up.

"How are you doing it?"

Freya raised an eyebrow, her face expressionless, her green eyes just looking back at Tom. "Doing what, Uncle Tom?"

"Saving people's lives who would most certainly have died, not least your own." Freya smiled. "No, Uncle Tom, that's what you do. You saved me, remember?

Tom shook his head. "We both know that is not true. Somehow you saved yourself, and now I think you saved your Aunty Rose, Mr Winter and last week , Freddy Piper!"

"Me, Uncle Tom? You saved me after the accident, you operated on Aunty Rose and Mr Winter, and I have never spoken to Freddy Piper! You are an excellent Doctor, everyone says so!"

Tom looked at Freya. She was very good. He would not like to play poker against her, he thought to himself, you just never know what she is thinking. He did not know that he was playing poker against her now. And losing. He tried again.

"Apart from me, there is only one other person who is connected to all those cases, and that person is you, Freya. Rose's appendix should have burst long before she got to the hospital, yet it did not. Mr Winter's leg would have moved more than it did, and one of the bones would have severed an artery and he would have bled to death long before he got to hospital. And the day after I met you outside Freddy Pipers house, he recovers from a terminal illness that no one in the history of medicine has recovered from. It has to be you, god knows how, but it does."

Freya said nothing. She just looked at Tom as he went on.

"In each case, there were faint marks on all three bodies. On Rose's appendix, on Mr Winters leg and on Freddy's hand. Marks like small fingers would make. I think they were your fingers, Freya. I know it sounds crazy, but I believe that somehow you are healing people. So, I ask you again. How are you doing it?"

Freya continued to gaze back at Tom, her face giving absolutely nothing away while her mind absorbed what he had said. So that's how he suspects me! Thanks for letting me know. "Have you told anyone else about your theory, Uncle Tom?" she asked.

Tom shook his head. "No. They would think that I had lost my mind and that I might be unfit to practice medicine. But I'm right, am I not? It all fits. Somehow it has to be you, impossible as it seems!"

Freya sighed. "Not only are you a superb Doctor and someone who I am so very close to, but you are also an excellent detective. Well done. Here's how it works. "And she held out her hands to him, while planting a thought in his mind. Tom could not stop himself from taking her hands in his, before immediately realising his mistake. Too late. There was a brief spark of triumph in his eyes, before he slumped back in his chair as a wave of fatigue swept over him. In that brief moment before he lost conscience, he knew that he had been right, and also knowing that he had lost. Freya rose from her chair and looked down at the sleeping man slumped in the leather chair. He would wake in a few minutes and remember nothing about marks on bodies, or of their conversation. It had to be this way. Freya looked around the room. The room where her letter to the old Doctor had been read and now where Tom sat in that chair. She moved around the desk and headed for the stairs, pausing for a last look at Tom. Softly she said to herself, "And now only I know the truth!" before leaving the room and going upstairs to join the others. She had been gone less than five minutes.

"Uncle Tom will be up in a minute," she said to Penny in the kitchen.

"What have you two been doing down there?" she asked.

"Oh just helping Uncle Tom make the right decision on something, you know what men are like!" said Freya with a wink. Penny laughed. "Where would they be without us?" she said. Freya smiled. "Not where we want them!" and she touched Penny on the arm and went out to the sitting room. Penny would not remember talking to Freya either.

A week had passed since her son had recovered. She could still not quite believe it. Every day he got stronger. He was eating and drinking more and more and keeping it down. The drip had been removed and once again he could enjoy the simple luxury of being able to turn over in bed. His other medication was constantly being reduced, and soon he would not need any! In a little while more they should be able to move his bed back upstairs to his room! She could not take it all in. She had steeled herself to losing her only son and facing the lonely years ahead alone. She had not dared to hope that he would overcome his illness, and yet a miracle had happened. Freddy would live.

She was walking around the village alone, just looking at things. It was all the same as it was before, yet it was all different. The air was raw and damp, there had been quite a good fog the night before and here and there patches lingered in the November air. She took some deep breaths and had never smelled anything better. The world was now a much better place. In the far distance she could see three figures making their way down into the village. A very large man, a smaller and slimmer woman and a girl with blond hair in a ponytail. A family. She had a family again. She was truly blessed.

She began to make her way home, her parents were keeping an eye on Freddy. She had just wanted to get out for a while alone. Next week she and Freddy were going to Abbotsbury to see the consultant and two top men who were coming up from London. Freddy's case had caused huge interest in the medical world. This had never happened before, ever. They wanted to know how he had done it. She didn't care how, just that he had been spared. What a Christmas they were going to have! It was a miracle.

She turned into Coleman Street and saw her mother talking to a strange man on the doorstep. As she approached her mother saw her. "Ah there you are, dear. It seems that news of Freddy's recovery has spread. This gentleman is a reporter!"

Astra was, as usual the first to read the local newspaper, as she was the one who carried it from the "Time Flies" public house after her weekly visit to see Lucy. Lucy would retrieve it from the bin and keep it for her friends up on the wold. This week's edition had on its front page the headline,

MIRACLE BOY!

There was a picture of a smiling boy called Freddy Piper and his mother, followed by the story of his miracle recovery, which had baffled the medical world. Someone had done their research and there was reference to a Doctor Tom Thornton, the local Doctor who had worked his magic two years earlier when he had saved another child who had been badly injured in a car crash. That child had been called Freya Olsen.

Astra read the rest of the story and was about to turn the page when she looked at the picture again and then froze. The picture of the boy and his mother had been taken at the boy's home in Elfington. To pass the time while he recovered, he had done some drawings, and one of them was just about visible in the picture. Astra's eyesight was exceptional, but to be sure she got a magnifying glass. Yes. She had been right. Seen in close up, the picture the boy had drawn was of a cat. A cat with spots on its coat, tufted ears and green eyes!

The green eyes of Freya Olsen had also read the story. She was so glad that Freddy was going to make a full recovery, but reading about herself had brought back the memory of the accident more vividly. She still could remember nothing about it, except that it had changed her life forever and started her on a new path here in Elfington. Soon she would be nine years old, and would spend her third birthday in England. She had already given herself the best present she could. The life of Freddy Piper.

She wished she could remember what had happened the night of the crash, but there was still a fog in her mind that hid the truth. What she did know was since that night she had been given powers that no one else had. Why? Why her? She did not know. It was all connected to the accident, about which she could remember nothing. She knew that until she could solve the mystery, she would not be complete. Maybe in the future she would remember, but until then she would live her life one day at a time.

She put down the paper and moved to the window, drawing aside the lace curtain and drinking in the beauty of the wold beyond. There was just something about it that stirred something inside her. Perhaps the answers she sought were there? She did not know that they were.

Time passed quickly and before anyone knew it, it was Catmus day! For Tog and Millie it was their first and after a lovely meal everyone gathered around the roaring log fire and retold the stories of how they all came to be here in the hideaway and their first meeting with the Cats. Hugo began with the chase, then Astra entered into it, telling of how she had seen her chance to escape the humans and be free. Jago came next and then Lucky, Barney and finally Tog and Millie. Lucy was not forgotten and Lucky told her story for her.

Tog and Millie listened wide eyed to the tale as it unfolded, fascinated by how it had all started. For both of them, it was the first time they had heard the whole story from the start. Millie, sitting next to Tog was spellbound. As she listened she decided that humans were not to be trusted, although she had yet to set eyes on a real live one. Tog had promised to show her some next year. Although Millie was only four months old, she was growing quickly and understood all of what she was being told. She could already communicate with all the others, although her vocabulary was still quite small, but like her was growing every day!

She was very respectful of the others, giving them the titles of Aunty or Uncle where appropriate. Tog was a special case. She called him father.

The first part of March 1965 had been wet and windy, but towards the end of the month the weather improved just in time for the end of the term holiday at Easter. Munch had recovered from his humiliation of the sugar cube inoculation saga and was back to his old menacing ways. He had gathered a new gang of three other would-be "hard cases" to go around with him. He had also started smoking. He had pinched the odd fag from his dad and his brother, but they soon began to notice so he was forced to buy ten of the cheapest fags he could find from the local shop, saying that they were for his dad.

The shop keeper knew at once that they were really for him, as his dad smoked a different brand, but sold them to him anyway. If the stupid sod wanted to ruin his health, it was all right with him! To fund his smoking habit, Munch needed cash. He helped himself to a few coins from his mother's purse when she was not looking, but dared not to take too much in case she noticed. So he and his gang would threaten selected children in school and around the village to give them money, or else! The usual demand was a threepenny bit, or depending who it was, a tanner. Since most children were like him and got no pocket money, he had to choose his victims carefully. But there were enough kids to keep him and his followers in fags and matches.

Freddy Piper was back at school on a regular basis and was really enjoying being there. It was so nice to be around other children and to feel so well. He and the other infants were kept separate from the older children and had their own part of the playground to play in. Freya had managed to introduce herself to him and with Miss

Foster's approval they would chat now and again, something that they both enjoyed. They shared a common bond that went far beyond what had been reported in the newspaper.

When the school term came to a close at the end of March, it was strange to think that the dairy and the railway had been closed for a year already, and that Lars had worked for that long at the Old Wood Farm. The job was now permanently his, as the man who had broken his leg had decided that claiming the dole was better than working and he had told Mr Briggs that he would not be coming back. Both Alan Briggs and Lars were delighted at that news and had a drink in the "Time Flies" public house with their respective other halves to celebrate.

Freya and Dutch spent as much time together as possible during the Easter break and one day they rode their bikes down to the old dairy where Lars had worked and then on to the railway station. They were both shocked at how they had both fallen into such disrepair in just one year. There were weeds everywhere and at the railway station the track had been removed, leaving just the imprints of the wooden sleepers in the stones. It was very sad to see these places that had been so busy and part of the village life to end up like this. As they had looked down at the station from the road bridge, Mr Lamb drove past in his car and tooted his horn at them as he passed, getting waves from the friends as he went by. He was as busy as ever, getting recommendations from satisfied customers who had told their friends. Both Penny and Rose had passed their driving tests. First time!

Soon it would be Tom and Penny's wedding, which was to be at the small church in Wallbridge, St Joseph's. Freya was really looking forward to her role as a brides maid, but before that there was the Easter holidays to enjoy, and of course, Easter eggs!

Freya was not feeling well, and had been under the weather for a few days. She had stomach ache and head aches and generally felt grotty, which was unknown for her, as she was never ill and had always been full of energy. She was also finding it hard to concentrate, which again was something she had always been able to do with ease. She felt unsettled. Something was wrong.

She had not mentioned it to either Lars or Rose, hoping it was only a temporary thing and would go away in a few days, but it had not. Today was the Thursday before Easter and the Doctor's surgery would be closed until the Tuesday morning after Easter, when it would be stuffed. She decided to go and see Aunty Penny and have a chat with her off the record rather than see Doctor Tom officially, which would have to include taking Aunty Rose with her as children did not go to see the Doctor on their own.

She made her way down to the village on foot and tried to avoid people where possible, as she did not feel like conversation at the moment, which was again not normal for her. Just as she entered an alley that was a short cut to the doctor's she experienced a wave of nausea and had to sit on a stone wall for a while until it had passed. Such was her condition that for the first time she was unaware that others had followed her into the alley until a shadow fell across her and a voice said, "Give me sixpence or we'll get you!" Freya had not even heard anyone coming up behind her. Munch. It would just have to be him sneaking up behind her on this of all days. From nowhere a dark rage like she had never known swept over her and in a blur of movement Freya was on her feet, hands making fists as she launched herself at Munch. A perfect left hook with a fist of steel landed on the side of Munch's head, and a right cross of equal power connected with the right side of his face a microsecond later. Munch went down like a sack of spuds, blood flowing from his nose and mouth. He lay on the path moaning, completely stunned. Freya whirled around to face the other three boys, fists raised and eyes flashing, ready if they were foolish enough to want what their leader had just got. They were not. They just stood there, in total shock as Freya asked in a low voice. "Anyone else want sixpence? You?" she said looking at the nearest boy. A hasty shake of the head.

"You?" another shake of the head. "You?" The last one copied the others. Freya lowered her fists and took a step closer to them. "Final warning! Stay out of my way, or you'll get what I just gave him. Got it?"

Three scared and pale faces nodded agreement. All of a sudden they had lost all interest in mugging people for money. With a last look at Munch, who was still on the ground, Freya turned on her heel and walked away down the alley on shaky legs, not looking back, knowing that the others would not follow her.

Turning around a bend in the alley so Munch and his mob could not see her, Freya stopped and leaned back against a wall and took some deep breaths to calm herself. It was then that she became aware of something wet trickling down her leg. In alarm she put her hand inside her trousers and gasped when she saw what it was. Blood. She was bleeding, but how could that be? She had not been injured just now. With a fresh purpose, Freya continued on to the Doctor's, praying that she would not encounter anyone else before she got there. She was lucky. With considerable relief she opened the door to the Doctor's waiting room to find it empty. Penny was sitting behind the open top half of the stable door of the dispensary and smiled as she saw Freya coming in, the smile fading quickly as she saw the distress on Freya's face. Quickly she opened the lower half of the door and came out into the waiting room and met Freya in the middle. "What's the matter, Freya? You look pale. "

"Aunty Penny, I feel sick and I am bleeding."

"Bleeding? Where from?"

"Down there," said Freya.

A look of understanding crossed Penny's face as she guided Freya into Tom's consulting room.

"There's no one here, Tom is upstairs, up on the bed with you and I'll have a look," said Penny, closing the door behind her. Leaving Freya on the examination bed for a moment, she went around to secure the dispensary, before returning to the bed. A quick examination confirmed her initial diagnosis.

"Well, Freya, I'm delighted to tell you that there is nothing seriously wrong with you. What has happened is you are having a period. This is what happens once a month when you start to change from being a girl to a young woman. Welcome to the club!"

Freya was staggered. "How can this be? I am only nine and a half, I'm too young to be a woman yet. Are you sure?"

Penny smiled. "Quite sure, Freya. Nine and a half is a little early, but I was not much over ten when I started, so let's get you cleaned up and we can have a cup of tea and a chat, as I am sure that you have many questions."

An hour later Freya made her way home, very aware of the towel she was wearing and carrying a bag in which were a packet of spare ones that Penny had given her. Penny had explained that ladies had to cope with this business once a month, and what had happened to her and what would happen in the future, both physically and emotionally, as her body continued to change into a woman. Freya had asked lots of questions and Penny was able to answer all of them with ease, being a woman and a nurse. By the time Freya left the surgery, she felt so much better now she knew what was happening to her, and was almost back to her old self once more. She had not mentioned to Penny anything about Munch and his gang and was starting to feel that she had over reacted. She did not regret battering Munch, he had had that coming for a long time, and if it had not been her, it would have been someone else.

Being a bully, you always ran the risk that you would pick on the wrong person one day, and he had learned that lesson this morning. Freya was disappointed with herself. With her gifts, she of all people should be able to use her mind and her femininity to control the Munches of this world without punching them. After all, she was a woman now and must conduct herself properly!

The alley was empty as she walked back home, there was only a few drops of blood on the path to show that anything had happened. She did not know if it was his or hers, not that it mattered. It was done, and could not be un-done. She was back home for lunch and told Aunty Rose about her adventures of the morning, leaving out the part about Munch. During the afternoon she went out into the garden and that was where Dutch found her when he called around. He pretended to be wary about coming into the garden, asking if it was safe.

It never ceased to amaze Freya how quickly news could travel around the village. Everyone knows everyone. Dutch had heard that Freya had beaten up Munch and had knocked him out. Clearly the tale had already undergone some embellishment. They sat down together and she told him most of the truth, leaving out the bit about her becoming a woman, knowing that he would not understand, as she would not have a few hours earlier.

When she had finished, he looked at her and told her he wished he had been there to protect her, not that it seemed she had needed his help. She surprised him by giving him a hug and a kiss, touched by his sincerity and believing that he really would have fought Munch to save her. She really was very fond of Dutch and always would be. Now she was turning into a woman, but she knew that he would remain a boy for some years yet. It did not matter to her. She would wait for him to catch up.

When Dutch left to go home for tea, he thought of what Freya had told him. What a girl! The child who had come back from the dead and gone on to rid the school of Mrs Hunter, had now sorted out the school bully. He had strong feelings for Freya and really wished he had been there to protect her. He knew that the name of Freya Olsen would go down in the village folklore, never to be forgotten. He also knew that what Freya had done to Munch would never reach the ears of any adult, but stay between the children of Elfington. Soon every school child would know what had happened today. All would come to the same conclusion. Don't mess with the Vikings!

Chapter Thirty-Six

Freya had made a decision. She would go to Munch's house and apologise for punching him. He had no right to go around with his gang threatening people, but she thought that she had over reacted. Just because she could beat him up, did not mean that she should. Violence was not the answer to the Munch's of this world, tempting as it was in his case. She was disappointed with herself. She of all people should know how to use the power of her mind to control the thugs of the village, and not to become one herself. By pure chance, Munch had caught her at a very vulnerable moment, and she had lost control of herself briefly. Now that Penny had explained what was happening to her, she would be able to deal with it again.

She was surprised that his parents had not been to her house to complain, but they had not. So on the Wednesday morning after Easter, and feeling so much better and back to her old self, Freya set off to Munch's house, a bar of chocolate in her coat pocket to give him by way of compensation.

The Wild family lived on a rundown small holding down a dirt track, not far from the Railway station. It did not take long to get there on her bike, as it was all downhill. She found the ramshackle cottage about half a mile down the track, and as she rounded a bend, a black and white dog on a long lead made of string started barking at her approach. Freya dismounted and looked at the dog, concentrating her mind on it, telling it that she meant it no harm and that she was only visiting, and asking permission to pass by. The dog stopped barking and sat down, its head on one side as if it was listening to her. Slowly, its tail started to wag. Freya knew that on a very basic level, she had managed to communicate with the dog. Freya waited for a moment before slowly approaching the dog, using her mind to talk to it, repeating what she had already said again.

The dog allowed her to stroke it and Freya looked around and saw a bucket next to a dripping tap in the yard. She went over to it and filled the bucket and placed it next to the dog, who immediately started drinking noisily. Leaving the dog to enjoy its drink, she approached the door of the house and knocked.

She waited a while and was just about to knock again when the door opened and a large woman stood before her with a surprised look on her face. The ruddy complexion and big frame told Freya that she had found Munch's mother.

"Yes?" It was clear that the Wild house did not receive many visitors.

"Mrs Wild?" asked Freya.

The woman nodded warily.

306

"My name is Freya. I go to school with Mun—, er Richard. I am here to see how he is. I am very sorry about what I…"

"Ah, yes," said Mrs Wild, smiling, cutting Freya off. "Come in, come in. I wondered if anyone would come. Such a business. Poor Richard."

Freya found herself in a large warm kitchen, with a large range taking up most of one side of the room. Opposite the range were two doors, which Freya instinctively knew no one but the Wild family went through.

For the few visitors, the kitchen was as far as they would ever go.

"Please sit down, er, Freda, so nice of you to come. Richard is out in the yard somewhere, but he will be in soon, I'm sure. He has not left the farm since his injury."

Freya pulled out a wooden chair from under the large kitchen table, its legs making a loud scraping noise on the red tiled floor. She sat down and tried again.

"Mrs Wild. I am sorry for what happened to, er Richard, but you see…"

"Yes I quite agree," said Mrs Wild, cutting Freya off again. "It's a sad state of affairs when an innocent child cannot walk about the village without being set upon by a gang of yobs!"

"Yobs?"

"Yes! Poor Richard. There he was, minding his own business as usual, when he was attacked by four louts from somewhere, demanding money! They were probably day trippers going up to Cropwell Manor for the funfair, I shouldn't wonder. He managed to fight off two of them, but he didn't stand a chance against four. Anyway, after he had knocked down two of them, the others ran off, they aren't used to people standing up to them, you see. I'm so proud of him!"

Freya slid the bar of chocolate she had brought with her back into her pocket. So. That's what he had told his mother! The lying little toad! And she had come here to apologise to him!

"It must have been quite a shock for you when he came home," said Freya, her mind working furiously. "I wonder, Mrs Wild, if Richard got a look at any of them?"

"I don't know, I don't think so, he said it all happened very quickly," said Mrs Wild.

"Yes, I'm sure it did. Well, I think you should consider reporting it to the police, after all, Mrs Wild, they could have attacked you!"

"You know, I never thought of that, maybe we should."

Just then, Munch came in. "Who's that bike out there belong to…?" he said, his voice trailing off, as he answered his own question when he saw Freya.

"Ah, there you are, Richard. Freda here has kindly come to see how you are, I was just telling her all about it. Wasn't that kind of her?"

Munch just stood there, rooted to the spot, the colour draining from his face, except for the blue, black, yellow and purple bruising around both of his eyes. The two green eyes that gazed back at him were as cold as the North Pole.

His mouth opened and closed, but no sound came out. He was in the shit up to his neck, and knew it.

His mother continued. "Freda here was asking if you got a look at any of those thugs who attacked you, as it might be wise to report it to the police. What do you think?"

"Police?" he managed to whisper.

"Yes, the Police, er, Richard," said Freya," I was just asking your mother, we just cannot have gangs roaming around the village attacking innocent people, can we? I mean, they could have attacked me! And I know what my Uncle would do if that had happened," said Freya, twisting the knife and watching him squirm.

Munch had started to sweat, and he looked desperately at his mother.

"No Police Ma! I told you I didn't get a good look at them, and they are long gone by now!"

Mrs Wild looked at Freya. "What do you think, Freda?"

Freya pretended to consider it, while her eyes bored into Munch's, watching him sweat, enjoying his discomfort. Making him wait.

Finally she said, "I think Richard is right, Mrs Wild," getting up and moving over to where Munch sat. Gently she reached out and took his face in her hand, turning it left and right as if examining the injury.

Her back was to Munch's mother, so only he could see her eyes and the expression on her face. Her message was crystal clear. In your face! Literally!

She released his face and turned to face Mrs Wild again. "By the time we go back to school, he should be back to normal, so perhaps it is best to leave things as they are. We will have to hope that the gang does not come back, or it will have to be a Police matter then."

Mrs Wild nodded. "I agree, would you like a cup of tea, my dear?"

Freya, who had been about to go, smiled. "That would be very nice of you, thank you. Are you having one, Richard?"

Munch shook his head, just wanting to get out of the room and away from her, before she talked his mother into enrolling him into Sunday school.

"Er, no. I think I'll go to my room now and have a lie down." He needed one!

Mrs Wild and Freya traded a "Men were such wimps" look between them as Munch opened one of the doors and made his escape.

As he climbed the stairs to his room, he realised for the first time in his life just how dangerous women could be if you crossed them, especially when they put their heads together! He also realised just how lucky he had been to get off so lightly. If Freya ever told his mother, or worse still, her Uncle what had really happened, he would be dead meat! The truth would come out, as the other three boys who had been there would crumble under questioning, no doubt blaming it all on him to save themselves.

He also had to admit that Freya had got guts. She had dared to come into his house, sitting on his chairs, and was even now drinking tea in his kitchen, with his mother! She could have dropped him right in it, no doubt about it. She had won. He knew it, and she knew it. He would watch his step in future, around her. Half an hour later, Freya said her goodbyes to her new friend Mrs Wild and went outside to collect her bike. As she wheeled it out of the yard she stopped as the dog came towards her, tail wagging furiously. Freya noticed that the bucket of water was already half empty, so she laid her bike on the ground and took the bucket and filled it up and put it where the dog could reach it. The dog was licking her hand and Freya walked to where there was a patch of sunshine and sat down, the dog sat next to her, having already detected the chocolate bar in her pocket. They sat together in the warm spring sunshine and shared the chocolate together, the dog having the lion's share of it, he was far more worthy than the person for whom she had intended to give it to. She hoped Munch would take heed of the thoughts she had planted in his mind, always assuming that there was a mind between his ears to plant thoughts into! He'd better! She sat with the dog for a while longer before saying her goodbyes to it and making her way home.

True to his word, Tog took Millie outside to show her what a human looked like, and the nearest place that there would be humans to see was the Old Wood Farm. It was spring and Millie was six months old and almost fully grown. She had not as yet asked Tog where she had come from and how she had come to be in the hideaway. When that day came, Tog had decided to simply tell her the truth.

Hugo, Jago and Lucky had asked Tog if they could come with them and so they set off and made their way to the Old Wood Farm. Just as they left, Barney was reminded of a poem he had read recently, by someone named Edward Lear, called "The Owl and the Pussycat"! He chuckled to himself all morning about that! The others, unaware of the humour they had created, had arrived at their destination and they found a good spot where they could see the farm yard and waited. They were lucky, as after only five minutes, two male humans appeared together. To Millie, they were huge, especially one of them, who was much bigger than the other. She was in fact looking at Lars and Alan. She watched them as they walked around, only using two legs to do so. Clearly they were powerful, but to her appeared clumsy and they wore coverings on their bodies, probably to keep them warm. She also noticed they had some sort of machines which they used to help them do things. She was somewhat underwhelmed by the two specimens before her, they had not lived up to her expectations. Eventually, the two humans left the yard and disappeared somewhere else.

Tog said that there was one other human at the farm, a female, who did not come outside much, so they might as well return home before it started to rain. So they made their way back to the hideaway and vanished back inside, arriving back in the main chamber in time for lunch. Lucky had read the latest copy of the local newspaper that Astra had brought in the night before from her visit to see Lucy. She pointed to a story inside on page seven. LOCAL DOCTOR TO MARRY NURSE. Millie read it with her and when she had finished, she looked at Aunty Lucky, not understanding its relevance. Lucky said, "When there is a human wedding, they invite lots of other humans to see it, young, old, male and female, fat and thin. A nice collection for you to have a look at. With Tog's approval, you and I are going to that human wedding and you can have a good look at them. What do you think?"

Millie was intrigued. "But, Aunty Lucky, how can we go to a human wedding?" she asked.

Lucky smiled. "I've got a plan!"

The Sixth of May was a Bank Holiday, and as luck would have it, actually a nice warm and sunny day.

Tom, Penny, Lars, Rose, Freya and Dutch had driven out in Tom's car to the country to have a change of scenery and had ended up at a pub for a lunch time drink. The pub was on the far side of Abbotsbury, on the edge of a place called Churchwell, a place that both Rose and Penny had got to know while out learning to drive with Mr Lamb. Although they did not know it, they were not far from Quentin Drummond's flat.

As the weather was so nice they sat outside on a wooden picnic table and relaxed. There were daffodils, snowdrops and crocuses in clumps on the lawn, adding splashes of colour against the green grass. The trees were starting to come into leaf and birdsong filled the air. It was a nice peaceful day before the wedding, now only a few days away. Everyone was excited, but Freya realised that had it not been for the accident that had taken her parents, none of them would be enjoying this lovely day together. That one terrible event had changed all of their lives and brought them to this place, on this day, at this moment in time. They were meant to be here, and soon they would realise why.

A few tables away and slightly behind a small bush were a group of three men, who were drinking and laughing loudly, and making comments, mostly about the women who were sitting nearby. Clearly they had been drinking for quite a while. Both Tom and Lars had glanced over to them more than once, when the swearing got a bit loud. As always seems to be the case, there was someone to try and spoil the purity of the day. A couple at the next table to the group had had enough and got up and went inside the pub, and as expected one of the men passed comment about the woman as she walked by, remarking to his pals that she had a "nice arse on her" and laughing with his pals at her discomfort. Clearly the men felt very confident in their group and did not worry about being challenged. The one who had made the crude remark looked over at Freya's table, and then spoke to the man who had his back to it.

"Roger, tell me I'm wrong, but isn't that what's her name that you used to go out with, the nurse?"

The man called Roger turned around and looked over, just as Penny looked up. For an instant, their eyes met. Quickly she looked down again while he continued to stare. Finally he turned back to his pals and said in a loud voice, "Yeh, I think it is," and joined in the laughter with the others. Penny had gone pale and Tom asked quietly, "What is it, Penny, are they bothering you?"

Penny turned to him, tears in her eyes. "Oh, Tom, it's him! Roger. I'm sure of it!"

The others were looking at Tom and Penny, wondering what had happened. Tom looked grim and reached into his jacket pocket and pulled out his car keys and handed them to Dutch.

"Dutch, would you be so kind as to escort these ladies back to the car and wait for us there, while Mr Olsen and I go and have a word with those gentlemen." He had spoken in his usual voice, but clearly he would not take no for an answer. Dutch nodded. "Yes sir."

Tom looked around the table. "Please go with Dutch, we won't be long," said Tom, his face quite calm, but again, not about to have a debate about it.

Everyone got up, and as Freya did so, she put her hand on Tom's, and said, "Take care, Uncle Tom."

She knew what was coming and had just increased his strength and reflexes three fold. He nodded, unaware of what she had just done. Penny also touched Tom's arm, her eyes pleading. "Tom, please ignore them and come with us, he's not worth bothering with."

Tom smiled grimly and kissed her lightly on the cheek. "Don't worry, I won't hurt him too much, although he deserves to be. Go with Dutch and wait in the car." Reluctantly, Penny turned away and followed the others across the lawn towards the car. Tom looked at Lars and said, "All I can tell you is that one of those men was very unkind to Penny before she met me, and if you could keep the other two away while I put some manners on him, I will be very grateful."

Lars nodded. He had heard enough. Penny meant a great deal to him as well. Together they walked over to the table where the three men were drinking. Lars tapped Roger on the shoulder and said, "My friend would like a word with you."

"Fuck off," said Roger, not bothering to even turn around to see who had spoken. Suddenly he found himself flying through the air and landed on the lawn close to where Tom was waiting. Lars had just picked him up as if he weighed nothing and thrown him across the lawn. "Wrong answer," said Lars, who then sat down in Roger's seat and looked at the other two. "Just sit where you are, and I won't hurt you."

The other two, suddenly stone cold sober, looked at the giant Viking sitting in front of them and his huge muscles. That and the look in his eyes told them all they needed to know. They remained in their seats. Roger was on his own.

Tom circled around Roger, who had got to his feet and was looking over at his table, wondering if he could catch who ever had thrown him with a sneaky punch from behind. One look at the giant sitting in his seat changed his mind. No chance. With no help from his mates he tried to talk his way out of trouble. No chance again!

"Look, mate, I'm sorry about what happened with Penny, but that's all in the past now, no need to get excited about it, let's just go our separate ways and leave it at that."

Tom just looked at him, then suddenly, he moved with lightning speed, surprising himself, and caught Roger with two hammer body blows, before moving away again. Roger grunted, and fell to one knee, pain radiating around his body. He got up with difficulty, his face set in a snarl.

"OK, if that's the way you want it, she was a tart, and got what a tart deserved. Now you are going to get yours." He swung a punch at Tom, who side stepped it and landed two more hard punches to the body, before moving away again.

They had moved quite away from the table, where the two others watched their pal getting systematically beaten up. Tom moved closer again.

"You piece of shit, you raped her. She pleaded with you to stop, begged you to stop, but you just did it anyway, then left her lying on the floor when you were done. I'm so glad we have met at last. A man should be accountable for his past." Roger had sagged again, but suddenly lunged forward towards Tom, who moved nimbly to one side and again unloaded two more hard punches to Roger's body as it went past. Being a Doctor, he knew where to hit someone. Roger was in considerable pain, but lunged forward again. Tom finished him off with a fist of iron to the solar plexus, and as the body came down, caught Roger with a jaw-breaking right cross to the head. Roger crumpled to the ground and did not get up again. He lay there, moaning in pain. Good.

Tom walked back to the table and touched Lars lightly on the shoulder. "Thanks, Lars, we can go and join the ladies now."

Lars nodded and looked at the shocked faces of the other two. "Stay away from Elfington and treat ladies with respect. Got it?" Two heads nodded. Lars stood and together he and Tom walked away back to the car, not a care in the world. The car park was behind a tall hedge and they had seen nothing. Penny hugged Tom and asked, "Are you all right, Tom, are you hurt?"

Tom smiled. "I'm fine. I don't know about you lot, but I fancy another drink! I think we should get to the "Time Flies" in time for one. I'm buying."

Dutch handed over the car keys and Tom said, "Thanks Dutch" and Lars gave him a pat on the back. Suddenly Dutch felt he had joined an exclusive club. As they drove along back to Elfington, he thought that if anyone tried to harm Freya, he would kill them, or die in the attempt. Freya, sitting next to him, reached out and held his hand, almost as if she could read his mind. She could.

Later that day, as darkness fell over Elfington, Penny sat on the bed she shared with Tom and looked at her reflection in the dressing table mirror, thinking about the events of the day. Her man had fought for her and tried to right, as far as that particular wrong could ever be righted, a wrong done to her almost seven years ago. Strangely, she felt a huge relief, like a great weight being lifted from her. Now she could get married. Tomorrow, Tom would become a healer again. But first.

She walked into the living room, and stood before Tom, who was sitting on the sofa. He looked up at her and smiled. She looked down at him for a long time, just as she had that first time at her cottage, the night she told him what Roger had done to her. He noticed that she had changed into a jumper. It was the same one she had worn back then. His mouth went dry as he realised what was about to happen. Slowly, she reached down to the bottom of the jumper and pulled it over her head, arching her back as she had done before, her breasts standing out against her ribs. She moved her hands up to them, but the nipples did not need much in the way of stimulation, and were already erect. She moved forward, her eyes never leaving his and carefully placed one leg on each side of his body and then sat on his knees.

Tom moved his hands up over her hips and cupped each breast in his hands, hearing her gasp as he did so. Finally he spoke. "I love you. Will you marry me?"

Penny smiled back as his hands started to move. "Yes. What are you doing on Saturday?"

Mrs Penny Thornton lay in bed next to her husband of a few hours, back in the flat above the surgery. She was twisting her new and unfamiliar wedding ring around her finger, too excited and happy to sleep, not wanting the day to end. She had just made love to her husband, just like that first time in his flat, after they had finally escaped from Abbotsbury Hospital after being marooned by the snow. Like that first time, she had tried to make it last as long as possible, wanting to please him, wanting to love him, wanting him to love her. He had and now the perfect day had just become a little extra perfect. The day had gone like clockwork, the ceremony, the photos, the reception, even the weather had been warm and sunny. It could not have gone better. An old friend and colleague from the A & E department at Abbotsbury Hospital had told her that a man had been brought in on the Bank Holiday Afternoon, which she had agreed to work in order to get the Saturday off for the wedding. He had looked vaguely familiar, and she remembered that he had gone out with Penny many years ago. Good job that she had not married him! The man had stank of drink and had been in a fight, and looked a real mess.

Penny smiled to herself in the darkness. Good job indeed. She turned over and cuddled up to Tom, feeling his warmth. She remembered again what Tom had said to her the night she had told him her secret. He had said that it was not her fault, just wrong place, wrong man and wrong time. He had been right, as he usually was. Now as she lay next to her husband she was in the right place, at the right time and with the right man. She had never thought that she could love anyone as much as she loved Tom. Tomorrow, they would drive to Blackpool for a week's honeymoon. But as she finally started to fall asleep, she was as happy as any woman could ever be. Out of something very bad, something very good had come. The circle of life.

As darkness fell over the wold, Millie sat in front of the glowing embers of the fire, and continued to tell Tog all about the events of the day. She had seen lots and lots of humans, all ages, shapes and sizes at the human wedding. She had sat next to Lucky, the Owl and the pussycat, in the branches of a tree growing in the churchyard of the small Church in Wallbridge and watched, fascinated at the goings on below her. The humans had assembled outside, and then all gone inside the church for a while, before coming out again. She had liked the organ music and the singing. After everyone had gone inside, she had climbed down from the tree and managed to climb up a sloping wall and look through the window at the ceremony inside.

It had surprised her that a cat could walk around where ever it wanted and no one bothered, whereas if Tog or Astra had done it, they would have been noticed, reported and captured. What funny things humans were. She had re-joined Lucky back in the tree when the humans came outside again and continued to watch what was going on. One human stood out much more than any other, and Millie mentioned it to Aunty Lucky. She also had noticed that particular human, and not for the first time. It was the girl from the sports day, and the one that Lucky had had brief telepathic contact with at the school. The girl had a much bigger aura than any of the others. While they looked at her, the girl looked up, directly at the spot where they were sitting, as if she had felt the weight of their eyes looking at her. Millie and Lucky knew that she could not see them, but it was strange that she had known where they were. Lucky told Millie that the girl had also looked at her perch when she was watching the sports day.

Both of them wondered if this human could be the special one the Gallownians had told them would come. They could not see the sign they needed to see, and anyway, this was the wrong place. Contact, whenever it came, would be on the wold. But still, that child definitely had something the others did not. They were right.

Freya had enjoyed the wedding immensely. As bridesmaid, she had got almost as much attention as Penny and Tom. She had, of course worn her special necklace, but the style of her dress had hidden it from view. After the service in the Church, there had been the photos outside. While posing for them, she had felt a sensation that someone was looking at her. Of course, lots of people were looking at her, but this was different, someone was *looking* at her.

Instinctively she looked up at a tree nearby, knowing that was where the look was coming from, just the same as the feeling she had got at the sports day. Freya never forgot anything. She could see nothing, but she was sure that there was some one, or something there. She was correct. She also knew that whatever it was would not harm her, the sensation she felt was a happy one. She turned back to the photographer and smiled.

The reception had been very good, but the music had been too loud, and on the way home, her ears were ringing. Dutch had looked very handsome in his suit. He had the job of usher, and he had ensured that everyone was in the correct pew and that they had an order of service and prayer book. She had sat with him and danced with him, and hoped that one day she would be the bride and Dutch would be the groom. But that would be in the future, after all, she had only just become a woman, and Dutch was still a boy. It was not the time. Yet.

It was very late when Freya climbed into her bed and Rose tucked her in. When she had gone to her own bedroom, Freya cuddled up to her Troll and was instantly asleep. As always, her parents were waiting for her, and she had much to tell them.

Chapter Thirty-Seven

Quentin Drummond lay back against the pillows of his bed and watched the woman get dressed. She was happy to let him watch her, as there was nothing he had not seen many times before. As usual, she had had a good visit to his flat and would return home to her other life a very satisfied woman and await her husband's return later that day from the same company that Quentin would return to when she had gone. As always, they would leave the flat separately and quietly. She slipped on her shoes, checked herself in the dressing table mirror and walked to the bedroom door, turning to blow him a kiss, which he returned. As the front door closed quietly behind her, Quentin swung his legs out of bed and reached for his trousers. He smiled to himself. What a woman! She had worn him out. When he returned to his flat later, he would have an early night on his own to recover. He would need to be well rested for tomorrow.

Because tomorrow lunch time he would be entertaining another lady visitor. Tomorrow Mrs Mary Marshall would be his guest! Ten minutes later, Quentin also left his flat quietly, not wishing to draw any attention to the fact that he had been home at lunch time. As he got in his car and drove away, neither he nor his guest had taken any notice of the red and white striped workman's tent across the road from the block of flats. In the tent sat a private investigator on a folding chair, together with a packet of sandwiches, a flask of coffee and a top quality camera on a tripod, which was aimed at the entrance of the block of flats. The man was wearing overalls with the logo of the G P O on the pocked. Satisfied that Mr Drummond would not be back for a few hours, he left the tent with a bag of 'tools' and a clipboard, every inch the general post office phone engineer he was pretending to be. He was wearing a wig and clear lense glasses. He was a professional and knew that the best way not to be remembered was to hide in plain sight.

He knew what number flat he was heading for, the information supplied by his employer for this assignment. He knew that there was no burglar alarm in the flat and he had noticed that all the properties had locks by the same manufacturer, to which he had a master key. He also noted that none of the flats had any 'spy holes' in their doors that looked out onto the landings. Good!

In the main door and up the stairs to the first floor to flat number seven, looking like an official from the post office with every right to be there. So long as no one came out of the other three flats on that landing, he would be alright. Unhurriedly, he approached the door of number seven, keys in his gloved hand, unlocked the door, and quietly let himself in. Once inside, he moved quickly. A rapid check of the one bedroom flat confirmed that he was alone. He went into the bedroom and removed a box the size of a box of man-size tissues from his bag of tools and looked around the room. Opposite the bed was a wardrobe, on top of which was a suitcase. Perfect. He placed the box on top of the case in full view, not attempting to hide it. The box was brightly coloured with red and yellow stripes. The box said 'MOTH REPELENT – DO NOT TOUCH' the box had three holes along each side, to let out the vapour. The box actually contained a state of the art miniature video camera from America. James Bond did not have access to better. The man positioned the box so that he had a good view of the bed. He knew that Mr Drummond had a cleaner. She was due later today. She would think he had put the box there. He would think she had. The simple things always worked the best.

The bed was pulled out and a listening bug was placed behind it. That, together with the camera on the wardrobe and the stills he had got from outside would do nicely. Less than six minutes after he had entered the flat, the man left, locking the door behind him. He went back to his striped tent across the road and looked into a monitor, which showed the bed clearly in flat number seven. He stayed in the tent for another hour, during which time the cleaning lady arrived. He recorded her cleaning the bedroom and change the sheets, they needed to be changed! A slight adjustment to the focus of the camera was required, then the tape was rewound for tomorrow. The bug picked up the noise of the carpet sweeper and the off key singing of the cleaning lady. All was ready. He smiled to himself. "Come into my parlour said the spider to the fly!" When the cleaning lady had gone, he took down the tent, and loaded it into his van with all the other stuff and drove away. He would be back tomorrow and every weekday lunch time for a couple of weeks. That should be enough for his client. The he would return to the flat to remove the bug and retrieve the mini camera. Nice work if you could get it.

While Simon Marshall waited for the results he had privately requested, he thought back to when he had become suspicious.

John Stagg had come back to Elfington for a few days to visit his sister and her family, and to see his old mates and have a good booze up. His family had been less than thrilled by the very short notice he had given them of his arrival on Friday afternoon. He had only telephoned on Thursday night. His sister Mary had hoped to see Quentin and had had to cancel it. Simon had fared better and had said that regretfully, he had to go to the office on Saturday morning to do some very important work, which had consisted of reading the newspaper in peace and quiet.

By lunch time Simon reluctantly prepared to go home, knowing that brother-in-law John would be in the pub for the first of two visits that day by the time he got home. With a little bit of luck, he might avoid him for the whole day! As he walked down the empty corridor he noticed that the door to Quentin Drummond's office was open and on impulse, he went in. It was bigger than his, of course, and with a better view from the window. In the corner of the room, behind the door was a golf putter next to the coat stand. Quentin liked to practice on the office carpet between his important meetings. Simon knew that John Stagg would be meeting him at the golf club on Sunday for lunch and yet more drinks.

There were a few papers on the desk, also bigger than Simon's, and he could not resist a quick look at them. Nothing very exciting he decided at he turned to leave. Suddenly, he looked at them again. One of the papers was a bill for some golf shoes that had been delivered to his home address. Flat seven, Windford Heights, Churchwell, Abbotsbury.

Why did that ring a bell? Then it came to him. Some months ago he had bumped into the lovely Nurse Penny Grey in the village, and she had mentioned that she had seen his wife in Churchwell while she had been having a driving lesson. She had said that his wife had been going into a block of flats and that what a small world it was! At the time he had thought little of it, Mary belonged to a few clubs and was out and about a lot. But… he joined the dots in his mind.

Was it possible that Mary had been seeing Quentin behind his back? He thought back to the first dinner party that they had attended when he had been promoted and remembered how Quentin had looked at Mary, and how Mary had looked back at him! Yes, it was possible, but there may also be a perfectly innocent explanation. He had no proof that anything was going on between them, and anyway, Quentin was a single man who could do as he pleased. And yet, and yet the more he thought about it, the more he realised that it could indeed be possible. It surprised him to realise that he did not care.

Simon left the building and drove home on auto pilot, his mind elsewhere. He hoped that he would have the chance to buy John Stagg a pint after all. Had it not been for his surprise visit this weekend, he would not have gone into the office and might never have known!

Miss Doyle's suspicions that Mr Fuller would be a terrible teacher and an even worse headmaster had been spot on. He was not there, as Mr Mitchell had been, because he was intelligent and cared about the children and their education. He was there because of his "connections." Worse still he was using his position to gain an advantage over Miss Foster, something Miss Doyle also suspected he had done before to other attractive but naive young ladies who were book smart and life stupid. Mr Fuller was so smooth, he would slide uphill with no difficulty. Mr Fuller was married, to a short and overweight but very nice lady, whose father was quite well off. Mrs Fuller had always led a sheltered life, protected from life's unpleasant side by wealthy parents who had themselves not been allowed to see the harsh reality of life. It had been a good move on his part, especially as she was quite happy to let him go to various meetings and other activities on his own, trusting him completely. Say no more.

It was none of Miss Doyle's business what he, or Miss Foster did or did not do, but she didn't want Miss Foster to be another victim of a smarmy pig like Mr Fuller!

The results of the eleven plus examinations were due in soon, and she was sure that once again, no one from St Martins School, her school, would pass. In fact, she had heard that Mr Mitchell had been the last pupil from this school who had actually passed and gone on to grammar school. She would do her best, as always, but next year's students were also unlikely to do it either, in her opinion, especially with Mr Fuller himself over seeing their revision and exam preparation. He did not encourage them to try too hard, and even seemed to suggest that they should be content to work locally, have a nice life, and follow in the footsteps of their parents. The year after that, there was one, maybe two students who really could pass. Freya Olsen and Gilbert Van den Berg. If they were able to pass, it would, of course make Mr Fuller look good, and he did not deserve to. But Miss Doyle could not care less about Mr Fuller, she did care about Freya and Dutch achieving the best results they could and doing well.

It was good that Mrs Hunter had finally gone, but Mr Fuller was a poor replacement for Mr Mitchell. It would be really good if Freya and Dutch could go on to grammar school before she herself left the school and moved on to other things. She knew that they would both try their best, and she would do all she could to help and encourage them.

Andy the greyhound had failed to live up to the expectations of his owners. He had been entered into two further races, but had not won, or even been close. He had in fact come last and second to last. He had turned out to be a bad investment. That was a pity. For him anyway. There were three choices for Andy's owners to decide on. One was to find him a new home, but the trouble with that was it might take some time, and time was money. Second was to take him to the vet and have him put down. But that again would have to be paid for, and Andy had cost them far too much already with nothing to show for it. The third option was much simpler, and the most cost effective. Dump him up on the wold!

Any reputable dog breeder would never consider such a thing, they loved their animals as much as they loved their children. Sadly Andy was owned by a breeder who was not reputable. So it was agreed. Andy had outlived his usefulness and had to go.

The next day when it was dark, Andy was put in a cage, the same one he travelled to the track in, his collar was removed and he was taken to the middle of the wold, miles from anywhere and released. He would never know that Tog had suffered the same fate a year ago, in exactly the same spot! Already weak and under nourished, he spent the next few days wandering around, just as Tog had done before him, getting weaker all the time. Unlike Tog, he had gone in the opposite direction and was actually on the edge of Elfington Village. Late at night he came to a road and paused on the verge, just about able to stand up. In the far distance he could see the white lights of a car coming slowly towards him. In his run-down condition his mind was all over the place, and as the car drew closer he imagined that his owners had realised their mistake and had sent the car to come and get him and take him home. He took a step forward.

Suddenly the lights got much brighter as they were switched to full beam and the car surged forward straight at him. Blinded by the lights, he could not react in time and the car struck him with a sickening thud, throwing his body high into the air and landed in the undergrowth. He was dead before he hit the ground.

The car drove on, the driver shouting out in delight, "Yes! Got the bugger, whatever it was!" John Stagg was a happy man as he drove away from the body at the side of the road, and not just because of the five pints he had drunk with his old mates. The dog's body lay still where it had landed. Andy the Greyhound had run his last race.

The school holidays began again, and Freya and Dutch were inseparable. They spent the summer holidays either up on the wold, or at the lake next to the Old Mill. The water and the steep hills of the valley reminded Freya of the fiords of Norway. Home. Would she ever go back there again? Not without money, that much she knew. She and Dutch would spend at least one afternoon a week working in Mr Winter's garden, something that they would both be happy to do for nothing, as they enjoyed his company and the stories he would tell them about his life on the island of Jersey.

But Mr Winter insisted that they accept a couple of bob each per visit for their work. Dutch, like Freya was saving up for a visit back to Holland one day, but like her, he was told that it would have to be next year. It was always next year. Like most of the other children in the Village, neither of them received pocket money, and did not expect to. They were both independent-thinking children and did not expect to be given anything for free.

Freya also got a sixpence now and then from Mr Benton, when she thought up a new slogan for him. She had earned a tanner this week as he wanted to shift a large number of joints of beef, which he had picked up cheap, and needed something different to draw attention to them. Freya had not needed long to come to his rescue. She had handed him a piece of paper on which she had written just two words. HAND SELECTED. Mr Benton was thrilled. The girl was a genius. Just those two words had changed the way his customers would think of the joints. As she put her sixpence carefully in her pocket, her green eyes twinkled with pleasure. Getting people to change the way they thought was just one of the many things she was good at. Although she did not know it, she was flexing her mental muscles in preparation for the next phase of her life. Mr Benton sold all his joints of beef in record time.

Freya was also flexing her muscles regularly in her back garden, doing the exercises that she had learned from Uncle Lars. She and Dutch, together with Rose and sometimes Penny would collect their folders from the shed, select the body parts they were going to work and then begin to do the exercises. Thanks to the early tuition that Lars had given them, he was happy for them to exercise on their own, confident that they knew what they were doing and would be safe and not injure themselves. Dutch concentrated more on his upper body than the ladies and the results were starting to show. Chest, arms and back were growing well, and together with a good diet and lots of rest, he was very pleased with his workouts. He was also very mindful of what Lars had drummed into all of them right from the start. Don't over train! He knew that doing too many exercises too often would not make him stronger, but actually weaker and more prone to injury. Freya knew why he worked his upper body hard. He wanted to be able to protect her and keep her safe from bullies like Munch. She never told him that she had special strength and could take care of herself. Freya was touched by his wanting to protect her and it just made her affection for him stronger than ever. She was mentally light years ahead of where a girl of her age should be and knew that beyond any doubt that Dutch was the best friend she would ever have or ever want.

The whole family and Dutch had helped out with the haymaking and Mr Briggs had got all his hay inside in record time. It was a joyful and happy time and Freya and Dutch added half a crown each to their savings. A week or so later a farmer on a nearby farm asked Lars if he would agree to Freya and Dutch giving him a hand with his hay, and after checking with Dutch's parents, was happy to agree, trusting them to be safe and to do a good job. The two friends were happy to help out and were reluctant to accept money from the farmer, but he was so pleased with their work that they went home with another half-crown in their pockets and straw in their hair. On the way home they met Freddie Piper and his mother who were out for a walk. There was a man walking with them, and Mrs Piper had her arm through his. She introduced him as a friend of hers that she had met at Abbotsbury Hospital while they had been trying to establish how her son had so suddenly got better. The man said he was a consultant surgeon and confessed that he, together with all his colleagues still had no clue as to what had happened. Freya could tell that Mrs Piper and the Doctor were perhaps a little more than just friends and she was delighted that Freddie's mum had found someone to be with and make her happy, after all the years of pain and heartbreak while Freddie had been ill.

Freddie had grown quickly and was a sturdy boy who was full of life and his mother's pride and joy. He looked so well, tanned by the sun and running around the village with his friends, enjoying the life he had so nearly lost. Freya was so pleased to see him so strong and free from the illness that he had had. He and his mother would never know the part that Freya had played in saving him and it gave Freya a warm glow inside to see the living proof of the powers that she somehow had. She still did not know how she had managed to save him, but only that she had. It was not yet the time for her to learn the secret of her special gifts, but the clock in her mind was ticking, along with many others, moving ever closer towards the time when she would know everything. As she and Dutch said their goodbyes and headed home, Freya smiled to herself again. The Doctor friend of Freddie's mum would never know that the village girl he had just met with straw in her hair was the one who could solve the mystery of Freddie Piper's recovery.

Occasionally, Freya or Dutch would earn a shilling unexpectedly. Mr Hargreaves, who was the postmaster at Elfington Post office, would sometimes need a reliable person to deliver a telegram, as very few people in the village had a telephone. There was one telephone box in the village, but it was usually not working, as the local yobs seemed to take great pleasure in vandalising it as soon as it got repaired. It didn't really matter, as most villagers did not know anyone with a telephone for them to call!

So when a telegram arrived, he would look out of his window to see if he could spot someone he could trust to deliver it. Dutch and Freya were on his list. Munch and a number of other village children were not. During the summer of 1965, Freya and Dutch went to the Cinema for the first time in their lives. A new film had come out that both Lars and Rose, and Dutch's parents thought would be suitable for them to see. Lars had a week's holiday from the farm, and on a hot August day, he took Rose, Freya, Dutch and his mum in his car to Pondford. They went after lunch and met Mr Van den Berg outside the Cinema at quarter to two, as it was market day in Abbotsbury, it was half day closing in Pondford and the barber's shop had closed at one p.m. Freya often wondered what had happened to the pig that had escaped from the market there two years ago.

Normally the Cinema itself would also be closed on a Wednesday afternoon, but as it was the summer holidays, they were able to draw enough people in to make it worthwhile. The Cinema was quite small and it was more than half full when they all sat down on the red covered folding seats, which squeaked when they were folded down. There were two films, the first a short western, which lasted about an hour, then the "Pearl and Dean" adverts, followed by the "Coming Soon" trailers.

Then the main feature began and as soon as it started they were all transported to another place and another country. The outside world did not exist, as the magic of the film did its work. The music, the story and the way the film was put together were magnificent and there was silence throughout the performance. It was something that no one would ever forget. The film was called "Born Free", about Elsa the lion in Africa. No one wanted it to end. Only when finally it did and the lights went up was the spell broken. Everyone shuffled outside into the bright sunshine of the real world, the seats once again squealing as they returned back upright. It seemed to Freya that the world outside the Cinema was somehow harsher than it had been before they had gone inside. The street noise seemed louder, the fumes from the traffic seemed to smell stronger and the sunshine brighter. They all made their way to the town fish and chip shop for another holiday treat and Freya told Dutch that she wished she was able to communicate with wild creatures, like they had in the film. She did not realise that she already had.

The village shop in Elfington was run by Willie Baxter and his wife Morag. They had moved down from Scotland and taken over the shop in 1962, the same year that Freya had arrived in Elfington. Morag Baxter did not take much interest in the day to day operation of the shop itself, content to do the books and other paper work, leaving husband Willie to stand behind the counter and deal with the public.

Everyone liked Willie Baxter, well, everyone except Mrs Hunter, but only a few could really understand all of what he said. Willie, in his turn, liked everyone who shopped in his store, particularly those who spent the most money. The exception was, of course Mrs Hunter. Whenever she came in to the shop, she was always complaining and finding fault with everything. Willie, never backward in coming forward, would have none of it, and gave as good as he got, and was known for his dry humour and quick wits. Rose and Freya were in his shop one Friday, near the end of the summer holidays, when Mrs Hunter came in. As usual, Mrs Hunter ignored them, still blaming Freya for her premature retirement from St Martins School. Willie was less than thrilled to see her and stood behind his counter and waited for the first complaint to come out of her mouth. He didn't have to wait long. As Rose was paying for her shopping, Mrs Hunter's complaining voice boomed down the aisle.

"These tomatoes are Spanish!" The way she said it you would have thought that they were radioactive.

Quick as a flash, Willie shot his reply back. "Yea supposed ta eat 'em, nay talk to 'em!"

He looked at Freya and winked. She and Rose tried hard not to laugh out loud. Mrs Hunter, trying to look indignant, headed for the door. "If that's your attitude, I'll take my custom elsewhere!" And out she went, banging the door shut behind her. Willie grinned. "Gud. But sadly, she will come back, even though she will not be welcome, but you, Mrs Olsen, and you wee lassie will always be, especially after you were instrumental in getting that auld witch out of the school. The whole village owes you for that."

He reached up and took down a jar of stripy lollipops from a shelf and removed the lid, offering the jar to Freya. "Take you pick, on the house, lassie!" Freya selected a red and white striped one and popped it into her mouth. "Thank you, Mr Baxter."

"Yea are very welcome. Mind how you go," as Rose and Freya left the shop and headed for home.

Mrs Hunter, meantime, had moved on to the Post Office and on entering was dismayed to see a queue of five people waiting to get to the wire grill, behind which Mr Hargreaves was dealing with the middle-aged woman in front of him. The woman, who everyone knew as Miss Bates, lived with her elderly mother on a remote farm near Withycoombe, and only came into the village now and then when she had to. Today was the day she had to, and she had several transactions to deal with. She was wearing a man's donkey jacket, held together with orange bailing twine, a green woolly hat that was obviously home knitted, and trousers tucked into wellington boots that were giving off a smell of cow shit. The postmaster, not for the first time, wondered why she was wearing her winter clothes in August. It never occurred to him that they were the only clothes she had.

Her mother's pension book came back under the wire grill, together with six weeks of pension money. The book and the money went into a pocket in the donkey jacket, and the button firmly closed. Next some bills that needed to be paid were produced from another pocket. Each bill was in an envelope with the exact money needed for it to be paid, held together with an elastic band, prepared by Miss Bates' mother earlier. One by one, the envelopes were passed under the wire grill to the waiting hands of Mr Hargreaves. Miss Bates had already been at the counter for ten minutes when Mrs Hunter came in. As the door opened, four heads turned to see who the newcomer was. Immediately the four heads turned back to face the wire grill and the conversation that had been going on stopped.

A minute later, a loud sigh was heard from the back of the queue. Mr Hargreaves looked up and over the top of his glasses on hearing the noise. What was wrong with that woman, he thought to himself as yet another envelope came under the wire grill. Soon, another loud sigh was heard from Mrs Hunter. Mr Hargreaves slowed down as much as he could, to keep Mrs Hunter waiting. After a third loud sigh, Mrs Hunter could wait no more and marched out of the post office, banging the door closed behind her. The four customers behind Miss Bates looked at each other, shook their heads and resumed the conversation again. Like everyone else in the village, they all knew about Mrs Hunter's "dead" husband, and no one would blame him for leaving. The only question they had was why the hell had he married her in the first place!

Rose and Freya were strolling along towards home, enjoying the lovely late summer weather when they heard the squeak squeak of Miss Bates' rusty bicycle approaching. The noise got louder and then as she went past them, shopping bags hanging from the handle bars, started to fade as the creaking machine headed home, carrying Miss Bates and the supplies with it. A simple soul perhaps, but like everyone else, Freya knew that she too had something to offer the world, a contribution to make in her own unique way. Anyone attending St Martins Church when Miss Bates was there would know that she could sing like an angel, knowing all the hymns by heart as she could not read the words in the hymn book.

The summer of 1965 was flying by, and soon the autumn would be with them once more and with it the activities that had to be done before the winter set in. Log collecting, potato picking, berries to be picked and jam to be made. It was Freya's favourite time of the year and she was very aware of time moving ever onward into the future. There would be a new intake of children into the school and everyone would advance by another year. Soon she would be ten and would only have one more year to complete before she would be in her final year at St Martins. In that year of 1965, Freya began to feel that she was on a special journey, heading towards something as yet still unknown, a destination she would eventually arrive at and find the answers to all her questions. It saddened her to think that she would be leaving this part of her life behind and moving on to a new school in a new place, but nothing stays the same for long, and she had this year already said goodbye to being a girl and had begun to experience life as a young woman. For Freya Olsen, aged nine, the summer of 1965 was a time of transition, of preparation for what was to come next in her extraordinary life, and gifted as she was, even she could not begin to guess at what lay in store for her. Only the Universe knew what lay ahead, and what destination she would eventually arrive at and what would be waiting for her there.

Chapter Thirty-Eight

Her first memories were of being pushed aside and of always being very hungry. Try as she might, she was not big enough or strong enough to get much in the way of milk from her mother, the others were just too strong. As she did finally begin to grow a little, she became aware of just how much bigger her sister and two brothers were, and how small and puny she was compared to them. She had no way of knowing then that it was because she was so small that she would live and the others would not. All she did know was that she was a she, and she, like her mother and siblings was covered in brown fur.

Her home, if you could call it that, was a cage. The cage was one of many, and like hers, contained more of the same small brown creatures just like her. She could see that every so often, huge strange-looking creatures would appear and suddenly there would be bright, white dazzling light that hurt her eyes. The huge creatures always brought food and water with them and there was plenty of it, but again, she did not get her fair share, the others made sure of that. When the food and water had been given out to all the cages, the bright white light would disappear as suddenly as it had appeared and it would be dark again, until the next time the huge creatures reappeared again and the process repeated. The routine was always the same. Bright light, the huge creatures appeared, food and water, darkness. When the others were sleeping, she would peer through the bars and look around her, curious about what was beyond, but all she could see were others just like her, eating, sleeping and most importantly, growing. She came to the conclusion that she was probably the smallest of all, and she would have been right. She noticed that high up there was a square shape above the cages that changed gradually from dark to light then back to dark again. The square shape fascinated her. How did it do that? Why did it do that, and what did it mean? She felt that she ought to know, that somehow it was important.

One thing she did know, as time passed, was that she, like all the others of her kind, as well as getting bigger, were slowly changing colour. She had been brown, but now her fur was changing to white. She wondered if this change was connected to the square shape she could see. It changed much more often, it was true, but it did change. She started to notice that the square shape was less light and more dark than it used to be. What did this mean?

Time passed slowly. Her sister and two brothers were now the same size as their mother, only she was smaller. Then one day, everything changed. The bright white light appeared, together with the huge creatures, but unlike usual, they brought no food or water with them. Instead they brought some sort of containers and one by one, they removed all the creatures like her and put them in the containers. She watched, fascinated. What was going on? She noticed that here and there, one creature, small like herself, would be left behind in the cage, and when they got to her cage, her mother, sister and two brothers were taken away but she was left and the cage door closed. It was the first time that the door had been opened. When the containers were full and the cages all but empty, the huge creatures took the containers away and the white light was replaced once again by darkness. She felt very unsettled and lonely, the cage suddenly big with only her inside, the room quiet. Where had the others like her gone? She did not know. Perhaps they would come back again, but somehow deep down, she knew that they would not. Where ever they had gone to, they would not return. She was right, they never did.

She wondered why she had not been taken. There were only a few like her left now. Her world, the only world she had ever known had suddenly changed. What would happen now? For the first time ever, she was able to eat her fill, then she curled up and tried to sleep, but it would not come, even when the square shape turned dark. So many questions and no answers.

The answers she craved were simple. She had been spared because she was small. Small and female. She would be fattened up, then put with a male to produce more of her kind. This would happen when her fur was brown again and the square shape was more light than dark. The process would then begin again. When her fur changed back to white once more and her babies were grown up, they would all go into the containers and never come back. Luckily, she knew nothing of what was in store for her. Her world was a cage in a room, with a square window high up in the wall. It was all she knew.

For she was a stoat. A stoat on a fur farm. Her fate was sealed.

Chapter Thirty-Nine

There was no moon that night as Lucy followed Astra along the track that headed up on to the Wold, leaving the darkened "Time Flies" pub behind them. It did not matter that there was no moon, both of the dogs could see perfectly well without it. Lucy was returning to the hideaway for the first time since she had been saved from certain death when she had been left, trapped in the stolen van that had been driven up on the wold and abandoned, under a hot sun. Only the prompt and timely action by Lucky, Hugo and Jago had saved her. That had been two years ago, and the special friends she had met that day had not only saved her life, but changed it for ever, and in so doing she had become part of their secret world. She was excited to be going back to where it had all began, and to meet her old friends and also the new arrivals that Astra had told her about on her regular visits to the pub.

She was returning tonight as she had important news to tell them, news that they all needed to know. For tonight, Lucy would be accepted as a full member of the special group of friends and would be telepathically connected with them all for the first time. She knew that she had been on a sort of probation, not knowing the location of the hideaway, or seeing anyone except Astra. But she also knew that there was another reason for the delay, and that the friends that awaited her also knew, and had been happy for her to take as much time as she needed to overcome her problems in her own way.

Such was the horror of the experience that Lucy had gone through, and the mental and emotional trauma she had suffered, that she had needed those two years to recover fully, helped by her special friend Astra, who had gently talked her through it, little by little as they had lay by the fire at night in the pub while the humans had slept above their heads. Lucy was very aware that without Astra's help and her special powers, she might never have recovered at all.

But now the demons that had troubled her for so long had gone and she was fully healed, ready to take her place with the others.

Lucy was very surprised to learn where the secret entrance to the hideaway was in the Old Wood. She had come up to the Old Wood lots of times with her owner and actually walked right past it down the gully while Mr Young had sat down on a fallen tree for a rest and she had explored the wood on her own.

The two dogs had sat together for a full ten minutes when they had arrived at the gully, listening and watching to make sure that they had not been followed or seen by anyone. When Astra was satisfied that all was well, she had shown Lucy where the entrance was and how to get in, and also how to erase their scent left behind in the gully to betray its location. Once safely inside, Lucy marvelled at the periscope that Astra had showed her, there was no blindfold for her now, Lucy was one of them, accepted and trusted, and she felt a surge of pride go through her as she realised that all the others would have had to agree for her to be shown these secrets and was aware of how much trust and responsibility they had placed on her by so doing. As she trotted down the tunnels with Astra, she told her that she would never let her and the others down. Astra smiled in the darkness. She and the others knew that.

Soon they arrived in the main chamber and although it was after midnight, everyone was there, sitting by the log fire, waiting to greet her and make her welcome. It was just as Lucy remembered it as she was reacquainted with Hugo, Jago, Lucky and Barney, and introduced to Tog and Millie. She immediately felt at home and could feel the positive energy being directed at her by the group. As she had been telepathically linked to Astra for a long time, her brain was quite able to connect to the others as one by one they found her frequency and communicated their thoughts to her. Soon she was able to talk to everyone easily, and Astra asked her to reveal the urgent news that had brought her to the hideaway this night.

Lucy began her story. On Thursday afternoon, two men had checked in to the pub as guests, saying that they were ramblers here for a few days to explore the wold. They looked like ramblers and had the usual equipment and clothing that you would expect ramblers to have.

But Lucy immediately sensed that they were not what they seemed to be, all of their stuff was brand new and there was just something about them that made Lucy doubt them. She was getting very strong negative energy from them. They had come down from their room and had a meal and drink in the bar and Lucy had moved closer to them and sat by their table and listened to their conversation. Straight away she realised that she had been right about them. They talked in low voices and had been sitting away from the other customers by the door, both had strong accents, and Lucy struggled to understand what they were saying at times.

Lucy took a drink of her tea before continuing, everyone was focused on her and what she was saying. The only sound in the cavern was the crackling of the logs on the fire. One of the men was questioning the information that they had and if it could be relied on, as they were taking a big risk by being here in England. The second man said that it had been told to a commander by a loyal member of the cause, a man of long standing who had proved himself many times during the struggle and could be trusted. This person had recently died of some illness and before he had done so, he had revealed to the commander the location of something that they would be able to use against the Brits if they ever brought their campaign to the mainland.

They were here to try and find what had been hidden, something left over from the Second World War, and they said that they wished that their leader would hurry up and join them so that they could get it over with and get back home. The leader was expected tomorrow, or rather today, as it was now after midnight and therefore Saturday morning. The leader had a much more detailed map than they had, and had said he should be able to find what they were looking for without too much sweat. As soon as he joined them, they would begin their search immediately.

Barney, who was very much into human history and had studied it in some detail, asked a question.

"Lucy, did either of those men use the word Cache, spelt CACHE, or the letters SOE?"

"Yes, Barney, they did, now you come to mention it. What does it mean?"

Barney looked grim. "If I am correct, and I think I am, it means we have a serious problem to deal with. Where did these men say that they would be searching?"

Lucy looked at the faces of her friends before replying.

"Here! Right here in the Old Wood!"

Everyone looked at everyone else. It was Millie who asked the unasked question.

"Uncle Barney, what do you think these men are searching for?" All eyes turned to look at him. Finally he answered.

"Guns, young Millie. They are looking for guns, guns to kill people with!"

They had been searching throughout the night, but without any luck. Thankfully Lucy had managed to get a quick look at map the men had, and was able to work out that what they were looking for was at the north end of the Old Wood, and not the south end, where the secret entrance to the hideaway was. At least they would not have humans poking around there. Knowing this information had narrowed the area down a lot, but there was still a lot of ground to cover, and not much time to cover it in.

So eight pairs of eyes, seven of which could see just as well in the dark as in the daylight, started to search for the hidden weapons. They had all agreed that they must find the guns before the men did, if only to stop them from killing other humans, not to mention any animals or birds that might get in the way!

As they had made their way to the north end of the Old Wood, Barney had briefly explained how the guns had come to be hidden there in the first place. When Britain had been threatened with invasion during the last war, small groups of people were trained to commit acts of sabotage on the enemy forces if they actually landed on British soil. Weapons for them to use had been hidden in various places in readiness. As it had turned out, the invasion had not happened and when they were sure that they were safe, the stockpiles of weapons were withdrawn. Or most of them had. Somehow, it seemed, one stockpile had been missed.

Millie had asked what the men Lucy had heard talking wanted the guns for. Barney replied that he suspected that the men were terrorists who had a grievance against the British government and if they could get their hands on weapons already here, they would not have to buy them from somewhere else and smuggle them in to the country and risk being caught. Millie thought about what she had been told, and decided that some humans were not very bright and appeared to be unable to get along with each other!

The Gallownians had been right. Humans were far from being ready to be contacted. If they could not get along with each other, how would they cope with aliens from another galaxy? Or animals and birds that had been augmented by them. No wonder it was vital that they stay hidden and undetected.

It was ironic that the only one of the friends searching that night that could not see much in the dark was the one that found the hidden weapons, or rather, they found him! Barney was forcing his way behind some large bushes when suddenly, the ground gave way beneath his trotters and he disappeared from view with a loud squeal! The others all came hurrying over to where he had last been seen and found him peering up at them from a hole in the ground that had opened up under him. In fact he had, purely by accident, walked over a wooden hatch that had concealed the entrance to a large cave below. The wooden hatch had, over the years begun to rot and it had been unable to bear the weight of a well-fed pig. If any of the others had walked over the hatch, it would have been strong enough to support them.

Barney had been lucky, the hatch had softened his fall and he was not hurt. Lucky flew down to join him in the cave and she could see at once that he had found what they had been searching for. There was an old lamp on a dust-covered table and they managed to light it so Barney could also see what he had found. The cave was stacked with boxes that were all marked with a sign like a big bird's footprint and the letters W. D. Under the letters and the sign, the contents of the boxes were listed.

Rifles, hand guns, mines, grenades, ammunition and explosives. Barney was careful to keep the lamp as far away from the explosives as possible. Just in case.

They found a ladder and propped it up against the hole in the hatch to let the others climb down. They all looked at the boxes in horror. There were enough weapons in the cave to support a small army! In the wrong hands they could cause a huge amount of trouble for humans and animals alike. They were surrounded by instruments of death and destruction. They had seen enough. Barney managed to climb out of the cave with some difficulty, as his trotters were not designed to climb ladders. Once he was safely out, the lamp was turned out and the others joined him on firm ground. Lucky perched on the branches of a nearby bush and summed up where they were. Phase one was complete. They had managed to find the hidden weapons before the humans. Now for the hard part. They had to think of how to stop the men with the map from finding them as well! They looked at each other for inspiration, but no one could think of a plan. They had been up all night and were tired. There was no way they could remove the boxes from the cave themselves, they were far too heavy. As they all racked their tired minds, Lucy noticed a faint light starting to appear in the east. Dawn was breaking and in a few hours the men from the pub would be starting their search. Time was quickly running out!

Lucy had to return to the pub before she was missed, and Astra went with her part of the way, leaving the others to make their way back to the hideaway. The two dogs chatted to each other as they trotted along the track, the sun rising slowly behind them in the sky. Lucy said that she hoped the collective brain power of the others would be able to come up with a plan. Astra agreed, then stopped dead in her tracks. Lucy stopped beside her and looked at her friend, noting the expression on Astra's face. She had seen that look before during their chats in front of the fire at the pub. Astra was thinking.

A few moments later Astra turned to Lucy and said, "Lucy, you just gave me an idea!"

"I did?"

"Yes. You said you hoped that the collective brain power of the others would enable them to come up with a plan."

"So?"

"So, I think it's about time we focused our collective brain power on to your owner, Mr Young, as I think we will have to get some human, good human involvement in this and we are going to need his help. This is what I want you to do."

Mr Young had just settled down in his favourite armchair to read the newspaper, when he felt something scratching at his leg. It was Lucy's paw. She was sitting right next to him. He looked down at her, then up at the clock.

"My word, Lucy, you're keen this morning, I was hoping to finish my paper before we went out!" Lucy just sat there, looking up at Mr Young and wagged her tail, and raised her paw to scratch his leg again, pretending that she had not understood what he had said.

"OK, OK, you win. We'll go now, I'll read my paper later when we get back, the news will still be the same! Come on then, girl.

Lucy needed no second bidding, heading for the door as Mr Young put on his jacket and cap. All morning, as soon as she had got back, she had been focusing her mind on Mr Young, following him around without him being aware of her, trying to plant a thought in his head. She had no way of knowing if it had worked or not, and was keen to get him outside where she knew reinforcements were waiting.

They set off together up the track that headed up onto the wold. Hidden up in a tree that they had to pass under were Lucky and Millie, both adding their thoughts to Lucy's, their eyes and heads turning as the man and dog passed below them. Further down the track, one on each side of it, Hugo and Jago lay concealed in the heather, their bodies perfectly still, only their eyes followed the head of Mr Young as he approached them. A little further on still, the bracken and gorse bushes hid the bodies of Tog and Astra, who also focused hard on the head of Mr Young. Lucy did not try and look for her friends, she knew they were close by and doing their best to support her efforts.

As the man and dog passed Tog and Astra, the track forked in two, one track heading to the south side of the Old Wood, where the gully and the secret entrance to the hideaway were. The other track, much less used, headed to the north side of the Old Wood where the weapons cave was. Ninety nine times out of one hundred, Mr Young would turn left and follow the south track. The plan that Astra had come up with would soon be seen to have succeeded or failed at that fork in the trail. Mr Young stopped at the fork, scratched his head and turned to Lucy and said, "You know, Lucy, let's take the north trail for a change, its ages since we went that way!"

Bingo! Thought Lucy to herself. They had done it. The thought that she and all the others had been transmitting towards Mr Young all morning had been a simple one. Take the north trail! And he had!

As Lucy followed Mr Young further up the wold, she knew that the others would be busy moving into position for what lay ahead. Phase one had worked. Now it was time for phase two!

Barney had been busy. While the others had been occupied further down the wold, trying to plant a thought in Mr Young's mind, something he had been unable to help with because he was just too hard to hide, particularly now that it was late autumn. Instead, he had managed to get his pink body back down inside the weapons cave without breaking his neck. He was working on the assumption that his friends would be successful in their mission, he had great faith in them, and that soon Lucy and Mr Young would be approaching the cave.

Working as quickly as he could, he had managed, with some difficulty, to open a box of hand guns and take one out, leaving the box open. After a quick study of the weapon, he had found the safety catch and ensured that it was set on "Safe". He did not know how to check if it was loaded or not. It probably was not, but probably was not good enough for him to take any risks. Guns had a nasty habit of going off and killing things! There was a lanyard attached to the handle of the gun, and carefully putting it in his mouth, he slowly climbed up the ladder, telling himself that this would be the last time he would have to do it! Once he was safely out of the cave and on firm ground once more, he left the gun on the ground next to the wooden hatch that he had fallen through earlier that morning and then made his way as carefully as he could though the thick bushes around the cave, and back to the gully on the south side of the Old Wood and when he was sure that he had not been followed, he let himself in to the hideaway and trotted off to the main cavern to treat himself to a well-deserved cup of tea and a bag of acorns. His part of the mission was now complete, and he would just have to wait for the others to return to find out how the rest of the operation had played out.

The others had managed to reach the weapons cave a few minutes ahead of Lucy and had found the gun that Barney had left out for them. Leaving Jago hidden under the bush next to the gun, the rest of them took up positions deeper inside the Old Wood where they could watch the action. Lucky had settled herself in the branches of a tree a little further down the track, where she could watch the approach of Mr Young and Lucy. From her perch, she could also see a bank of fog in the distance, rolling in over the Wold.

Lucy, who had also noticed the fog, kept herself ahead of Mr Young at all times, hoping he would not look back and see it, and perhaps turn back too soon. It would be such a shame if all their hard work and planning was spoiled by fog! Slowly, Mr Young and Lucy approached the cave, passing under Lucky in her tree for the second time that morning. She heard Lucky wishing her well and telling her that everything was going to plan and that Barney had done his part. When they were finally level with the bushes that concealed the cave and Jago, Lucy suddenly ran into the bushes, as if she had seen something and was giving chase. Once safely hidden in the bushes, she approached Jago and lay down next to him, the gun between them. Peering through the bushes, they could see Mr Young standing on the track, calling for Lucy. He had seen the fog and was keen to start back.

Lucy waited a little longer, then putting the lanyard firmly in her mouth, she made her way out of the bushes, pulling the gun behind her as she had just found it, which in a way she had. Jago went the other way and joined his brother in the wood. When Mr Young finally saw Lucy emerge from the bushes, he said, "There you are, Lucy! Where have you been, you naughty girl, we must start back now, there is fog coming in!" As Lucy got closer to him, he frowned as he saw she was dragging something behind her. "What have you got there?" he asked, as if Lucy could understand him. His frown deepened as he saw what Lucy had brought him. Gently, he took the lanyard from her mouth as she left the gun by his feet. Mr Young bent down and carefully picked up the gun, his face grim as he looked at it. Like most men his age, he had served his time in the Army as a national service man, and knew immediately what Lucy had brought him. A Browning 9mm pistol!

"Where the hell did you find that?" He asked Lucy, who just sat on the track and wagged her tail. A long-forgotten memory surfaced in Mr Young's mind and automatically he found and checked that the safety catch was set on safe, then ejected the magazine from the gun, already knowing that it was empty by the weight of the weapon. Running on auto pilot now, Mr Young cocked the gun to check if there was a round chambered. Satisfied that the gun was not loaded, he pointed it up in the air, moved the safety catch to the off position, and pulled the trigger, letting out a sigh of relief as he heard the click he was expecting. His Army weapons' instructor would have been proud of him. Putting the magazine and the gun, now set back on safe, into his coat pocket, he turned and walked towards the bushes that Lucy had dragged it out of.

He tried to force his way in to the bushes to try and see if he could find out where Lucy had got the gun from, but in the twenty five years since the cave had been sealed, the brambles, briers, gorse and hawthorn were just too thick and thorny for him to make any headway. Returning to the track and brushing himself down, he said to Lucy, "Lucy, old girl, you have no idea what you have found, do you?" Lucy just kept wagging her tail. If only you knew, she thought to herself. "We must get back home quickly, I have a phone call to make!" said Mr Young, setting off back down the track at a brisk pace. Lucy trotted along behind him, acknowledging the praise that the others were giving her from their hiding places in the Old Wood as she passed by. Soon they were lost to view in the fog, and the friends started to make their way home to the hideaway for a well-deserved meal and a rest. Phase two was now complete and they could do no more. What happened next was down to Mr Young.

Two miles away and hidden in the fog, three men stood huddled together and peered at their map, trying to make sense of it, but all they could see was greyness all around them, and until it lifted again, they were not able to see any landmarks to guide them in the right direction. Time was passing and they were getting nowhere fast. A glance at their watches told them that it was eleven a.m.

It fell to Inspector Pitt himself to answer the phone, as Sergeant Smith was busy instructing a newly arrived constable in a very important piece of police work, namely how to make a decent mug of tea the way they liked it!

"Abbotsbury Police Station, Duty officer speaking."

"Good Morning. My name is Mr Young, and I am calling from the "Time Flies" public house in Elfington. I have something rather serious to report."

"Oh, what's the problem, Mr Young, somebody been pinching the beer mats?" said Inspector Pitt in a light tone of voice, knowing that nothing rather serious ever happened around there, especially on a Saturday morning.

"I'm afraid it's much worse than that," said Mr Young.

Something in Mr Young's voice made Inspector Pitt start to take the conversation seriously. "My apologies, Mr Young. I'm Inspector Pitt, you'd better tell me what has happened."

So Mr Young did.

Ten minutes later, Inspector Pitt put the phone down, closed his notebook. Forgetting to drink his rapidly cooling tea, he waved Sergeant Smith over, the calm of the Saturday morning shattered. Shit!

Up on the Wold, the fog was lifting quickly and the watery sun was making an appearance at last. The three men could now make some sense of the map and could now see the way they should go, the Old Wood now visible in the far distance, and they set off in that direction at a brisk pace, trying to make up for the time lost.

Inspector Pitt sat in Mr Young's private living room at the 'Time Flies' and looked at the pistol on the table in front of him, as Mr Young came to the end of his story for the second time, the new constable he had brought with him writing furiously in his note book. When he had finished, Inspector Pitt asked two questions.

"Do you have a safe, Mr Young?" and got a nod in return.

"Right. Please put that gun in it and lock it up, and I'll have the key, and do you know someone with a chain saw that can be trusted to keep his mouth shut?"

Another nod.

"Right, go with this officer and bring him back here, with his saw as quick as you can, and don't take no for an answer. Tell him that it's official police business and he will be paid for his time."

As Mr Young and the constable left, Inspector Pitt glanced at his watch. It was quarter past twelve.

The three men had arrived at the Old Wood and were again studying their map. They finally agreed that they were indeed at the Old Wood, but that they were on the south side of it, and needed to be at the north side. After lighting a cigarette each, they moved off again, eager to make up for the earlier delay in the fog, the prize they had come for getting closer with each step they took.

Inspector Pitt had not been idle while he waiting for the return of his officer, Mr Young and the man with the chain saw. From the telephone in the sitting room, he had rung his boss and declared a major incident, telling the Superintendent what had happened so far. He was promised more officers and resources, and that this would be quickly passed up the chain of command, before joining him later at the pub. Inspector Pitt immediately requested that his boss and the reinforcements go to a picnic area that had a large car park about half a mile away, so not to attract too much attention. His boss agreed, better to keep the whole thing quiet and definitely away from the press.

The last instruction the Superintendent gave him was that he should use his discretion, Inspector Pitt was the officer on the ground and he would support any decision that he made. As Inspector Pitt put the phone down, he smiled grimly to himself. Using his discretion meant that if things went well, the Superintendent would claim the bulk of the credit, if things did not go well, he, Inspector Pitt would get the blame. Such is life.

Just then, Mrs Young came in and inquired if the Inspector would like some more tea. She had been told nothing by her husband, only that he had seen some dead sheep up in the Old Wood and had rung the police to report it. For the second time that day, Inspector Pitt had reason to be grateful to Mr Young. He declined any more tea, and told her that as soon as her husband returned, he would be going up to the Old Wood with him to have a look at the dead sheep for himself. She nodded, and said she had to go and see to her guests' bedrooms, as they would be back soon from their ramble up on the wold. Such nice men, she added, from Ireland.

Inspector Pitt, who had not been paying much attention, suddenly looked up at her. "Ireland?"

"Yes," she replied, "from the south I believe, Cork, I think they said they were from, although I have to admit I have trouble understanding them at all, not that they say much. They keep themselves to themselves. My husband says he would put money on them coming from Ulster with their accents, not that I would know the difference."

Inspector Pitt nodded as she left the room with the tea tray. Alone again, he picked up the phone and dialled. He had been a copper for far too long to ignore his instincts, and his instincts were telling him that when you have someone finding a gun on the moors, and possible men from Northern Ireland checking into a nearby pub, there was a connection and he was taking no chances.

A voice on the other end of the phone finally answered. It was Saturday afternoon, after all, and everyone knew that nothing important ever happened on a Saturday afternoon. Inspector Pitt only said five words to the operator. "Get me special branch. Urgent!"

Mrs Young happened to look out of her guest's bedroom window as her husband, the Inspector, the constable and old Ned Jenkins headed up on to the wold, following the track that would lead them to the Old Wood, with Lucy following behind. As she turned back to her work, she did not see a large bird silently take to the sky and fly off, also towards the Old Wood. Lucky was heading home to alert the others. Mrs Young finished cleaning and polishing the room and went into the next one to do the same, quite forgetting that Inspector Pitt had asked her not to touch either of them until some other policemen arrived to check them over. Just after Inspector Pitt had made his request, the phone had rung, and it was her friend Betty calling, saying that she had had trouble getting through to her as the phone was always engaged. After chatting for half an hour, Mrs Young had completely forgotten what the Inspector had asked her. It was only when three more policemen, in plain clothes arrived later on, each carrying a large case, did she recall his request. Too late. Mrs Young could not understand why they wanted to look into her guests' rooms anyway. They would be back soon for their meal. Surely they could not have been involved with the dead sheep, could they? They were such nice gentlemen. She had by accident, wiped away the fingerprints of two very dangerous men. It was all Betty's fault!

"You're sure that this is the spot?" asked Inspector Pitt to Mr Young, as the group of men came to a halt. Mr Young nodded, rubbing his back as his body let him know that he was exceeding his usual activity level.

"Yes. Lucy went into those bushes, and a few minutes later she came out pulling the, er, item with her."

Inspector Pitt turned to Ned and said, "Right, Mr Jenkins, I want to see what's behind that lot!" pointing to the huge mass of brier, gorse and hawthorn bushes that stood twenty or so feet to the right of the track on which they were standing. Ned was just to ask why, but the look on the Inspector's face made him decide against it. Instead, he opened the large bag he had brought with him and removed his chain saw, a can of petrol and two hedging hooks, curved steel blades on stout wooden handles. Helped by the constable, he moved towards the tangled mass of branches.

Inspector Pitt, who had been wondering what story he could dream up to tell Ned, suddenly had a brainwave. "Make sure you keep yourself up wind," he said to the two men. They both stopped for a moment and looked back at him. "Sir?" asked the constable.

"I'll brief you both later on, but it's best if you stay up wind, got it?" said Inspector Pitt.

"Yes, Sir," answered the constable for both of them as they moved to their right a bit before starting to hack their way in. Inspector Pitt beckoned a puzzled Mr Young to do the same and as they moved, he began to talk to him in a low voice. When he had finished, Mr Young looked at the policeman with new admiration. Inspector Pitt was wasted as a policeman, with an imagination like that, he could have a career as a writer. Or a member of parliament!

The three men heard the sound of the chain saw quite close by, but thought little of it as they moved forward. It was the countryside after all, and farmers were cutting things down all the time. As they rounded a large tree they saw two men directly ahead of them on the track, then two more to their left, cutting down some bushes. Two of the men were wearing policemen's uniforms. For a moment they hesitated, not sure if they should go on or go back, but they had been seen and the leader hissed "keep going" to the others and they continued on. They were all armed and were sure that the men ahead of them were not. If they had to, they would simply kill them all and drag their bodies into the bushes. One thing was certain. They were not going to be captured.

"Afternoon, gentlemen, enjoying your ramble?" said Mr Young, above the noise of the chain saw, as he recognised two of the three men. They all nodded and smiled as they passed by, but did not speak. Mr Young turned to Inspector Pitt and said that two of the men were the ones staying at the pub, but again, the noise of Ned's chain saw stopped the Inspector from hearing him. The three men were soon lost to view as they continued on down the track. Once they were sure that they could not be seen, the leader called a halt.

"I don't know how, but the bloody police have found the guns. They must have, they were right where the map said the cave should be. Fuck. There must be a leak somewhere, or someone has talked. That's the mission aborted. We must get the hell away from here now, before the coppers up there realise who we are. Come with me now, don't go back to the pub, leave whatever is there. Move it!"

The other two needed no encouragement. At a very brisk walk, they followed the leader away from the weapons cave and down the track and off the wold. They arrived in Elfington village and caught the bus to Abbotsbury. They then made for the railway station, where they split up. The two who had stayed at the Time Flies caught a train to Derby, changed there and made their way up to Edinburgh. A week later they were back in Belfast. The leader caught a train to Stoke, then on again to Liverpool via Manchester. There, he was safe. He did not return to Northern Ireland. He had a job on the docks and simply turned up for work on Monday morning as usual. He would bide his time. He was determined to strike a blow against the British somehow. He smiled as he walked to work. He may have missed out on the hidden weapons, but he still had his Sniper's rifle!

Ned and the constable were making good progress in the brambles, able to saw off large chunks of bushes with the chain saw, once they had hacked their way in. The bushes were moved off to one side, well out of the way. Inspector Pitt called a halt after half an hour and ordered his men to move clear and have a well-deserved fag. Making sure that they could see him, he took his scarf from his overcoat pocket and tied it around his face, covering his nose and mouth before moving into the area cleared by the men.

Ten pairs of eyes watched him disappear behind the bushes. Three pairs were human. Seven were not. Once out of sight of the others, Inspector Pitt pulled the scarf down and moved forward as far as he could to peer between the remaining branches. He could just about make out a hole in the ground, and dropping first to his hands and knees, and then to his stomach , he managed to carefully wriggle his way up to it and peer down inside.

"Holy shit!" he said to himself, as his eyes adjusted to the gloom of the cave, grateful now for the bright sunshine. He could see boxes and boxes, stacked up on top of each other, all marked with W. D. and a short arrow, like a giant bird's footprint. Like Mr Young, he had also done his national service after the war, and knew a box of weapons when he saw one. With considerable difficulty, he wriggled his way out of the bushes, narrowly avoiding poking himself in the eye as he did so. Pulling up his scarf again, he re-joined the others, brushing himself down as he went, and taking his cap back from the constable, his hair still showing traces of bits of twigs and small brown leaves.

He approached Mr Young. "You were right. My instruments show the same readings as yours did."

Mr Young nodded, playing his part, his face grim.

Turning to the other two, he moved closer to them and lowered his voice, as if fearing he might be overheard. There was in fact no one within two miles of them, well, no human anyway.

"What I'm about to tell you is classified Top Secret," began Inspector Pitt. Ned and the constable nodded. "Only we four, and the boffins from the ministry know the real story…"

So," concluded Inspector Pitt, a few minutes later. "We will all stick to the dead sheep story, right?" Heads nodded. "I don't need to tell you that it is a serious criminal offence to mention what you know to anyone. Ever. So no loose talk. Got it?"

"Yes, Sir," said the constable and Ned together. Mr Young nodded also. God, he was good. I almost believed it myself! He thought. "So now we go back and I set the wheels in motion. Constable, you stay here and keep guard, I'll send someone up to relieve you soon. Keep up wind and stay alert. You have done well, and my report will reflect that!"

The young constable, only just out of training, swelled with pride. Who said that it was quiet in the country? "Thank you, Sir!" he said, as the other three began to head down the track and make their way to the pub. When they had gone, and careful to keep up wind, he settled down to do what police officers the world over spent a lot of their time doing. He waited.

Inspector Pitt arrived back at the Pub to find his superior waiting for him wearing civilian clothes, having just come from the golf course. All right for some! With him were two special branch officers, dressed as ramblers, who were waiting to have a chat with the Irish Gentlemen when they returned from the moors. Taking the Superintendent to one side, he brought him up to date, on what he had found, what he had done and what he wanted to do next. The Superintendent approved all of his suggestions and went to his car to use the radio to set things in motion, while Inspector Pitt went to find Mrs Young.

"Your guests, the Irish ramblers, where are they now?" he asked without preamble.

"Well, as far as I know, they have not returned yet from their walk, unless they came in without my seeing them. Have you seen them, dear?" She asked as her husband appeared with Lucy at his heels.

"Not since they passed us earlier up on the wold," said her husband.

Inspector Pitt's face fell. "They passed us, up on the wold and you never said anything?" He said to Mr Young.

"I did say something, but you were looking at the, er dead sheep and I don't think you heard me, what with the saw going and all."

Inspector Pitt took Mr Young to one side and beckoned the two special branch officers over, the need for them to pose as ramblers was now invalid. He would bet his pension that they would not be coming back here. Not now. Leaving Mr Young to give his colleagues a description of the two men, Inspector Pitt went over to his boss and updated him again, knowing he would be less than pleased. He was right.

Later that afternoon, as Inspector Pitt waited for the finger print men to arrive, he sat in the empty bar with the now relieved constable from the Old Wood, and thought about the day's events. He had achieved his main objective, in so much as he had found where the dog had found the gun from, and in so doing, he had found the weapons in the cave, and ensured that they were secure, without anyone knowing that they were there. There were four officers up on the wold now, guarding the weapons cave, although they did not know, and never would, what exactly they were keeping watch over. His instincts had been right. The "Irish ramblers" had been here for the weapons, and now they had seen him and the others earlier, they would be long gone. Shit! How they had come to know that there were weapons up there at all he would never know. Hopefully the finger print boys would turn up something, thank god he had asked Mrs Young to not clean their rooms. The descriptions of all three men had been put out and the bus, train, seaports and airports would be watched, so with a bit of luck, they might yet get their hands on them.

All in all, he had done his best and now he would head back to Abbotsbury to write up his report, as soon as the finger print men completed their work. The system would now take over and he could get back to the station for a bit of peace and quiet, and a nice cup of tea. That would be the end of the matter, and he was quite sure that he would never come across any of the "Irish ramblers" again. He was wrong.

"Officialdom" can, when it wants to, move very quickly and as darkness fell over the wold, it swung into action. Army trucks, moved along the dark country roads, all heading for the large car park next to the picnic area that Inspector Pitt had wisely chosen earlier. It was the nearest point to the weapons cave and well away from prying eyes, as road blocks had been set up to ensure no one would see what was happening, complete with signs proclaiming that "Army exercises" were taking place up on the moors that night. The trucks were full of troops, who were immediately put to work, and were guided down a trail by police with torches and up to the Old Wood. The troops had no idea where exactly they were, or what they would be doing, having been brought in from Nottingham, and told nothing. As usual. It was dark when they arrived, and would still be dark when they left. All they knew was that they were on a moor somewhere. And if you have seen one moor, you have seen them all.

The remaining bushes had been removed from around the cave, and once again, thanks to Inspector Pitt's quick thinking, the way it had been done, from the side rather than from the front, which was directly in view from the track, meant that unless you looked hard, you would not notice much had changed. All through the night, box after box was brought up from the cave after being wrapped in hessian to hide any markings, taken into a tent to be checked by bomb squad officers, and when declared safe, were taken out of the other end of the tent by different men, and carried down the trail back to the car park and loaded on to a special truck. Before dawn, the cave was empty and just left as it was, the need for secrecy gone with the last of the boxes. The troops climbed back into their trucks and were driven back to their barracks, never having known where they had been, or what they had been carrying. The weapons were taken to a special depot and secured. As daylight came on Sunday morning, everything was done. Apart from an area of well-trampled grass and a pile of cut bushes, everything looked much as it had done before. Almost.

Sunday morning found Inspector Pitt back at Abbotsbury Police station, finishing his report. The story he had told Ned and the new constable about toxic gas being detected by Mr Young, who was a secret monitor, employed by the "Ministry" to keep a check on what was believed to be old second world war gas bombs, dropped by an enemy bomber that had been off course and later shot down, would ensure that they kept their mouths shut. And even if they did talk, it would not be about what had really happened. Only a handful of people actually knew the whole story about a cave full of weapons and Irish terrorists sent to find them. And a group of special creatures who had set the whole thing in motion to begin with, and had watched everything from the darkness.

Later that day, just as dusk was falling again, after the friends had slept and had had food and drink, they returned one more time to the now empty cave for a last look at what the humans had done, as Barney had missed most of the action due to his light colouring. But now he was able to venture out during the day light as he was wearing something that Astra, helped by Millie had made for him from something that had been found in the cave and removed before the humans took the guns away. It was a camouflage cape, and at the moment just tied around him with string. In the days ahead, Astra and Millie would tailor the cape to fit him better, but even in this crude form, he blended into the background as well as the others did and it greatly increased his ability to go out and about in the day time. Barney was a very happy pig.

Everyone was relieved that the horrible weapons had gone, together with the men who would have used them to harm others. The plan that Astra had thought of had worked very well, and they now knew that they had the collective brain power to actually plant a thought in a human's mind. It was a very good outcome to the events of the last few days. Just as darkness was beginning to fall, and fog was beginning to form was again and they were about to make their way back to the hideaway, they all heard a faint noise at the same time. Seven heads turned in unison towards the pile of bushes that the humans had dragged deep into the wood, trying to identify what had made the sound. A little while later, the noise came again, weaker than before, but definitely from the pile of bushes. Something was in there. Something that was injured and crying out for help.

Millie, being the smallest and the most flexible, agreed to check it out and squirmed her way in to the pile of branches. Deep inside the pile, she found the source of the noise. A tiny red squirrel, only a few days old lay injured, and was calling for help. Somehow, the tiny creature had managed to fall out of its drey high above them in the trees, and but for the pile of branches to break its fall, would have died. But although injured, it was alive. The second thing that Millie noticed was that tiny creature was clutching something in its little hands, and as Millie watched, a little pink tongue licked at the brown object it held so tightly to it. Sensing movement, the squirrel opened its eyes and focused them on Millie. It was not afraid, never having seen a cat, or indeed any other creature other than its mother before, and did not know that cats were best avoided if you were a squirrel and wanted to live!

Millie quickly communicated what she had found to the others, and they all helped to make it easier for her to gently extract herself and the baby squirrel from the branches. It was clear that it would not be able to be returned to its drey, and that it was injured and very weak after its fall. Once again, Astra took control and decided that the baby squirrel would have to be taken quickly to the hideaway and nursed back to health. The others agreed and a piece of Barney's cape was torn off and the squirrel was placed in the middle of it, and the corners gathered together and placed firmly in Lucky's claws, and she immediately took off and headed towards the viewing room, while the others made their way home as quickly as they could, Millie getting a ride on Barney's back. But even when they were moving quickly, they always kept a good look out.

When they arrived back at the gully, Hugo and Jago stayed outside for twenty minutes after the others had gone inside the hideaway. They just sat and watched and listened for any sign that they had been followed. It was foggy, dark and a Sunday but even so, they waited. Finally they were satisfied and vanished inside the tunnel and joined the others. Lucky had put the newcomer in Millie's basket and moved it next to the fire and started to heat some milk. As soon as Millie had arrived back, she climbed into her basket and the baby squirrel, feeling her warm body, cuddled up close. When the milk was ready, it was only then that the tiny hands let go of the brown object it had been holding and gripped the bottle that Astra held instead and drank thirstily before going into an exhausted sleep.

Tog examined the brown object the squirrel had been licking. It was part of a round chocolate sweet, and must have been dropped by one of the soldiers while he was moving the bushes and lost in the darkness. The squirrel owed its life to that dropped chocolate, without which it would have starved to death. Although the chocolate had been licked a lot by the squirrel, the name stamped on it was just about still visible. The friends looked at each other and realised that this tiny creature had been destined to join them. There were just too many coincidences, and they all knew that nothing happens by accident.

During the days, weeks and months ahead, the squirrel recovered and grew stronger. It became clear that it must have bumped its head when it fell from its drey, as it found it hard to communicate with the others other than at a basic level, but that was enough. A simple soul perhaps, but one that brought joy and happiness to the hideaway as he scampered around the tunnels during the long winter months. He was accepted and loved by all and after only a short time, the friends could not imagine life without him.

The squirrel was named by Millie, as she had accepted the role of being its mother. She called it after the name on the chocolate that had been with it when it was first found, and it seemed to suit the cute little chap with the bushy tail and tufted ears. She called him Rolo.

Chapter Forty

The board of governors' meeting, held in St Martins School, had come to an end, and the members went to collect their coats from the pegs that the children used during the day. As Headmaster, Ken Fuller had had to be there. Miss Fiona Foster, as a student teacher, did not, but she had been allowed to "sit in" on the request of the Headmaster so as to better understand the workings of the school outside of the actual teaching.

As Ken saw the board members out, Fiona went to the ladies to "powder her nose" before she too headed home. A few minutes later she came out, looking the same as she had before and put on her coat. She thanked the Headmaster, who was chatting to the last two board members by the front door, for letting her attend, then left the school and walked down the dark street and into the late autumn night.

Soon after she had gone, Ken Fuller ushered the last two members out and putting on his own coat, turned out the lights and secured the school, and headed for home, also alone.

A little later, he turned into an alley that led from the school road up to the playing fields, little used even in the day time. One side of the long alley was taken up by a high stone wall, which was continuous save for one or two recesses which gave rear access to gardens. As it was a Monday night, no one was about. A little way into the alley, Fiona Foster was waiting for him. After a quick look around, they embraced and kissed, before moving further down the alley to their usual spot half way down, where they could see both ends of the alley at the same time. It was while they were kissing that they failed to spot a figure enter the alley from the far end and move silently down it towards them, then quickly slip into one of the recesses. The figure had, due to their superb eyesight and night vision, seen and identified the kissing couple instantly, and like a shadow vanished into the recess without being seen. The figure would wait for them to go before proceeding further. Luckily, the recess had four steps up to a stout wooden door and as long as there was no movement, the extra gloom of the recess would hide them.

The hidden figure could hear the two figures walk closer and closer, but then stop opposite to where the hidden figure was motionless in the recess. The hidden figure could see that the woman was facing the recess, while the man stood in front of her with his back turned. The alley was quite dark, but the clear night and full moon did give some light As well as having superb night vision, the hidden figure also had fantastic hearing as well, and could hear the whispered conversation that the couple were having with ease.

"You took it off, Fiona?" asked Ken Fuller, as Miss Foster unbuttoned her coat.

"Yes, Sir, and I did not wear any perfume this evening. I know the drill! I'm all ready for you," she giggled.

"Great. I've been looking forward to this for ages. I thought that meeting would never end. Now, let the dog see the rabbit!"

"Your wish is my command, Headmaster!"

Miss Foster opened her coat wide and then pulled up her jumper, revealing her firm, full, naked breasts to Ken, who lost no time in holding one in each hand and start to fondle them and pull at her nipples, which were already standing out due to the woollen jumper rubbing against them and the cool air she could feel around her chest. Her bra was in her handbag. While Ken squeezed and then sucked her breasts, she continually looked left and right to check that no one was approaching. She did not look into the recess. The jumper stayed up on its own, so Fiona just held her coat open for Ken to take his pleasure.

He murmured to her in a breathless voice, "My God, Pussykins, even in this light I can see what a fantastic pair of tits you have," before continuing sucking one and squeezing the other.

"You always say that, Kenny baby. Oh, that's nice, keep going!"

He needed no encouragement. The squeezing, pulling and sucking continued, as the hidden figure in the recess looked on in amazement. Pussykins? Kenny baby? My, My, My!

Soon one of his hands moved lower, across her flat belly and on to the curve of her hip. Fiona knew the sign, and letting go of the coat, she reached down and unfastened the belt of her trousers and unzipped the zip, before opening the coat once more. Breathing heavily now, Ken placed both of his hands down to her waist and continued, sliding them down over her hips and bottom, taking her trousers and underwear with them, until they were half way down her thighs. Her almost naked body gleamed pale in the moon light as she moved her legs as far as her clothing allowed her and took a wider stance.

Ken ran his hands over her bottom, holding one buttock in each hand, squeezing the smooth firm flesh and pulling her cheeks apart, murmuring to her all the time. "Soon we won't have to do this in an alley, soon we can be together all the time, my pussykins. Be patient my angel and we will be able to be happy together. Just a little longer, I promise."

Fiona gasped as his hand moved down between her legs. He had not asked her to go "All the way" yet, and she would not let that happen until he had left his wife and they were together. She knew that he was very well connected and he had promised that he would use his contacts to secure her a good teaching job in a top school. He said that he loved her and she believed him. She knew that she loved him. His wife didn't understand him and there was no intimacy between them, he had said. So she was happy to do what she could to comfort him. So she stood, semi-naked in a back alley in Elfington while her Headmaster enjoyed her body.

She continued to check left and right as he kept one hand between her legs and the other moved from her bottom to her breasts and back again. The weather was fine and dry and so Ken took his time while she held open her coat and kept watch. Finally he had had enough. He gave her a final kiss and stepped back, letting her pull up her knickers and trousers, and pull down the jumper and gratefully button up her coat.

When she was ready, they said their good nights and he went down the alley to his home, and she went the other way to the room she rented in the village. The figure in the recess waited a full five minutes before being sure that they had gone, before emerging and silently heading home. Well, Well, Well!

Ken Fuller arrived home and found that his wife had already gone to bed. Good. He decided to join her but after getting quietly undressed, he went into the bathroom to relieve himself in more ways than one, as he was still aroused by the passion of the evening. That done, he went into the bedroom and turned out the bedside light and slid between the sheets next to his wife, who was snoring, as she usually did.

Before Ken fell asleep, he marvelled at Fiona Foster's stupidity. She was very compliant, and did what he asked her to do without question, one of the best he had had, and he had had a few, and what a body! He looked forward to the next phase of the seduction, the part when he told her he could not leave his wife just yet, as she had been diagnosed with a serious illness and he must see her through it and get her better. That usually worked quite well. He drifted off to sleep, tired after a very enjoyable day's work.

Fiona Foster arrived back in the room she rented from an elderly couple, glad to see that neither of them were using the bathroom that she shared with them. She put a shilling in the gas meter and ran a bath.

When it was full, she lay back in the hot water and reflected on the events of the evening. Her breasts, nipples and between her legs were tender, the result of being squeezed, pulled and poked too roughly for too long.

Still she had pleased him, and she had enjoyed it herself, although he could be a bit rough sometimes.

Soon, once she was a fully qualified teacher, he would help her to get into a decent school and they could be together. It never entered her naive mind that no school would touch either of them with a barge pole if they found out, and they would find out, that he had left his wife to run off with a student teacher after having an affair with her. Fiona Foster was an educated young woman, graduating near the top of her class at University, but when it came to real life, and in particular real men, she should wear the dunce's pointed hat.

The alley, which had seen so much action that evening was now deserted, well, almost, so no one saw a second shadowy figure climb down from a tree that overlooked the alley and drop lightly to the ground before making its way home! From the tree the figure had had an even better view of the couple below and had also heard the conversation. It had also seen the first figure enter the alley, spot the couple and slip silently into the recess, then emerge later after the couple had gone. Finally, the alley was really deserted and would remain so for the rest of the night, after the last of its visitors moved on and vanished into the darkness.

It was the custom at St Martins School for some of the older girls to work in the staff room during the mid-morning, lunch time and mid-afternoon breaks. They would be required to make the tea or coffee and wash up afterwards. Today it was Freya's turn and she was alone in the staff room drying the cups, saucers and spoons just before the start of afternoon lessons.

She finished the last cup and was just about to leave when she noticed the handle of a teaspoon on the floor, just visible under the long table cloth that covered the table, dropped by the last girl to do the job before her. Freya dropped to her knees to pick it up when at that exact moment, the door at the other end of the room started to open. Freya froze for a moment, and then, for reasons she could not explain, instead of just standing up again, she stayed where she was on her hands and knees and silently crawled under the table, hidden by the long table cloth.

Two men had come into the room, one was Mr Fuller, the headmaster. Even before he spoke, Freya knew it was him by his shoes. The other man was a stranger. They began talking in low voices when they saw the room was empty, or so they thought. The stranger was saying, "Right, Ken, this won't take a minute. I've just had lunch at the golf club and had a word with the secretary. He confirmed to me that he can get you in as a social member in a few weeks, if I give him the nod. I've also got a pal on standby to second your application, so all I need from you is your word that you are prepared to honour our agreement."

Mr Fuller said, "It's not going to be quite as easy as I first thought, John. All the other teachers have said that they want Freya Olsen."

Under the table, Freya frowned. What did the other teachers want her for? She had not asked them for anything. She soon found out.

The stranger, John was saying, "Forget her, she's foreign and worse still, poor. Appointing her will do your career no good at all, and well you know it. Anyway, you're the headmaster and you will have the final say. If you want to be a member of the club, you know what you have to do. Make my niece head girl for her last year, and my pal's son head boy. It's as simple as that." Mr Fuller was quiet for a moment as "John" continued.

"You know that there's a waiting list of over a year to join, and you also know who goes there, and what mixing with them could do for your career. I don't need to tell you the old saying, it's not what you know but who you know, do I?"

"No," said Mr Fuller.

"Well then, nothing more to be said then, is there?" I'm going back home down south in the morning and might not be back up here until well into next year, so I need to be sure we can agree on our deal, or I'll have to let the club secretary know that he can give the membership slot to someone else."

Under the table, Freya was staggered. She had given no thought at all about who would be appointed head girl. All she knew that whoever it was, was chosen from children in their last year at the school. She was very surprised to learn that the other teachers wanted her. Clearly, being foreign and poor did not seem to be a problem for them.

Ken Fuller, as usual thinking only of himself, made up his mind.

"OK, John, It's a deal. I give you my word, your niece will be appointed head girl. My hand on it!"

The two men shook hands.

"Well done, Ken. I always said you were smart. As soon as I hear that you have made the announcement, I'll put the word in. I'll even stand you lunch when I see you in there. Right then, I must be off, I'll leave it to you."

Freya heard the door open and then close again. Under the table, she could see that the room was empty, the two pairs of shoes had gone. Slowly she crawled out from under the table, just as the bell went to start the afternoon lessons. She left the staff room, the corridor outside it was empty, and headed for her next class. She had a lot to think about.

Driving away from the school, John Stagg smiled to himself. His sister Mary would be so pleased, and anyway, he was sure that Daphne would make a splendid head girl!

The year of 1965 was drawing quickly to a close, and Freya and Dutch had celebrated their tenth birthdays, in September and November. As usual, they had given each other a small gift on the appropriate day, but what they continued to give each other the rest of the time was their friendship, on which no price could be put.

Next year they would begin their final year at St Martins School, and sit their eleven plus exam. Dutch felt he might be able to pass, while Freya knew beyond any doubt that she would pass, although she did not say it. What worried both of them was the potential cost of going to grammar school. There were scholarships available, which would pay for their education, but the cost of everything else would have to be paid for by their families, and they both knew that it would be a struggle. Farmers and Barbers were not known for being rich. They were too young yet to get a weekend and holiday job at the nearby Cropwell Manor, where quite a few of the villagers and some of the older children worked, either in the canteens, cafes, boat rides or fun fair. Both had their ears to the ground to see if they could get a paper round, and Dutch thought he might be in with a chance to assist the new Milkman on a Saturday morning, when most people paid their milk bills, something that Freya had done for free when Uncle Lars was doing it. Both of them had a little savings and would try to add to them as and when they could. Freya's savings had a new coin in them, an actual Crown, brought out after the sad passing of the war time leader, Sir Winston Churchill.

On 30 January, Freya, Lars and Rose, like millions of others had watched the funeral on the TV at home. It had been on a cold January Saturday afternoon and would stay in their memories forever. The service at St Pauls Cathedral, the procession through the streets, the boat ride on the river Thames, the crane's dipping their jibs on the riverbank as the boat, the 'Havengore' had sailed by, and the train leaving Waterloo Station heading for Oxfordshire. It came as no surprise to Freya that the train had left from platform eleven. It just seemed right that it had. Freya wished that she could have known him. She knew that she would never spend her special Crown, but keep it as a reminder of these days and of Sir Winston.

One thing they did know, they would manage. Somehow. So long as they had each other, that was all that mattered, such was the depth of their friendship. Freya had discovered numerology and she explained it to Dutch, who was quite surprised to find how often the number eleven came up. Freya was not surprised.

Dutch was born on 27 Sept 1955, so that was $2 + 7 + 9 + 1 + 9 + 5 + 5 = 38$. $3 + 8 = 11$.

Freya already had 2 x "11's in her birth day and month, and the year was also 55, which was 5 X 11.

Dutch lived at No 47, $4 + 7 = 11$.

Freya lived at No 29, $2 + 9 = 11$.

Next year they both would be 11, in year 66, which was 6 x 11.

Freya knew just how important the Number eleven was to her, it was not just "a number". It was the lowest two digit prime number, a master number. Her special number, and although she did not know it, it was also the number of the Gallownians. They knew the perfection and clarity of thought and mind that the number eleven could bring to a very special gifted few, and equip them with exceptional mental and physical power, a unique consciousness and instinct, and emotional discipline, being able to be open to external stimuli of any kind, being unconsciously "tuned in" to things very few others would ever know existed, let alone be able to detect.

The Cats, Lisa and Bob, had been part of that elite group, and it was why they had been chosen to visit Earth again and check on the progress, if any, the humans had made in their development. The Cats had been near the end of their visit to Earth when they had become aware of Freya. Although they had been miles away, underground in the hideaway, and asleep when the car crash had happened, they had both awoken and immediately realised they had received that unique stimuli that they had thought only their kind could send and receive, not only on this world, but in this galaxy!

So when they both received a weak signal from a new source, they knew at once that a member of their special elite group was in need of their help, such was the depth of mental connection that they had. Tracking the signal, that started weak and was getting weaker, they arrived at Abbotsbury Hospital, climbed the fire escape that was next to the intensive care ward, and found a very badly injured human girl, called Freya Olsen.

But Freya did not yet know she had this special gift, but was becoming ever more aware that she could do things others could not do. Saving Aunty Rose, Mr Winter, and Freddy Piper were things she could just "do", without knowing how or why she could. It was the same with going out during the night and being able to see perfectly clearly. Again, she just knew that she could do what others could not. Soon all would become clear to her, and the clocks that still ticked away in her mind would come to a stop, and the fog that still lingered over the details of the car crash would melt away and she would finally know everything. But until that time came, she would just have to be patient a little longer.

Meanwhile, time was passing by and before anyone knew it, it was Christmas again, and everything shut down for the long holiday. In Elfington, Freya, Dutch and their families spent time with each other, together with Penny and Tom. Mr Winter was once again guest of honour for Christmas dinner at Freya's house. He had insisted on walking there on Christmas day, and when he arrived, the reason he had done so was clear. He had brought with him a new, bigger, adult size bicycle for Freya, who hugged him so hard he was almost crushed when he gave it to her. Everyone had a lovely family day, with lots of food, drink, laughter and love. Mr Winter really felt he was an important part of the Olsen family, and he was right, he was.

In the hideaway, the family of special friends celebrated Catmus day together, except for Lucy who had to stay in the pub. She had been surprised, when late on Christmas eve, and the pub was closed and Mr and Mrs Young had gone up to bed, she had heard Astra's voice in her head, asking her to come outside. Letting herself out of the cat flap, she emerged into the garden to find all her special friends sitting on the frozen lawn, waiting for her! As she went to greet them all, it had started to snow, so she and Astra had gone back inside and opened the back door and let all the others go inside. They all trooped into the main bar and sat in front of the fire. The back door was closed but not locked, just in case someone came down from upstairs, but with nine pairs of super sharp ears, they would have plenty of time to leave without being seen. As Christmas eve became Christmas day, a group of unique creatures sat in front of the fire and enjoyed its warmth. A watcher, had there been one, would have seen two Foxes, three Dogs, an Owl, a Cat, a Pig, who was wearing camouflage clothes and a Squirrel warming themselves on the hearth.

They were silently chatting between themselves and admiring the decorations that the humans had put up. Rolo in particular was quite overcome with it all, and almost forgot to give Lucy a large acorn he had brought for her. She thanked him and put it in her basket, saying she would eat it later. The friends stayed for two hours, and as the fire died down, they rose and made their way back outside and said their goodbyes. Lucy let them out and again with Astra's help shut and locked the back door, before Astra went through the cat flap which Lucy secured after her. Returning to the main bar, Lucy jumped on to a seat and put two paws on the window ledge and peered out into the darkness. The snow had stopped, and although she tried, Lucy could see no sign of her friends. They had vanished as silently as they had come.

Chapter Forty-One

It was so much quieter now the others had gone. In a strange way she missed her family, even though they had not been kind to her. She would be happy to share the food and water with them now. Time passed even more slowly. Now she was alone in her cage, she could eat and drink as much as she liked, and was at last getting bigger and stronger.

She continued to watch the others that were like her, the ones she could see from her cage anyway. She could not see above or below, but guessed that it would be the same as what she could see opposite. All the others that had not been taken away were female, just as she was. Why? She also watched the strange huge creatures when they brought the food and water. There were always four of them, and they seemed to have a set number of cages that they looked after. The one that came to her cage was bigger than the other three, and the noises that came from that one were of a lower tone than the smaller ones. She decided that that one must be a male, and the others female. She was right. She also worked out that the male looked after the cages that were higher up because he could reach them more easily. Again, she was correct. This information was stored away. It might be important. So the routine continued day after day, week after week, and she ate, drank, watched and waited.

She noticed that the square shape above was now dark a lot more than it was light, but over time she noticed that the dark time was slowly getting shorter and the light time was slowly getting longer. At the same time, but in reverse, she and the others like her were also changing colour, and just like the square shape, the change was gradual. When the square shape was light more than dark, their fur was brown again, but before, as the light in the square shape grew less and the dark more, they had started to change to white. She remembered that when she was born, her fur had been brown, and when the others had been taken away, it had been white. Without knowing why, she had correctly linked the changes made by the square shape to the colour of her fur. Instinctively, she knew that this information was very important, and again she was right.

So, she reasoned, when her fur became white again, she would be taken away in the containers, like the others had been. But before that, she correctly guessed that she would be forced to produce a family of her own, as would the others. But she did not want to have babies, only for them to be taken away by the strange huge creatures. But how could she prevent it from happening? This she did not know, but as the light in the square shape grew more and her fur changed back to brown, she knew that time was running out. So she ate, drank and watched. It was all she could do. For now.

Her fur, like all the others of her kind was now fully brown again and somehow she knew that she was as big as she would ever get. The light in the square shape was much more light than the dark and she knew her theory had proved to be correct. But knowing what was probably coming her way did not help her to prevent it. Then, one day something momentous happened. From where her cage was, she had noticed that one of the creatures like her that was on the opposite side appeared to be unwell. Like her it was now alone in its cage and did not eat, drink or move very much, and after a few more changes in the square shape she saw that one day it was not moving at all and lay completely still on the floor of its cage, the food and water untouched. Although she had never seen a dead creature before, she was sure that's what had happened. The next time the huge creatures came and the bright light appeared, and the male huge creature got to that cage he stopped and peered inside, and noticed that the food and water had not been touched.

The cage door was opened and he reached inside and poked the brown fur. Seeing it still did not move and he made a noise, withdrew his arm and turned away and disappeared from her view, leaving the cage door open. She stared across, her mind spinning with the enormity of what she was seeing. He had left the cage door open! The other three female huge creatures took no notice and continued to service their cages. A while later the male huge creature returned and hurriedly serviced the remainder of his cages, hers included before finally removing the body and putting it into a bag. The cage door was left open, as if to remind him that the cage was now empty and he disappeared and the darkness returned again.

For a long while she remained where she was, just looking at the empty cage with its door wide open. As much as she could, she looked around the room at the other cages to see if any of the others had taken any notice. They appeared not to have, and although she was sad that one of her fellow creatures had passed away and would never know life beyond this room, it had given her what she had been looking for. A way to escape. Out of something bad, something good had come. Although she had no way of knowing, the Universe had spoken, pointing out to her the way she should go. Her spirits soared as she began to make her plans. The square shape was ever more light than dark. It would have to be very soon, time was running out!

After there had been five more changes from dark to light and back again in the square shape, she was ready. Since the death of her fellow creature, she had eaten and drunk a little less each change, but so far as she could tell, the male huge creature seemed not to notice, just topping up the food and water and moving on to the next cage. She supposed that to him, the cages were all the same as were the creatures in them. Again, she was correct.

As the bright light appeared and the huge creatures began their work, she was ready to put her plan into operation and lay as still as she could on the floor of her cage, facing away from the door as her dead sister in the other cage had done and hoped she looked the same. Her food and water had not been touched. She could hear the male huge creature coming closer and closer to her cage and prayed that she would not show any signs of trembling as she was absolutely terrified. It was a leap into the unknown, as she had no idea what was beyond this place. It had been her world since she had been born and she knew nothing else. But she knew she had to try and escape. One way or another she knew that she would eventually leave this place, either in a container with her yet to be born family to a fate unknown or hopefully on her own, free. So she lay there, hardly daring to breath, her body completely still, but her mind was whirling at super speed. So much could go wrong. What if he just ignored her completely? What if he didn't even notice? What if he failed to leave the door open? What if... Too late. He was outside her cage. This was it.

She held her breath, trying to imagine the huge male creature peering through the bars at her. She heard him make a noise and then she heard the most wonderful sound she had ever heard before, the sound of the door of the cage being opened behind her. Although she was expecting it, when he reached his arm inside and poked her body, the force of it still came as a shock and it took all her will power to keep still, as her body was pushed across the floor of the cage. She heard him make another noise and then move away, but there was no sound of the cage door being closed! Her heart beating like crazy, she made herself wait a little longer, keeping very still, giving him more time to move even further away. Taking a couple of deep breaths, she made her move. She leapt to her feet and turned to the cage door. It was wide open, the huge male creature nowhere to be seen. In a flash, she was out of the cage door and running along the ledge on which her cage sat, passing several other cages on her right, her route worked out in advance. She jumped down to the next ledge, and then the one below that and then one more until she was near to the floor before leaping the final bit and landing on it hard, but keeping moving, desperate to make good her escape before the huge creatures could react.

Her timing had been perfect. Two of the female huge creatures were servicing the cages opposite to hers and had their backs turned. The other female huge creature was looking the other way! Amazingly, no one had yet noticed she had got out! The massive door that let the huge creatures in and out was open and she shot through it and out into what lay beyond, leaving behind the only world she had ever known, out into the unknown and freedom!

Such was her speed as she ran out of the room that had been her home so far, she was hardly able to stop herself hitting the wall of the corridor in which she found herself, her feet skidding on the slippery tiles. A glance to her right showed her only a dead end, so she turned left and shot down the seemingly endless corridor, keeping to the side to avoid the huge feet of the other huge creatures that moved about in it. As she finally neared the end of it, she could see an even bigger door than the one that she had just ran out of, and her heart sank as she approached it. It was closed. It had all been for nothing. She had failed.

But by sheer good luck it started to move slowly towards her as she got closer and she quickly moved to her left to avoid being squashed by it. As soon as it was open enough, without hesitation she ran out between the massive legs of a huge creature that was on the other side of it, before the door could be closed again. Breathless and weak from the huge effort she was making, she continued to run as fast as she could, realising that she was actually outside the building for the first time in her short life, but with no time to look around, her only focus was on what was in front of her. She did notice that she was on a dark strip of something, which opened out on to a huge flat area which was the same colour. She saw a number of massive things lined up in rows ahead of her, and had to quickly swerve to avoid one of them that somehow was able to move on its own, making a very loud noise as it did so. In avoiding it, she had put herself directly in the path of another one that was coming the other way. With no time and unable to avoid it, she just froze and waited for the impact. The noise was deafening as the massive thing passed directly over her head, a dark round thing just missing her. As it moved away she started running again and headed for some lighter coloured spiky stuff that lined the dark flat area. The spiky stuff was soft and springy under her feet and as she moved through it, became much taller until it was way over her head. Unable to run anymore, and completely out of breath, she could go no further and had to stop.

Quickly she turned around and looked back to see who was chasing after her, sure that there would be a lot of huge creatures hot on her heels. To her utter astonishment, there was no one at all! As her breathing slowly began to return to normal, a wave of pure euphoria swept over her, as her eyes continually swept around searching for danger. She had actually done it! The plan had worked! She remained where she was and continued to look back the way she had come. None of the odd-looking things were moving now and there was still no sign of any huge creatures close by. In the far distance she could see the huge door that led outside. It was now wide open and flat against the wall. The reason for it sent a shiver through her. Next to it on the dark strip she had run down were a big stack of cages, and the cages were full of small brown furry creatures, just like her. As she watched the cages were carried inside and the huge door closed. The new batch of breeding stock had arrived, and the cycle would start all over again. She suddenly felt a new sensation sweep over her. Guilt. She knew what was in store for them and felt desperately sad that she could not help them. She would never know that she was the only Stoat that had ever escaped from the fur farm. She had got out just in the nick of time!

She stayed in the long spiky stuff for a while longer, making certain no huge creatures were after her and when she was satisfied she began to look around more slowly, forcing herself to calm down and get her racing mind to concentrate on the here and now once again. A slight breeze wafted over her, ruffling her fur. It was a nice sensation, a new sensation, one of many that she would experience now that she was free. The breeze was full of strange fragrances and she took several deep breaths, enjoying the smell, savouring the smell of the outdoors. The smell of freedom. But now she had to keep that hard-won freedom, she owed it to the others of her kind who were still inside. So with a final look around, she turned her back on that dreadful place and carefully moved off, heading away from it and its memories, keeping inside the long spiky stuff that she did not know the huge creatures called grass. She had no plan to follow, no idea where she was or where she was going. She did know that she was not alone. The world outside was full of wonder, of new and exciting things. As she travelled, she came upon many strange creatures, very different to her. Some could somehow move through the air, others were enclosed in vast areas and spent their time eating the short spiky stuff that seemed to be everywhere.

There were strange noises she could hear and she could see tiny little things that hovered in the air then shot off where ever they liked. She was in awe of everything, the sheer vastness of it all was almost too much for her to comprehend. It was indeed a world of wonder and excitement. She had always thought about what lay beyond, but she could never have dreamt it would be like this. It was all so new and fresh. She came upon a dip in the ground that was full of liquid that looked to be the same as what she had been given by the huge creatures. Suddenly very thirsty, she took a sip. It tasted the same, but much colder and she drank long and deep from the puddle she had found. When she was full, she burped and for some reason she thought this was funny and she found herself shaking with laughter, another new experience for her, there had been nothing to laugh about before.

She moved on, the fur farm lost to view far behind. The long spiky stuff stopped suddenly and she gazed in wonder at a new sight before her, a large area of impossibly tall things that towered above her, blocking out some of the light. Slowly she moved among them, touching one here and there, they were hard and round at the bottom, but as she looked up at them way, way above her head, she noticed that they divided into many smaller and smaller parts at the top, she could feel the coolness of the air and hear the sounds they made as they swayed slightly on the breeze. She moved deeper and deeper into the wood and as the light began to fade, she found one of the tall things had fallen over and as she went to look at it, a wave of fatigue swept over her, the stress and strain of her escape and the wonder of all the new things she had seen suddenly catching up with her. She came upon a hollow in the ground under the fallen tree and crawled into it and curled up and was instantly asleep, invisible to anyone, a brown thing under a brown tree trunk that lay on brown earth. It was her first night of freedom and as she slept, she missed seeing the sun going down and the night taking over. It did not matter, it would be there for her to see as much as she liked from now on. She had sort of seen it before anyway, but only through the skylight in a room full of cages.

She awoke just before the dawn, and for a moment did not realise where she was. Then it all came flooding back. The escape, running and running. Hiding and the wonders she had seen on her journey here. Freedom. She stretched and crawled out from under the fallen tree, just as the sun began to rise in the east. She turned to watch in absolute wonderment as it appeared and started to spread its warmth and light to the earth below it. She was spellbound at this new spectacle unfolding right in front of her very eyes and a feeling of deep peace swept over her as the new day began. She had had no idea what she would find beyond her cage, but what she had seen so far had exceeded her wildest expectations. It was all so big, so different, so colourful from what had been before. She felt very small, yet somehow part of it all, like she was meant to be here.

When she had finally had her fill of the wonder of the sunrise, she walked over to the puddle she had found the day before to have her fill of water. She drank deeply, enjoying the cool refreshing water, listening to the sounds of the birds as they sang in the trees all around. Just as she raised her head, she looked at her reflection in the remaining water and wondered what the new brown shape was that had suddenly appeared on her left and was growing bigger very quickly as she looked into the water. A sixth sense surfaced from deep within her and she threw herself to her right, just as the sparrow hawk landed in the puddle with a splash, claws extended to grab her. She bolted for the fallen tree where she had spent the night and threw herself into the hollow beneath it, turning in time to see the young hawk launch itself back into the air and fly away in search of less wary prey. She had been very lucky, for had it been an adult hawk, her life would have ended there and then. She stayed in the hollow for a long time, shaking with fear. That had been very close. But she had learned the lesson the Universe had needed to give her. In the midst of all this beauty and wonderment, there was always danger around, and she would keep her wits about her from now on and not assume that the world in which she now lived was always a friendly place. But hunger drove her movements now and with great care she emerged from the hollow and continued her journey, moving from cover to cover, slower but safer now, using the senses that she had never known she had but had saved her life.

She continued on for a few hours, getting weaker and light-headed through lack of food when she heard a strange new sound, which got louder as she went forward. Moving even more slowly now, and feeling the air grow much cooler she wondered what lay ahead. She stopped and peered through the branches of a small bush and gasped at the scene before, her hunger forgotten for a moment. The new sound was being made by liquid, a vast amount of liquid that was somehow moving along a groove in the ground and making a swishing, gurgling sound that was very pleasant to hear. She just sat behind her bush and looked at it, enthralled at this new phenomenon in front of her, but also remembering to check around from time to time, the lesson of the morning well learned. The ground beyond the bush she was hiding behind was bare of anything, the ground sloping gently down to the edge of the moving liquid. One of her needs had now been met, she now had access to what she was sure was drinkable water, but her other need was still to be dealt with. Food. She badly needed food, but where could she get it? As she sat and thought about it she did not see the figure of a huge creature approaching in the distance. Although she did not know it, her second need was about to be met. Food was on its way!

She watched the huge creature get closer, ready to run if she needed to, but to her amazement, the male huge creature stopped right in front of her and began to unload the many things he had carried with him. When she had first noticed him approach, she had at once thought that he was out looking for her, but realised that they had no idea where she had gone and besides, they had plenty more like her to deal with. No, the huge creature was here for another reason. When he had got all his things arranged around him, he began to assemble a long stick with something very thin hanging from the end of it. When he was finished, he flicked the end of the stick towards the liquid and then holding the other end in his massive hands, he sat down and waited.

She watched and waited with him, wondering what would happen next. But nothing did. A long time went by but he just sat there, facing the liquid and holding the end of the stick with the other end pointing out over the water. She was just about to move away when he reached down into one of his packs and pulled out a smaller container and opened it, and put something white, the same colour as her fur would change into, into his mouth. The breeze was blowing from him back towards her and she could immediately smell the aroma of something very nice. Her mouth watered as she hungrily watched him put the food into his mouth. Soon his giant hand reached down into the container and pulled out another white thing. Just as he was about to take a bite, something happened in the liquid, and the stick started to bend! He immediately put the white thing down on top of the container uneaten, and stood up his attention focused on the water. Before she could stop herself, driven by hunger and all caution gone, she shot out from the bush, ran right next to the huge creature and grabbed the white thing, which was half as big as she was, in her paws and ran for it back behind the bush with her prize! She knew she had taken a terrible risk, but she was desperate and had had to try. The huge creature had noticed nothing. Whatever had bent the stick had got away and he sat down on his stool and still watching the water, reached down for the food.

She was tucking in to the food straight away, not knowing or caring what it was, while she saw his hand move around left and right for the food that was not there, only looking down when his hand had not made contact with it. He made a noise, and looked all around but the sausage sandwich he had made was just not there! He never thought to look behind him, not that it would have done him any good, as she was invisible in the undergrowth, one small brown thing among many others. He gave up looking, made another noise and then continued to gaze out over his stick once again. She continued to watch as she ate over half the sandwich in one go and when she could eat no more, curled up and fell asleep, clutching what remained of it tightly to her with her paws.

The sound of the huge creature packing up awoke her and she peered through the bush again watching him, feeling much better, no longer dizzy and weak. When he moved off with all his equipment, she waited until he had disappeared into the fading light before emerging from her bush and after another check around, went down to the water's edge and drank, then ate the remaining food while she could. It was while she was eating that she noticed that there was a big piece of tree that had floated down on the moving liquid and had somehow managed to come into the bank and get trapped there. It was as if it had come into the bank just for her and was waiting for her to work out what to do with it. She looked at it, deep in thought. It was quite a big log, big enough for her to climb on. Just then there was the sound of some unseen creature calling out deeper in the wood, the sound making her jump. She had no idea what had made the noise and was not going to stay and find out! Using the log to travel on the water would take her further away from the place she had escaped from and would be easier than staying on the land with whatever had made the noise! She had no idea where the water was going to, but then she did not know where the land would take her either. It was almost dark, but just as when she was in the cage, she could still see very well. She had not found the moving liquid by accident, nor had the log arrived right next to her at this exact time by chance. She realised that this was the way she should go and see where the moving liquid would take her, and she pushed the log out into the water and jumped on as it moved away from the bank. Using her claws to keep herself steady, she soon got used to the motion and began to look around as the log moved gently along in the current, the little bay she had started from already lost to view as the log went around a bend in the river. She was unaware that the Universe was once again guiding her to where she was destined to go. The river, like the darkness that concealed her from danger, was her friend. The river had a name. It was called the river Elf.

The river she travelled on was a small one, deep in parts, shallow in others, with the odd mound of stones appearing in the middle now and then, with the water parting to go either side. The log took its time, going where it wanted, following the current as the water meandered this way and that, allowing its passenger plenty of time to gaze at the land on either side as it slid by. Sometimes the banks were high and she could see nothing, then the land would slope down and she could see buildings in the distance, some with the glow of a light in them. There were plenty of trees lining the banks as she passed by. After a while she saw a group of very large creatures right by the water's edge, drinking from the river. Fortunately, they were on the far side, away from her and took no notice. They were yet another new set of creatures that she had not seen before. She kept a wary eye on them until she had passed by, leaving the strange creatures with the black-and-white blobs on their bodies and two horns growing out of their heads to enjoy their drink.

She had travelled a long way, much further than she would have done had she stayed on the land. And it was such an enjoyable experience, just gently floating along, invisible to the huge creatures that seemed to rule things here. Above her head, where ever she looked, were tiny specks of light that twinkled as she gazed up at them, adding further pleasure to the experience. What were they? What did they do? There was so much to see, even in the dark. Everything was just so big!

On and on she travelled, putting many miles behind her, just drifting along, alone in the darkness. But she began to realise that it was not so dark as it had been, perhaps it was time for the light to return, but it seemed that the darkness had not been there long enough. The light was coming from behind her, but she dared not turn around, in case she fell off the log.

The new light was different from the other light, much dimmer and as the river suddenly swung sharply to the left, almost doubling back on itself, she saw what was making the new light. A huge dull white disk had appeared, directly in front of her, like a tunnel into which the water would surely flow. The disk had slightly darker blobs on it here and there as she sailed towards it. Yet another magical event had occurred right before her eyes. At that moment she felt very small indeed. Closer and closer she went, so close that she reached out a paw to try and touch it. Then she noticed that the bottom of the disc was actually above the land, not resting on it as she had first thought. What could it be? She just gazed at it in total wonder, until the river swung to the right and the huge disc that glowed moved behind her once more.

She did not know that she was witnessing a wondrous event. It was a full moon. She got a few more glimpses of it as the river continued to twist this way and that, and when she could, she just looked at this magnificent, magical and mysterious occurrence that was her companion as she travelled, lighting the way as she moved to her unknown destination . It was much cooler on the water, with new smells for her to experience and new sounds for her to hear. For her, whose whole life had been spent in a cage in a room, it was almost overwhelming to see so much wonderment at one time.

The light was changing again, but this time she knew that it was the bright light that was approaching now, and the disc that had been her companion had dimmed and moved away. It meant that she could not travel much further. As if reading her mind, and for the first time the log drifted from the centre of the river and moved to the right, heading for a shallow bank, as if it knew that its passenger must now leave it behind. The log drifted gently into the bank and grounded on the stones. She jumped off on to the bank and turned to see the log immediately move out into the current once again to continue its journey alone. She watched it go, silently thanking it for bringing her here, wherever here was. When the log was lost to view, she climbed up the bank and carefully looked around her. In the distance she could see a large structure, but somehow it looked odd. She could see no lights on or any sign of any of the huge creatures who might live in it.

For some unknown reason, she moved cautiously through some spiky stuff that was wet with moisture towards the structure, ignoring her instincts that told her to stay well away from anything connected with the huge creatures. As she drew closer, she could again hear the sound of moving liquid, but louder, as if it was angry and quite different from the sound of the river, and she could now see why the structure looked odd. Part of it was missing and had fallen down, the huge slabs lying on the wet spiky stuff. The loud noise of moving liquid was also explained. It was flowing very fast down the side of the structure in a narrow channel, eventually joining the much slower-moving liquid that had carried her here.

To the front of the odd structure was a wide strip of more spiky stuff and then a huge area of still liquid all in one place, it was from this that the fast-flowing liquid was coming from. She made a decision. What better place to hide than in a structure abandoned by the huge creatures, they would never think of looking for her in there. Sure that the structure was empty, she squeezed between the giant stones and moved inside. A quick check around confirmed that the inside was indeed empty, and seemed to have been so for quite a time. Finding a dark corner that was warm and dry with a good line of sight to detect anyone who might approach, she curled up and was instantly asleep, sure that no one had seen her. But she was wrong. Someone had!

Lucky had flown out of the hideaway early to stretch her wings in the cool of the early summer morning. She had flown around the skies in the pre-dawn darkness, alone and free to go where she wished, thinking once again just how fortunate she was to have been found by Hugo, Jago and Astra and to be part of the unique family of creatures that lived free of the fear of humans and could live their own lives together in peace. As was usual, she ended up down by the Old Mill and had perched in her favourite tree, the one she usually used to keep a look out when her friends had used the boat tunnel and were below, gathering in supplies. It gave her a very good view of all the approaches to the Old Mill, the lake, which had a little mist hovering above its still surface before the heat of the sun burned it off, and the secret entrance to the boat tunnel that led up to the magical cavern. Her super sharp eyes scanned the ground below as dawn was breaking. It was very calm and still before the activity of the new day had begun. The sun had not yet reached the surface of the lake, and it was still in shadow, but the first rays of the sun had already found the river Elf and were glinting off its surface. Her eyes focused on the river, as movement on it caught her attention. A log was floating down stream, still some distance away, but as she looked at it, she noticed that there was something very odd about it.

She watched the log as it came nearer, and realized just what was so different about it. To her great surprise, she could see a small brown creature of some sort riding on it! As she continued to watch the log approach, it started to move from midstream as if being steered by an invisible hand, and approached the near bank, heading for a small inlet just above the point where the water from the mill race joined the river. As the log ground on the shallows, the small creature jumped off on to the bank, without getting its feet wet, and the log immediately moved off again towards the centre of the river, caught now by the flow of the mill race water. Lucky watched the newcomer take its time to carefully look all around, nodding her approval. Apparently satisfied that there was no danger, the newcomer headed cautiously towards the Old Mill, using what cover there was, but unable to stop from leaving a clear trail in the grass, wet from the morning dew. After another look around, the visitor eventually went into the ruin of the Old Mill, squeezing between the fallen stones as the sun began to climb higher in the sky. Lucky correctly guessed that the mysterious creature would rest inside during the day. It had cleverly used the cover of darkness to get here. Clearly a highly intelligent creature, but one she had not seen before. She wondered where it had come from, and why it was here, but first she needed to find out what sort of creature it was. On silent wings Lucky the Eagle Owl left her branch and flew back to the hideaway for breakfast, knowing that nothing ever happened by accident, and she had been meant to see it. She had much to report to the others when she got there!

Everyone waited while Barney looked at his book of animals and birds, one that the Cats had left behind for just this situation. He had the image in his mind already, given to him and the others by Lucky, together with the story she had told. Finally he closed the book and looked up. "It's a Stoat!"

Lucky nodded, as did all the others. They were all there, waiting to find out more about the newcomer. No one asked if he was sure, knowing that if he was not, he would have said so, such was the bond they all shared, and the trust they had in each other. Rolo jumped up and down in excitement, at the thought of having another friend to play with. "And," he added, "Clearly not just any Stoat. They are not known to use logs as boats and sail down rivers during the night. This one had worked out that it can travel much further by using the river, save energy in so doing, avoid possible predators and not be seen by humans, all at the same time. So I think we should consider trying to make contact with it."

The others thought about it and came to the conclusion that, as usual, he was right. If the creature did not want to make contact with them, or was not able to be contacted, then no harm done. And if contact was able to be made and the creature wished to continue its journey at some future time, then its memory of them and the hideaway would be erased. The same choice had applied and still did apply to any of them. No one was forced to stay if they did not wish to, but as each new member had joined the group, all had been more than happy to remain and be part of their special family, adding their own unique skills and knowledge to the others. The question that they had to think about now, was who would do it, and when.

The "How" question did not need to be asked, as that was already known. Contact would be made telepathically, it was just a question of finding the right frequency. As they were not sure if the visitor was a male or female, something very important when trying to establish first contact, two friends would go, one of each gender. They also knew that the chosen ones should have the strongest telepathic skills, which meant that it would have to be two of the three "Originals", Astra, Jago or Hugo, as they were the only ones who had actually met and connected with Bob and Lisa, the Gallownians. Astra and Hugo agreed to go and try to make contact with the Stoat and see if it might wish to join them, if only for a while to rest. Jago suggested that food and water be taken to give to the Stoat, which must be hungry and thirsty after its journey.

There was a feeling of excitement in the hideaway about the mysterious newcomer. They would let it rest during the rest of the day, sure that it would not leave until it was dark again. They all knew that nothing ever happens by chance. The Stoat had been meant to be here, and Lucky had been meant to witness the event. It was just the way of things.

It was late afternoon when the twins and Astra set off from the magical cavern, Tog had joined them to help Jago with the boat, and they were waved off by all the others except Lucky, who had flown out earlier, back to the Old Mill to keep watch in her tree, as it was quite possible for humans to walk around the lake and the Old Mill on such a nice summer's evening. Tog remembered when he had first joined the hideaway, how strange everything had been at first and how he had felt unworthy to have a place with them, and wanted to come and reassure the Stoat that it was welcome, and was meant to be with them. By the time Jago and Tog tied up the boat and went to peer through the periscope behind the closed doors that led out on to the lake, Lucky was already in position to give the signal that all was clear, her super sharp eyes detecting the slight movement of the log, in which the end of the periscope was hidden, and briefly fly down from her high perch to a lower branch and nod her head. Quickly, one door was opened and the boat slid out behind the curtain of branches of the willow tree that concealed the secret entrance. In no time at all, Jago guided the boat along the bank to the ramp, watched his brother and Astra jump ashore and tugged on the rope to signal Tog to pull him back inside the tunnel and close the door. They would wait there until Lucky gave the signal that it was safe to venture out again and hopefully collect three passengers for the return trip.

As soon as their paws hit the ground, Astra and Hugo moved into some undergrowth and waited for Lucky to give the all-clear again for them to enter the Old Mill. It was awkward to lie down, as they had the food and water tied to their bodies, so they sat instead. So far, so good. It was up to them now to try and make contact with the stranger. They realised that it was almost four earth years since the two of them had met, up on the wold and made contact with the Cats. That encounter, like this one had been meant to be. Right place, right time. During that four years, so much had happened, now there were nine special creatures living in the hideaway. Would the mysterious Stoat hiding in the Old Mill be number ten? Only the Universe knew that. So they waited and watched the shadows grow longer until Lucky reported that a pair of humans she had been keeping an eye on were now far enough away for them to move off. This was it!

She had slept the whole day, mentally, physically and emotionally exhausted by the journey of the night before and it was only the smell of food that woke her. Her nose twitched and her mouth watered by the smell that greeted her as she opened her eyes. For a moment she thought she was dreaming, then she noticed a pile of white things on a square of paper, next to a bowl of water that had been placed near to her. She had not heard a thing. Her heart sank. She had been found. After all she had gone through, all the planning, the stress of the escape and the journey, it had all been for nothing. The huge creatures had tracked her here. It was over. They had won.

Keeping still, she scanned the large room carefully to see if there was still a way out. The escape route she had planned to use if necessary was still clear. Then she noticed in the far corner, lying on the floor, she could see two shapes. One larger than the other, but both a lot bigger than she was, but certainly not the huge creatures. They were, like her, motionless, just lying there, waiting. Then she heard a voice, faintly at first, then clearer. It was a voice she could somehow understand. But the voice was not speaking out loud, it was somehow inside her head! The voice spoke slowly, in a low, calm and friendly tone. As if reading her mind, the voice answered her un-asked question.

"Do not be afraid of us, we mean you no harm. We have come here to help you. But if you wish to leave, you can do so at any time, the way is clear and there are no humans nearby." Before she could stop herself, her mind answered the voice in her head of its own accord. A part of her brain that had been dormant had just activated itself.

"Humans?"

"Sorry, you call them huge creatures, but they are known as humans. We also have to avoid them, like you. We were like you once, in fear of what they would do, but now we are able to live in a safe place, a place they do not know of. We have brought you food and drink, you must be hungry and thirsty after your journey, please enjoy it, it is all for you."

She could not resist the smell any longer and quickly ate all the sandwiches and drank most of the water. The sandwiches had tasted delicious.

"Why are you doing this? How are you doing this? How are you able to talk to me, in a way I can understand and not make any sound? I have never been able to do this, even with my own kind."

Astra replied. "I am using the power of my mind to communicate with you, it is a gift that I and my friends have been given, you are already starting to use your gift to reply to me. All creatures should be able to do it, but only a very special few actually can. You are one of those special few. We saw you arrive earlier on the river and come in here, so we waited for you to rest and knew that we must try to help you. Please trust us, we mean you no harm, we only wish to help."

"What is a 'River'?"

"It is what you call the moving liquid that brought you here," replied Astra. "My name is Astra. My friend here is called Hugo. As I said, we have a safe place to live, away from the humans. You are welcome to come and see it and stay with us while you decide what you want to do. You can leave whenever you wish, but we hope you will stay. There are other creatures there who also have escaped from the humans as you have."

Suddenly, in a flash, deep inside her, she knew that she could trust these new strange creatures, and a wave of relief swept over her when she realised that she was not alone any more. These last few days she had learned to trust her own judgement, and now every fibre of her being was telling her that these two strange creatures that had found her were trustworthy. She had no idea what they were, having never seen a fox or a dog ever before, and if they had wanted to kill her, she would be dead already. But they had made no threat against her, and all their actions had so far been ones of kindness, they had given her food and water. She realised that somehow she had arrived at the destination that she had not known she had been seeking. There was just something in that calm, friendly voice that she knew was genuine. She would be safe with these creatures, she could trust them, and all that she had been told was true. She already felt a real and deep connection with the creature called Astra, and that was only after a few minutes. She had made it. This was where she had been heading for. This was where the Universe had guided her to. Now she was really free.

Lucky was so pleased to see the Stoat emerge from the Old Mill with Astra and Hugo, who looked up at her as she reported that all was still clear. She moved down to the low branch again and nodded to the periscope log, knowing that Tog was watching from the tunnel. The boat emerged as if by magic and silently made its way along the bank to the ramp, and every one climbed in before it vanished once again behind the Willow tree and into the secret tunnel. Lucky took off for the hideaway to inform the others that the mission had been a success. She smiled to herself as she flew through the darkness. Now there were ten!

"This safe place, where you live with the others, does it have a name?" the newcomer asked as she sat in the boat. Astra nodded and smiled. "Yes. We call it the hideaway. Home."

Chapter Forty-Two

1966 was flying by, a new radio station was launched called Radio 1, the United Kingdom had won the Eurovision Song contest with a song called "Puppet on a string" sung by Sandie Shaw, and England had won the world cup, much to everyone's delight. Dutch was pleased that England had won, but he had wished it had been Holland instead. Now summer was here once again and it was the end of the school year. For those who were leaving, it was a bitter sweet moment as they would not be returning as pupils again. Miss Doyle had been correct in her prediction. No one from St Martins School had managed to pass the eleven plus exam.

On the last day of the summer term, there was no morning assembly, but everyone came together just before lunch in the hall and it was the tradition that the headmaster would announce the names of the new head boy and girl to start in September. There had been much speculation on who it might be, both Freya and Dutch were favourites, but Freya always shook her head when it came up in conversation, saying she did not think it would be. She did not let on that she already knew who the head girl was going to be, and had a reasonable idea who would be head boy.

Mr Fuller kept everyone waiting until the end of the assembly to make his announcement. The outgoing head boy and girl were already up on the stage behind him, together with all the other teachers, and they had received a round of applause from the school for their efforts during the last year. Mr Fuller glanced down at his notes for effect, as if he did not already know who it was going to be.

"John Hardy, I'm going to appoint you head boy." As John made his way up on to the stage, Freya nodded to herself as she joined in the applause. John's dad ran the local haulage company, Hardy's Haulage and employed a few of the local men as drivers. He was also a school governor. And a member of the golf club. A few of the children looked over at Dutch, surprised that he had not been chosen. Miss Doyle also looked over at him, as if she too was expecting his name to be called. Although he did not know it, Dutch had been the choice of the majority of the teachers when they had been asked their opinions. John had received his badge and stood next to the ex-head boy and awaited his partner.

"Daphne Marshall, I'm going to appoint you head girl." There were gasps from the children and teachers alike as Mr Fuller finished speaking, not least from Daphne herself, who had not been expecting it. Dutch whispered to Freya as subdued applause broke out. "He's mad. She will be a terrible head girl. Everyone thought it would be you!" Daphne had gone pale and had to be literally pushed up on to the stage to receive her badge and to stand next to the ex-head girl, a dazed look on her face. Freya felt sorry for her. She had absolutely no idea that her uncle had arranged it for her. Mr Fuller could feel a pair of eyes on the back of his head as Miss Doyle glared at him. He could also see a pair of green eyes calmly looking up at him from the floor. He quickly brought the assembly to a close, wished everyone a good holiday and signalled for the lunch to be served.

Miss Doyle sat through lunch with a face like thunder. She already had a low opinion of Mr Fuller, but this was too much. Like Freya, she also had known who the head boy and girl were going to be, and was not pleased. She would never forgive Mr Fuller for this, and was thankful that her time at the school was short. She felt someone looking at her and turned to see Freya's eyes on her. Freya raised an eyebrow and Miss Doyle shook her head slightly in reply. But there was nothing either of them could do. The decision had been taken and the announcements made, and that was that. Mr Fuller had bartered away Dutch's and Freya's appointments so he could join a golf club, and mix with the "right" sort of people! Freya sighed. Such was the way things seemed to be in the adult world. Ability did not seem to count, and it appeared that it was better to have a completely unsuitable person from the "right" background, rather than a competent and clever one from the "wrong" one.

The meal was eaten quickly as everyone wanted to start the holiday. Soon the dining room was empty and the children were streaming down the high street on their way home. Dutch was telling Freya that he was hoping to be able to earn good money during the holiday, as it was hay making time and also Mr Winter was bound to need them in his garden. Freya nodded, only listening with half an ear, the announcement of Daphne Marshall as head girl had hurt more than she had let on. A car swept past them down the high street. The new head girl was telling her mother about her shock appointment and showing her the badge she had been given. Her mother nodded in approval. It had not been a shock to her.

That night, Freya was restless, a rare thing for her and she had made sure that Uncle Lars and Aunty Rose would sleep long and deep when they went to bed. She waited until two in the morning and then dressed and went out of her bedroom window, down the tree and out into the darkness. Her old friend the night was waiting for her and as usual she stood quite still in the alley beyond the garden wall and tuned into it. The air was full of the smells of the earth in summer and she could see and hear the creatures of the night going about their business. When she was ready, she moved silently through the darkness and patrolled her territory, as cats liked to do, letting the night calm her and dissolve the pent-up frustration that she had felt earlier. As usual, she came across other cats, also patrolling their patches, some of which overlapped with hers, but they were used to seeing this strange cat/girl from time to time and had accepted her as one of them. They knew her and she knew them and they co-existed together and shared a bit of their territory with each other.

After an hour, Freya was her old self and began to make her way home when she spotted a new cat far in the distance. It was black and fluffy and appeared to be heading towards the Old Mill. As Freya watched, it stopped and seemed to sense her presence, even though they were a long way apart, and turned to look directly at her, as if to let her know that it knew that she was there, before continuing on its way. Freya watched it go and resumed her journey home, having a strange feeling that somehow she knew the new cat, even though she had not seen it before. Ten minutes later she was back in her room and ready to sleep, her old friend the night had once again worked its magic. As she drifted off to sleep and joined her waiting parents, the new cat she had seen was sitting in a boat being pulled along a secret underground tunnel with some of her friends, silently telling them about the strange cat/girl she had seen in the village.

Millie had her own secret territory which she did not have to share with any other cats. For now anyway.

Mrs Hunter was fed up and grumpy. Nothing unusual about that, she was always fed up and grumpy, it was her natural state. If things did not go her way, she would become more fed up and grumpy, but if things did go her way, she would not become less fed up and grumpy. She was never actually happy.

When she had been "requested" to leave St Martins School and not return, she had not gone quietly, it simply was not her way. She never did anything quietly. So, with time on her hands she had written to everyone she could think of to try and get reinstated as a teacher again, including the new Headmaster, the board of school governors, her MP, the Secretary of State for Education, the Prime Minister and Her Majesty the Queen! And when that had not borne fruit, telephoned them all as well. But to no avail. She was not going to get her job back and that was definitely that! And to her complete surprise, the school had continued to function without her! The only crumb of comfort that she had was that she managed to bring down that fool Mitchell with her.

From what she had heard, the new headmaster seemed to be much more to her liking and had, so the village grape vine said, reintroduced the cane back into the school, something she very much approved of. Children needed discipline, and Mrs Hunter was a great believer in them being seen but not heard, and preferably not seen either. The trouble was, she did see and hear them, especially that foreign girl, Freda Olsen, who she blamed completely for her being asked to leave the school. It never entered her head that it was she herself that had been the architect of her own downfall and no one else. No. It was all that foreign girl's fault! If only she could get her own back, but how? Mrs Hunter reached for the gin bottle, even though it was not yet lunch time. A nip or two would help her think, it always did. Something would come to her sooner or later, and when it did, it would be payback time!

The summer of 1966 flew by so quickly, as summers tend to do when you are young. The haymaking had been done, Mr Winter's garden looked fantastic with not a single weed to be seen. There had been a family visit to Abbotsbury market and one to the cinema at Pondford. They had seen the new James Bond film, "You only live twice" with its haunting theme tune sung by Nancy Sinatra and really enjoyed the film with all the gadgets, including "Little Nellie"! Freya was very impressed with the way that the villain, Blofeld had cleverly hidden all his men and equipment in a volcano, right in plain sight of everyone. Of course, 007 had won in the end, but it was an excellent film. Once again, as they emerged into the summer sunlight, it seemed that the film world was the real one, and the real world was artificial.

During the summer Dutch had helped the milkman on a Saturday morning now and then, and Freya had got an unpaid job of taking the dog that belonged to Mr Young who ran the pub "Time Flies" out for a walk on a Saturday morning as Mr Young had hurt his foot when he dropped a barrel of beer on to it while working in his cellar. Both Freya and Lucy were delighted with this arrangement and went either up to the Old Wood or down to the Old Mill. Lucy was able to carry on chatting to her secret friends which ever place they went to and catch up with the news and learn how the Stoat, which had been called "Flux" because of its continual change of fur colour, was settling in. Lucy found Freya a very enjoyable girl to be around and would listen to what she said to her, being able to understand every word.

When at the end of the holiday, Mr Young was able to take Lucy for a walk himself again, Freya asked if she could continue her Saturday morning task as she had become very fond of Lucy and taking her for a walk was so enjoyable. Mr Young was more than happy to agree, he could read his newspaper!

And so the summer passed by and soon it was September once again and Freya and Dutch returned to St Martins School for their last year, little knowing that it was going to be a year to remember, for more reasons than one!

The preparation was at an end, the revision complete, and today was the day of the eleven plus examination. Freya, Dutch and the rest of their class filed into the assembly hall at St Martins School to find tables and chairs set out in long rows, and strange faces were waiting for them. On the stage there were some chairs set out each side of a giant clock that was resting on a table. It was a Saturday morning and it seemed very strange to be in the school on this day, the playground and corridors empty and except for them, the coat pegs bare. Freya could tell that some of her classmates were suddenly nervous, hoping that the revision they had done, or not done would be enough for them to do well. Most however seemed unconcerned, sure that they would be going to Pondford Secondary Modern School next year anyway. Everyone did, except for a few rich kids whose parents could afford to pay for them to go to Abbotsbury Grammar School. No one from this school had actually passed the exam since the old Headmaster, Mr Mitchell had, many many years ago.

The invigilators were all strangers, here to supervise the candidates for the exam. As everyone took their seats, Freya made sure that she sat behind Dutch, telling him with a smile, it was to make sure that he did not try to copy her answers! It wasn't, as she knew he knew very well. Just before the chief officer began to speak, Freya whispered "Good Luck" to Dutch, who gave her a thumbs up sign without turning around. As the rules of the exam were explained to them, assistants moved down between the rows of tables, putting the question papers and answer books in front of each child, face down. When the chief officer had finished his speech and dealt with a couple of questions, he moved over to stand next to the giant clock and said, "You may turn over your question papers now, and good luck to you all," and pressed a button on the giant clock to start the red second hand moving, before taking his seat. The exam had begun!

In a little under two hours, Freya had finished. As per the advice she had been given at the start of the exam, she had spent time reading all the questions quickly, then starting with the shorter, easier ones first, before attempting the longer and more complicated questions later. When she had done everything, she rechecked her answers again, just to be sure. It was done. As was her habit, and remembering Miss Doyle's whispered advice on the day she had defeated Mrs Hunter, not to attract too much attention to yourself, she had deliberately made a few minor errors here and there, knowing that if she had worked to her full potential, she would have got one hundred per cent, which certainly would have got her lots of attention. She had calculated that she would probably get a eighty five to ninety percent pass mark. It would do very nicely. She was not conceited or over confident. She just knew that she had passed. Her photographic memory and enhanced mind had made sure of that.

Now that she had finished her work, she turned her attention to Dutch. Freya knew full well that he was more than capable of passing as well, but she also knew that he was worried about the cost of going to grammar school. The scholarship would pay for the tuition, but all the extras would be for the account of his family, and like Freya's, they were poor, and he did not want to burden them with the expense that going to grammar school would bring. Freya looked forward and noticed that he had stopped writing. She looked down, as if she was thinking, while her eyes focused on the back of Dutch's head. After a few minutes, his hand moved and he started writing again and did not stop until he too had finished all the questions and rechecked his work. Freya smiled to herself and looked down again. She had not given him any of the answers, he already knew them. What she had done was to give him the confidence to do his very best and worry about the costs later. Somehow, they would earn enough money to be able to afford all they needed without putting too much strain on their families. Freya had no intention of going off to grammar school without him.

Soon the three hours were up and the exam over. The answer books and questions papers were collected and lunch was served. As expected, the talk was all about who had put what as the answers to the questions, and a few began to realise that they may have gone wrong. Munch did not worry, knowing before he had begun that he had no chance of passing and not caring anyway. He was going to work on a farm when he left school and had no need of qualifications to do that. So long as he could milk a cow and bale hay, that was enough for him.

Dutch was confiding to Freya that he had known the answers, but had decided to get them wrong and go to Pondford, not wanting to put pressure on his parents with costs they could not afford. But near the end, he suddenly had a thought come into his mind that he should give it his best shot and sod the costs, as he would find work from somewhere to pay for most of it himself, and anyway, he did not want to be apart from her, knowing that she was sure to pass, and would need him to look after her at the new school.

Freya smiled at her special friend and said, "Let's hope I do pass, or you will be on your own!" For a moment, Dutch looked at her in horror and said, "You did try to pass too, didn't you?" Freya smiled again. "Of course I did," she said, reaching under the table and to squeeze his hand. "I don't want to be apart from you either, we're a team, right?"

Dutch smiled back at her and squeezed her hand. "Right!"

Simon Marshall sat at his desk in his office, deep in thought. So it was true. His suspicions had proved to be right. It was all there in black and white, contained in the report that lay open on his desk, written in precise terms as if for a court case, which it might well end up as, if his wife decided to be difficult when he used it to divorce her. His wife. Mother of Daphne. How could she have done it, and with him!

Dates, times of arrival, times of departure, location of vehicle etc., etc. There were lots and lots of photographs to support the written evidence, as well as a tape recording of various conversations, together with a good quality colour cine film of about twenty minutes which had been taken from a high position looking directly down on to the bed, which showed the viewer everything that had taken place below. Simon wondered just how the private investigator had managed to get such a film without the subjects knowing it.

It was a first-rate piece of work, he had to admit, done by a professional who knew what he was doing. In a strange sort of way, it was almost too good, as it left no doubt at all that his wife was having an affair with his boss, Quentin Drummond in his flat and behind Simon's back. It raised more questions than it answered, the first of which was why? Why was Mary doing this? Had he not tried his best to please her, to give her everything that she had wanted and more besides? He had not worked hard to pay for all that she had asked for, large house, luxury furniture and carpets, fashionable clothes, shoes, her own car.

She had wanted for nothing and yet here she was cheating on him. He felt betrayed, humiliated and used. The colour film had been bad enough, showing them having sex. But the audio was much worse, as they laughed at him, calling him a plodder and a doormat while they lay on the bed naked, touching each other with the bedroom curtains open so as not to attract attention from the neighbours, and her car parked a few streets away. They thought they had thought of everything. Everything except that he might find out! If it hadn't been for that lovely nurse, Penny Thornton, he probably would not have. One part of the audio tape, Quentin had asked Mary why she stayed with him. She had replied with a yawn, that he served a purpose, paid the bills and gave her respectability and so long as he did as he was told and continued to be a good father to her daughter, she would keep him on, adding that he would be nowhere without her and her connections!

With a sigh, Simon closed the file and locked it in his safe, to which only he had the combination. So. What to do now? He had had the report for quite a while already and had been going to confront his wife at the start of the summer holidays when quite unexpectedly, Daphne had come home from school, wearing the Head Girl's badge, and he had hesitated. Daphne was the one good thing that had come out of his marriage to Mary and he did not want to spoil her last year at school, so he had decided to wait a little longer before he wielded the axe.

After Christmas would do, better still, early in the New Year. Yes, that would be good. One last Christmas together as a family. So it was decided. He had always had a secret building society account, in which was a couple of thousand pounds, his "running away money" as he liked to think of it. By the time the legal side of things had been completed, Daphne would have finished her time at St Martins. January 1967. That was when he would confront her. He smiled, it would be a late Christmas present to himself! Ho Ho Ho!

A few weeks later, during the half-term break in late October, just before Halloween, Mrs Hunter found what she had been looking for. Elfington was built on the side of a valley and as such there was no shortage of hills, most of them steep ones. While on a rare walk down by the Old Mill, she had seen Dutch and Freya on their bikes in the distance, further down the same track she was walking on. Freya had spotted Mrs Hunter long before she had seen them, and had turned off the track at the first opportunity and headed down another to avoid passing her. No doubt, as it was Halloween, Mrs Hunter had come out for a spell! The new track took them along the front of the lake and passed the Old Mill itself before joining the road again that led back into the village.

Mrs Hunter saw them turn off and scowled to herself. Bloody foreigners. She walked on a little further and as she did so something high up on the bank, a fox probably, dislodged a small stone which tumbled and bounced its way down the slope through the undergrowth before dropping on to the track ahead. It landed quite a way from her and was no bigger than a tennis ball. As she had watched the stone rolling down the bank, a thought came into her mind and gave her the idea that she had been looking for. She turned back at once, and made her way slowly home, moaning to herself about the steep hills, but with a very rare smile on her face. Today had turned out to be a very good day indeed!

High up on the bank, Rolo and Flux watched the human down below. They had been chasing each other along the bank and really enjoying themselves. Rolo had wanted to come here and put some acorns in a pile to be collected later and Flux had come with her friend just to enjoy the outdoors and be close to the spot where everything had changed for her when she had made contact with her new family. They had been allowed to come, so long as Millie came with them. She was lying on a branch of the oak tree beneath which Rolo and Flux were scampering about. She had watched the stone they had dislodged roll down the bank, but as it had not hit anything, all was well. From where she was, she could see the grave of her siblings across the lake, it was nice for her to be close to them. She had also seen the two human children and recognised Freya, the cat/girl and her friend, and noticed the older human female and even from here, she could see the red negative energy aura emanating from her. No wonder Freya and her friend had turned off the track! Still no harm done. But for once, Millie was wrong.

"And so, Headmaster, I could have been killed or badly injured, and it was only sheer good fortune that I was not. I insist that you take the strongest possible action against those two lunatics!" Mr Fuller tuned back into what the visitor to his study at St Martins School was saying and looked at her, surprised that she had finally stopped speaking. He had been on the receiving end of at least half an hour's worth of non-stop verbal battering. He had tried to interject, but Mrs Hunter just talked over him as if he had not spoken and carried on in her usual booming and penetrating voice, not seeming to breathe at all. He thought that it was like a record which once started, had to reach its end without interruption. After this, he would have to visit Dr Thornton, or better still, his gorgeous wife Penny and get his ears checked for damage. Mrs Hunter did not talk to you, she talked at you. All the stories he had heard about her were true. Thank god she was not teaching at this school now. His school.

"This is a very serious incident," he said gravely, "you could indeed have been quite badly hurt." Pity you weren't, he thought to himself. He had not believed a word that Mrs Hunter had said, but as an ex-teacher of this school and, more importantly, still a member of the parish council, something he intended to join as soon as he could for the contacts it would bring him, he would have to do something, knowing if he did not, Mrs Hunter would give him no peace until he did. "Right then, Mrs Hunter, please leave the matter with me. After Friday's assembly, I'll have them both in here and give them a good talking to." He sat back in his big leather chair and put down his pen, a signal intended to show that the discussion was over and that she should take her leave, thinking that would do the trick and the stupid old bat would go home. He was sadly mistaken. The signal, if received at all had bounced off her. "A good talking to, Headmaster, falls far short of what is required! I have come to you with this in the hope that you will take the appropriate action. However, if you are unwilling to do the necessary, I will have no choice but to report this incident to the Police and let them investigate. But that, I'm sure I don't have to tell you, would not reflect well on this school, or you as headmaster, would it?"

Mr Fuller nodded, knowing he had been easily out manoeuvred by a professional. Last week had been Halloween, and he was sure the old Witch had been out on her broomstick! "What would you consider to be the appropriate action in this case?" he asked, already knowing the answer he would get.

He was not disappointed. Mrs Hunter did not hesitate in replying. "I want those two children caned, Headmaster. Nothing less is acceptable to me." Mr Fuller nodded again. If that's what it would take to get rid of her, then so be it. All he wanted was a quiet life, and so, like many others had done before him, he gave in to her demands. "Very well, Mrs Hunter, I agree. For something as serious as this, the cane would be appropriate in this case. You have my word. Freya Olsen and Gilbert van den Berg will be caned."

"When?"

"Today is Thursday. Tomorrow. I'll do it tomorrow."

Freya had seen Mrs Hunter walk up to and then go inside the school that Thursday morning from her desk by the window, something that she had thought she would not see again. Immediately she could sense the negative energy coming from her even across the playground and wondered what had brought her back here. Nothing good, she was quite sure. Forty minutes later, she noticed Mrs Hunter cross the playground and leave the gate open, something she would always shout at the children for if they did it, and make her way down the road, a smug look on her face, replacing the usual scowl she had arrived with. Miss Doyle, who was taking the class instead of Mr Fuller, who had had to deal with his visitor, also noticed the arrival and departure of Mrs Hunter and the changed expression on her face. Clearly she had got what she had come for, no surprise there she thought to herself, most people gave in to Mrs Hunter, just to get rid of her, except perhaps Mr Baxter from the village shop.

Miss Doyle frowned. Where ever that woman went, trouble was never far behind. During the lunch break she would make a few discreet inquiries and find out what was going on. Miss Doyle had her special way of finding out what she wanted to know!

Mr Fuller was, at least where the school was concerned, a man of habit, something that Miss Doyle was counting on. She now knew what Mrs Hunter had come to the school for, and what Mr Fuller proposed to do about it, and had managed to work out a strategy to counter it. In fact if all went to plan, she intended to kill three birds with one stone, metaphorically speaking.

Friday morning saw Miss Doyle up and about earlier than usual, as she set about putting her plan into action. The school morning passed as it usually did and it was not until eleven forty-five that Freya and Dutch were called to the Headmaster's study. Everyone knew that if the cane was about to be used, this was the day and time that it happened. Munch knew this more than anyone else. But everyone also knew that Freya and Dutch could not possibly be going to his study for that, it was just a coincidence, nothing more. Dutch was at a complete loss as to why Mr Fuller had sent for them. Freya was not.

After keeping them waiting outside in the corridor for several minutes, the door opened and they were told to come inside and close the door behind them. They could tell from his face and demeanour that they were here for something serious. The clock behind Mr Fuller's desk showed eleven fifty-two as a tall, slim girl in a much-washed and mended dress, and a smaller boy in shorts and a much-washed shirt with frayed collar and cuffs stood together in front of the large desk, behind which sat a man wearing a new suit, white shirt and smart tie. Without preamble, he began to tell them the accusation against them, watching Dutch's face go pale, while Freya's did not change at all, remaining blank and expressionless, her green eyes locked onto his.

In her classroom, Miss Doyle also glanced at the clock. Eleven fifty-five. Not quite time yet. At that exact time Mr Fuller concluded his case. "Well?" he demanded. "What have you got to say for yourselves?"

"We didn't do it, Sir, nor would we ever dream of doing it," said Freya for both of them.

377

Mr Fuller stared back at them in disbelief. "So, Mrs Hunter is a liar, is that what you are saying? She just decided to make it all up and come up here and take up my valuable time for the sake of it? Well?"

Dutch was very scared now and it showed. "Honest, Sir, we did not try to hurt Mrs Hunter, we saw her, but she was a long way away from us," his accent coming through stronger than normal.

"So, you were there, down by the Old Mill at the same time as Mrs Hunter?"

"Yes, Sir, but as Gilbert has just said, we were a long way away and down on the same track as she was, therefore we could not have not have dislodged a stone from high up on the bank."

Her steady gaze and calm demeanour was making Mr Fuller uncomfortable. She should be as scared as the boy, but she was not. She was as calm and relaxed as if they were talking about the weather. He had always thought there was something about that girl. She was always so sure of herself.

The clock now said eleven fifty-six.

"Well, I've given you the chance to own up, but you have not taken it and continued to lie. If Mrs Hunter, a well-respected lady of high morals and a former teacher in this very school, says you did it, then you did it, and I believe her, and that's all there is to it." Dramatically, he slid open a drawer in his desk and took out the cane and placed it on the blotter in front of him, noting Dutch's eyes going wide, and his chin starting to quiver, following his every move. Freya's expression had not changed.

Eleven fifty-seven. Time. Miss Doyle handed over the class to Miss Foster, who had been assisting and headed down the corridor to the headmaster's study, a grim look on her face. Show time!

Mr Fuller picked up the cane and flexed it, getting to his feet as he did so. He turned to Dutch. "Hold out your hand!" Dutch turned to Freya, clearly terrified. She moved closer and put her arm around him. "Don't worry, Dutch, no one is being caned today."

Mr Fuller was just about to speak when the door suddenly opened and Miss Doyle swept in to the room, without bothering to knock or wait to be asked inside, taking in the scene in one glance. The cane in Mr Fuller's hand, the outraged look on his face at the interruption, Dutch trembling and close to tears, partly due to the cane, but mostly at the sheer unfairness of it all, that anyone could ever think that he would ever hurt anyone. And Freya with her protecting arm around him, calm and about to speak.

"Miss Doyle! What is the meaning of this? I was…" Miss Doyle ignored him as if he was not even there. "Run along now, children, there has been a dreadful mistake. Go and see cook and have a glass of milk, she is expecting you, while I have a word with the headmaster. Don't go back to your class, it's nearly lunch time anyway. Off you go now," and Miss Doyle ushered them out in to the corridor and closed the door behind them, turning back to face Mr Fuller, her smile gone, replaced with a look of utter contempt. "We need to have a little chat, you and I, and we are going to have it right now," said Miss Doyle, sitting down in a chair in front of his desk and folding her arms, the universal signal of one who is not going anywhere.

Out in the corridor, Freya and Dutch began to make their way to the kitchen, but stopped after a few steps as Dutch was shaking so much. Freya gently took him in her arms and held him close, talking to him as she did so. "It's all over now, Dutch, Mr Fuller has been given false information, that's all, and Miss Doyle is sorting it all out for us. Don't worry, you know I'll never let anyone hurt you." Dutch hugged Freya tightly, feeling her warmth and strength spread through him, calming him. It was a good job he could not see Freya's eyes as she looked back at the door to Mr Fullers study!

Dutch finally released Freya and said, "Thank goodness Miss Doyle came in when she did. Mr Fuller was going to cane us and we didn't do anything wrong, did we?"

"No Dutch, we didn't do anything wrong. I'm sure Miss Doyle is explaining the facts of life to Mr Fuller right now. So let's go and have that glass of milk and leave her to it!"

Mr Fuller was beside himself with rage and was just about to give Miss Doyle a mouthful of abuse when she said, "I wouldn't say anything rash, if I were you. You see, I know about you and Fiona Foster, or should I say pussykins?"

Ken Fuller's eyes widened in shock and they seemed about to pop out of his head, his face turned bright red and his mouth fell open. Miss Doyle looked at him calmly. "Do sit down, er, Kennybaby, you don't look very well." He sat as she continued. "And while we're about it, put that thing away, no one is going to be caned from now on, as long as I'm in this school."

Mr Fuller looked at her, regaining some of his composure. "Miss Doyle, let me assure you that there is nothing going on between me and Fio, I mean Miss Foster, how dare you say such a thing!"

Miss Doyle raised one slim eyebrow. "I was there, Kennybaby, in the alley when you were groping Fiona, or Pussykins as you seem to like calling her. I've known about you two for quite a while, but I've said nothing. But when I heard that you were going to cane those two children for something we both know they have not and never would do, I thought it's about time we had a little chat."

Mr Fuller was silent for a while, his mind working furiously. Then he smiled slowly and leaned back in his chair. "Good try, Miss Doyle, but no deal! Those two will be caned and I will enjoy doing it even more. No one will believe you and your tittle tattle. So that's it. You are now finished in this school, and I want your resignation by the end of the d..."

"Look out of the window, Kennybaby and tell me what you see!"

Mr Fuller turned in his chair and saw his wife walking through the school gate and across the playground. It was twelve fifteen. Miss Doyle glanced at the clock. She was right on time.

Mr Fuller swung back to face Miss Doyle again, his face draining of colour, as Miss Doyle continued.

"I asked her to come, as I thought you might take that attitude. I'm sure she would be interested to learn about you and pussykins!"

Mr Fuller looked at her. He had badly underestimated Miss Doyle, but he was not about to give in now. He had one more card left to play, and he played it now.

"You're good, Miss Doyle, I'll give you that, but still no deal. It's still your word against mine, and my wife will believe me, so by all means, let's get her in here and get it over with."

Mr Fuller sat back again, the smile back on his face. He had won.

"You know, Kennybaby , you really are a smug bastard, but although you might be able to talk your way out of anything, how long would Fiona survive under questioning before she cracked and told the whole sorry tale? Not long I'd say."

Miss Doyle glanced at the clock again. Mrs Fuller would be here in a few seconds. Perfect. "I've asked your wife to join us here, and Miss Foster is also en route as we speak. So, it's make your mind up time, Kennybaby!"

Miss Doyle sat back in her chair, noticing that the smile had gone again from his face. Miss Foster was not on her way here, but he didn't know that! Finally he spoke.

"You're bluffing. This would ruin your career as well as mine, not to mention Fiona's!"

Miss Doyle rose from her chair, put her hands on the desk and leaned across it, her face inches from his. "Try me!"

Mr "Kennybaby" Fuller looked into Miss Doyle's eyes. She would do it, he realised, if only to spite him. He sighed. He had lost.

"Very well, Miss Doyle, very well. You win. "

Miss Doyle kept her gaze on him for a few seconds more before returning to her seat.

"Thank you, headmaster. Now before your wife comes in, this is what we will do. I will keep my mouth shut about you and Fiona, she has no idea that I know, and never will. I will agree to leave the school at the end of the Christmas term. I will say nothing to your wife, or anyone else, you have my word on that. You, in return will not get that cane out again while I'm still in this school and you will not punish Freya or Gilbert in any other way for something we both know they did not do. Mrs Hunter is a lying, spiteful, bitter old woman who still blames Freya for her having to leave this school and has no doubt dreamt up this whole thing and used you as a fool to do her dirty work for her, and you fell for it! If there was any truth to her story, she could go to the police, but she won't, believe me, because it's all a pack of lies. So, do we have a deal? Your hand on it?"

Mr Fuller nodded, knowing it was the best he could hope for. He reached out and took the outstretched hand and shook it briefly. Miss Doyle smiled. "I will have to hope you don't go back on your word, because if you do, I will not hesitate to have a chat to your wife, not to mention the board of school governors, so bear that in mind. And by the way, you may not realise it, but I've actually saved your miserable neck. "

Mr Fuller looked at her. "How so?"

"Freya's parents are both dead, have you ever met her uncle?" Mr Fuller shook his head. "No."

"Well, if you had, you would have remembered it. He's six feet five inches tall, nineteen stone of pure muscle, due to his body building work in the gym in his back garden, and if you had caned his niece for something he would know she had not done, well, I can only say you had better like hospital food, because that is where you would end up. Vikings are very protective of their womenfolk."

There was a knock at the door, and Mr Fuller went to open it to find his wife standing outside. "Hello, dear," she said, "I understand you have got Miss Doyle in here?" Mr Fuller nodded and opened the door wider. Miss Doyle got to her feet. "Yes I'm here, Mrs Fuller, thank you so much for coming, but I have a new knitting pattern which I just know you're going to love, so as we have finished our discussion, I'll run along now, with your permission of course, Headmaster."

Mr Fuller managed a smile and said, "Of course, Miss Doyle, thank you for your input."

He watched them go down the corridor together and into the staff room, chattering away, just as the bell rang for lunch. He went back inside his study, closed the door and sat back in his chair, deep in thought. He took a long breath and let it out slowly. That had been a close call and no mistake. He would just have to hope that cow Miss Doyle kept her gob shut, as he was getting to the stage in his relationship with Fiona when he would suggest she joined him for a weekend away, while his wife enjoyed her new knitting pattern and thought he was away on school business.

A wave of anger swept over him, he hated losing, especially to a bloody woman! It was all the fault of that stupid old bag Mrs Hunter, coming in here with her fairy stories, and he had fallen for it. He pulled open the desk drawer with a jerk, removed the cane and snapped it into two pieces and threw the two halves in the general direction of the waste paper basket. They both missed and landed on the carpet. He sighed. It just was not his day!

After lunch, Miss Doyle was on playground duty, and found Freya and Dutch together, as usual. She leaned back against the stone wall that surrounded the playground and waved them to come over to her. Freya was her usual self, calm and confident, but she could see that Dutch was not himself, quiet and wary. Miss Doyle smiled at them both. "Just to let you know, I've spoken to the Headmaster and he's now of the opinion that you were telling him the truth all along and that Mrs Hunter was mistaken. No further action is being taken and the matter is closed. I'm sorry that you were accused of this, as everyone knows you would not do anything of the sort."

Freya smiled and nudged Dutch. "See! I told you Miss Doyle would sort everything out!" Dutch looked very relieved and Miss Doyle reached out and ruffled his hair. "You're a good boy, Gilbert .Now you and Freya run along and stop worrying. It's all over and done with. It was all a silly mistake. "

Miss Doyle watched them move away and join Freddie Piper by the shed in the corner of the playground. She continued to look around the playground and sighed. She would really miss this place, but she was really tired now. She had stayed much longer than she had planned to, but in a few short weeks the reason she had had to stay would no longer exist. She thought back to the events of the morning. Her timing had been very good, except when she had entered Mr Fuller's study. Freya had just been about to reveal she had also been in the alley that night and seen Mr Fuller and Miss Foster together and try to blackmail her way out of avoiding the cane. But as luck would have it, she had arrived just in time to prevent Freya from doing so.

No one needed to know about Freya's nocturnal wanderings! Over by the shed, Dutch and Freddie were chatting about the World Cup, but Freya was watching Miss Doyle. She had done well to sort out Mr Fuller and make him see reason, guessing correctly that she had used the same strategy that Freya herself was just about to deploy when Miss Doyle had stepped in. Getting Mrs Fuller to come to the school had been a master stroke, she had to admit. But it was better this way, no one, except Miss Doyle knew that she had been in the alley that night. Freya smiled to herself, her green eyes twinkling. Poor old Kennybaby had never stood a chance! She tuned back into the conversation between Dutch and Freddie, which had now changed from the World Cup to Dr Who and the Daleks. Freddie admitted that he had watched the last episode from behind the sofa and Dutch confessed that he had as well. Boys!

Freya looked at them both with mock horror. "Daleks don't scare me, they can't climb stairs, go outside or move over uneven ground, and with only one eye on a stick, they would be so easy to sneak up on. No, Daleks are nothing to worry about. Cybermen, on the other hand, they are the scary ones!"

Later that day, and alone in his study again, Mr Fuller reflected back on the events of the morning. There was something about that child, Freya. Something different. Then he realised what it was. Her eyes. They were like a cats. Her eyes spoke volumes, but said nothing. It was impossible to know what thoughts lay behind them, but her facial expression that morning would suggest that the thoughts were far from happy ones. The warmth and friendliness that were almost always there had gone, to be replaced by something else, something much colder. He had seen the look she had given him somewhere before. Now where was it? Oh yes, it was on one of those wildlife programmes on the TV, from Africa where one of the big cats had crept up on a herd of antelope and had selected a young one for dinner, and the camera had caught the look on the cat's face as it had a last look around just before it started its attack.

The Cat's eyes were devoid of pity, of compassion, of mercy. They were totally focused on the here and now, on its prey which was blissfully unaware that its time on planet earth was rapidly running out. The eyes were like twin laser beams, locked on to its target, ready to strike.

He shivered. And just like the young Antelope, his fate had been sealed. He wondered what she had been going to say before Miss Doyle had burst in. He would never know now. So with as much dignity as he could muster, he would let the matter drop and move on. But this young antelope had been allowed to escape. This time. It would live to fight another day. But it was a very stupid young antelope and it had learned nothing. It would be its undoing.

Chapter Forty-Three

Dutch and Freya stood on opposite sides of the road that led out of the village and on to Beggars Cross, each holding a small Union Jack flag on a stick in their hands, ready to wave when a very special lady passed through Elfington Village in her car on her way from an engagement in the Potteries. It was a week after Miss Doyle had stopped them from being caned and Mrs Hunter was out for revenge.

They were the last two children to line the route, put there by Mrs Hunter, who had found out that that spineless excuse for a headmaster had not actually caned them after all, as he had promised to do, she had used her position on the parish council to her own advantage, and secured the job of senior route marshal and allocated the children their places. The other members of the Council were more than happy for Mrs Hunter to do this task, anything to get rid of her and keep her happy. Their classmates had been placed further down in the village, where the road was steep and twisty, and the special car would have to slow to a crawl in order to navigate the narrow road, giving them a much better view of the lady who would be inside. Where Dutch and Freya had been put, the road was straighter and not so steep, so they would see less as the car would start to gather speed as it left the village. Mrs Hunter had made sure that they had the worst view of all, as they were only foreign children anyway, and she did not like them, so that was that!

Everyone in the village was lining the streets, especially the High Street, which gave the best view, and were eagerly waiting like the children for the car to come by. But where Dutch and Freya were standing, there were no houses or people, only Mr Winter, who stood at the end of his drive leaning on his walking stick, waiting for the VIP to go by. Freya and Dutch had waved to him and he had waved back. They did not mind where they stood, as they were close to the Old Mill, Freya could see its roof in the distance if she turned around and looked through the trees. They had been standing there for three quarters of an hour, and soon after her arrival, her attention kept being drawn to a large oak tree that stood in a small clearing back from the road. There was nothing special about the tree, it was one of many she could see from where she stood. Dutch had his back to it, as he was facing her across the road. Freya glanced down the road to see if she could see anything, but there was no sign of the motorcade yet. She recognised Inspector Pitt, who was standing closest to them, twenty yards away, having placed his officers further down the route. Freya thought he looked very smart in his best uniform, ready to salute as the car went by.

Again, Freya's gaze returned to the Oak Tree across the road. She frowned. All her instincts were telling her that something was wrong, and that tree was part of it. She was correct. Sitting near the top of the tree was Lucky, and below her, lying flat on a large branch, was a man with a rifle! Lucky had come to see the lady in the car, she had read about it in the paper, but when she had settled in the tree, she had immediately spotted the human below her. It had been a human with a rifle that had shot her. Then she had seen Freya, the blond girl from the sports day and later the classroom in the school, where there had been a brief contact between them. Quickly Lucky focused her mind and her eyes on the girl, trying to re-connect to her. Freya kept looking at the tree, but the distance was too far and Lucky had not remembered the correct frequency yet. Still she kept trying, knowing that she could not allow the human with the rifle to harm anyone, not least the lady in the car.

As Freya gazed at the tree, a gust of wind stirred the branches, just a little, but enough for her augmented eyes to see that there was a figure, very carefully hidden in camouflage clothing in the tree, and the figure had a weapon, and it was pointing straight at her, or rather where the car would be when it passed by. Out of the corner of her eye, she saw the flags start to wave and a cheer went up from the crowd. The car was approaching. She had to do something. Quickly she ran across the road to Dutch. "There's someone in that tree with a gun, I think they are going to shoot at the car, quick, run and get the policeman and tell him!"

"Are you sure?" asked Dutch in alarm.

"Yes, trust me. I'm going to try and distract him while you bring the policeman. So hurry!"

"Be careful!"

"I will, now go!"

As Dutch ran down the pavement as fast as he could, behind the crowd, all eyes were on two motorcycle outriders that had just turned the final corner, blue lights flashing. No one took any notice of him.

Breathless, he ran up to the police man and pulled his arm. Inspector Pitt, who had been getting ready to salute, looked down in annoyance at Dutch, who had to shout in his ear above the noise of the crowd.

The Inspector looked at the boy in horror. Please God, he thought to himself, let this be a joke.

"Are you sure about this?" he asked as the motorcycles approached him.

"Yes, sir. My friend Freya is going to try and distract him until you get there!"

The name "Freya" got his attention. He was sure that there was only one person with that name within a hundred miles. The still unsolved hit-and-run case. Inspector Pitt did not hesitate any longer and, having no radio, began to run up the pavement with Dutch hard on his heels. Again, all attention was focused on the road and no one saw the two running figures behind the crowds.

They were still ahead of the car, which had slowed to almost a crawl to swing around the final tight bend in the road, but not by much. The royal car was behind another police car, which was behind the motorcycles, with a final car behind. All began to slowly gather speed as they headed out of the village. They could not see the two running figures racing up the hill ahead of them!

Freya had reached the tree and was looking up into its branches. The man was very well camouflaged, but once you knew he was there, he was quite visible. She shouted up to him, telling him to come down and to put his gun away, but he did not react or respond. His prey was coming closer. He had missed out on the stock of weapons hidden up on the wold, and had no intention of letting this chance pass him by.

Freya decided not to try and climb up, but to try and distract him and get him to come down to her. She could hear the cheering getting louder and knew that she would not have been able to reach him in time anyway. With her mind working frantically, she grabbed a rock and threw it at the man in the tree. She had fantastic hand-eye coordination and always hit what she aimed at, another gift from the cats. This time was no exception. The rock hit the man on the side of his head just as he fired the gun at the car. It was enough to spoil his aim, and save the life of the very special lady. The high velocity round from the silenced rifle hit and went through the rear left side window of the royal car, which shattered but remained in place, and embedded itself in the back of the leather seat, inches from the head of the royal passenger, who instinctively threw herself sideways across the seat and into the lap of her lady-in-waiting, who was sitting next to her.

The driver reacted at once, as he had been trained to do and put his foot down and the powerful car surged forward, flashing his lights as he did so, and caught the leading secret service car, which seeing the flashing lights from the royal car and seeing it surge forward, also leaped forward itself and they flew down the road to Beggars Cross, over taking the motorcycle outriders, who, fortunately were not riding close together, and not noticing Mr Winter waving his flag. Soon the motorcade was gone, carrying their badly shaken, but still alive royal passenger to safety.

Back at the tree, the gunman was already trying to make his escape, not knowing if he had killed his target or not. He swung down from the tree, the rifle slung across his back on a sling. As his boots hit the earth, another rock hit him in the face, stunning him and drawing blood.

He looked at Freya with hatred as she threw herself at him, catching him unaware. Freya pummelled him with her fists, catching him on each side of his face with hard blows. The speed and power of the blows made the gunman stagger back. He could not believe a mere girl could hit him that hard. He lashed out at her, managing to hit her with one punch to her head and knocking her down. For a moment she lay on the ground stunned, but saw his boot heading her way as the gunman tried to kick her in the head and she rolled away. Quick as lightning, Freya grabbed the boot as it passed

386

her head and twisted with all her might. The gunman, unbalanced now and again caught unawares by the speed of Freya's moves, crashed to the ground, just as Freya leaped to her feet and gave him a mighty kick between his legs. He rolled over on to his side, clutching his groin and groaning in pain.

Out of the corner of her eye, Freya saw Dutch and the Policeman running towards her. She went to give the gunman a final kick in the ribs for good measure as Dutch and the Policeman drew close. It was her one mistake. The gunman, not as badly injured as he had made out, grabbed her foot and pushed, sending her sprawling, while in one fluid move, he brought the rifle on its sling around to the front of his body while raising himself to one knee and fired, hitting the Policeman in the left chest. He flew backwards and lay still. The gunman recognized him from the time when he and his group had come so very close to getting their hands on a large cache of weapons hidden up on the wold after the Second World War.

Payback time! The gunman rose to his feet and pointed the silenced rifle directly at Dutch. He did not want any witnesses. "Your turn" was all he said as his finger tightened on the trigger again. Dutch's eyes went wide as he faced death. The gun in the man's hands looked as big as a cannon and the end of the barrel seemed as wide as a jam jar. Thoughts flashed through his mind at lightning speed as he waited to die. He was frozen with fear. The gunman had shot the policeman without hesitation, now it was his turn. He could not miss! He wondered if it would hurt. He turned to look at Freya, a look of profound sadness on his face. He did not want to die and leave her. Not here, not like this. The gunman fired.

Time stood still. There was a blur of movement as Freya leaped up with impossible speed to throw herself in front of Dutch at the gun went off. The bullet meant for him hit her, saving his life. The bullet struck her special necklace, which was reacting to the impulses it was receiving from its life host, the golden "11" suddenly glowing bright red in the blue stone, as it placed a protective shield around itself and Freya, and the round ricocheted off, as Freya, now infused with superhuman power and rage, landed next to the gunman and with a fist of steel struck the gunman on the side of his head. He was unconscious before he hit the ground. His last conscious thought was that no human could move that fast or punch that hard. He had never even seen the blow that knocked him out. He lay still at Freya's feet, the silenced rifle trapped under his body. Sure now that the danger was finally over, Freya moved over to Dutch and held him close to her for a moment, as the glowing red "11" of her necklace returned to its original golden colour. There was not a mark on it, or her.

Dutch drew power from Freya's embrace and she released him, knowing that he would never remember what he had just seen her do, and together they moved over to where Inspector Pitt lay. There was blood everywhere, pumping out of the entry and exit wounds. Freya unbuttoned his tunic and then his shirt, while Dutch kept an eye on the gunman. Freya slipped her hand inside Inspector Pitt's shirt and found the entry wound. The bullet had gone straight through his body and out of his back. Dutch helped her to lift him up while Freya's left hand went around his back and under the blood-soaked shirt to find the exit wound. She put a finger in both of them to stop the bleeding. It was all she could think of to do.

Dutch just helped to hold the policeman up, his child's mind unable to comprehend what he had just witnessed. He put his free arm around Freya, drawing strength from her. And that was how they were found by the police who came looking for Inspector Pitt. The officer nearest to him had seen him running up the road and had reported it to his Sergeant. An unconscious gunman, their fallen comrade with a gunshot wound that was being plugged by a blond girl who was covered in blood and dirt and who had a bruised and battered face and a boy who was holding the policeman and the girl upright. It was over.

As luck would have it, it was a Saturday afternoon and the doctor's surgery was closed and empty. Tom and Penny were just finishing lunch, having decided to miss the goings on in the village. That was about to change. There was an urgent knocking at the surgery door and Penny went down to answer it, to find a plain-clothed policeman holding up his identification and asking if the doctor was home. When she answered yes, he spoke into his radio and minutes later, the casualties came in.

First was Inspector Pitt, who was in the back of an unmarked police car together with Freya, who still had her fingers in the bullet wounds to stop him losing any more blood, he had lost far too much already. Dutch was also there. They were taken inside and the years of working in the casualty department of Abbotsbury Hospital paid dividends that afternoon. Tom and Penny swung into action, not knowing or caring what had happened, just dealing with what was before them right now. Freya told them he had been shot with a rifle, and she was stopping the bleeding as best she could. Tom and Penny knew immediately that she had saved his life by her prompt action. His tunic and shirt were cut away and only then could Freya step away from him and let Tom and Penny do their work.

It was obvious that the policeman needed to be under the care of a hospital and after stopping the bleeding and starting a drip, he was taken by police car to Abbotsbury Hospital, who were forewarned by telephone that he was coming in. A secret service man went with him. This had to be kept quiet. Once he had gone, Freya and Dutch were attended to. Already in the consulting room they lay on a bed each. Dutch was unharmed, but grubby and badly shaken. Freya had a rapidly closing left eye and was covered in blood and dirt, her hair matted and dirty. Everyone was amazed by how calm she was. Lars and Rose, who had been collected by the local police, arrived together with Gilbert senior and Beatrice Van Den Berg, relieved to see their children safe. Lars and Rose were shocked and alarmed when they first saw

388

Freya, fearing the worst. They had been told little, only that there had been an accident and that they should come at once. Penny, seeing their expressions and knowing what they were thinking, quickly assured them that the blood she was covered in was not hers, but that of a police officer that she and Dutch had helped, and was now on his way to hospital. They were very relieved to hear it. Memories of the crash that had taken Freya's parents was still fresh in their minds.

They had all been in the crowd and had walked up to where Freya and Dutch had been standing, only to be told by a police man that the road was closed and they should find another way home. When they asked about their children who had been standing there, a secret service man in plain clothes appeared, identified himself and requested that they should come with him, quietly. They did so.

The gunman, now conscious again was taken away by the police and the secret service men, who had taken over, and had quietly and calmly organised themselves so as to attract as little attention as possible. As a result of their training, the whole business was kept as quiet as it could be. Elfington was a small village, after all.

There was a policeman in the patients' waiting room to stop anyone coming in while the children were being treated, and as Tom and Penny were checking them over the door opened again. Tom spun around, angry at the intrusion, thinking that it was the policeman. "I said no one was to come in while I'm treating..." He stopped in mid-sentence when he saw just who it was who had come in. Lars, Rose, and the Van Den Bergs all gaped in surprise, getting to their feet. Only Penny recovered enough to curtsy.

Her Majesty Queen Elizabeth, the Queen Mother came in and said in a quiet voice, "Please, please do not get up, and doctor forgive my intrusion, but when I learned more of the details of what had happened, I just had to come and see these brave children for myself and to thank them for saving my life today."

Her Majesty was accompanied by three royal protection men, who quickly checked the room to make sure it was secure. Two of them then left, leaving one behind. They were taking no chances. Doctors usually had sharp instruments. The man stood by the door and said nothing, just watching. His eyes kept moving all the time. Lars wondered if he was armed. He was. Dutch's parents looked at Lars and Rose, dumbfounded. So this was the "minor incident" that they had been told their children had been involved in! The Queen Mother moved over to Tom and asked, "Doctor, please tell me that they are not injured and will recover quickly." Tom nodded.

"They will, Your Majesty, nothing broken. They just look a mess, especially that one!" he said with a smile and nod towards Freya, who looked like she had just done ten rounds with Henry Cooper.

Her Majesty moved over to Dutch's bed and turned to Tom and said, to everyone's surprise,

"This child could do with a hug, don't you agree, Doctor?"

"I think it will assist his recovery, Ma'am," he said with a smile.

Her Majesty put her arms around him and gave him a long, gentle hug, and a kiss. "Thank you so much for all you have done for me today, you are a very brave boy and I am very grateful to you."

Dutch nodded. "You are welcome, Madam, we could not let that bad man harm you and get away."

"Quite right," said the Queen Mother. "Now lie back and rest while I thank your friend."

She turned to Freya's bed and for a moment her composure almost deserted her. Her eyes filled with tears and her chin quivered. Freya was battered and bruised, clothes covered in blood and dirt, her face and body cut and scraped. But one green eye gazed up at her.

"Dear God, child, you have been in the wars," and gently bent down and gave her a gentle hug and kiss as well.

Freya said, "Be careful, Madam, I am sorry that I am not very clean at the moment."

The Queen Mother smiled. "Then we will have to see about that!" She turned to Penny. "Do you have a wipe I can use, nurse?"

Penny began to say, "Let me, Ma'am, you shouldn't..."

But her Majesty simply held out her hand and said, "Please, I must do something after all they have done for me, let me help just a little bit."

Penny handed over a packet of wipes and the whole room watched as the Queen Mother very gently took Freya's hands one at a time and wiped some of the grime off them, touched at the gesture she was making.

When she had finished, she said to Freya, "Well, what do you think?"

Freya examined her hands, turning them over. Then, with a smile she said, "Much better, thank you."

Her Majesty took the newly cleaned hands in hers. "Thank you again for what you and your friend here have done for me today. I must go now and get out of the Doctor's way, but I will be in touch again soon."

Her Majesty shook hands with Lars, Rose, Gilbert senior, and Beatrice, saying what marvellous children they had, and then with Penny and Tom, thanking them for their work. Then, she was gone and the door closed behind her. Her Majesty left Elfington Village as quietly as she had come, in an unmarked car with tinted windows. There were no sirens or flashing lights, and no one saw her leave, just as no one had seen her come.

Back in the consulting room, everyone looked at everyone else, unable to take in what they had just seen. The Queen Mother had taken the trouble to come herself and thank Freya and Dutch for what they had done, and at that point in time none of the adults actually knew what exactly they had done. The secret service man only said that there had been a "minor incident", a typical British understatement, and that Freya and Dutch had assisted the police and had received some minor injuries, and had been taken to the doctor's surgery for a quick check over. Only later did they learn the full story, and what a story it was. Both Dutch and Freya could have been killed by that gunman. They were all interviewed at great length by detectives, before all being sworn to secrecy.

Only Freya knew the whole truth. She had told the police a slightly different version of events, knowing that the gunman, Dutch and Inspector Pitt would actually remember very little. She had touched them all, ensuring that they could not. So she played up their parts and played down hers. As always, trying not to attract too much attention to herself. The only other creature who had seen the whole thing was Lucky the eagle owl. She had a very different story to tell, but not to the police, but to her friends at the hideaway!

Dutch was allowed home after Doctor Tom had checked him over. His mother gave him a bath and a good meal, then it was straight to bed. He did not resist. He felt drained of energy. What a day it had been. Before his parents had left his bedroom, he was fast asleep and he dreamed of stars and moons. He slept for twelve hours and awoke feeling much better, but unable to remember much about what had happened the day before. Tom and Penny called in to see him and he asked about Freya. They told him that she was also resting at her home and like him, was none the worse for her adventures.

Freya had also been allowed home and like Dutch she had a bath and tucked into a meal, although chewing was difficult, as was talking. She also did not resist as she was tucked into bed by Lars and Rose, who told her how proud of her they were. Freya looked back at them with one eye and smiled weakly. They kissed her goodnight, on the right side of her face and then went downstairs.

When they had gone, Freya climbed out of bed and went to the window. She opened the curtains and the window itself and looked out into the night. The breeze gently blew her blond hair, together with the lace curtains as she breathed in the cool night air. As usual she looked up onto the wold, and could see the craggs standing out in the moonlight.

Tonight was a blue moon, the second full moon in the same calendar month. There was not a cloud in the sky, which was full of stars that twinkled back at her. She could only see a tiny, tiny fraction of the Universe from her window. How much more was out there, she asked herself. She felt as if she was between worlds, living on earth, but also belonging somewhere else as well.

For a long time Freya stayed looking out of the window and into the night. It was the same window that Bob and Lisa had climbed through to put her special necklace in her coat pocket on their last night on earth. She was holding the necklace in her hands. She raised it to her lips and kissed it.

"Thank you," she said to it and to the night beyond.

She looked at the eleven sided blue stone in her hand, and the golden "11" running through it. Eleven was her special number. Her birth date and her birth month. She saw the number "11" many times each day. Her parents and the Universe were always close to her.

"Where have you travelled from to be here with me?" She asked it. "How did you find me? How did you give me such energy and power today?"

The stone said nothing.

"I am on a journey, from where and to where I do not know. You were given to me to help me on that journey. We will travel together and see where the journey takes us," said Freya to the stone and to herself.

She closed the window and the curtains and climbed into bed, cuddling up to her Troll. Soon she too was in R E M sleep and with her parents. She had so much to tell them tonight!

In the viewing room of the hideaway, many pairs of eyes gazed out into the night and down at the twinkling lights of Elfington in the distance. Somewhere down there in those lights was the human the Cats said they would one day meet, the one they could trust, and the one who would, sometime in the future, be drawn to the wold to find them. They would wait for the girl with the blonde hair and green eyes they now knew it to be.

Her majesty Queen Elizabeth, the Queen Mother attended the charity concert in Derby on schedule, shaking hands and putting people at their ease, as she always did. She was still very shaken by the events of the afternoon, but no one would ever guess. Her advisors had urged her to cancel the engagement and rest. The Queen Mother however, was having none of it. She would not disappoint all the people who had gone to a lot of trouble to perform tonight, for a charity she was patron of and who needed the money.

A lifetime spent in public service was ingrained in her. No one noticed any difference in her during the event, but her thoughts were elsewhere during the performance. She was thinking of a brave Police officer, a brave Dutch boy and a brave Norwegian girl, all of whom had risked their lives to save hers. The concert drew to a close and she headed off to a hotel for the night.

Later that night, and finally alone, the Queen Mother knelt by her bed and thanked God for sparing her life and sparing three others. The tears came then and she wept.

Seeing the children lying in the doctor's surgery brought back memories of the Second World War, when she and her husband, King George the sixth, used to go to the east end of London and do what they could to try to raise the spirits of the people, who had suffered night after night of bombing.

Oh, Albert, I miss you so.

She stayed there, kneeling by her bed for a long time. Unbidden, a thought popped into her mind.

Trust in the bounty of the Universe!

Now where did that come from, she asked herself, getting to her feet and climbing into bed. She knew that she would not sleep, not after the events of the day, but to her surprise, she drifted off at once, something that had not happened for a long time. Quickly she entered R E M sleep and began to dream. And what dreams they were.

She saw exquisite planets, moons and stars, vivid colours swirling around each other as she travelled through space between them. They were stunningly beautiful, breath-taking in their complexity. It was exhilarating as she swooped effortlessly around them. They were real, and she was there among them, free of the restraints of the earth and her position on it. She had seen much in her life, but she had never experienced anything like this before. She awoke the next morning after eight hours of uninterrupted sleep, rested and refreshed. As always, she got out of bed carefully as not to aggravate a back problem she had had for years, but to her astonishment, it had completely gone!

As her senior lady in waiting entered the room, Her Majesty was ready once again to serve her country.

It was October twenty ninth. 1966.

Amazingly, virtually no one noticed anything that could not be explained away easily. A few villagers noticed the Royal cars speed away quickly after passing through the village, later explained that Her Majesty was running late for her next engagement.

The police were also seen running up the road after the motorcade had gone. Again, this was because the police had received reports of a cow on the road, and they were keen to recapture it quickly, in case it got into the crowds in the village. That was why they had had to close the road.

One or two people said they saw an ambulance parked near the Old Mill. This was explained away as being called to treat one of the policemen who were looking for the cow, who had managed to twist his ankle!

And that was it. In the days that followed, all involved in the "incident" were debriefed, and sworn to secrecy. The official secrets' act was brought into play and the few who really knew what had happened kept their mouths firmly shut!

The gunman, after treatment was charged with two counts of attempted murder, together with a whole host of lesser offences. He was facing a very long stretch at Her

Majesty's pleasure, and Her Majesty was not best pleased that he had tried to murder her mother!

Inspector Pitt made a slow but full recovery and received a long overdue promotion to Chief Inspector. He was also awarded the top bravery medal the police could get, in a secret ceremony by no less a person than the Queen Mother herself, who made a special visit to the private room at the hospital, again unseen by anyone. He knew he could never wear it in public, of course. But it was in his file that it had been awarded, which would do his future career no harm at all.

The press never got wind of anything and never would.

The day that Her Majesty Queen Elizabeth, the Queen Mother drove through Elfington went down in history as a great success and would be long remembered by the villagers...

And by the special friends in the hideaway. Lucky, who had played a key role in saving the life of the Queen Mother, had watched the events unfold below her. She had been able to attract Freya's attention and bring her to the tree and thus expose the gunman. She had also seen Freya move to save her friend from being shot. She knew that no human could move that fast, yet the girl called Freya had been able to do so. And she had seen, clearly seen, the necklace that Freya had been wearing. When it was all over, she had flown back to the hideaway and when all the friends were there, she recounted the story to them, and showed them the detailed drawing she had made of the necklace she had seen.

Jago, Hugo and Astra looked at each other. They had always known that this day would come. Astra left the chamber and returned with a piece of paper, on which the Cats had drawn a picture of the special piece of jewellery that would identify the one and only human they could ever trust. A human known to the Cats and approved by them. Everyone watched as Astra put the paper she had brought, face down, next to the drawing Lucky had made. Then she turned the paper over. The two drawings were identical. They had finally found the special human the Cats had said they would.

A Norwegian girl called Freya Olsen.

The three hand written envelopes arrived, first class, at three different addresses in Elfington on the same day. The hand writing was the same on all of them. One was addressed to Master Gilbert Van den Berg. One to Miss Freya Olsen, and one to Doctor and Mrs Thornton. The postmark was Derby. Freya and Dutch did not recognise the handwriting, nor did they know anyone who lived in Derby. Neither did Tom or Penny.

There was nothing else different about them from any other letters. But what was inside the envelope was. Written on the finest vellum, and with the Royal coat of arms in colour on the top of the page, was a hand written letter on the sender's private stationery.

Her Majesty Queen Elizabeth, was personally inviting Freya and Dutch and their families, and Tom and Penny to join her and the Queen Mother, plus other members of the Royal family for a few days, starting on December twenty seventh. At Sandringham. The final guest and his wife, had received their invitations from the Queen Mother herself, when she had travelled to a private hospital in Derby to award Chief Inspector Pitt his medal in a special private ceremony.

The Queen very much wanted to meet them, and thank them all personally for saving the life of her mother, but informally and privately.

She had signed the letters simply with one word

ELIZABETH.

Chapter Forty-Four

It was finally here. The day she had been waiting for all her life. Her eleventh birthday. She had been feeling more and more excited as the special day drew closer. And now it was actually here. It had fallen on a Saturday and as tens of millions of people around the world would turn their thoughts to remember those who had not returned home from the wars that had been fought, and to those who had survived but had been injured. Each of the adult guests at the Olsen house remembered the years of the Second World War in their own way. Lars and his brother Anders had been young boys growing up in Norway during the occupation, and he thought about him and his wife Marit, and of his late parents. Gilbert and Beatrice Van den Berg had also been children in Holland and had also been occupied, they too remembered the fear, the hunger and the rationing during those dreadful years. The guest of honour, Mr Winter, had spent the war on the Island of Jersey and his thoughts also took him back to that terrible time of occupation when he had lost his entire family. He alone could also remember the equally terrible war that had been fought before.

But they were not gathered at twenty nine Druids Way on this day to remember the dead, but to celebrate the birthday of one very alive and special girl, who had, mostly unknown to them, changed all of their lives in her own unique way. Rose, helped by Penny had provided a buffet for the guests and everyone enjoyed salmon, ham, and cheese sandwiches, pork pies and sausage rolls and all the other goodies that filled the table. Lars was a very proud man as he watched his wife and niece that day. Since Freya had come into their lives, everything had changed for all of them. His house was full of happy people, genuine friends who meant a lot to him and his family, so different from before, when no one ever came, or wanted to. There had been a surprise visitor earlier that morning, Chief Inspector Pitt had called in with his wife to bring Freya a present, looking thin and pale and different in his civilian clothes. He had only been out of hospital a few days but had wanted to come and thank her again for saving his life. They were invited back in the afternoon and agreed, so long as they called him and his wife by their first names, which were Clive and Jenny. He now sat by the fire chatting to Tom, a plate of food on his knees, while his wife talked with Beatrice, Rose and Penny. As Clive Pitt looked around the room, he was very aware that but for Freya, he would most certainly be dead, and his wife a widow. He caught her eye and smiled, knowing that she too was probably thinking the same thing.

Mr Winter sat on the other side of the fire, enjoying its warmth and the company around him. Freya and Dutch were making sure that he did not go short of conversation, or hungry and his glass was not empty for long, as well as circulating around everyone else. Outside the cottage on this dank November day, darkness had fallen and fog had begun to form around the street lamps, but inside there was laughter and happiness, friends and family together to honour a special young lady who meant such a great deal to them all. They had all sung "Happy birthday to you" for her and gave her three cheers. Freya had thanked them all for their presents and their company on this special day for her. It had not escaped her notice that including herself, there were eleven people there that afternoon! She was really enjoying her special day, surrounded by all the people who mattered to her, feeling the genuine love and friendship that they were sending her way, she felt truly blessed.

None of them could know that later tonight, when they had all returned to their own homes, Freya Olsen would receive another gift. A gift no other human being either alive or dead had ever had, a gift from the Universe itself, to augment and enhance much further , the gifts that she had received on the day she had almost died, gifts that had saved her life, and in so doing , had saved most of theirs as well. The date was the 11/11/66.

By ten o'clock that night, Lars and Rose were ready for bed, aided by thoughts planted in their heads by Freya, and after they were thanked, hugged and kissed by her for such a wonderful day, every one headed up to bed. Lars and Rose would sleep long and deep throughout the night, as they always did when Freya wanted them to, never knowing that Freya had left the house.

By ten-twenty they were both fast asleep and Freya, having changed into warm outdoor clothing was ready to go. Silently out of the window, as always pushing it almost closed, down the tree, being extra careful on the wet and slippery branches, that dripped with moisture, and across the garden and over the garden wall, all without making a sound. Now the fog was really thick and she took deep breaths of its unique damp fog aroma as she waited for a few moments in the alley behind the cottage, tuning herself in to the night. She smiled to herself. The Universe had sent two old friends to be with her on this special night and as they wrapped themselves around her like a cloak, she made her way up to the Old Wood with them as company. She made good time, sure-footed and confident. Familiar trees and bushes loomed out of the dark and fog, but with her cat's eyes it might just as well have been daylight. She felt no fear what so ever, for this was her natural habitat and she was fully tuned into it. She had no idea why she must go to the Old Wood this night, or what she might find there. She only knew that on this night of all nights, she must go, had to go. It was her destiny.

By ten to eleven she arrived at the gully, knowing that this is where she had to be. Without knowing why, she un-zipped her coat and took out her special necklace from inside her blouse, so that it hung outside her jumper and was visible. Then she just stood quite still in the centre of the gully and waited. What she was waiting for she did not know, only that she must. This was where she needed to be on this day and at this time. Suddenly, from nowhere, a breeze blew through the trees and cleared the fog away, magically revealing the biggest moon that she had ever seen. It was a "Super Moon", a rare occurrence when the moon was at its closest point to the earth and therefore much bigger and brighter than normal. But this was not a normal night, and its bright yellow glow matched the yellow eleven in her necklace. Freya just looked up at it in fascination, drinking in its beauty, letting its beams wash over her, feeling its power, one planet amongst billions of others. Without looking at her watch, she knew that it was eleven o'clock. Exactly. It was time. Her time. The time. She turned around.

Whatever she had been expecting, it was not this. Freya could not stop herself from gasping at the sight that greeted her as she completed her turn and stood with the huge super moon behind her. Even with her advanced hearing, she had not heard a thing. Ten creatures sat in row and looked back at her. One of the creatures was Lucy! Some of the other creatures she knew she had seen before. The cat from the village street, late at night, the pig, much bigger now, but she knew it was the same one that she had helped to escape from the market at Abbotsbury over three years ago, and the large bird she had made brief contact with on the day she had got the better of Mrs Hunter at school. Immediately Freya could sense a powerful warm energy, and a friendly aura emanating from them and could hear the faint buzz of many voices murmuring in her mind, as if she was in a crowded room of people. But the Old Wood was as silent as it had been before, only the gentle breeze stirring the bare branches of the trees that looked on. The voices that she could hear were inside her own mind, not outside in the air. One voice was much clearer amongst the murmuring of the others, and she just knew that it was the large bird from the school that she could hear. But who were these creatures, where had they come from? What did they want? Surely this could not be really happening.

The bird was speaking to her, in her mind. "Hello, Freya, and happy birthday. Welcome to the Old Wood. We have been waiting for you. We are real and you really can hear my voice in your mind, it is called telepathy. It is just one of many gifts we have in common. We always knew that one day you would come here to us on this special day and at this special time. The Cats had told us you would. As you now know, I am the bird in the tree from the school, and I was also at your first sports day and at the human wedding. More recently, I was in the tree that held the gunman who was trying to harm the important lady. My name is Lucky, and I am what the humans call an Eagle Owl. Do not be afraid, we are your friends. We have known of you for a long time, but it was only when I saw your necklace that we were really sure you were the special one we had been told to expect. Allow me to introduce the others. Lucy I think you already know!"

Freya was truly amazed, but not in the least afraid. They knew her name, and that it was her birthday! They had been expecting her to come here, on this day and at this time. They had waited for her. How could they know? Who had told them? What did this mean? Then it hit her, and she knew. The Cats. They had arranged all of this. Now everything was clear. Bob and Lisa. They were the link to all of this. Somehow she could communicate with the bird called Lucky, but not by speaking. How could this wonderful experience be happening? Humans could not communicate with each other without speaking, let alone by using their minds. Even with her enhanced mind, it was a lot for her to take in. Still no one had moved. They just sat and waited as the bird called Lucky continued.

"I know what you are thinking, but everything will soon become clear. Once you have connected with all of us, we can tell you more about ourselves and answer your questions. May I continue?"

Freya nodded. Lucky began. This is Astra…

And so it began. Each animal was introduced to her and quickly tuned themselves into her mind, enabling Freya to hear them clearly. It was a truly empowering experience, a connecting of like minds as each unique creature established a pathway of communication with her. The last two were more difficult, as Flux was still quite new to the group and her mental pathways were still being developed and Rolo's were limited due to the injury he had when he fell out of his drey. But contact was able to be made and Freya felt a great sense of harmony with these most unique of beings, a giving and receiving of a very precious gift, a union of warm emotion unlike anything Freya had ever experienced before. When the connecting was complete, Rolo came forward with a large acorn in his little hands and he offered his own gift to Freya. She took it from him, thanked him using her new gift, then knelt down and scooped him up in her arms and cuddled him, holding him close to her. He loved it. That signalled the others to come forward and Freya was surrounded by her new friends, eager to get close to her, and she reached out to stroke their fur, feathers and coats, further enhancing the bond already growing between them, all the time keeping hold of Rolo. Enormous waves of pure joy and emotion swept over everyone as Freya was welcomed, and the super moon cast its glow down over the glade and the eleven members of the new species below. This was what they had all waited for, this was what everything had been moving towards for the last few years. Finally all the pieces of the Universal jigsaw were in place, fitting together perfectly. Just as they should.

Finally, as if by a secret command, the friends moved apart and Astra let the way down the gully, Inviting Freya to follow them. Setting Rolo down on the ground, Freya got to her feet and moved along with them, wondering where they were going. She did not have to wait long, as to her astonishment, half way down the gully, each of her new friends turned towards the bank and appeared to simply walk into what looked like a solid wall of earth! When all of them had vanished, Freya heard Lucy's voice asking her to part the ivy in front of her, and step forward through it. For just a brief moment longer, Freya hesitated as she recalled a memory from long ago, when she had had to leave her parents behind the big closed gates and go on alone without them, stepping into the fog and whatever lay beyond, then as now, on the threshold of something unknown. But the moment passed and she parted the curtain of Ivy and found a short tunnel behind it, at the end of which Lucy sat waiting for her. Taking a deep breath, Freya stepped forward and entered a world within a world, a world that only eleven special beings would ever share. The door was closed behind her and the gully was empty and the super moon alone once again. The moon did not know or care that on this eleventh day of November, the time on the planet below was exactly eleven – eleven.

Freya found herself in a large chamber made of solid rock, only the floor was different and covered with a film of light sand. A lamp had been lit and it cast its warm glow around the cave. It was not really necessary, as everyone could see very well in the complete darkness, but the importance of the event seemed to justify it. Freya looked around and was surprised to see three wooden trucks parked to one side of the cave. They were just like the ones the village children had, made from pieces of wood, but with wooden wheels. One of the trucks was fully loaded with fire wood from outside, another was full of potatoes from the nearby fields. The third truck was empty. One of the foxes, Jago told her that they were preparing for the winter, and Freya replied that she and her family were doing exactly the same thing, there were logs and spuds everywhere around the house!

Freya suddenly realised how easily she had started to use her telepathy gift and communicate with her new friends. It just seemed so natural to do it, so obvious. Flux, Rolo and Millie were climbing on to the back of Barney to ride on him to where ever they were going, and as they settled themselves, he turned his head and said, "If it was not for you, Freya, none of us would be here tonight, safe and secure in our secret hideaway. We all owe you so much, it is such a pleasure to meet you at last!" Freya knelt down and gave him a hug, careful not to disturb his passengers, telling him that he and everyone was most welcome , and how happy she was to have found them and be part of their secret world, and be accepted by them. She got to her feet and then they all set off down the wide tunnel, Freya had the lamp in one hand, and Lucky had asked if she could perch on Freya's shoulder, something which she was more than happy to agree to, knowing that the Owl, like the others just wanted to be close to her. She wanted to be close to them as well. Freya did not ask where they were going, or why they were going, just knowing that, like everything else that had happened so far on this special night, it was just necessary for them to. Everything would, she was sure, unfold just at the Cats had meant it to.

The tunnel meandered its way, left and right, always slightly upwards, rarely going straight for very long, and Freya and her escorts left foot prints in the sand that no one else would ever see, chatting between themselves as they went, enjoying getting to know her. Freya had never felt so happy, so completely relaxed and content as she did now. This was where she wanted to be, needed to be, with these special, unique creatures that the Universe had gathered together. Here she was at last whole, complete and accepted.

As they moved around another bend in the tunnel, Freya could see a faint light in the distance, which got brighter as they drew nearer to it. They were arriving somewhere. All of a sudden they entered a very large chamber and as one they all stopped dead in their tracks, unable to accept what they were seeing, even on a night with so many surprises. There, sitting next to the roaring log fire and enjoying its warmth, were two creatures that all the others had heard of, and some of them had actually met. Everyone knew immediately who they were. It was Bob and Lisa. The Cats had come back!

Finally, all the greetings had been exchanged, the introductions and connections made, the hugs enjoyed and the questions answered. All except one. It was now time to ask it. Why had the Cats returned?

The answer was simple. It was time. Time to complete what had begun four earth years ago. Or to end it.

The gifts that they all had, the telepathy, the enhanced sight, hearing, smell and brain function and much more were only temporary, and if not made permanent, would soon start to degrade over time, and they would all gradually return to being an ordinary member of their respective species, rather than a member of a new and special one. Freya was the exception, she could not ever fully return to being an ordinary female again, as the damage she sustained during the car crash that killed her parents, and that the Cats repaired could never be truly undone, to do so would mean her death. But she would not evolve any further, her gifts would remain at their present level. She would always be a very bright and gifted woman, one of a small elite group, her powers capped forever where they were.

But what the Cats had returned to ask was, did they want to take the final step, to make their gifts permanent and for ever, and to enhance them yet further still? The foundations had been laid, the basic pathways established and they all had had some experience of what they could expect life to be in the future. But it was a decision that each of them would have to make alone. To go forward would mean that for ten of them they could never go back to what they had once been, the final step, if chosen was irreversible. It also meant that they would age very very slowly, and live for many earth years more than ordinary animals.

The Cats had thought that the inhabitants of this planet called earth would not be ready for this to happen for many centuries to come, and had been almost ready to leave when they had received a unique signal from Freya that told them that there was indeed an advanced being on this world after all, but that the being was dying and in need of help that only they could give. From that event, everything else had flowed. And now there were eleven advanced beings here with them. That was why they had returned on this special day. The day that bore the number eleven, the special number that the species called the Gallownians held so dear. The decision must be made on this day. So. Forward or back. To create a new species, a new form of life in the Universe, or a return to what already was.

The Cats rose and made their way back to the fire and sat next to it once again and waited. The only sound to be heard was the crackling of the logs as they burned. For a few seconds, the only contact between Freya and her new friends was eye contact. They all looked at each other and then as one voice the decision was made. They would go forward. Together!

And so it began, like most things do, with a circle. Each participant was placed with great care, the strong next to the not so strong. Bob was next to Rolo, Lisa next to Flux, male next to male, female next to female. Millie next to Freya, Tog beside Barney, the twins, as always next to each other, and Astra, Lucky and Lucy completed the circle. The Cats took turns in speaking telepathically, preparing the others for what was to come, their voices, always calm, gentle and soothing. There was no need to rush. All eyes were closed. All breathing was deep and regular. All bodies upright yet relaxed. They were ready.

"Clear your mind, relax your bodies, and concentrate on the sound of our voice. Concentrate on the here and now, on this place, on this room. Everything is still, everything is quiet. Nothing else matters, only here, only now, only this. Concentrate, concentrate. Time has no meaning here, there is nothing else, nothing beyond this place. Relax, relax. Listen to the sound of our voice. You are safe, your minds are drifting, drifting, come with us, trust us, concentrate, there is no need to hurry, share our thoughts, we are one, there is unity, we are together, relax, relax…

And slowly it began, minds melding together as an unseen protective sheath of pure energy began to form around them, surrounding them, protecting them, the energy was gentle, warm, as it swept over them, nourishing them. They felt peace, tranquillity, warmth. New pathways were forming in their minds, knowledge, wisdom and information flowed down the paths, like a new trail through a forest that once travelled down, was easier to do the next time, building layer upon layer. Time stood still. Each of them was different, each was given only what they could deal with. Clocks were set to release knowledge gradually, over time in the future, as and when they were ready to receive it. Rolo had more clocks set than the rest, as his brain injury had to be repaired first, then the curtain that had prevented him from progressing was lifted for ever and when he was ready, he would be able to move forward and achieve his full potential. But he was still the same loveable Rolo he had been before, but renewed, repaired, enhanced.

On this most special of nights, a new species had been born, a new form of life created. They were the first of their kind. Unique, special, bonded together, telepathically linked. They were the first eleven. The Hendeca Association was born. Just how long the melding actually took, no one knew. The fire had burned down low, as they slowly became aware once again of where they were. The Chamber was just the same as it had been before. They were different. It was time for Freya to leave. Farewells were exchanged and she was escorted home by the Cats themselves, while her new special family settled down for a long and necessary sleep, to allow their minds to adjust to its new configuration. Freya did not remember much about the journey home, and before she knew it, she was back in her room, safe. The Cats had briefly come into her bedroom and she had knelt down and hugged them, silently thanking them again for saving her life, and for all the gifts they had given to her. The Cats purred gently and licked away the tears that ran down her face, as she realised that she would never see them again. Their work was done, and with a final hug from Freya, they went out of the window and down the tree as silently as they had come, vanishing into the fog that had formed once again. It was over.

Freya was in the staff room at school, just after lunch, and the room was full, except for Mr Fuller, of course. She was chatting with Miss Doyle, while she dried the cups and saucers. It was the Monday after her birthday weekend, and Miss Doyle asked if she had had a nice birthday. Freya told her all about it, the party at her house, and later her trip to the Old Wood and the new friends she had found there, and about the wonderful gifts they had all received from the Cats.

Miss Doyle was so pleased for her and said that she would miss her terribly when she left, but now that Freya had received her final gifts and met the others, she did not need the protection that she had stayed on to provide for her, and anyway, she could not hold this human female form for very much longer, enjoyable though it had been. Her visit to this world had, unexpectedly been a complete success and now it was time for her to go home to Gallownia with the others.

Miss Doyle put down the newspaper that she had been pretending to read and left the room, leaving Freya to finish her work and tidy up when the other teachers went back to their classrooms. They had not spoken a word. Freya had found another Gallownian, who had needed to stay behind to ensure that Freya would receive her final gifts. Now her work was also complete and she would soon leave the school and the planet called Earth and return to her true home.

Chapter Forty-Five

Once again, it was time for the school Christmas carol concert, traditionally performed by the children in their final year at the school. Dutch and Freya had asked if they could produce and choreograph the show, rather than take part in the singing. Miss Doyle, who was organising this her final concert had agreed. The three of them had got their heads together and came up with a plan for the concert that would be remembered by all those who saw it for a very long time.

Miss Doyle, a keen cinema goer, had drafted in a friend of hers to help. He was the projectionist at Pondford cinema and a keen film and slide maker and editor called Len. He in turn, had provided many items of equipment and his time and energy for free. He had quickly understood what Miss Doyle, Freya and Dutch had in mind, not least because Miss Doyle and Freya had put their ideas directly in to his mind. Together, they had worked hard, and Len had proved invaluable to them, with his seemingly endless contacts in the film world. But finally and after several run-throughs, they were ready. Miss Doyle had chosen the carols and had trained the boys and girls to practice singing them separately. Only four people knew how the whole show would be like.

Mr Fuller had been happy to let Miss Doyle handle the concert, if it was a flop, he could and would blame her for it. All he cared about was that she was leaving the school soon after it. Of course, if it was a success, he would claim all the credit, as she would not be there in January to say otherwise.

All through the day of the concert, the four producers had been busy. Len, the projectionist had arrived during the morning with his van full of equipment, some of which had been "borrowed" from the cinema at Pondford. Dutch and Freya had been excused lessons for the day and could be seen by the other children helping Len and Miss Doyle carrying in mysterious looking boxes into the assembly hall. During the lunch time, more than a few children had tried to peek behind the closed curtains on the stage at what was going on there, but Miss Doyle, who seemed to have eyes in the back of her head, had made it clear that there was to be no peeking. They would just have to wait for the show this evening. This just added to the excitement of what was to come later.

The school was buzzing with anticipation, as the one thing they did know for sure, was that no scenery had been made or painted this year. The canvas and paint that was always used was still in the shed in the corner of the playground. How could Freya and Dutch put on a concert without scenery? Even the children who were going to sing the carols could shed no light on it. They did not know. No one knew. The whole school could not wait for eight pm to come.

The audience began to arrive just after seven in the evening. As was the custom, the head boy and girl would be waiting by the front door to greet them, before passing them on to others in their final year to take their coats and guide them to their seats. Daphne had reserved a seat next to her parents for her Uncle, who was driving up from Hampshire, where ever that was, to see the show and stay with them for a few days. Freya thought that she would at last see him in person, having only seen his shoes when he had come into the staff room to buy for Daphne the Head Girl's job. Freya did not know that she had in fact already met him once before.

It soon became clear that extra seating would be required, and Miss Doyle, who had anticipated this, organised the setting out of folding chairs brought in from the Village hall. One of the first to arrive had been Mr Lamb, of Lamb's Driving School fame. He had wanted to park his car right outside the school gates so everyone could see the signage on the car's roof as they went in. He now had a second car to cope with the extra demand and that was also parked outside the School gates, facing the other one. He also had arranged for a special leaflet to be put behind the wind screen wipers of every car in the area. He had learned from his association with Freya the power of advertising and was using the concert to recruit more students for next year.

Inside, the hall was packed to capacity. Everyone was there. Word had got around that this concert was going to be a cracker. They were right. Chief Inspector Pitt, wearing his best uniform was seated in the front row with his wife Jenny. He was starting to look much better now, and would be back on duty in the New Year. Tom and Penny sat next to them, chatting to their new friends. Nearby were Willie and Morag from the shop, who were chatting to Mr and Mrs Benton. Mr and Mrs Briggs from the farm were talking to Lars and Rose, who had collected Mr Winter and escorted him to his seat next to them. Larry Lamb could be seen chatting to Mr Hargreaves from the Post office. Mrs Stratton, the Infants' teacher, was playing softly on her piano while the guests were still arriving. The noise of the conversation was almost drowning out her efforts. Even Miss Bates and her mother were there, having been told by Mr Hargreaves that she should not miss it. They were wearing their Sunday best clothes and for once there was only a very slight smell of cow muck coming from their shoes. Sitting upright at the end of the second row and talking to no one, was Mrs Hunter. She had at first decided that she would not attend, but curiosity got the better of her, and she had come, hoping that it would be a shambles. It would serve that toad Mr Fuller right if it was. And that cow Miss Doyle. And as for those foreign children, well, they shouldn't be allowed to organise the concert anyway, this was an English school!

By eight o'clock, the hall was completely stuffed. A record attendance. Daphne's Uncle John had just scrapped in in time to take his seat at the end of the front row. He could have been there much earlier, but had been in the golf club for a drink or three before the show. He had got a lift from the club with an old pal, as there was no parking to be had for more than half a mile around the school. He sat in his seat sucking polo mints, which did not really hide the smell of the brandy he had drunk. He jumped as a bell sounded loudly three times from behind the curtain. Len had thought of it, as he knew that's what happened if one went to the theatre. If one was putting on a show, one had to do it right! The conversation tailed off further as he rang the bell twice more a minute later. One minute after that, he rang the bell a single time. This was it. Show time!

The lights dimmed, the switch having been installed by Len that morning and what little conversation there was died away and then stopped as the curtains opened to reveal a gigantic white screen that filled the whole of the back of the stage. Suddenly it flickered into life, showing thousands and thousands of stars twinkling brightly in the blackness of space. Len gave the audience a full thirty seconds to admire them before nodding to Miss Doyle who ushered the first group of children on to the stage, singing "Silent Night" as they walked on. Mrs Stratton accompanied them on the piano, adding a few flourishes of her own as she played. The audience looked on with appreciation, many of them singing along with the children. When the carol came to an end and the children moved silently off stage and into the wings again, the stars on the screen began to fade Music could be heard, coming from large speakers placed at the sides of the stage. A large rock, or asteroid came into view, tumbling endlessly through space, on a timeless journey through the icy blackness. As it went along, a faint light began to appear far in the distance. The audience were silent as they watched the asteroid head relentlessly towards the dim light. As they watched, the rock grew smaller and smaller as it moved in front of a creamy white object. The object itself started to move backwards on the screen, until its shape could be seen. The asteroid had vanished completely against the vastness of the Moon that was pulling the asteroid towards itself, to form yet another crater on its surface.

Now the moon was on the move again, sliding upwards and to the right on the giant screen. Suddenly, a very bright light appeared, bathing the room in its glare before it too moved to the right side of the screen, taking the place of the moon, which had vanished now that the Sun had arrived. Even Mrs Hunter was impressed. Another shape now came slowly into view in the bottom left of the screen. It was a small round blue ball. Slowly it continued to move to the centre of the screen, gaining in size as it did so. Everyone knew what it was. Earth. Their own planet, seen from space. The Earth continued to grow in size, and soon the continents could be recognised. Africa, Asia, Europe, they were all moving away as the Earth continued to turn and grow.

Soon the shape of the United Kingdom was clearly visible, growing ever larger as if the audience were in a hot air balloon that was descending down to the ground. It soon became clear to most people what part of the country they were looking at. Smoke from the chimneys and kilns of the nearby Potteries, where some of the audience worked could now be seen.

The ground was getting ever nearer as hundreds of pairs of eyes watched in silent fascination at the spectacular events unfolded before them. From the vastness of space, they had travelled through the Universe to a small part of the North-west Midlands. Below them was Elfington. Home.

The journey was now complete. The image on the screen was now that of the Wold, with the Craggs thrusting up majestically into the grey winter sky. Moving ever more slowly now, the camera finally came to a stop above a flock of sheep grazing. The flock of sheep grew smaller, their baaing could be heard through the speakers. The light faded even more as darkness fell over the land. Suddenly, with a wumph, a fire appeared in the middle of the screen, so real it seemed as if it was actually there, and the next group of children walked on to the stage and sat on the floor as if they were sitting around a real fire. In the distance figures moved around the sheep. Only those with sharp eyes noticed that the distant figures seemed to have horned helmets on their heads and clogs on their feet! Freya and Dutch had not been able to resist doing that! The floor of the stage had been marked for the singers in chalk and as they sat down, Mrs Stratton began to play and the children sang "While shepherds watched their flocks by night".

Behind the curtain, Miss Doyle looked over at Dutch and Freya and smiled. The three of them looked at Len, hunched over his control panel as he projected the images on to the screen.

He had done a superb job. Feeling their eyes on him, he looked up and smiled. Miss Doyle put her hands together and silently clapped them together, indicating her appreciation. Len gave a slight bow and returned his attention to his box of tricks. He had more surprises in store yet. But there was a limit to what even he could produce from this primitive human equipment. But he was pleased with how things were going so far. Who knows, it might give the more artistically-minded among them a few ideas for the future!

The fire dimmed as the children once again moved off the stage. As soon as the fire had died away completely, a building filled the screen. It was a very old picture that Len had found in the files of the Abbotsbury and Pondford Times. The building looked vaguely familiar, and Mr Winter was the first to realise what it was. It was the Old Mill, but not as it was now, but how it had looked soon after it had been built, in 1802. Then it was called "Deca's Mill", named after the owner, Ken Deca, when the Mill, and later the Railway, were the centre of life in the Village. Another picture replaced the first, showing horse-drawn carts making their way up the track towards the mill, where groups of men waited to unload the crops, so they could be ground by the mill stones. More pictures followed, showing the great Mill wheel turning and more horse and carts heading away from the mill, loaded with sacks. All the while the pictures were being shown, a sound track could be heard, muted voices, the snorting of horses, the noise of the carts as they came and went, and above all the thrash, thrash, thrash of the giant mill wheel as it turned and turned. The pictures had all been taken at harvest time, and it had been a welcome relief from the cold and grey of winter.

The pictures and the sounds had given the audience a real glimpse of what life had been like in the village all those years ago, and just how important the Mill had been. The last picture brought everyone back to winter again. It showed the Mill covered in snow, the lake frozen and the area silent and deserted. The picture remained on the screen as Mrs Stratton began to play the notes of the next carol as the children returned to the centre of the stage, each carrying a branch of the green and prickly bush to link in with the music. The harvest had been safely gathered in. Now it was time to rejoice and give thanks. The carol was "Deck the halls with boughs of Holly".

And so it went on. Old pictures of the Village continued to appear on the screen, the Church, the High Street, the Railway station and many more, including the finger post at Beggars Cross as it had changed over the years. One picture was of a newspaper headline in the year 1929. "STOCK MARKET CRASH!" Many of the older people in the audience well remembered those grim years of the great depression, they had been children themselves then. Another newspaper headline filled the screen, its one word speaking volumes. "WAR"! Again, those looking up at the screen well remembered those terrible times, only twenty five years ago. More pictures followed, many were of the railway station as the men of the area headed off to war.

There were a few pictures of evacuated children next to the trains that had brought them to the village, each with a bewildered look on their faces and a brown luggage label tied to their clothes. More than a few of the audience saw themselves on the screen. They had stayed in the village after the war had ended, having nothing and no one to go back to. Many in the School that evening were thinking the same thing. They should never have closed the Railway. Everyone had used it, some had worked on it, everyone missed it. The sounds of the trains, so familiar to them all, was now gone forever. Without it, the Village was not the same. The trains had brought the holiday makers to visit the nearby Cropwell Manor, with its boating lake, gardens, cafe and small fun fair. Some of the villagers worked there during the summer. But not as many as before the Railway closed. The Village was slowly dying. The final image of the war era lifted their spirits again, and was of yet another newspaper headline. "VICTORY!"

The final series of pictures were of the School in which they now sat. Len had managed to find a very old picture of when the School was being built, and this was followed by others, showing the School through the years ending with a final picture of the School as it was now. While these old pictures had been shown, Mrs Stratton had played a haunting piece of music on the piano, evoking emotion from many looking on. It had been edited perfectly to end as the last picture had been on the screen for thirty seconds. As the music died away, the children returned to the stage for the final time. As if sensing the sombre mood of the crowd, she immediately swung into "Happy days are here again", and everyone joined in, filling the hall with sound, while the children stood in front of the screen and waved small Union Jacks to the audience, who did not want the magic to end. Almost as one, the entire hall rose to its feet as the song came to an end, and gave the children deafening applause, Mrs Hunter reluctantly among them, as she would have been the only one still seated. A few glanced at their watches. It was nine thirty. An hour and a half had gone by and no one had noticed, so engrossed had they been in the show. The concert had brought out the community spirit in them all, and everyone would long remember this night in the years ahead.

Mr Fuller took to the stage and gestured to the children and asked for another round of applause, joining in himself. He was beaming with goodwill. The show had been a huge success and he would make sure that he got the credit for it. But he could not take quite all of the credit, so he waved the audience back to their seats and thanked the children again for their outstanding performance, Mrs Stratton for her beautiful playing and arrangement, which gave rise to another round of applause. Finally Mr Fuller asked the audience to welcome to the stage the masterminds of the whole show, Mr Len Weaver, Miss Doyle, Gilbert Van Den Berg and Miss Freya Olsen! Even before he had got the last names out, the audience was on its feet again, applauding even louder than before. Mr Fuller greeted them all in turn with a hand shake and a beaming smile, and then joined in the applause as the four of them moved to the front of the stage, and took bow after bow to applause that would not stop. What a show it had been!

Freya stood next to Dutch and looked out at the hundreds of happy, smiling faces and let the waves of emotion wash over her. The show had been a huge success, and the aura of the audience was a sea of warm blue. There were only two specks of red among it. One was Mrs Hunter. No surprise there. So Freya turned to see who the other red aura belonged to. Her gaze travelled along the front row, past Uncle Lars and Auntie Rose, Mr Winter and Daphne's mother, who had gone pale, and her father to stop on a large fat man standing next to them, Daphne's Uncle, but she could not see his face as he was looking down and to his left towards the door, as if he was eager to leave. The applause finally began to subside and the children started to leave the stage, moving to their right towards the steps that led down to where Daphne's Uncle was standing, to join their families. Freya, wondering why his aura was red, kept her eyes on the man as she moved closer to him, and just as she reached the top of the stairs, he made his second mistake of the evening and glanced up at her. Freya stopped dead in her tracks, frozen, her gaze never leaving the large man as the colour drained out of her face, standing right above her own family in the front row below her. Somewhere, she had seen that face before, but where? Suddenly, in a flash, it all came flooding back. The car crash, the pain, the smell of the petrol leaking from the wrecked car. Then a man had appeared in the distance, walking towards her as she peered over the back seat of the smashed car that was slippery with her blood. The driver of the other car that had caused the crash had walked back. For a moment he had stood there, right next to the car, just looking down and Freya had had a momentary clear look at him. She had reached out her hand and cried for help, but the man had just turned and walked away, leaving her and her family to die.

In the audience, Lars and Rose noticed Freya's expression and started to look worried. She seemed to be in a trance. The look on her face was like nothing they had ever seen before. It was a mixture of recognition, shock, anger and horror all at once. A chill seemed to descend over the room. Those who had started to rise and move from their seats stopped, the noise dropping away as they realised that something was very wrong. A strange hush came over the crowd as they felt the emotion in the room. Miss Doyle moved over to Freya and said quietly, "What is it, pet, what is the matter?" although she alone knew what was going through Freya's mind now.

Now the room was completely silent. Waiting. Finally Freya spoke. It was just a whisper. "You," She said pointing at the large man who had gone very red and was again looking towards the door. Everyone turned to look at who Freya was pointing at. "It was you. I remember now. You came back after you had hit our car. I saw you. You came back. I looked at you, asked for your help, but you just stood there. Then you turned and walked away and left us to die. You could have saved us, but you walked away. It was you!"

Freya's voice had got steadily louder as she spoke, the last three words coming out as a shout. As she said the last three words several things happened at once. Freya jumped off the stage like a cat and threw herself at the man, but quick as she was, Lars Olsen was quicker still. The man tried to get to the door that led to the corridor but found his way blocked by an even larger and more powerful man with blond hair and murder in his blue eyes. A massive fist smashed in to the face of the man with such force that he was knocked to the floor. Lars lifted the twenty stone man up with one arm as if he weighed nothing and was about to hit him again when a voice behind him shouted, "Lars! Stop!" The voice had such authority that Lars paused to look around, already knowing who it was. Chief Inspector Clive Pitt walked forward and gently touched Lars on the shoulder. "No, Lars, no. Let me deal with this. Please. This is a police matter now." Lars looked back at him for a long moment. "He killed my family, left them to die, now I will kill him."

"No, Lars, you will not. You are a much better man than him. We all know that. Please, let him go. I will give you my word that he will be put on trial for what he has done. Now, my friend, please, step back." Lars looked at him, then beyond him where Freya and Rose stood together. They both nodded slowly. Lars turned back to the man, who he still held up by one arm, and let him go. He crumpled to the ground and lay still. Tom and Penny moved forward and bent over him, as Lars allowed Clive Pitt to lead him away, with Freya and Rose following.

Miss Doyle stepped forward and gently took him from the police man. "I'll look after him, you go and do your duty." Clive Pitt nodded. He moved back to where the man was now sitting up on the floor and said in a crisp voice, "John Stagg, I am arresting you for the murder of Anders and Marit Olsen."

Chapter Forty-Six

It was quite late by the time Freya, Lars and Rose got home. Penny and Tom had come with them. The fire had long since gone out, so Rose put on the electric stove, then went with Penny to put the kettle on. No one had spoken on the way home. Lars sat in his chair with his head down, trying to calm the swirling emotions surging through him. He remembered what one of the men from the dairy had said to him once years ago, "If you ever lose your temper, you could easily kill somebody." He had come very, very close to losing his temper a few hours ago. If it had not been for Clive Pitt, he may well have. Tom sat nearby also saying nothing, but just being there for his friend. It was Freya who knew that she must break the spell. She moved over to her Uncle and knelt before him and gently took his giant head in her hands and lifted it until he was looking at her. A pair of calm green eyes gazed into a pair of troubled blue eyes. Nothing was said. It did not need to be. Gently Freya put her arms around her Uncle, who looked so like her father, and pulled him close to her. Lars put his massive arms around his niece, who looked so like Anders and Marit. And then Freya's control crumbled completely under the huge weight of suppressed emotion, and they wept together. They had each other, and finally they had closure. Finally it was over.

It was past midnight when Penny and Tom headed for home, and Rose, Lars and Freya went to bed. It had been quite a day. Freya felt mentally and physically drained as she climbed into her bed. For the first time in quite a while, Lars and Rose tucked her in and kissed her. When they had gone and turned out the light, Freya had one more thing she had to do. She reached for her Troll and held him close to her and quietly spoke to him. She told him about the events of the evening, and that she now remembered one final part of the story. She told him she remembered being dragged from the car just as it caught fire, her heels making grooves in the soil. She told him she remembered being laid down safely on the ground, out of harm's way. She told him she remembered looking up and seeing the face that had saved her life. It was his face. The marks that Inspector Pitt had found but could not identify belonged to him. Somehow, he had come to life and saved her. She told him she knew what he had done. She told him that she would never forget. She told him that she loved him, as she had always done. The Troll said nothing. It did not have to. He knew she loved him, and he loved her. He was her guardian. He was real. The stories about Trolls were true. Now both of them knew it, they always had. And as always, they kept their secrets to themselves. Freya fell asleep while her Troll kept watch over her as he had always done, and always would.

Chapter Forty-Seven

The next morning there had been more than a few callers at the Olsen house, and Lars, Rose and Freya had been touched by the genuine concern that the villagers had for them. Mr Winter and Dutch and his mother had arrived early and had been welcomed inside gladly. Lars did not go to work, Alan Briggs had told him to take as much time off as he wanted. He had also called at the house earlier, another true friend. Lucy would have to miss her walk up to the Old Wood today, but Freya knew that she would understand. Just as Freya awoke, Lucky had arrived in the tree outside Freya's bedroom window and had told her that her secret family were all thinking of her, as she knew they would be.

Strange as it seemed, after Lucky had gone back to the hideaway, Freya lay alone in her bed for a while, just thinking about the events of the night before. Her Troll sat where he always sat during the day, on a chair next to her bed, where the sun would not reach him. She smiled, as she knew that she had not put him there. She felt as if a great weight had been lifted off her. Knowing the whole story now had made a huge difference. It did not change the past, but now she could start to put it behind her and move forward.

It was just approaching noon when there was yet another knock at the door, and Freya went to answer it to find Clive Pitt standing there looking like he had not slept much. He hadn't. Freya welcomed him inside and he sank gratefully into a chair by the fire in the front room. When everyone was ready and he had taken a sip of the tea Rose had given him, he told them the news he had brought. John Stagg had been taken to Abbotsbury Police Station, and put into a cell. He had said nothing, except that he was an innocent man and that he would enjoy suing the Police for wrongful arrest and Lars for assault. He had great trouble saying anything at all, due to his swollen face. It was the next piece of news that shocked them all.

Also in a cell at the Police Station was Mary Marshall! The mother of Daphne and sister of John Stagg.

Everyone looked at each other, and it was Mr Winter who asked the question on all their minds.

"Why is she in there, Clive?"

Only the crackling of the logs on the fire and ticking of the clock could be heard as Clive Pitt sipped his tea again. "I was just about to go home when we got a call from the Fire Brigade, asking us to attend a fire at the Marshall's house here in Elfington. Naturally, after what had happened last night, I went myself.

The fire had been put out by the time I arrived, it had been in an out building away from the house. The Fire Brigade told me that they were fairly sure that the fire had been started deliberately, so we had a look inside the outbuilding to find out what was in it." He took another sip of his tea before continuing.

"What we found was what Mary Marshall had tried to destroy. We found a car. A red car, under a cover and hidden behind a load of boxes and other junk. A red car that was damaged at the front and had green paint scrape marks on it where it had hit another vehicle. I would bet my pension that those paint scrapes will match the green paint of a Morris Traveller. A car that was registered to one John Stagg. It is the car that my officers and I have been looking for since the crash. It was there, all the time, right under our noses. Mary Marshall had tried to destroy the evidence against her brother, without which we would have had a hard time proving our case in court. Now we have that car, we can place John Stagg at the scene of the crime. Everyone thought that he had simply taken the car down to Hampshire with him when he moved down there!"

There was silence in the room for a while, as everyone digested what they had just been told. Clive Pitt drank more of his tea then continued again. "I arrested Mrs Marshall on the spot, and she will be charged with, among other things, perverting the course of justice. When we got back to the station, I arranged a little show for our guests, and went to see Mr Stagg, leaving the cell door open a bit. He immediately started to tell me how sorry I was going to be for arresting him, when I said, "We have found the car, John, we have found the car." Just as I said that, my lads moved Mrs Marshall past the door, so he could see her. And that was it. As soon as he saw his sister, he knew that the game was up. When I left to come here, he was making a full confession." He finished his tea and looked up at Lars and Freya.

"So, it's over. They will remain in custody until they go to trial. If only he had stayed away from the concert, we might never have found that car. When I asked him about it, he mumbled something about he had to see his niece as she was head girl, and she had told him that the concert was going to be a special one. If you hadn't got your memory back, he would have got away with it."

Freya looked back at him and smiled. "You have to trust in the bounty of the Universe, Uncle Clive, that's all!" As usual, she was right.

Epilogue

The Easter of 1967 would long be remembered by many people in and around Elfington for reasons not connected with Easter eggs and Easter bunnies. The Abbotsbury and Pondford Times had produced a special edition for the Easter weekend, as there was so much local news to cover.

The front page was reserved for the biggest story of them all. It was the conviction and sentencing of John Stagg and his sister, Mary Marshall. In large type and in bold letters, the paper proclaimed its headlines,

GUILTY!

"John Stagg, formally of Elfington, but now living in Hampshire, was today (Tuesday) convicted of two counts of murder, and one count of attempted murder at Stafford Crown Court. He was also found guilty of several other lesser offences, including driving while banned and driving with no valid Insurance or M O T test certificate. His sister, Mary Marshall was found guilty of perverting the course of justice, and aiding and abetting her brother to conceal evidence."

The paper then went over the details of the case at length, concluding with the dramatic events at the Elfington School concert, where Freya Olsen, the only survivor of the crash, suddenly regained her memory and recognised Stagg in the audience. Stagg was arrested in the School by Chief Inspector Pitt, who was also attending the concert, and taken to Abbotsbury Police station for questioning. Mary Marshall was arrested at her home later that night, after she tried to set fire to the car that Stagg had been driving on the night of the fatal crash, and had been kept hidden by her in an out building. Her husband, Mr Simon Marshall had helped to put out the fire and had called the police and fire brigade. He had been questioned by the police but was later released without charge. They were satisfied that neither he or his daughter had had any idea that the car had been hidden in the out building, and they had in fact been away the weekend of the incident, visiting his mother in Manchester.

The case had raised questions about the need for a police station to be opened in Elfington, as the village was increasing in size every year.

Stagg was found guilty on all charges and sentenced to life imprisonment. Mary Marshall was also found guilty on all charges and sentenced to fifteen years' imprisonment. Commenting later outside the court, Chief Inspector Pitt told waiting reporters that after four years, justice had finally been done. Once the vehicle involved in the crash had been found and examined, the case against the defendants was conclusive. Two dangerous criminals had been removed from the streets and the residents of Elfington could now feel safe again.

Freya sighed and put the paper down and gazed into the fire that burned cheerfully next to her. Now everyone knew what had happened that fateful night, her first in England. Just as it had been then, today was a Saturday, and as usual she had collected Lucy and they had come to visit her secret family under the Wold. They were all close by, to give their support to her at this difficult time, and to let her know that she was not alone and never would be. She was part of their secret world now and Freya could feel the positive energy being directed her way and was very glad of it. As the paper had been read by all the others, Freya threw it into the fire and they all watched it burn. It was over and done with. Freya looked around the chamber at the others and smiled at them, letting them know she was OK. It was strange, but if the crash had not happened, she would not be sitting here now, and neither would any of them. All of their lives would have taken a different path.

The Cats would have returned home after yet another fruitless visit to earth, and all the lives she had saved by using the powers that they had given to her would have been lost. Soon, another wonderful event was about to happen. After the magical three days that she, Dutch and their families, together with Clive and Jenny Pitt, and of course Tom and Penny had spent at Sandringham with the Royal family, Her Majesty the Queen had wanted to give them something to show her personal gratitude for saving her mother. Her Majesty had come up with a gift that only she had the power to grant. In two days' time, on the Easter bank holiday Monday, they were driving to a place called Castle Donington, where, waiting for them would be two private jets. One would be heading south, taking Dutch and his family back to Holland for a week's holiday to see their relatives and friends. The other would be heading north east, to Oslo, Norway. Freya and her human family were going home. Back to Norway, to the place where it had all begun almost five years ago.

At the time, everyone had said that they could not possibly accept such a generous gift, even from the Queen. But Her Majesty, as she usually did, had got her own way. Everyone had seen a side of Her Majesty that very few ever saw. She had called Dutch and Freya toward to stand before her, then, in a very un-Queen-like manner, had slid from the couch on which she had been sitting and knelt on the carpet and gently pulled them to her, hugging them for a long time, thanking them again for saving her mother's life, and risking theirs in the process. She had explained that while even she could not insist that they accept her gift, she was enjoying the Christmas break with her dear mother, instead of having had to attend a state funeral. It had been a very emotional moment, a private moment. A special moment. Her Majesty had sat back on the sofa, and invited Dutch and Freya to sit on either side of her, and after she had removed something from her eye, that had somehow caused it to water, had asked Lars, Rose, Gilbert and Beatrice to please accept her gift, as it would personally mean a lot to her if they did so. Four heads nodded agreement. It was a done deal. Tom and

Penny had looked on, so glad to be part of this special moment. In Penny's handbag was a cheque, drawn on Her Majesty's private account at Coutts and co, London for seven hundred and fifty pounds. To be used as Tom and Penny saw fit to buy or replace equipment or furniture at the Elfington practice. Next to that cheque in Penny's handbag was another, for the same amount, but this time drawn on the account of The Queen Mother.

Her Majesty's "People" had made all the arrangements , and taken care of the travel documentation , passports, hotels, everything. Home. She was going home. To see her old friends, visit her old school, return back to the house that she had used to live in, and to visit the graves of her parents. But it was not really home. Not now. Elfington was her home. England was her home. The secret hideaway in which she now sat with her special family was home. But it would be nice to go back to where it all begun. It would bring closure. She rose to her feet and she and Lucy said their goodbyes before heading down the tunnel to the Old Wood entrance. All the others came with them, to see them off.

For them all, out of something very bad, something very good had come. The circle was complete. The circle of life.

Simon Marshall sat in the office that had once been occupied by his former boss, Quentin Drummond, and put down his copy of the special edition of the local paper on the desk. He had not been reading the main story as he, more than anyone, knew all there was to know about that. Simon had been looking near the back of the paper at the pages reserved for the estate agents. His own property had made its debut there this week, and as the paper was a special, he knew that more people would see the picture of his house than usual. By the time it had been sold, Daphne would have left Elfington Primary School, and the new house he hoped to buy in Abbotsbury would be handy for the Grammar School he would be sending her to in September. Even now, people were viewing his house, which was one of the reasons he had come to the office on this Easter Saturday morning.

He had noticed that a flat had been sold in the Churchwell area of Abbotsbury, a first-floor, one bedroom apartment. He smiled when he saw the address. Flat seven, Windford Heights, Churchwell, Abbotsbury. The paper did not say that the seller had moved on as he now had no employment in the area.

Simon smiled again, he smiled a lot these days, and opened a drawer in his desk and withdrew a file, the contents of which he knew by heart. The file had been created from a larger one that he had in his safe, where there was also a video and audio tape. After the events at the school concert, he had not needed his file after all. Mary had remained in police custody until her trial, and now she was beginning her fifteen years jail sentence. Her brother would be spending considerably longer as a guest of Her

Majesty. Good.

Simon leaned back in his leather chair and let his mind go back to January. It was then he had been summoned to head office in Manchester to see the Chairman of the board of Directors.

As he had taken the train from Stoke Station to Manchester Piccadilly on a cold but clear winter's morning, he had a copy of that file with him, plus a special video and audio tape that he had had made from the original in his safe. He had guessed correctly what would be ahead of him when he got there, and he had come prepared. After the Christmas and New Year holiday were over, the arrest of his wife and brother-in-law had been big news, both locally and even nationally for a while, so it had come as no surprise to him that he had been asked to attend head office.

At head office he had been made to wait for almost an hour, before being ushered into the presence of the great man himself. Coffee was not served. The Chairman had got straight down to business. Although everyone knew that Simon had had nothing to do with the death of those two people, the publicity that the forthcoming trial would generate would not look good on the company, he did not want to have the company name associated with "that sort of thing", and so, the Chairman suggested that Simon might like to look for employment elsewhere. A good reference would, of course be provided, together with money in lieu of notice.

It was, as the Chairman put it, "For the good of the company, of course".

Simon had nodded, smiled and opened his briefcase. He handed over a file, a video and an audio cassette and suggested that the Chairman read, view and listen to them in private and behind a locked door. As he rose to his feet, Simon said that he was going to take an early lunch and asked if perhaps the Chairman would be kind enough to spare him a few moments at say, two o'clock, when he had had a chance to re-consider his position. Without waiting for a reply, Simon saw himself out and headed for the nearby park, where he sat on a park bench and enjoyed the cool and crisp air, ate his packed lunch and fed the ducks and seagulls. After many years of being forced to eat in overpriced pubs and restaurants, he did not want to set foot in one again.

Still with a little time to spare, he took a slow walk around the duck pond before making his way back to the head office, arriving at quarter to two. The receptionist was looking out for him and emerged from behind her desk and asked him if he would be kind enough to make his way to the Chairman's office right away. Simon smiled at her and stepped into the waiting lift that had been held for him by a messenger. On the eight floor, he alighted to find the Chairman himself waiting for him, ready to shake his hand. Simon's coat and scarf were taken and he was guided back into the office that he had left two hours earlier to find tea, coffee and biscuits awaiting him.

Simon listened as the Chairman informed him that he was now of the opinion that the company should publicly stand behind one of their up and coming executives at a time like this, and to assure him that his position in the firm was quite safe, unlike someone else's. Simon nodded, and assured the Chairman that he could keep the file, video and cassette, that he had no intention whatsoever of telling anyone else about any of this, and assured the Chairman, who now insisted on being called Tony, that he had had the file, etc. made because his own wife was also a visitor to the flat of Quentin Drummond and had only found out about the others by chance. In fact there were no "others", save for his and the Chairman's wife, but it did no harm to let Tony think that there may be other board members wives being naughty as well. Tony looked up from pouring the coffee and met the steady gaze of Simon. Nothing was said, nor needed to be. An unspoken deal had been done, for the good of the company, of course.

That had been three months ago, and Simon had travelled back to Elfington a happy man. He had cooked a nice meal for Daphne and when she was tucked up in bed, Simon had got very drunk. As he now rose from his desk and put the file back into the safe, a thought crossed his mind. His promotion had, once again been due to John Stagg, but this time, he did not mind. For him also, out of something bad, something good had come.

Miss Fiona Foster did not return to St Martin's School for the spring term. She had decided that teaching was perhaps, not for her after all. Since the time she had been observed by Miss Doyle and Freya in the alley, not that she would ever know it, she had not met 'Kenny baby' Fuller there again. A week later, she had ended her relationship with him, belatedly realising that he was only using her.

This thought had suddenly come to her one lunchtime while sitting in the staff room. How could she not have seen it before, she asked herself? There was one other person also in the staff room that day who could have answered that question for her, but chose not to. After the Easter break was over, Fiona was going to start training to be an air hostess for B. O. A. C.

Ken Fuller was cross that he had not been able to go "all the way" with Fiona, but hey ho, that was just how it went. Anyway, he had his eye on a rather nice young barmaid up at the Golf Club, so he would get over it quite quickly. Pity about Quentin though.

On Good Friday, Penny Thornton sat by the fire in the living room of the flat above the surgery, while Tom was downstairs catching up with his patients' notes after the Thursday morning and evening sessions, which had been much busier than usual as the surgery would be closed until the Tuesday after Easter holiday. Open on her lap was the bumper edition of the newspaper, and she had only glanced at the lead story, already knowing in great detail the facts of that case. Freya, Lars and Rose would be coming round for Sunday Lunch before they went away for a week's holiday.

She turned to page five where there were other stories of lesser importance, and gave a gasp as a name from the past leaped out at her. The story read, "The trial has begun at Stafford Crown Court, of a local man, accused of the attempted rape of a fourteen-year-old school girl who was walking through a local park on her way home from the shops in January. The man, named as Roger Dorling, of no fixed address, attacked the girl on a Saturday afternoon after dusk, and had dragged her into some bushes. She was saved by a passer-by walking his dog, who heard her screams and went to her aid. The man ran off, but was arrested the next day by Abbotsbury police.

Dorling has pleaded guilty, and asked for twenty-six other offences to be taken into consideration. He remains in custody and the trial will continue next week".

Penny put down the paper and gazed into the fire, remembering. Thank goodness that the girl had been saved by the man and his dog before he could do anything else. The girl would, in time get over her ordeal, but she would never forget it. Like she could never forget what he had done to her. Penny sighed. The story had brought it all back to her again, not that it had ever really gone away. The twenty-six other offences should be at least twenty-seven, as she had never reported the time that Roger Dorling had raped her. How many others like her she wondered, had also not reported being sexually assaulted by him?

Probably too many. Fear of being named, fear of the shame and the stigma that would be on them and on their families, but not on the attacker. They would still have to live and work in the local community, the looks and comments made by people who did not understand and never would. After all, they would nudge each other and say, that's her, she must have asked for it. How hard did she fight? And so on.

Suddenly she felt movement in her belly and put her hands on the ever-growing bulge as her baby kicked out as it turned, as if letting her know that it was here and understood. She smiled. She was expecting her first child during the summer. Tom's child. Created by the love that they shared, a love that was true and deep. A love that had begun the night that she had watched Tom try so hard to save the lives of Freya and her parents when they had been brought into Abbotsbury casualty department on that August night.

After four years of being alone after she had been raped by Roger Dorling, she had decided to do something that she had said that she would never do again. Trust a man. They were all the same, she had told herself, only after one thing. No. Never again. But watching Tom, the young, quiet and brilliant doctor who would not give up trying to save the lives of Freya and her parents, she had made a decision.

And it was a decision that she had never regretted. For with him, she knew beyond any doubt that she was safe. Safe and loved, fulfilled and truly happy. Tom had loved her back to life. Everything had begun again for her the night that Tom had saved the life of a little Norwegian girl called Freya Olsen, who was a very special part of the life she now led and had thought she would never have.

Now the man who had hurt her so badly was behind bars and would remain so for a long time. The paper slipped from her grasp and fell to the floor as she dosed off in her chair, a smile on her face as her hands held the new life growing inside her. It was indeed a very good Friday.

Two thirds into the newspaper, and away from the main stories that filled the front pages, was the "Births, Deaths, Marriages, Congratulations and Situations Vacant" page. In the "Marriages" section the paper reported on the Marriage of Belinda Piper to Professor George Brewer at Abbotsbury Registry Office. The bride had been given away by her father, best man had been Dr Thomas Thornton, and Chief bridesmaid had been Mrs Penny Thornton. The happy couple were enjoying a short honeymoon in Blackpool with their son, Freddie.

In the "Congratulations" section were a few names of pupils who had passed their eleven plus exam and among them were Freya Olsen and Gilbert Van den Berg. There were congratulations for them both from Uncle Lars and Auntie Rose, Mum and Dad Van den Berg, Clive and Jenny Pitt, Mr Winter, Tom and Penny. And someone called Aunty Lizzy. This was how Her Majesty the Queen Mother has asked to be known by Dutch and Freya. Her regular hand written letters to them were always signed off with that title, and their letters to her were addressed in the same way. Freya and Dutch had acquired a new Aunty. And Aunty Lizzy intended to be a good aunty to her special niece and nephew, for whom she would always have a special affection.

In the "Death" Section, one of the names listed there, was that of Mrs Edna Hunter, of Elfington. Mrs Hunter had been a teacher at St Martins' School for many years and had also been a member of the Parish Council until her death. The notice did not say that her body had lain in her house undiscovered for two weeks.